Curio's Christmas

(The Curio Chronicles)

Robin John Morgan

First published (Paperback) in the UK in 2022 by Violet Circle Publishing.

Manchester, England, UK.

Print ISBN: 978-1-910299-38-8
Digital ISBN: 978-1-910299-39-5

British Library Cataloguing in Publication Data.
A catalogue record for this book is available from the British Library.

All paper used in the production of this book are sourced only from wood grown in sustainable forests.

www.violetcirclepublishing.co.uk

Also by Robin John Morgan.

Heirs to the Kingdom.

Book One, The Bowman of Loxley.
Book Two, The Lost Sword of Carnac.
Book Three, The Darkness of Dunnottar.
Book Four, Queen of the Violet Isle.
Book Five, Crystals of the Mirrored Waters.
Book Six, Last Arrow of the Woodland Realm.
Book Seven, Bridge Of Sequana.
Book Eight, The Circle of Darkness.

The Curio Chronicles.

Part One, Abigail's Summer.
Part Two, Curio's Summer.
Part Three, Curio's Christmas.

Other works.

Rise of the Raven.
Han's Cottage.

Even in the middle of the darkness of the worst night,
there is the reassurance, that dawn will bring back the light.

Be the light, and bring hope.

Without understanding why, or how, I had started to grow up and mature, and it all began during the heat of that glorious summer. So much has changed since that time, I can see that now. I suppose that is the point, we cannot see what is around the corner, we really do not know what comes next. We can jump on the road of life, and run at high speed with the pack, or we can slow down and admire the scenery.

(Abigail Jennifer Watson)

Chapter 1

Home.

"Ladies and gentlemen, this is your Captain speaking, welcome to Flight 1527 From New York to London. We are currently flying at 42000 feet with clear skies, and it is now safe to undo your seat belts. Please relax and enjoy the flight, it is 10 o'clock New York time, and we will be airborne for approximately 7 hours and 18 minutes, and will be on time to arrive at Heathrow at 22: 20 hrs UK time, do not forget to reset your watches." Katie gave a long sigh, and unclipped her belt.

"I fucking hate flying, are you sure you don't want to, you know, sneak back and help calm us both down, it's your last chance Deadly?" I gave a chuckle.

"Well, I have got to say Katie, I admire your dedication, you are more persistent than a Uni rugby player, but for the hundredth time, this snatch is Birch only." She gave a giggle.

"You cannot blame a girl for trying Deadly, okay then, I will frap alone, see you in a minute, I am about to become a mile high masturbator, unless... Oh yeah, now she is really cute."

She made her way to the back of the plane, and I relaxed, and undid my belt, I am not a fan of flying, and all I wanted was to touch earth, and touch Birch, God, I have missed her so much. I settled back, slipped on my ear phones, closed my eyes, and hit play, and Avril burst into song.

Getting what you want is overrated, and thanks to some over bloated, self indulgent posh, celebrity twat, on social media, I am now an American best seller. Yep, James Deakins, famous stage artist, and renowned English literary genius, loved and admired throughout all the world, absolutely hates Seeds of Summer. His tweet of 'lewd, crude, vile, and utterly, distasteful, piece of garbage @Abigail Jennifer Watson' got everyone talking, and actually the daft shit, sent my sales skyrocketing, which is what you get for being a jumped up dickhead.

I laughed when I saw it, this from a man, who nine years ago, got caught trying to shove his manhood into his twenty two year old nephew, and he had the nerve to try and publicly shame me.

Three weeks of North America, is just too much, for this quiet village living hermit. I am not complaining really, the hotels are lush, and provide everything in the way of comfort that you can possibly need. Nothing is too much to ask, and everything appears to be twice the size of everything at home, especially meals, never in my life have I seen such huge portions. I will not deny, I have eaten very well, especially if you look at what was my flat toned stomach, which now has a little wobbly belly.

I have signed books, smiled, and had short conversations with some very lovely and especially polite people, and also had some very strange stares, from those my books offended, but in general, I have found Americans to be quite lovely, if not a little out of step with us more forward thinking people.

New York terrified me, and I have decided, I frigging hate outdoor people. If there is more than ten, I am legging it. You have no idea of the joy of walking in Wotton, where at most, on a normal busy day, there are eight people on the street. New York is filled with thousands of insane people, how the hell they survive the human stampede every day, amazes me?

I stepped out of the door of the hotel, and spent the next two hours, lost, and apologising, as I was utterly mowed down, by people who did not even look at me. I ended up sobbing in my hotel room, whispering 'I want to go home, I want to be alone in a room with just Birch.' Oh god, the next seven hours are going to feel like the longest of my life.

Mind you, for a time every lesbian on the planet hated me, and then suddenly, thanks to the British press, who somehow acquired a picture of me kissing Birch, at Deb's wedding two years ago, and plastered it everywhere, I am now an American gay icon, how messed up is this world?

Once again, to the press, who I sleep with, has far more importance than who I am, or what I write. Dad is not talking to me again, it was bad enough after the wedding, when he saw me with Birch kissing, and now with a picture of his daughter all over the papers, not only has he felt publicly shamed, the whole village knows, and that is simply too much for him to deal with. It is so stupid, what does it matter as to who makes me cum, isn't it the deep bond, and love that matter?

So, life has yet again moved on, and as I now completely understand, just like Birch has always said to me, 'you don't stop playing because you grow old, you grow old because you stop playing', which was something two years ago I failed to understand, and to be honest, for the last two years, my life has been such fun. Birch is a dream to live and be with, and of course, the rest of the Curio's, with our hidden secret life at home, it has simply been the best.

It is strange for me to look back, I have been here in the good ole US, talking about a book, which is pretty much my own life seven years ago. Okay I have renamed everyone, my lead character is Bram, and her crazy mate is Willow, and everybody gets them, they really understand Bram and her struggle with her attraction to Willow, so I have to question, why the hell did no one understand me?

I have been on TV shows, done adverts, sat in hotel rooms for days talking to the press, and all of them really understood what it is like to be victimised, and yet, nothing is ever done about it, they shake their heads and agree, yet no one speaks out loud enough to end it.

I mean, it is there in black and white, and they all have sympathised with the characters, and yet nothing ever changes, people still do not speak out, and suicide is still on the rise in young adults, in both the UK, and the US. It is mind boggling, I must admit, I cannot wait until they read the shoots of summer, which is the half written book, I have on the computer at home. I thought it was just Wotton, you know what, it is not, it's the whole bloody world.

Wotton has changed a little bit, Amanda the Florist, has a boyfriend, well I say boyfriend, I mean he is forty two, so I suppose he is more of a man friend. She is a lonely adulteress no more, and actually they look really cute together, he turns up on Saturdays and helps put the flower stands out.

Amie Bosworth finally divorced Andrew, the landlord of the

Hunters Arms, claiming domestic abuse, and she is shacked up next door to Hatty, with a guy named Dennis, who treats her lovely, she deserves that, and it is nice to see her without black eyes. Denise, Deb's assistant is engaged to Roy, a plumber from Oxendale, and as you can imagine around us, there are a lot of pipe jokes about him, although to be honest, he is about as much fun as a toothache.

Low and behold, Marion the queen of urination, and oldest spinster in the village, has actually started dating, Sydney, a banker from Oxendale, and so we all assume, she is no longer taking the piss out of Ronald. She is a lot more tolerable since, and she does spend quite a lot of time in the bookshop, and yep, she is really into wet knicker novels.

The bookshop is booming, and has become a massive success for Deb's, it does help that Jimmy often is in the shop when not touring, and Battered Taco fans call in and he advises them on the best Steam Punk novels. You know I must say, listening to the lyrics of the band, it is hard to believe he is so well read. Rumour has it Deb's has helped write a few new lyrics for forthcoming songs on the next album. Deb's is Deb's, she has not changed much, she is as sweet as always, and I do love popping in the shop for coffee mornings with her.

The biggest surprise I would say, is probably Curio Life. The site just went bonkers, and got bigger and bigger, so much so, we moved the whole operation into Sweetie's Retreat, onto yet another larger server. It has at least ten thousand videos on it, and is now more a national than a local site.

Izzy felt it was better run full time from the practice, and I must admit for all of us, it was a welcome relief. It is now a registered charity, that serves mental health issues for young adults, and has in a way absorbed the Tarts program into it. Edwina still maintains it, and we all still have a presence on it, and all of us make regular updates, but it is now managed on a day to day basis by Aden Jenkins, a really talented twenty five year old computer geek, and occasional bed partner of Edwina, and Chloe if she is not looking.

The huge news to rock the village of late, was that three months ago, Derek Werrington, who had a bit of a drunken public row with Marjorie on the green, was raided, and arrested shortly after for antique fraud. He has recently been sentenced to five years in prison, and all his property has been seized, his shop is empty at the moment. It really does not take much to work out that yet another anonymous tip off, came from pretty much the same Wotton source, and that is currently located on the old Sutton Farm Estate.

Marjorie I am sad to say is alive and well and hates me even more, because now she knows I screw Birch, and have written a lewd book of filth, which delights her to show she was proven right. She drives past every day on her way to the village, to sit in her usual spot, at the Tea Rooms, and complains about the moral decline of us whores. She is still absent from the Parish Council, and has been very vocal about her opposition to female vicars, but in many ways, she has gone underground, and still has her hands on the pulse of the village, hence, I am still as unpopular.

Nigel married possibly the worlds stupidest woman earlier this year, we all know it was an arranged marriage, I mean, after all who the hell would be stupid enough to marry him? Actually, that would be, Primula Rosebanks, or as we like to call her, 'Prude Prim.' Rumour has it, she does not like sex, although considering the video we all still watch on a regular basis, for shits and giggles, as we all know, it is probably his pencil size penis she does not like, she is probably not even aware he has slipped it in her.

Milton retired, which Madge has still not forgiven him for, and we assume is still getting it good from his club members, with a ten inch dildo. Izzy who is a club member, keeps her activities on the low down, and all we really know is the new club is on our lane, but we have no idea at which house. I mean, we know it's not my dad's, or Bradley's, but one of those buggers up the lane, has a full size kink dungeon in the basement.

To be honest; we take the mentality of if they are happy, leave them to it. I mean, who am I to question others? I spent seven years trying to be someone I was not, and hide the fact I was madly in love with a woman, something this village and my father will not forgive me for. If they want to dress in rubber, or whatever it is, and bang the shit out of each other, with huge rubber toys, for fun, I am not going to condemn them.

Peter and Mary have taken a bold step, encouraged by Celia,

who has been a regular sun worshiper in our garden this year, and according to Birch's emails to me in the states, we have all been invited to a Christmas naturist meet and greet, at the Oxendale Sun Club. Who would have thought it seven years ago, when they lived in fear of being shamed by Madge? I think it is really nice, and I think we will probably go, more out of curiosity, although Birch is quite clear, she does not join clubs, as the politics become far too complex and spoil the fun.

Speaking of politics, the Parish Council, is now vibrant and fun, Anthony and Edwina have both made massive contributions, much to the shock and horror of Madge, when she discovered a Pride Tent at the Summer Fete this year. When I left for the States, Anthony was organising Christmas lights for the village, something that has always been a little on the thin side, and he was on a crusade to make the village sparkle, as Oxendale Council have again cut the budget, and reduced what they were prepared to spend. He has been fundraising for six months, and I am actually looking forward to seeing what he can do. This really is his first time to fully shine, and we are all behind him.

Edwina was added to the council, more for I.T. capabilities, and in that she has been amazing, the village web pages are so much better, and through it, she has run an initiative to give all the local business's a discount, on their own web sites, all of which are linked to the main village site. Shopping online in the village has become a god send, and as a result, several young people have been full time employed delivering goods bought online from a local village store.

Edwina has proved to have been a wonderful all round aid to the council, she gets involved with most things, with a happy smile and great enthusiasm, and she has in many ways become a very popular part of the council. My mum and Celia are a brilliant team, and have become such good friends, and to be honest, because of their efforts, they are unlikely to be unseated any time soon.

Deb's and Jimmy are really doing well, her wedding was amazing, and the real credit should go to Birch, because honestly, she could see it in her mind, and through that she made it happen. Deb's shot off to Bali, and came back as brown as a stick, and proudly informed us, she had no tan lines, which Jimmy highly approved of. She talked for weeks about her honeymoon bless her, although she completely freaked out Chloe, when she showed her pictures of her and an octopus. Chloe watches too much rude Anime, and so saw tentacles in a completely different way to us.

Mum is doing fine, although a week before I left for the states, she told me her and my dad were still in separate rooms, and honestly, I have no idea why she will not simply admit she is unhappy and file for a divorce. I have no understanding of her, or why she even puts up with him, he is rude and nasty all the time, even in company, and I have had more than my fair share of arguments with him, in the last year about it. Yeah, I am less popular than ever, but I sort of realised that after Deb's wedding.

To be honest, the Curio's have changed a little, I suppose living in the house we have finally found a routine that we all have slipped into, and we all just go about our days doing what we need to with a lot of wise cracks and giggles. I feel we have grown up a little, although we can still be silly and wild if we need to, if anything I think such is our ease, we are more open about ourselves at home.

There is a reason most of this has happened, and also why I have finally got a decent selling book. It really is down to the one wonder that is Birch, my absolutely bonkers and beautiful lover. I have spent so many hours of the last seven years with her in my thoughts, it is quite ridiculous, and yet it isn't really.

Years ago, at Uni, I knocked on her door, hoping I was not lost on my first day of Uni, and a naked, alabaster Amazonian opened the door, smiled, and said, "Hi Sweetie." And I think I have been in love with her ever since. Her inner strength and acts of kindness have not only changed my world, but the world of everyone she connects with, and I think all of us secretly see her as a true angel, albeit a sexually deviant and utterly bonkers one.

I have so much love in my heart for her, something for a such a long time, I tried to deny, and yet two years ago, after almost having a breakdown, I finally faced myself, and admitted the truth, which was, I could not fall in love with anyone else ever, because I was totally devoted to her. Here, sat on a plane approaching Heathrow, she is the only thing in my thoughts. I have been so lonely and miserable, in the states for three weeks, batting off her sexually predatorial friend Katie, just yearning to be back in her arms again, and with a little luck, tonight I will be.

Flying is an unnatural act, so the bump of the wheels and the screech of the tyres, was a welcome, if not jittery feeling. Katie was sat in her seat, with her hands clenched firmly on the arm rests, and had her eyes closed. I cannot deny, considering she jets off all over the world with Roni, she has not instilled me with a great deal of confidence in flying.

It was good to be back on land, and walking through arrivals, with my yearning to be home growing even stronger, I was relieved, although I still had to get out of London and back to Wotton. Pulling my pull along suitcase, next to Katie, I made it through to the arrivals gate, where long lines of people stood holding signs, containing the names of people they had to collect. Katie shook her head.

"Seriously!?" A loud squeal, echoed at the far end of the line and I looked up.

Before me was a line of multicoloured looking garden gnomes, each holding a sign, I read along the line. 'Deviant, Slut, Smut Writer, Whore,' and the biggest sign of all 'SWEETIE.'

I almost wanted to cry, there she was in her robe, with that amazing long white hair, with black patches, those gorgeous green sparkling eyes, and the most beautiful loving smile on the planet. It was utterly unexpected, she dropped her sign as she saw me, and opened her robes wide, and she was stark naked, and on her tummy was written 'Attention Needed,' with an arrow pointing down. Katie was laughing her heart out, I smiled, and wanted to cry. God, I have missed her so much.

She closed her robe, ducked under the barrier, and came hurtling down to me, her robes undid, and became wide open, and swayed behind her, and I let go of the handle of my case, as she hurtled into me, and smothered me in her boobs.

"HI SWEETIE, I MISSED YOU!" Oh god it felt so nice to just pull her close and hold her tight, and smell her soft perfume.

"Oh Birch, I have missed you so much."

She loosened her grip, and I looked up at her, she beamed with happiness, bent forward, and pulled me into a long passionate kiss, and it felt so good, I just did not want to stop. The flash bulbs informed me, I was going to be back in the papers tomorrow, daddy will be chuffed. The press have become my version of the Shrew Crew on a national level, I think the only thing they write about me is my name, it is according to Anthony, the price we pay for fame, yeah, sod that, I hate them. Honestly who cares, this was all I really wanted, and they could print what the hell they liked, none of them would ever understand, what being in her arms was truly like.

We separated, and I held her by the waist and just looked at her, and smiled, her eyes were alive and sparkling, she was smiling, and she was so beautiful.

"Hi Sweetie." I lifted my hand to her cheek; the tears came and my eyes blurred.

"You have no idea how much I have missed you, I frigging hate America. I am doing no more of that shit unless you come too." She took my hand.

"Let's go home Sweetie... Oh, hi bitch, hope you failed miserably with my Sweetie." Katie smiled and hugged her.

"Fuck you slut, I will get her one day."

Birch gave a loud cackle of a laugh, and holding my hand, we walked back to the others, for a round of hugs and cuddles, Deb's almost crushed me to death.

Leaving the airport was not a quiet thing, as a billion questions came my way, and I asked a billion back, as the press ran along at our side, taking yet more pictures. We finally made it out of the doors where a parking warden was looking at the time on the meter, we were five feet away when the machine expired and he pulled out his pad, Chloe shouted, and waved at him.

"Whoa... Wait we are here." He slipped his pen out of his pocket. She shook her head. "Come on, we are here."

He looked at her as if deciding what to do, it was clear he was going to write a ticket. Having no alternative, Chloe resorted to what she does best, she pulled apart her robe, and walked right up to him. He froze and looked at her slim naked sexy body, she winked, he smiled.

"Hey Mr Parking man, how about we make a deal?" He looked at her suspiciously.

"What kind of deal?" She winked.

"If you can go longer than three minutes, you can give me a ticket, if not, we are free to go." He frowned; Edwina rolled her eyes.

"Christ, not again?" Chloe pushed him up against the door of Petal, her hand slid down his uniform, and she moved in real close.

"GIRLS!"

Edwina sighed. We all knew the routine, to be honest, she freaks me out at times. Deb's Birch, Edwina and myself formed a shield and stood round Chloe with our backs to her. To be honest, I never wanted to watch her, as it weirded me completely out. She went down, and the sound of a zipper announced her intention. The warden's eyes bulged, Edwina looked at her watch, and hit the stop watch.

"GO!" The warden suddenly jerked.

"Oo!"

Edwina counted the seconds as they ticked past. The warden's arms spread across the door, and he went bright red, and he started to breathe in a very strange manner, as he made little high pitched squeaking noises. We started to giggle, the one thing we all knew about Chloe, was she was good, there was no way he would make it past 2:20. He gave a loud 'Squeak!' and then gasped, Edwina stopped the watch.

"2:16, Chloe you are slacking, but we are free." The sound of his zip going up announced her task was complete, she stood up and smiled, and kissed him on the cheek.

"Yummy!" He looked shocked and relaxed, and gave a smile, she took his hand, and walked him slowly back to the curb, and smiled as she let go.

Birch opened the driver's door, and made sure this time, to step over the deposit Chloe had spat out, and climbed in. The last time was funny as hell, but also made us all shudder, and feel queasy. I jumped in the passenger side giggling, and everyone else climbed in the back, where Anthony had already loaded my case. The warden just stood staring at us, his ruffled shirt above his belt, I smiled.

"By sweets." Petal lurched forward, Anthony screamed, and we shot off in the direction of home. Anthony looked at Deb's with a panicked expression.

“I thought you were driving?” Deb's gave a smile.

“I drove here, and Birch wants to be up front with Abby.” He looked forward and screamed.

“ARRRGH.... BIRCH... HEADLIGHTS!” She looked down.

“Oh yeah!” She smiled and hit the switch, and turned to look back, she smiled. “Thanks Sweetie.” Chloe, Edwina, Deb's and Anthony all screamed.

“LOOK AT THE FUCKING ROAD!” She turned back, and they all sat back, white faced, holding their chest, and gasping with relief.

I sat back in my seat and slid my hand onto her thigh, her robe was open slightly, and I could feel her soft white skin, I slid my hand up it. Deb's leaned over in between us, and turned to me.

“I am warning you Abby, if you even try to finger her, while she is already trying to kill us by driving, I will put your frigging head through the window.” Birch giggled, and I started to laugh, Birch turned round.

“You know Deb's Sweetie; you were much more daring before you got married.”

“LOOK AT THE FUCKING ROAD.... ARRRGHHHHHHH!”

“Oops! Sorry Sweetie's”

God, it was good to be home, I had really missed this.

Chapter 2

Home for Christmas.

I lay back in the pillow, gasping for air. “Holy shit Birch, you really did miss me.”

We had been at it for hours, my legs were broken and weak, I had given her at least three massive orgasms, but in all honesty, and judging by how sensitive my clitoris was, I had been given a hell of lot more. She crawled up smiling and flopped on my shoulder, her face was red and hot.

“Deads Sweetie, I am dead, you killed me.” I smiled and put my arm round her, it was so nice being home again. I gasped in more air.

“Birch, I need liquid, if I cum anymore I will turn to dust, and blow out the window.” She gave a giggle and lifted her head up.

“If you can still walk down those stairs, I am losing my touch, and I am screwing you again.” She gave a cackle of a giggle. “Let’s go find beer.”

I wearily, and feeling a little unstable, slipped off the bed onto the floor, my legs were weak and still trembling. Birch was equally as bad as we came very slowly down the stairs, Edwina came out of the library and chuckled.

“Ha, that is what too much fun gets you bitches.” She walked towards the kitchen, I leaned over the banister and smiled.

“Jealousy is so unattractive Edwina.” She giggled and gave me the finger.

I had only two objectives when I arrived in the kitchen, the first being sit down, the second was acquire a beer, at the moment the cellar steps were out of the question. I made it to the island, and perched gingerly on the stool, holy shit my vagina was so sensitive, the cool vinyl felt nice, but the tingles it sent down my legs, made me sit up straight.

Birch sat down opposite me and leaned on the island and

giggled, I was assuming she just had the same experience. Edwina put two bottles down on the island, and smiled.

"I haven't the heart to make you get your own, but don't expect this all the time, you know you two are just sluts for each other don't you?" I smiled.

"You are an angel; I will repay you one day." She sighed.

"God I am jealous, it's been two weeks, I need to find a man, or a woman, a tongue or dick about now would suffice. God, when people say dry patch, I never thought it would be a desert. They said run your own business, it will be fun, what they never told me is, I would be sat at a computer for the rest of my life, miles away from anything remotely sexual." Birch lifted her head off her arm.

"What about Aden, I thought he was your gap filler?" She shrugged.

"He is meeting his gamer mates, apparently, they have a big WOW battle planned, you see this is the bloody problem with modern gamers. Luke would bend me over and screw me with his controller on my back, now he was a serious gamer.... Oh, actually!"

She picked up her phone. I watched as she dialled, and winked at me. Birch smiled as I glanced at her, she was looking very spacy at the minute, but her eyes sparkled with happiness, and I loved that. Edwina stiffened.

"Luke... Hi it's Weena." She sighed. "Weena... You know, Banger Bobbles?" Birch sniggered, and looked at me.

"Banger Bobbles?" I smirked, she was going red.

"Yeah Luke, I was wondering if you had any free time... Girlfriend, oh... Is she there? No, good, look I have a few projects on the go... Yeah freelance, are you interested in a deep coding session, the pay is good.... Oh yeah, I can pay that way too." She looked at us both and raised her eyebrows. "Yeah, number three... Cool, I will be here." She ended the call, and looked at the ceiling. "Thank you, god." I gave a laugh

"I take it Luke has some major coding to do?" She smiled a huge smile.

"Oh yes, Luke is going to be decoding my mattress, and rebooting me all night, thank god for Luke, for a moment I was even finding Percy attractive."

It was a sobering thought, sharing men is one thing, but sharing Percy, Chloe's secretly perverted teddy? Even for this house, that was way too screwed up to contemplate.

Several beers later, and the wonders of liquid back in our systems we were upright and able to walk, we wandered down the hall and into the living room, Deb's and Chloe were both curled up on the sofa reading. Deb's was reading Wuthering Heights, again, Chloe never disappoints, she was reading 'Butt Action Magazine.' I cannot deny I was intrigued, I leaned over to peek.

"Holy shit Chloe, where the hell do you find this stuff?"

She was looking at a double page spread of a very ripped looking guy, who was fully stiff, and my god, it was bigger than even Milton could handle, she turned it too me.

"Do you think that is photoshop... I mean that is bloody huge, no man could possibly be that big in real life?" It was hard to even contemplate, and weirdly enough, I could not take my eyes off it, Birch leaned in and giggled.

"That will make your eyes water, it's surgically enhanced, they have a cut that frees the skin to make it even longer, so yes, it really is that big." I looked at Chloe, and she winked.

"Sad thing is he is gay, I got this off Anthony, it only uses gay models. I like some of the articles in it." Birch sniggered.

"Yeah, I can see the article you are studying; it is very informative."

I had to chuckle, Deb's phone bleeped and she picked up. She sat and read the message, and then gave a long sigh. I looked at her and could tell instantly she was upset. She typed back looking really upset, a moment later her phone bleeped, and she gave another long sad sigh.

"Is everything alright Deb's?" She looked up, I thought she was going to cry, her voice was low and squeaky.

"They want to extend the tour. Abby, I really wanted him home, it's supposed to be our first real Christmas together, but they have been offered a live Christmas Day gig. Loads of bands are doing it, but they have the headline spot." She gave another sigh.

"Am I being selfish Abby? It's just with mum and dad going away, this would have been our first real Christmas together, you know just him and me. I just wanted us to be our own little family. It is why we chose not to go away with them, I wanted to be completely alone with Jimmy." Birch gave a sigh.

"Well my mum and dad are off with yours, this will be the first Christmas, I will not be home with them, so I suppose we are in the same boat. I have not seen them since last July, and I was really looking forward to it, so I really get you Goggles." I turned to Birch.

"Why don't we make it a Curio Christmas then, I mean we are a family, aren't we? Anthony's dad has turned on him for coming out, which means he won't see his mum, Edwina and Chloe have always gone home. If I am honest sitting in my mum's house with my dad ignoring me is not going to be fun. Last year we did not even decorate, because all of us were not here, because Anthony ended up at Delphine's. We can do a Christmas for us. The Pemberton's can come for dinner, I could invite mum and dad, although I don't think dad will come, I am sure Delphine will come." Deb's went from depressed, to instantly excited.

"Can we have a tree and lights and streamers, oh god, I would love that?" She bounced up and down on the sofa, Chloe gave a huge grin.

"Oh, I am so fucking in for that, my dad is a right boring old shit at Christmas, he just eats and then sleeps. Can we have house lights and mistletoe, and snogging and stuff? My dad hates all those things, and I have always wanted to do it... Please guys, can we do this?" I looked at Birch.

"I cannot deny, I am getting excited about this, my dad is so dull at Christmas, and to be honest, it would be nice to wake up in bed here, and share the day here, it would be really special for me."

Alright and now, I am playing dirty, Birch loves to see me excited and happy, and I wanted to see all the girls and Anthony happy, but I also wanted to be here at home with her. I wanted to sit in bed alone with her and give her my gifts, and just watch her open it. It simply and probably is, very sad and soppy, but to be honest, for me it would mean everything. She looked round the room at the happy smiling faces.

"I am a pagan, if I am honest, I don't really get Christmas, I love Yule, and watching the sun, I have never really had a Christian type Christmas. I spent one year with Raven Moon, she had a holly tree, and candles, and food things. My mum and dad never really did the tree and baubles things, so I am not sure what to do. I mean, I see it everywhere; it is yet another example of how much power the Bell Twats have, but it looks like for you guys this is a really big deal, and this is your home, and I have never stopped anyone expressing their happiness." Chloe nodded.

"So that is a yes then?" I giggled and Birch smiled at me.

"I want to do a Yule for you, and so if I do, you can all do a Christmas for me, is that alright?"

The room was suddenly filled with screams of joy. Deb's hit a level of mad happiness I had not seen before. Chloe put down her gay porn mag, which just shows how bloody happy she was. Both of them started talking at a fast pace, and it appeared plans were in the making already. It was crazy to watch, and I leaned back, and Birch snuggled into me, and kissed my neck, the tingles shot through me, she gave a giggle.

"So, is screwing under the Christmas tree really a thing, or is it an urban myth?" I gave a sly smile.

"I say we try it and find out." And suddenly Birch was really excited about Christmas.

The obviously very loud Chloe and Deb's attracted attention, Edwina appeared to investigate, walking like she had been horse riding for days. She was greeted with the news, and was very happy, although she did appear like she had a ride or two left, before her coding session was over.

Anthony came down, to enquire as to what could make Deb's and Chloe so bonkers, and soon there was excitement all around, and the plans for a full on Curio Christmas were hatched. We would go wild, have a crazy Christmas, and have guests round for a big traditional dinner, and a huge Christmas Party.

Anthony was already stressed out over the lights for the village, but Chloe was keen, and so we all agreed, she could lead the way for outdoor decoration, and we would help out where needed. All of us wanted to be a part of the tree, and we agreed it would be a group effort, as Deb's explained, it was the one aspect of Christmas, all families should partake in. I sat back with a big smile.

"You know what this means don't you guys?" They all stopped talking and looked at me.

"We have nothing, and so that can only mean one thing... Shopping." And those were the magical words of motivation we all loved to hear.

The excitement level grew, Anthony got really into it, Edwina returned to her room, in the hope Luke had got his stamina back, and chatter flowed with the drinks. The jet lag was kicking in, and the sudden tiredness hit me, I was still on US time, and feeling the effects of a seven hour flight.

Birch took my hand and guided me to bed, she snuggled into me and it felt so good, for three weeks I had struggled to sleep. I even put pillows behind me to help, but suddenly having her there, and feeling her soft breasts pushed into my back, and that familiar heat from her body flowing into mine, made everything right again. I pushed back, and her arm came round and cupped my boob, and my world was again perfect.

"I missed this so much Birch, god you have no idea how hard it was to sleep without you."

Her soft breathing sounded in my ear, Christ, she was already asleep, maybe she had missed this as much as I had too? I closed my eyes, and let it all drift away, nothing in the universe mattered, this was all I needed.

I was warm, snug and quiet when I opened my eyes, I really needed a pee, but I did not want to move. I had rolled over in the night, and she was lay on my shoulder breathing softly, with her hand between my legs, my god, was she a dream groper?

No wonder I wanted a pee, she was pushing down on me. I smelt her scent, and looked down, into a mass of birch bark hair, I lifted my hand to stroke her long mane, it has grown so much, apart from a few trims by Anthony, it now touched the bottom of her bum, when she was standing, mine just made it four inches past my boobs.

She moved, and snuggled more into me and gave a happy sigh, she was wakening slowly, she moved her hand, and I tingled.

"Mm, Sweetie... I have missed this so much." She lifted her head, and looked at me with dreamy eyes, and smiled. "Hi sweetie." I smiled.

"Hey you, sleep well?" She gave a long contented sigh.

"I have hardly slept since you left, what time is it?"

"One o'clock, we slept much longer than I expected, I need a pee and coffee, you want one."

"Coffee yes, pee not so much, you go first."

It was November, and the heating was turned up. Outside the sun was shining, there had been frost on the grass, but we had missed it. Deb's poured us both coffees, as we sat yawning, oh god it was so nice to drink proper coffee, I am not sure if it is the water, or if it is their coffee, but it's felt like weeks since I had a really good cup.

Chloe was in her studio, humming Christmas carols, as she painted, Deb's sat down and lifted her cup, she smiled at us.

"Are we doing real or fake?" I blinked trying to find some semblance of being awake before the coffee kicked in, I failed.

"Huh?"

"Trees, should we have a real one or a fake one?" Birch blinked.

"In order to protect you, it has to be real, and blessed by the forest spirits." I turned and looked at her.

"Huh?" She gave a giggle.

"The pagans believed that if you bring an evergreen into your home at Yule, it has been blessed by the spirits and wards off evil. I would like real, they smell nice too, and you need to keep them wet." I looked to the studio.

"Do you think Chloe has been blessed by the forest spirits, she is permanently wet?" Deb's giggled.

"I like real, I have always wanted one, mum always said they were messy." Birch nodded.

"Spruce are messy, their needles are in little cups that dry out in the heat, that is why they shed, you want a fir, they grow right out of the branch, and drop less." She was impressed.

"How come, if you are a Pagan, you know so much about Christmas Trees?" Birch shrugged.

"I don't, I know trees, and how they grow, I love trees, they make me happy."

Yet again the simplicity of her love of nature, was teaching us all, and so it was decided, we would go and find a good tree this week. Deb's got very excited, she ran off looking for a tape measure, she was going to measure the room height, so we could pick the perfect tree for our living room. I looked at Birch as she lifted her cup.

"You know the ceilings are pretty high here, she is going to want a bloody huge one?" Birch smiled.

"We are Curio's, if we are going to do this, we may as well do it big and bold, I mean to be honest Deads, Wotton expects it."

She was right, this would be our first proper Christmas here, and we should go full out.

After coffee, scratch that, after several coffee's, I headed upstairs and back to my desk, I had been away for three weeks and had a lot of mail. I switched on my computer, and picked up my phone, I had a message from mum, with a photo, and yep, the papers had as predicted, splashed Birch and me across every paper. Actually, it was a pretty good pic, that showed the partially dressed, Birch, showing just about everything, kissing me with passion.

Dad was not happy, again. Birch walked into the room looking at her phone, I smiled. "We made the papers again." She nodded.

"My mum sent it me; I actually think it is a good picture, do you think they do prints? The story is pants, I might ring them and correct them, it wasn't a medical examination, I am not that kind of a doctor. It was lust, complete and utter lust, I saw you, and I wanted you, so I took you. I wish they had not put black squares on it though, I think my boobs are good enough to look at." I sat back in my chair.

"This is life now as a best seller, are you okay with this, I don't want you caught up and hurt by this?" She sat on the bed.

"Deads Sweetie, I am a sex therapist, this makes me look brilliant, if anything this is really good for business, I mean look at it, I don't just advise, I prove I practice it as well." She giggled.

"My dad is pissed off about it." She shrugged at me, and gave a sigh.

"When is he not pissed at us, he hates the fact we are sexual, look Deads, what choice does he have? He can either ignore you forever, of grow the hell up and live with it, at the end of the day your mum is cool with it, and that is really all that matters, isn't it? We are both consenting adults, it has bugger all to do with him. I am going to run a bath; will you be joining me?"

"Like you need to ask." She giggled.

It felt really strange to me, and I must admit I had struggled with it for two years. That summer seven years ago, Dad knew we shared a bed, he saw how close we were, and how her staying at Uni, left me sad, alone and depressed. From the moment Birch came back, the change in me had been instant, how could he not see how much I loved her? It boggled my mind that he could not honestly believe for a minute, that all of that would have not led to us being sexual. I suppose the good thing is he has not played the nudity card as much; he is now hooked on the sex.

Just over a year ago we travelled to London, and did the World Naked Bike Ride, and yep, you guessed it, the Curio's were in the papers, all naked and covered in body paint cycling past the queen's palace. He hit the roof and screamed about how disgraceful we all were, although mum did say she found the video on the internet still open in his browser, so he obviously had no problem seeing Birch, Deb's, Chloe and Edwina naked, what a hypocrite.

The nudity is less of a bother to him now, as he has found out Birch and I have sex, it's crazy, Mum pretty much worked it straight out, and yet he missed it, and it was another reminder of where I lived, a village where how it looked on the outside, was far more important than it was on the inside.

The opinions of all those bigots that had attacked me for years, was far more important to him, than my happiness, and that really pissed me off, and it made me really open my eyes. I sat in the bath leaning against Birch, and told her what I was thinking about his reaction.

"You know Birch, his behaviour has really made me think. If you remember, I told you back then, that I told my dad what Martin did, and he refused to believe me and took his side. I know it sounds mad, but I really think my dad does not ever want me to be sexual. I think the thought of Martin screwing me, or as was the case trying to, or the fact you have sex with me, I think it is beyond his ability to comprehend, I think he seriously sees me as none sexual." She pushed me forward and washed my back with the new fluffy sponge.

"You could be right; I have certainly counselled men who refused to accept their daughters even thought about sex. It is a possibility, maybe you should tell him you have screwed men, and see if he applauds." I giggled.

"I do think it is weird, I am twenty six years old, surely he must know I have had sexual partners, I mean he has seen them pick me up from the house?" She gave a sigh.

"I doubt he will talk about it Deads, but I do think at some point you both need to, this ignoring you is childish."

Chapter 3

Confronting Truth.

Clean from our bath, with the bed stripped, and in the washer, Chloe confirmed that she had spoken to her mum and dad, and they would be delighted to be guests for Christmas Dinner, after all, it meant saving money, so her dad was thrilled. Anthony also informed us Delphine was overjoyed, she had been planning a Christmas alone. Deb's asked if we would be inviting Hatty and Clive, I cannot deny it had crossed my mind, my problem was dad, I had to face that hill first, and see if I could conquer it.

There was no avoiding it, I had to go across the road and see my parents, it was Sunday, so I knew my dad would go to the pub before coming home, so that would give me time to talk to mum. Birch was not letting me go alone, and so we dressed, which sucked, and went over, we walked in and I shouted out.

"Hi Mum."

"In the kitchen."

We walked in, and she was cleaning, but there again, she is always cleaning, it is a Wotton house wife thing, she smiled.

"This is a nice surprise; I hope you're staying for coffee?" Birch sat at the counter.

"Flick we only came for the coffee."

She giggled, mum switched the kettle on, I sat down next to Birch. This felt familiar, we had witnessed some fun here, all sat together over the years. Mum made the coffee, and sat down with us; I was happy she was alone.

"Mum we are thinking of doing a full Christmas at our place, and we wanted to know if you and dad would come over for dinner with us, you know, give you a break, and let us take care of you for a change? Chloe's mum and dad are coming, so is Delphine, and because Jimmy has been booked, Deb's will be there too?" She gave a sigh.

"Your dad is really unhappy at the moment, Abby I would love too, but I cannot say he will. I am sorry, I really am; it would mean so much for me to see your family together, having a proper Christmas meal, and I really do wish things were different." I understood, I hated it, but I knew well what he was like at this time of year, honestly, he made the grinch look pleasant.

"I want to talk to him, and to be honest mum, whether he wants to come or not, I still want you there. Look mum, I hate to butt in, and it probably is private, but you guys are still not sleeping in the same room, and have not for seven years as far as I know. Be honest, the only thing you still do with him is the Council, apart from that you live separate lives? So just come, have some fun, and enjoy the day, if he hates me that much, leave him here, I want you at my first real Christmas at home." She looked concerned.

"Abby I just want a peaceful Christmas; you know how difficult he can be?" She gave a sigh. "Can I think about it?" I stared at her.

"I really bloody hate the fact you have to ask me that, I am your daughter, okay so I screw a woman, does it really matter that much?" She reached over the counter and grabbed my hands.

"Abby, I love both of you, you know that, Birch is like a daughter to me, I have no issue with your sex life or even your nudity, I thought you understood that?" I felt really angry.

"Of course, I know, which is why I don't understand why you cannot come alone."

The front door banged and I turned with a jump, I felt my heart beating in my chest, but it had to be faced. A few seconds later my dad arrived through the kitchen door, he took one look at me, stopped, and then stared.

I had not seen too much of him of late, after the huge row I had with him after Deb's wedding, and one over my investments, I had kept my distance. He looked older, greyer, colder, his eyes looked dead as he looked at me, and they reminded me of the many times in my life, when I faced him as a child to be disciplined, which actually made me nervous.

It was clear he had been drinking, he always got that red glow to his face when he had a few whiskeys. I had hoped we could sort this out, but as I looked at him, as he stared at me, I became unsure. He reached inside his jacket, and pulled out a wrinkled newspaper, he lifted it up and shook it at me.

"HAVE YOU SEEN THIS? You two are all over the bloody papers again, everyone is talking about it, have you seen how you embarrassed yourself?" Birch slipped off her seat, I pushed back my hand and stood up.

"No Birch, this is for me to deal with, it is time it was done."

She looked really nervous; my mum looked terrified. I walked towards him slowly, I will not deny, even now he still scared me, but this time I was not running away. I looked him straight in the eyes, and faced him full on.

"My lover missed me and met me, and kissed me, why is that a crime? I saw plenty of people hugging and kissing their loved ones returning from being away, no one seemed to care much about that. Does it really matter that much Dad, just because I sold a few books that the gutter press follow me? I am a writer Dad, it was bound to happen. You know, I always hoped you would be happy I was truly loved, but obviously not?" He pointed at Birch with the paper.

"It is completely unacceptable for public behaviour Abigail; you know better than that. She was bloody naked in the airport, in full view of everyone." I could see his face reddening, well going redder than it was, the booze had started the process. I took three steps forward.

"Actually, Dad she was wearing a robe, but it came open as she ran to me, sadly the news only printed that picture, they took plenty more of us all fully dressed, but there again they took enough to choose the most sensational. I don't care what they print, I am not ashamed of Birch, she is the love of my life, they can say what they like, anyone who cares for me knows they only print bullshit and lies. You know I have got to say Dad, I always thought you were smart enough to understand that?" He got redder and waved the paper more.

"She was bloody naked, and she was kissing you, you have a reputation to maintain, do you seriously know how bad that looks?" I stared at him, and shook my head.

"Dad, I wrote a sex and body positive book, and I back up every word in it, because I actually do believe it to be right for young and old people. It does not matter whether her robe came open or not, they were there taking pictures, they would have put one in either way with a sensational headline. That is what they do, they are like vampires sucking the life out of everything." He shook his head, and his eyes opened wide; his face was going even redder.

"You looked like a whore, with her hanging from your neck, she was kissing you, have you any idea of the damage this could cause to this family? Abigail, she was naked for god's sake." I felt the sigh pass my lips; I really could not believe him being this entrenched in today's modern world.

"That is all you care about isn't it, if it had been a naked guy with his dick out, it would have been fine, you would have laughed, and boasted to your friends, look how heterosexual my daughter is? I was not naked, I was dressed, Birch is not your daughter, so why are you so upset? Her parents have not hit the roof, they understand how that paper only prints to sensationalise and ridicule, so why worry about it? It is not like we don't all know, Dad I screw a woman and I absolutely love her, and I am going to screw her tonight, and tomorrow and every day I am with her." His eyes bulged wide, and he exploded.

"HOW DARE YOU USE THAT CRUDE VILE LANGUAGE IN MY HOUSE. YOU WILL SHOW ME RESPECT." God, I think I was starting to hate him even more, I was really getting pissed off with his narrow mind, and village life morality.

"I am twenty six, I am an adult, show me some fucking respect, and I will show you some. Why is it you cannot accept me for who I am, why Dad, I am your daughter, your flesh and blood? I remember a time when you talked of Birch as a daughter, and yet now she is eating my pussy, you are insulted, hell that gives you more in common, doesn't it? I mean come on Dad, you had no problems eating your secretary, did you forget I saw that? I was fourteen, did you care what I thought, I mean, you wasted no time chewing her face off, what else did you eat that day? Seems to me like you, Birch and me all like the same taste." I heard my mum snigger behind me.

He stood there shaking, red in the face and still pointing at me with his paper, I could see his anger getting even stronger.

"It's not normal, women are not supposed to do that to each other, for you or her to do it is shameful and disgusting. I cannot believe you would shame me like this, how could you do that to me?"

I could not believe him; I shook my head, just staring, unable to even comprehend him, this wasn't some other girl, this was me, his own bloody daughter.

"This is not about you Dad, I am old enough now, you have not been responsible for me since my 18th birthday. I did not go out of my way to shame you; I did what you did years ago. I met a person, I had no idea who they really were, and I fell in love with them, honestly, I denied it for years. I refused to accept I could fall in love with a woman, but you know what? I did, and eventually after five years of heart break, and pain, I admitted the facts. I had, I did not intend to, it was not deliberate, it just happened. I would say that is what you did isn't it when you met mum, you fell in love." He shook his head.

"She was a woman and I was a man, there is a difference Abigail, it is not the same. Publicly kissing her is wrong, and you should have known better, it has shamed all of us." My god talk about entrenched views, I felt so angry, but also heart broken.

"I came here Dad, because Birch and me want a real family Christmas, and we want you and mum there, even now, listening to yet more of your bullshit, I still want you at my first Christmas table, because it means something to both Birch and myself. Dad this is who I am, and you know what, it should not matter, because I am your daughter, and yet you called me a whore, that is familiar. I can now see how you worked with Marjorie for so long on the committee, because you are as big a hypocrite as her. You have the nerve to call me, how many office workers have you screwed behind mums back, have you any idea how much that shames her or me, God do you honestly think we did not know, do you even care? What Dad, is that alright because it is you, have you ever cared about the shame you have brought to this house Dad, what are you seriously telling me, that screwing half of your staff is not shameful?" His face went almost purple and he started to shake. He pointed at the door with the paper.

"GET OUT, GET OUT OF MY HOUSE, AND TAKE YOUR LESBIAN SLUT WITH YOU!"

That impacted on me and really hurt, and my eyes teared up, the anger in me just boiled up like milk in a pan. I walked up to him and faced him square on, as he shook with anger. I lifted my hand and SLAP! He rocked back on his heels.

"DON'T YOU DARE EVER CALL HER THAT IN FRONT OF ME AGAIN, SHE WAS NOT A SLUT WHEN YOUR EYES HUNG OUT OF YOUR FACE, WHILST SHE SUNBATHED IN YOUR GARDEN NAKED. YOU FUCKING HYPOCRITE, I AM UTTERLY ASHAMED YOU ARE MY FATHER, EVEN JERRY IS MORE WORTHY THAN YOU, HE MAY BE A PERVERT, BUT HE IS HONEST ENOUGH TO ADMIT IT!"

I turned, and walked out, and headed for the front door. Birch stood staring with tears in her eyes, as she stared at my father, she gave a sob, her voice cracked with her pain, as she breathed in another massive sob.

"I saw you as a father, I felt such love for you, and that was what you were thinking?"

Felicity reached out to her, a look of heartbreak on her face, but Birch stepped out of her way. She burst into tears, and ran past him, and through the door. She ran into my arms and sobbed; I pulled her close, as she sobbed deep bitter sobs into my shoulder, and I hated my dad even more.

"He is hateful, he is just another Madge, do not listen to him Birch. Come on, we shall go home." She looked up at me, her eyes filled with tears and her lip trembled, it was heart breaking to see it.

"I am so sorry Birch; I am ashamed to be his daughter." I pulled her close and guided her through the door.

Felicity stared at him down the kitchen, her cool blue eyes burned with her anger.

"How could you say that, how could you Edwin, this is not some random woman, it is Birch? My god you are hateful, she is the best thing that has ever happened to Abby. You cold vicious nasty evil man, you stand there, pretending to be decent, and honourable, after years of betraying me and your daughter. You have lied and snook about, skulking around, at least Abby has been open and honest about her activities. I am tired of this Edwin, you cast your lascivious stare everywhere except where it belonged, how the hell did you think I felt? I am done with you, I have had enough, if I am so unworthy, then just leave me the hell alone. I want you out of this house Edwin, I want you gone, I hate you for what you just did, and I will never forgive you for it, get out, get out of my sight, you disgust me." Edwin stood frozen staring at her, Felicity lifted her phone and dialled. Chloe picked up.

"Hi Mrs W, sorry Abby nipped out a while back, she left her phone on the kitchen island."

"It's alright Chloe, will you do me a favour, just tell her I will be there for Christmas, Edwin is not coming, so I will be coming alone."

"Yeah, no probs, it's going to be magic Mrs W, we promise."

"I know Chloe, that is why I am coming. I will talk to you soon."

"Yeah, talk soon, kettle is always on if you need one, bye."

Felicity ended the call, and stared at Edwin. "Why are you still here, GET OUT!?"

He blinked, turned, and walked through the door. She leaned on the counter and took a deep breath, finally, after all of these years, she had found the courage to say it. She walked across the kitchen, and bent down, she opened the cupboard, slid back the bag of flower, and with trembling hands, pulled out the bottle of raspberry flavoured gin, she grabbed a glass and poured a good measure.

Taking a big swig, she screwed up her eyes, and shuddered as she breathed out, then refilled the glass, and took a deep breath. Felicity closed her eyes and leant back on the counter, as she gathered her wits about her, it took her a little while before she felt composed enough, and her hands stopped shaking. She lifted her glass and drank the contents, and gave another shudder, then breathed out a long sigh of deep breath. Felicity reached for her phone, and opened her contacts, she pressed the button, and held it to her ear.

"Hatty... I just told him to leave, are you home, I could use a place to talk, until he has gone?"

Hatty stood still in shock, the voice on the other end spoke. "Hatty are you still there?" She nodded.

"I am still here Flick, just shocked, I am always here, you know that." The call ended and Hatty looked at me, as I sat beside Birch.

"Abby she is coming over, she has just asked your dad to leave, she wants to be here until after he has gone."

I cannot deny, I have seen her suffer so much over the years. In the last couple of years, she has spent a lot of time with Birch and me, and I did not blame her, my dad has changed so much in the last few years, he has become colder and nastier. I know I have not seen it all, but considering what he said about Birch, I know I will never forgive him, I pulled Birch closer, and looked at Hatty.

"She has always stayed to make things stable for me Hatty. I am a grown up now, she should leave him, and you should help her, because I will." Birch had stopped crying, she looked at me with red surrounded eyes.

"Deads, I get it I do, but honestly, you should not be a part of this. Look, I know he has hurt you; I know what he said really cut deep, but Deads he is still your dad, do not take sides. If your mum leaves, it is her decision, actually it needs to be only her decision, let her take this moment, let her own it, trust me on this. Support her by all means, but do not get between them, it is up to them now to sort all this out. We should go, we should not be here."

I knew she was right, I looked at Hatty and she nodded in agreement, I gave a sigh.

"Okay we will leave, and you can talk to her, take her out to the studio, so we can sneak out, because if we leave now, she will see us." I took Birch by the hand, and led her upstairs and waited. I pulled her close and hugged her, and spoke quietly to her.

"I am sorry he said those things, you know they are not true right?" Birch pulled me closer into her.

"I know, it just really shocked me to hear him say it, honestly Deads, I never thought he would. Now I think of it, you hurt him with your words, what choice did he have, except to hit you in your weakest point? He is not blind Deads, he sees how much you care, in order to fight back, he targeted me, because you left him no choice. It was the only way he could hurt you; I do not honestly believe he meant it." I shook my head.

"I could have said more, and yet I held back, he taught me that Birch, he should practice what he preaches." I heard my mum come in downstairs, she shouted.

"Hatty are you there?"

"Out here Flick." I waited a few minutes until I heard them

talking in the studio, and then as quiet as mice, we snuck out of the house and walked home.

It is funny when you look back, and suddenly you finally see the truth. For all these years I had refused to accept his coldness, his cruelty, his lack of emotion. I wondered, is this what we do, is it some sort of pattern we all fall into to excuse their behaviour for no other reason than they are a parent? It feels like society puts so much pressure on us to love our parents, and yet they were shitty, they did not live up to the same standard. They could abuse us, but society says, we must love them. Society is screwed up, and I am not having any of it. We walked towards Waterside Lane, and I gave a sigh.

"How many people go into therapy because their parents screwed them up Birch? Think of all the money spent every year by people who find it hard to handle life, because their parents cannot handle it. I mean look at Anthony, he should be with his family for Christmas, but his dad cannot accept him as he is. It is wrong Birch, you know him, he is one of the nicest, kindest and most caring people I have ever met." She smiled and squeezed my hand.

"Anthony will be with family at Christmas Deads, he will be with us, and we love him, and we care about him. You are right though, I have spoken to a lot of young people whose lives have been messed up, for no other reason than their parents were cruel, or cold. It is a sad fact of reality, it is not pleasant, but there are a lot of people out there suffering. Look at Curio Life, all those videos, I watch every one of them as they are posted, how many of those people would be happier, if their parents would just accept them? We are all creatures of nature, and in some things, we have no choice, it is natural." I gave a sigh.

"The world is so screwed up, you and Izzy have your work cut out for you, that is for sure." She gave a chuckle.

"We have a good case load each, there is no doubt about that, I have thought I should bring in more counsellors in the New Year. The biggest problem we have today is most people who qualify in psychology, go on into the advertising industry or social media, very few end up in mental health, there is a real shortage. Sadly, the big business's pay much higher wages, so mental health loses out. I think it is a sad reflection of society, that selling things is a higher priority than a person's emotional health. We see companies spend millions, to sell a product that is deliberately targeted at shaming people into hating themselves, so they buy it. All adverts are is carefully crafted subtle insults to gilt trip people into believing they need a product; I hate the way people are manipulated for profit. That is today's world, it is so wrong Deads, and yet it is allowed." She was so right.

"People like the Shrew Crew reinforce that with their shaming, it is like a vicious circle, just going round and round hurting more and more people. God, it is so wrong, you see that is yet another reason to not bring kids into this world, I mean why subject them to that?" Birch nodded and then frowned.

"What is the Shrew Crew?" I looked at her and giggled.

"It's Chloe's pet name for Madge and her cronies, she got cornered in the post office by Agnes Whetherton, Henrietta Cole Denison, Marion and Bethany, the other day, she said it was like Madge had her own alternative for the Parish Council, she calls them the Shrew Crew." Birch giggled.

"Yeah, I know who you mean now, they do run round frowning and scowling a lot with Madge. Shrew Crew, I really like that, I think it fits perfectly."

We walked through the gates, up the drive, and in through the doors, we were home and safe, and back in the madness, were from the library, there was a debate in progress.

"Oh, darlings it has to be coordinated, I mean, red and gold, or blue and silver. Oh dear, Chloe my dear girl you are hopeless, one does not just splash colour everywhere, my god, I thought you were an artist, think of the composition, it has to reflect the whole feel of the house?" Chloe gave a frustrated sigh.

"Anthony this whole fucking house is about colour, look at our robes, or the chairs, we all have different colours, and our tree should reflect that. Honestly we are not dressing hair, we are dressing a tree, I say we go big bright and bold." Anthony gave a gasp.

"Oh... There is simply no winning with you, Chloe, darling, I hate to point out the obvious, it's called dressing a tree... Dressing... You have forgotten how to; it's been so long since you wore clothing. My God girl, if we used you as the influence, we would put nothing on it, the poor thing would stand there green and nude."

I leaned in and saw them all sat around the computer, Deb's looked up and rolled her eyes.

"Tree dressing, not as easy as you would have thought." Edwina sat with her head phones on typing, and ignoring them all. I grabbed Birch's hand, and walked to the kitchen.

"You know, they are busy, and will be for some time... In the States, I did a lot of remembering. Do you remember that day when we were just moving in?"

We walked into the kitchen, I turned to face her, and slipped my hands down to her jean's buttons, she looked down, and frowned.

"Didn't you say something about sex on a table?"

I pushed her back slowly up the kitchen until she bumped into it, she gave a big smile, as her jeans slipped to the floor. I pulled up my top, and tossed it onto the floor. She gave a giggle.

"I do believe we said something about having the conversation again later." I pulled her top up over her head, and I nodded.

"Yeah, I think it is time we spoke about it again." She gave a giggle and then breathed in quickly.

"Oh Deads." She lifted herself up and slid back onto its cool surface, I climbed up.

"Hmm, where were we... As I remember...?"

"Oh Deads... OH GOD... OOH SWEETIE!"

Chapter 4

Lights.

Birch leaned over the bed, and kissed me softly, I opened my eyes and gave a happy little moan, as I kissed her back. Her eyes were bright and happy, as she leaned back with a huge smile.

"I am off to work Sweetie. Anthony has a free day, and he is going into the village to meet the electricians. Edwina is still in bed, and Chloe is very much wide awake and getting very festive, so be warned."

She leaned in and kissed me again, I lifted my arm, and held her in place, and kissed her softly and slowly back, she gave a soft moan. She lifted her head back, and bit her lip.

"I do wish you would not do that; I am still turned on from the kitchen. Oh, Deads, I want to stay here now." I giggled.

"I just want to remind you what is waiting at home for you." She took a deep breath.

"Oh, you dark little beastie, that is so unfair, I will be wet all day now." I raised my eye brows, and smiled.

"Good, you will be ripe when you get home." She smiled, and shook her head.

"You play way too dirty at times. Okay I have to go, there is a coffee there for you." She slipped off the bed, walked to my chair and picked up her brief case, she looked back and bit her lip.

"You can be a real meanie at times Miss Watson." I gave a happy sigh.

"I am touching myself too." She watched as the duvet moved; I gave a soft moan.

"Stop it, oh, you are so unfair, I hate working." She looked at her watch. "I have a session at eleven." I winked.

"Oh god... Oh... Oh Birch I am so wet, and it's only eight thirty... OH!" She dropped her case, and slipped off her jacket.

"You bitch, I hate you, but I love you." I giggled as she undid her blouse, I threw back the covers, and I showed my two fingers buried inside me, I moved them and gasped.

"Oh God!" Her pants hit the floor, and she ran over, and jumped on me with a squeal.

"Okay you dark little beastie, you win." I smiled and pulled her close, feeling her soft warm body against mine.

"Hmm, yummy!" She attacked me with passion.

Deb's, looked at her watch. "Where is Birch, I thought she was leaving?"

"OH DEADS.... OH GOD!" Chloe looked up at the ceiling and giggled.

"She is probably going to be a little bit longer." Deb's, rolled her eyes.

"Christ, we spent years wishing they would shag, and now... Now I am wishing they would stop." Chloe sniggered.

"You are one to talk.... OH JIMMY!" She giggled.

"It's not that bad." Chloe stared at her, and she smiled. "Well okay maybe a little."

It was a little while before Birch had finished her quick shower, got dressed and was once again ready to leave, she came up to the bed where I lay naked and sweating, and smiling, she shook her head, and grinned.

"You are a wicked girl Deads, but I kind of like that about you." I winked.

"I could go again." She stepped back and wagged her finger.

"NO... Oh no, no, no." She chuckled. "I have definitely got to go; I have a client." I pulled my lip down.

"Not for another hour." She stepped back.

"Sweetie, I have to go, behave now." I sat up, and she giggled, and stepped back. "Deads I mean it, I have to go to work." I jumped forward, and she squealed, turned and ran for the door.

Chloe came down the hall from the kitchen, as Birch came squealing down the stairs at high speed, I stood at the top laughing, as she made the door, she looked back, looking giddy.

"I will see you later."

I jumped onto the top step, she looked panicked, screamed, grabbed the door, yanked it open, and ran screaming through it, I started to laugh, Chloe looked at me and smiled.

“I love seeing you two so happy.” She pointed. “You are dripping by the way; fuck she is good.” I looked down, and saw the shiny on my legs, and shook my head.
“No, I think that is hers.” Chloe gave a giggle, and headed into the library.

I needed to work, Shoots of Summer was still a rough draft, and I still had half of my fourth book on my vampire tale to finish. I headed back to my room, I was not in the mood, I saw the wrinkled sheets on the bed, and walked over to straighten them, I was knackered, I flopped down on the pillows, and breathed in her scent, I loved my life.

Ker chunk... Ker chunk... Ker chunk, Ker chunk, Ker chunk, Ker chunk. I opened my eyes, outside my window was a ladder, a pair of legs, and a very neatly shaved vagina, I blinked and rubbed my eyes, I saw the blotches of paint. I sat up, still feeling groggy. Ker chunk... Ker chunk... Ker chunk.
“Chloe what the hell?” The ladder moved, and more of her appeared, she leaned over.
“Sorry, did I wake you, I was trying not to. I am decorating the house, the lights we ordered have come, and I thought I would get a move on. God Abby, I love this sort of stuff.” I smiled, I was awake, so I figured I would help her.
I got out of bed, pulled on my thick robe, and walked over to the other patio window, and slipped through onto the balcony, Chloe had actually done more than I realised. She was up the ladder using a shot gun stapler to pin the lights in place. I looked at the four tall apex that rose up above all the windows, she had done three.
“Chloe how the hell did you get up there, those apexes are a bit bloody high?” She looked down from her ladder.
“I got on the roof.” Okay, she was freaking me out now.
“How?” She clicked another light strand into place. Ker Chunk! And then looked down.
“I went into the attic, and out through the side window, and onto the roof tiles, then just walked across.” I frowned not really understanding.
“We have an attic?” She nodded. Ker Chunk!

"Where?" She stopped and looked down at me.

"Fuck Abby this is your house, you have owned it for two years, have you even actually explored it? I went up the first day we were here, I was hoping it was floored, but only half of it was done, I thought it would make a cool darkroom for photos and stuff. I mean it's a bit dusty, but with some work, we could do a decent enough job." I did not have a clue.

"Show me." She gave a sigh, and came down the ladder.

"You know what, you and Birch are the only people I know who would buy a house and not explore, because you were too busy shagging, and this is me telling you."

I followed her out of the bedroom to the stairs. The stairs led down four steps from both sides of the upstairs hall, then met on a landing, from which the central stairs go down to the entrance hall. The two long halls that run from the door to the kitchen, have a landing above them, and it is on those landings that there are doors to two of the front bedrooms.

I have never really walked down them, as they are just guest rooms. On the left side I noticed another door near the large windows, Chloe walked down and opened it, revealing a small staircase that went up four steps and then turned, and went right up into the attic space, I had never even realised.

"You know, I always thought this was just a linen cupboard, I never realised it was stairs?"

I followed her up into what was a high filthy room, she clicked the light on. I looked round in wonder, it was massive, and at both ends there were sash windows. One was open, she pointed at it.

"I climbed out of that one onto the roof, and then just walked over to the edge to staple the lights on." I felt an adventure arriving, she gripped my arm.

"Whoa hold the rush, look."

She pointed at the floor. There was an eight foot wide strip, which ran to the window, but apart from that and the large square we were stood on, the rest was joists.

"Stay on the boards or you will fall through okay, and it is a long drop if you are over the stairs."

We walked up to the window and Chloe climbed out, I poked

my head through, she was stood on a steep side that sloped right to the edge of the side of the house, and it was a bloody long way down. I felt my stomach twist and my head swirled, and pulled my head back.

"Screw this, I am not that curious anymore." Chloe looked back at me and smiled.

"You are scared, oh wow you pussy, come on it's fine, in bare feet you have great grip." I shook my head.

"You are frigging mental you know that?"

I leaned out; it was a bloody steep slope to the edge. Chloe leaned on the side of the window, and pointed, round what was the small bay window section I was stood in.

"Look it goes up to the main roof, and that is pretty easy, I suppose this is the scariest bit, but once you are up there it's fine." I shook my head and my stomach lurched again.

"Yeah great, you can bugger off, I want to live." She shrugged.

"It's your loss, you can see for miles."

I was happy, I had no need to look out across the village. I decided to have a look on the inside, where the floors were even, and not sloping into the abyss of oblivion and death.

There was not a huge amount to see, it was really dusty, I saw a pile of something, and walked down to the other end of the house, there were some old wooden crates, some old bedding, a few plastic bags, but little else, I turned and walked back to the stairs as Chloe came in through the window.

"If I am honest Chloe, I think you have guts, I really could not go out there. I am sorry, ladders I think I can do, but roof walking, I would panic and fall the hell off." She shrugged.

"It's okay, I have done most of it now, the front is done and we just have the two big trees in the front to do, I was thinking Anthony could help with those. I don't like prickly trees."

I closed the window, and we came back down, and I helped with the ladder, well I held it, and she climbed up it, and fixed the lights on. We did over Birch's balcony, and then Deb's balcony, I had to keep a wary eye open, Chloe spotted Phileas sat on the bed. I kept checking, just to make sure he was still there.

It was cold, even with my robe on I was shivering, I looked up at her naked bum.

"Are you not cold, I am freezing?" She looked down and shook her head.

"Not really, but I have been pretty busy, so I suppose that is keeping me warm." I felt another huge shiver run down my spine and shivered again, she giggled.

We were finally done, and went down to the kitchen for drinks and to wait for Anthony. He arrived after several gin and lemons, we grinned happily at him.

Chloe grabbed the boxes of lights and the ladder, she put on her dungarees, and I found Birch's, they were a little baggy, but they smelt of her, so I slipped them on. I pulled a top and a thick jumper on, and then I joined them in the front garden. Chloe had the ladder up against the tree, and was feeding the long wire of lights up to Anthony, who was looking really shaky, and unsteady, I looked up to watch.

"Wow you have a really cute bum Anthony." He looked back, panicked as he wobbled, and grabbed the ladder.

"Oh, Abby darling, please, don't distract me, by pointing out my finer points." Chloe pointed.

"We need them higher Anthony, if we don't do the top, it will look fucked up." He looked up.

"Chloe, are you sure this is safe?" She stared up at the tree.

"Those branches are thicker than the ladder steps, just grab on to it and climb on, it is not that hard." He looked up nervously, and swallowed hard.

I will not deny, it was brave, I would have shit myself and said no. He reached up, and grabbed a branch, and then nervously lifted his leg. Chloe watched.

"Yeah, that one, just a bit higher, and you will reach the top, just drape the lights on." He looked up; I could see he was sweating.

"Just so you know darling, I may have the long light hair and reasonably good pecks, but I am not ruddy Tarzan." He stretched up, and the tree moved, he squealed. "Oh! Oh! It's bending."

The tree leaned slightly forward, and he clasped his knees onto it, and held on for dear life. It rocked back as he moved, and swung the other way, I tried, honestly, I did, but it looked like he was screwing the tree, and I could not hold back the giggle, it swung again. Chloe watched.

"Oh! Oh! Oh! OH! OOH!"

"What the fuck are you doing Anthony, decorate it, don't fuck it?" I sniggered. He looked down and squealed, as he swung round at the top of the tree.

"It's wriggling around, it's wriggling around Chloe, you have to stop it, Oh, oh, oh, oh." She looked at me strangely.

"What is he talking about, is his willy wriggling?"

"I think he means the tree is swaying."

She understood, she looked up as the tree swayed under his weight, he came backwards and then swung sideways and then forwards, he looked like he was on a bucking bronco.

"Anthony, stop riding it, and just wrap the lights round." He shook his head.

"I cannot let go, oh, I am not letting go, oh, save me Chloe, oh, oh, oh, MOTHER!"

Chloe looked at me, and rolled her eyes, she gripped the ladder and quickly ran up. I watched nervously; it did look a little comical as he swung about up there, whilst the top of the tree swayed. Chloe climbed up behind him. She hung on with her right hand, and then slipped her left round his waist.

"Anthony for god's sake, stop pissing around and let go, or we will be up here all night."

He clung to the tree, she pulled, he looked back looking panicked, Chloe sighed. Suddenly he swung round and grabbed onto her, she wobbled, and I held out my hands, and then realised.

"Shit, if they fall, I am legging it, not catching, or getting squashed by them."

Anthony had his arms round Chloe's neck, and his legs wrapped round her waist, and crossed behind her, it looked like he was trying to bang her up the tree, I started to giggle. He had his eyes closed tight, Chloe slid her leg down the trunk, feeling for a branch, she checked her footing, and then clinging to the trunk, she slowly descended towards the ladder.

"Fuck Anthony, it is usually me sat like this in the guy's lap."

Birch walked in through the gates, and looked up the tree, and then at me. "What are they doin?" I giggled.

"Anthony ran out of courage; Chloe is saving him."

Chloe finally found the ladder, and carefully stepped on. Anthony clung to her, as Birch watched on, she looked at me with a strange look, I frowned, she looked back.

“Has Anthony got a hard on?” Chloe stopped on the ladder, and looked down.

“Is that what that is?” She looked at his groin. “Holy fuck Anthony, am I turning you on?” He opened his eyes and looked horrified.

“Oh my god NOOO!” Chloe looked at him.

“Your lump is rubbing my muzzle, and it’s growing, holy fuck have I overridden your gayness?” He looked horrified.

“Chloe darling do not flatter yourself, I am scared, and when I get scared, I get hard.” Birch sniggered and gave an evil smile.

“I am so going to scare him as often as I can now, and measure the results.” I sniggered.

Chloe made her way down to the bottom, and Anthony flopped to his knees and pushed his head on the floor, he looked like he was praying, I giggled at him as he gasped in air to calm down. Maybe it is just me, but I was curious.

“If you are scared of heights Anthony, why did you go up?” He looked up at me, and gave a gasp.

“I did not know I was, until I got up there.” It made sense, yep, I could live with that, I turned to Birch, she was gone, I looked around for her.

“Hi Sweetie... Hold on, are those my dungarees?” I looked up and saw her at the top of the tree wrapping the lights on.

“Wow Birch, you have a killer ass.” She smiled.

“Why thank you... Hang on, don’t change the subject.” I smiled.

“If you want them, come pull em off me.” She giggled.

“Oh, I will, just you wait my dark little beastie, once we have done these, you are coming out of them.” I chuckled.

“I am making a brew, who is up for one?” I shivered; November was not my month.

I left them to it and made coffee, as Anthony and Birch helped Chloe run the long leads into a wall mounted waterproof box just outside the porch, ready to light up.

Finally, they all came in happy; the lighting was done ready, and darkness was already coming down, all we had to do was wait for Deb’s coming back home, and then we planned the lighting up ceremony. A text from Deb’s announced she would be home soon, so we decided to cook and eat first, to let it get really dark.

With Chloe and Birch in the kitchen, food came fast, and as Deb's arrived home, we all sat down to eat. I am telling you, the greatest thing about living in this house, has to be the cooking. Two years with Chloe, Edwina, and Birch as teachers, and Deb's and me had even improved, every meal time was a good experience, and with the great company, because we had grown together like sisters, and a brother, it made each day wonderful.

I think if anyone ever asks me, what I have gained most from living in this house, I think I would instantly say, these wonderful people. Anthony is like a brother, and Chloe, Edwina and Deb's, they are my sisters, I feel a bond with these people that is unbreakable.

I know them like the back of my hand, I know their loves and lives, their kinks, and their inner most secrets, and I will stand and fight to protect all of them, because I love them with all my heart.

Once we had eaten, we all mucked in with the washing up, drying and the putting away of everything, is it weird that everyone expects us to be messy? Even I have to admit, the house has always been a lot cleaner than I ever thought it would be, well, except for Birch's room, and maybe mine.

Finally, we all trooped outside, which for half of us meant clothes, and as Chloe prepared, we stood across the road, and waited for the big light up. She shouted over the wall.

"ARE YOU READY?" We all yelled back.

"LIGHT THEM UP!" And poof, on they came, wow it was blinding, I looked at everyone.

"Holy shit how many lights have we used?" Birch shrugged, with a huge smile on her face, and her eyes sparkling as she looked at them.

"Isn't it pretty, it is so colourful, I really love it guys." Debs was tilting her head from side to side, I looked at her, she turned to me.

"Is it just me, or do those sets of white lights, round the windows, all look dick shaped?"

I turned and looked, the lights came up the sides of the downstairs window, up the sides of the upstairs windows, and then went out sideways before rising up in a bell shape, on the front of the large apex. Oh my god she was right, there were four huge penis shapes drawn in lights on the wall in white, whereas everything else was in coloured lights, Birch started to giggle.

"I love it, we have Christmas penis's care of Chloe, only she would think of it. Wow guys she is so lovely, it is perfect, we have our whore house, and plenty of dick." Chloe came out with a huge smile on her face and walked across the road to stand beside us. I giggled.

"Nice Chloe, nice touch, especially the dicks." She gave a smile.

"I figured it is us, and if I am honest, I am going to spend the whole of Christmas screwing some." Deb's, rolled her eyes.

"So same as normal then Chloe?" We all started to laugh, and then decided to go look at the back.

I have to say, Chloe did good, not only was the roof covered, she also did the balconies, the kitchen doors, and the beach house, it was bright to say the least, Birch looked at her.

"Sweetie, I think it is beautiful, although it's winter, I am not sure we will be out here much." Chloe shrugged.

"If it snows, I will be, I will be making snowmen." Birch jumped up and clapped her hands, and her eyes exploded with sparkles.

"DO WE GET SNOW HERE, I LOVE SNOW?" I gave a shudder, I frigging hate the white stuff.

The good thing about Wotton Dursley is that it does not often snow around here, and to be honest, I was really hoping it did not. I cannot deny, I like warmth, I like comfort, I adore the fact we can afford to turn the heating up, so we can live naked.

Underfloor heating as far as I am concerned is man's greatest invention, if you have not had that joy, your life is not worth living. Nothing is better than slipping out of bed to feel the heat in your feet, or to lie back on a deep fluffy carpet, that is warm and snug, it is luxury, and I really do consider myself spoiled rotten.

Talk of snow was unsettling, Birch was off telling stories of Uppermill and the deep drifts on the moors, and it made me shudder. The village had a whole range of things prepared for Christmas, and because mum, Edwina and Anthony had played a huge role in organising them, I wanted to be there to support them, oh god, please do not let it snow.

We walked back to the house, everyone was excited and happy, in a way this was the start of our Christmas, our next big project would be the tree, and decorating the hall. Deb's, had talked to Birch, and it looked like they were going to do it, I headed in through the doors.

Anthony followed me in as I headed for the drinks, he stood at my side as I poured and topped up the glasses. His voice was low.

"Abby... I hate saying it, but I really, really hate snow. I don't want it to snow, I have too much to do, the lights go on next weekend, and I don't want to stand in a blizzard to do it." I turned and leaned on the island to face him.

"I get you Anthony, I frigging hate it too, it's cold, wet, and miserable. I mean, I like sitting inside nice and warm, watching it, but if I can, I avoid it. Just so you know, if it snows, you won't be able to drag me out of the house." He gave a sigh.

"Oh please Abby, don't say that, I want you to do the big switch on, I was going to ask you, you know you are famous now, people will come to see you." I shuddered.

"How do you mean switch on?" He looked at me.

"I asked Birch, she said you would love it, we will have a little stage, you say a few words, and then press a button, and they all come on. Oh god have I done this wrong, they have printed the posters, and everything?"

Talk about boxed in and caught, I should have known it, whenever Birch is involved, I end up shafted. Anthony looked really nervous, and I knew, there was no backing out, I gave a long sigh.

"Okay I will do it; how long do I have to talk for?" He gave a big smile, and pulled me into a hug.

"Oh, Abby darling, thank you, it means the world to me."

I saw Birch stood by the door, her eyes were sparkling, and she was smiling, I looked at her, and she knew.

"You owe me so many orgasms for this." Anthony jumped back.

"Excuse me, oh Abby darling, live in vain, I am sorry, but if that's what you want, I am most definitely not your man." I looked at him.

"Seriously Anthony, I was talking to her." He turned around, and saw her leaning on the door, she waved.

“Hi Sweetie.” Anthony gave a huge sigh of relief; I noted the bulge in his jeans.

“Wow, you were that scared?” He looked down.

“Oh god... You know, I hate Chloe at times.” Birch sniggered.

“You got him at least five inches frightened Deads.” I started to chuckle.

Chapter 5

Tree Spirit.

"Chloe, are you ready yet? I mean it, if you are shagging Percy again, I am going to be really pissed off."

It was Thursday, I spent all day yesterday with mum talking, she had stayed a couple of days with Hatty. She was back and constantly apologising, to which I told her, it was not her place to do it. The way I saw it, he had two choices, apologise to Birch, or stay the hell out of my life, he chose wrong. She is doing good, having got over the initial shock of actually standing up to him, she was actually feeling very happy. I was so proud of her, she has suffered for a long time, and I felt it was now time to let her hair down a little, and enjoy life on her own terms, ooh, that sounds familiar.

Today we had to head into the village, Edwina was already at the bookshop, Birch had a free afternoon, and Deb's had found a place not far from Millington, near the lake we used to visit, ten miles out from the other side of Oxendale.

We could walk around a big place, and pick out our own Christmas tree, which we all loved the idea of, although this was a group thing, and we all had to like it to buy it. I will not deny, after watching the debate on how the tree was to be decorated, I was feeling a little uncertain as to if we would all agree on one. Last night we had all helped fix a new roof rack to Petal, which Birch had ordered under the guise of using it for the tree, which let's be honest, is bullshit, she is obsessed with these vehicles and wants all the accessories for it. With Denise looking after the bookshop, we were going to find our Christmas centrepiece, well I hoped so, I had to coax Chloe out of her room first.

The decoration war had ended, or at least there was a rough deal in place, when we had a house meet, and Chloe told us how in her house, every year, each person bought something they liked to hang on the tree. It blew away any concept of coordinated colour, but it made every single item on the tree a precious personal memory, and everyone instantly agreed. Well, I say everyone, I was not completely convinced Anthony is on board, he does have a flare for decoration. I finally pulled up outside the practice, jumped out, and walked towards Sweetie's Retreat, Chloe headed next door to get Edwina and Deb's.

I walked in and Alex smiled, Gill gave a wave, Alex pointed behind her. "Go on through, she is in the office."

The waiting room was pretty full, I saw Birch through the office window talking to Izzy, and held back just inside the doorway to reception. Birch looked up and I waved, she gave a big smile, and then waved back. I turned and looked back into the waiting room; this place certainly attracted some strange types.

Pat came down the stairs talking to a man she named Bobby, she was chatting away. "Now remember Bobby, we have worked on it, and you are doing well, but being conscious of it is key."

He nodded and looked at me, I shuddered, he had thin hair scraped over his head, big glasses, and a long coat. Honestly, if he turned out to be a flasher, I would not be surprised, if there was a type that exposes themselves, this had to be him. He stared at me all the way down the stairs. Yep, I was completely freaked out, and I got goosebumps everywhere.

They reached the bottom of the stairs, and I suddenly felt very nervous, he had to pass me to leave. Pat smiled, and as he walked past me, he stopped leaned in, and took a long deep intake of breath. Okay I was freaking the hell out, why the hell was he smelling me?

He took the smell, sniff whatever the freaky frig he was doing in, and then turned and looked right through the window at Birch. Cold shivers ran down my back, he smiled what I saw, as a sick and twisted smile, Pat looked at him.

"Bobby, this is exactly what I mean, you have to be aware of it, to stop doing it." He put his head down and walked past the gate, I breathed a sigh of relief, Pat smiled.

"See you next Thursday." He headed for the door, Pat looked at me, and lowered her voice.

"He is harmless, he has a strange if not very keen sense of smell, he recognises any woman by sniffing her, he says he can smell their vagina odour, and can identify any woman from their scent, it's really fascinating. He used to go down on his knees, which was problematic, but he has come a long way in the last year."

She headed for the break room, as I stood there and smiled, whilst my inner voice in my head screamed, holy shit did he smell Birch on me, okay, I was really freaking out now.

There were about ten people sat in the waiting room, all of them were dithering rapidly. I could hear their feet vibrating on the floor, and some of them were humming, it was more messed up than I was ready to cope with especially after Bobby.

I don't want to be impolite, but they were, how can I say this, larger than most of us, and less attractive than Milton and Nigel. As I watched, I found myself dithering my own legs, I realised, panicked, and pressed my feet firmly into the floor, whatever they had, I hoped to hell it was not catching.

That thought alone unsettled me, actually scratch that, they freaked the shit out of me. My mind became very aware of locking my legs, as I watched them all vibrate in unison. I focused my mind, but it was really hard, I shit myself, when I almost started to hum along with them. Izzy came out of the office talking with Birch, and nodding, they split, Birch walked up with a smile.

"Hi Sweetie, just let me get my coat, I won't be a second."

She ran off up the stairs, God, her ass looked great in black pants. Izzy winked as she walked past into the reception area. She grabbed a file, and looked at the whole room.

"Okay group session, this way."

Every one of the dithering, humming, patients got up, and looked instantly excited, as they headed to the gates, like a vibrating herd of excited buffalo, and came through. I stepped back, some of this lot were big, and then suddenly it hit me, holy shit it was Thursday! Birch appeared at the top of the stairs, pulling on her coat, she came down smiling, and looked at the group heading into the Meeting Room, with Izzy, and I shuddered. Birch leaned in and kissed me.

"Hi Sweetie." I smiled, and looked at her seriously.

"That's them isn't it, Deb's worst nightmare, that is the group, it's Thursday?" Birch turned to see the last ones squeezing in through the doorway.

"What, the masturbation group?" I heard Alex snigger, I shuddered.
"Holy shit, no wonder they wank, no one is ever going to touch that." Alex sniggered again; Birch looked at me.
"Deads, they are lonely, don't be cruel."
A low set of moans came from the bottom of the corridor, I shuddered, and went ice cold, my right leg started to dither.
"Okay that is really frigging unsettling, can we please go now, I am suddenly terrified of hearing moans?" Birch gave a giggle, and we turned to walk out, Alex had a fixed smirk on her face, I leaned in to her and whispered.
"They are off, I am legging it before the climax." She put her head down, and snorted, Birch shook her head.
"You two are terrible." Gill gave a giggle.

We jumped in Petal, the Shrew Crew were out and scowling at us as usual, I turned the key, as Deb's leaned over, I looked at her, and smiled, she looked suspicious.
"What are you up to?" Birch looked at me, and she knew exactly where I was going, she started to giggle.
"Deb's it's Thursday, do you know who I just met?" She slipped back into the back of Petal, as her face turned pale, looking terrified.
"Do not even say it Abby, I mean it, it's horrible, some weeks you can hear it through the wall, it freaks Denise out."
Birch gave a snort and started to laugh, I turned round, and Chloe and Edwina were looking at me puzzled, Deb's narrowed her eyes at me.
"I mean it... Oh please don't Abby, don't let her know, I beg you." Chloe stared at me.
"What... What am I missing?" Birch turned and smiled.
"It's nothing Sweetie, it is just Izzy's group session, nothing much." I giggled; I loved the tact. I drove off from the curb.
"Yeah Chloe, you would not be interested, they just sit round talking and masturbating." Deb's, squealed.
"ABBY?" Chloe looked stunned, as she looked back through the rear window, and back down the street.
"Fuck Birch, you have a masturbation club, holy fuck why didn't

you tell me... Can I come?" I laughed, as Deb's squealed.

"See... See what you have done, is it not bad enough with her headboard, I do not want to hear her frigging off next door at work too?"

Birch gave a loud cackle of a laugh, and the fun began, this was the start of what would be our best Christmas ever, our first real Curio Christmas.

We decided on route to go into Oxendale first, we had nothing, so we could buy baubles and tinsel, and other decorations, then head for the tree farm, and that was my biggest mistake ever, think about it, what is Christmas?

Christmas is about shiny, and cuddly, need I say more, baubles and tinsel, and both Birch and Deb's are wet, and buying like overly confident stockbrokers. Fluffy Christmas teddies, and suddenly, Chloe is a huge pile of mush that loves and hugs everything, and I had brought them into a seasonal shop dedicated to Christmas. My only sanity was Edwina, the eldest, and most stable one amongst us.

Edwina is calm, easy going, relaxed, and oh shit, computerised sound to light units, for outdoor lights, and now she is exploding with joy, fondling the boxes and talking so fast I need an interpreter. I panicked as I looked round trying to keep tabs on them all.

I could not win, Birch was running round, going bonkers wrapping herself in tinsel, hanging baubles from her ears, and picking up bright shiny baubles, with whoops and cheers. She gaped with sparkling eyes and bursts of joy and excitement, and everyone is looking at me like I am the carer for the special needs people. Actually, scratch that, I bloody am!

I was sure Chloe was trying to do something perverted with a teddy, so I walked quickly away in pursuit of Birch, who had so much tinsel wrapped round her, she was starting to look like a gay version of the frost fairy.

They spent hundreds of pounds, I bought one bauble, it was in the sales rack left over from Halloween, and it had a skeleton on it. Back in Petal with it half full of bags, I had wondered whether or not, I needed the roof rack for the baubles? We hit the road, and headed for the tree farm, which was in the back of beyond, and comprised a bloody huge hill filled with trees, this was a tree farm? Nope, it was a frigging big mountainside forest.

We parked up next a wooden cabin, come office, and were met with a merry old chap called Phil, Deb's took the lead as she had spoken to him on the phone. He knew what she wanted, and had an idea, of where we would find the tree. We were joined by Gordon, a six foot tall, well built guy with a chainsaw. Edwina and Chloe, instantly flanked him, I gave a titter.

"Holy shit, one smell of a new penis, and they are around it like bees to a honey pot."

We trudged up the side of the hill looking at tall trees. Deb's, had the exact size and knew what we needed, and knowing her as well as I did, I left her too it. Birch was in the woods wrapped in tinsel and wearing a huge smile, she loved trees, and so for her this was less of a shopping trip, and more of a return to nature. I think had it been warmer, she probably would have stripped on the spot, and ran naked through the woodland, dancing and singing.

Actually, I am not that convinced she won't, and was glad to know that the influence of her friend Raven Moon, had not been great enough, to make her want to strip, and rub her private bits all over the trees. Although, she has been known to snap, and go all into the wilds on me occasionally, so I watched her carefully. She was all smiles and fairy dancing at the moment, so for now I was safe.

It took forever, and was getting dark, when Deb's finally committed to a tree, I felt like we had walked for miles, as my calves screamed at me. I leaned back on the trunk of a tree, sweating like mad, and gasping for air, Christ, I need to get fit. Birch smiled as she pointed to the tree. She looked so thrilled and filled with love for it. Her eyes were huge and bright, her long white hair flowing from under her hat, lifting softly off her shoulders in the breeze. She turned with the softest smile, a look of complete love on her face.

"Deads, look, it is so beautiful, I really love it, do you?"

I had to smile, she was staring at the green bushy tree with absolute love, like it was the most sacred tree on the planet, she stroked its foliage, and gave a happy little smile.

"Oh Sweetie, it's so soft and lovely, I could sit forever just being one with it."

I stood up straight, and took a long breath in, my lungs were relaxing, and not quite as strained as they had been. She came over towards me, and I slipped my arms round her, and leaned on her shoulder.

"I really love it; I think it is perfect. Let's hope all the others agree." She turned her head. and her green eyes shone with happiness.

"It's perfect, isn't it?" I leaned in and kissed her, it was, she was right.

There was finally all around agreement, this was going to be our Curio family Christmas tree. Phil measured it with a tall cane, that had tape rings on it, and gave a nod, and so Gordon stepped up, and suddenly reality kicked in.

My beautiful nature loving, spiritual, Pagan girlfriend gripped my arm, like a pterodactyl, squealed out in shock, and fell apart on the spot, as Gordon fired up the chainsaw, and with a flick, powered into the tree, and it fell, and Birch stared with absolute horror, and burst into gushing tears.

"WE MURDERED IT!"

She looked away and wept on my shoulder, Chloe who admittedly loves Christmas, and all things Christmas sparkles and fluffy stared at her.

"What the fuck did you think we would do, decorate it here, and all sit round it for dinner freezing our tits off?"

Birch turned with eyes full of tears, looked at Gordon with hate, then looked at the tree, and with a very sorrowful voice said.

"I am so, so desperately sorry," to it.

Chloe was now convinced she was completely mental. Gordon spun it around on the floor, and walked ahead, dragging it back down the hill. Birch gave a low squeal, let go of me, and skipped behind him, sobbing and asked him to.

"Don't hurt it." Debs shrugged, and her usual soft caring demeaner, was replaced with the Christmas gremlin.

"It's fucking dead already, get the fuck over it Birch." The Christmas spirit is so touching at times, it just warms the cockles of the heart?

At the bottom of the hill, Gordon put the tree through a netting machine, and whilst he did that, Old Phil took the weeping Birch by the hand, and led her across the field, he pointed.

"Look love, you see that hill over there, well last year we cut five thousand trees off it, but we planted ten thousand back. I love how you love these trees, but the truth is, those over there take more filth out of the air than the big ones do. You see, your lovely tree will make your house beautiful, but the ones I replace it with, will make the world nicer, and cleaner." Birch gave a sniffle, and dried her eyes and smiled, she gave a nod.

"I like the idea of that." He nodded.

"Don't you worry, we won't cut the whole hill, we leave some big ones in, just to look after the small ones, and that is how it should be, it's the natural way, and good woodland management. It is never a nice task, but sometimes, you have to cut out the old and the dead, to give the space for the young to grow, and let's be honest, one of them is a hell of a lot better for the world, than plastic." She smiled; he was right.

After much grunting and gasping, as Chloe and Edwina played helpless females, Gordon came over and lifted the tree up onto the roof rack, while they smiled and batted their eyes. Poor sod, he had no idea what predators he was dealing with, that look he saw in their eyes was not devotion, they were looking at him, like a starving man would look through a window at a freshly roasted side of beef.

The tree was strapped to the roof, and as darkness descended completely, and shivering, I drove back to Wotton, and home. Chloe had bought some super weird metal stand with clamps, that could be filled with water, and once off the roof of Petal, which involved almost giving Deb's and early orgasm, when she bent over as we lifted, we all staggered in with our tree.

Furniture was rearranged, to ensure maximum access, and the tree was then placed in the front centre of the large window, and the net cut off. It sprang open slapping us all in the face with a pine flavoured kiss, and we spent the next two minutes spitting and wiping our tongues round the inside of our mouth. It was eight and a half feet high, and thick and bushy.

Chloe crawled under and showed Birch how to fill the stand with water, to keep the tree alive, rather like a huge cut flower, and Birch swore it would never run dry. I did a quick hoover, because by now we were all sweaty, and so therefore barefoot and naked. The dressing of the tree commenced, with Chloe, Deb's and Edwina leading the way with lights first, followed by baubles, and then Birch was given the sole task of tinsel to finish the tree off.

Anthony arrived home with a bag full of baubles, he had nipped out in his lunch hour, and had also ordered a load online, and he added his decorations. With one last clean up, because even with fir, needles get snapped off, the mission was complete, and we all sat in a long row on the sofa, and waited for Deb's to flick the switch. The room was in darkness, as I held Birch's hand, all of this was new to her, even if a little traumatic. The lights came on, and whilst everyone gasped and cheered with delight, I watched her face.

The coloured lights, and the shiny baubles, cast light all over her soft white skin, her eyes twinkled with delight, and she took a small sharp intake of breath. She was mesmerised, and looked so incredibly beautiful, and there it was. Even after all these years of knowing her, that childlike innocence that was so natural in her, which just shone right out of her. I smiled as she sat staring, not moving. I leaned in, and spoke quietly.

"Do you like it?"

Her eyes did not move, she gave a soft smile, and her voice was so soft and quiet, and filled with innocence.

"Deads, it is so beautiful, I want to cry." I kissed her cheek.

"Happy first Christmas ever." I picked up my phone, and sent a text, I had another small secret plan on the go.

It was a strange thing to know someone had never actually had a Christmas tree of their own. They say Christmas is for children, and I disagree. I mean, firstly if you could see Debs, Chloe and Anthony at the moment, you would see it is not. Looking at Birch, I could see the child come out of her, the tree switched on, and in that instant, the child within her rose to the surface, and shone out of her brightly. I left her to sit and admire the tree, and after a few quiet words with Edwina, I went to the kitchen to prepare drinks.

Birch disappeared, and then returned to the living room with a rolled up black mat, she moved the large low coffee table into the centre of the room, rolled the mat across it, set up some candle sticks and incense, sat on the mat naked, muttering to herself, as the lit candles around her flickered. Chloe and Deb's were interested.

Birch sat in the centre of the table cross legged with her eyes closed, a circle of candles burning around her, Deb's looked at Chloe who shrugged, she looked back at Birch.

"What are you doing Birch?" She kept her eyes closed, and softly spoke.

"This tree means a great deal to all of us, yet it had to die, so, I am communing with nature, and thanking the tree for giving its life to us, so that we will be safe and protected throughout this season." Chloe did not quite get it.

"So, Witchcraft?" Birch opened one eye.

"It is respect Chloe, for the world, nature, this tree, I think it is right and meaningful to show it."

Chloe understood that, and sat in front of the table and closed her eyes, Deb's did the same. Birch smiled, and then focused her thoughts.

A tap at the back door set my operation in motion, Edwina stepped into the living room, and quietly closed the doors, and held them shut. I held my finger to my lips, and thanked Norman; he nodded and gave a big smile as I handed him the money. He whispered quietly.

"Daisy got the best one we have." I whispered back.

"Thank her for me will you, I will see you both at the switch on."

I had to work fast, so I sprang into action, and off I went at high speed, the living room doors were closed as I hurriedly passed, and staggered up the stairs. Talk about panic, I worked hard and fast, to prepare something very special.

I had thought about it all day, but it was only when I saw her reaction in the woods, that I fully made up my mind, and as Old Phil talked to her, I got to work on the phone, and who better to ask than Norman and Daisy, two of the loveliest people in the village, and they were delighted to muck in.

Finally sweating like crazy, and with my heart beating, I made my way downstairs, and Edwina winked as I walked into the living room. Chloe was sat in the circle of candles drinking, Birch was sat on the floor with Deb's looking up the tree, at everyone's different baubles.

Edwina handed me a glass, and I finally got to really look at the tree. It was huge and full, and actually really beautiful. I sat on the chair and watched them all, whilst I cooled down with a drink, Birch saw me, came over, and cuddled up into me. I lifted my arm to pull her round, and got a whiff of myself.

"I stink, I might have a bath, do you want to join me?" She looked up at me.

"Yeah, that will be the perfect end to this night, I love the tree, I was blown away by it. I never understood why people had them, but I can see why now. You know Deads this is not a Christmas thing, this goes back thousands of years before Christ, and the tree worship of the early pagans, this is a purely pagan thing. I do love it, and I love how the room smells, it makes me feel closer to nature." She was so lovely.

"Okay, I will go run the bath, and will come get you when it is ready." She smiled and nodded, I got up and walked to the door, I looked back at Chloe.

"Wow this witchcraft thing really works, look Chloe you are floating." She panicked, her eyes snapped open, and she looked down in shock, Edwina burst out laughing, I shook my head.

"She is so easy." I headed for the stairs; Chloe yelled.

"I fucking hate you at times Abby, you freaked the shit out of me."

Half an hour later, I found Birch once again sat staring at the tree, I took her by the hand and led her upstairs to my room, and into the bathroom, where I had surrounded the bath with candles, she smiled as she slipped into the hot water filled with soft bubbles, I slipped in behind her and she lay back.

"You spoil me."

The truth was, out of all the things we had done together since I had known her, bathing was one of my favourite things to do. I loved to wash her gently, and enjoyed the tracing of the contours of her body. Long before I admitted that I wanted her sexually, this had been my only way of being close and touching her, and even now, I still found it a massive turn on.

She relaxed and gave a happy sigh, as I washed her hair. We swapped, and she did me, which was my second favourite thing, and feeling relaxed, calm and clean, we made our way into my room, and I dried her hair, and then she did mine. When we were done, I looked at her?

"Can we sleep in your room tonight?" She shrugged.

"If you want to."

I took her hand, and led her back through the bathroom, her room was in darkness. As we walked in, I heard her breath catch in her throat. Out on the balcony was a four foot tall tree, decorated in traditional pagan symbols, and decorations, its tiny lights twinkled in the darkness, and it had one tiny bauble in black, with a skeleton on it. She looked at me stunned, and I gave her a soft smile, leaned in and kissed her.

"This one is in a pot, it has roots, you can grow it forever. Norman and Daisy cater to a pagan community, they make a lot of wreaths and decorations, and so I got them to send me enough, to cover your tree. You can save them, I am not sure if I had to put them in a certain order or anything, but you can always rearrange it. The good thing is, you can use them next year, it is sort of a meeting of two ideals, it's Birch like." Tears streamed from her eyes, as she looked at it.

"Oh Deads, it is the most beautiful tree ever, I am not touching it, I am leaving it just as you have done it. Oh Deads, I love it so much." I opened the doors, so she could see it better.

"Norman told me it is better out here, they like the cold, that way it will stay fresh, and keep growing, but this one is yours; it is your forever tree."

She stepped out and looked at all the decorations, with five pointed stars, and Celtic knots, I must admit, I was quite proud of myself, I thought I had done a pretty good job, she crouched down, and wiped her eyes.

"This is a blessing tree Deads, some of these symbols protect all of us, Norman and Daisy know their stuff." She stood up and came in, after all, we were both naked, and it was freezing, I pointed to the switch on the wall.

"It is on a timer to come on and off." She looked at me.

"I don't want it to go off, I want to keep it lit, it will shine and light the way for all of us this winter." I bent down and flicked the switch.

"There you go, it will stay lit all winter." She snuggled into me, and I wrapped my arms round her.

"Deads, I really love my tree, I love you so much, thank you, it is the most perfect thing anyone has ever done for me."

She took my hand and pulled me onto the bed, I lay back and she lowered onto me, and we started to kiss, it was soft, caring, and gentle, and had so much meaning to it.

Downstairs, Chloe walked into the living room.

"Who ate all the orange cream biscuits, I bought five packets of them?" They all looked at each other, and shook their heads, none of them had. Edwina frowned.

"You know that is weird, because I was sure this morning, we had half a chicken for the stir fry, but when I went to get it, there was nothing." They all looked at each other and shrugged. Deb's, looked up from the floor.

"Did Izzy have it, she loves chicken, and she can eat, I mean wow, she packs it in good?" Edwina shook her head.

"I am not sure, it's possible, I mean the woman can eat, especially after a club meet."

Chloe disappeared, and then walked in with the chocolate biscuits, and flopped down on the chair, and lay back.

"I am knackered, I am going to eat these and then crash, it has been a busy day, and I am helping Anthony with the grotto set up for Santa tomorrow." Edwina looked at her, she was in charge of the queue outside the grotto.

"I thought Bill Smedley had a heart attack last week?" Chloe nodded.

"Yeah, he died, Anthony is on the prowl for someone a bit younger to replace Bill. He wants someone with some stock to them, he thinks that way they will outlive the kids. I must admit if I was a bloke, I would do it, it must be fun having all them kids on your lap, telling you their secrets." Deb's, looked up at her.

"God Chloe, even when you say it in a happy voice, it still makes you sound like a really messed up pervert."

I lay back on the bed gasping for air, wow she is good, she curled into me and rested her head on my breasts. I lay back, breathing in air and stroking her long white hair, I glanced down, she looked so happy, her eyes sparkling, as she stared out of the window, God she was stunningly beautiful.

"Happy?" Her eyes moved to look up at me.

"This is the happiest I have been in my entire life, yes Deads, I am very happy." I smiled, and her eyes slipped back to stare at the tree. I had a feeling; this was going to be an unforgettable Christmas.

Chapter 6

Easy Misunderstandings.

I feel like for the last week I have slept, I am not sure if it was jet lag or just Birch wearing me out. I have had a lot of really wonderful and deep sleep, maybe it was just seeing Birch so happy. I am not sure, but I woke to find her sat in bed drinking her coffee, looking through the window at her tree, I cannot deny, I feel really good about how it turned out.

Today is Friday, and the lights are due to be switched on Sunday evening, so it was all hands on deck. On the Village Green, a special green marquee had been set up, with a fence around it, and Anthony and Edwina were in charge of making it look like Santa land.

In a bit of a desperate bid to replace our recently deceased previous Santa, she had talked Luke in covering. He was tall and broad, and pretty ripped, not that the kids would ever see how ripped he was, although considering Edwina's choice of payment, we figured she would, so it counted.

The marquee had to be divided into two sections, one for the grotto, and one for changing and storage of gifts. A wooden floor was laid down inside by Ronald, to stop dampness, and allow for the stacking of boxes, and fake grass was rolled out over it. Chloe and myself erected the dividing curtain and doorway, then built a platform, for the big golden chair of Santa, which had been built by the amateur dramatic society. It was really wood and plaster painted with gold paint, it looked pretty effective, and he would be sat on it, looking the part of kindness and joy, Santa was supposed to be.

Another back drop was put up, which created a small area behind Santa, to shield the doorway for Santa swaps. Then we set to work on decoration, which involved, plastic Christmas trees, large polar bears, penguins, reindeer, and lots of toadstools, which was weird, do mushrooms even grow in the Artic? We sprinkled lavish amounts of fake snow all over the place, and hey presto, sweating, two and a half hours later, we had Santa Land.

Edwina was very happy, we had been under pressure all day, and even though it would open tomorrow at ten, this afternoon as part of the start of the celebrations, a specially selected 100 children from the village, would have a special invite to meet Santa. Anthony was as always panicked, he had the job of loading the boxes into the back, and making sure everything ran smoothly.

Everything was going to plan as Chloe and myself, now dressed as elves, worked out on the grass outside, erecting more fencing. I cannot deny, Chloe was the sluttiest elf I had ever seen, with her obvious braless chest, and very tight green tights and no underwear, as she flirted and flaunted with every male that passed.

It was 4:30, and Luke had not shown up, Edwina was texting, and Anthony was in melt down, he dramatically paced up and down the tent.

"I knew it... I knew it, I told her you know, we need more than two? Ralph has gone down with the flu, and Luke is not here. We will be ruined... Oh, Oh, we are looking at ruin before it even starts. I shall be a laughing stock, the only gay to not pull off something extravagant and fabulous!" Chloe sat on a pile of boxes, pulling the tights out of her vagina.

"Chill the fuck out Anthony, Edwina is a really good shag, Luke will be here." He stared at her, and became hysterical, I tried, but could not help giggling.

"Chloe, I cannot run a village event of this importance, based on your sister's ability to use her vagina, and sate men's lust. I am sorry darling, but how well her hips move, and the velocity of her thrust, are not a proven formula for our guarantee of a Santa." She rolled her eyes.

"God, drama much?" Anthony looked distraught.

"I cannot allow a failure; I need a Santa." He whipped round, and walked out of the tent in a panic, Chloe looked at me and sighed.

"He needs to chill, Luke will be here, I told him I would do him too." She smiled, and then winked.

Outside, Edwina was watching, she saw him, and gave a sigh of relief, he ran over with his bag, sweating and gasping for air.
“I am so sorry, shit bloody car packed in.” She was happy just to see him, she smiled and reached up and kissed him.
“I don’t care you are here, that is all that matters, get ready, and then I will blow you to warm you up.” He gasped for breath.
“Hell girl, this is worth more than a blow job, for this I want you and your sister, and I really need a drink.” She gave a giggle.
“Well Chloe won’t refuse, but are you sure you will be able to handle her after me? Get ready, and I will go get you a coffee.”
The time was getting closer, and I must admit, I was worried, when Luke entered through the flaps, and collapsed on the boxes gasping for air. I gave a sigh of relief, Chloe smiled.
“I am screwing you later… Abby come on, we need to get things ready.” Luke dropped his bag and pulled out his red costume.
I slipped off the boxes, and followed her into the Santa side of the marquee, we made sure the sacks were loaded with the colour coded presents, and everything was in place, and then we took up our positions and waited for head elf Edwina. In the back Anthony arrived with another Santa, he gave a sigh.
“Oh thank god, come on we need to get ready, we start in five minutes, and Luke dear, you owe me. I have aged because of you; I will have crow’s feet in the morning.”
I peered through the flap as Edwina hurried over the grass with a coffee, she slid in quickly and saw Santa sat on his chair.
“Oh hell, this was a close one, alright, we have five minutes, wait until I give the signal, then let them in.” Outside the children were gathering with their special tickets.

Edwina rushed over to the Santa seat. I got your coffee, and you have time to calm down a little, so relax, oh God it is cold in here, the coffee will warm you a little, but just in case, I think you have earned a little extra warming, and my gratitude.” She pulled at his pants, and slipped her hand inside.
“Whoa, Christ you are really cold; the poor little bugger is hiding.” She gave it a warming massage, and looked up at his hairy white beard and red hat.
“Oh Santa, you are so going to cum more than once this year.”

That did the trick, Santa started to grow, she pulled back his pants, and saw it growing inside.

"Oh, he is looking much warmer now, come to Mommy Claus for a good warming."

She leaned in and started to use her mouth to warm it, I looked back and saw her head bobbing. I patted Chloe on the shoulder, and Chloe turned back to look, we both sniggered, wow this guy was getting paid well.

He leaned back and gripped the arms of his chair, and gave a long slow moan, Edwina moved her eyes and saw him, with his head back on the rest. She would have smiled, but that was not really possible, she gave a happy little moan, as she swirled her tongue round. I was watching with Chloe and giggling, Chloe nudged me and sniggered.

"Santa is about to cum to Wotton."

I laughed as Anthony walked in dressed like an elf, to check we were ready; he walked round the chair and saw Edwina sucking off Santa, and gave an almighty squeal.

"OH MY GOD EDWINA, ITS HO, HO, HO, NOT BLOW, BLOW, BLOW, WHY THE HELL ARE YOU DOING THAT TO RONALD?"

I froze and looked at Chloe.

"Huh?"

Chloe looked at me, and then down the room towards the seat, her jaw fell open, she suddenly realised, and then she started to scream with laughter. Edwina was frozen on the spot staring at Anthony with a mouth full of Ronald, he turned his head and pulled down his beard.

"Antonio don't stop her; I am almost there."

Edwina shot back across the floor, away from the chair, and stared with abject horror as Ronald winked.

"Wow, if I had known helping the committee was this much fun, I would have volunteered years ago, you are much better than Marion." Chloe fell to her knees, gasping for air in hysterics, as she looked at me and pointed.

"She blew the piss king Abby, it's not fucking Luke, it's Ronald."

Edwina's head snapped round, as she turned purple, I was trying so hard to not laugh, Chloe was holding her sides, and screaming with laughter. Santa pulled up his pants, then his beard, and sat and smiled. Edwina jumped up looking horrified and ran into the back, with a shriek. Ronald leaned back in his chair the happiest Santa I have ever seen, and roared into the air.

"Ho, Ho, HO, MERRY CHRISTMAS." One of the parents, on the other side of the tent flap, looked at her children.

"Did you hear that kids, Santa is coming?" I started to giggle.

"He would have if Anthony had not interfered." Chloe fell back on the floor laughing.

For the rest of the night, which was our only night, as the regular volunteers would be starting tomorrow, the children trooped in to meet the happiest elves, they would ever meet. It was cold, and our costumes were thin, as most of the fathers noticed when they looked at my chest, but every time it felt remotely miserable, I just looked at Edwina, who was redder than Rudolf, and I was warm and happy all over again. She walked towards the door and stared at us both as we smirked.

"Luke can never know about this, I mean it guys, he can never know, you tell that drama laden hairdresser, one word, and I will shave his head, and cut off his prick in his sleep."

I tried not to giggle, honestly, I did, Chloe put her head down, and joined me. Edwina stared at us with the evillest eyes an elf has ever possessed.

"I mean it, not a fucking word, and Birch must never ever fucking know, I will never live it down." Chloe looked up and grinned.

"Okay Edwina, but I screw Luke first." She seethed at her with hate.

"Okay... Shit, I really hate you two."

You will not believe how long it takes to get one hundred kids through a marquee, and onto Santa's lap. To be honest I could not tell Ronald and Luke apart, Chloe managed the solution, Edwina had left Ronald very horny and hanging, so if the kid looked really uncomfortable sat on Santa's lap, that was probably Ronald.

I gave it some thought, and it made perfect sense to me. I was counting the minutes as I slowly lost feeling in my bum cheeks, the temperature was falling, and I was shivering like crazy, when we finally got the last kid through. Birch slipped in, as we prepared for the close. She smiled.

"Oh Deads Sweetie, can you take this costume home, I think it is really sexy?" I was shivering.

"Oh god I am so cold, I cannot feel my bum cheeks they are so numb."

"Oh Sweetie, why didn't you say."

She slipped her arms round me, and then slid her hands down inside my tights, her hands were so warm and lovely, and I felt the heat of her body flow into me. I just stood there shivering, slowly feeling life come back to my body.

The night was not over yet, we had packing up, and moving out all the spare stock to do, and Birch joined in. Once everything was packed up, we walked back towards home, Birch was disappointed I had got changed. Edwina was quiet, I thought she was listening, just in case I said anything to Birch. Chloe leaned into Luke giggling, I sort of felt bad for Edwina, I could not imagine what it must have felt like to suck Ronald off by accident, then have to cope with letting Chloe sleep with Luke first. I looked at Birch, hell I was glad I did not have a sister.

I suddenly noticed something, and looked round and stopped, Birch looked at me.

"What's up Sweetie?" I looked back up the main street.

"Where is Anthony?" She smiled.

"Oh, he is fine, he is getting instructed on wiring diagrams." I frowned.

"Come again?" She giggled.

"If he is lucky, he will... The wires guy Michael, is giving him some extra tips on his wires." I gave a chuckle.

"That is nice, good for him, I am really happy for him." She appeared happy.

"Yeah, it is nice, he has been alone too long."

We hurried along watching our breath swirl out of us in clouds through the cold night air, I made a mental note not to forget to buy gloves for Sunday.

We arrived home, and I swung the door open, and stopped, I looked behind at the door number, just to check we had the right house. The stairs were decorated with wide red velvet ribbons, interwoven with thick swags of green, decorated with bead chains and baubles. There was holly and poinsettia's, it looked like a Victorian Christmas palace, I was blown away completely. Birch stood with tears in her eyes just smiling, Deb's sat in the centre of the stairs looking a little worried, she looked at Birch.

"I am so sorry Birch, I got bored, I was going to wait for you to help, please do not be mad with me." Birch walked onto the stairs, and lifted her up, she pulled her into her arms and hugged her.

"Oh Sweetie, it is so pretty, and so lovely, and I love it completely, how could I be mad?"

It was pretty amazing, and she had done all through the living room, and the library, to match, I was really impressed with her amazing ability, to pull shit off. I mean, why was I surprised though, she was the most intelligent, and capable person I knew? I watched Birch, who was so happy and Deb's, with that wonderful naïve smile, that hid her deviant little self. In a way that was the real value of what Christmas stood for, the simple joy, of making each other happy.

Chloe was all smiles as she walked into the living room, Edwina walked past me.

"I am going to brush my teeth and gargle." I could not help giggling, Birch looked at her.

"Edwina Sweetie is everything alright?"

Her head snapped back to me, and I put my head down, and tried to stifle the laugh, Deb's narrowed her eyes as she watched me. Edwina walked on up the stairs, I looked up, and made eye contact with Birch who was looking suspicious. She came slowly down the stairs, watching me.

"Okay Sweetie, something is going on, what have I missed?"

I saw Edwina stop at the top of the stairs and look back in horror, she had no idea how much I was fighting the urge. I was saved when Chloe walked in, looked up and saw Edwina staring down at me. Chloe looked at Birch.

"We had a mishap, and Edwina blew Ronald off by accident." Deb's, frowned.

"Bugger off Chloe, how stupid do you think I am, now tell me what really happened?" Chloe shrugged, and walked back into

Luke in the living room.
"Suit yourself."

I headed to the kitchen closely followed by Birch, I needed a drink, and a hot bath, just to warm back up. I flopped down at the island, Izzy was sat drinking scotch, she looked well ahead in the game, she raised her glass in salute.

"I saw Andrew Bosworth earlier, Deadly, he was complaining about your dad, he said he is drinking too much." I looked at her.

"So?" She shrugged.

"Just saying, don't shoot the messenger." I gave a long sigh.

"How bad is he?" Izzy put her glass down.

"He told me it is not so much him, but the noise him and his friend cause, it is upsetting the other customers."

It is great isn't it, not one of those lot has stood up for me in the last seven years, but when the shit hits the fan, they call me to help them. I understood. I put down my glass and stood up. Birch got up, I looked at her.

"It is not worth you coming, he will just attack you again, and I don't want that." She shook her head.

"You are not going alone Deads, try to stop me, I will still be there." I nodded, I knew it was pointless to try, Deb's touched my arm.

"Will you be alright Abby?" I patted her hand, I knew of her feelings, her dad had been really violent to her and her mother back in our school days.

"It will be fine."

I grabbed my thick black coat off the rack, and slipped it on, Birch pulled hers on too, she smiled and took my hand.

"Come on Sweetie."

I have not been that frequent a visitor to the Hunters Arms Hotel and Bar. I have always found it attracted the kind of people who hated me. Andrew came from behind the bar when he saw me with Birch.

"It is good to see you Abigail, thanks for coming, I appreciate it. I would have called you, but not that many people seem to know your number."

I looked round the old pub with its original beams, old oil

paintings, and brown velvet seats, it never really changes, just like the village. It is not a bad place, it is quite tasteful really, I am just not a fan of the people who drink in it.

"It is alright Andrew; it is better if I deal with this. Where is he?" He pointed to the back room.

"I asked them to sit in there, it is harder to hear their laughing and jokes about your mum. I am sorry Abigail, I really am, your mum is a good woman." No mention about me I noted, that was probably just Andrew being polite.

Andrew took us through to the back room, where my dad sat with Angela his secretary, who was looking more than a little bit cosy. I unzipped my coat, and dropped my hood, and stood right in front of him, he looked up and scowled, Angela did not even seem to care.

"Oh god... Look, the daughter of shame has returned." I was not enjoying this. My dad leaned into Angela's ear and whispered, not that quietly.

"That is her lesbian friend."

He started to laugh, I stared at her, and she looked embarrassed, after all she knew me well enough, she had been to the house plenty of times on business. I stood right in front of them, trying to find words that would resonate with him, I did not want a slanging match like last time, Birch hovered just behind my shoulder.

"The customers are complaining Dad, they say your behaviour is getting out of hand, and I was asked to come and talk to you. Trust me, I do not want to be here anymore than you want me to be." He looked up; his eyes looked hateful.

"Does your lesbian friend have to go everywhere you do?" I shrugged.

"Yes, does your whore follow suit?" Angela looked offended and stood up.

"Now just you wait a bloody minute, I..." Birch stepped in.

"Oh Sweetie, trust me, neither of us want to be here, why don't we just go sit over here, and let's be calm, polite, and quiet, while Abby and her dad sort this out? You know, you would look so unattractive with your head bashed in with a large pot ashtray."

I glared at her with hate, she understood, and moved quickly away. I looked down at my dad, and gave a sigh.

"Why are you still here, I thought you had an apartment in the city?" He took a drink.

"I have taken a week off to sort things out with your unreasonable mother, she wants the house, and I want to sell it. She will not play ball, as soon as it is done, I will locate to London full time."

To be honest, I never thought he would sell the house, I guess, I wanted to see if he had at least one small shred of decency in him, but it was clear, my hopes had been in vain.

"What happened to you Dad, you were never this cold and cruel, mum does not deserve that, no matter what has happened, she has always stood by you? The house is all she has, she has invested a lot into it, I get you own half, but all the work that has been done on it, has been paid for by her, just give it her, you can afford it." He took a deep breath.

"You won't understand this, but we had an agreement between us, she cannot buy me out, and I want the capital to invest in a new project."

I shook my head in disbelief, what a piece of work he has become, over thirty years of marriage, and all it comes down to is liquidating assets, for a deal.

"You will never get her to sell that house, it is her life. I get you do not understand that, I mean why would you, after all you were never really there were you? She tolerated your bullshit for years. Christ Dad, she has earned that house the hard way, just give it her and go, live your life, bang Angela, and let her enjoy what little she has left after you broke her."

He stared up from the table, once again he was red faced from the booze, he looked cold and cruel with his grey hair and hard face. It was crazy really, but I hated seeing him like this, I had no idea what had changed in him, all I knew was, I hated how greedy and cruel he had become.

"Abigail it is now valued at two and a half million, I have not been unreasonable, I offered her a buyout for just one million, that takes into account fairly all the work she has done on it, I am actually trying to be decent here, I am trying."

Well, he wasn't screaming at my lover, and calling her whore and slut, so that was an improvement.

Birch looked at Angela, she was not unattractive, if anything she was Flick like, just with the curled blonde hair, and the bright blue eyes. Birch guessed she was mid to late forties.

"So, Angie, the word on the manner is you were screwing him when Deads was in Uni, so this for you is quite a long term relationship. I hope you have had plenty of gifts, being the other woman should be rewarded, especially for that sort of dedication?" She looked really uncomfortable.

"Not that you would understand, but I love him, and my name is not Angie, it is Angela, and you should mind your own bleeding business missy." Birch giggled, and her eyes sparkled.

"Oh, you are so cute... Can I just point out something, because there has been a slight misunderstanding?" She frowned at Birch.

"What misunderstanding is that, because I am not aware of one?" Birch smiled.

"Aw, bless you, Sweetie." She leaned right onto the table. "I think you got the impression it was Abby who would beat you stupid with an ash tray, and your mistake was in your thought. It was the wrong one, that would be me Sweetie, so be nice." Angela went white as she stared at Birch.

"You are a psychopath." Birch giggled.

"No Sweetie, but oddly enough, I am the one person in this village you could meet here, who does actually know where to get one for you... SURPRISE!" She gave a huge smile. Angela slid back away from her looking terrified.

"You are frigging mad." Birch gave a slight smile, and nodded.

"Keep it up Angie, and enjoy being pretty while you can."

I looked at my dad.

"If you get the money, you will leave mum alone, no problems or nothing, you will just sign the papers to make the house all hers, and go?" He gave a nod.

He is such a shit, I knew he could smell the money, and he knows me well enough to know, I would defend mum to the death. I looked him deep in the eyes.

"I have another book ready, and with what I will get from the sponsorship deals off my tour of America, and with what I have now, I can raise the money, sign over the house to her, and I will give it you. Just leave mum alone, and do not make waves, I just need a couple of weeks." He looked impressed, he looked down at his drink, smirked, and then looked back at me.

"The problem is Abigail, I need the cash now, two weeks will be too late." He was a slippery shit bag when it came to cash, I gave a frustrated sigh.

"Dad work with me on this, you have millions stashed abroad, stop acting like an arse, you know this is nothing compared to all your other assets. Give me some time, you know I am good for it, after all, you were doing my books until last summer, you had them long enough to see what has been flowing in."

I saw that glint of recognition in his eyes. I had to wonder if that was what this was all about, the fact I had moved my trust fund, and accounts, to Birch's mum's company, was this revenge?

"I am in the deal Abigail, I am sorry, I need it now." I gave a sigh.

"Nothing changes when it comes to money does it Dad? You would even screw your own daughter over to make a profit?" I watched as he smugly sat back.

"Business is business Abigail, this is not personal, it is simply a deal, I thought they taught you that at university?" God, I hate him. I shook my head.

"You are a real piece of work, not personal, how bloody personal could this be? You are my father, you are supposed to give a shit and protect me, and yet here you are, trying to fleece me. You know I have the cash, and you also know if I give you the full amount now, it will crash my trust fund, and I will have nothing left to live on, and yet, you would happily take that away from me. I made my offer, in two weeks when the cash transfers from the states, I can pay you, it will damage my fund, but I can do it. If mum and me ever meant anything to you, then..." SLAP!!

Birch leaned over at my side with a hand on a cheque, placed firmly and flat on the table, her voice was angry yet quiet.

"Do not beg this piece of shit Deads, you are worth a thousand times more than that." Birch glared at him.

"One million cash, in your name, sign the bloody papers, and give Flick complete ownership you frigging snake, or I will make your slut so ugly, no one will ever want to look at her."

She grabbed the large decorative heavy ashtray off the side.

Angela saw it, and screamed at the top of her lungs, looked at Birch with utter terror, and ran from the room begging for help. Birch lifted her other hand, and there was the cheque, Birch stood up.

"I want those papers signed by midday tomorrow, and Flick never needs to know anything about this, as far as she is concerned, you did the decent thing for once in your miserable life. Give the signed papers to her solicitor, and then piss off to London, and leave us all the hell alone. Come on Deads, we are leaving."

He smirked, and I felt sick to the stomach. She tossed the ashtray on the seat at his side, grabbed my hand and pulled me away. I watched as he calmly lifted the cheque, read it to check it, folded it neatly, and slipped it into his pocket and smiled, what a cold hearted predator. I could not believe this was the same man I grew up around, if I wasn't so furious, I would be heart broken.

Outside in the ice cold air, I felt queasy and light headed, and took a moment.

"Birch let me breathe." I leant against the wall, and took deep breaths in and out.

"I will pay you back Birch, every penny, you will have it all." Birch slid into me, and pulled me close, her eyes were close and looked huge, there was so much love in them.

"No, you won't, I won't take a penny off you. I did that for mum, not for you, she has been there for me, and watched over me ever since I first came here. Two years ago, when I was falling apart, she was my guardian angel, and behind the scenes, she did a lot for me, like keep my mum and dad updated. Deads, she watched me like a hawk, and she showed me such love, and when we needed her most, she stood at our side against this village. You fell in love, and I fell in love, and it was not what either of us expected, and once again, she accepted it all, and encouraged us to be us. I have loads of money, I bloody well hate it, I try to spend it, and it all just piles back in the pot with interest, I have no other use for it." I lent on her shoulder.

"It's a million quid Birch, and I frigging hate him for taking it, he should have just given it to her." She squeezed me tighter.

"Honestly, he knew I had the cash, that is what this was all about Deads. Screw him, let him choke on it, all I know is she needs us, and I will not let her down. If this gets him off her back, and gives her the freedom she wants, then I am happy to do whatever it takes, the way she did for us. This is not about cash, this is about love, family, and what that means to us all, and sadly, in that your dad is clueless." I kissed her cheek.

"Thanks Birch." She turned and looked at me, and her eyes sparkled.

"I will never let anyone who is not your mum, you or me, buy that guest house, that is the place I made love with you for the first time to show you my love for you, and we are not letting it go." I chuckled.

"I hate to point it out, but it is way bloody cheaper to just keep the bed." She giggled

"Shit, I never even thought of that."

She smiled, and kissed me, then took my hand, and we walked away from the Hunters, in the freezing cold darkness, and headed towards Waterside Lane, and the warmth of our home.

Chapter 7

Deceptions.

When we got home, I was frozen, I went into the living room where Chloe sat with Deb's. These two had grown really close over the last two years, they were hardly apart these days, but it was nice. I suppose in many ways, Birch had taken up a huge part of my life, and being married, Deb's split her life between Jimmy and us, she just naturally gravitated towards Chloe, because they were often alone together.

I curled up, in what is considered my spot, the corner of the sofa in the centre of the room. I was surprised to see Chloe downstairs. I flopped down and looked across at her.

"I thought you would be with Luke?" She leaned back in the chair and stretched.

"No... I was mainly joking around, he has got a great body and all, but to be honest Edwina is more into him. I actually think she has feelings for him, but will not admit it. I let him go up to her, he is more a Banger Bobbles sort of guy." She smiled; Debs was interested.

"You think she really likes him that much?" Chloe gave a wicked grin.

"Don't say anything, but when we lived at home, I read her diary, oh wow it was mind blowing." Deb's looked shocked, and then a little frightened.

"You have not read mine, have you?" I gave a chuckle.

"Something to hide have we Deb's?" She looked at me and turned scarlet, Chloe leaned round, and looked up at her.

"Wow it's that filthy?" Deb's turned her face away.

"I would not write those things in a place people would find them." Chloe chuckled.

"So, she has, and now she wants to throw us off the scent." Chloe put her arm round her. "Deb's this was years ago, I would never do that to you, no, I just read Edwina's." I had to admit I was a little intrigued.

"So, come on then, tell us, what was in it?" Chloe leaned forward in her seat, and grinned at me, as her eyes twinkled.

"It was filled with pages about Luke, I mean, this thing goes back years, since they were in school together, she has been crazy about him for like forever, and she has done some really smutty stuff with him, I can tell you. That is why I wind her up about him, you know she is really tough minded, it is not easy to rattle her, but bring Luke up, and it's a whole different story." I have to admit Chloe's smile was wicked, and naughty, I made a mental note of it for a book.

Birch arrived with drinks, and we curled up, she sat enjoying gazing at the room and the tree, it made me smile, she was like a little kid at times, anything that is shiny or sparkles and she is there. I relaxed and my mind drifted, as the memory of my dad sat in the pub came back to mind.

I was really disappointed, and it hurt to think he would try to hurt me financially, was Birch right, was this his way of extracting her cash? He had tried many times to get her accounts, but her mother had been adamant they stayed with her firm, and I think I could understand why. Birch used a group called the EFG, Ethical Finance Group for everything she did, even Edwina and Chloe were audited by them, it made me think. I looked at her, as she stared dreamily at the Christmas tree.

"Can I ask you something private Birch?" She turned and smiled.

"Sweetie there is nothing private between us, ask me anything you want, I am an open book for you." I loved how transparent and trusting she was with me.

"Your accounts firm the EFG, why is your mum so adamant you stick with them?" I noticed Deb's staring at me. Birch leaned back.

"I suppose simply put they are ethical, everything is UK based, all accounts are straight, taxes are paid, and they are environmentally based. They donate a lot to charities that save the planet, or help the poor, and they invest in green projects. Mum likes the way they work, and so do I, which is why I use them, and helped you move over to them."

"Does your mum think my dad is a crook?" She smiled.

"Sweetie, what is done is done, look it is all sorted, and your mum will be happy." I gave a sigh.

"Good dodge Birch, and skilful too, you turned that around smoother than a freshly shaved vagina." She turned and looked at me, her eyes were so green.

"Deads Sweetie, I have never lied to you, and I won't now. I do not know about your dad, he could be clean, he could be dirty, I honestly have no idea, but there are some not so nice rumours about his partner. He is not a very nice person by all accounts, and it has been implied, he does some dodgy dealings on the markets. That worried mum, so after your dad was really rude and horrible to you, I advised you to move, I was trying to look out for you, that is all."

I understood, I knew she would never lie, and that was enough for me. Deb's was still staring at me, I frowned at her, she looked upset.

"What Deb's?" She looked really uncomfortable; her voice was a little strained.

"Abby, my dad heard some things that really bothered him, so much so, last month he moved everything for the whole family, and company, to the same company as Roni. I know it has hit your dad's company hard, my dad was his biggest client. They had a huge row at our house, your dad went really insane, and honestly, I thought he was going to get battered. Dad's security threw him out, I am so sorry Abby, I didn't want to tell you because I did not want you upset." I took a deep breath.

"Wow, Roni advising against him, and now your dad, probably the most honest person I know, outside of this house has moved away from the company, that pretty much says it all. Thanks Deb's, I am glad you told me, I really am, I have seen sides of my dad recently I never thought I would, you have actually helped me."

She still looked really guilty, but she had not realised how much sense she had made. It did not take much to work things out now, he was putting the squeeze on, because he needed a deal to stabilise his company, and one million would go a long way to helping. I looked at Birch, she was watching me with concern in her eyes.

"Are you really okay Sweetie?" I stoked her long hair off her shoulder, and smiled.

"My Dad is in trouble, and it threatened mum didn't it, you had an idea, and that is why you stepped in, you really have saved her?" She gave a light sigh, and smiled, her eyes sparkled.

"Mum has told me stuff, I knew about Bradley, Deads, if that paperwork goes through tomorrow, her home will be safe, and that is all that matters. If he has no claim to it, then that protects her, I did not lie, I did it for her, because like you, I really love her too."

Just when you think everything is settled and life is normal, she just sits up and does it again, and she blows me away, and changes my life forever. I cannot deny, I have never met anyone like her, she is without doubt a one off, it's a Birch thing for sure. Birch stood up and took my hand.

"Let's run a bath and relax Sweetie." I slipped off the seat and followed, as she led the way, Deb's gave a sigh.

"I wish someone would bathe with me; they are so lucky." Chloe turned to her.

"It is just two people sat in hot water, what is the big deal?" Deb's stared at her.

"Chloe it is nice, you know having your back washed, someone doing your hair while you talk to them, it is really nice, it feels special." She shrugged.

"As I said, it's just washing, I mean hell Deb's if you want it that bad, I will share a bath, I am covered in paint. I could probably do with washing it off, I have nothing better to do." Her eyes lit up.

"Really? Chloe I would love that." Chloe stood up.

"Come on then, we will use your bath, it's bigger than mine."

Birch lay on the bed staring out of the window at her bright little tree in the darkness, whilst I sat on the edge of the bath, and watched it fill, it was slower tonight for some reason. The reason was Deb's was filling her bath, as Chloe lay on Deb's bed, making dreamy loving sounds as she hugged Phileas.

Deb's lined up the soap and sponges, with shampoo and conditioner, and threw in a bath bomb, and as the water level rose, the room filled with exotic relaxing scents, she was really excited over the idea.

I walked into the bedroom, and climbed up on the bed, and sat on Birch's nice round bum, I leaned forward and kissed the bottom of her neck.

"Come on, leave your tree to grow, and slip in the bath with me." I climbed off her, and she rolled over smiling.

"I really love it Deads, I know it sounds silly and childish, but I cannot help myself, I have to watch it, and admire it, it is so beautiful Deads."

I pulled her hand, and she reluctantly left the tree viewing, and followed me into the bathroom, and then slid in behind me and relaxed. I leaned back into her, and closed my eyes, it had been so cold today, and it was nice to feel the heat pass through my whole body. Birch lathered her sponge and started to wash me; this really is my idea of heaven.

Chloe slid into the bath behind Deb's, her whole body was covered in small blobs of dried paint.

"Wow this actually feels nicer than I thought it would." Deb's smiled, as she leaned back.

"I remember sitting on the toilet talking to Abby, and Birch just slipped in, and I thought, I wish I had thought of that, it has always looked so much fun." She passed Chloe the sponge. Chloe rubbed the soap on it.

"What didn't you think it was gay, I mean, you know those two, they wanted to bang each other years before they did it?" She shook her head.

"This was way back when Abby was still in Uni. It is just so normal and natural, like this, I mean we are great friends, and we are here washing each other. To be honest Chloe you need a bath, I saw all the paint on you." She leaned forward, and Chloe rubbed the sponge on her back.

Chloe looked down at her boobs, and saw the paint, she rubbed them with the sponge, they swished around in the water, and tiny little streaks of bright coloured water ran off them as the paint dissolved. Deb's lifted one of her own legs out of the water, and washed it with the other sponge.

The room was filled with the steam of the hot water, and hung heavy with the floral scent of the bomb, and Deb's felt calm and relaxed, as she leaned back against Chloe's soft boobs. Chloe reached over with the sponge and washed the sides of her neck, and her throat, she rubbed gently, washing Deb's who had her eyes closed, with a dreamy look on her face, and made her way down. Chloe was relaxed and just enjoying the moment, when she looked down and saw she was rubbing Deb's boobs.

Deb's lifted a knee in the water and turned it inward, and Chloe stopped rubbing.

"You better not be cumming? I mean it Deb's, stop it." Deb's opened her eyes, and looked up.

"I was just deeply relaxing." Chloe dropped the sponge.

"Yeah, fuck that, sit up, and I will wash your hair, you wash your own front."

Deb's sat forward and Chloe grabbed the shampoo, and started to wash Deb's hair, she ground her fingers into her scalp, and rubbed hard, Deb's gave a little moan.

"Oh, I love it when someone else washes my hair." Chloe's fingers stopped.

"Why?"

"It feels nice, don't you think so?" Chloe frowned.

"Just nice, not turned on?" Deb's turned round, and looked at her.

"God Chloe chill out, it just feels nice." She gave a sigh of relief and then continued.

With her hair washed and rinsed, Deb's ducked so Chloe could straddle over, and then slid back and opened her legs for Chloe to sit down. She grabbed the sponge, and started to wash her back; Chloe relaxed.

"You are right, this feels really nice, I have never done this before, you know wash, I have screwed guys in a bath, but they have never washed me."

Deb's squeezed the sponge, so the hot water ran down her back rinsing her off, and then Chloe leaned back as Deb's lathered up the sponge and started to wash her shoulders and higher chest.

Chloe closed her eyes and relaxed, the heat, the smell of the soap, the soft motion of the sponge, it all felt really wonderful, Deb's looked down at the water.

"Your legs are covered, they will take some scrubbing, wow

Chloe, my nipples only get that big in the cold." Chloe opened her eyes and gave a gasp, she sat up and covered her boobs with her hands.

"Do my hair now."

She leaned forward and lifted her knees up, grabbed the sponge and started to rub them. Deb's rubbed in the shampoo, and Chloe stopped, and let her head fall back.

"Oh god that feels so wonderful." Deb's smiled.

"See, I told you, it feels really good, it makes me remember being a kid when my mum washed my hair." Chloe smiled.

"Yeah, I get that, I really do." Deb's rinsed Chloe's hair, and ran her fingers through it to free some of the knots out.

"You have really nice hair, it is really fine, I love the way the colours run down in waves, it's really pretty." Chloe stood up, and Deb's looked at her bum. "How do you get paint all over your ass, God Chloe, is there any part of you not painted?"

She grabbed the sponge and started to rub, Chloe wobbled and leaned forward and put her arms out to the wall, Deb's rubbed really hard.

"How long has this been on here, it's really hard to wash off?" Deb's knelt up, as Chloe stood bent over.

"Honestly you need taking in hand, so you are taken better care of." She rubbed more soap on the sponge and started to rub harder, Deb's tutted. "It's bloody everywhere, open your legs, it's all up your inner thighs." She slid the sponge in between her legs and rubbed really hard.

"You should be nicer to yourself, and take better care of yourself, you are such a pretty girl, and you have a lovely body, treat it better Chloe."

She vigorously rubbed up and down and across her inner thighs, Chloe put her head down and let out a little gasp, her breathing was a little faster than it had been, Deb's realised and stopped and stared at her.

"Oh my God, you are going to cum?" Chloe tensed, and looked back, her face going scarlet, Deb's eyes opened wide as she looked at her.

"Oh Christ, this is turning you on, isn't it?"

"NO!" She giggled.

"I was turning you on, I almost made you cum." Chloe stood up straight, her face was going purple.

"NO, YOU WEREN'T!" Deb's giggled.

"It's alright Chloe we are friends, you can admit it." Chloe stepped quickly out of the bath and walked backwards away from her, shaking her head.

"It wasn't... It wasn't you are wrong." Deb's gave a mighty laugh.

"You were totally going to cum." She giggled. "You liked me rubbing you." Chloe shook her head.

"No, I didn't, it's not true, stop saying that." Her face was going redder.

Birch leaned back, and gave a happy moan as I pulled the brush down through her long hair.

"Ooh Sweetie that is so nice, I love having my hair brushed by you."

"YOU WERE!"

"I WASN'T!"

"WERE!"

"WASN'T!"

I put the brush down, and sighed. "Oh god, what are they up to now?"

"ADMIT IT!"

"NEVER!" Birch stood up.

"Honey, the children are off again."

She walked over to the door, and I slipped off the bed and hurried behind her. In the hall Chloe was walking backwards, dripping all over the place, her hair hanging soaked, and her face red as a beetroot. Deb's was staring at her as she walked forward pointing at her, she looked red with anger.

"I heard you moan, you liked it." Chloe shook her head fast.

"No, I didn't, I was dry." Birch looked at them and gave a sigh.

"What the hell is going on now?"

Deb's looked at us both stood watching at the door as she slowly advanced, and Chloe took more steps back. Debs was pointing right at Chloe, she smiled as she looked at us.

"We shared a bath, and because she was covered in paint, I washed her bum, and between her legs, and SHE WAS GOING TO CUM!" Chloe turned redder than a beetroot and shook her head.

"I wasn't, I am straight, I am really straight, you know how straight I am, I wasn't honestly, she is lying, it's not true, girls don't do that for me. She was telling me how pretty I was, that is all, it was nice I liked it, I like being told I am pretty, most girls hate me that is all." Deb's looked really annoyed.

"OH YEAH, EXPLAIN TO ME HOW NIPPLES GET THAT BIG IN A HOT BATH CHLOE?" Chloe gave a squeak and her hands flew up to her chest, she shook her head.

"I was thinking of Percy, that's all, I thought after the bath I would do Percy because I am frustrated."

"NO CHLOE, YOU WERE FRIGGING TURNED ON BY MY SPONGE. THAT IS WHY YOU WANTED TO DO PERCY, BECAUSE I WAS MAKING YOU CUM!"

I must admit the mere notion of Chloe being frustrated just does not compute, I mean this is Chloe after all, and yes, she does have Percy as back up. Birch smiled at Chloe.

"Sweetie why are you so red, it is alright, it does not matter if it was a girl or boy, it's nice to be washed there. Deads did it to me earlier, and I liked it a lot, I am going to screw her brains out shortly because of it, just admit it was nice, it is safe here." Chloe looked terrified.

"Birch, please not you too, I was not going to cum, I just got wet that's all." Birch smiled; Deb's gave a look of sheer delight.

"I KNEW IT!" Deb's stopped and folded her arms looking smug.

"I made you my bitch Chloe." Chloe realised what she had said, turned and ran down the hallway and into her room. Debs gave a huge grin, and I could not help but giggle.

"Poor Chloe, that must have been terrifying for her." Birch giggled.

"It was a good experience; she now understands all of us better." From her room loud moans came through the door, I looked at Deb's.

"I think Chloe is imagining you as a teddy right now." She shuddered.

"Screw you Abby, I shave." Birch slipped her hand in mine.

"We have hair to finish, and then sex by the tree." I smiled and waved bye, bye, to Deb's, she chuckled, and walked back to her room to dry off.

I sometimes wonder why when you have a bath and get all nice and clean, Birch gets really horny, and we end up hot, sticky and sweaty, and in need of another bath? I was sleepy, and now my mind was awake, so I left Birch to stare at her tree, and walked through to my room. Sunday was the big switch on, and I had to say a few words, and so I thought I would try to gather my thoughts and find a few things to say.

I wrote about ten different speeches, and none of them felt like me, I deleted them and opened a new project I had been working on. I had started it two years ago, and had adding bits each time I felt inspired, so I wrote some more of a chapter I was constructing, most of the book is written, I just need the final chapters. By the time I got to bed, Birch was sprawled out, and breathing softly, I slid in and cuddled up, and soon the day's events, and all the feelings I had felt about my dad, melted into my brain, and I slipped off into oblivion.

Considering Friday night, I actually woke up early for a Sunday, it was 10:57, Birch was still fast asleep, she does sleep better at the weekends these days, but there again, she had hundreds of thousands of pounds of soundproof materials, poured into the walls, so I am quite sure that is the reason. Anthony was already out, actually I am not completely sure he came home last night.

I sat in the kitchen and quietly drank coffee, yes, I am privileged, as I enjoy the finer points of life, and there is no finer privilege than an empty kitchen, devoid of my psychopath house mates, with a full coffee pot. I got so carried away, I made toast, and opened a new jar of green and yellow jam.

We have eaten all our jam, and so we are down to the last thirty jars of Birch's jam. I spread it on my toast, it smelt nice, and as I scraped, I could almost hear her overly happy voice in my head. 'The taste should be distinct, so distinct, you do not need a label Sweetie.' Not going to deny it, I had a taste, I have no idea what flavour it is, but I do like the taste, it's yummy.

I wandered down the hall and popped my head round the library door, no Edwina, so it appears Luke did not go home. I headed upstairs with my toast, and my extra large cup of coffee, in the direction of my desk. Birch was flat out, lay on her back, with a massive happy smile on her face, and her legs spread wide.

I left her to it, and walked back into my room to my desk.

I opened the recycle bin, and restored all my files from the previous day, and read through my notes, I cannot deny, I hated all of them. At four in the afternoon today, I have to say something, and honestly, at this moment in time I am devoid of words that would be appropriate. I sat back and sipped my coffee, and drifted into day dreams, as I considered everything I had learned about my dad, and I could not deny, things appeared to pop up in my brain.

Two years ago, at Deb's wedding, on the dance floor in full view, Birch made the most unbelievable commitment to me. It had been a rough time before that, I got lost and confused in everything, and it almost destroyed what we had, but we came through. She said those words and I knew then, this was real, it meant something, and as we swore to stay together, we kissed. Phew just thinking about it gets me so hot. Birch kissed me, and I reached up and held her in the kiss, oh god I am so wet, I might go and wake her up.

Phew I need to change this train of thought fast. Okay, Dad saw me with her on the dance floor in full view, and hit the roof. The following day was like D day, talk about full on war? We did not speak, and Seeds of Summer came out a month later, and once again he hit the roof saying it was lewd and disgusting. He made his opposition to it well known, and our war of silence continued. Then the picture emerged as I was attacked by people accusing me of attacking the sexual orientation of people, combined with the moral brigade hell bent on banning my book as filth, and so the war continued.

His company doubled their fees, as my income stream rose, and I got pissed off and drove to London, and we had yet another public row, where he called me a slut, and attacked my lesbian whore girlfriend, talk about taking a leaf out of Marjorie's book?

I was ignored at Christmas, so spent it in Manchester with Birch's family. Then I was surcharged by his firm in July, and it was at that point, I got so pissed off, I met with EFG, and transferred everything from Watson/Banner Accounting and Investing, to them.

He exploded at me, and stood out on the street in front of my house screaming through the gates like a lunatic. Shortly after that my Aunt Phillipa died, leaving me five hundred thousand, he tried to get mum to let him handle the transaction, but I declined, and let EFG do it all for me, the way I saw it, my trust fund was performing better than ever, it made sense to slush it all together.

After finding out last night, Bradley his biggest client, had moved to EFG also, it really shocked me. Bradley and my dad went far back, so if Bradley had moved, I have to ask myself why? It bothered me all yesterday, and it is the reason I am up so early, and here I sit, and have to ask a question, which is something I never thought I would, and yet none the less, after watching his greedy little paws maul that cheque Friday night, I am asking, is my dad a crook?

It is horrible to consider it, because even now after all the nasty things he has done, or said to me over my life, I don't want him to be. I really don't, but I am beginning to think he is, and I do not know how I feel about that at the moment, apart from sick to the stomach. I think I really regret eating all the toast now.

Chapter 8

Mum's Time.

I was lost to reality in my own little dream world, trying to find just one single reason, to like my Dad enough to ever talk to him again. I was sipping my coffee, staring at my screen, not even aware of what was written on it, when my world cracked, and through the gap left by the splinter that fell out, I heard 'tap, tap, tap.' I blinked, and saw mum leaning on the doorframe, she smiled.

"Is it okay to come in?" I dropped my feet off the desk, and spun round in my chair, almost sloshing coffee all over me.

"Daft question, you know you are always welcome."

She walked in and looked round the room. Little changes with me, there are less knickers on the floor since I stopped wearing them, but apart from that, clothing was flung everywhere. Mum sat on my sofabed next to my desk.

"I have just come from Church, Patrick Brimley was waiting outside for me, he had an envelope, in which was the completed paperwork for the house transfer, it appears that overnight Edwin changed his mind, and has signed it all to me. Abby I am now the full owner of the property." I smiled.

"That is good isn't it, that is what you wanted?" She looked at me with that I am your mum, and I know you did something look, I tried to feign ignorance.

"You do not seem too surprised Abby, I had a hell of a row with him Friday afternoon. He would not budge an inch, he threatened all sorts of legal action, and now suddenly, he has signed the house over and agreed to sign a none fault divorce as soon as it can be legally presented. All of that in a matter of just over twenty four hours. Abby he personally delivered these to Patrick's home first thing this morning."

I sipped my coffee trying to look innocent, and probably failing completely. She looked tired and worn, the last week had been a rough one, I know that experience well, when dad did not get his own way, everyone suffered, I tried to look for a positive, to cheer her up and hide my involvement.

"You have been married a long time mum, maybe he has sat back and thought about it, and changed his mind. Mum it was not all bad, you did have some good times."

I felt really awkward, I hate hiding things from my mum, I mean hell, that is why she is getting divorced, the man she married has hidden everything from her, she looked a little lost, or maybe she was trying to understand. She gave a sigh.

"Abigail."

Oh shit! I am in trouble; she used my full name.

"I know Edwin better than anyone, and especially that polished and prim excuse for a woman he has been with all these years. The hussy has not got a clue about him. Edwin does not change his mind when it comes to money, it would take nothing short of a tsunami to achieve that." I nodded my head.

"Yeah, I think you are right."

She turned and looked right at me with those piercing blue eyes, that could read the deepest corners of my soul. I cannot deny, I was starting to panic a little, my mum has the capabilities of a bloodhound when it comes to sniffing out hidden plots.

"Abigail there is only one tsunami I know of with such power, half of it is looking at me, and I am assuming the other half is in there sleeping?" I gave a sheepish grin.

"Nice compliment, but I will pass on that."

She stared at me, oh crap, what do I do she is onto me? I honestly thought I would get away with it for at least a couple of weeks, maybe this whole business has sharpened her ninja powers right up.

"Hatty saw you." I gave a gasp, and slouched in the chair.

"SHIT!" She smiled.

"She didn't really, she was with me, she came to the house after your dad left, I just guessed. This has Birch stamped all over it, so I knew you were involved, but had no proof." She gave a giggle. "You shot yourself in the foot."

Christ am I really that easy to con? Actually, scratch that, I see a list in my head already growing, of candidates, which contain the likes of Martin, James, Doug, Kyle, and Daniel. I made a mental note, never play poker with mum. I looked at the floor and thought for a second, how could I put this, in a way that got me off the hook? I looked up at her and smiled.

"Okay, yes, I got a message saying he caused a few problems at the Hunters, Andrew wanted me to go over and sort it out. I saw him, and we spoke, and yes, I told him he was a shit bag, and to stop playing games and hand the full ownership of the house to you. I pointed out we all know he has millions stashed away in offshore accounts." She gave a slight nod to note her understanding, her eyes fixed on me.

"He did not take any of your money did he, because he would if he could get to it?" I shook my head.

"My money is safe and out of his reach." She gave a sigh, and looked really relieved.

"I am so glad to hear that, I was so worried he would try to take your inheritance from Phillipa, he was angry when she left it to you, he always thought it would go to him."

"As I said mum, we all know he has cash offshore, he has boasted about it enough."

Mum sat back on the sofa and relaxed a little, she understood him far better than I realised, so he had been after Phillipa's cash, my instincts were to a degree, right. I sat back and relaxed, I think I have got away with it, I could see her trying to puzzle it out. It sounds crazy, but I just wanted her to think that a little of the man she married, had surfaced for a second, and relented.

I have spent my life watching her serve him, she was a good wife. Actually, my mum was a great wife, she was hard working, dedicated and loyal, and all the moments of happiness in my childhood were with her. I suppose it was important to me, because I know she has suffered terrible loneliness, and pain through his coldness, and in a way, I wanted her now to make up for it and live. Weird as it sounds, if she thought that just for one second, she had maybe managed to bring a little of the old Edwin back, it might be enough for her to move on and be happy.

Birch has talked often about the women who marry cold, abusive, unloving, husbands. They do so, because the guy was like prince bloody charming in the early days, bombarding them with gifts, and constantly telling them how much they loved them.

They were literally the kindest most loving men you would ever meet.

The poor women never realised it was all just an act, just a way of securing a pretty wife to have pretty children, to make their public image and profile better. They were cold, narcissistic, abusive men, who were driven by power, money and praise, and once the women married them, they were trapped, unable to do anything as their husbands dropped their act, took control of everything, and kept all the details of themselves, the house, and the money secret behind passwords.

She talked of the many women she had worked with, who would tell her, 'I know I can get through to him, and bring that side of him back.' They honestly believed that if they loved more, did more, tolerated more, it would eventually change them back, to the kind loving men that they had been when they married.

The simple truth was, there was never ever any hope, these kinds of people were set in their ways, and in complete control. They already had what they needed, they had the token wife and child, there was no need for them to change. Oh yes, they would do something shitty and the women would break down, but all they had to do was turn on the charm, shed a few crocodile tears, and promise to change, and the women would accept every kind of abuse you could throw at them. They would always forgive their newly reformed loving husband for everything. Sadly, it never lasted more than a week. These cold cruel men, are incapable of change, it is in their DNA, they are natural narcissists, who can only see themselves and their own needs, their wives and their children's needs are invisible to them.

These people are incapable of loving, they can pretend, because they know the words, and they certainly will spend money on gifts if it is absolutely needed to patch things up, but apart from that, everything has a monetary value. They squirrel away hiding their cash, acting self important and creating a fake image, of the perfect husband and the perfect father, and dutiful son, and everyone praises them as an upstanding citizen. It makes me sick to think about it, because it is all a charade, a mask, that hides the cold, sadistic, uncaring, and unloving monsters they really are, and I realise now, my dad was one of them.

I had often thought as Birch talked, she was telling me all this so that I would understand my mother and father, and today sat here after Friday night, I could see she had been. Birch had warned me in advance of what was to come. I had to admire her, I think Friday night she was far more informed than I realised when we entered the Hunters, she must have worked my dad out a long time ago. She had no bag, so she must have slipped her cheque book and pen in her coat knowing, and was sat poised, and ready to jump to my aid. Only this time it was not for me, it was for my mum. I think I love Birch even more today, just because of what she has done for my mum, she never ceases to amaze me. My voice was soft.

"Are you going to be alright mum, this must be really hard for you?" She was sat leaning back on the sofa head rest.

"Abby, I have cried a lot of tears over the years, and I will not deny I have been lonely, some days have been gruelling for me. Your Uni years were the toughest, but having done them, I am not going to do any more. I know he is your dad, and I am not going to tell you what to do about that, you are a big girl, you know what is right for you. But I have to tell you Abby, I am going to live, just live and enjoy life. I think I will paint more, cycle more, and read more. I put so much on hold to live up to his standards, and so I am going to take them off hold, and do a few things I want to do." I smiled.

"I hope I can join in with you, I would love that." She smiled at me, and it was such a soft loving smile.

"I have made so many mistakes Abby, I really messed up and thought I had lost you forever at one time, I am so glad Birch helped us both find our way back together. You know, I am so proud of who you have become, I just finished reading Seeds of Summer again, and I have got to say, I love your honesty. You take the truth and just smack everyone in the face with it, as you point out the hypocrisy of society. It really is an amazing little book, I have learned a lot about me, and you also, from reading it. I love the fact, you chose Birch in the end, for a time I was afraid you wouldn't. Abby, you made the choice I was afraid of, and here I am, it took a long time for me to understand my life, but now I do, like you, I am just going to live it."

I was so happy to hear her say that, there are so many women out there today that fall apart, having made their entire life about their marriage, and serving this one ungrateful man. Too many women give up what makes them truly happy, my mum gave up painting, I always hated my dad for that, he just made it impossible for her. I cannot count how many times I sat in the garden at home, and wondered how many amazing pictures she could have done, if only he had allowed it. I think it is the cruellest thing he ever did.

"I am really happy to hear that mum, and just for the record, both of us are proud of you too. Birch really loves you mum, you are like another mum to her, you will not be alone, and the door is always open. You know Christmas Day, why not come over Christmas Eve, and spend the night here. We have two rooms, you sleep in here in my room, and then we can all be together first thing in the morning, it will just be like it used to be. Although in a strange way, you will have four extra daughters, and a son to contend with, because mum we are all one big family here, and you are part of that. The only real difference will be, it will be here in my house for the first time. I would love that; would you think about it?" She smiled.

"If Birch finds out, she will hound me until I say yes."

"Too late I know, so say yes... Hi Sweetie, say yes Mum."

She giggled as Birch stood in the door scratching her head, her hair standing out in every direction, she rubbed the sleep out of her eyes, and blinked.

"I need coffee... Oh, and a pee."

Wow Birch can really pee loud... And for ages, how much did we drink last night? We headed downstairs for coffee. Edwina had finally risen, and yep Luke stayed, they were already sat at the computer in their underwear, drinking coffee and talking code. I lingered at the door a moment and watched them; it appears to me Chloe was right. Edwina would talk, and ask him what he thought, and then just stare into his eyes as he answered, oh boy she is hook, line, and sinker into him in a major way. I think that it is so sweet, and actually looking at her smile, she is so happy.

In the kitchen Deb's was getting ready, we sat down and I looked at her.

"What ya doin?" She gave me a big smile.

"I own a bookshop, and my favourite author is making a rare

public appearance, I am opening up, there are books to be sold."

It is one of the many things I love about Deb's, she is so supportive. Since the release of Seeds of Summer' she has had a huge poster of me, which okay I find weird as hell. No one likes walking into a building, and seeing a huge five by four, picture of themselves, but I cannot deny, seeing the whole section filled with my books, all with my name on the spine, is a huge thrill. I am shameful I know; I sometimes go in the shop on the pretence of seeing how Denise is, just to see the display of my work.

We made coffee and sat round the island, Deb's opened a packet of biscuits, and immediately, Chloe's head popped round the studio door, she saw the ginger nuts and came out to join us. She walked up the kitchen, and I stared at her.

"What the hell are you wearing?"

She looked down, she had on red laced panties, with white fir around the waist band and the legs, she looked at me like I was mental for not knowing.

"Christmas Panties!" I looked at Birch, as she sipped her coffee.

"Do you have Christmas Panties?" She looked down at her slightly fluffy vagina.

"I only have one pair of panties, the one's I bought for Deb's wedding, and I am not sure where they are." Chloe shrugged.

"It's winter guys, it gets cold, so I thought I would wear something warmer."

Okay it is not just me is it, I mean she is wearing only panties, and the house thermostat is set to warm enough for Satan? My mum grasped the stick, she understood my thoughts.

"Chloe you are still 98% naked, do panties make that much of a difference?" She looked down.

"I like it kept warm; you know just in case." I looked at her in disbelief.

"Of what... It starts raining dicks?" She shrugged.

"I don't know what will happen next, I mean seriously, did you ever think Edwina would give Ronald a blow job?"

My mum spluttered, and coughed, her coffee went everywhere, Edwina who was walking down the hall with two empty cups, turned on the spot, and headed back to the library. Mum coughed, and her eyes watered, I gave her a large pat on the back, Deb's stared at Chloe in shock.

“That was true?” Chloe frowned and nodded.

“Yeah, I told you.”

Mum continued to cough, and Birch handed her some kitchen towel. We helped clean up, and mum stopped coughing, and then we explained to her how mistakenly she had thought Santa was Luke, but in his panic, Anthony had grabbed Ronald, dressed him up and sat him in the chair. She giggled when I told her how grateful Ronald had been, and how Edwina was redder than his suit. Chloe nodded looking very serious.

“So, remember guys, always check under the beard first.” Deb’ stared at Chloe suspiciously.

“Jesus Chloe, how many Santa’s do you intend to blow, I mean is this a thing you do?” She shrugged.

“I keep all my options open.” I looked at her.

“Wow you are such a slut.” She smiled.

“I know, it makes me happy.” My mum just sat giggling.

“Is it like this all the time here?” Birch looked up from her cup.

“Pretty much.” The coffee was working, and Birch was coming to life.

It was nice to just sit around the island in the middle of our vast kitchen and talk, and have fun. We talked of life and love and dreams, and all five of us added our thoughts, mum appeared to be really enjoying it, I think she needed it. Just listening to us, all aged in our mid twenties, reminded her of the life she once dreamed of, she put her cup down and smiled at me, she had a faraway look in her eye. She turned the cup slowly on the unit and looked down at it, and gave a long sigh.

“You girls remind me so much of a younger me, learn from me girls, don’t give up your dreams and your soul for another person. I have so many regrets, do not make the mistakes I made.”

“Bullshit.”

We all gasped and looked at Birch, mum looked up at her, Birch’s eyes shone bright green.

“That is such crap Flick... Look we all have choices, we can be who we think we are supposed to be, or we can be who others think we should be, that is a choice, and one we all make. You chose to be the woman Ed wanted, there was no gun to your head, you openly and freely made that choice. You gave up a lot to be the model wife in the model village, do not regret it, bloody own it." I looked at her not understanding why she would say that, mum looked hurt.

"Jesus Birch, aggressive much?" She turned to me.

"Oh really, you tell me, was she a good or shitty mum?"

I felt panicked, I did not want dragging into this, everyone was looking at me, and I swallowed hard. I looked at my mum, and then turned to Birch.

"That is unfair Birch, she is my mum, you know better than any how I feel about her." She smiled, and her eyes sparkled.

"I do, I know how much you love her, I saw how much it ate you away at Uni because you parted on bad terms. I saw how you fought to rebuild that bond when you came back, and I saw how much you truly loved her the other night, as you negotiated on her behalf. Your love for your mum is a huge part of who you are, so you tell me, was she wrong to do what she has done, would life have been better or worse had she taken a different route?" I frowned; it was a stupid question.

"That's stupid, had she taken a different route I would not be here." Birch smiled at me, and her eyes sparkled even more.

"Exactly... I would not be sat here with the love of my life, Deb's would not have the wedding of her dreams, and Chloe would be sat in a flat starving to death, because none of this would have happened. Ed is a prick, Hatty is right, but it does not change the fact, that some great good has grown out of what your mum and dad did. Look, a lot of it has been painful and has taken its toll, but that is life, tell me Deads, you are not married, has your life been any easier, because of that?" My mum smiled.

"I see your point Birch, actually you have such a beautiful way of seeing my life, I am feeling very touched." Birch turned.

"Flick I am so glad you met Ed, because that gave me Deads, and also another person I see as a mother. I get it, life sucks at the moment and you feel you have lost everything, but trust me you have not. Flick those things we feel do not go away, they are all there inside you, they always have been, you are still you, and I think in the weeks to come you will see that. If you do not like the woman that was married to Ed, boot her out, make a different choice." Suddenly her outburst made sense, she looked round at all of us with those big green beautiful eyes.

"Look at us... Society is full of shit, it says by this time we must be educated, by that time we must have a job, or by this time we must be married with kids, but it is a crock of shit. All of us sat here can be and do anything we want. look at Chloe, she is happy, all she wants to do is paint and screw, society says that is wrong, but why? She is happy, Deb's was obsessed with a vocalist she wanted to sleep with, she did it, and four years later he married her. Society says that was improper, but look how happy she is. Society says Deads should love all women, or all men, but she doesn't feel attraction to them all, she chose me, and I chose her. We are both happy regardless, because we made a choice that was right for us. You are free now, make a different one that is in tune with you." Chloe sat back; her eyes were wide open.

"Oh wow, you just totally mind fucked me... In a good way." Birch reached across the table and took my mums hands in hers.

"Flick you are only as old and only as free as you choose. The way I see it, this could be the best thing for you, because having devoted your life to your husband and daughter, you can now devote the rest to yourself. If it feels good, just do it, and enjoy your time, that is all we are doing."

I watched as my mum's eyes sparkled, it was like suddenly she understood everything, and her smile, was probably the most beautiful I had ever seen. She squeezed Birch's hand.

"Thank you... You know, you are all my daughters, I really do love all of you so much." Chloe smiled.

"I totally get that, what's not to love mum, we are fucking wonderful?" She started to laugh; Chloe looked round at us all. "What?" Deb's leaned over and kissed her cheek.

"You are simple, but very lovely." Chloe looked down; Deb's frowned.

"What are you doing?" Chloe looked at her.

"I am checking you out to make sure you don't have a sponge." I started to giggle, Deb's winked and looked at mum.

"I got her so wet last night it was unbelievable." Chloe looked at her with a furrowed brow.

"I was damp, the rest was the bath, it was Percy who got me really wet."

"Oh, you liar." Mum looked at me. and I shook my head.

"Just don't ask, it's safer that way."

Time was ticking on, and Deb's had to go open the shop, I was the guest for the main event, which felt strange. I needed more clothes than the big baggy top I was wearing. It looked really cold outside, and standing outside in it was not my idea of fun, so I decided to head upstairs and find something warmer to wear.

I put on long socks, and slipped on my black heavy canvas pants. I slid on a vest, velvet top, and a big heavy jumper, and walking downstairs in a house already hotter than hell, as we did live in few clothes at home, I felt I would melt. I slipped on my thick coat, as Birch came clumping down the stairs in heavy snow boots, I smiled, she had two jumpers and a scarf wrapped round her neck. She pulled on her heavy coat. Chloe appeared wrapped to the nines, and we all joined mum at the door and set off.

It was cold, as we walked down towards Manor Road, I linked my mum's arm, and she gave it a squeeze.

"I have had fun today, Abby." I breathed out and watched my breath drift upward.

"I am glad you did, mum you are part of us, and always welcome to come and just hang out." Birch who was holding my other arm looked across me.

"Flick if Ed has gone, what will the Parish Council do, he was the accounts member?" She gave a sigh.

"I have someone in mind, the hard part will be convincing them, they are most certainly qualified, the problem is they are hostile to the council." Birch gave a giggle and shook her head.

"I wish you luck, but I have to say Flick, if you can get her, that would be a mighty move for this village." I looked at Birch, feeling confused.

"What, do you know who mum means?" She giggled.

"Sweetie have you not worked it out?" I shook my head.

"No, who is it?" Birch looked at my mum and gave a big smile, I turned to mum, and she winked at me.

"We are talking about Hatty, Abby."

I looked at her feeling completely surprised, and gasped out my words with utter surprise.

"NO WAY?"

Chapter 9

Lighting Wotton.

Wotton Dursley was preparing for the Christmas season. Shops were opening later, a large Christmas tree was in the centre of the Village Green, and every shop had a small tree, either outside on the path, or on a wall bracket fixed above the doors, or windows. The Hunter's Arms was decorated with coloured lights, and had five lit trees along the wall.

Santa's Grotto was busy, all the new staff were doing a great job, I noticed a good few elves, who looked way less slutty than we had. Outside the Church Hall a wooden stage, ten feet high, had been erected, and decorated either side with two giant trees. It had a large steel framework with lights on it, from which hung a huge Merry Christmas banner, it looked much bigger than I expected.

Green Street was again closed, and the Tea Rooms, which was open until late, had outdoor heaters that blew warm air onto the tables, and was serving hot chocolate, with marshmallows. Louise and Stacy were dressed in warmer looking Christmas uniforms, and they were busy.

The village was really busy, I must admit, I had not seen it this busy before. Kids were all over the place, there were food vans serving chips and burgers, which were parked up in front of the empty antique store, and the dress boutique, had long lines of families, as we walked up the side of the green towards the church, I turned to mum.

"Mum this is pretty amazing, I cannot believe there are this many visitors, I have never seen it this busy before." Birch giggled.

"You are silly Sweetie." I didn't understand.

"Why am I silly, can you see all this, it is mad busy compared to last year? I tell you what, Anthony has done a first rate PR job. I really hope all the new lights are worth seeing, or there will be a lot of disappointed people." Birch gave a chuckle as my mum just smiled, she leaned into me.

"Just keep your hood up until we are inside Sweetie, we would hate you to be stampeded." I turned and looked at her.

"What the hell are you talking about?" My mum started to laugh, she looked at Birch.

"Bless her, isn't she lovely?" Birch giggled as her bright green eyes twinkled.

"She is my Sweetie Flick, she has always been special, that is why I love her."

Okay so these two lunatics, were making no sense at all. I hate it when they do that whole Runestone talk with your brain business.

We arrived at the Church Hall, and Birch walked me in, Anthony saw me and came rushing over.

"Oh, you got here unnoticed, thank god for that, I was having kittens worrying about you getting mobbed before you made the door." I looked at him as I pulled my hood down.

"Are all of you bonkers, why the hell would I get mobbed in Wotton, it's the most boring place on earth?" He stepped back and rested his right hand on his chest, his eyes looking at me like I said something ridiculous.

"Oh, Abby darling, you really are so adorable." He laughed. "I was about to send out search parties, fearing that lot out there would rip your clothes off." I was understanding nothing at all, I think he is mad too.

"Anthony you are mental, the only person who wants to rip my clothes off is Birch." She leaned in and gave a giggle.

"I think Nigel would like too also." I cringed, and a cold shiver ran down my spine.

"Do you have to, Jesus Birch you are twisted?"

What I had failed to notice in my introverted hermit like life as a writer, was my book was a best seller. I mean, a picture of me with my semi naked lover at the airport, splashed all over the papers should have been a hint, but I did not see the world like others. In an attempt to make the Wotton lights popular, my mum and Anthony, had very craftily arranged for a lot of press, to show the author of Seeds of Summer, was their guest for the light up. I looked at mum as she explained it all to me, and apologised, for being underhanded.

"Mum I am not that famous, trust me, you might get a dozen or two more, but don't get your hopes up." Birch gave me a big cuddle.

"Sweetie, Anthony is right, you are adorable." She planted a huge kiss on my lips.

I had an hour to go, and was informed that I was best off removing my coat, yeah that boat did not float, I am a creature of comfort. We agreed the compromise of hood down, hair on display, and unzipped, which left me with a warm back and arms, it was a push, but I could live with it. To fill the time, I sat with Birch, and had a coffee, Anthony kept on coming in and telling me how there was a crowd building, I was not that convinced.

The night and the lighting up would take the setting of a few carols with the Church Choir, then mum as Parish Council Chair will make her announcement's, and then I get to say a few words, and then hit the big red button, not exactly the hardest thing to do. Birch told me how much she admired my confidence, and that Deb's had roped off the seats in the shop, as she wanted me to sign a few books. I shrugged, I had no problem with that, as long as I was not facing the giant poster of me, I was fine.

Marjorie sat in the Tea Rooms, with her usual Shrew Crew.

"I must admit, this is all very suspicious, what are they up to? I think it is disgraceful that they have spent so much money on a huge platform like that. It is a gross negligence of their position, she swans round the village these days like she is the queen, there needs to be some big changes in this village, and one of them is that Felicity Watson needs to be ousted."

The choir arrived, dressed in their gowns, with Gail, I had not seen her for a while, her hair had really grown long, it made her look prettier. She saw me and came over.

"Abigail, how are you? Nervous I bet, playing the home crowd is never easy." I frowned.

"I am fine Gail, love the hair it looks really good, you have not been in our garden for a while, I take it things have been busy?" She gave a sigh.

"Yeah, I feel some days like there are so many things going on, I need another vicar to help cope, I will make it at some point. I was hoping to pop by over Christmas." I chuckled.

"They are on tour all Christmas, they have a gig Christmas Day, so he will not be back until New Year."

She looked disappointed. Gail had a big crush on Floyd, the guitarist of the Battered Taco rock band, she had slept with him four times that we knew of. I must admit, it was really messed up to actually know a vicar who was also a rock groupie.

The Choir went out to sing their carols, and I sat back and relaxed, outside there was a lot of clapping, Birch slid her chair closer to me.

"I will be right with you at the side of the stage, don't be nervous, just breathe in, then say your piece and hit the button." I nodded.

"Birch, I know what to do, I will be fine, stop worrying."

I sat back and listened to the carols as the Choir sang, it reminded me much of my early teens of when I was a part of it all. It is strange in a way, because I do not miss the choir at all, but I do love to listen to them. The choir's set of carols ended, and the applause was a lot louder than I expected, I leaned back in my chair.

"Wow they really liked that." Birch smiled at me, she pulled on my arm.

"We are up, come on." I gave a sigh and got up.

"Let's get this done and over, I want to get home, get naked, and then get drunk and have my wicked way with you, in a warm and steamy environment." She gave a gasp.

"Oh, I want that too now, I want bath sex, you know, I have wondered if we should have a sauna added." I smiled it was a great idea, I was into anything hot, especially in this weather. I leaned in to kiss her, Gail appeared.

"Anthony says it is almost time, he wants you out by the stage." Birch took my hand.

Outside the doors, a large cloth wall had appeared, to screen the doorway off from the street. We walked up behind it, to the steps that led up to the stage. Anthony stood smiling, I could hear my mum welcoming everyone, announcing some of the events that would be coming up over the next few weeks. Birch took my hand, and Anthony gave the signal, we walked up the steps to the side of the stage, I saw mum stood at the microphone. I also saw some of the crowd and gripped Birch's hand tight.

"OH CRAP, THERE ARE MILLIONS!"

The crowd was huge, I could only see from here to the shops on Church Rise, and there was not an inch of free space, it was literally packed with people, hundreds of people. I felt myself falling apart, as my legs started to shake, I turned to her, and looked into her green eyes.

"Birch there are too many, I cannot go out there, I am really sorry, I just cannot do this."

My heart was racing, and I was starting to sweat, I could feel my mouth drying out, my mum was coming to the end of her announcements, and my stomach had started to churn, I was feeling desperate, I grabbed Birch's jacket, and pulled hard.

"Birch why are they here, I want them to go home?" She smiled.

"Sweetie, they love you, Deads, they are all your book fans, these are the people who have read Seeds of Summer." I felt my jaw drop, as the wind ran out of me.

"They are fans... They came to see me?" She smiled.

"Yes Sweetie, they really love what you write, that is why they are here." I was as my northern friends say 'Gob Smacked', I looked back at them.

"But Birch, there are so many." She pulled me into a hug.

"Of course there are Sweetie, you are Abigail Jennifer Watson the author of the Hand of Death vampire series, and Seeds of Summer, who do you think buys them all?"

I honestly never realised, it just never actually dawned on me, I had money flowing in, but it just did not compute in my brain, that it was from book sales. People bought my books, lots of them, and it looked like a lot of them had come here. Birch slipped off my coat, and then lifted her scarf from her neck and wrapped it loosely round mine, it smelt of her perfume, as she lifted my hair out and arranged it on my shoulders.

"Deads, go talk to your fans, I will be here, but you will also have something of me round your neck to keep you safe and warm. Deads, you earned this, oh Sweetie you earned this the hard way, go out there and enjoy it, and switch on those lights." I took a deep breath.

"Kind of over the top Birch, but you are right." She leaned in and gave me a soft kiss, I felt my toes curl, and I gasped as I broke free.

"Wow!"

"That is for extra sparkle, but I know you will sparkle brighter than any lights tonight, you always have for me." I think I blushed; my mum was stood next to the mic.

"Ladies and gentlemen, thank you so much for your patience, I stand here tonight a proud mum, as I introduce our guest for tonight, because she is my daughter. Ladies and gentlemen, please welcome to the stage, Miss Abigail Jennifer Watson." Birch screamed, and bounced up and down clapping.

"Deads, that's you."

I took a huge breath, turned and walked nervously onto the stage, and heard the deafening noise of applauding people.

It was really scary, as I looked out on a sea of faces, I have never seen Wotton look like this, there was not a place anywhere empty. The green was gone, the roads the pavements everywhere was packed with happy smiling faces. I stood by the mic, and I was blown away completely, I could feel tears in my eyes, as I stared at them all. Their cheers were deafening. I suddenly felt really awkward, and waved.

"Hello... Hi... Er... I am Abigail, welcome to my village home."

My voice sounded so loud through the speakers; it was so weird hearing myself like that. It was blinding under the big spotlight, and cameras flashed from every direction. I had no idea what to do, hell I get nervous talking to some of my neighbours, but this... This was beyond belief. I took another deep breath and smiled, as the crowd roared into the air, it was terrifying, and also pretty amazing, I could feel my legs shaking.

I wish I had prepared more, but honestly, I just never expected this, I was shaking like a leaf as they all looked to me. I looked back, and saw Birch, she was stood with her hands clasped on her heart, smiling, her bright green eyes dancing in her face with happiness. I looked out at the masses.

"Wow you guys, this is mind blowing, I wondered who bought

all the books." There were so many happy smiling faces, it was overwhelming, and I felt tears form in my eyes.

"This is too much; wow you guys are amazing."

I looked back and saw Birch smiling, my legs were shaking like crazy, I had no idea what to say, they were yelling how much they loved me, and it just blew me away, I was trying to think of smart words to say, but it was just too much. I leaned into the mic.

"Seeds of Summer has become a huge success thanks to you all." Cheers again rose into the air, and I smiled.

"You really are, absolutely amazing, and looking out on all of you, actually stood in the village I based the book on, is so overwhelming for me, but it is also the most wonderful thing I have seen here for a long time, thank you, all of you."

The roar of the crowd was deafening, and all I could do was smile and laugh, even though I was terrified I would pull a Rosie, because honestly, it was very intimidating.

"Most of you think I made Seeds of Summer up, and some of it I did, but most of it was quite true to life, especially that wonderful character called Willow." I looked back at Birch, she was stood smiling with tears in her eyes, I turned back to the crowd and cheering smiling faces.

"What you do not know is, I based her on a very amazing and special person, she told me, 'Be You.' Does that sound familiar?"

The audience erupted, and I felt the laugh rise up, and bubble out of me, this was actually a lot of fun, and I was starting to feel a little calmer. I giggled.

"Would you like to meet her?" They roared out, and I laughed and turned and held out my shaking hand to her, she looked utterly terrified, and shook her head. I leaned into the mic.

"Birch, Willow, please?" I looked back at the crowd. "She is a little nervous, I don't blame her, it scared the shit out of me walking up here." The crowd made a ton of noise, Flick pushed her hand into Birch's back.

"She needs you, get out there." And she shoved hard, Birch staggered onto the stage in full view. I grabbed her hand and pulled her towards me, the crowd roared with deafening delight.

"If you don't recognise her, it is because she is dressed tonight."

Laughter roared up, and she came to my side, she looked so terrified, it felt good to finally get my own back and catch her out.

I held her hand tight. I stood by the mic.

"Seeds of Summer, is a story of hope, of understanding who we are as people, as we try to understand the hate in the world that surrounds us. I think all of you truly understand that, which is why you are here. We all face so many challenges in life today, and we have to overcome the ignorance of those who cannot see us as the people we are, and so we endure their shame. Christmas is a time when we should try to just accept each other, and allow our humanity to flourish, and not judge. Be you, and be nice to each other."

The crowd roared in applause, and even though my heart was pounding in my chest, I felt excited inside, this was like nothing I had ever known, I turned to Birch and she was smiling and watching me, I squeezed her hand, as I turned back to the mic.

"Seeds of Summer is also the story of how I found this amazing human being, and how she has changed my life, and my writing. It is as much her story as it is mine, and because of that, tonight in our home village, I want to throw beautiful light over everything, and illuminate the world we share." I pulled Birch, and we moved slightly to the podium next to the mic. I then reached over to the big red button holding Birch's hand.

"Ladies and gentlemen, tonight we will light new lights that have been funded by many donations, it has taken a long time to raise these funds, and we do have buckets around for more donations. I hope you will help me support this village, we are so proud of it, and as you know, Willow loves all things that sparkle."

I looked at Birch, and smiled, her eyes twinkled. I took her hand in mine and lifted it up above the button.

"I hope all of you have a really wonderful Christmas, and thank you for taking the time to come and meet us, it has really made our year. I now declare the Wotton lights officially lit."

I pushed both of our hands onto the button and the whole village suddenly lit up with a million lights, I gasped as the crowd roared. It looked so beautiful; I could not believe it. All the buildings were decorated, there were lines from lamp post to lamp post, they reached across the road, and went right round the Village Green.

Everything was just so colourful, and I think this was the

prettiest I had ever seen the village. Every lamp post had a Santa, or snowman, or reindeer lit up on it, and it all looked simply beautiful.

Both of us stood and waved from the stage, for a good few minutes' smiling, and then slowly walked off to huge applause, my mum was all smiles as she walked back onto the stage and up to the mic.

"Ladies and gentlemen, Miss Watson will be available to sign copies of her books at Cog's and Wheelers Bookshop shortly, we have a line roped off, if you wish to purchase or meet with her."

I came down the steps feeling really happy, Birch was giddy and happy, I turned to her and pulled her close, and gave her a huge kiss.

"That was really scary, I started to panic a little, thanks for being there. It felt so strange and weird, but Birch it was amazing, they all came to see us, wasn't that just the best?" She just looked at me with those beautiful eyes.

"Sweetie it was your stage, you did not need to share it, they came here to see you." I knew that.

"Birch, I wanted to, I could not have written it without you, I was also terrified, but once I felt your hand in mine, I was fine." She put her hand to my face and her eyes sparkled.

"Oh Sweetie, you have no idea how great a writer you have become, you stopped living, that was all, but you are more alive now than I have ever known, you are so beautiful." A tall guy in a black shirt with security written on it tapped my shoulder.

"Excuse me Miss Watson, but I have to get you to the book shop, there is a long line." Birch pulled on my coat, lifted my hood and zipped it up, I felt really happy.

I have got to say, walking down the middle of the road, peering out through my large hood, was a really strange experience. The line went from the bookshop right up to the post office. Two large guys in black were stood on the door. From under the hood, I looked at the long line of people, aged from young teens into their thirties. I pulled Birch close, she was loving this, and staring up at the millions of lights across the street.

"Deads, this is so pretty; I love living here."

People in the line were happy and smiling, it felt so surreal, had they really all come because of my books? I could hear secret excited voices asking 'is that her?' Oh man this is so messed up, I must admit, it does not feel real. I spent four years alone in my tiny house struggling, and then feeling the disappointment when my stories did not sell, and so just seeing this, here in Wotton, was mind blowing.

As I arrived at the shop, I dropped my hood, and flicked my long hair back, and there was an instant explosion of flash cameras, and a murmur of excitement in the line. I walked in through the door with Birch, and Deb's was flustering, she already had about forty people in the shop. Luke was carrying out boxes filled with books, Edwina and Denise were at the till, taking payments, and Chloe was stood on watch by the two seats, she was in control of a red rope that had been used to section off the seated area, there were already four excited people there holding books.

Chloe winked, and leaned towards us with a huge smile and whispered to us.

"There is a box of pens, and a tall glass of courage on your table." She looked back and gave a sly smile.

"There is a guy at the back, I told him I was the inspiration for the crazy artist girl, and he did me good in the toilet, although don't tell Deb's I admitted it, I am not sure she was happy about it." She wore a very big and happy smile.

I took off my coat, and folded it neatly, and placed it down by the side of my chair, the shop got silent the moment I had walked in, and there were people stood silently watching me, holding my books with the pages open. It was as Birch would say, 'unsettling.' I looked at the young girl waiting at the front of the line and I smiled, she was holding a copy of 'Sanctuary Arch,' which was my latest book, it felt so odd to see it in her hand.

I sat down in my seat, and Birch took over on the rope, and let the first girl through, she gushed with excitement, as I wrote her name, and asked for a selfie, and that for the next three hours was my life. I was absorbed with writing nice things in books, and signing them, and endless selfies. The glass was soon empty, and Chloe provided a refill. Outside the hordes of visitors were having a great time, the brass band was on the stage playing carols, and all the shops were busy, and having the best night of the year sales wise.

I left home at two thirty, and it was almost ten when I was finally finished. My last fan was a young girl called Kerry, she beamed with delight, as she sat in the chair, at my side.

"I am so happy Miss Watson to finally meet you, I want you to know that you and all the Curio's are so special to me." I looked at her as I wrote in her book.

"You have seen the Curio site?" She nodded.

"I wanted to kill myself, I was being bullied so badly at school, and I heard about it, and went on and posted a message, that was about two years ago."

I stopped writing and looked at her, it felt shocking to actually hear someone say the words out loud, she smiled such a loving smile.

"You and Chloe answered me, and I cried for days I was so happy. You both really got me, you just understood everything. We talked for six months, and things got so much better for me, I just want you to know, what you guys did was amazing, and it made such a big difference to me. I made quite a few friends on the site forum, and we all met up, two of them are my best friends now."

She was so sincere, and yet so alive, I felt a lump in my throat, and had to swallow, to try an overcome the huge emotion that was swirling inside me. She looked at me and held out her hand.

"It has been a real honour to meet you, all of you, and I just wanted to thank you in person." I could not help it, my eyes filled, and tears ran down my cheeks, and my voice got all squeaky.

"I am so glad you came on the site, and I am glad you did not do something daft; I have been there Kerry, I know what that is like, and how bad it feels. You don't need to thank us; it is actually our pleasure." She smiled.

"It is probably cheeky of me, but all of you are here, do you think they would have a picture taken with me?" I gave a sniffle and looked at Birch, tears were on her cheeks too, she smiled and nodded.

Five minutes later, I handed my phone to Luke, he already had Kerry's, as we all gathered together, and smiled, the pictures were taken and she hugged all of us and gushed happy thanks. I hugged her for an age with tears in my eyes, it probably sounds crazy, but it felt like I was hugging my younger self. She left happy and Deb's locked the door, Birch was really happy, she looked at us all, her eyes full of life and sparkles.

"We did good guys, things were getting really tough for all of us, but look at us, and look what we did. Kerry came to see us, and is alive because of our web site, we saved a life, and she is so lovely, we really did good."

She was right, it is so crazy to think about it, we were just trying to get through, fighting back so we could be left alone, tired of being called and bullied. We still were not there, even now after two years, but out there, people had been watching, and as a result it had saved others, and I felt so good about that.

Walking home was noisy, and I made a mental note, don't let Chloe supply the drinks at big events, I was starting to feel giddy. Izzy had joined us, and was telling us about stories of her cases in Manchester. One woman came in to talk because her husband would only have sex, dressed in a raincoat and wellies, and he made her wear a fisherman's hat. We all started to giggle as she chuckled about the case, and then she looked at us all, and told us.

"I am telling you, there are some people out there who are really weird, even for me." I looked at her.

"Seriously, wow you are so accepting of everyone's kinks, how could anyone be too weird for you?"

Izzy gave a chuckle, and then told us about a really weird guy who wanted to join the club, he liked to have sex with loaves of bread filled with mushed bananas. Chloe was laughing and staggering all over, Deb's looked appalled, which set me off. Izzy and Birch were really serious about it all, and Luke was looking panicked at Edwina who just shrugged. Izzy was fascinated.

"Yeah, we scooped out the centre, and then filled it with the fruit, and microwaved it for a minute, you know, just to get them warm enough, and then he just got hard as a rock and attacked it." Deb's shuddered.

"Izzy no matter how you look at it, that is seriously frigging messed up." She smiled.

"I must admit it smelt lovely; I think I will bake banana bread tomorrow." Chloe looked at me with a worried look.

"You heard her story; seriously can we trust her? If you eat some first, I will." We reached the gates as I started to giggle, Birch stopped and looked at the house.

"Who was the last one home?" I frowned at her.

"We were why?" She looked at me.

"Deads, it was daylight, we did not have lights on, did we?" I shook my head.

"Nope, well not as I remember, does it matter?" She looked at me.

"Then who put all the lights in the house on?"

I turned to the house, everything was lit up, I looked at the others, they all shook their heads, no one knew. Okay so that is really weird?

Chapter 10

Past Feelings.

I have felt I was on cloud nine all day, it was crazy, but my whole body was filled with a level of excitement I had not felt since I was a child. Hatty emailed me a video, as always, she had been on photographic duty, documenting everything for the Parish Historical Society. Even though it was impossible for me to make anyone out in such a huge crowd, she had set up her tripod and filmed me on stage. There were several really wonderful close up shots of Birch and myself waving to everyone.

Edwina was at her computer, Luke had finally gone home, she was in a video chat with Aden, whilst working on the site, she was wearing her head set with a face mic, and it was funny as she would randomly say stuff, and I kept looking up and saying 'What' then realising what she was doing, I giggled.

My computer bonged, I looked at the screen, Chloe messaged me from her laptop. Edwina had set up an in-house message system. To be honest, when she first did it, I thought she was nuts, my normal approach was to just yell, and I always got an answer, but on some occasions, it was actually really helpful. Deb's used it a lot, to talk to me from her room privately, as did Chloe from the studio. Most of the time we would all meet in the kitchen and talk, but when it came to sharing music, and pictures, it was really useful.

I read the message. 'Need to talk, I am in the kitchen, come alone.' It felt odd, just like me, normally she would just yell. I typed back. 'On my way.' I grabbed my cup, and got out of my seat. I arrived in the kitchen, Chloe was sat at the island with her laptop, she looked up as I walked in. I put my cup down, and sat in the seat opposite.

"What's up?"

She slid her laptop round, and showed me an email. She grabbed my cup and went to fill it, I looked at the email. It was from Oxendale Victim Support. I read through it, and felt a cold tingle in my back, Martin Hinkley had been released from prison. Chloe sat down and put my cup in front of me.

"They have let him out Abby, and honestly I am not sure how I feel about it." I looked at her sat watching me.

"I did not know you had victim support?" She shrugged, and tried to smile.

"Only Edwina knew, I kept it quiet, I did a year of counselling, I was embarrassed because I had nightmares and panic attacks." I was completely thrown.

"I wish you had told me Chloe." She smiled a sad smile at me.

"Abby, I wanted us to be such good friends back then, it is hard to explain, even now I get all mixed up about it. I was a total bitch to you, and yet you saved me from him, and I could see how much you were struggling with everything that was going on. I guess I talked to my counsellor a lot about you, and she really helped me understand everything, and that helped me in a strange way help you. Abby, I wanted so badly to make up for the shit I did to you, the counsellor helped me do that, and come to terms with what he did. I guess being around you, I could see you were doing alright, and I was there, just in case you had a tough moment."

I understood, in a way I had done the same thing, I had watched her to see if she was doing alright, I smiled.

"I remember admiring you for handling it so much better than I did, you were pretty strong and confident, and that really helped me, I wanted to be like you." She reached out across the island and grabbed my hands.

"Abby, you have no idea how strong you are, I got to tell you, I had a real girl crush on you back then, I mean in a very none sexual way, you know that right?" I chuckled, she smiled.

"Abby the sex was not the problem, honestly, screwing me would never have hurt me, one hot bath and he would have been gone. What scared me, and it took a long time for me to get over it, was how helpless I was, he was just too strong, and that made me so scared. You know, I bullshit a lot, but I am always in control of the sex I have, that night he was in control, and that really terrified me, because I could not stop it." I swallowed hard and took a breath, that I really could understand.

"I really do get that Chloe, the powerlessness of me around

him, I mean, I fought him off more out of panic than control, but after, when I got home, he had already told my dad I was masturbating in church, and my dad believed him and not me. I think that scared me the most, it is why I stayed quiet, if I could not convince my dad, then no one else would ever believe me." She squeezed my hands.

"We have each other Abby, and we both know our story is true, that is all that matters now. Abby he may come back to Wotton, and we may see him, can you handle that?" I felt a flutter inside my stomach.

"I have not thought about that, how do you feel?" She looked down at her cup.

"I am not in a rush Abby, I am all better now, and stronger inside than I have ever been, but honestly, I am secretly shitting myself. I am really afraid that if I see him, I will pull a Rosie, and just shit my pants."

"I was really hoping you would not say that, I feel the same, I was hoping to steal some of your courage. Shit Chloe, let's just hope he stays away from us, I mean he knows not to mess with us, right?" She gave a nod.

"Yeah, I am not sure he will be in a rush."

Birch walked quickly down the corridor towards the spare counselling room with Izzy.

"So what do we know?" She opened the door and they entered. Izzy was holding a yellow file; she sat down and opened it up.

"He came out yesterday, he has been a model prisoner, although there have been one or two incidents, it was suspected he was sexually assaulted, the signs were there but he refused to comment. His registered address is in Oxendale, his ex wife Julia, moved out of the area, she has an eight year old son, and has remarried, she has a court supervision order on him, as a registered sex offender he is only allowed supervised visits done through Social Services. Janet told me he has made no application for a visit, so at the moment it looks like he is making a clean break of everything." Birch sat down and took a deep breath.

"Okay all we can hope for is he stays the hell away from Chloe and Abby, be extra vigilant at the house for me Izzy, if anything feels off, I want to know straight away. I remember that coldness in him, and I cannot deny, it scares me Izzy, if he so much as comes within ten feet of Abby, I will kill him, I will." Izzy smiled.

"Hey, you are the calm one, remember? Jemi, I am all over this for you, Janet has become a good friend and she is on the ball, they have their watchers on him, just relax, we are on this." Birch nodded, she looked strained, Izzy smiled.

"I can cover, if you want to go to her, go on get out of here, just go to her Jemi, once you hold her you will be fine." Birch teared up.

"I couldn't handle it if anything happened to her Izzy." Izzy understood that better than any.

"Yeah, I have seen that mess, go to her... Go on get out of here, you are useless to us today." She wiped her eyes and smiled.

"I have no idea what I would do without you, honestly I really don't."

"Yeah, I have seen that mess too." She gave a giggle.

Chloe had phoned Rick, yeah, I know, I have not got a clue either. Her way of dealing with fear and stress, was to bang her way through it. I felt it was probably a really good method, sadly my girl was working, so I sat on my bed and relaxed sipping coffee. It is a tried and tested method I know also helps; I have studied it thoroughly for years.

The truth was, I was not sure how I felt about Martin, when it first happened it completely screwed my head up, and I managed to get myself through it alone. The last time I was confronted with it, I was saving Chloe, and I also had Birch, Roni, and my mum, and that made it easier.

It was now ten years on from when he first tried to rape me, and I had changed a great deal. I was not that shy, scared teenager, I was in fact a young woman, and I had seen so much in the last ten years, and grown stronger because of it. The truth was, I was not sure how I would react if I saw him, I suppose I would know in the moment. The last time I saw him, I had rushed into the church, only to be paralysed with fear, as I saw him prepare to rape Chloe, my thoughts were bouncing all over the place.

I put my coffee on the side, and lay back in the pillows and closed my eyes, I suddenly felt exhausted, and I just wanted to drift, float, and escape the moment, and the darkness swept into my mind, and I felt lighter than air, now this was what I really needed. I cannot deny, this transcendental state, whatever it is, is my idea of heaven, the world stops just for a short time, and it is like taking a time out, and just letting go of everything and being at one in peace.

Celia was stood talking with Lillian when Marjorie arrived, flanked by her Shrew Crew. Bethany, Agnes, Henrietta, and Marion walked to their usual table, and Marjorie walked up to the counter, where today, Louise was managing service. In her usual fashion she snapped out her order, like it was some form of military command. She slowly viewed the tables, taking note of who was in, and her eye landed on Anthony talking with Felicity, she instinctively scowled. Louise stared at her stood by the till.

"Mrs Wallace... I did say that will be six pounds and fifty pence please."

"What... Oh yes, here, bring the change to the table."

She walked off as Louise started to set up the tray for Stacy to serve. Marjorie had her eyes fixed on Felicity, as she walked past her own table, and continued on to the back.

"I want to speak with you Felicity Watson." Her voice as always, was loud and brash. Anthony looked terrified as Felicity turned and gave a polite smile.

"Madge, is there yet another problem?" She stood with her arms folded, staring at her.

"Yes, there dammed well is, what right have you got to spend valuable funds, building a stage for your daughter to prance about with her whore on, in the middle of the village? It is a shocking waste of our money, and have you seen the litter this morning, it's disgraceful?" Felicity slid round in her seat.

"The litter is not unsimilar to that left after every village fete, and as you are well aware, we have a system designed by yourself as I remember, in place to deal with it, which as I have noted, is happening as we speak."

"Well, what about that monstrous thing you built, that costs money, good money, and we do not part with it to waste on the likes of your daughter and her whore?" Felicity bit her lip and took a deep breath; the whole place had fallen silent.

"Madge, as it happens it was a remarkably good investment." She stood up, and faced Marjorie.

"Most of that stage was designed and built by Ronald, and the armature dramatic societies handy men. They have requested new timber for their productions, and we did a deal with them, we supplied them new timbers, bolts and fastenings, and they recycled the rest, from their own supplies. I will grant you there were costs, which were a little over one thousand pounds, but that is also an investment to aid the societies future endeavours. All the lighting and metal framework, the hall already has, so we borrowed them."

"It is still a lot of money, one thousand could be used in better ways in this community." Felicity smiled.

"As I said, it was an investment, we put buckets out, knowing that readers of Abigail's books who are big fans would be here, and I am sure you heard her make a request of those people for support? Well, it paid off, because last night we raised a little under twenty two thousand pounds for the village fund." Marjorie looked astonished.

"Well, if that is correct, I shall withdraw my objection, I am assuming Edwin will confirm this at the next public meeting?" Felicity took a deep breath; this was the moment she wanted to avoid.

"I suppose you should know, after all it will get out sooner or later. Madge, Edwin and I have separated, and he has moved to London, he will no longer be acting as Accountant on the committee, I hope to replace him shortly."

Telling Madge was not easy, but she realised it was better if she said it first, rather than let the gossips spread false rumours. Marjorie was shocked, and actually looked a little distressed, her voice lowered.

"I am very sorry to hear that Felicity, I really am, and I am sorry, this must be a very difficult time, please forgive me. I know you two had some rough patches, but I always thought your drive and determination would bring you both through. I am very sorry to hear that, I hope things will work out for you." Felicity smiled, and tried to fight back the tears.

"I appreciate that Madge, I know we have often sparred, but to hear that from you, is actually very much appreciated." Marjorie lifted her hand to her shoulder.

“We have known each other a long time Felicity, we have had our fall outs, but I have always admired your pluck, so you hang in there, you will come through this, you will see.” Felicity gave a nod.

“Thank you, Madge.” She looked at Anthony.

“I don’t approve of you, but credit where it is due, the lights this Christmas are the best for forty years, well done.” She turned and walked back to her table, Felicity sat down, as Anthony shook from head to foot. He looked at her across the table, his face was white.

“Did that just happen? Honestly Flick, I am not sure my bladder is cut out for committee business, excuse me a moment.”

I smelt her perfume long before her lips touched mine. They were soft and warm and just moist enough, and I gave a happy little moan, and responded kissing her back. I opened my eyes, and looked at her bright green eyes, and she smiled, her voice was almost a whisper.

“Hi Sweetie.” I smiled.

“This is a nice surprise.”

She leaned in and kissed me again, and I felt her soft warm skin press into mine, I instinctively spread my legs and brought them up her sides, and she nestled into me.

“Oh god, I have no idea how you know, but I really wanted this?” She slid down and kissed my neck softly and I felt the ripples run through my body. “Oh Birch!” She gave a soft sexy moan.

“I want you my dark little beastie.”

I took a long breath in, as my skin came wildly alive, oh she was so going to get it, I could feel the beast inside me waking up. I looked down at the mass of white hair, patched in black, she looked up, and her eyes smouldered with lust, I felt my heart jump, God that look really turned me on, I smiled.

“Oh yeah Birch, let me see your beastie too.” She gave a giggle, and took my nipple softly in her teeth and growled. Oh hell, that was it, my whole body exploded with tingles.

Hatty walked into the Tea Rooms, she saw Marjorie and sighed,

Stacy came up at her side.

"Felicity has paid for your drink, sit down and I will bring it to you."

Hatty gave a nod, and turned towards the back table, Marjorie looked up at her, but said nothing which was strange, it did make a nice change, she arrived at the table and sat down.

"How are you doing?" Anthony pushed his chair back.

"I will leave you two to talk, I have an appointment in ten minutes." Hatty smiled.

"Thanks for sitting with her, and great job, I really love what you have done with the lights, and picking Abby was a really smart move, you deserve far more credit than you have been given." Anthony smiled; he was clearly pleased.

"I love working for the council, I think everyone should try it, thank you Harriet." He made his way out, and Hatty looked at her.

"So, you look tired, did you even sleep at all last night?" Felicity gave a sigh.

"I am fine, and yes I slept very well, I spent most of yesterday with Abby, and watching her last night was a joy, I really think she was lost for words when she walked on, she never expected that." Hatty gave a chuckle.

"Yeah, I was filming her, she looked a little lost for a moment, but I think she handled it well, even if she did need Birch at her side." Stacy arrived with two coffees, Hatty smiled at her. "Thanks Stacy." Felicity lifted her cup.

"I think if that had been me, I would have wanted you there too, they are so like we were." Hatty gave a chuckle.

"I am not sure that is such a good thing Flick, we served up our fair share of chaos in our time. I have to say, I think they are perfect for each other, on paper they should not work, and yet, just like us, they fit perfectly together. I am actually quite proud of them; I think I am growing maternal towards them." Felicity gave a titter, just the thought of Hatty as a parent was funny in itself.

"Speaking of paper, it is why I invited you, I have a proposition for you." Hatty looked at her suspiciously.

"Okay so now I am worried, what plot are you hatching in that devious mind of yours?" Felicity looked her right in the eyes.

"I want you to take over the accounts and replace Edwin, I want someone I can trust, and work with in comfort. Hatty, I have worked at his side for years, and honestly, the thought of someone else doing it... Well frankly it terrifies me, I trust you, I have little trust of the others who would be suitable."

"Damn!" Felicity blinked.

"What on earth is the matter?" Hatty narrowed her eyes.

"You know damned well what is the matter, you always phrase things so I cannot say no without looking like an utter shit?" She smiled.

"Look you taught mathematics for five years before you got the art class, something like our simple accounts is a breeze for you, and it would be nice to work with you again." Hatty gave a sigh.

"Always the impossible deal... I will only do it on one condition, and I mean it Flick, this is a deal breaker if you don't do it." She was curious.

"Go on, what is it I must do for you, I think we are a little too old to sleep together." Hatty shrugged.

"I still fancy you, I always have, I am open to it, but no that was not my deal, I kind of wish I had thought of it though. Flick I want a canvas, a decent size one, at least four by five, I want you to paint me a picture for my home gallery, do that I will stay, you get a freebie until it is finished, I would say March next year, if it's a no show, I hand the books back." Felicity gave a chuckle.

"God you never quit do you, alright, you have a deal, is there anything you want me to paint?" She leaned back in her chair, and looked at her as she considered.

"Paint me something that makes you happy, something that really brings out all your joy, and I don't mean a dildo, you are not getting off the hook that easy." Felicity looked shocked.

"For god's sake Hatty, we are in the Tea Rooms." Hatty gave a laugh.

"I bet at least 90% of the customers in here own one, they will just never admit it. Is it a deal Flick, there is no backing out?" She nodded as she lifted her cup.

"I hear you; I won't be backing out." Hatty smiled.

"I cannot wait, I am really excited now."

Birch flopped back on the pillow and looked at me smiling.

“Oh god, I needed that so badly.” She lifted her arm and stroked the hair from my face, her own face was red and she was panting for breath.

“You okay Sweetie?” I smiled, as I looked at her.

“I am now you are here; I take it you heard the news then?” She chuckled.

“Was I that obvious?” I swallowed; my throat was so dry.

“Just a little bit, it is alright, I am glad you came home early, and hey, extra sex, I am never going to turn that down. Thanks Birch, I did not want to disturb you at work, but I did want to be close to you.” She smiled.

“I love you, Sweetie; I will be here when you need me. Does Chloe know, is she going to be okay?” I nodded.

“She got a message telling her he was out, and she showed it me, we talked for quite some time about it, she will be alright, we are both here together, so we will look out for each other.” Birch sat up and gave a sigh.

“It is always one thing after another, I sometimes wonder if life will ever run smooth?” I sat up next to her and slipped my arm round her waist.

“Birch stop worrying, we will be fine, we stay in groups until we know more about what is going on.” She nodded.

“You keep your phone with you at all times, I mean it Deads, even from room to room in the house, and especially outside the house. Izzy has eyes on him, so they will let us know what he is up to. If I am honest, he is on parole, so the odds are nothing will happen, but you know me, I like to cover all bases just in case?” I kissed her shoulder.

“I will be very careful, so don’t worry.” She nodded.

“Okay Sweetie, I need food, let’s go and make something, I need to recharge for round two.” I gave a happy giggle as I slipped off the bed.

“So, there is going to be round two, oh wow you spoil me.”

We headed downstairs and started to cook, and suddenly Edwina and Chloe with Rick were with us, and by unanimous vote, it was sausage butties all around. The Sausage Butty, is a thing of great wonder I discovered in Uppermill when I was at Uni. I had never had them before, and was freaked out when

Birch first made me one, but one bite, and I was hooked forever. She likes red sauce on hers, but I prefer brown.

We all sat round the island eating like greedy rats with a hunk of stale cheese, and in the library the usual tune of a video call sounded, the problem with that was we all had computers in there, so all of us had to run to the library to find out. It was for Birch, she jumped in her seat and clicked the icon to connect, the screen went dark for a second and then filled with the green haired image of a happy smiling Bev. She waved.

"Hey Jemi." Chloe and Edwina both shot their hands to their lower parts.

"Guard your vaginas." I giggled, and walked round to the side of Birch and waved.

"Hi Bev." She gave a huge smiled and waved.

"Hey Deadly, good seeing you, nice boobs." She looked at Birch. "Jemi, I want to ask you a big favour?" She gave a happy smile, and leaned forward.

"Bev Sweetie anything, what do you need?" She fidgeted a little.

"Well, you know Breeze Yet, she has some mates coming home from her land, and we promised to show them a good time. They are coming to London, and we want to know if it would be okay to come see all of you over Christmas. I mean your folks are gone, and me mam has not forgiven me for buying a house and living with my bird. We will stay at that posh hotel and stuff, but will hang out with you guys, if that is okay? I reckon it will be brill." Birch looked up at me, I had no issue with it, I loved her to bits.

"I have no issue with it, she is lovely." Bev gave me a thumbs up, Birch turned and smiled.

"Bev Sweetie, you are always welcome, you know that?" She bounced around on her seat.

"Fuckin score, Oh Jemi, this is going to be banging, we will bring shit loads of stuff, you know booze and food, her mates are bringing loads of that frog food shit, but some of it is tasty, it will be like old times. I got to tell that fat bloke at the Hunting pub that we are having his rooms. I have a sort of sensitive problem to solve, but I will talk about that when I get there with you, it is a kind of side by side not for video thing." Birch gave a smile.

"Okay Sweetie, you know me, I am here, let me know when you are near us."

"Ta Jemi, you are a fucking legend, give Deadly a good shag for me ha ha ha." I leaned in.

"Oh Bev, she just did me good, and you have no idea how naughty she has got, she just...."

I walked away from the screen, and Birch started to laugh, I heard Bev in the background.

"Deadly, what the fuck, tell me you bitch, I wanna know, Jemi what you doing to her, go on tell me all the dirty stuff?" Birch just laughed at her.

"Bev Sweetie, some things need to be said in person, not online." Bev gave a sigh.

"I will get me own back; you watch." I laughed as I headed back towards the kitchen.

Chapter 11

Trash Talk.

I heard the door bang, and opened my eyes, Birch was curled round me, we had gone back to bed, and exhausted each other, and then slept. It was dark and the little tree on the patio was lit up and bright. I could feel Birch's breath, as she breathed out on my shoulder, I was warm and snug and closed my eyes, and just drifted in this wonderful feeling of happiness.

I started to slip back into sleep, listening to the soft pace of Birch's breathing, when BOOM, BOOM, BOOM! My eyes snapped open.

"CHLOE, I WANT HIM BACK!" Birch disturbed, and rolled on her back.

"I MEAN IT CHLOE, GIVE HIM BACK!" I sat up and gave a sigh.

"What the hell now?" Birch sat up at my side.

"Having kids is a frigging pain, I am definitely going to go and rip out my uterus, when I am not as tired as I am now." She turned and slid off the bed, I followed.

BOOM, BOOM, BOOM! "CHLOE!" I opened the door, and saw Deb's standing by Chloe's bedroom door.

"Deb's what the hell, I was sleeping." She turned and she looked really angry.

"Phileas has gone, and I want him back." Edwina came out of her room.

"For god's sake Deb's, put a bloody sock in it, Chloe is not here, she has gone to collect a paint order from the Post Office." She walked up the hallway. "Why are you trying to kick her door in anyway?"

Deb's looked so angry, but I could see how worked up and upset she was getting, Phileas was really special to her, I looked at Edwina.

"She has lost Phileas." Deb's snapped at us.

"I have not lost him, he was taken, I make my bed every morning, and I always sit him on my pillow. I came home and he is gone, she has got enough teddies of her own, so I want Phileas back." Edwina gave a sigh.

"Deb's, Chloe knows how precious he is to you, she would not do that to you, trust me, she feels the same about Percy, and she really treasures you as a friend. Chloe would never do anything to hurt you." Deb's looked at me, and her eyes filled with tears.

"Abby, tell her how important he is, it has to be her, you know how much she loves him, she has tried to steal him once before." Talk about a rock and hard place?

"Deb's if I am honest, all she has ever done is hug him, you know what she is like, she just grabs and hugs. It is bloody messed up, but if I am really honest, Chloe really loves you, I really do not think she would steal him. I don't think she would want to hurt you like that." Birch agreed.

"Yeah, she is screwed up with those things, I really don't get all that rubbing and hugging and shit, but Deb's we are talking Chloe. She feels really close to you, I know, she has told me many times, I just do not think she would do this to hurt you." Deb's wiped her eyes.

"Birch no one else here would do that, Chloe adores him, she is the only one here who would take him." I understood her point, I looked at Birch.

"You know what, something is not right here, I mean it is not just Phileas, Izzy asked me if I had seen her panties two days ago, she said she had put them in the wash, but I emptied and folded all the laundry, and there were no panties in it. Chloe is always bitching someone ate her biscuits as well. I am telling you; I have wondered a few times if something was not right." Edwina gave a nod.

"Yeah, someone ate all the chicken, yet no one appeared to know who, and earlier Chloe was losing her shit because she had left her keys on the tray in the living room, when she went to get them, she said they were gone. I got tired of arguing with her and just lent her mine. I got to say, I checked her room and her studio, there was no sign of them." Debs frowned.

"They are on the tray, I just put mine on top of them." Edwina shook her head.

“That is not possible, I checked right after Chloe, and they were not there.” Deb’s gave a shrug.

“I know what I just saw, they were there Edwina.”

She could not believe it, she turned and walked downstairs, I could not deny, I wanted to know, so I followed her, Birch and Deb’s tagged along. True to her word, there were Chloe’s keys in the tray with mine, Birch’s and Deb’s. Edwina shook her head as she looked at them.

“No, I am not having it, I took my keys out, and gave them Chloe, and the tray only had two sets in it. I don’t care what anyone says, I am not wrong on this. Guys something weird as hell is going on, I do not know what, but something frigging weird is definitely happening.” Deb’s looked at us.

“Guys no one else comes here, well apart from Luke.” Edwina turned on her.

“I hope you’re not suggesting this is him Deb’s, because let me be really clear here, his dick has either been in my mouth, on my tits, up me, or at my side for every second he has been here. I have a shot with him, and this time I am not blowing it, I am showing him levels of affection that will blow every woman he has ever been with out of the water completely... Deb’s, Luke is my Jimmy.” She looked upset.

“I am sorry, I was not suggesting he would do this Edwina, but you know what, I am really happy for you, honestly I really am.” Edwina blushed a little, and her voice dropped.

“I love him guys, I have for a really long time. I buggered things up a good few years back, and I have another shot, and I am really going for it.” Birch pulled her in and gave her a hug.

“Oh, Sweetie that is so lovely, but we all kind of know, your sister has a big mouth, although she is really rooting for you at the moment, and we all think it’s really sweet.” Somehow the conversation was drifting.

“Guys, we are losing the focus here, I need a beer, I say we grab a beer, and put our heads together, and see if we cannot find some sort of logical answer.” Birch agreed, although her loyalty is tied to alcohol, so that probably was her motivating factor.

We moved into the kitchen, the fridge was almost empty of beer, Edwina went down to the cellar, whilst Birch and myself opened a cold one, and sat down at the island. I opened the tin,

I would much rather be lay in bed with Birch about now, she sat next to me and took my hand in hers. I turned and looked in her eyes, she looked really happy, I leaned on to her, and she felt lovely and warm. Edwina came back up the steps.

"Guys rather than take two out of the box, just bring the full box up, and put all of them in the fridge." The front door banged.

"I AM HOME!"

It was Chloe, she came down the hallway carrying a large box, she staggered into the kitchen and put it down, she looked at us all.

"Okay, now that is not the welcome I was expecting, what is going on?" Deb's was right off the mark.

"Phileas has gone off my bed." Chloe looked instantly upset.

"Well, where is he, we must find him, Deb's where have you looked, I will help you find him?" Deb's looked guilty, and put her head down.

"I thought you had him." Chloe looked at all of us, and shook her head slowly.

"Guys, come on you know me, I would not do that to Deb's, I love her, she is one of my best friends. Alright he is one of the cutest bears I have ever seen, and I love cuddling him, but I would never take him." She looked at Deb's.

"Look at the other night, I gave him loads of cuddles when you ran the bath, but I put him right back on your pillow when you called me into the bathroom. Deb's I would never take him away from you, he is like my Percy." She looked at us, she was clearly upset.

The atmosphere was tense, I had never known it feel this tense in this house, I looked at Chloe, she was clearly close to tears.

"I don't think it was you, I just don't think you would hurt Deb's like that. I have no idea what is going on, but something is not right." Birch agreed.

"There is something very strange happening at the moment, I am not sure what either, but we all need to be alert. It worries me that it is happening inside the house, when it is locked and sealed, and when we are also in it, and also when we are out. I will not deny, I am still bothered about all the lights being on when we got home, I cannot explain that, I hate not being able to explain everything."

Okay so now we were all a little bit freaked out, Birch was our staff of reason, which is a little insane considering, and she was struggling to work out the other unexplained happenings, Chloe did not help.

“Oh fuck, I hope it is not Gwenda again.” Deb’s looked at her.

“Sod off... Just bugger off with all that Gwenda shit, I am not doing it, not again, you scared the shit out of me that night.” Birch sniggered.

“To be honest Deb’s, we cannot rule out anything, including the supernatural.” Deb’s spun round.

“And you can bugger off too Birch, and do not even talk Abby, you can bugger off as well, I am not doing Gwenda again, and that’s final.” Birch giggled.

“It’s alright Deb’s, you can sit this one out, on your bed... Alone... With no Phileas... and we will find out, and hope we make it back to protect you. At least we will try, I would hate for us to be dead, and you left alone in your room, with no Phileas.”

I had to turn away, and not look at her, as I fought down my giggles, Deb’s voice trembled.

“I don’t want to sit on my bed alone, and I don’t want you guys to be murdered in horrible ways by Gwenda.” Edwina shook her head.

“You guys are horrible, it is alright Deb’s, spirits are not known for taking trophy’s, no, that is more likely to be a serial killer.” I looked up.

“What? Screw you Edwina, I am sitting on Deb’s bed with her.” Chloe nodded.

“Yeah, me too, I have seen the Halloween movie, fuck that shit.”

Izzy walked in the far side door of the kitchen, carrying a paper, everybody jumped out of their skin, Chloe held her heart.

“Fuck Izzy, have you not heard of footsteps, what the fuck, did you float? I almost pulled a Rosie?” She shrugged, and threw the paper on the island.

“Read that, we are in the spotlight again.” Birch slid the paper over, and I leaned in to look at it.

The Oxendale Mail, had an article entitled. ‘Sex Author’s House of Depravity.’ I felt my breath catch in my throat, I read the opening line.

'Recently top selling author Abigail Jennifer Watson hit the headlines, when she was met on her return from the US by her naked lover Dr Jemima Dixon, pictures of her kissing her nude partner, at Heathrow Airport, caused almost as big a stir as her controversial book, Seeds of Summer, and it appears her source material for such a lewd publication, came from her own home in Wotton Dursley.' I looked at Birch, feeling shocked.

"Why would they write this?" She stared at the article.

"I need to read this Sweetie, and then we will talk." Chloe Deb's and Edwina tried to crane their necks to see it. I looked down to read more.

'We have been given reliable information from an inside source, which has informed us of wild sex parties, fuelled by alcohol, in what they have termed as a den of lesbian and gay lust. Our source, has talked of cupboards filled with sex toys, sacks of condoms, and even kinky cuddly sex toys. They went on to describe partner swaps, swinging activities, and depraved sado-masochistic and fetish fuelled romps. They even have their very own torture chamber in the cellar, with chains on the walls, behind the wine rack.

Miss Watson accompanied by her lover on stage gave a wonderful rendition of a shy, little goodie two shoes just nights ago, when she switched on the Christmas lights in Wotton, but we are not buying it and neither should you. One resident has been having sexual relations, with a man she knows to have a serious long term girlfriend, and we approached said girlfriend for comment, she was heartbroken, she refused, but did tell us, his days with her would be through when she saw him.

One can only ask what kind of immoral happenings are going on, as we only just scratch the surface, and with the wife of rock musician Jimmy Blazer, currently staying there, we have to ask if this is just one big rock and roll household, after all, the band Battered Taco have a long record for debauched living.'

I could not read anymore, and felt the tears, and pulled away, I turned to Deb's, as the tears filled my eyes.

"Don't read it, I don't want you hurt, please Deb's it's all lies and bullshit, do not get any of it in your head." She slid her arms round me and pulled me close.

"Alright Abby, but if it has upset you this much, then I don't want to." I hugged her tightly.

"Deb's call your dad, tell him to read the Oxendale Mail, and tell him to have Margret on standby." She looked up at me.

"Is it that bad?" I wiped my eyes.

"You know what sucks?" She shook her head. "That piece of shit was written by Ben Shepperton." She looked at me confused.

"You mean little Ben from History?"

"Yeah, that little shit we protected through the year nine, well he just stitched us good, and I know just what I am going to do about it. If he wants to print lies about me, I will write the frigging truth about him." I grabbed my phone, and dialled, Debs looked really worried. The phone connected to the answer phone.

"Hi Tomas Jennings, Oxendale Reporter, I am sorry but I am out on a job, leave a message and I will ring you back." I wiped my eyes and took a deep breath.

"Hi Thomas, it's Abigail Jennifer Watson here, I am assuming you have read that trash piece of bullshit and lies in your rival today? How would you like a response that is pure truth, about a young fourteen year old boy called Ben, who was forced to suck his bullies off and swallow their semen, and was saved by two female classmates called Debbie and Abigail? If you are interested, call me, I am writing it now." Deb's gasped, and her eyes looked huge.

"Holy shit Abby, I am not sure you should do that, Jesus Abby, I mean he pissed his pants twice, and shit himself a couple of times, but being forced to suck dicks. Holy shit, telling the rest of the world that, I mean Christ, that is scary shit." Her eyes were growing so big in her face, I was afraid they were going to explode, I nodded, feeling the anger inside me.

"Wow, swear much Deb's? It is, isn't it? But it is all true, we saved him from the bullies, and sexual abuse, and yet he has become just another bully, and he is bullying us. I am done with that Deb's, I took on Marjorie for peace, and now this shitbag is starting it all again. That piece of crap is out there, Deb's, everyone has read it, well I am tired of it, and I aim to stop it."

I grabbed my can, and walked into the library, and sat down at my computer, and opened a new document, and started to write.

I know a lot about being bullied, I wrote about it in my book,

Seeds of Summer, so you can imagine my surprise, when today I read an article written by someone I called friend, in the Oxendale Mail. I speak of Ben Shepperton lead reporter for the newspaper, and someone I know has been bullied equally as badly as I have.

The betrayal I feel as I read this piece of absolute garbage, which is apparently from an unnamed inside source, which I find suspicious to begin with, is nothing but an endless tirade of bullshit and lies, and I resent his piece deeply. I am in a sexual relationship with a woman, an immensely successful and respectable doctor, who has already suffered at the hands of the press due to a wardrobe malfunction. Ben appears to delight in this brief mishap, where her garment came open, and yet he fails to remember many of the mishaps he had in school.

Unlike Ben, I write truth, and I am sure that many of the classmates that bullied him, for his frequent soiling of his trousers, in class at age fourteen, or misadventures in games, when he wet himself out of fear of the teacher, on a regular basis, would back up my story if questioned. I find it sad that on one very painful occasion, he was rescued by myself, and Debbie Wheeler, now wife of Battered Taco vocalist Jimmy Blazers, as we saved him from a prolonged period of sustained sexual assaults.

He appears quick to put pen to paper, to make money by trashing me and Debbie, two of his loyalist friends, but how likely is he to name the boys, who forced him to suck their penis's until they ejaculated down his throat? Or would he like me to post the video interview I did with him for Seeds of Summer, and let all of you see how he blatantly asked me to sleep with him, telling me he has always had a crush on me? He is quick to throw mud at my housemates for their dating choices, and approach their so called long time partners, for comment, so could I publicly ask his wife if she was aware of his crush on me, or the fact I refused to sleep with him when he asked? I have the tape, and would be very happy to post it for her.

I will be seeking legal representation, and be filing a law suit against the Oxendale Mail, and will obviously be happy to provide all my proof to corroborate my own article on him. Tell me Ben how does it feel to be back in my shoes, and bullied by a person you never thought it possible of?

You know how to get me, I am sure the long spate of sexually charged emails you sent me have my address on them, oh yes, I am printing them now, to publish, and they do. Abigail J.W. Deb's stood back.

"Holy shit you cannot give that to the Reporter, they hate the Mail, they will print it." I looked at her and smiled, Birch came in, and she leaned over my shoulder to read.

"Wow Deads, is all that really true?" Debbie nodded, and looked really white.

"Every word of it Birch, Abby and me saved his ass, we told the boys we would tell the whole school they were all really gay if they did it again, and they left him alone after that." Birch looked at me.

"It is your call Sweetie, if you want to publish it, I will stand with you." I loved the loyalty, what a shame Ben did not have it. I sat back in my chair.

"Just wait a little longer, Tom will do some checking first." Deb's phone buzzed, she looked terrified, it was a strange number. "Answer it Deb's." She held it to her ear.

"Hello, this is Debbie Battersby, who is calling please?" She listened and took a deep breath.

"Yes Tom... No, it is all true, that really happened... She is, wow that is scary, I would hate that... Abby does not lie, not ever, she never has, when she tells you it's the truth, you can bank on it... Jimmy is doing great, he is in Japan... I am sure I could arrange a meeting when he gets back, but that depends on how all this goes... Oh yes, I am already talking to our family solicitors, everything he has written is lies, and we are suing the paper. I believe so is Dr Dixon. Ring Ben and ask, I am sure he will tell you, but I can tell you this Tom, we are all the best of friends, you have seen the Curio site, now you tell me, do you honestly think anyone inside this house would do that?" She smiled.

"As I said, there is no one in here who would do that, we all look out for each other, the whole story is lies... Alright... Bye Tom."

She ended the call and smiled, Chloe, Izzy and Edwina came in to the library and waited. I watched her as she took a deep breath.

"Guys someone offered the story to them, but Tom showed his editor the Curio site, and as soon as he saw that, he told Tom to leave it alone. It looks like whoever it was, must have gone to the

Oxendale Mail, and they must have bought it, apparently this guy wanted five thousand pounds for the scoop. Oh, and it was Ben who took the picture at my wedding, and sold it to the daily papers." Edwina stared at us.

"It is not Luke, I just talked to him, his ex-girlfriend, because he did dump her last week, has only been dating him three months, and all she had done for the whole time is whine about his gaming. I mean okay I am at fault, but you know what, I don't care, I really love him guys." She started to go pink and Chloe giggled.

"Banger Bobbles is in love guys." We all chuckled as she went beetroot and smiled, I lifted my can and took a swig. Izzy looked at me.

"So, what do we do now, are you going to give this scoop to this rival?" I shook my head.

"No... I am not like that Izzy, I bloody hate Ben at the moment, but it is not my way of doing things. I know Tom, he has given me some good and fair press, he will do his job properly, which means, he will call Ben, and then we shall hear from him. I would imagine it will not be much longer, in the meantime, we need to find out who this person is that is selling a story on us, because someone has done it, and no, I do not for one second think it is Luke, or Brent, he has not been on the scene for a while." Edwina hit her keyboard, Birch slid Deb's out of the way and jumped on hers.

"It is someone who has been in the house, because how do they know we used to have a sex dungeon in the cellar, and the chains are still there on the walls, the question is who?" I sat back and watched my phone propped up against my screen.

The minutes ticked by, and I sat and drank, the moment came and everyone stopped, I sat forward in my chair and hit the answer button, and then pressed record as I put the phone to hands free.

"Abigail."

"Hi Ben you cocksucker." The phone went quiet.

"Abigail I just talked to Tom; he says you are writing a piece on me from school?"

"I write a lot of stuff, you know based on all the sordid sexual shit I have seen and done in my lewd life, why are you bothered?"

"Abigail, that is not fair, it is private, come on you are a public figure, people have a pop at you all the time."

"Yes Ben, my name goes on printed books, yours goes on printed papers, both are published and earn us money. So do the pictures you take, of me and Doctor Dixon, so by that chalk, you too are a public figure, so I can have a pop at you too."

"Abigail, I have a wife and kids, I am asking you not to do this." I laughed, and reached for my mouse."

"You do not even know what I have written, and yet you are begging me, wow you have a nerve Ben, especially after that lying trash piece you did on me. Here I will send you the draft, and by the way, I have a serious and committed relationship too, not that you gave a shit?" I copied it into a new email and then clicked send.

"You know Ben, you were not that worried about your wife as I remember, when you were trying to get in my panties six months ago, why the sudden concern now?" There was a long silence, I assumed he was reading the piece.

"HOLY SHIT ABBY!" Yep, he was reading it. "Abby if you give this Tom, he will destroy me and my family."

"What like you are trying to do mine, oh there is irony?"

"Please Abigail, do not send them this, what do I have to do?"

Birch was watching me very carefully, her eyes were bright and sparkling, her long white hair hung over her shoulder framing her face perfectly, she gave a small smirk of a smile, I blew her a kiss.

"Ben, you will write an apology, to each and every member of this household, that is one article per person, and explain how misinformed you were. I want to see a full retraction also in the Oxendale Reporter, after all you will owe Tom big for this, and I also want the name of your source. Give me that in the next issue, and I will not send this off, am I clear?"

"Abby, I cannot divulge the source, I am sorry but I cannot."

"Okay then Ben, let me see. Copy... Open new mail.... Tom's email address... Title, hmm, er, let me see, how about, response to that cum swallower at the Oxendale Mail, by Abigail Jennifer Watson, yes, I like that. Okay body text, that would be paste, and dear Tom, please find article in response to that shit bag at the Oxendale Mail, as agreed, I look forward to reading it Abby J.W.

Okay all I have to do now is move my mouse up here to the right top corner of the page, and click..."

"ABIGAIL WAIT!"

"Do you have something to tell me Ben?" We could all hear him sigh on the other end of the phone.

"He was called Rodney, that is all I know, he would not give us more, he was paid in cash." Birch looked really alarmed, and leaned over.

"Ben this is Doctor Dixon, can you describe this man?" I looked at her, why did she care?

"He was scruffy, he had lank hair, a bit smelly, he said he had been forced to live rough, we put him up in a hotel and got him some clean clothes, he had a wash and looked pretty normal after that. He sat on one of our laptops and wrote everything down, and when my editor saw the detail in the content, he paid him the difference from the deductions of clothes and hotel and he disappeared. We have another ten pages of stuff for a back up piece, but if it's all bullshit, we have been screwed." Birch nodded.

"You have been screwed alright; the guy escaped from a secure hospital two months ago, he is a known mental patient with a record of violence, and delusions."

"Shit... My editor will fry me for that." I looked at Birch, then back at the phone.

"To be honest Ben you deserve to be fried, just for sending that picture of us at the wedding to the daily press. If you proceed, not only will I write about you, I think you will find three law suits on your door step the following morning, and these will be the very big legal boys. I want to see those retractions, if I do, your paper will survive."

"Yeah, I hear you, for what it is worth, I am sorry. You and Debbie really helped me at school, that was a tough time for me, and yes, your piece was right, I became what I hated, I am sorry for this, I will put it right for you."

"That is all I ask, you know the stupid thing is Ben, if you needed a story that bad, we would have given you something far better than that trash, and now you have blown it."

"You always were mentally tougher than me. I will fix this, have a good night. Good night, Dr Dixon." The call ended and everyone gave a sigh of relief. I looked at Birch.

“Who the hell is Rodney?” She looked at Izzy, who was very pale and suddenly I remembered. “Oh Christ, Cupid is out.” Chloe frowned.

“Fuck I hope not, Edwina already looks like a soppy bitch, that fucker can keep his arrows away from me, I don’t do all that soppy cuddling bollocks, it’s fucked up.” I stared at Birch with amazement.

“Says the bear cuddle master with the soppy expression.” Chloe smiled.

“Teddies are different, they really love back.” Oh man she is beyond messed up.

Chapter 12

Lock In.

Ever feel like you take one step forward, only to get dragged ten steps back? I sometimes feel that it would be so much simpler, to strip my hair back to its natural colour, get it French plaited, buy blouses, and slacks, and a nice little old lady's jacket, and wear sensible shoes, just to live here.

If I was to publicly announce I had given up alcohol, living naked and sex, would they all finally leave me alone? I somehow think not, and that is the problem with living in Wotton. I knew it at Uni, and it still applies today. I was targeted by Marjorie all those years ago, and because of her, I am still targeted now, and I really do not think there is much I can do to change things. Birch sat back in her seat and looked at Izzy.

"We knew he was out, but how the hell did he find you here?"

She leaned against the big table, up against the window, and gave a frustrated sigh. I watched her carefully, I know the story of Rodney, and honestly, the thought of a love sick maniac running loose with a bow and arrow, bothered me a lot.

I have always seen Izzy as strong, but suddenly she looked weak and vulnerable, and that really frightened me. This guy had really put her through the wringer, and considering he killed her cat, set fire to her car, and burned her flat down, I am not going to deny, I was becoming pretty rattled. Izzy stood up looking pale.

"I need something stronger than beer."

It had been a rough day all around, and the weirdness of everything was really getting to me, I agreed, something stronger than beer was required. It was a popular suggestion, so we all made our way back towards the kitchen, Birch walked slower than the rest, and slipped her arm round my waist.

"Are you okay Sweetie?" It was a good question, and not one I was sure I could answer right now.

"I am not going to say I am completely fine with this Birch; I am not. Just the stories of this guy rattle me, what are we going to do, are we going to tell the others, or not?" She stopped and turned to face me; she lifted her hand to my face.

"Deads, I will do everything I can to keep us safe, you are everything to me, but I think safety in numbers at this point is our best advice. I think we should all know the score, they live here too, they have a right to know." She kissed me softly, and I really needed it.

Round the island sat with vodka's, Birch and Izzy, filled in the others on Rodney and his antics with Izzy, which led to his eventual arrest, prosecution and containment in a secure facility for the disturbed. The others sat listening sipping their drinks, looking a combination of amazement and fear, Birch was stood by the windows with her back to them, outside it was pitch black.

"So, guys, as you can see, he is the one who has been watching us. I think it is safe to say, he is more interested in revenge on Izzy, but he looks to be using us as a way of getting to her." Edwina gave a long breath out.

"Shit. I really wish I had kept my mouth shut; this guy sounds like a frigging serial killer." Chloe slapped her.

"Shut the fuck up bitch, I was shitting myself enough thinking Gwenda was back." Birch gave a giggle.

"We need to use every ounce of our will power as possible, and focus all our thoughts, this guy is slippery, he escaped from a very secure mental institution, so we need to seal and protect all our boundaries." She reached out her arms pointing to the doors either side.

We were all looking at her, and suddenly outside, the garden lit up with a bright purple flash, Birch stiffened, her hair looked snow white, and the sudden flash, made her eyes look eerie, and to be honest, sexy as hell. Chloe almost fell off her seat.

"HOLY SHIT, ARE YOU USING WITCHCRAFT?"

"Huh?"

The thunder rumbled, and from nowhere, rain lashed down filled with chunks of ice that blew into the windows creating millions of tiny clatters. I must admit it was impressive, and looked like a perfectly timed special effect. Deb's shook, she was terrified of thunder. Birch turned and looked at the ice pieces hammering onto the window.

"Okay we need to get this house locked and checked, I want everything sealed, so nothing gets in and nothing gets out." Edwina looked round the room.

"Small point guys... If Deb's teddy went missing today in the house, does that mean he is already inside?" Chloe turned and slapped her again.

"What the fuck is wrong with you, shut the fuck up, I am scared enough as it is?" I looked at Edwina.

"We need to make sure the cellar is secure." Chloe's head snapped round, and she pointed.

"You can fuck off and shut up too." I looked at her.

"Chloe, we need to make sure, someone has got to go down there." She shook her head.

"You see that is the problem with bitches like you, with your smart arse ideas, I have seen Halloween, the fucking smart ass bitch always gets it first." Birch leaned over her shoulder.

"The one screwing always gets it second Chloe, have you locked Percy away?" She turned white.

"Oh fuck, I have to give up sex until they catch him." Edwina looked to Birch.

"Are we splitting up or staying together?" Chloe shook her head.

"Nope we stay together, every fucking ripper movie shows that when you split up, they get you, it makes it easier for them to pick you off." Deb's turned on her.

"Chloe you really need to be quiet, this is like Gwenda all over again, I am fine and doing okay, and then you talk, and my nerves start to rattle. So seriously, I love you, but shut the hell up." She looked at Birch. "We stick together, just in case she is right." I sniggered.

Birch turned and started to slip the small bolts up the windows, to lock them.

"Izzy lock and bolt the front door, Chloe push the locking bolts up in your studio, Deads, check all the downstairs windows with Edwina, make sure they are all locked." Deb's looked round.

"What do I do?" Chloe smiled.

"Stand there and try not to pull a Rosie."

"I am already doing that, give me something to take my mind off it." Chloe suddenly looked excited.

"We need weapons, have you still got that taser?" Deb's nodded.
"It's in my bag." Chloe's eyes sparkled.
"Cool, go and get it." She nodded.
"Brilliant idea, yeah I am getting it."

She turned and headed off into the hallway. I was in the library checking all the window locks, two were not secure, so I locked them down. I came out of the library, as Deb's came towards me looking focused, she walked past me, towards the door acting very determined. I headed towards Birch, who was locking down the second set of doors in the kitchen. Deb's came back down the hallway.

"Nope, nope, nope, nope, nope." I looked at her unsure of what exactly she was doing.

"Deb's are you alright?" She shook her head.

"Nope... I want my taser, but it is in my bag... On my bed." I laughed.

"Deb's we will be fine, calm down, come on take my hand, I will go with you, we can check the upstairs windows at the same time." She gave a gasp of relief.

"Will you, oh Abby, thanks, I am really scared?" I pulled her hand.

"Come on."

We walked back towards the hall, Chloe came out of the studio with a hammer, and followed us, I shook my head, it was pointless saying anything. We walked quietly up the stairs; the hallway light was out. Whether it was Chloe or Deb's I am not sure, but even I was starting to feel jittery. I found my ears were straining to pick up every sound. Chloe looked down the long dark corridor, the lightbulb, above us was missing, Chloe swallowed hard, and her throat made a glugging sound, we all jumped. She peered through the dim light, and whispered.

"Sorry, be glad it was not a Rosie, because honestly, at this current moment, I am not completely sure which of my bodily functions is in control." Deb's sighed.

"Well, we know it's not orgasm." She shrugged and smiled.

"Actually, I am really wet, that is not too fucked up, is it?" Deb's rolled her eyes.

"This is not the frigging supermarket, Jesus, do you even have dry days?” She frowned in the dim light.

“I am not sure; I don’t actually remember one.”

“You are such a slut.” I sniggered; Chloe smiled.

“Pretty much.”

“Serial Killers can smell arousal.”

We all leapt in the air and screamed, I turned round rapidly, my heart almost exploded out of my chest.

“Edwina what the hell, you scared the shit out of me?” She giggled.

“Sorry, I thought you heard me, I came up to check the rooms upstairs.” My heart was racing, and I was breathing in air at a good rate.

“Let’s just get this bloody done.” She nodded.

“I rang Luke, he is coming over, I gave him a brief outline of what the problem was.”

I was actually relieved, Luke is a pretty big guy, and we could use a little heavy support, normally I would rely on Izzy, but she had gone very quiet. Although considering what Rodney had done in the past, I did not blame her. We were getting nowhere, so I took the lead.

“Okay, Edwina, you go with Deb’s, both your rooms are down there, and check the guest rooms. Chloe come with me and we will do our rooms, and Izzy’s up here, meet back here when we are done.”

Everyone agreed and separated, and I suddenly realised I had drawn the short straw, I got Chloe. We checked out Birch’s room first, I locked and bolted the patio doors, Chloe went all gooey when she saw the tree.

“Abby it is gorgeous, I did not even know you guys had your own little baby tree, I want one, god you guys are too cute.”

I left her to ogle, and headed into my room, it was really dark, I cannot deny, I was shitting myself as I reached for the light switch. Okay, so I write horror books, as well as smut, but at this point in my life, the gothic horror writer took over my brain.

I froze on the light switch; I mean, how many times have you seen a movie, where they click on the light, and there is something nasty and unnatural standing there? Yep, that is what it is like to be me, welcome to my head. I stood in the dark, scared shitless of the dark, with my hand on the light switch, scared shitless of turning it on.

"Oh crap!" I took a few deep breaths.

"Come on Abby stop being a pussy. Oh shit, and I just talked to myself so the serial killer knows where I am."

I took a deep breath and then froze, 'what was that?' Oh bugger, my bedroom door was slowly opening, there was a glow on the wall, holy shit what was that? My heart started to beat really fast, I panicked and held my breath, the light flicked on, and flooded into the room, and I screamed for blue murder.

"ARRRRGHHHH!"

"Hi Sweetie.... Oh, sorry did I frighten you?" She had her hands up to her face, and looked upset. I gasped in air as my heart romped around my inner cavity.

"Holy shit Birch, do not do that, I almost pissed on the floor."

She ran over and pulled me close; Chloe came legging it in screaming, and looking terrified, waving her hammer. Birch's boobs were pressed into me, and she could feel my heart hammering, as it tried to escape through my boobs, I just stood there gasping in air, and wishing I never ever met Chloe.

Birch held me tight apologising, as I slowly calmed down, I looked at her green concerned eyes.

"Do you remember that day two years ago, where we stood here in this house, for the first time? Let's all live together it will be fun we said, well we were so frigging wrong, this place has become a mental institution, and currently the inmates are all loose and rampaging." She giggled.

"It has been fun though, hasn't it?" I took another deep breath, I looked at Chloe locking the windows, with a hammer held tight in her left hand,

"That one there, Birch, she is the biggest frigging psychopath in here." She loosened her hug and smiled at me.

"It has been testing Deads, of that there is no doubt, but honestly, it has been the happiest time of my life living here with you." I smiled, I could not deny, we had certainly had a lot of fun, I nodded and gave a gasp.

"Okay we are almost done, let's get this finished."

We went into the hallway and I locked my door, Izzy had gone to check her room. Birch had checked the other guest room, so all that was left was Chloe's room.

I have to admit, I have lived here two years, and the last time I was in her room, was the day before she moved in. She flicked on the light and my first impression was 'Wow.' Her room was really neat and clean, and littered with teddies, every unit had the top packed with them.

Her walls were filled with her artwork, I had never seen any of these, and they were mainly naked men, although there was a stunning one of Birch and myself, sunbathing together on the lawn at my mum's house, we were lay face down side by side looking at each other talking. She noticed me looking at it.

"No, not even for a million, I will never sell that one." I turned to her.

"Chloe it is beautiful." She came to my side and smiled, as she looked at it, her voice went really soft.

"It is more than that Abby, it is alive. That is my best ever picture, because I managed to capture the two of you, as you really are. When I was trapped in that shit hole in Oxendale, I would look at that, and cry, because I really missed you guys so much it was painful. It also made me happy, because you inspired my best work. It is probably my most precious possession."

"More precious than Percy?" She turned and looked at me, her eyes were so sincere.

"Yes... Yes, Abby it is, because that summer, that was the happiest time of my life, until I moved in here, it was a really special time for me, because that was the summer, I decided who I was going to become." I smirked.

"So, you lay in my garden naked in the sun and thought, I am going to become an artistic slut?" She gave a big beaming smile and nodded her head.

"Yeah, pretty much." I laughed and pulled her into a hug.

"It is an amazing picture, and actually Chloe, you are an amazing person." I squeezed her hard.

"Yeah, still not going to screw you Abby, I am so fucking straight its untrue." I laughed and slipped back, Chloe turned and opened her wardrobe door.

"This is Percy by the way." I stepped back with a gasp, and my heart leapt in my chest.

"Holy HELL!!"

There was Percy, he was a full size teddy, wearing a strap on with a massive black rubber dildo on it. She smiled, and stroked her finger down its shaft, I felt my legs twitch.

"Abby meet my lover, Percy." I stepped back; I was actually afraid of him.

"Oh Chloe, I love you I do, but you are so many different levels of messed up, I have no idea where to start."

I came out of her room at high speed, and leaned against the wall; Birch chuckled, as her eyes sparkled.

"I see you met Percy?" I looked at her.

"Can you still see the horror in my eyes?" Her eyes twinkled, as she started to laugh, I shook my head.

"That is the first time in my life, I have been truly intimidated by a frigging teddy bear, there is so much screwed up in that room, I am struggling with reality."

Chloe came out and locked her room, and I was relieved, the way I saw it, the whole bloody house was safer if Percy was captive.

We made our way back to the top of the stairs, all the upstairs was secure, and I felt a little calmer. We stood in the gloom waiting for Izzy, in almost darkness, quietly watching for her to come out of her room, Deb's turned to me.

"What was that?" Chloe turned and pointed at her.

"Fuck off... Fuck right off Deb's, I mean it; I am not fucking doing that shit again." I didn't understand.

"Chloe what the hell?" She shook her head.

"Abby do not fall for it, the last time she did that, Gwenda came up the fucking walls, and I ended up pissing myself in the cellar." I looked at Deb's she was stood frozen listening for something, Chloe dithered on her feet.

"I warned you; I fucking warned you; I mean it if...."

'SQUEEEEEEEK!" Chloe closed her eyes.

"Oh fuck, I heard it too." She looked at Deb's. "I fucking hate you, and those bat ears."

Birch was looking around, not much of the light came upstairs, she furrowed her brow, lifted her arm, and pointed.

"I think it was over there." Chloe whimpered.

"Oh no it's the fucking attic, everyone always dies in the attic." Birch looked at me with excited eyes.

"We have an Attic?" I nodded.

"Yeah, have you not been up there?"

"No... I love attics Sweetie; I want to see mine." And she was off, Chloe looked at Deb's

"Now look what you have done, it's the fucking mad witch, and the cellar all over again." I looked down, and noticed.

"Shit Chloe, you are wearing knickers?" She looked down and smiled.

"Yeah, I put them on in my room, you know, crazy psycho stalker and all that, I thought if he tries anything, they will slow him down." Deb's pointed at them.

"How, they are crotchless?" Chloe stared at them.

"Oh shit, wrong pair... I was in a hurry you know?" Edwina shook her head.

"How the hell are we even related?"

"Sweetie look, I found steps!" I panicked, I moved quickly towards her.

"Birch, slow down you cannot just rush up there, it is not completely safe." I caught up with her, and she was gushing with excitement, I grabbed her hand.

"We have to go slow, only a small section has floor; the rest is dangerous." She gave a giddy nod.

"Show me... Oh Deads, this is so exciting."

The fact there could be a murderous serial killer up there had completely evaded her. I leaned in and instantly wanted to change my mind.

"Oh hell, it is really dark in here." The sound of the rain felt really loud, obviously there was no sound proofing up here.

I held Birch by the hand, as she followed all giddy and happy, and I reached out into the total blackness with my other hand. I swallowed hard, oh Christ, I am not happy at all, I really hate this shit, why out of all the women I could fall in love with, did mine have to be mentally unstable?

I could feel her all bouncy and excited behind me, I reached out until I felt a step. I gasped for air; I could feel the sweat on my head. I moved forward slowly, and felt the next step, I could literally see nothing, and all I could hear was Birch's giddy little squeaks of excitement. I made a mental note, if I live through this, go see Roni for a full mental evaluation, because to be doing this, I was definitely missing some screws.

I went up another step, I could hear everyone behind me breathing. Have you any idea how bloody freaky it is to be in a dark enclosed space, unable to see anything, and all you can hear is others breathing? I can assure you it is messed up. We went up another step, I reached out with my hand, and touched something furry.

I kid you not, the scream that came out of me was deafening, and of course, when you have five nervous women in a tight enclosed, very bloody dark space, the ripple effect is instant. Everyone screamed with abject terror.

"Oh fuck... guys I am so sorry, it just came out again."

"It's okay Sweetie, I did too, it happens." Deb's gave a cough.

"Yeah, me too, you twats are naked, I am still dressed... bollocks!"

"Fucking dirty bitches, I am fucking drowning in piss down here, and these are new shoes."

"Oh, Edwina Sweetie I am so sorry."

My heart was thumping like mad, I really bloody hate mice, rats, actually anything small and furry that scurries. Birch felt my fear.

"Are you alright Sweetie?" I took a deep breath.

"I touched something hairy." I felt her shudder.

"Ergh! Please Sweetie that is unsettling, where is it now?"

"Birch, it's pitch bleeding black, how the hell would I know?" I instantly felt the tension in the air rise behind me.

"Deads Sweetie, I really need you to find out. I love all things, but not creepy little hairy ones that run about in the dark." Chloe gave a titter.

"Birch is scared of rats and mice."

"No I am not, I just do not like things that are known to run up your legs, and gnaw at your parts."

"Huh... Holy fuck they do that? Abby, find that fucking thing and fast." I heard Birch quietly snigger. The truth was I did not want to know what it was or where it was.

"Do I have to; I have already touched it once?"

I literally felt the air move, as they all shuddered in the dark. I took a big deep breath, and Birch gave my hand a squeeze. I leaned forward, and suddenly behind me a light came on, I stopped frozen, staring at the hairy beast.

"Phileas!" Yep, Deb's was spot on, Izzy was stood at the back with a massive hand held light.

"Sorry everyone, I have a few unpacked boxes, I thought we may need this, but it took a few minutes to find which box." I gave a sigh of relief, Izzy looked down.

"Christ you are all dirty bitches; I have got bare feet."

I grabbed Phileas and handed him to Birch, she passed him back to Deb's who hugged him lovingly, I still think it is seriously messed up. With some light, I could see the stairs, and so made my way up to the top with a very excited, if not damp legged Birch. I held her tight, I wanted more light, before she wandered off.

The group came up and looked around, Izzy highlighted the floor problem. There were two windows up here, one at each end, and the one Chloe had used was open, which was weird because I distinctly remember her closing it.

The rain outside was pouring down and bouncing off the roof, I shivered, and Birch moved in closer as she looked around with wonder.

"This place is beautiful, with some stain and some work, it would make a great play space." I looked at her not understanding.

"Define play space, I mean, you are not like going to build a model railway or something are you?" She gave a chuckle.

"Nice thought, but no... Deads, can you imagine it, with carpet, bean bags, and low tables? We could have parties or chill out sessions, and even a small gym set up. I mean look how tall it is, and there is so much space up here. Yeah, I could make this place amazing." Chloe leaned in.

"Abby, she means shag place, you know for orgies and stuff." I looked at Birch, and her eyes sparkled, she smiled.

"That was not what I meant but when you think about it, we do get off watching each other screw, it could be fun." I shook my head.

"You know Ben was not far off the mark with that article, we are becoming more deviant by the day." She giggled. Chloe walked up the loft to the window.

"I will close and lock this one, someone check the other."

We all watched as she followed the boards, none of us noticed the hands hanging on to the sill, well not straight away. Chloe was ten feet away, when up popped the head of Rodney. Everyone screamed out in terror, but Chloe screamed louder, her reaction was instant, she swung the hammer and, SMACK!

It came right down on his left hand, Rodney screamed, and we all screamed in horror, Deb's turned and buried her face in my boobs.

He let go, and his head disappeared, as he hung by one hand, over what I already knew was a very steep pitch in the roof. Chloe dropped the hammer, and grabbed the window, with both hands, and yanked it down. He let go just in time, and she watched him slide off the roof. We all hurried to look out, but by the time we got there, the roof was empty. I looked at Chloe, she was as white as a sheet, and shaking like a leaf, and her lip was trembling. I pulled her over, and held her tight as she violently shook.

"Is... he... You know... dead?"

I really had no way of knowing, from here you could not see the floor below, but it was a long drop into darkness, he would at the least be very badly injured.

"You did nothing wrong Chloe; he was attempting to hurt us." She clung to me shaking, Edwina slipped in and hugged her from behind.

We calmed her down the best we could, which when you think you just killed someone, is not much. We walked her slowly back to the stairs, and Izzy held the light, so we could see our way down. She stayed to check out the loft area, Chloe was really badly shaken, we got her in the kitchen, and sat her down, Birch broke out the brandy, and we all had a glass. I was rattled and terrified, somewhere down the side of the garage, there potentially was a body, I looked at Birch as she calmed Chloe down.

"We need to check Birch, holy shit what do we do if he is dead?"

I was trembling, so was Deb's, in truth all of us were really shaken even Birch. Chloe nodded and looked at me.

“Abby, I need to know, if I did it, I will face it, but I need to know.” I nodded rapidly, I understood her, I cannot deny, I felt as terrified as she looked. Birch came over to me and pulled me into a hug.

“I am just waiting for Izzy Sweetie, we do not have floodlights down the sides, we need a torch.” I nodded into her.

“I am sorry, I am really scared.” She squeezed me harder.

“Me too Sweetie.” She kissed my head. It was probably only a few minutes, but it felt like an hour, before Izzy appeared.

“He has been sleeping up there, I found a bin bag filled with biscuit wrappers, meat bones, beer cans, just about everything we have been saying was missing, I also found these.”

She opened her hand, and there was a set of freshly cut keys, my heart rate increased its beating, just the thought of knowing he had been in the house was so scary. I was trying not to think about it. Birch took them, and put them in the kitchen drawer.

“Izzy, we need to check, we need to find if he is injured or if... You know, it was a long drop?” She gave a nod

“Yeah, I have been thinking that too.” I looked at all the others.

“All girls together yes, we stand, we fall, we fight together?”

I won’t deny that a part of me really does not want to go out there, but I think I have to. One reason being, I want to stay by Chloe, and the other, I need to know the result of the fall, just so I will actually sleep at some point.

We all grouped together, and headed for the front door, Birch pulled out the bolts, and then undid the lock, she looked back at us, as she gripped the handle.

“Are we all ready?” We nodded; she pulled the door open.

“ARRRRGHHH!”

We all screamed like hysterical maniacs, as the tall wide wet figure of Luke was silhouetted in the doorway, he looked absolutely terrified.

“What the fuck is wrong with all of you, that scared the living shit out of me?” Edwina rushed through and leapt into his arms, and burst into tears, he wrapped his large arms round her.

“Oh, babes I am sorry, I didn’t mean to shout.” Birch smiled.

“Stay here with her Luke, we have to check something out.” He gave a nod, and pointed at us.

"You guys know you are naked and it's throwing it down yeah?" Birch smiled.

"It is alright Sweetie; it will wash the piss off."

He nodded as if understanding, we all smiled, as we trooped past heading for the side of the garage. I felt really panicked, as we approached the corner, it was really dark up the side of the house. Izzy shone her torch, and we all sheepishly looked round the corner. I followed the beam with my eyes, as it moved up the side, it went right to the back fence, there was nothing, she swung it across the side garden, and again there was nothing there. Chloe looked distraught, and she put her hand to her head.

"Oh shit, you see the movies don't lie, it's fucking Halloween all over again. They fucking shot him and he fell out of the window, and yet when they look, no fucking body. Oh shit, guys there is going to be a sequel, Rabid Rodney two, screw this I am going hiding with Percy." She turned and legged it, Debs looked at me.

"I am with Percy too, see ya."

She shot off, and I will not deny it, as messed up, perverted and intimidating as he was, I would rather share a cupboard with Percy than a house with Rodney.

Chapter 13

After Shock.

Sleeping was not the easier of things, the good news was, somehow Rodney had survived. We hurried inside and locked the door, relieved to know he was out there, and we were in here. Deb's slept in Chloe's room, both of them were shaken, and under the proviso that Percy stayed in the cupboard, Deb's crawled in to keep Chloe settled, in a none gay and very straight way.

Luke, Edwina and Izzy checked out the cellar, and made sure the metal outer door, was closed tight. Izzy then phoned the authorities to let them know Rodney had been spotted, bulbs were checked, and replaced, all over the house, and a reasonably normal state returned to our home, so we got drunk, took baths, talked, and staggered to bed. I wanted to sleep in Birch's bed, I know it sounds silly, but the lights on her little tree give me comfort.

My mind swirled, with Martin, Ben, and Rodney, and it was probably me just being paranoid, but it felt like every set of eyes were on me again. I lay there gazing at the tree, with Birch snuggled into me, tired, but unable to settle.

I needed to do something, anything, I could not lie here all night staring at a tree, even though it was really pretty. I slowly unravelled myself from Birch, and slid out of bed, the thermometer moved on to a different setting at night, so the house was cooler. It was not cold, this was a house that was never cold, which was one of my favourite things about it, and I walked down the stairs to the hallway.

I noted the groans, and looked into the living room, Luke was in his Santa's suit, and was half under the Christmas tree, Edwina was straddling over him, and thrusting, she had her eyes closed, and looked like she was in heaven. Isn't there a song about screwing Santa under the Christmas tree? If there was, I am sure Edwina knows all the lyrics. I walked into the library and sat at my desk, and turned on my computer.

The Curio site had a lot of new posts, and I started to read them one by one, and write a response to each and every one, it still surprises me how many new people come to the site. The world is so horrid, and it feels like adults are nastier than ever to each other, and their children. In a way, this site allows me the chance to try and do some good, even if that is just to lift the spirits of a student, or young struggling adult. In my mind, Christmas is coming, and isn't this the time to all be nice to each other? I was reading forum posts, and then.

"Sweetie... Sweetie..." I opened my eyes, and she smiled. "Hi Sweetie." She is so lovely, so beautiful, she makes me so happy, and I loved her.

"Hi."

Her eyes were so bright, I nodded awake, I was still at my desk, I must have fallen asleep in my chair. I sat up and yawned, she took my hand.

"I made breakfast, you should eat, and then probably get some more sleep."

I got up out of the chair, oh god, I ached. I followed her into the kitchen where bacon sandwiches awaited me with coffee, I sat down and got stuck in.

Mornings have not changed much in two years, everyone rushes around in various stages of dress, hair is brushed, make up applied, and bags are packed, and in between, there are frequent trips to the kitchen, where coffees are slurped, and toast is crunched, and all at high speed. At 8:15, everyone gathers in the hallway, and poof, through the door they go, and the house suddenly feels very quiet.

I sat drinking coffee, when Chloe wandered in, she flopped down, and I reached for the pot and poured her a coffee, she lifted it and sipped, I relaxed and refilled my cup. We sat there in silence for a little while, I could see her looking at me, and it was clear something was on her mind.

"What, just ask me Chloe?" She looked at me.

"You love Birch, I mean really love her, don't you? You know, you guys have something huge and massive and everyone sees it, you know, you really love her?" I lifted my cup wondering where this had come from all of a sudden.

"I think our record is clear on that, but yes, I have something with her I have never had with anyone else. I am closer than close with her, more honest with her and myself. When I am around her, she does provoke desires in me I never knew were there before. If that is love, then yes, I am deeply in love with her." She thought about what I said carefully, and nodded to herself, she looked up at me.

"Did you just know, I mean how can you tell if it is love? Abby, I love sex, I cannot live without it. It inspires me to paint, but I worry at times, because I see you, and Deb's, and even Edwina now, and you all knew, it is like you just woke up and knew this person is the one. I guess I wonder how you knew?" She fingered her cup handle.

"All this with Martin, and then last night, it has made me wonder. You know, I could have killed him without thinking, and my life could have changed so badly overnight. Abby I am really trusting you here... You know Deb's stayed with me last night?" I nodded, she was struggling with so much, and it was clearly getting to her.

"Did something happen between you two?" She looked at me, it was clear something did, I could see her considering whether or not she should tell me.

"Chloe if it did it is fine, we can talk about it, I won't say anything to anyone." She smiled.

"I know that... Abby the night of Gwenda in the walls, and last night, Deb's was scared, and she climbed in with me, and it was okay because I was jittery. I am still a bit, so it was good for both of us. You know there was no sex, it was just sleeping... The thing is, both times, when I woke up, I was cuddling her, you know like arms right round her, pressed up real close kind of cuddling." I nodded, I could understand that, she looked down at her cup and stared into it.

"The thing is Abby, I really liked it."

I gave a sigh, if I am honest, I was not surprised, all of us were partnering up, except her, I had wondered if at some point, she would realise.

"Chloe it is okay to enjoy being close to someone, you know Deb's and you have grown very close, she really does care a great deal about you. I don't think there is anything wrong with cuddling up with her. I remember when I came home from Uni and Birch and me shared a bed, I would wake up with her clamped onto me, and just lie there feeling her warmth and listening to her breathe, and I loved it, it made me feel so good." She smiled and gave a sigh.

"So, it is okay to enjoy sleeping with someone you like all night in a bed, it is not gay or anything? You know, because with the whole bath thing, which I still do not understand if I am honest, I thought I might be falling in love with her, which as you know for me is kind of fucked up?" I chuckled, she has no idea how complicated everything can be, maybe this was her looking inside to see what is next.

"Chloe only you will know if that is how you feel, if I am honest, questioning your motives is a good thing, but also be aware, it might not be about Deb's, it might just be you want that more often. You know, to actually wake up with someone? All I can tell you is if it is love, you will know sooner or later, because you cannot hold that back, it just grows inside you, and you have no idea why this one person becomes everything, you just know, and my advice would be don't doubt it, trust it."

"Yeah, I understand that, thanks Abby, that really helps."

I smiled, and in a way, I felt privileged because she trusted me enough to ask. We sat quiet for a few moments, I could see she was thinking, and she quietly spoke.

"Can I ask you something else, because it made me wonder?" I lifted my cup.

"May as well while we are here." She looked at me, and lifted her cup.

"You went to America for three weeks, I heard you and Birch talking, and she told you it was okay to sleep with someone over there, you asked if she meant Katie. So, I guess I am curious, did you sleep with her, or someone else?" I gave a chuckle.

"Honestly Chloe, Katie started to really piss me off, she was relentless for the whole three weeks, she just would not drop it. I didn't want sex with her, I don't see her as attractive like that." I stopped and had to think, Chloe sipped her coffee and watched.

"Look at it this way, when I look at Birch, I don't just see her, I feel her, it is not just the boobs or the ass, which are pretty bloody sexy, but there is a feeling I get. It builds inside me; I really cannot find the words. With Katie I am aware she has a killer body; I mean she was batting off men and women in the states, left right and centre. But when I look at her, I feel neither sexual, or feel those sort of feelings inside me, and without that, I cannot get turned on. It probably sounds cruel, and I don't mean it that way, but looking at Katie for me, is the same as looking at Nigel." She gave a shudder.

"So, you went three weeks without any sex, ouch, that must have been hard?" I shook my head.

"Birch wasn't there, and I missed her so badly, don't tell anyone, but I actually cried quite a lot when I was alone, because I was so lonely without her and you guys. I knew I had been contracted for ads and talks, so I just gritted my teeth, got everything right first time round at the events, and counted the minutes until I could hold her again." She smiled.

"I think that is really sweet, I hope I have something like that someday."

It was clear as day to me, just not her, she was so like Hatty at times, it was clear she was not in a rush to settle down, but she also wanted something a little more consistent. I thought she had that with Max, she had been around him most of the summer, but he had always gone home after sex.

Chloe was feeling insecure, I really understood that, I was too, the last few days had just felt like one long onslaught. I had Birch, she had no one, and I think she was starting to feel that. She was nervously fingering her cup; I reached across and took her hands in mine.

"Chloe, there is someone for everyone, yours has not appeared yet, but they will. That painting last night, I told you how much I loved it, and you told me it was because it was alive. That picture gave you an internal feeling, you feel it, and so I will say this to you, if you ever feel like that around anyone, sleep with them all night. Wake up next to them, and enjoy it, that picture is exactly how I feel about Birch, exactly, it took my breath away to look at it." Her eyes opened wide.

"Holy shit, really?" I smiled.

"Chloe, it is the most beautiful picture I have ever seen." She smiled a huge wide smile.

"Wow, coming from you Abby, that means such a lot, I really want to paint something now." I stood up with my cup, and went to fill the pot.

"When I feel like that, I write, so go paint." I turned round and she looked nervous, I frowned.

"Is something else wrong?" She looked down.

"I am afraid to, the whole wall is glass, what if he is watching? I tried to kill him, and I am afraid to go in there."

That really hit home, the names Nigel and Martin spring to mind, if anyone understands that feeling it is without doubt me. I put the pot down, and pulled open the draw, which I knew had a coil of wire, I saw it and pulled it out.

"Come with me, you need to paint."

I walked into her studio, I could see what she meant, the whole wall was glass, you could see the whole garden from here, which meant, anyone in the garden could see in. I grabbed her hammer, and took a nail out of the box. Standing on a stool, I hammered it in about seven foot off the floor. I did the same on the other side, and then tied on the wire, and pulled it right across, getting it as tight as I could, and wound it on to the nail. I looked at her and smiled.

"Right, you now have a curtain wire, so get all your back drop sheets, we have loads of paperclips, so hang the fabric, and block all the outside out, and get doing what you do best, paint."

She gave a nod, and with a big smile she ran to the library, to grab the pot of clips. I sat in the kitchen, and drank coffee once we had done it, and watched through the open door as she started to paint. Before long, she started to hum, now that is the Chloe I know and love.

It was only December second, and already Christmas had a cloud over it, and so I headed upstairs to sort out my month. I sat in bed with a pad and started to make lists of what I needed, and also what I wanted to buy people. It was not long before my tiredness caught up with me, and I drifted off.

Izzy sat on the phone talking to Willington Institution, they had been contacted by Manchester, and one of their teams was liaison with the recovery of Rodney for the police. She gave all the details of the days previous events, and helped them with the changes in his description.

Birch was out at the front with Gill going over the appointments, she was bent down looking at the screen, when a van pulled up. A man jumped out, reached into the side of the van, he pulled out a large paper bundle and walked into the practice, and dropped it on the floor, Birch looked up and frowned.

“Excuse me, but what are you doing?” The man looked at his clip board.

“Love, I got two bundles of fifty for this address, they are free copies, and I do what the ticket says, there is one, I will get the other one.” He walked out, and went back to his van, Meg walked round the front of the counter, and pulled on the brown paper, she looked up.

“Why do we have free copies of the Oxendale Mail?” Birch smiled as she walked round, the guy came in and dumped the second bundle down.

“Could you sign here please?” Birch took the pen, and scribbled her name, he smiled. “Cheer’s love.”

He turned, and walked out. Birch bent down, cut the string, and pulled out a copy, she opened it up, and there on page two, was a full apology to each and every member of the Curio’s.

“Wow Deads, you can be very powerful if you put your mind to it.” She looked at Meg.

“Give everyone who comes in today a free paper, I am going to nip out, I am free for an hour, so I will take a few of these with me.”

Ten minutes later, Birch walked up the street with a large pile of free papers, she handed them out to the few people she met. Her main target was the Tea Rooms, she knew they put a paper out for customers to read. She walked in and smiled at Celia. She saw the papers and turned her nose up.

“I did not think you would read that rag?” Birch smiled and handed one over.

“I do today, especially page two, actually we were hoping you would give a few copies away for free.” Celia looked at the page.

“Put as many as you like out, I am glad to see this. I won’t ask how you did it, I have known you long enough to know not to ask." Birch smiled, and shook her head.

"This was not me; it was my dark little beastie; she can be a very persuasive little powerhouse when she puts her mind to it." Birch put a large stack down on the paper table. "Thanks girls, as always you are looking very tasty." Lillian gave a giggle.

Five minutes later, she walked into the Salon, and handed copies to Delphine, and walked over to Anthony who had just finished a client, she handed him a copy.

"Just in case you read it last night, here is the rebuke." He took the paper.

"Birch darling, I heard what he wrote, Michael read it to me. I have never read that rag; I cannot deny, he has a nerve, I remember school, Abby was really good and helped him when others saw him as a laughing stock. I hope you girls are not bothered by it? Birch darling, it is trash." She gave a giggle.

"Nevertheless, he pissed off Abby enough to respond, read page two." He gave a slightly cheeky look.

"Our little gothic doll got feisty, oh dear, this I want to read." He took the paper and opened it, and started to read, he gave an excited titter. "Oh, he has pulled the plug, whatever did she do?" Birch gave a giggle.

"She wrote a wonderful article, and sent it to him, telling him she was printing it with the Reporter. It freaked him out, I have to say Anthony, it was pretty impressive." He gave a giggle. Birch reached up to his arm.

"Anthony, we have not seen you at home for a few days, we miss you. You do know Michael will be made welcome. It is your home too, and you can have guests stay over whenever you want." He patted her hand.

"You are such a darling Birch, I know, this has been very new to us, and I have been enjoying it, you know, just getting to know him? Oh, trust me darling, I want to show him off, and you can bet I will be soon." She gave him a soft smile.

"Okay, we will all look forward to welcoming him, very soon. I have to go, I have work, but it has been nice to see you and just check in with you." He gave a bright smile.

"Always playing mother, I think it really suits you." She shook her head, and made her way to the door, Anthony watched her leave, he lifted the paper, and looked at it. "Abigail, you really are so exceptional, I hope now you believe it?"

The G5, or Gamers Five, are a group of five male gamers, who have played together for a long time. All of them are well known in the gaming world, and the IT community, where they did security work. The word hackers had been flouted in the past, but to date no proof has been found. Luke had seen what had happened, and heard a great deal of detail from Edwina, and as the leader of the G5, he called them in for support.

The four other members appeared at the door, they were a varied group of highly intelligent, computer specialists. They arrived and went to work, and within minutes, they were inside their van, pulling out ladders and boxes of tech, and it was not long before they were up ladders fitting cameras, right round the whole house. Luke sat back with Edwina.

"I want you safe, the boys will make sure of that. Everything will be Wi-Fi fed, so there will be no wires to cut, and you will all be able to monitor every part of this house. One click, and you will have eyes everywhere." She snuggled into him.

"I owe you big time, let us know what it costs, we are not short of cash Luke. This is what you do, so give us an invoice, it will be paid straight away." He looked at her.

"That is not why we are here, this is not a cheap ticket job, Weena, I am worried about you, this will make me feel more relaxed when I am not with you."

"Okay Luke... So, are you planning on staying around for a while, because I would be okay with that, you know, no pressure?" He chuckled.

"Always worrying, relax Weena, I will be around for a long while." She cuddled up to him.

"Good, I could use the attention." He chuckled.

Chloe sat painting on the floor as normal, when a tall thin guy walked in through the studio door, she froze and stared at him.

"Who the fuck are you... EDWINA!?" He raised his hand and waved it.

"Whoa chill out girl, I am here with Leveller, we are helping him out." Chloe slid back across the floor.

"I have never fucking heard of him...EDWINA!" She appeared

at the door.

"Chloe it's fine, honestly you are safe, these are friends of Luke, they are helping by fitting a better security system, no one will hurt you, these are the good guys." She nodded rapidly.

"Okay I get you, he just walked in, and it freaked me out, no one comes in here when I am working." She gave a nod.

"I know, I forgot to tell them, I am sorry. Chloe you will be fine, I promise, I am doing everything I can to make all of us safe." She relaxed a little.

"Okay Edwina, I am sorry, I just got panicked." He looked at her.

"I really am very sorry; I do this for a living. I don't want to hurt anyone; I want to protect people. I am sorry I scared you, I truly am." She nodded.

"Yeah thanks, sorry I yelled." He gave a long sigh, sized up the room, and then went back in the kitchen for his gear. Edwina crouched down in front of her.

"Chloe, are you going to be alright, I can call your counsellor if you need me too?" She shook her head.

"I have Birch if I need it, I am alright Edwina, I just got scared because I did not know him, that is all, I will be fine now." She gave a smile and lifted her hand to her sister's cheek.

"I will be in the library, so if you get scared again, come to me, or just yell out, I will be here for you Chloe, I will always be here for you." She nodded.

"Okay."

She got up and walked out, the guy with the ladder came to the door, he knocked, Chloe looked up and saw him standing there.

"Hello Miss Pemberton, my name is Terry Meddler, my mates call me Bosh, I am a security consultant working with the G5 group. I am here to fit special cameras to improve your security?" She gave a little giggle.

"That was stupid, I already knew you were here." He gave a slight chuckle.

"I wanted to do it over again, and this time get it right. I have two cameras to put in here, I won't get in your way." She nodded, and he brought his ladder in, and set it up near the door.

"I see you have put a line up; you know, I have special blinds that go up and down if you want some? They are good in the summer for keeping the light off your work, the sun can fade the paint you know, it is not good for your art, which by the way, is brilliant?" She looked up at him, as he prepared the camera for fitting.

"Thanks, I face all my paintings to the wall in summer, it keeps the light off them, I have a web site where I sell them." He nodded.

"I will look you up... By the way I hate to bring this up, but you do know you are naked, don't you?" She giggled, and looked down.

"I live and work naked as much as I can, I paint better without clothes, I feel happier and free like this." He screwed the camera into place.

"Never done it myself, work naked that is, in this game it is probably not the best, a lot of very straight laced people out there. I got to say, I admire your ease, you appear really comfortable in your own skin?" He came down the ladder. "Okay that is one done, the other will focus on the door, and keep some eyes on there for you." She moved back to her painting, and looked at it.

"Thanks for being so nice, I needed it, I had a pretty scary night last night, I am a little jittery today." He understood.

"I heard some of it, it is why we are here, I promise you will feel safer now, you can relax." She felt a little calmer just knowing that, he came down his ladder and smiled.

"All done, see I told you it would only take a second." He slipped a tablet out of his bag and looked at it, he showed her.

"See there you are all safe and secure, we have not done everything yet, but when we are finished, you will have a little hand set in each room, and you will be able to pause filming for an hour at a time if you want privacy. It will also have a panic button, if you get worried, you will be able to use the intercom to talk to others on it. You will never need to be afraid in here again." He winked and gave her a smile. She felt a massive sense of relief.

"Thanks Terry, that makes me feel a lot better." He winked.

"There are four of us on the job, so you may see some of them, we all these T shirts on, so don't be alarmed, we have a lot to fit, we will be here most of the day. I will come back later when it is set up and show you how to use it." She nodded and gave a smile.

"Thanks, I am really glad you are here, and thanks for being so nice, it has helped me." He winked again.

"Okay onwards and upwards, I have the upstairs floor to do next." He grabbed his ladder and walked out, Chloe leaned over slightly to watch him, she nodded approvingly.

"Nice butt."

Birch sat at her desk in her office, holding the phone to her ear.

"Edwina, I understand your concern, I am watching both her and Deads, but you have to understand that both of them today will be a little rattled, hell we all were. Deads will sleep it off and then talk, Chloe bottles things up, and she will either let it out in anger, or she will have sex and let it all out there. I know of her counsellor, she has a great reputation, and yes, she would be a help, but I am sorry, but that has to be Chloe's choice. She may come to me or Izzy, both of us can handle it, but we will have to wait for her to ask. Give her some space and let her paint, and watch her okay?"

"Alright Birch, she is fine at the moment, she is painting, Abby helped her hang some curtains, so she is completely private now, and that has helped. Abby has gone back to bed and she is asleep at the moment, to be honest I wish Chloe would, I think sleep would do her good, but you know Chloe, she lives to paint."

"If that is what she needs to do, let her do it, Edwina she is a very resilient person, she will come through this, and if she struggles, we are all there supporting her. As I said it is only a day after, give her a little more time, look I will talk to her tonight alone, and see how she is doing if that puts your mind at ease?" Birch could hear Edwina give a sigh of relief.

"Yeah, if you could, it would really help put my mind at rest, thanks Birch. I know I am like an old woman, but she has never had my strength, she has always been a bit soft hearted like dad. I know she acts tough, but she really isn't, I actually love that about her, just knowing you are keeping an eye on her does help."

"Edwina, we all love her, she really is very special, I will always watch over her. Go do your thing with Luke, and relax a little bit yourself. Okay Sweetie I have to go; I will talk with you later."

"Okay thanks Birch, see you after work." Birch put the phone down and sat back in her seat.

"Where are you Rodney, I want you off my property and back in care as quickly as possible? We all need calm, and you are making big waves."

She closed her eyes and just rested a moment, she felt so tired, last night had been draining. This was not how she had expected Christmas to start at all.

Chapter 14

Gamers Five.

December had not started easily, Birch and Edwina had employed the services of G5, and as a result, for two days, the five guys, one of which was Luke, walked round the house fitting camera's, and checking out all locks. The outer door on the garage side of the house, which led down into the cellar, was replaced with an air tight security door, and their last task, was to build a security hub, to connect the whole system together.

Everything was to be wired into Edwina's server, the problem was it was not really big enough, and so after some thought, Chloe and myself were recruited, and we set to work in the attic, cleaning. Andrew Mortenson aka Morty, was an electrician, and he massively improved the lighting, and as we cleaned, Bosh and Jeremiah Wilks aka Creamy, fitted brand new flooring and insulation. By mid week, we had a huge new room, and I mean huge.

With spot lights, and the whole space being completely sealed, it was very bright and warm. Luke who the guys called Leveller, worked with Edwina fitting a new large private server at the far end above her room, everyone was very excited. To me it just looked like a large shiny box, with lots of flashing lights, and fans that hummed, like something out of a space movie. The G5 assured me it was the 'dogs bollocks' of computing, and who was I to argue, after all, my skills were simply editing pictures and word processing.

Birch made the final addition, which was box after box of carpet tiles. Chloe and I received them when they arrived, on a pallet. We then spent the day carrying them up, which took forever, and ended with us both, naked, sweating, and gasping for air on the pile of boxes we had moved. It felt like an exhausting day, but it had also been great fun. The guys had great spirit, and were really easy to get along with, and there was a lot of banter, and as the days moved on, Chloe and myself felt a little more like our normal selves.

I decided on a bath, and went up to my room. As I walked down the hallway, I noticed Chloe's door open, and I could hear she had someone in there, so nothing unusual about that, I went to open my door when I heard Chloe's voice.

"Terry I am twenty six, it is not up to Luke, I really like you, and I want to do a bit more than kiss, Luke has no say in that." I stopped and stood for a second, I heard Terry.

"Chloe I really do like you, honestly, I am a little bit crazy about you, I really am, but Luke made all of us promise we would not hit on any of you. It is kind of part of the deal, I will get my ass kicked just for kissing you, if he finds out."

"He has no right, this is my body and my life, and I say who I date, not fucking Luke."

I had to admit, I agreed with Chloe, I walked over to Chloe's door and leaned in, Chloe was looking upset.

"Guys, it might be better if you shut the door, and just for the record Terry, if you really do like her that much, you would risk everything for her, so close the door, get your kit off, and put a smile on my best friends face." Chloe smiled.

"See, even Abby says it is okay."

I pulled the door closed and left them to it. I cannot deny it did annoy me, I decided to ask about this, and so headed back downstairs. I found Luke in the kitchen with Edwina, and two of the other guys, I looked at them and smiled, and then turned to Luke.

"Is it true there is a rule that none of the girls in this house are to be touched by your crew?" Edwina looked at him, he squirmed a little.

"Yes... I thought it would make the job easier if the guys did not get distracted with you girls, and also considering recent events, I thought it would make it easier." I nodded, and looked at Creamy and Bongo.

"Have you ever screwed girls on other jobs?" They both looked really uncomfortable, which pretty much said it all. "I will take that as a yes guys, thanks." I looked back at Luke.

"We have a rule in this house Luke, which is the girls always have a say in their own lives. We are open minded, free thinking women, and as much as I get why you tried to protect us, your job was to boost security, not tell us who we could or could not be friendly with. As far as I can tell the job is complete, all we need is the invoice and you will be paid, which means at this current moment, you and your team are guests here. You are a bunch of great guys, and we appreciate everything you have done for us, honestly, we really do, but baby sitting us is not part of your job, we are quite capable of doing that ourselves, please remember that in future." He looked embarrassed, and gave a nod.

"Honestly Abby, I was trying to look out for you, that is all." I understood that.

"Are your guys a danger to any of us?" He looked surprised.

"No, these guys are as straight as they come, I would vouch for all of them, they are decent respectful guys." I nodded.

"What about Terry?" He smiled.

"Terry and me go way back, he is the best out of all of us."

"Good, because Chloe is really into him, and this no involvement rule is causing problems, because he is really into her. I told them they could screw each other, you know, considering at the moment you are working for me, this being my house an all, which makes me your boss, so I overruled you." Edwina burst out laughing, Creamy and Bongo sniggered. I nodded and turned.

"I am going for a bath." I walked up the hallway with a smile, as they all started laughing, I heard Edwina speak to Luke.

"Overruled by Abby, you soft pussy."

I smiled, as I headed up the stairs, and then down the hallway and felt like a queen. I giggled quietly to myself, I walked up to Chloe's door, opened it and leaned in, Chloe was on top of Terry ripping his clothes off.

"Luke has been told, you two are free, although, I can see Chloe gave a convincing argument, carry on." I closed the door with a giggle, and walked over to my room, and headed for the bath.

Fifteen minutes later I slipped into the bath, and felt the hot water kiss my whole body.

"Oh, this is nice." I closed my eyes and just relaxed.

"Hi Sweetie." I opened my eyes and smiled.

"Hi, I thought you were working later?" She smiled as she stood holding two large glasses of wine.

“We finished everything a lot quicker, Gill really has trained those girls well, so I came home as quickly as I could, so I could be with you, and I found you bath cheating, shame on you.” I started to giggle, as she handed me the wine glasses and started to strip.

“Is bath cheating even a thing?” I looked at the wine.

“Are we going up market?” She chuckled as she pulled off her pants.

“It’s Christmas, and the clients are all bringing a couple of bottles in as a thanks. I have been giving them out to all the staff, seriously Deads, we have so much, I am not sure the staff will be sober after Christmas until at least February. I brought twenty home tonight… Shuffle up.” She slid in behind me, and I handed her the glass, she leaned back in the tub.

“Oh god Sweetie, this is nice.” I leaned back into her and sipped my wine.

“We are such spoiled bitches, you know that?” She chuckled.

“Amen to that.” We chinked glasses.

As I think I have said before, life is best, when you are relaxing in a hot bath, and yet, a problem occurs when the water goes cold. Having relaxed and talked, as this was our favourite place for the small important chats, we sat on Birch’s bed, and she looked out of the window at her tree, whilst I brushed and dried her hair. I must admit, I was really happy with her response to the gift, I had caught her quite a few times sneaking off to sit in the dark and stare at it.

It did not matter how many times I told her; Birch shouldered the burden of everything that happened in the house. In a strange way, which only Birch understood, the tree helped her to focus and think, and as a result, it destressed her, the little tree was her way of letting things go. I ran the brush through her hair and turned the dryer off.

“All done.” I stroked her hair, I love how fluffy and full it is when it has been washed, she leaned back.

“I love that Sweetie; it feels so nice.”

I looked down at her as I knelt up, and she leaned back into me, her bright happy eyes stared up at me. She lifted her hand and touched my cheek.

"You look tired, this has taken its toll on you, I want us all to make this a really wonderful Christmas, but so far we have been hit with troubles, will you be alright, I am worried about you?" I smiled at her.

"This is what I need, just this, you and me, this is my world, that out there, that is just stuff going on in the back ground." Her eyes sparkled up at me.

"I love you so much Deads, and yes, it is these moments alone I cherish the most." I leaned down and kissed her, she snorted on my chin and I giggled. She started to chuckle. "Okay that was messed up." She laughed.

"Please tell me there is no snot on your chin?" I giggled and her eyes danced, she turned to face me, and pulled me close. "Okay let's try that again." She leaned in and kissed me softly.

Part of the deal with the G5 was we cooked them a proper meal, so while Birch took Luke into the library to settle the bill, Chloe, Edwina, and myself got stuck in on a full roast beef dinner. In the living room, the guys hooked up a games console to the large TV, and started a round of fighting games. Beers flowed, and laughter echoed down the hall, it felt nice to hear it, and in truth, we all needed it. Deb's set up the table, and laid everything out, and by the time everything was ready, all of us had consumed enough alcohol to have us all in very high spirits.

We really hit high level, as the guys all sat round the table, and feasted on hot food. It was crazy to see them eat, it was like they had never been fed, as they spooned mash, roast potatoes, peas and carrots on to their plate, with many thick slices of beef. I looked at them all stuffing themselves.

"Do you guys not eat proper food?" Bongo shovelled more mash on his plate.

"Not like this we don't, I'm telling you, if you cook like this for us again, I will do any jobs you want for free, this is bloody lovely."

All the guys nodded, as they shovelled the food in. Birch grinned across the table, I always thought she could eat a lot, but her plate looked empty compared to the guys.

The atmosphere was really relaxed, the last few days had been fun, and we had all got on really well, they were a good group who answered our endless questions. They mainly lived alone, but crashed at each other's flats, they pretty much got so involved with games and coding, they forgot to eat, and like us, they had each other's backs.

G5 was created by Luke, it was his business, and they handled mainly security work, like they had done for us, they also did a lot of IT work beefing security for business. Currently only Luke had any kind of relationship, but as I had discovered, they had encounters on private jobs that took care of them. I suppose we were as curious about them as they were us, and eventually we got down to their gamer names. Terry aka Bosh, answered us.

"Most of us have names from our gaming, you know, Luke is a titan in gaming, and he is known for running in and shooting the shit out of everyone, he also levels up faster than any of us. Bongo, here he does a lot of mods for games, and he always has lots of drum beats in the background to really get the heart pumping, his games are like immersive as fuck." Bongo smiled, and Chloe frowned.

"Immersive as fuck, how do you mean?" Terry smiled and bobbed his head.

"You know, like your art, you just get drawn in and swallowed by it." She stared at him and went bright red, she sounded really surprised.

"My art does that to you?" He smiled and looked round the table.

"Well yeah, I just thought everyone saw it like that, you are a brilliant painter." She smiled a really shy smile, it was such a nice moment, I patted her leg.

"See, you have no idea how good you are." Terry nodded agreeing with me.

Deb's looked at Jeremiah, who was a broad guy of Nigerian origin.

"I am not sure how to ask this, because I don't want to offend you, but why are you called Creamy, you know, it is not really obvious to me?" Edwina sniggered, and all the guys put their heads down, Creamy looked panicked.

"I... Er... Well!" Deb's looked at him, looking flustered.

"It's okay, you don't have to answer, I don't want to embarrass you, I don't mind if you don't want to answer."

He smiled and leaned on the table, I must admit looking at the guys who were all looking at each other and smirking, I wanted to know now, and it was clear Birch was more than interested. Creamy looked at Luke who smiled, he shrugged, and looked at Deb's.

"It is a little delicate, but funny as hell Deb's." Okay, so I was really interested now, he looked at Creamy. "Should I tell them?" He shook his head.

"Why not, you tell everyone else, it was bound to come out sooner or later." Edwina sniggered again. Luke looked round the table, we were all obviously very interested at this point. He gave a giggle and patted Creamy on the shoulder.

"You see girls, our mate here is a healthy young buck, if you get me, and he is well known in the equipment department." Okay we had seen the bulge, so we pretty much were ahead in that game. Luke smiled, the others looked down and tittered.

"You see, we were on this job, working for this really rich guy in Hampstead, and he had three daughters, who were to say the least, hot, and very flirty." He gave a long sigh.

"That was a hard job, well the thing was it was driving us all wild, they were really coming on strong, and we had a big job on, and the more we tried to work, the harder it got. Well for Creamy here, it got a lot harder if you catch my drift?" Terry sniggered.

"Well, the thing was, it was really hot, and so we were in shorts, and as you know, there is not a lot of room in those things, it gets a bit cramped, and we were all struggling. Creamy here, he was in pain, oh dear, it was very bloody obvious, I mean his shorts were close to ripping."

Edwina gave a titter and Birch started to giggle, I was smirking, and Debs was just staring at Creamy, holding her fork full of mash in front of her face. Luke looked round the table, with a smirk.

"Anyway, this one girl came into the kitchen where Creamy was working. I mean, the day was hot, and with all the ovens on cooking lunch, it was like a boiler room in there. So, he has this pantry cupboard open, and is feeding cable through, to link the system into the room next door to me, when he suddenly feels this hand on his equipment, and it starts to softly rub. He jumps up in surprise, and there is the girl in a thong bikini, and she is hot, I mean sexy as hell, and all smiles. Anyway, she tells him how much she would like to see it. Well as you can imagine, his junk had been stroked and is expanding, and it is painful. This girl slides up onto the table, opens her legs and pulls the thong to one side and starts to rub herself, and she tells him how hot she feels, and how she likes to watch guys take care of themselves."

Creamy was starting to look very uncomfortable, Chloe was hanging on every word with big wide eyes, loving every minute of it, Edwina still tittered. Deb's was transfixed on Creamy. I had to admit, I really wanted to know what happened. Luke smiled.

"So, my mate here who is rapidly expanding, says, he cannot because it will be messy, as he is known to produce a lot, you know, the batter? So, this girl, who by this point has two fingers inside herself, and is moaning like crazy, just grabs a glass and gives it to him. He looks round, and there is no one anywhere to be seen, so he whips out the old soldier, and she goes wild, and she starts really going at herself, which drives him nuts. So, he starts whacking away, and as is always the case, he reaches that moment as she moans like crazy, cumming all over the place and bang, he fires into the glass and God dammed almost filled it. And to be honest after the day we had been through, it was a great relief."

"So what happened?" Deb's, was a little more into this than I had thought she would be, Luke looked at her.

"Her mum came in, so Creamy turns real fast, flips the soldier back, and zips up his shorts, and the girl puts down the glass, and pulls her thong back. So, he is in the pantry sweating and panicking like mad, and the mother starts preparing the meal for service. She mashes the potatoes, and then tells her daughter to grab some cream, when low and behold she spots the glass. My mate here shits himself, as he watched her pick up the glass, and she dumps it in the mash, she whips it up into a good fluff, and then shoves in her finger, has a taste, and looks all dreamy eyed, and says to her daughter, who is also freaking out. 'Oh, so creamy.' And with that she carries it off to the dining room."

Birch giggled, but apart from that there was utter silence as the guys had their heads down, with their shoulders shaking, and we all just stared taking it all in. Chloe spoke first in a very impressed and stunned sort of way.

"Holy fuck!" Birch sniggered.

"Deb's Sweetie, close your mouth we can see your mash." And the room erupted into mad laughter. Deb's looked at Luke.

"Did they eat it?" More laughter erupted, Luke wiped his mouth, as he chuckled, and nodded at her.

"Yeah, we were all outside, pissed off because the mean old bastard did not ask us to join him, although, once we found out what happened, we were pretty bloody glad he hadn't."

All the guys laughed hysterically, and Creamy did eventually laugh, even if he did look a little embarrassed, Deb's looked kind of repulsed and impressed at the same time. The night after that became more fun. We all finished our meal, and the guys mucked in and helped us wash up, the jokes were flying, and I could secretly see Deb's checking out Creamy's bulge. Birch noticed too and winked at me, and I giggled as I wiped the plates.

We were pretty drunk when we remembered Birch had floor tiles, so we staggered up to the attic and unpacked the boxes, and found every box had a different colour tile in it. I should have known, she likes colour, it's a Birch thing.

Have you any idea how hard it is to lay floor tiles, which are every bloody colour of the rainbow, whilst drunk? Oh, you have no idea how much it screws with your head. Half way through, I felt dizzy, and was filled with uncontrollable laughter. To make it fun we started in each corner with four teams, and raced to the centre, the whole attic was filled with hysterical laughter, and after two and a half hours of hysterical cross eyed laughter, I lay on my back in the middle of the attic, having placed the winning yellow tile, gasping for air with sore sides, as I looked up at Birch, as she stood marvelling. She clasped her hands together and held them close to her heart, as she looked round swaying, with a big bright smile.

"Guys it is so pretty, I love it."

Chloe sat by the window sweating, and Deb's was already passed out. We lounged about talking, and I lay on the floor next to Chloe, I reached over and patted her thigh.

"You alright?" She smiled and raised her glass.

"Yeah, I am doing okay... I talked with Terry, I told him I do not do boyfriends, but I would be interested in more than just one night, I like him. He lives in a shit hole, so I told him if he needs me, I will make him a priority, and he can stay over." For Chloe that was a big move forward, I squeezed her leg.

"That is really good, I am happy for you." She smiled.

"He is staying tonight." I winked.

"Good for you."

We finally staggered down the stairs carrying Deb's, and we put her to bed. Terry slipped in with Chloe, Luke followed Edwina into her room, and with a spare room, plus my room, we let Creamy and Bongo take the twin bed guest room. I looked at Morty.

"You can sleep in my bed." He raised his eyes and looked me up and down with a smile. I gave a giggle and pointed behind me.

"I sleep with her, in her bed." He looked disappointed; Birch giggled.

"Oh Sweetie, did you want her too, sorry?" He gave a sigh.

"Win some lose some, maybe next time?" I kind of felt bad for him. I showed him into my room, and kissed his cheek.

"Sleep well." I walked through to Birch, who was already in bed, pretty drunk and full of fun.

"Hi sexy Sweetie." I giggled as I pulled off my t shirt.

"Poor Morty, he is so disappointed because you can have me any way you want me." She giggled.

"Oh, I really want you in every way possible." I smirked at her.

"I want to be had every way possible." Her eyes twinkled with delight. From the room next door Morty shouted.

"I CAN FUCKING HEAR YOU, AND IT IS JUST NOT FAIR!" I climbed on the bed, and crawled towards her, I looked back at the door.

"THERE IS A GLASS ON THE SIDE." Birch burst out laughing, and I pulled the duvet towards me revealing her long pale legs.

"Oh yeah, now that is what I am talking about." She slipped them open, and I bent down and kissed her thigh, she gave a soft gasp.

"Oh god, I need you Deads." I started to kiss my way up, she gripped the sheets and slid forward towards me.

"Don't make me wait, I really want you." I chuckled, and slipped backwards. "Oh Sweetie don't tease me, I want you so bad." I looked up at her, she was already breathing a lot faster.

"Wow you are really horny tonight." Her eyes were partially glazed, she gave a gasp, and bit her lip, I could actually feel her whole body vibrating, and I had hardly touched her.

"Oh Deads, please don't make me wait, not tonight, please Sweetie."

I smiled at her and lowered my head, and gently kissed her outer lips, she moaned and instantly bucked forward. Wow she was soaking, I slipped out my tongue, and ran it gently upward from the base, and she gave a long loud moan, and leaned back. I liked this, I slid my hand up, and poked out a finger, I traced down her moist slit, and her legs twitched as she moaned.

"Oh god, Oh Deads... Take me baby, I need you." I pushed and my finger gently entered her. "Ooooh!" She was trembling, I had never seen her like this, I pushed her legs wider and she smiled.

"Oh god yes please." Morty walked into the room in his boxers.

"For fuck's sake Abby, just fuck her, you guys are driving me mental." I looked back and saw the huge bulge in his shorts.

"You going to watch?" He smiled.

"I would bloody love to, I just didn't think you would let me." I looked at Birch, she was past gone.

"I just want you to screw me now Deads, I really need this." I pushed my head down and entered her with my tongue, she thrust up on the bed.

"Oh, GOD!" Morty had his shorts off, and walked over to the bed for a better view, he was stroking himself.

Birch was lost in her deep smouldering lust, I worked my mouth, teasing every inch of her, she looked down at me, gasping.

"Let him have you, let me watch." I looked up.

"I am busy, I want you." She gave a loud gasp.

"Deads, he really wants you; I saw you out there, let him take you now, I want to see you happy." He gave a nod, as he looked at my naked ass waving. I pushed my tongue in harder and she squealed.

"Top drawer, condoms."

He grabbed the handle and pulled it open; I could see his fully erect manhood; he grabbed the packet and tore it open. I continued to work my mouth, I slid down and entered her, banging her with my tongue, she was going wild, clawing at the bed and rolling her head around. I had never seen her this turned on, and it was really getting me going. Morty climbed on the bed behind me.

"Are you sure you are okay with this?" I pulled out, and looked back.

"Jesus, just do it already."

Birch looked at me, she was shaking, and sweating, and smiled. That was all I needed, I dived back in, Morty slipped in easily, I was soaking wet, and with each stroke, I bounced into her, and she jerked and gasped, I moved around inside her while Morty took me, and it was hard to focus.

My eyes closed, oh god it felt good, it had been a while, and I was cooking already, my temperature was rising just watching Birch. Morty pounded into me and Birch looked at him with smouldering eyes.

"Faster, you pussy." I was barely keeping it together, I wanted so badly to cum, but I wanted Birch to cum first.

I moved on her harder and faster and she squirmed and writhed on the bed, and all the time my face was pounded into her almost as if Morty was screwing her himself, Birch let out a wail, and my whole body responded, she clawed at the bed.

"Deads, I need to cum."

I was doing my best, she was so wet, in all our time I had never known her be like this. Morty was gasping for air, as he thrust in fast and deep, oh god my body was on fire and my legs were twitching, it was taking everything I had to control myself.

"Cum for me baby, Birch cum for me."

I thrust my face into her harder than I ever had, and Morty slammed into me, I could feel him throbbing, he was so close, and I was on the edge, he pounded again and I jerked, clawing into Birch's legs, she rose up a little off the bed and wailed, and that was more than I could handle, my insides exploded, and I went full tilt nuclear orgasm.

I wailed into Birch, and jerked and she exploded like the flood gates had opened with a squeal. Morty pulled back on my hips, and then grunted, and the throbbing inside me created yet more ripples, and out of nowhere Birch flooded into a spray.

I felt myself get dragged back into Morty, as he jerked with his climax. He slid his hands on to my breasts, and squeezed, as I came really hard, and Birch pretty much washed us from head to foot with a loud squeal. I just hung there, held up by Morty spasming, and lost to everything, as Birch writhed on the bed moaning.

Morty flopped out of me, and fell off the bed onto the floor, and just lay on his back gasping for air. I collapsed unable to stay upright onto Birch, and she weakly pulled her arms round me as she gasped for air. Birch slowly regulated her breathing and looked at me.

“I have never done that, I have always wanted to, I got you to do it, but I could never do it for you, and Sweetie, I did it, I did it for you.” She smiled and looked so happy. I gave a slight giggle, I was exhausted.

“Baby, the bed is soaked, but thank you, it was frigging amazing.” She flopped back into the pillow, and gasped in more air. I leaned over the side of the bed, and looked down at Morty.

“Are you okay?” He opened his eyes and looked up at me.

“You guys are wild, I am knackered, leave me to sleep here, honestly, that was insane, and amazing.”

I finally came round to reality, my whole body was tingling, Birch sat up, and reached for my hand. She slipped off the bed and pulled me, I simply followed on shaky legs.

In the bathroom she turned on the shower, and we stepped in. it was hot and steamy, she lathered her hands and began to wash me, I was still on fire, and my head was still pretty buzzed from the booze. She slid her hands over my breasts, and they started to grow again, I was hyper sensitive, and as the hot water flowed over me, she leaned in and began to suck and nibble at them. My body exploded again, and my legs shook, she slid her hands over me, as she sucked, and I leaned back against the tiled wall, panting, as my body tingled all over, I had cum once, I was not sure I could cum again.

She worked her way down, and started kissing my stomach, her hand moved between my legs, and ran up to my butt cheeks, my legs spread, as I began to feel my whole body vibrate, and I let out a loud moan, she moved lower, kissing and nibbling, I was gasping for air, I was not sure I could take this, my vagina was already so sensitive. My arms shot out to the sides of the shower;

my legs were wobbling.

"Oh god Birch, I don't think I can take this."

She moved in between my legs, and I felt a blast explode through my body, my arms snapped down to her head.

"Birch no, I cannot take it, I am too sensitive."

She thrust her tongue inside me and my eyes flashed and sparkled, I felt my legs giving way, bolts of shock exploded in my vagina, I squeezed her head.

"Oh god... OH GOD!"

I could not take anymore, I never felt anything like it, I could not breathe, she was wild tonight. I was shaking, and she just did not stop, the power inside my body was building and building and I could not handle it, I leaned back on the wall, and BOOM! I lost complete control, as my head and vagina exploded, and I just hung there in the hot water, jerking and shaking unable to even speak.

She moved back, and I slid down the wall, Jesus this woman was going to kill me, with her insatiable lust.

I don't even know how I made it into bed, when I came round properly, but I was in my own bed, nice and dry and warm, and Birch was sat on my lap watching me, filled with happiness and smiles. I looked at her and gave a weak smile, her eyes were dancing.

"Sweetie, you made me squirt; I am so happy."

Christ this woman is a maniac, and some sort of sex ninja, how could she be so alert?

"I am really happy for you, I am, but Birch, I think you broke me." She giggled and leaned forward; she kissed me slowly.

"Deads, Sweetie, I love my life with you, I have never been happier than I am at the moment. I really love you."

I lifted my weak arms round her, and just held her, I was so tired. She snuggled into my neck, and I held her close. I relaxed as I floated, I felt amazingly happy, but so tired. I closed my eyes with a smile, and I remember very little afterwards, I was gone into the land of happy loving dreams.

Chapter 15

The Author.

It was Friday morning, and everyone was rushing around, I felt tired and aching, Birch had pretty much worn me out last night, and yet she was loud and happy and more alive than I had ever seen her. I had to be up, as I was expecting a call from Katie, I had one more event booked for the year, it was a sci fi fantasy convention, in London, where I was booked to make one of few public UK appearances.

The venue was at the Hopkins Theatre, and we would be staying for one night at the Phillips Hotel. I was to be interviewed by Gordon Stimes, a pretty famous TV personality, as part of a gothic revival feature for the convention. I had insisted Birch was part of this, I had hated America without her, and so both of us were to be collected, and driven there by chauffer, which in itself would be weird.

Birch had helped me pick out a new outfit, although Katie had suggested I look at a few designers on her books, and I ruled that straight out. A package had been sent by courier, which had all access stage passes, and event passes in it for us, Chloe admired them, as she turned them round in her hand.

"You know it is sort of really weird Abby, because you are actually pretty famous, and yet we hang out and get drunk, and screw in front of each other like normal people." I gave a chuckle; I loved her to bits.

"Chloe are you sure normal people live like we do?" She gave a shrug.

"Everyone fucks and gets drunk, but you know what I mean? Abby you are this really cool person I live with, it's like, it's you... You know you; I mean look at us, I am naked, and you only have a t shirt on, and we are just sat here chatting and drinking coffee, whilst everyone else is running round like maniacs getting ready for work, it is weird, Abigail Jennifer Watson, is like this huge well known writer."

I could understand her, it was something I still found strange, but it was a fake image, because actually, Chloe got to see the real me, the gothic writer was some ideal everyone else had, I was just me.

"Chloe, you are one of a few people that I can trust, you are a best friend to me, this here, this mess, this is who I am, this is the real me. Actually, you know that mess I become when I am writing, you know, that zombie who forgets to eat, and does not leave the house, has messy hair and is smelly? That is actually Abigail Jennifer Watson the famous writer, that is the real me." She smiled.

"I love to listen to you when you write, I have peeked in your room and watched you, you look like a painter, just with a keyboard and no brushes." Now that I got, I had watched her paint many times.

"That is who I am Chloe, not all that frills and fancy stuff, I don't like it, it makes me uncomfortable."

"Yeah, I could see that when you were on TV from America, Birch cried when she watched it, she got really worried about how unhappy you looked."

"Chloe Sweetie, you said you would not say anything." She twisted her mouth as she looked at me.

"Oops, I forgot." I looked at Birch.

"You cried?" She gave a sigh.

"I was missing you, and then I saw you and it just all came up, because you were as unhappy as I was." She looked really apologetic. "Sorry, I know I promised I wouldn't, but three weeks felt like a life time." I smiled, and nodded, I understood that.

"Now do you understand why I want you with me, I hate it too, even if it's only one night?" She came over to me and leaned in and kissed me softly.

"Deads Sweetie, I get it, I do, and I will be there. I have to go to work, so I will see you soon, watch out for the bean bags, they are being delivered today, okay?"

The door banged, silence descended, and Chloe and I sat sipping our coffee. The moment I had been waiting for arrived, my phone rang, and I hit speaker phone.

"Hi Deadly, you sexy little minx of cuteness, how are you doing, are you and the slapper ready for Sunday?"

"Hey Katie, yeah we are packed and ready, the passes came so we have everything."

"Okay the car will pick you up, it is all in the itinerary, all you really need to do is get that sweet sexy cute little ass of yours in, and we will do the rest. I take it your slapper is still happy with everything?" I gave a sigh.

"Birch will be with me, and she is fine, yes."

"Such a waste of a hotel and double bed, but hey those are the crosses we have to bear, if you need extra, I will be two doors down." She chuckled. "I will go through everything once you make it here, be warned, the press has been asking about you, so there will be cameras, wear your mirrored glasses, it fucks with the flashes. Okay you sexy little sweetness, I will see you Saturday, with your yummy little ass, for drinks in the lobby."

"Okay we will see you there." I hit the button and ended the call; Chloe filled my cup.

"I see what you mean, she is pretty full on. Abby, I am not like that am I with guys?" I smiled.

"Not that bad, the difference, is you take no for an answer." She sat down and lifted her cup; I could see she was thinking about it, she looked at me, and her dark eyes sparkled.

"Abby, I know she is Birch's friend, but you know what, get rid of her, and replace her with Edwina, or another agent. I can see how she gets to you. You looked really uncomfortable then, honestly it is not worth it, if she does not respect what you and Birch have, give her the push." I sat back; I cannot deny I had thought about it.

"To be honest if she would drop all the shit about sleeping with her, I would have no problem, but in America, she would not quit, and I had reached my limit when we got back. I am only doing this because Birch is going to be with me." Chloe gave me a nod, she understood, and I smiled.

"I like our talks Chloe, I like that I can be normal with you, it means a lot." She smiled at me, and I had to giggle.

"I really like the fact that you are famous, and I don't want to fuck you." She giggled and I started to laugh. "Seriously I am so straight it's unbelievable."

Did you know bean bags come in boxes, because I didn't? Birch being Birch bought fifteen, and yep, everyone was a different colour, some were even multi coloured, and the attic was starting to look like one big acid trip. We carried the boxes into the kitchen, and unpacked the bags, then took them up to the attic. It was good fun throwing them at each other, and then, when we got tired, we lined them up and collapsed on them, they were really comfortable.

Ripping up the cardboard took forever, armed with box cutters, we chopped it into small enough bits to pack the wheelie bin, it was pretty cold outside, so we did not hang around, the wind was blowing really cold now. Winter was on us big time, and the garden looked bleak.

The pool was covered and still heated, it had a large hooped top over it, which these days was permanently condensed, Edwina was the only one who still used it. I had considered a swim a few times, but watching the trees sway in the cold wind, soon put me off. I guess I like my comfort and heat too much.

Evening arrived, everyone came home, including Anthony, I had really missed him, and hugged him to death, and he loved being the centre of attention. It felt right having him back, even though I knew he was really enjoying his relationship with Michael.

Everyone relaxed, and I felt a little more introverted than normal, I think it was just nerves about the up coming event. We ate in the living room, Birch loved sitting on the floor next to the tree, and after we had eaten, it was movie time, Deb's and Chloe were going through the guide, Chloe looked at Deb's.

"It's not Christmas until cousin Eddie shows up." She did not agree.

"Seriously, you are a beginner, everyone knows it is when Hans Gruber arrives?"

I left them to it, and slunk off up to my room. I had washed all the bedding, so remade the bed, and flopped on it with a pad to make notes, Birch came in with a drink, she slid onto the bed at my side and handed me a drink.

"Something is on your mind; do you want to share it?" She was getting to know me a little too well, I felt shitty. I looked at her and gave a long sigh.

"Birch, I am really sorry, I know Katie is your friend, but I have been doing a lot of thinking, my contract is up in February, and I am thinking of moving agencies. I really don't want to cause any problems, but I think I want a new agent." She lay back on the pillows.

"I cannot deny Deads, I have expected this, are you really that unhappy?" I put my drink down, and lay back on my side to look at her.

"Katie is the best at her job, and she has done wonders for me, I am not ungrateful Birch." She appeared to understand.

"But?" I gave a frustrated sigh.

"We will never have a threesome with another woman, and I will never sleep with another woman, it will never happen, I don't want that, not ever." She nodded.

"She is getting too intense? I completely understand, I have been there, I know what it is like. Deads talk to her." I gave another frustrated sigh and sat up.

"It is like talking to a brick wall, it just gets worse Birch, she is frigging relentless and it's driving me mad. I spent three weeks in the States telling her no, and she just kept coming. Birch I am tired of it, all the snipes and digs, you know she does not want me, that is the mad thing, it is not me she even gives a shit about." Birch frowned, and sat up.

"Okay I am confused, what do you mean?" I looked at her with utter disbelief.

"Frigging seriously, you don't know? Birch, she only wants me because I am yours, if I was sleeping with any other woman, she would not give a shit. Because I got you, and she didn't, she has to have me, to prove a point. It is frigging Tony all over again, you would not screw her, and you have left her, and moved on with me, so she needs to have me now. What is she going to do, take a cast of my vagina as a trophy?"

I felt so shitty, but it was what I was feeling, she looked shocked, I leaned forward, and put my head on my knees, and wrapped my arms round them. It all was starting to feel like it was too much, and all I wanted to do was just stay at home and avoid her.

"I am sorry, but it is really getting to me, I will do this weekend and be a good little girl, but after this, I have honoured every part of my contract, and I think I am going to walk away. I feel so shitty Birch, I really do, but I have had enough."

Birch gave a long sigh, and she put her hand on my back and gently rubbed. I closed my eyes, and pushed my face into my knees, I felt horrible and mean, but I had just reached that point where it felt easier to walk away rather than endure any more.

"I have to admit Deads, I never thought of it that way, but actually that makes so much sense. Look I am behind you one thousand percent, you know that, and if it is getting you this wound up, then yes, this is not good for you. I can talk to her if you want me to? Actually, I would not mind playing the jealous lover, it could be fun, I could go all green eyed monster on her, if you need me to get involved I will." I gave a sigh.

"The mad thing is she is amazing at her job, she believed in me when no one else would, and I loved her for that, but I am just tired of all the inuendo. I can handle some good jokes, but they are none stop, she needs to quit and go stalk someone else. I just don't find her attractive, I just don't it is that simple... By the way, you already have the green eyes, and sexually, you can be a very naughty little monster." I giggled, she leaned over and put her arms round me.

"Do the weekend, and I will sort this out for you, I promise, I will get her to back off." I nodded.

"That is all I want, everything else is fine."

"Okay Sweetie, leave it to me."

I felt better having talked, yet I still felt guilty, but I relaxed more, and for the rest of the night I snuggled up with Birch and talked. Eventually we curled up in bed, and I drifted off into sleep, feeling warm and safe in her arms.

Getting up nearly killed me, Anthony was ready at eight in the morning, to sort out my hair, the tips were still pretty vibrant, but needed a touch up, and my roots needed doing, I had grown a white stripe down the centre of my head, which to be honest I liked, so I sat in the chair and he went to work, as I consumed more coffee.

I have never had an author website, most of my promotion was done on social media, and Edwina has been building one for me, which would launch today. At the top of the page, in the side bar was my glowing endorsement for Anthony's business, and a personal recommendation of how I could never let anyone else touch my hair. I owed him that, I considered it repayment for his kidnap, and his first ever ride as a passenger with Birch. He finally finished as I dozed in the chair, and Birch giggled as I jerked awake.

"Hi Sweetie, you look beautiful." I smiled at her, as I came slowly round.

"Hi baby, I think you are so pretty and lovely too, and I love you." Her eyes sparkled and she smiled. Anthony gave a sigh.

"Oh dear, honestly you two make everyone's else's love look ridiculous and pale. Right darlings, I have people to please, so Birch, you squeeze those designer black jeans on that seat, and for the love of us all, put her down, you can play later."

I smiled and got out of the seat, Edwina handed me more coffee, and I sat back, and watched Anthony work his magic on Birch. It took him forever, which was good because I got to drink more coffee and wake up. After hair, came make up, I was aware that because this was a convention, the press would be there, and also a lot of gothic fans, and to be honest that was the one part I was looking forward to the most.

I sat in the bathroom, watching Birch as she did my eyes, it was kind of strange, because she was doing my eyes, and I was staring into her eyes. Birch wanted the red, I loved the black, but I cannot deny, when she used dark red, my bright bules really popped, and it looked surreal. I looked in the mirror and smiled, it had been quite some time since I done the red, and it was pretty sexy,

Once mine were done and looking fantastic, it was my turn to do hers, and I wanted to try something different. Birch was not goth, she was pure natural, pagan, warrior, witch, and so I broke out a dark green I had bought specifically for today. I did her eyes full on dark goth, but in the deepest of green, and oh my god, with those bright green eyes staring though at me, I was instantly turned on. I leaned back and looked at her.

"Holy shit, Birch baby, I really, really want to screw you right now, those are the sexiest eyes I have ever seen." She looked in the mirror.

"Oh Sweetie, you have found my true inner spirit, oh my god, I want to bang myself, have I got time to frap?" I giggled.

"The car will be here soon; we need to get dressed." She pouted.

"I wanted at least a quickie with you, nothing too fancy, you know some quick finger play?" I sighed.

"Birch the car will be here in a short time." She giggled and got up and walked towards me, I panicked slightly. "Birch, I mean it; we have to get ready."

My heart was already beating, I could not deny, she looked amazing, and I was really wet, but we had to be ready on time, she moved in really close and those eyes came up close, and my heart skipped a beat.

"Oh, Birch please, we have... Oh God, oh Christ Birch we don't have time... Oh Baby yes."

Her fingers were exploring, and my body was reacting, I slid my hand forward between her legs, and she gave a happy gasp.

"Oh yes Sweetie I need this, I need you."

Both of us were too far gone now to do anything but absorb each other, I was backed up, and sat on the sink with my legs wide apart, she was between then, her leg raised slightly on the toilet seat, her wrist working fast, and I had my hand on her, with two fingers just inside her, and she was gasping and biting her lip.

I was so turned on, looking at her eyes, I could not see anything else, just the bright green of her pupils, surrounded by the dark green mystery, of who her inner self truly was, a force of nature. I leaned back, I was so sensitive after last night, and I was building up fast, I leaned back against the wall mirror.

"Oh Birch, I am going to cum, I cannot take this." She grinned.

"I know, that is why I wanted you now, I want to look you in the eye when you blow." I was panting.

"Hell, you call me dark little beastie; you are pure underworld." She giggled, and I thrust up hard with my hand, and she gave a sudden gasp.

"Ooh shit!" I smiled.

"The dark little beastie just woke up, you got her attention, now get ready." She gasped as she tried to laugh.

Downstairs, Chloe sat sipping more coffee and holding up the conference passes, Edwina was making toast.

"I wonder if I will ever make it and become as successful, you know, get really well known in the Art world?"

Edwina looked back as the toast popped out, and saw her holding the pass as she slowly turned it in her hand.

"Chloe you are an amazing artist, but be honest, we both knew it would take time. You know Abby did years of feeling like she was getting nowhere, but she stuck at it, and eventually her patience and determination paid off. It takes time Chloe." She gave a nod and sat back.

"Yeah, I know that, but I have been thinking I should do more, you know I have a lot of stuff, maybe I need to find other ways to make it more available."

Edwina cut her toast and put it on her plate, she moved to the island and sat down, and lifted a slice.

"It never hurts to try, once people see your work and know your name, they will share stuff about how good your work is, try it." Chloe nodded and looked up at the ceiling."

"It is getting late, I hope they are not screwing again, the car will be here soon." Edwina smirked.

"Wow who are you and what have you done with my sister? You worry too much, Birch is never late for anything, she is a stickler for time keeping."

I leaned back as my climax hit me, my legs shook, and stiffened, and she gave a long low moan, and I felt her throb inside, she was there. She lurched forward and pulled me into her, I threw my arms round her, and hugged her tight. I shook in her arms, as the waves crashed over me, she hung on to me making little squeaks in my ear, and shaking, it was crazy, but oh my god it was so sexy.

Both of us just hung onto each other as our climax raged, and then came the calmness as we breathed in rhythm with each other, slowly coming back from our high. I gave a laugh.

"Oh my god you are so mental at times Birch." She took deep breaths

"I needed that, I wanted our scents on each other when we leave, trust me, our bond is tighter now than ever before." I flopped on her shoulder.

"I never doubted our bond Birch, I doubted we would be ready in time for the car."

She gave a cackle of a laugh, and I started to giggle, I lifted my head and looked at her, oh crap that was probably a mistake, she had a red glow and those sultry eyes, I leaned in and kissed her softly, and slid forward.

"We need to get dressed, my legs are buggered, I am glad it is a long drive."

We were finally ready, I had on a top that laced at the top, which obviously I left shamefully loose, a long heavy black flared skirt with frills round the bottom, my knee high black suede boots, and a long black lace coat. I grabbed my round purple mirrored shades, and my black parasol. Birch was wearing a low cut long green top, a full circle green tied dyed skirt tied with a shawl, and a cream lace over shirt. We both slipped our passes over our necks, and let them drop, I handed her my best green mirrors.

"If they are using flash, look straight at them, it reflects the light, and screws with their pictures." She smiled as she slipped them on.

We pulled our cases out of the door, and a very well groomed tall man, in black greeted us with a bow, and took our cases. He showed us to the long black limo, and opened the door for us, we climbed in feeling like rock stars. Chloe stood at the gates taking pictures, and waving as we pulled away.

The dark windows let us see out, but no one see in, and as we drove through the village, everyone stopped to watch, it felt fun, just seeing them watch us, of course they had no idea who was inside.

The limo was huge, we had space to stretch out, and relax, we had music, and a mini bar, this was a level of luxury travel I had never had before, it even rivalled America.

As we drove towards London, Markus, our driver for the event, lowered the window, and filled us in on what Katie had told him. There was going to be press, and a few fans had gathered outside the hotel entrance.

Barriers were up to hold them back, as there were a few high profile guests staying there. We were to get out, and try to avoid answering questions, even if they asked offensive things, we were to just ignore them. Press were not allowed inside, and so we were to get in as quickly as possible, where we would meet Katie and be taken to our suite. I understood and thanked him. Birch sat back all smiles, as she poured a gin from the mini bar.

"Sweetie isn't this fun?"

I sat back, my legs were still twitching, I closed my eyes and just drifted, remembering every moment, of those green eyes staring at to me, as we both climaxed. It is the most intense thing I have ever felt, pure love, desire, and trust, and I felt more alive inside than I ever have, that was without doubt, the look of pure love, God she was so special, and not even aware of it. We had been driving for a while, when the partition slid down, and I opened my eyes.

"We shall be there shortly Miss Watson, so be prepared. I would advise that you allow Dr Dixon out first, and she can shield you from the cameras. Dr Dixon keep your eyes down, and focus on Miss Watson, it will hide your face from the cameras, and also show the crowd how close you are to each other, trust me, it works wonders with the fans, leave the bags, they will be brought up to you." He smiled.

"Thank you, Markus, I really appreciate your advice, I am quite new to all this, and feel a little like a fish out of water." He nodded.

"It is my pleasure, take a card, and if you need advice, or the car, call me." I saw the little holder and took two, and handed one to Birch.

"Right, we are here, wait for me to open the door, and I will shield you the best I can, get ready for the flash cameras, watch out for the steps, no one wants to fall in front of the press." I took a deep breath, and reached out for Birch's hand, she smiled and gave it a squeeze.

"Sweetie, this is another adventure for us, so smile, be happy, and let's giggle like crazy bitches all the way through it." I smiled and chuckled.

"Thanks... You know, for coming with me."

She leaned over and kissed my cheek, the car rolled into place outside the entrance, and flashes were already going off. Markus opened his door, and stepped out. Birch gave a sigh a relief, leaned to one side and let a huge rasping fart go, she gasped with relief.

"Oh, thank god for that, I have been holding that in since we left Wotton." I could not help myself, as I started to laugh, as Markus came round the side, and the door opened.

The first thing that hit me was the sudden noise, inside the car we were insulated, and then suddenly the noise roared into my ears, and it was cheering fans, my fans, it was insane.

Birch slid out giggling and stood opposite Markus to create a safe space, it was flashing like an electric storm out there. I took a deep breath, and slid across the seat, and as rehearsed, I lifted my parasol, and pushed it out first. As I got to the edge of the seat, I pressed the button, and as the mass of flashes that went off, they were absorbed as the parasol popped up. I stood up and the fans went crazy, the noise was deafening, and all around me people were screaming my name.

Cameras were going off everywhere, and some of them were fans. Reporters were shouting 'Abigail... Abigail...Abigail'

I ignored them, as Birch took my arm, and Markus stepped back, and I could see the twenty five feet of wide steps to the glass doors. The press were mainly to my left, on the right were waving fans, and they were all ages, waving books and pictures crammed up against the barriers. Birch was on my left, and steered me towards the fans, I was so blown away and happy. I could not help but smile, I walked towards a young girl, who reminded me so much of Deb's, she was waving a copy of Sanctuary Arch.

I got closer, and she was all smiles and so excited, she held out her book and a pen, I took them, as Birch grabbed my parasol, and she just bounced around.

"Miss Watson, you look so beautiful, and your partner is stunning, I love your books." I smiled and leaned into her.

"What is your name?" She gasped with surprise.

"I am called Marie, oh thank you so much, I love your books." I signed the book, I felt so excited and full of energy, Birch leaned in.

"Marie, do you have a phone, give it me, and I will take a picture." Her eyes exploded in her face.

"Would you, oh my god, that would mean everything?" Birch handed me back the parasol.

I moved close to the rail and leaned in, carefully tilting my parasol, and blocking out most of the press. Birch took the picture and handed the phone back, she had tears in her eyes she was so happy. Moving towards the door was slow, I could see Katie inside, and she looked a little pissed off, but I didn't care, these people had stood here waiting for a glimpse, and it was the least I could do, and I did not care what Katie thought, I was really enjoying myself.

I signed books and pictures, and just blank pages of note books, in a sea of happy faces, Birch was chatting with the fans either side, and both of us were smiling. People who I had never met were telling me they loved me, and they loved my work, and when I think back to those dark times, this made all the suffering worth it.

For the whole time, the press screamed at me and Birch, I was almost at the door, when a guy in a baseball hat with a camera shouted.

"Abigail, is it true you host gay orgies?"

I looked up and he clicked, Birch yanked on my arm, and dragged me up the last few steps to the door, I waved and smiled at everyone who had stood waiting, and the cameras finally got a clear shot, and flashes went off everywhere. I got dragged through the door towards Katie. She looked at me, and was clearly not happy.

"I said walk straight in Deadly." I laughed; I was feeling like a million dollars, as I folded down my black parasol.

"Yeah mum, I know, but I wanted to talk to my readers, they have stood out there waiting, and they buy the books for all this. Why is that a problem?" She frowned.

"I am trying to shield you from the press, please Deadly, you were not like this in the States, just follow my lead." I looked at Birch and giggled, she sniggered, and bit her lip. She shook her head, Katie sighed.

"I knew bringing her would be trouble, okay let me get you signed in, and I will show you your room."

I walked with her to the reception desk, and the book was already there for me and Birch to sign. I looked round at the foyer, it was really modern, bright, and very relaxing. Birch was fascinated with the colourful art, the lights, and comfy seats, it was open, spacious, and the whole atmosphere felt warm and inviting. Birch admired the low colourful comfy seats; I laughed as we walked towards the lifts.

"Forget it, the attic is full." She giggled.

The suite was mind blowing, it was more like a large flat, and bigger than the guest house. It had a kitchen, a table, and full size luxury sofa. I gaped at it, and turned to Katie.

"Are we paying for this?" She smiled.

"No, this is paid for by the convention society, you are their guest of honour and main attraction, you really need to get use to this Abby, this is who you are now."

I understood people liked my books, but this was not me, no, this was not me at all, if anything this was a treat for me, it made me smile.

"This is not me really Katie, if you want to know who I am, talk to Chloe, she knows." Birch looked at me and smiled, Katie did not really understand. She put the key card down on the table.

"I have a few things to sort out, so settle in and relax, and I will be back in a bit."

I walked round the room, and Birch headed for the fridge, and got really excited, it was full of drinks. She grabbed two gins and a bottle of lemon. I laid my parasol down, and slipped off my lace coat, this place was mind blowing.

I wandered round the place, the bed was a double, and in the bathroom, it had a rainfall shower, and a spar bath. This was high class luxury, Birch handed me a glass, and we sat down on the sofa in front of the massive high rise windows, she smiled.

"I loved that, seeing you talk and take time out for your fans, Deads they loved you, did you see how happy they were when you walked over to them?" I relaxed and sipped my drink.

"I wanted to cry, honestly, I did not expect that, and they were so nice to me, so lovely, and they loved you. Birch, they accepted us for who we are." I smiled and looked at her. "Did you see how happy and excited they looked?" Birch held up her phone, there was the picture of me and Marie.

"They looked as happy as you did, I am so glad I came Sweetie, just seeing you like that, was the best thing I have seen this year." I sat there smiling remembering it all.

"It made me so happy Birch."

"Deads, you have wanted this for as long as I have known you, it is so nice, because you supported me and backed me, and I got my dream. I wanted to cry today too. To be honest I still do, because to see you finally get what you have dreamed of, was the most precious thing I could witness. Sweetie you are without doubt a writer, I know this, because I witnessed your fans, and they love you."

I felt choked up, it was really weird, I was so happy, but listening to her soft words, really hit home, I made it, I finally made it. America had felt surreal, it did not really impact on me, but here in my country, to see that, it was so amazing, all those faces waving my book, with my name on it, it meant everything to me.

In America, everything was business, Katie was on time, on schedule and very efficient, and I always arrived underground and out of sight. I was picked up, and whisked from one place to another, the only real time I got to talk to people, was when I did book signings, and then I only really got a minute or two, today having Birch with me made it fun and special. I could stop and talk and really communicate with those people who actually bought the books, and it meant the world to me, I looked at her and smiled as we relaxed.

"I will never forget today, Birch; it will stay in my heart for the rest of my life."

Katie returned and we headed downstairs, into the convention, where we were whisked off into a book signing session, and once again I got to meet yet more smiling and happy fans. They came up to the table and got their two and a half minutes, Katie frowned as I held up the line by asking questions of my fans, and stretching the time out a little. It really amazed me that Katie did not understand how important these people were to me, she just did not get it, they were my readers, and that meant the world to me.

After the signing, we were taken to a guest panel, where I sat with another writer and two actors, and again, fans got to ask questions. I loved it, I had more time and could enjoy the reaction of the people asking the questions, and how they were really cheered on by answers. I cannot deny, having this chance to actually talk with them, was so amazing, never in a thousand years would have dreamt my life could be this wonderful.

It felt like a long day, and my hand was sore at the end of it, but I got back to the hotel room happy, because I had met and talked to fans, and I loved them as much as they loved me, and I felt really good inside.

It is so easy to forget the darkness of days alone in the guest house these days, but I never will. When my books failed to sell, it was heart breaking, I had worked so hard on them and given my all. I do not think anyone truly understands the devotion and love a writer puts into a book, they have no idea of the sacrifices we make to get the thing right, or the crashes of confidence we go through, it can be soul destroying.

Being a writer has been my dream for as long as I could remember, and when my books failed to sell, that dream smashed on the floor around me. It was never about the money, I really did not need it, my dad had seen to that, but I did want to be taken seriously, and my darkness grew out of the fact I had not been, and it crushed me completely.

Today, was the first time in my life, I really did feel like I had earned the recognition, to call myself a writer, and it is a day I will never forget for as long as I live. Those happy smiling faces, and the genuine kindness of all of them, I do not think I have ever been happier.

Chapter 16

True Fans.

I relaxed in the bath with Birch, feeling the heat soak into me, last night had been late, drunk, and very sexually charged, but I had been dragged out of bed way too early, and now after a long day at the convention, it was hitting me. I lay back against her, and just enjoyed the feel of her, as I relaxed and unwound.

"Jemi, Deadly, are you in here?" Birch leaned her head back, as I slid down in the water, and felt my heart sink.

"In here Katie." She came into the bathroom; I closed my eyes.

"Oh, very nice, is there room for another?" I opened my eyes and looked at her.

"Yeah jump in." She gave a bright smile, and started to unbutton her blouse. I stood up, and reached for my robe.

"I am really tired, I have not had much sleep, you two soak for a while, try the spar Katie, it is wonderful."

I pulled on the robe, and walked into the bedroom, and sat on the bed to dry. Katie slipped off her pants, and closed the bathroom door, she got into the tub and faced Birch.

"Okay what is going on, she has been off with me since we got back from the states, and I am working my ass off for her?" Birch closed her eyes, and relaxed.

"Katie, she is a hot property, especially now she has almost finished Shoots of Summer, and she has half written her next gothic novel. Tell me, is she worth a lot to the organisation?" Katie relaxed.

"Oh, this is so nice, I only have a shower in my room. Deadly, has just hit a million sales, it is not for one book, you know, it is across the board with all her books, but people are talking about her a lot. America was a smart move, the deals she did brought in a lot of revenue, I would say currently, her and your mum are the two biggest assets this company has writing wise, why do you ask?"

"Katie, you are going to lose her, her contract is up in February, and she is talking of moving to another company." Katie opened her eyes.

"Stop her then, you are a major shareholder, protect your assets, and make her see reason." Birch gave a sigh.

"I won't do that, because she is not the one who needs to see reason, it is you." Katie sat up quickly and the water sloshed around the bath.

"What the fuck, I broke my back to get her off the ground, fucking look where you are sat. All of this is because of me, I have done everything in my power to get her name out there, how the fuck do I have to see reason?" Birch looked at her intensely.

"Katie, stop with all the sexual passes and inuendo, she is tired of it, she is never going to sleep with you, so just stop, she is not Tony." Katie looked really angry, she lifted her hand and pointed at Birch.

"Just you fucking hold on Jemi, this is not like that, that was a sport fuck for fun."

Birch looked at her.

"Really? I remember Marianne, telling you time and time again, she was straight, and to stop, and she did exactly what Deads is about to do, so you screwed Tony to get your own back. Katie, I love you to bits you know that, but you are going too far, and it is upsetting her. We are together, it is deep and it is strong, and neither of us will ever sleep with another woman. She is really happy with you as her agent, she genuinely thinks you are amazing, but the constant hints and jibes to sleep with you, are pushing her away from this company, so I am asking you to stop."

She was not happy that was pretty obvious, and gave a frustrated sigh, she stared at Birch across the bath, and her face softened.

"I think the world of her Jemi, I loved touring the States with her, we had some amazing conversations, but you know what I am like, I really fancy her, and it is not because of you, it is because she is as fit as fuck."

"Katie, we are together, we are strong, and this is a mega thing to both of us. She wants you to be her agent, she does not want to sleep with you to keep you, she would rather walk away. Trust me, her next book will be massive, I have read most of it, and it is way better than the first. Back off a little, and cool things down, we want to keep her with us, do that, and she will stay." Katie shook her head, and gave another frustrated sigh.

"Okay I am sorry; I did not realise she felt this deeply about it. Wow, I never thought I would see the day you warned someone off your patch, and especially not fucking me. Is it really that serious between you two?" Birch nodded.

"Katie, she is my everything, and she is my future." She nodded, although she did not look very happy at all.

"I get it, okay kid, I will change my approach, honestly, I would never do a thing to hurt her, I love her to death. I love working with her more than anyone else, but I am telling you now, I am not calling her Miss Watson, like I have to do with that mouldy old bitch Morley." Birch smiled.

"Katie, just be yourself like you are with mum, and call her Abby, she will love that."

"Okay I got it, I will talk to her and apologise, honestly, I did not realise... How the fuck do you cope with this, my tits are boiling?" Birch gave a laugh, as she stood up, and reached for the towel, she looked down.

"Last chance to munch a soapy biff, I am not stopping with you, fuck that would be dull, I like my banter with an old slapper like you." Birch chuckled.

"Get out, you soft soapy tart, you have been licking too much southern pussy, and it is rubbing off on you." She laughed as she dried herself down.

"I love you; do you know that, you slag?" She chuckled.

I do not remember them coming back into the room, I was flat out. I woke with a start wrapped in Birch, she smelt of soap, and it was really nice. I slipped out of bed, it was ten in the morning, I pulled on my robe, and walked through to the living area, and yawned, there was a soft tap on the door. I walked over and opened it, and a young guy with a trolley smiled.

"Miss Watson, your late breakfast as ordered." I stood back, I hadn't ordered anything, he wheeled it up to the table.

"Would you like me to serve, or are you happy alone?" I gave him a pleasant smile.

"It will be fine; my partner is not up yet." I grabbed my bag and slipped out a twenty, it was all I had in notes, and I handed it to him, he appeared very happy.

"If you require anything else, just let me know Miss Watson." I gave a happy nod.

"Thank you I will." He left pulling the door closed. I excitedly ran into the bedroom and jumped on the bed.

"Birch get up, we have breakfast on a trolley, come on there is bacon." Whoosh, she sat up and sniffed the air with her eyes still closed.

"Bacon, I love bacon."

The TV appearance was to be recorded live, and I was nervous as I slid on my black velvet bootcut pants. I had on a long black, flowing top, that split to the navel, with laces. I looked in the mirror, it was open enough to reveal my orange sized mounds, but not enough for them to be on full show. I had suede black ankle boots, and a thin red silk scarf loosely round my neck, which matched my freshly done hair. It looked stylish, and a little sexy, and with the red eyes redone, I was a complete dark little beastie.

The theatre was a small intimate little theatre, decked out in red and black, which was a surprise, we were given the tour as the crew prepared. Gordon Stimes was there and shook my hand, he was about mid forties, lightly greying, and very relaxed, he reminded me a little of William Dixon. We talked of the books, and I was surprised to find he had read them. I liked him, he was very well read, and was very respectful and gave my books high praise. Birch chuckled as she watched us talking, I think I was so surprised, it made her laugh.

The front central row had been reserved, and Katie and Birch would sit there, with some other VIP's, and when announced, I was to come down the left staircase from the back, and walk up onto the stage to take my seat.

I would be wearing a radio mic, and my assistant for the day would be Monica, a thirty five year old technician, she was witty and made me giggle, and very down to earth. She had really short black hair, which made her brown eyes really stand out. We did several walk through's and mic tests, and then we were taken into the back, it was almost time. I felt the nerves, as the introverted side of me wanted to run away, and I fidgeted with my hands. There were 446 seats for this live special, and they had been drawn from a pool at the convention, so only really lucky ticket holders would be in the audience, which came as a relief, as that meant they should all be fans.

Waiting in the back room was the worst part, I sipped a drink of weak gin and lemon, Birch was close and holding my hand, Katie was talking to the officials, when Monica appeared.

"Okay almost time, everyone is in and we are standing by, this is a live show, and will be filmed in one take, but broadcast will be delayed, for an hour, so just relax, enjoy yourself, and take your time. You will be introduced, and the music will start. I will tell you when, and the doors will be opened, and just walk in, and smile. The fans will definitely want to shake your hand, do a few, as you move down, and then get on the stage sit down and relax, alright?" I nodded and took a deep breath; I was shitting myself.

The signal was given, Birch and Katie walked round with me, up the back stairs and back around to the outside doors, where there were three large security guards. Birch hugged me.

"Sweetie you will be fine, I will be right there in front of you." She kissed me softly and stepped back. Katie winked at me.

"Be yourself, honestly you got this kid." I took a deep breath.

"I am terrified Katie." She leaned in to me, and kissed my cheek.

"Remember the states, you were just like this, all shy and nervous, but once you hit the stage it was gone?" I took another deep breath, and nodded, she winked. Birch and Katie went through the doors to their seats, and Monica checked my mic, it was working fine.

"Okay almost time, and just for the record, everyone is like this before they go on, even Gordon, it is all part of the show. Smile, it makes you look sexy as hell, and your lady is waiting down there to see you." I smiled, and she winked. "Stunning."

The audience applauded and Gordon came on stage, he stood at the front of the stage, and looked at the cameras.

"Tonight, I will be hosting a particularly lovely guest, and a new phenomenon. Not only has she written the best selling book,

Seeds of Summer, a modern slice of life fiction, she is also the author of the very successful Hands of Death series of books, and her success, has brought back into fashion, the gothic horror fantasy novel, and I must admit, I for one am delighted about that."

He smiled, and the audience appeared very pleased indeed, the tension in the room was rising, as he moved closer to his seat, and gave a big smile to the cameras.

"Ladies and gentlemen, would you please give a warm welcome, to Miss Abigail Jennifer Watson."

The audience burst into applause, and the speakers fired up with Avril Lavigne's, Dumb Blonde, it was the tune that had been used in the States, I did not even know that it was to be used here. It is a cool tune and I do love it, I mean honestly, when it comes to Avril, what is not to like?

Monica nodded, and I took a deep breath, she counted down, three, two, one. The doors opened, and I walked forward, and into the theatre where everyone stood clapping, and it was so loud. I walked onto the steps smiling, and it was genuine as people reached out and patted my shoulder, a guy grabbed my hand and shook it, he had heavy black eye liner, and was as white as a ghost, I gave him a big smile and nodded a thanks.

I walked slowly down, smiling and shaking a few hands, aware a camera was on me, and I finally reached the bottom. I walked across the short space, and onto the low stage, the music faded out, as I faced the crowd and saw Birch, and smiled.

The biggest shock came when I saw Roni, Will, Hatty and my mum, all stood with beaming smiles applauding, and my face exploded with even more smiles. Gordon waved his hand to the chair, and I turned and sat down and made myself comfortable, as the applause faded, and everyone else sat down. He smiled and shook my hand, and turned to the crowd.

"What a wonderful and amazing welcome, I think you have a fan or two in tonight, would it be alright to call you Abigail?" I smiled, seeing so many people watching me, it made me feel a little shy, and I was trembling slightly with nerves.

"Abigail or Abby, I am fine with either." He gave a nod; I smiled and waved at the fans. It was weird, but sitting there, I was terrified, and yet, seeing all the smiling happy faces, really made me feel liked.

"I have to say Abby, you look amazing tonight, I love your hair, and to be honest, you look like you have stepped right out of one of your own books. I cannot tell you how happy I am to see a resurge in gothic horror, what made you want to write it?" Birch winked, and my mum was all smiles, I looked at her.

"It is all my mums' fault." The audience laughed, I looked at Gordon.

"Her favourite book was Dracula, but I was not allowed to read it, I was just a child and did not realise it was a collector's edition and valuable. So, one day I misbehaved, and I borrowed it without permission, and snook out of my house on to the canal. There is an old ruined mill there that had large stone arched windows, most of them were smashed, but there is one intact left, and I used to sit there and read. It was there under that old arch, I fell in love with Bram Stoker, just like she had." He smiled and looked at my mum.

"So, you are to blame, are you? Well thank you, because your daughter has pulled off a miracle, and got thousands of new younger readers, into traditional gothic horror again." I laughed and my mum blushed, as the camera panned on to her. He looked back at me.

"So, you sat under an old arched window, from I would imagine the mid to late Victorian period, and you read Dracula? Oh how simply wonderful, I cannot think of a better setting. Now I could be reading into things too much, but would that be the inspiration for the arch of protection, that you write about in Sanctuary Arch?" I nodded, I really loved that he had read my books.

"You noticed, I see?" The audience chuckled.

"Yes... It is a very sacred place to me, when I was younger, I would go there, it was a place I saw as refuge, a place of safety. It was also the place where I really first understood who I was, and opened up to a very special person for the first time. It has a lot of sacred memories attached to it, which is why I made it a place in the books, that no vampire could be harmed under it. I think the arch is so powerful in my thoughts, that when I needed some place to save Willis, the young vampire, it just drew itself in my mind, and I wrote it into the book." He nodded and appeared to really understand me, and I loved that.

"Now, Willis and Gabrielle are separated in the book, and because of that, Willis feels such pain, he wants to die, and starves himself of human blood, and yet the thought of Gabrielle, keeps him alive, and he fights between life and death, and in doing so discovers his humanity. I have to say I loved every second of reading it Abby, what was it that prompted you to evolve such a tale?"

I saw her, and I smiled, but I could not say her name. She was watching me, her green eyes shining at me across the space, her long lovely white hair, with those unique patches, and that soft loving smile, Gordon realised and looked at Birch and smiled

"A person very close to me, once told me the reason vampires love so much, and so deeply, is because, they have lost the gift of life. The more I thought about it, the more sense it made to me, she told me that she thought the reason they lived off blood, was because it fed the heart, and as long as their hearts beat, they would retain that wonderful part of humanity, which is love. I found that so powerful a message, especially when you consider it was the living, that showed the least humanity and love in their treatment of the vampires, that it was very ironic and yet poetic." He looked really surprised, and he turned and looked at the audience, they were hanging on to every word.

"That Abby is actually a very wonderful concept, the most humane was the dead, and the most inhumane, were those alive, and therefore their ability to love, was increased, by that standard, that actually would make Dracula a classic love story." I nodded and smiled.

"It is an amazing idea don't you think? Without blood there is no life, and if the heart dies, we lose love, but the vampire can take love even into death, love truly is eternal." He sat back, gasped, and looked at the audience.

"Isn't she absolutely amazing ladies and gentlemen, such a keen mind, and yet such a simple logic, and none of us saw it until now, but she did, and has revived an entire genre. Abby, I have to raise my hat to you, I am rarely blown away, but I am tonight, I love it, I really do, it is a remarkable concept."

I was starting to enjoy myself, and relax as my answers got longer and more elaborate as I unravelled the plot twist of my first two books. Gordon was so into it, I no longer noticed the cameras or the audience, it just felt like two gothic geeks chatting books and plots, and I felt really relaxed. I was lost in the conversation, the time just slid past, until he smiled and looked at me.

"Now I have to ask, because I know you support a very worthy cause, which I believe is called Curio Life, tell us all a little about it." I was a little surprised he asked, wow he really did his research.

"Curio Life is something very special to a group of close friends, who two years ago, had suffered a great deal, from judgement. We felt lost, isolated, and we were struggling to understand ourselves, and our life. We wanted just to be us, to be allowed to grow and develop and not be shamed." I looked at the audience. "I am sure a lot of you guys really understand that, look at us all, we are beautiful, we are natural, we are who we want to be, and the price of that is to be bullied and shamed, and victimised." It really hit a note with the audience, I saw the look in the eyes of many of them as they nodded, I smiled.

"See, they all really get it, they understand."

Gordon smiled and turned to look at the audience, and it was so clear to him, as they all sat watching with black eyes, white faces, and crazy hair, he nodded gently as I spoke.

"We set up the website for our community, so we would all have a place, a voice, somewhere to tell our side of the story, a way of knowing we are not alone, and that it is okay to be who we want to be. We never thought it would grow so big, but there are a lot of people suffering and killing themselves because of being shamed. We truly understood that, and so tried to reach out and simply tell them, be curious, be inspired, be yourself, be a Curio. Today the site funds youth recovery programs to help people aged 18 to 30, and it has made a huge difference to a lot of people."

Gordon clapped, and the audience gave a cheer, and joined in, I felt so happy seeing the reaction, Roni sat smiling and gave me a nod. The Audience settled down, and Gordon was all smiles.

"I commend your friends for their bravery, and for what they have done, thank them on my behalf." It was quite touching to see his sincerity, and I gave a soft smile.

"I will, thank you." He gave a sigh and smiled at me.

"Oh Abby, I could talk all night, we are almost coming towards the end, and I have to say, I am a little disappointed, so I have to ask, as I know you are working on the fourth in this series. Gabrielle is on sacred ground, which is impossible for a vampire to walk on, will Gabrielle and Willis find their way back to each other, because honestly, I am dying to know?" I gave a huge giggle.

"Gordon, now that would be telling, I like to keep everything secret until the release date." He held up his hands and smiled at the audience.

"I had to try, you all are just like me, and you cannot wait." The audience laughed with him; he gave me such a wonderful smile.

"Abby, you have been a delight, and I do feel very honoured, because I know you seldom do interviews, but before we go, I do believe today is the launch of your new website?" I gave a nod.

"It is, I have not seen it live yet, I have been a little busy." He chuckled. "It has been built by my friend Edwina, we have spent a lot of time on it, and my other friend Chloe Pemberton, whom illustrates my covers, has drawn some amazing artwork for it, you should check out her site, she is an amazing upcoming artist. I am really spoiled as I have a house full of her work. I will be giving regular updates on all my stories through the site, so yes, as soon as I get back home, I will be logging in to see it myself, I am really excited for everyone to see it." He smiled.

"Do you know the URL?" I lifted my hand to my mouth.

"Oh yes, I am so excited I forgot, it is Abigail J W . co .uk, all lower case."

"Fantastic, I will be looking it up myself, as soon as I am back home." He looked out into the audience. "I hope you all do too." Gordon turned back to face me and smiled, he leaned forward and took my hand.

"Abby, this has been such a pleasure for me today, you are truly a lovely person, and such a delight to talk to. I hope you will come back when your next book comes out, so we can talk more, I am so grateful you agreed to come on the show." I gave a broad smile.

"I won't deny, I was terrified when I walked out, but I have really enjoyed it, and yes, I would love to come back when the next book is ready, thank you, and thank you everyone for loving my stories, it means the world to me."

Gordon stood up, and beckoned me to stand, he held my hand gently, and we faced the audience, and they all rose from their seats, and cheered and whistled, it was just overwhelming. I was so happy my words were liked, no one could possibly know how much it means, to see others love your books, as much as you love other authors books. The show music started as the audience continued to clap, and Gordon smiled and turned to me.

"Abby, I have interviewed a lot of people, but tonight, I think has been my most enjoyable, and if I may be so bold, your lady partner has not taken her eyes off you once, now tell me that is not Bram and Willow?" I gave a giggle.

"You are too wise Gordon." He started to laugh, and the director shouted.

"CUT!" We were off air." I gave a deep breath out; I had done it.

Birch came over with a beaming smile, members of the audience were loitering, they had their phones out, Gordon held out his arm.

"They are your fans; you can go and talk to them."

Birch took my hand, and I walked to the front row. I noticed four large security guards move in from the sides, all of them watching carefully. I walked up to the rail, where there was a line of people holding copies of the book out. Monica came up to us, and she handed me a pen with a smile.

It was crazy, as I took copies of my book off the smiling people, who were surprisingly all ages, and a lot of them female. One guy handed me a book and asked if I would sign it for his daughter, I smiled as I signed the inside cover, and he took pictures. Birch was at my side talking to the fans, who asked her as many questions as they did me, they were really interested in knowing as much about her as well.

I glanced to the side as I signed a book, and saw her happy and smiling, her eyes sparkling, as fans told her how lovely she was, a few even commented that they could see where I got Willow from, which delighted her. People thanked me, and said such lovely things, and when Monica reappeared to take us back stage, I was a little disappointed I could not meet and talk to more of them. We both waved as we were guided back to the stage, Monica leaned in to me.

“Don’t hug guys, I am sorry about this, just follow me, some of that lot are press looking for a trophy up there, It pisses me off, they were not supposed to have tickets. Come on, let’s get you safe in the back room and get these wires off you.” She clicked the pack on my back off. “Okay the mic is dead, you are safe to speak now, follow me.” We walked off back stage into the reception room, and Monica stepped back and looked at me.

“Well bloody hug then, I don’t have all day you know?” Birch slid into my arms.

“I am so proud of you Sweetie, you were wonderful, it will make such a great show.”

“I did okay then; I didn’t say anything stupid?” She kissed me softly.

“You were simply you, and the whole world will love you for it.” I gave a sigh of relief.

“I am happy, I didn’t want to do anything that would embarrass you.” Monica gave a chuckle.

“To be honest love, she met you in an airport with her chuff and tits on display, you would have to work pretty bloody hard to beat that.” Birch gave a cackle of a laugh, Monica was right, that would take some beating.

I had all my wires and mic removed, and I was finally cleared by the producer to go, he was very happy with the take, and thanked me repeatedly. Katie appeared, and led us by the back way to a restaurant, where everyone was waiting. William came forward to meet me, and gave me a huge hug.

“My goodness Abby, you were simply delightful, I was so proud of you.” I loved William, he had very Birch like qualities, he stepped back and cupped my face.

“Abby, I heard about your dad, just know, you are like a daughter to me, and I will always be there if you need me, and Roni feels the same.” It was touching, he had that look in his eye of genuine love, just like Birch.

“I love you like a dad too Will, and right back at you.” He smiled and patted my cheek.

Mum and Hatty snatched me together, I thought they were

going to fight, and tear me in half, both of them were so excited. They talked at the same time and I kept looking from one to the other, it was like talking to Deb's and Chloe when they got excited. All I could do was smile, they were proud, I got that much. I was saved by Roni, who swept in, and pulled me into a huge hug, it felt so nice, I had four of my favourite people with me, and Birch, it was such a good day. A young waitress stood watching, and I noticed her, she smiled, I pulled away from Roni.

"Miss Watson, your table is ready, and there is a complimentary bottle of Champagne awaiting you, compliments of the house. Would you and your party care to follow me?"

All of this was so overwhelming, it was a lot to take in, but I was happy and going with the flow, and that was all I wanted to do, just enjoy the day. We walked through the restaurant to our table, where two staff waited to seat us, we all sat down and the bubbly was opened and poured. I have got to say, it was nice of them, but yuk, this stuff was like piss, I am not a fan, I could see by Birch's reaction, she was no fan either, I waved the waiter over, and ordered two gin and lemons, much to Birch's approval.

The meal came and we all relaxed, it was nice to see Roni and Will, they were going to stay at the Hunters for a night, but Bradley had insisted they stay with him, like us, they would be driving back later. Mum told me how proud she was and how much she had enjoyed it. Hatty was gushing praise, and it was lovely it really was, but what I really wanted, after all the nerves and excitement of the day, was to get home, and relax with Birch. I leaned on to her and smiled, she slipped her arm round my waist, and smiled at me.

"You looked so happy, it made me happy, all those people Deads, and all the ones that watch, they are so glad you woke up. I am really glad you woke up." I looked into her eyes and could see her love.

"You want to give her a quick snog for me love?"

I turned and there was a guy with a camera pointing right at me, I lifted my hand up, to hide my face, and my stomach twisted. Will stood up and stepped in front of the man.

"What the hell do you think you are doing? Get the hell out of her face, she is having a meal for god's sake." Two large men in all black appeared, the photographer sneered, as they grabbed him.

"She makes her living fucking like a slag, and writing about it, I make mine doing this, she is fucking hot property. I can eat for a year with one good shot." I had my head down, Birch leaned down to me.

"Deads Sweetie, don't let them get to you, this is part of our life." I shook my head.

"No Birch, it's not, I should be allowed a meal with my family, out in the street I get it, it is just like Nigel, but in here, what next, them climbing the fences, and photographing my bedroom, like he did? It's just madness with them, they don't care." She held my face.

"No, it is not fair, neither is Marjorie, or Martin, or all the other shit we have been through, the world isn't fair Deads, but we still have to find a way to deal with it, and we do that by saying screw them."

"Er, excuse me, I am really sorry, but please do not get upset, he is just an idiot. Miss Watson, I was there today, and I watched and listened. I am here with my family having a meal too, and I want you to know, that yes there are horrible men like that, but there is also an awful lot of people who love you, because you write such wonderful stories."

I turned from Birch, and looked up at the young girl, she was about seventeen, she smiled, and I dabbed my eyes with the paper napkin.

"What is your name?"

"I am Karen Braydon." I gave her a smile.

"Thank you, Karen, thank you for being there today." She smiled.

"You were wonderful, and I hope you don't mind me saying, but you and your lady are really pretty, she makes me think of Willow." Birch gave a chuckle and leaned over and whispered.

"You know Karen, she based Willow on me." She gave a wide smile.

"As soon as I saw you, I thought so, but Miss Watson, you are really pretty too, you should write about a female vampire, it would be great to read that." I gave a nod.

"I may well do that at some point, and if I do, she will fall in love with a human and be called Karen." She gasped, and I nodded, everyone at the table was smiling. She looked at me.

"I better go back, I just wanted you to know how much those of us who read, love your stories."

"Thank you, Karen, it is so sweet of you, and it has really helped."

She waved goodbye, and stepped back, and walked to her table. I watched her feeling better and had a sudden thought. I grabbed another paper napkin, and pulled out my pen, and I wrote quickly on it.

'To Karen, I solemnly promise, at some point, there will be a character in the Hands of Death series, and her name will be Karen, thank you for really caring. Abigail Jennifer Watson.'

I looked round and saw her with her family, they were looking over and smiling, I winked at Birch, and slid back my chair. Her Mum saw me coming and nudged her, I walked up to the table and handed it to her.

"Keep it safe, if I don't keep my promise, you can take me to court." She opened the napkin and read it, and she almost exploded with excitement. I looked at her family.

"You have a wonderful daughter, she is very sweet and kind, and you are a lovely family." I winked at Karen and then walked back to the table, as I sat down, I could see her excitedly showing everyone, even those on the table behind her, wanted a look.

Once the meal was done, we headed up to our room to collect our things, I pulled Birch close and just held her for an age, and breathed, it all felt exhausting, and exhilarating, but I was ready to go home. Before we left, we met and had coffee with the organisers, who were delighted. From the moment I was announced as the TV event guest, ticket sales had rocketed, which had put the whole event into a very good profit. I was pleased, but to be honest, I still found it a little strange, as I did not in the remotest way feel famous.

It did not take very long before we were back in the lounge area downstairs, waiting for Katie. She took me to one side.

"Abby, I owe you an apology, I have spoken to Jemi and she has filled me in, and I want to clear the air between us. Look Abby, you do have some of this wrong. I will not deny I am very highly attracted to you, but it has nothing to do with Jemi, you are not another Tony. If I sleep with you, it will be because you are worth sleeping with. I like you, not just your body, but your mind, your kindness and a whole lot more. I love working with you, and I now understand I overstepped the mark, and I am big enough to admit that. I don't want to lose you Abby, I want you to stay on, because I really believe in your work. I will back off and respect your relationship, and I am truly sorry, you should have said something Abby, and then you would not have felt so bad for so long, so... Friends again?" She held out her hand. I gave her a smile and took her hand in mine.

"I don't want to leave, I really don't, and I love working with you, but I am with Birch, and I am not attracted to other women, honestly I don't know why, I am just not." I shook her hand and she smiled.

"Okay then, new deal, me and you, and your next book, twice as big as this one." I felt a huge relief, and grinned.

"Deal."

Once everything was sorted out, Markus pulled up outside, our bags were taken, and loaded, and then Katie hugged me goodbye.

"I will see you soon, now this time, just walk, no stopping, get in the car and get out of here."

She walked to the doors, and the attendant opened it. I walked out into the flashes of cameras linking Birch and headed for the open door, two large guys walked at our side, the press were shouting out my name. Birch held my arm, and I kept my head down, and just as I reached the door, a voice shouted out.

"Miss Watson how does it feel, knowing your dad is under investigation, for fraud and tax evasion, will you visit him in prison?"

It caught me completely off guard, I stopped and looked back.

"What?"

It felt like a thousand flashes went off, and I was blinded, Birch gave me a push, and stepped in to block the camera. I was lost for a second, my head spun, I jumped in and she clambered in behind me, and Markus shut the door. Cameras were pressed up to the glass, and went off, Birch leaned over me as I hid my face, my mind was spinning. Markus jumped in, and we sped off away from them, Birch sat up and I looked at her.

"Is my dad in trouble?" She shook her head.

"Honestly Sweetie, I have no idea, but we can find out." Katie turned at the door.

"Shit, I almost pulled it off, I should have known that big mouth twat, Peter Ford, would fuck things up." She walked back into the hotel; it was too late now; the cat was out of the bag.

Chapter 17

Normality Returns.

Chloe jumped up out of her seat. "SHE SAID MY FUCKING NAME, DID YOU SEE THAT, SHE FUCKING SAID MY NAME ON TELLY!?" Edwina sighed.

"Big bloody deal, she said mine too, now shut the fuck up, I want to hear her." Chloe was beaming with happiness, Deb's giggled, as they all focused back on the TV screen. Chloe sat down and whispered to herself.

"Thank you so much Abby, god you are a brilliant friend." Edwina's phone rang, she picked it up, it was Aden.

"Have you seen the broadcast? The web site is being smashed, the traffic flowing to it is off the charts, we may need to boost the servers before they overheat, I cannot get hold of Jemi, but if this keeps up it will crash the site."

"Okay Aden, we are expecting her back at some point tonight, as soon as I see her, I will talk to her, if the site crashes there is not much we can do until tomorrow."

"Yeah, I am tracking the progress from home, I am telling you, Abby has no idea how influential she is becoming, she is a little wonder, she really is. Okay I will keep you up to speed, see you tomorrow." On the large TV screen, Abby stood waving and smiling as the audience applauded, Chloe sat back with a big smile.

"That was blinding, she was awesome, it is so messed up, she is like huge, and yet she sat here this morning in a t shirt with no knickers on, eating toast with us, is that what it is like for you Deb's?" She giggled.

"It is a little bit, but to me he is just Jimmy, at home he is a really normal guy. I don't see him as this huge rock and roll singer, he is just my hubby, my Jimmy, we cook together and mess about together, he is just a regular guy." Chloe winked,

"Yeah, but you get to suck his rock star dick though, don't you?"

Deb's blushed, and looked shocked.

"I don't talk about what we do together Chloe." Chloe gave a snigger and raised her eye brows.

"You do though, don't you?" Deb's turned beetroot, and lifted a pillow to her face and giggled.

"Chloe... Stop!" Edwina laughed.

"Yep, that is a definite, she does, and she likes it." Deb's threw her pillow across the room at Edwina.

"This is who you are now."

I sat in the limo, as those words echoed around my brain. It is so strange, for so long I have yearned to be me, and it has been such a struggle, such an exhausting fight, as I have spent years living in doubt.

I arrived at Uni a perfect country naïve, almost virginal lost figure, I knocked on the door of what I hoped was my dorm, as I had spent over an hour lost, to find this wonderfully lovely person was my roommate. I did not really know her, she was stranger than any one I had ever met, not at all like me, and yet with just a smile, I knew I had found a friend.

She had strange ways and strange ideas, and yet so much of what she said resonated deeply inside me, and slowly I began to find my own way. That was the most wonderful thing about Birch, she never told me who to be, she told me, look and see. As a result of almost a year of inner change, one drunken weekend, I took the plunge and dyed my hair. I knew straight away, this was who I wanted to be, it was so crystal clear to me, and then I returned to Wotton, and it started a war.

I spent all that summer fighting for my independence, and fighting my feelings, that were growing within me. I confronted myself, the new me and I loved it, but there was one preconceived notion I denied, and I regret that now. I fell in love with the most unexpected person, and then hid it, and I suffered because of it. I had embraced every other aspect of me, willingly, passionately, and with complete belief, and yet my feelings for Birch were buried.

My second year at Uni was the most amazing, I lived a crazy wild free life, and I studied hard and lived with Birch. We slept together, but were none sexual, and I was so unbelievably happy, it was insane. Then I had to come home, and leave her behind. Her work load tripled as she headed for her doctorate, and I was suddenly alone in an empty bed, living with the regret of not telling her how I felt. I was in love, and still tried to deny it, and it ate me away as I ached to be with her, so much so I wanted to die, because life alone was destroying me. My friends all had jobs, and had moved on in my absence, and the loneliness became too much to take.

I was blind, and stubborn, and as soon as she returned, which took a further four years, I knew the truth of who I was, and it was not who I had set out to be. I told her, I broke down and screamed at her, and told her I was in love with her, I finally said it, and in an instant, I felt whole again. The months that followed were bliss, even though I was still fighting to be who I was, yes, I had some doubts, a lot of people appeared to play on them, until one terrible night at the end of summer, my doubts took over, and she walked away from me, and my world collapsed.

Those few days changed my life forever, I knew who I was, who I wanted to be, and all I had to do was admit it, be honest about it, and embrace it. That fateful night I did, and I have not looked back, and my life has changed as a result, and it is all for the better. My writing has improved, my story telling is better, and my sales have risen. I did a three week tour of the states and they embraced me, and I really loved it, but today, I sat on a stage and felt the warmth and the love of people from my own country. Birch was just feet away watching and smiling, and it meant the world to me.

I have money coming in, I am recognised in public, my books are available in shops. I walked into a high class, high cost hotel suite, and Katie told me, this is who you are now. It wasn't, she was wrong, and she should not have just stuck a label on me like that, because I am something completely different. I am not into all this glitz and glam, I don't want to use prestige, as control like they do in Wotton, I am not so self obsessed, I have to maintain an image like my mother has had to, I am nothing like this at all.

I am plain, simple, and ordinary, just like my readers, I am not special, I am me, the girl Birch cuddles, or Chloe has coffee with. The girl Deb's sits with in the garden to tell me about her life, you see that is who I want to be. I live in a house with the most talented and amazing people in Wotton. We are loud, noisy, naked and get drunk, and act like complete kids, and I am so fine with that, because in that house I am Abby, and everywhere else I am Miss Watson, and that was where Katie went wrong.

"Sweetie we are here, we are home."

"Huh?"

"We are home Sweetie." Markus was smiling holding the door open.

"Oh shit, right, shit, sorry." Birch giggled; and Markus smiled.

"I will bring the bags, get yourself inside." I slid out of the car with a smile.

"Thanks Markus, I appreciate it, here, on your day off, treat yourself." I handed him fifty, he looked at it in his hand.

"Miss Watson, you do not have to do that." I shrugged.

"You won't believe this Markus, but a lot of people call me rotten, and then there are some who are lovely, and kind, and they make me feel special. People like you, and so I want you to do the same, use my money for something special for you." He smiled.

"I could not possibly refuse this now." I giggled.

"I am a writer; I am that good with words."

He broke out into a huge belly laugh, and escorted me to the door, before returning to the car for our bags.

My arrival was announced with screams, Chloe came from nowhere and leapt on to me, and almost strangled me.

"Abby I am so grateful, I have had seventy hits in the last hour, I love you so much, in a completely straight way of course." I giggled.

"Well of course, I mean I love you in a totally gay way, but hey that is me." She suddenly looked really serious.

"Fuck, do you?" I pointed at her face.

"Ha Haaaaaaa!" She smiled.

"Fuck you bitch." Deb's snuggled in to me.

"You were amazing, I loved it, I have watched it twice already."

It was nice to be home, Markus brought up the bags and gave a bow, and left, I still had his card, and we all wandered down to the kitchen, and the drinks were opened. It was so nice to see familiar walls and faces I love. This was my safe zone, the place I was at ease, this was my comfort zone, and where I was happiest. I spent the night being asked a million questions, and Birch and myself told them all about the room, and the hotel, and what it was like in the theatre. By the time we got into bed, it was late, and both of us were exhausted. She snuggled into me and I smiled, I loved to be home, and alone with her. I closed my eyes, felt her warmth, and heard her softly breathing, now this is the real Abby, happy and contented in the arms of Birch.

Is it weird that Chloe was bouncing around like Tigger on crack, because I said her name on television? My God, she was loud this morning, and had more energy than a nuclear power plant. She was adamant we shop in the village, and I must admit I was not terribly keen, but I am talking Chloe, and when she gets like this, it is hard to say no.

We walked down the lane towards the village, well I say walked, to be honest walking a Springer Spaniel puppy, would be less exhausting. I did not know it was humanly possible to even talk that fast.

We arrived a lot quicker than I wanted, and Chloe headed into Jessops for paint, and I sauntered up the main street towards the Post Office. Peter Saxon was outside, restocking the news stand, he noticed me and smiled.

"Wow, our own little Abigail, who would of thought it?"

I smiled, and looked at the stand, and caught my breath, my face was everywhere, I mean, my picture was plastered across every daily newspaper, I stood at his side, and he put his arm round my shoulder.

"We are really proud of you Abigail, we watched you last night, and the papers were right, you were elegant, sophisticated and genuinely likeable, we are so proud of you this morning."

It felt weird, all the papers were saying really nice things about me, and so was Peter, but hey this is Wotton, and that rare occasion of someone saying something nice about me was happening, and I was taking it.

"Thanks Mr Saxon, it was a really nice experience." Chloe came bouncing up the street like Tigger, she saw the papers and screamed.

"OH MY GOD ABBY, LOOK AT YOU!" She beamed at Peter.

"Mr S, I want one copy of every one of them!" She turned and ran into the shop; he gave a chuckle.

"She appears a little excitable today." I shrugged.

"It is Chloe, she gets like this, I mentioned her because she is struggling to sell her art, and her website got smashed, and it is the most hits it has had. It means a lot to her, I mean, no one has bought anything yet, but they looked, and she is so over the moon that they did." A few minutes later, she came bouncing out with an arm full.

"Let's go for a coffee."

I must admit, the thought of adding caffeine to Chloe, freaked me out a little, she was already at warp speed, I was not sure going to caffeinated light speed was a wise move. I was jerked sideways, as Chloe dragged me up the street, I waved goodbye to Peter who was laughing.

I sat in the corner of the Tea Rooms, whilst Chloe rabbited on at high speed, and showed every daily paper that had been printed in the UK today, to Lillian and Celia. Stacy smiled when she put the coffee down.

"I really loved last night, you looked lovely, and you were so natural, I have downloaded it, but you know what, I really loved the fact you plugged your friends, that was really sweet." I smiled up at her.

"She is a great artist; more people should see what she paints." She nodded at me and looked back towards Chloe excitedly talking at the counter.

"I looked at her website, she is brilliant, she will get there you know, talent does not go unnoticed? Look at you, it took a while, but last night you saw all your hard work pay off."

Chloe bounced up to the table and sat down with a smile, Stacy returned to her work. I must admit, she was hard work, but she was so happy, and I was not going to stop that. We sat talking and were not aware of the Tea Rooms, when Agnes, Henrietta and Bethany walked in.

"Oh, isn't it amazing, one night of TV, and suddenly she is out and about, we hardly see her otherwise, although considering the news, I am amazed she would show her face." I realised the Shrew Crew were talking about me, Bethany tutted.

"Well, what do you expect, like father, like daughter, nothing good has come from that family."

Chloe gripped my hand, I was so tired of this shit, was it ever going to end, I mean, what do I honestly have to do, just to be given a fair shake? Chloe shook her head softly.

"Leave it Abby, we can just leave, honestly it is not worth it."

I nodded, she was probably right, and I stood up, Celia and Lillian were looking worried, Stacy stood frozen by the counter, Louise was stood outside and everyone was looking at me. I took a deep breath, and tried to compose myself. Henrietta threw me a dirty look.

"Well, what do you expect, brothels and fraud, and god knows what, she will end in prison like her father, and I say good riddance, this village has no tolerance for criminals."

Chloe shook her head, but I could feel the anger inside me burning up, I kept my voice low, and took the three paces to the table. I am so sick of it, and although Birch has told me many times to weather the storms of them, I was not letting them spoil Chloe's day. Chloe took my hand and pulled me to hurry, but I stood firm.

"No one in my family is a criminal, and I do not run a brothel, so I would ask you to kindly get your facts right if you wish to yell them across this establishment." I turned and walked towards the door.

"Well not yet, but he will be convicted, and as for you madam, we are only repeating what was clearly written in the Mail, all your fornicating filthy ways have shown we were right all along. If you are so dammed decent, why were you fawning all over that whore you live with last night? You are always flaunting it round the village, it is disgusting, and against the scriptures."

I let go of Chloe's hand and turned, I could feel the rage inside me, I hated these women with a passion, I was trying, I really was, but it was so hard. I had been happy, Chloe had been happier than I had seen her in ages, and they just had to spoil it. I took a deep breath and walked back to the table, and looked down at the three of them sat looking smug.

"Firstly ladies, Ben Shepperton, printed full apologies for that article, because it was incorrect, and as for my father, he is not a criminal. There is an investigation into his partner from what

I have heard, but not my dad. So, if you want to shout at me, get your facts right, yes, I am out here today, as company for my friend, and not because last night I did an interview. I have just spent three weeks in the USA, doing the same thing there, because believe it or not, I have sold over a million books, people ask me for these interviews because my stories appeal to them, nothing more." Bethany looked smug.

"You should watch the news, it clearly shows your father going to the police station, if he was not a criminal, then why would he have too?" She smirked. I stared at her, honestly, I wanted to slap her face. I resisted the temptation, and smirked at her.

"Really, because I heard on the news that Wotton was filled with vicious, sadistic, two faced old prudes, who had never been able to get laid they were so foul, and yet I still came out with my friend." Celia and Lillian tittered in the background. Agnes looked outraged.

"How dare you, I have never been so insulted in my life, you vile mouthed harpy." I stepped back, and looked down at her.

"Oh right… Oh I see, and I thought the news was all lies, but that was you three was it? I think in that case, I need to get my friend home; she is obviously not safe out." Bethany gave a gasp as she looked at Agnes, Celia snorted a laugh, there were titters all around the room, I smiled.

"You really hate it don't you, you can dish it out, but you cannot take it? Wotton is changing ladies, and you are falling out of step, and that is why you hate us isn't it? We have a best selling author, the most successful bookshop ever, and a therapy centre, with one of the most qualified doctors in her field. A brilliant new artist, and a computer genius that outshines all her rivals, and now we have the most talented hair stylist this area has ever seen, and we did it all in a couple of years. Tell me ladies, what have you done here in the last forty, apart from sour the cream in every shop you have passed with your faces?" They looked stunned; I gave a smirk.

"Yeah, I thought as much, bugger all." I turned and walked to the door. "Come on Chloe before the cream sours." I winked at Lillian, walked out and breathed in; Chloe took my arm.

"Just walk… Holy fuck Abby, how did you not scream?" I kept on walking.

"That is what they want Chloe, they want us to show ourselves up, and I will not let them win. They are just the same as the reporters, all they want to do is spread lies and hate, if we rise up to them, we give them more ammo, and I will not do that anymore."

We crossed over the street and walked down towards the book shop, Bradley's car pulled in outside of the Practice, and Birch came out, I waved and shouted to her, and she stopped and smiled, but she looked worried.

"Deads, why are you out here?" I did not understand.

"I was helping Chloe shop." She looked at Bradley, then back to me.

"Sweetie, get in the car, and keep your head down out of sight, you need to get home."

She gathered her hair into a bun, and pulled a woollen hat over it. I did not understand, she looked round checking the street.

"Come on hurry up and get in." Okay, so suddenly I was panicked.

"Birch what is happening?" She shook her head.

"Not here."

Chloe did not need telling twice, she pulled the back door open and slid in, Birch jumped in the front, and I slid in next to Chloe, Bradley drove straight off. Honestly, it was like we had committed a crime, and Bradley was the getaway driver.

Waterside Lane was packed with vehicles, four of them were police cars, and the rest were press. Photographers were lined up on mass outside my mum's house, I felt my stomach twist, what the hell was going on?

Chloe saw the cameras, and pushed me down in the seat, I resisted her, but she shoved me hard, she pulled up my hood, and leaned over me, and I felt the panic course through me, I was starting to get really frightened. Bradly drove up to the gates, and Birch, with her head down, pressed the button on her key ring, and the gates swung open, Bradley drove straight up to the door.

Chloe jumped out, stepped into the porch, and opened the front door, and then Birch and myself made a mad dash in to the house. I stood in the hallway, confused and disorientated, trembling and feeling really scared. I looked at Birch, she looked a little rattled, she looked over my shoulder, I took a deep breath.

"Birch what the hell is going on?" A deep voice sounded behind me, Birch's eyes looked at me and then shifted to back over my shoulder.

"Miss Watson, Doctor Dixon?"

I turned and saw the uniform, and felt my heart lurch, why were there three police officers in our living room? A large sturdy officer smiled at me, and I swallowed hard with fear.

"I am Sergeant Mondale, and these two gents are detectives from Scotland Yard, could we have a minute of your time please?"

What the hell was going on? I looked at the official looking guys, I had done nothing wrong, why would they want to see me, and why were the press gathered on mass outside mum's house? I turned to Birch, feeling panicked.

"Birch what is going on, Birch I am scared?" Birch took my hand, and gave it a squeeze, she gave me a soft smile, and her eyes held her concern for me, her voice was soft and quiet.

"It is alright Sweetie; they just want to talk." She looked up. "Hello Sergeant, I am Doctor Jemima Dixon, and this is Miss Abigail Watson, how can we be of assistance?" I turned back round.

I was lost for words; my head was spinning, I don't want to assist anyone, I want someone to tell me what is happening. He smiled at me.

"I don't want you to be alarmed Miss Watson, we would like a chat, nothing more."

Okay so he wants to chat, but about what, could he not be clearer? Birch gently guided me, as I felt the panic inside me, as my heart pounded.

We walked into the living room, and sat down on the sofa, the three of them sat on the other side, and pulled out some paperwork. Birch held my hand, but I will not deny, I felt intimidated by them. One of them was a tall man about early forties, he had a good sized beer belly, which protruded in front of him as he sat, his legs slightly apart, to accommodate it. He introduced himself as Det Sgt Jon Bancroft, he looked at me like he despised me, I had seen that look on Marjorie many times.

His partner looked a little younger, and looked like he worked out, he was introduced as Det Sgt Eric Bishop. He appeared less stern, but I got a really cold sensation from him, like this guy wanted to know everything about me. I felt a cold shudder run down my spine.

I looked at them both, Bancroft and Bishop, it sounded like a cheesy 1990's cop show. I sat there not knowing what I should do or say, I had no idea what was going on. Bancroft leaned forward, and I tensed, my throat felt restricted.

"We would like to ask you a few questions about your father Miss Watson." Bradley stepped into the room, I looked up at him, he looked worried, and that really frightened me.

"Excuse me gents, but if you do not mind, could you wait a few more moments, Miss Watson and Dr Dixon's legal representation has just arrived. I am sure you understand, especially with Miss Watson being as high profile as she is at the moment? We would be more at ease if her counsel were present."

The detective gave a sigh, he was clearly not happy, I must admit I felt happier, Birch gave my hand a gentle squeeze, I glanced at her.

Birch was sat watching everything about them, I had seen her do it so many times, as she read all their movements and gestures. I was hoping she would see something I was not, because at the moment, I felt scared and helpless.

There was a tap on the door, Edwina opened it, and in walked Margaret. Oh shit, the Shredder was here, that did not bode well, if we need her, then what the hell did they want? She was on my side and I still shit myself, she walked in like she owned the place, and came right over to us, my leg was slightly trembling, she looked down at me, and I felt real fear.

"Take your coat off Miss Watson and make yourself comfortable, and just relax, there is nothing to fear."

I nodded, I was sweating, and as much as she terrifies me, I felt a little more relaxed, I was actually glad she was here. She looked at Chloe, who was stood in the doorway.

"Miss, could you hang up their coats, and I think coffees, would be welcome."

Chloe came over as I slipped my coat off, she looked as scared as me, she touched my shoulder as if to say 'I'm here.' I smiled at her and she nodded. Margret opened her leather bag, took out a pad, and clicked her pen.

“Right Detective Bancroft, you may proceed.” He looked at me, I felt my heart pound harder.

“Miss Watson, could you tell us what your current relationship to your father is?” I looked at the Shredder, she still terrified me, she nodded I could answer, I looked at Bancroft, actually, why did that matter?

“Why are the police interested in knowing that, what goes on between my dad and me is private?” Margret gave a smirk, Bancroft looked upset at my response.

“I have to ascertain the facts of communication between you two, it is important.” It felt unusual, but I had nothing to hide, it was no secret we did not get on.

“It is not good, it has not been for two years, he does not agree with my choice for a partner, we hardly speak.” The Detective gave a nod.

“I take it by the way you are holding hands, that your partner is Doctor Dixon?”

“Yes.” He made a note on his pad.

“Is it a sexual relationship.” Margret growled, I swallowed hard, Christ she is scary.

“That is irrelevant to this case Bancroft, ask only what is required for your case, not your grubby little reporter friend Ford. Be aware, if you disclose anything of this case to the press, I will have your badge, you should have learned that from last time.”

He looked at her with distaste, I had no idea what last time was, but I got the impression she chewed him up, and spit him out, he was certainly no fan of her. He looked at me, in a cold way.

“I apologise Miss Watson… Earlier this year you transferred several large accounts away from your father’s company, and moved them to EFG, would you like to explain why?” Margret turned to me and leaned in, and spoke quietly.

“You do not need to answer that, but be aware if you do, they are looking for reasons to pin on your dad.” I nodded, I looked at Bancroft.

“He has been horrible to my partner, and me, he cannot accept our relationship, and we have barely spoken accept to argue. I wanted to punish him, I did so by moving everything away to another rival firm." He wrote it down.

"That is the only reason, there is no other reason?"

I looked at him, I didn't like him at all. This probably sounds crazy, because I really hate a lot of things about my dad, and yet sitting here, I want to protect him from this horrible man.

"I am a spoilt little rich girl, and daddy pissed me off, so I pissed him off back, go on, write that down." Birch squeezed my hand, and smirked. He looked at me, he clearly did not like my answer, he made no note, but suddenly changed the subject.

"You bought this house in cash did you not?" I was really hating this, I decided to give as little as possible.

"I don't understand why that matters?" He gave a sigh as if working with an idiot.

"Miss Watson, I have to investigate all income related to your father, you bought this house cash, did you not?"

"My money is earned by me, and is not my fathers. No... I did not buy it." He looked confused, and looked at his partner, then back to me.

"I was led to believe you purchased this house." I shook my head.

"You were misinformed, it happens a lot around me, people speaking lies, you should not listen to the rumours, especially those in the press."

Margaret looked very happy with my progress so far, Birch bit her lip, and looked down to hide her amusement. He flicked back through some previous notes, and found what he was looking for.

"It says here you own the house; how can you own it, and not buy it Miss Watson?" I gave a smile and turned to Birch.

"My partner bought it and gave me half, we share everything, it is why she is my partner, and why I love her, and why daddy is pissed off. He does not like women who fuck each other." Birch's mouth crinkled, and she looked down, he looked very confused.

"She gave you half a house?" I smiled at her as she looked up, her eyes were bright and sparkling, I saw a little crease at the base of her eye, she was enjoying this. I gave a nod.

"She did, isn't she adorable, and very sexy too?" Birch jerked and gave a slight snort, he looked very uncomfortable. I must admit, I was feeling a lot better. He gave a sigh; he was clearly irritated.

"Alright, you are only a half owner; I will move on. I believe you had a show down with your father a short time ago, and words were raised, could you tell me about that?" I shrugged.

"Nothing to tell, he was getting drunk and rowdy with his tart of a secretary, who he has been banging behind my mums back, and is why she threw him out. The landlord had gotten complaints from his regulars, and asked me to try and quieten him down, I spoke to him, and told him to go to his flat in London."

"That is all, no shouting at all?" I shook my head, and just stared at him, he turned to Birch.

"Doctor Dixon, Mr Watson received a payment of one million pounds off you, could you explain why you would pay a man who allegedly hates you so much money?" Birch leaned back and crossed her legs, and placed her hands in her lap.

"I do not think he hates me; he just hates the fact I fuck his daughter, and she really likes it." I put my head down and sniggered. "I bought out his share of number six." He looked at her.

"Could you elaborate?" She smiled.

"About what, the sex or the house?"

Edwina stood in the doorway and turned away, I could see her shoulders shake, I was fighting the need to laugh, oh my god, she was so cool. He looked really pissed off.

"I would appreciate it, if you just spoke of the house, please." She smiled.

"You are missing out on some juicy stuff trust me, Abby is a wild little beastie, but in regard to that aspect of this, he wanted to sell his share of the property. Mrs Watson didn't want to lose her home, which is what the cold fish wanted, so I bought out his share. It was a fair and reasonable deal, and it is all legal and above board, I have been informed by text on route here, copies of all the papers are already on your desk in London, for you to inspect on your return." He frowned, and gave a sigh.

"Do you often just randomly buy properties Doctor Dixon?" She smirked.

"I was not aware it was random, and I believe there is no law against it? Do you like to buy dull shoes and tacky suits, or was that a random purchase also?" He gave a frustrated sigh.

"Please Doctor Dixon, would you please answer the question, it is important?" She gave a smirk, I looked down, and bit my lip. Birch stared at him; her intense stare made him uncomfortable.

"I like to buy things, I too am a very lavishly spoilt little girl, as you can see by my taste in houses and women."

Margret tittered, wow the Shredder laughed again, that is twice I know of, I checked the ceiling for cracks, nope, all is good. He looked like he was not really having a good time, Birch leaned forward, and I thought oh shit, she has learned what she needed, and here she goes. She looked right at him, and her eyes sparkled bright green.

"Detective, why don't we both cut the games and bullshit out, I am a psychologist, and I see games when they are being played. So, let's just cut to the chase, Edwin, as far as we know is an honest man, yes, his daughter is very pissed at daddy, but the truth is, he involved none of his family in his business. Miss Watson lived at home, with her mum, and hardly saw her dad, and when she did, he spent money on her, lots of money on her out of guilt. He was a shitty parent, but so are a lot of others, and sadly that is not against the law. You are wasting time looking for a rope to hang him with here, because in truth, neither of us know anything about how he made his money. Okay are we done, or do you have more, would you like to know how often we fuck, or where I hide my vibrator, because this is a false lead and you know it?"

Oh hell, she is braver than me, God, I am so turned on by her right now, he was clearly unhappy, but he knew she was right. He looked at his partner, who shrugged, and turned back to Birch.

"For now, that is all, if we have more questions we will be in touch, thank you both for your time."

He stood up, and the other two followed, I stayed sat down, and Edwina showed them to the door, he stopped and turned.

"This is an active investigation, so please stay put, just in case we have more questions, you know, stay in the country." Birch gave a laugh.

"With all your press friends outside, it is hardly likely we will be able to leave the house, let alone the country." He nodded and walked out; Edwina closed the door. I flopped back and gave a gasp.

"Okay that was intense." I looked at Bradley. "Is my mum alright, I want to see her?" He smiled.

"She is fine Abby, Roni and Will are with her talking to the police, I believe Harriet is there with her too."

I gave a sigh of relief, I was glad to hear Hatty was there, she would not let them give her any shit. I looked back at Bradley, he saw me staring at him, and he smiled, I guess this was what he was waiting for.

"Mr Wheeler, is my dad a crook, is that why you moved your accounts?" I think he expected it.

He walked over, crouched down in front of me, he took my hand in his. I love his eyes, they are so kind and caring, I totally get why Deb's loves him so deeply, he has to be the nicest guy I know.

"Abby, I moved the accounts because I heard a few things about Graham I did not like. It bothered me, but honestly in all my years of business, I have never once heard a bad word against your dad. I have always thought he was as straight as they come in business. I think he has failed at life, but that is not a criminal offence, that is stupidity. Do I think he is guilty, no, actually, I don't?" I smiled.

"You are a really great dad, mine could learn a lot from you. I am angry with him for being so nasty to Birch, but I have never thought he was a crook." Bradley squeezed my hand.

"Keep thinking that, because I think that too."

I smiled at him, I trust Bradley, because Deb's loves him so much, and that says everything I need to know about him, and if he does not think my dad is a crook, he isn't.

Chapter 18

Reporter.

Chloe watched from her bedroom window, the police were at mums for another five hours, the press came and went. The thing that worried me the most, was that a police van backed onto the drive, and police carried a lot of things out of the house, everything was boxed, so it was hard to tell exactly what. Once they had left, mum rang me. I had sent her a few messages, but when the call came, I ran up to my room, and sat at my desk.

"Mum what is happening, the police have been here asking questions, what is going on with Dad?"

"Abby, I do not want you to worry, your dad regardless of what they say is not guilty of anything. Look I know things have not been good between him and me, but if there is one thing I know about him, it is that he is honest in business. I have spoken with him, and he asked me to tell you not to worry. Graham has been involved with some things that your father was not connected to, and they are pretty shady to say the least. Your father voluntarily went to the police station to cooperate, he has opened the company to them, and given them complete access, he is hiding nothing."

I was relieved he was alright, and was helping, I had worried he had been arrested, it came as a relief to know he had not.

"Mum, I want to help, is there anything I can do?"

"No darling, we have to sit tight, and just ride this out, and let your dad handle this, he understands all of it, and he is in the best position to sort this, all we can do is wait for the outcome. Abby the news and papers are saying some terrible things about him, but they are not true, that wicked man Peter Ford is making a lot of things up, so please try to ignore them." It felt frustrating, but I knew she was right.

"Mum, I never read those papers, and I hardly watch the telly. If you talk to Dad, tell him good luck from me. I hated what he said about Birch, and I really wish he could see how much she means; I never wanted a war between us, but I don't want him to lose everything, he worked hard for it all."

"I know darling, I feel the same way, when I talk to him, I will tell him. Abby there is a lot of press here, please, stay away from here, do not come over, they will use your dad to get to you, and if they hurt you, that will get to him too, so just for now, keep a low profile and let this blow over."

That was easy to say, but knowing she was alone, was hard for me, I would rather be there with her.

"I don't like you being alone over there, I want to be with you."

"Abby I am fine, Hatty is here with me, and she is going to stay, so please don't worry about me. The house phone is ringing all the time with the press, so only use my mobile, I have switched the answer phone on full time. I will call you on my mobile if I hear anything alright?"

"Yes... Okay mum, just keep talking to me, or I will worry about you."

"I will darling, and don't worry, everything will be fine, I will talk soon."

"Bye mum."

I sat back in my seat and gave a sigh, I was hating this, but it was out of my hands, I had to trust dad, which at the moment was not the easiest of things for me, especially after the way he manipulated me to get to Birch.

I did not feel much like socialising, so I clicked on my computer, the best thing at the moment for me was work, we had been having such a good day, and first it was the Shrew Crew, and now this, everything felt like it had just slipped right back to normal, and it felt like it was just the same shit, different day.

I often wonder if it will ever end, we were all working hard to create a fun Curio family Christmas, and it felt every time we had fun, something came along to crash in and ruin it. I sat staring at the file on my desk top, it was difficult to think of writing, I needed to get my head straight. It suddenly hit me.

"I have a website."

I had completely forgotten, everything had been so crazy, I had not logged in, I hit my internet browser, and opened it up, and smiled. Wow Edwina had done such a great job, she had redone the top image with a picture from the theatre, and it looked amazing. The icon was red, I had messages and comments, I clicked it, and I had hundreds of comments. I gasped in surprise, how could there be so many, it had only been live a couple days? The very first comment on my site was from Birch. 'You inspire me with your words, I love you.'

I felt a tug at my heart and sat smiling looking at it. Suddenly my world was brighter, as I went down a massive list of some really nice and lovely comments. I sat in my room and read every one of them, and wrote thank you messages to all my fans, which was strange, as I was talking to a mass of strangers, who liked me, because my words in a book, gave them hope, or happiness.

It was late when I was finally finished, and I just undressed and slipped into bed, I felt happy, but tired, I drifted off, and at some point, Birch slid in with me, and cuddled up.

My life is so strange, half of the world feels like it hates me, and the other half loves me, my whole life is love, hate, I have got to say it feels bizarre. I woke early, which is weird for me, and headed down, for the crazy run around, that was mornings in this house. It was December 15th, and we had ten days before our family Christmas Day.

Chloe informed us there was only two news reporters now, camped out in their cars, I find it strange, because there is no way my dad would come back here, he has had everything related to his business taken by the police.

Chloe sat as usual with me, as we drank coffee, it was nice to see Anthony in the house, and even nicer to see Michael. I had not actually met him yet, he had been here whilst Birch and I were at the hotel, so the others were already used to him.

He was quite tall, and the contours of his shirt, showed he was pretty buff. He has short very neatly groomed hair, although he was with Anthony, so I suppose that is to be expected. His eyes were bright blue, and looked kind, his face was round and caring, I liked the look of him, his voice was surprisingly deep, and to be honest, he was pretty good looking, I am quite sure Chloe would not pass him up.

He sat down at the end of the island and smiled, I raised my cup to him, Edwina poured him a cup, apparently, he had been briefed by Anthony, who had told him, 'do not speak to Abby until she actually starts to talk, she is very sweet, but wakes up grumpy,' Anthony knows me so well. I had drunk three coffees' so I was feeling sociable, I looked at Anthony.

"Are you coming tomorrow, it's the Sun Club Christmas Party, and we have all been invited, I have to let them know the numbers today?" He stopped and looked at Michael, I looked across the island and smiled at him.

"What do you say Michael, do you fancy joining us?" He looked at me a little worried.

"Er... Isn't that one of those... You know?" Chloe leaned over the island.

"Nudist clubs, yes, we are having Christmas dinner and a bit of a dance, so are you up for it?" He looked nervous; Chloe shrugged.

"You are going to have to get used to it Michael, as you see, we hardly wear clothes here." Chloe was almost naked today; she did have on her special Christmas panties. Michael looked at Anthony.

"Will everyone be naked?"

He looked on sympathetically, he knew us all so well, and he knew it would not take long, before we had Michael nude.

"Mikey, it is not that bad, once you do it, you will wonder why you were so worried, but if you don't feel comfortable with it, we can skip it." I looked at him in his tight t shirt and jeans.

"You look like you work out, and have a nice body, be proud of it and don't hide it. I can tell you now, I am only wearing a t shirt because I knew you were here, and wanted to give you time to get used to me, but I live and work naked most days." I could see he was thinking about it, he glanced at us all, and we smiled.

"Abby, it is alright if I call you Abby? You are really famous, are you not worried what others will say?" I gave a titter.

"I am sure you have heard what people already say about me, Michael, I could go for dinner at the golf club in a nun's habit, and people round here would find fault with it. Michael, all of us in this house are unique people, and we are true to ourselves, in this house we do not hide who we are, what you see is what you get, and we do not apologise for it. I may be well known, but I can assure you, I am just an ordinary human female like all the others. If you want, I have a sarong, you can wear that, but we are going out as a family, because that is what we are, and you are now one of us. It is up to you?" He nodded.

"Okay yeah, I would actually love to come out with you all, it is nice of you to include me, thanks." I smiled.

"Wonderful I will let them know." Birch staggered in yawning; her hair stuck out everywhere.

"Sweetie why didn't you wake me?" I got up and kissed her softly, and she smiled. "Oh, I am awake now."

"I was about to, you were so peaceful, I thought I would give you a little longer." We both sat down as Edwina poured coffee.

"I am sorting out numbers for tomorrow night, and Michael is going to join us, so it should be fun, I am going to go and see Peter and Mary today." She put her cup down.

"Sweetie is that wise, there are press all over the place?" I was a little surprised to hear it, Birch had always faced everything head on, and never shied away from anything, and yet she appeared to think I should.

"Birch I am not going to hide, I have done nothing wrong, and I do not believe my dad has, they can only write if I talk. Birch, they will not make me a prisoner in this house, Marjorie couldn't, and neither will they." I could see her concern, but I needed to do this, I was not going to hide. She seemed to understand.

"Okay Sweetie, just be vigilant and avoid them."

Twenty minutes later I walked into the village with Birch, both of us wore large woollen hats, and thick scarves, and I had my hood up. It was freezing cold so did not look out of place, and I had my thick coat with a big hood. I walked Birch to the door of the practice, and left her, and walked up towards the Post Office. I knew better than to talk to Peter about the Sun Club, I had written everything down for him, and I handed him the letter.

"I wrote it all down for you, so there is no need to talk, you have no idea who is listening at the moment." He looked around.

"Hmm, there are too many strange faces in the village at the moment, be careful Abigail, they want to lynch your father, and they will you too." I understood that.

"I am aware of them Mr Saxon, but I am not going to hide, I

have done nothing wrong, this is my home, and I am a part of life here, and not Marjorie and her group or the press will drive me out of it." He smiled.

"I can respect that Abigail, you know, we think you have grown up into a very nice person. Mary and myself consider you and your friends an asset to this village. I understand not everyone sees it that way, but you belong here, and I wish you, and all your friends, nothing but good things."

It was nice to hear that, this village was my home, and for seven years, I have fought so hard to be a part of it, and to be recognised for that, felt like a small victory.

I left Peter and headed for the gift shop, I was almost there when suddenly in front of me was a man in a thick padded coat, he looked about mid forties. I tried to side step him, but he matched me, and blocked my path. I felt my nerves twinge, I looked at him, he needed a shave, his face had a mix of brown and grey bristles.

"Excuse me please, I am trying to pass, if you do not mind?" He smiled a grisly smile.

"I knew it, you can hide your hair, but that voice gives you away, it's a little bit too well spoken for most young women round here. So, Abigail, would you like to tell me about how it feels to have daddy arrested?" He lifted his hand and was holding a small digital recorder, I felt my insides lurch, he was more than a little intimidating.

"Could I have your name please?" He laughed.

"I am a nobody, answer the question."

I stared at him, and noticed Edwina holding her digital camera standing just to the side of him, with a boom mic clipped to the top, I had no idea where she had appeared from, but I felt a little relieved, I looked at him.

"Regardless of your status, I would still like to know your name, I think I can guess, but would prefer you address yourself." He smirked.

"You will not talk if I tell you my name, so just answer the question."

"I am not going to answer your question, because how I feel is none of your business." He leaned into me, and I took a step back, his breath stunk, and his eyes looked cold, he was really frightening.

"Look here Abigail, you are better off answering, because I have so much about you on file, and I can write up a storm and destroy you. So, how about you start talking, or I will start writing, and your career as a writer will end tomorrow."

"Are you threatening me?" He laughed.

"Of course, you do as I say or I wipe you out overnight, have you any idea how powerful I am, do you think that little sweet stunt you pulled on TV will wash after I have finished with you? Sweet little innocent Abigail, please, who are you trying to fool, now talk into the recorder and stop fucking pissing me off?" I felt my legs shake, and raised my voice.

"Write what you like, I am saying nothing to you or any reporter, my private feelings are exactly that." He shook his head.

"Wow you really are a stupid bitch; I am going to destroy you, say goodbye to your career bitch." I had taken as much as I could, and felt the upset rising inside me, and I swallowed hard, and lied to him.

"You do not frighten me, now get out of my way." I side stepped him, and pushed past him hard.

"Leave me alone." I put my head down and just forced my way past as he laughed at me, as the tears filled my eyes, I squeezed my eyes hard, and tried to force them back.

"Yeah, that's right, run away Daddies Girl, he cannot save you, I will destroy him as well as you."

He had not realised he had his back to Edwina, she smiled as she paused the video and walked quickly behind me, she caught me up.

"Are you alright?" I felt the anxiety in me, and was gasping for air, and shaking.

"I will be, I didn't cry, I fought it, and I didn't, it was him wasn't it, that is Peter Ford of that paper that puts up my pictures?" Edwina slipped her arm round my waist.

"Yeah, that is him, he is a nasty bastard, you did good and kept your cool." I nodded my head as I tried to breathe.

"Why were you there Edwina?" She smiled.

"Birch asked a few of us to keep an eye on you, she admires your independence, but she knows what that toe rag is like, we have been around since you left the house." I stopped and looked at her.

"Around, you mean following me?" She grinned.

"It is probably more a stake out, Birch figured if Marjorie could have transient watch, we could have a writer watch." She smiled; I looked round.

"But I don't see anyone." She gave a shrug and smiled.

"That is kind of the point of a stake out, I was in the car watching, when I saw Ford heading towards you, so I grabbed the camera and jumped out ready. I filmed the whole conversation, and got every word he said. If he tries to attack you, we will strike back in Curio fashion, with the truth. Abby, we love you, we have your back, remember, all girls together?" I looked back up the street, Ford was nowhere to be seen.

"I am afraid of him Edwina, he is going to hurt my dad, and then he is going to destroy me, and I really do not understand why, but I feel it, I felt it then."

I did feel it, the look in his eyes, and the stare he gave me, I knew without doubt he hated me, but I had no idea why? I had never met him, I did not know him, as far as I could tell I had done nothing that could even remotely offend him. I could feel my legs trembling, and my stomach twisting. Edwina took my arm.

"Abby, you have to understand, that this really has nothing to do with you, it is what he does, he just picks a target, and then goes out of his way to attack them, that is how he makes his money, he is just sick. Let's get you home, he is gone, but it is better if you are not out in full view. Abby, you have been out and been seen by the village, so go home now and relax, come on get in my car and stay out of view."

I agreed, suddenly I wanted to be home, and out of reach of everyone. I followed her to the car and got in the back, within moments Chloe appeared and moments later, Luke, they both jumped in and Edwina drove off, Chloe pulled me into a hug.

"You okay?"

I nodded; I was glad to be in the car where no one could get to me. I felt a bit stupid, I should have listened to Birch, although once again she was ten steps ahead of me, and watching over me. We drove down Waterside Lane, and he was there again, stood outside my mum's house, I felt a cool chill run through me, Chloe pulled my hood up. The gates opened and we drove in, Chloe looked back, and watched him.

"What does he want, there is nothing here for him to use?" Luke looked back.

"This guy does not care about the truth, do you remember Alison Williams, she had a great career until he took a dislike to her? She was a great actress, but he targeted article after article, and she swore it was all lying, but directors and produces dropped her like a hot potato, and it killed her career." I shuddered, was I next?

It was nice to get inside the house, I ripped off my coat and hung it up, and headed to the kitchen, my hands were still shaking, I reached for the gin, and Chloe put her hand on the bottle.

"Abby, you are safe, reach for the kettle, because that is not the answer." I looked at her and felt the tears as I swallowed.

"Chloe I am scared." She pulled me close and hugged me.

"I know, but you are not alone, you know, you and Birch have always been there for us, it is nice that we can be there for you. Abby do not worry about that twat; he is not as invincible as he thinks." I gave a sniffle, she just held me and it felt so nice.

"Chloe, I have worked so hard, and he can take it all away."

"No Abby, not this time, he too has a lot to lose, and to be honest, he really has underestimated all of us. Trust us, and trust Birch." I pulled back and looked at her as I gave a sniffle.

"Why trust Birch?" She smiled.

"God, you have no idea how much she loves you, whilst you were in bed last night, we had a meeting called by Birch. She saw this coming, and she prepared like she always does. Abby, trust us all, we are ready to fight for you." I did not understand.

"But Chloe how can we fight, he has some very influential friends?" She clicked on the kettle.

"Yes, he does, but he kisses their ass, none of them know who he really is. Abby all you have to do is show them the real Peter Ford, and then sit back and watch the rats abandon ship." Chloe made coffee and I sat down, and tried to calm down, Edwina and Luke came in and refilled their cups.

"Abby, G5 are in your corner, we have been very busy since last night, I don't want you to worry about this Ford guy, he has far more to lose than you do."

I was starting to understand, there was a lot going on, and I was out of the loop, and I understood why. I could not touch any of this because of my father, as it would look like I was covering up for my father's bad behaviour. The buzzer went, and Edwina pressed the button, and walked to the door. Two minutes later Morty arrived, he came into the kitchen and winked at me, he handed a portable hard drive to Luke.

"Oh boy, this guy is a piece of work, I got documents, emails, pictures, and a shit load of MP3 interviews. He has three pieces written and they are all assassination jobs on Abby and her dad, and all bullshit. He quotes sources, and one of them might interest you. He has an interview he recorded with a Marjorie Wallace, and it is pretty damming stuff, so once I had copied everything, I slipped Bangers Asian Dragon through the door before I closed it." Luke smiled.

"Nice job, that will slow him down." I looked at Morty.

"What is an Asian Dragon?" He grinned and looked at Edwina.

"Banger Bobbles, here wrote a piece of code a few years back that creeps round your system, and haunts any exits such as USB, Email send buttons etc. Anything that he tries to take off that computer, the first three words will be in Chinese, the next three in Taiwanese, and the next three in Arabic, and then it repeats. The good aspect of it is, as long as he is writing his shit on his computer, he is fine, but the moment he tries to copy it or send it out in an email, it will all arrive on the other end unreadable, and password protected. I set the password as 'I am a wanker,' all lower case with no spaces, the way I see it, only if he is truly honest will he think of that, so he is screwed." That was scary, I looked at Edwina.

"God, you wrote that. Hell, you live with a writer, do you know how that would kill me?" She smiled.

"Abby, I love you, I would never do that to you, but you know, just in case, be sweet with me." She smiled.

"Whoa, suddenly I am really nervous again, you can be bloody scary when you want to be." She giggled.

"Abby, it will only slow him down, once he realises, he will use another computer, but that will buy us all some time to do some digging. Morty give me that hard drive, I want to start digging straight away."

For the rest of the day, Edwina, Luke and Morty, sat in Edwina's room and analysed everything. Morty sat with head phones on, listening to recorded interviews, Luke went through the emails, and Edwina looked at the written articles. I supplied coffee; they were adamant I was not to be involved. Chloe was painting, so I headed to my room, and curled up on the bed with a book, it was not long before I drifted off to sleep, probably more out of boredom, than anything else.

I woke late afternoon; the house was quiet, and it was already dark. I wandered downstairs, Chloe was still painting, I made a coffee, and walked through into the living room, the Christmas tree was lit, and it shone with all its colours, casting shadows on the wall. I sat in front of it, looking into the branches, at all the different kinds of baubles and decorations, this tree was us, everything we were as a group, as a family, and it was beautiful.

It made me think of all that we had done together, naked summer, the fun at the fete, the lake, and our crazy shopping trips. I remembered those days from that summer, when we all sat on the floor in my tiny little guest house, drinking beer and laughing and talking, and I realised how lucky I was to be loved by such amazing friends.

I heard the door, but didn't really notice, I was lost in my own little world of memories, and then I felt two arms come round me, and snapped out of my thoughts. Birch was sat on the floor behind me, her head rested on my shoulder, her arms round me, her voice soft and quiet in my ear.

"Hi Sweetie, you looked so lovely sat here lit by the tree, I wanted to be close to you." I leaned back into her.

"I was thinking about us, all of us, all the fun we have had, and all those moments that made us the family we have become." She kissed my neck.

"That is nice, it is so easy Deads to let everything negative overwhelm you, it is at times like this you need to remember, you are not alone, and surrounded by love." I put my hands on hers, and gave them a squeeze.

"I know how much I am loved Birch; I feel it every moment of each day." She squeezed me hard.

"That is good, I am glad to hear it, where is everyone?" I gave a contented sigh.

"They are all busy looking at stuff they have hacked out of the horrible man's computer, and Chloe is painting." She slid her hands up inside my t shirt, and started to softly stroke my nipples.

"Good, how about we get our freaky Christmas on? I have wanted you naked and alone under this tree since we put it up." She pinched hard and I felt the tingles shoot into my stomach.

"Oh god Birch, you know how that drives me wild."

She chuckled as I turned and pulled her into a kiss, and suddenly, I am naked, half under the tree, and tingling like a crazy tuning fork, looking up at the branches and lights, smelling pine, and writhing in ecstasy.

"Oh god... Oh god... Oh god... Merry bloody Christmas!"

Chapter 19

Like Minds.

Both of us lay half under the tree facing each other and smiling, I winked at Birch.

"So, did it live up to your expectation, is sex under the tree all it's cracked up to be?" She gave a chuckle.

"I cannot deny it Deads, it is very sexy and really pretty, I loved seeing you lit by the tree, so I think yes, I am very happy."

Grabbing her clothes, we finally got our breath back, and arm in arm we headed to our rooms for a shower, and to prepare for tonight's event. It had felt like a tough day, but as I stood in the shower, and let the hot water wash over me, I felt more light hearted. I walked into Birch's room rubbing my hair with a towel.

"What do we wear tonight, I mean we cannot travel there naked, so what do we put on, I have never been to one of these things?" She sat with her dryer, running her fingers through her long white hair, which had black patches in it.

"I know we have to take our own towel, for sitting on, but I don't think there is any kind of preferred clothing to travel there in. I am wearing my thick robe, that way it is just one item, Petal will be heated so we should not be cold." I had not thought of that, it was a good idea.

"Will you be taking your bag?"

Birch looked at me, yeah, I should have known better. In all the time I have known her, I had not known a time where she did not take her large cloth bag with her. Chloe and Edwina always joked that it was Birch's survival kit, but in a way they were right. I knew it always had alcohol, money, and a large knife in it, baby wipes, condoms, and she even once pulled a dildo out and gave it Deb's, so yeah, I was inclined to agree with them.

Birch dried my hair, and brushed it, which left me feeling calm and relaxed, and we grabbed towels, slipped on our robes, and headed downstairs. In the kitchen Chloe was sat cross legged on the floor facing Deb's, she was painting her breasts with body paint, and painted them as Christmas puddings. Anthony was walking round with a candy cane that curled on his stomach, that headed down, straight down to what he called his sweet bit, I had to chuckle. Chloe smiled as she painted Deb's breasts, her own were painted as baubles, I loved it, and looked at Deb's firm large breasts that looked like puddings.

"Guys that is so cool, I want to do it." Debs smiled and looked down.

"Cool, aren't they? We were talking about how everyone dresses up for Christmas, and we are not going to be wearing anything, so we thought we would decorate our skin." I loved it, Edwina had hers painted like elf hats, I undid my robe, and sat down next to Deb's.

"Do me next." Chloe smiled.

"What do you want me to do?" I looked down at my small round balls.

"I am not sure, whatever you do, you won't need much paint." Deb's gave a titter, Chloe smiled.

"I can do you two lovely red apples; I am not sure snowballs will look that good." I looked down.

"I like fruit, I eat a lot, so do me some apples, small, sweet, and yummy, that is definitely me."

Chloe finished Deb's, and then started on me, Birch came in with a strand of tinsel round her waist, and two rings of tinsel round her boobs, she had a head band of tinsel, and she looked very bright and sparkly, so pretty much typical Birch.

The time was ticking, and so when we were all ready, we grabbed our towels, slipped on our robes and trainers, and Michael wore a tracksuit. Deb's was driving, much to the relief of Anthony.

Michael ran Petal on the drive to warm her up, Birch grabbed four bottles of wine, we now had forty in the wine rack, she felt it would be polite to provide a gift. With hoods up, we waved goodbye to Izzy, and climbed into the back of Petal. Deb's clicked the button, and the gates opened, and we headed out on to the lane.

The drive took twenty minutes, the club was set outside of

Oxendale, in the countryside. The club brochure, informed us it was a six acre site, that contained some woodland, a lot of lawns, camping pitches, a swimming pool, tennis courts, some gardens, and a large man made pond, deep enough to wild swim in.

We arrived at the gate, I looked out from under my hood as a floodlight came on as we drove up, I noted the CCTV. The gates were large wooden gates of at least eight feet, the fencing was the same. There was a lot of trees, and dense cover up the side of the road, it appeared to be very private. Deb's leaned out of the window and pressed the button on the intercom, a cheerful voice came back.

"Hello." Deb's leaned towards the intercom.

"Hello, we are the guests of Mr and Mrs Saxon, the Watson party of seven."

"Oh lovely, come on up and park near the meeting house."

The electric gates opened, and she drove in, we made our way up the long driveway, and pulled up in front of what they called the meeting house. I climbed out of the back, and looked at the large brick building with big windows. We walked up the glass panelled door, and were met with a large busted mid fifties looking woman, with very short dark and grey streaked hair. Her name was Glenis, she only wore a big smile, and was really happy and jolly, as she opened the door and welcomed us all in.

"Oh wonderful, hello, Happy Christmas, please, please, come in, you are all so welcome. Oh, I love your robes, they look so warm, come this way, we have a really lovely changing room." Birch was all smiles.

"Isn't she lovely, so full of fun."

We walked along the hallway to a door marked 'Changing,' and walked inside, and there was a bank of lockers, and benches. I must admit, I liked the idea of this, but I had no idea what to expect. We slipped off our robes and Glenis gave a squeal of joy.

"Oh, you look amazing and so festive, what a wonderful idea." Chloe smiled; she was really relaxed.

"I am an artist, I did bring them if anyone would like something doing, we thought it might add to the party spirit, as long as that would be alright with your club?" Glenis was overjoyed.

"Oh, I am sure this will be very well received, it looks like great fun."

It is a strange experience, all my life, I have gone into a changing room to change clothing, and come out wearing something different, this time, I was coming out wearing nothing. Glenis led us down to the main room, which was actually a really big room with a kitchen attached. There was plenty of seating around the room, at the far end a large table had been set up with festive cloths and floral arrangements, at the side of which was a large potted tree, decorated for the season.

As we came through the door, Peter came up to us and welcomed us with a smile, I must admit it felt weird seeing him naked, with his dick hanging out, and he was so brown and suntanned, and uninhibited. Mary spotted us and came over, she gave me a hug, her boobs were frigging huge. She hugged all the others, she again was so relaxed, and she took my hand, and led me with the others towards a group of twenty odd people of all ages, from around early twenties, to at least sixties. Birch leaned into me.

"Fascinating isn't it, I love the human body, we all have the same bits, just the proportions are all different?"

It was an eye opening thought, as I looked round. There were fat, thin, tall, short people, some a deep dark brown, some just off white, boobs of all shapes and size's from flat, to puffed up and round. Then there were the penis's, which to be honest were so varied, from long and thin to short and fat, one large guy, was so large and round, his looked like a small turtle's head just peeking out. Chloe came up at my side and saw me looking round.

"Oh man I wish I had brought my sketch pad, look at it all, it is a nude painters paradise." I smiled.

"No cameras allowed; you will have to memorise it all." She gave me a nod, and a cheeky grin.

"I would love to get those guys all erect and take pictures." I gave a giggle.

"Yep, and that would get us banned for life, stick to body painting them, and try not to arouse them with your brush." She chuckled.

"I am going to mingle, and see who will volunteer to be sketched in the New Year." And off she went into what for her, was penis and boob heaven. A small really well toned up, and sun burned woman, with long red hair introduced herself.

"I am so glad you all came, I am Martha, current Chair of the club." We all introduced ourselves, Birch presented the wine, which was very well received.

Martha introduced us all to the club, and encouraged us to mingle, Mary and Peter, were so different inside the club, they were much more relaxed and friendly, as they walked me round and introduced me. I met Alan, the vice chair, Maureen the Catering manager, Scott the accountant, and Victor, who was in charge of organising the grounds. All of them were welcoming and very enthusiastic about our visit, I must admit, I wondered if they had ever been visited before. A young woman approached me with a big smile and offered her hand.

"Hi I am Paula, it is nice to see so many younger people here, you guys are awesome, love the body paints." I shook her hand; she was very bubbly and enthusiastic.

"I am Abby, Chloe is the body painter, and she did bring her paints, just in case, I am sure she will do something for you." I looked round the room and spotted her multi coloured layered hair. "There she is, it looks like she has got Glenis into it."

We wandered over, and Glenis was all smiles, as Chloe skilfully painted two reindeer faces, on her boobs, I looked round the room, Anthony was talking hair with one of the women, Birch was chatting and smiling with a mixed group, Deb's was sat with two women, and Edwina was checking out the DJ set up. It looked like she was giving him some tips on his computer, even Michael was engrossed in a conversation with the groundsman.

It felt strange, we had only been here a short time, and yet we were happy and relaxed, and felt so welcome, and yet not a soul was dressed, well except Michael, who had on a sarong, which in all honesty hid nothing of his manhood. Alan wandered back over towards me, and offered me a glass of wine.

"It is so nice to have another club visit, and good to know young people are taking up the cause of naturist living. Peter has told me how you and your friends embraced naturism openly. I know your village well, and I cannot deny, that must have been some up hill struggle?" I gave a laugh and took a sip of the wine.

"You have no idea, but there again, if you know Birch, you will find she does not hide who she is, I think she has been quite a challenge for the village." He smiled, I loved the eye contact he gave me, to be honest he was at least fifty, and never once did he look at my body.

"You know I am not sure you are aware of this, but your little Curio group has done wonders for Peter and Mary, they felt judged and afraid to disclose their lifestyle for a long time, but your example has helped them be more relaxed about it, it has done them wonders."

"They are nice people, I have known them all my life, no one should have to hide who they are, it is sad so many feel they have too." He raised his glass.

"Well, you will find everyone here agrees with you, we love this lifestyle, and if I am completely honest, I have found nothing but kind caring people within it... Aha, finally, it looks like your friend, has managed to help Kenny sort out the music."

The music started to play, and people swayed their hips as they talked, they appeared to be a really happy and friendly bunch. I walked with Alan over to the main group, and slipped in at the side of Birch, who was laughing and joking with a large group, she smiled, and slipped her arm round my waist.

"This is fun, are you having a nice time Sweetie?" I smiled and nodded.

I was, I was actually really fascinated by it all, maybe it was me, but I had somehow thought naturist clubs were all quite cliquish, and all rules, but this really was no different from some of our garden days in the summer, except we lacked sunlight. The wine flowed, and everyone relaxed more, and soon we were all smiling and laughing when Maureen announced the meal was almost ready for service.

We were all seated down one side of the table, so we could face club members, and be central to the conversation, and we placed our towels on our seats and sat down. It was nice to see quite a lot of the members had some form of body paint on them. Then all of the ladies from the kitchen came out looking hot and red, and wearing aprons, carrying plates, and the meal was served, it was a full traditional Christmas dinner.

I was hungry, and had drunk quite a bit of wine, so I tucked in.

The conversation round the table was so similar to all of us at home, just fun chat, and we were all drawn into the conversation with questions from the others, who appeared genuinely interested in us.

I suppose we live naked and relax naked, and do open our home up to other naked people, so they were quite intrigued by us. It was amusing that we were referred to as the Curio Group, like we were some organised club. Little did they know that two days of exposure to Birch naked in the garden, seven summers ago, has pretty much corrupted all of us into the lifestyle.

Chat was abundant across the table as we ate, Birch was studying every aspect of them, like she was studying for a research paper, she was talking to Scott, the late thirties accountant for the club.

“The thing is Birch, most people fear us because we can do this, they simply cannot imagine walking around naked, and so they sit in judgement.” Birch agreed.

“But their fear is unfounded, most people really enjoy showering, they report it calms them down and helps them feel relaxed. One psychologist I spoke to at Uni, told me they felt it was because they were replicating nature. It was their theory that it was actually the nudity, and the feeling of water running down their body that was the cause of the calmness, as their body felt like it was in its natural state, and the process of washing was irrelevant. I find that notion really interesting, because if that is correct, then most people do not realise, they enjoy being naked, and should be naked more.”

I was really interested, was this right? I had no idea, and yet I had to admit, I loved showering. I always felt really relaxed and calm afterwards, was it my nakedness, I had no idea? The meal moved onward, and I was feeling calm and relaxed, as I chatted with Paula and Martha, I found the thing I loved the most, was no one had talked once about their job, or my career as a writer.

It is strange to meet people who understood my struggle for acceptance. Ever since I had returned home from university, I had found it hard, nothing I did appeared acceptable to a large percentage of those living in my village. The simple truth was, I could not live the life I wanted, and it was crazy, because I did not want that much.

I wanted to be sexual when I wanted to be, I did live naked in my home, I was not walking the streets nude. I wanted to be able to choose the colour of my own hair, I was not dictating everyone do it, in truth I did not want everyone copying my hair, it was what I liked, and what I wanted, nothing more. Yet for seven years I had been forced to fight, no matter what good I tried to do. I was called for it, and that looked like it would even be spread to the national stage, as people like Peter Ford tried to use my lifestyle, as a means for my destruction. I really understood why these people hid their naked life.

As the meal ended, the table was cleared, as other members joined in the big clean up. We all offered to help, but were told we were guests, so we relaxed with drinks, and Kenny returned to the music, and the floor was free for dancing.

To be honest the music was not that inspiring, I have nothing against old classics, but in all honesty, they do not really pump up the Christmas spirit. I wandered over to Kenny, where Edwina was already looking at his laptop music selection, I looked at the list.

“Is there nothing a little more uplifting we could play?” Edwina was scrolling down the list.

“I am looking, it is all Christmas classics, just nothing we have ever heard of.” She clicked the internet browser open. “Don’t worry, we will get this place jiving, we just need some new stuff, leave it with me.”

Glenis and Paula were up dancing with a very bubbly Deb’s, Birch grabbed my hand and pulled me close.

“Can I interest you in a dance young sexy lady?”

I looked at her bright smiling face, yep, she was tipsy, she held my waist as we swayed, her eyes dancing, and her long flowing white hair sparkling, with her tinsel crown, she breathed softly, as if calm in every ounce of her body.

“This is nice, these people are nice.” She smiled as she looked around the room.

“I am glad I came, as you know I did not want to? Having met all these people and spoken to them, I can see we are not so different, it is nice to know we are not alone.”

The music suddenly changed, and a conga came on, Deb’s gave

a scream, and suddenly everyone was getting up, and joining on the growing line. Birch spun me round, and grabbed my hips and we joined the line. The room was suddenly filled with "Oi!"

We all laughed out loud, and made our way hopping and dancing, round the whole room. There were wiggles and jiggles and bouncing in the most unexpected ways, and yet I loved it, this was the human form in its most authentic, and what I loved the most, was the women did not care, they were having fun, and the fact their bodies were bouncing to the music, just made it more fun for them.

For over an hour we danced, and sung our hearts out, and the club revelled in it, Paula was in her element, as she looked red in the face and cut in to dance with me.

"This has been the liveliest event I have ever seen here; wow you guys are amazing; I am so glad you came. Normally everyone is ready to go home at ten, but look at them, they are having the time of their lives, thanks Abby for doing this." I smiled.

"It has been really fun, all of us have been made so welcome, we have had a great night."

There was a yell from the corner, and Chloe came out with three hula hoops round her waist, she danced a wild gyrating dance, as the hoops spun round her, and everyone started to clap.

Chloe slipped a hoop down to her knees, I was blown away by the way she swirled her hips, she was way more supple than I thought she was, although when I thought about it, she knew every sexual position invented. One hoop hit the floor, as the two remained on her waist, she stepped out of it, and Birch gave a wild scream and ran to it, she stepped in and spun the hoop, and her hips began to gyrate.

Holy shit, she looked good, I watched her waist slowly moving, I had seen her do that as she ground down on me, I could feel myself becoming aroused, I was getting really wet watching her. The rest of the room was on their feet clapping and cheering, as Chloe and Birch side by side spun their hoops. Chloe gave a wiggle and another hoop dropped, Glenis gave a scream and came running across the floor, and jumped into the hoop, all the club members cheered, it was getting really loud in here.

The clapping continued, and Glenis bless her kept that hoop

going, I could not have kept it going that long, I started to laugh, enjoying the fun, and watched Birch, and clapped along. She was smiling and her eyes were sparkling with joy, she looked at me and blew me a kiss, I giggled and blew one back, she was amazing.

Chloe was having the time of her life laughing and smiling, and gasping for breath, she blew a kiss to everyone and the hoop dropped to the floor. She staggered over breathing heavily and sweating, Paula ran out and jumped in, and started to spin the hoop on her hips. It is funny really, in that moment, all I could think of was Birch seven years ago sat on the lawn at my mum's house.

"Deads, it is not that big a deal, so okay, people take a few minutes to adjust, it is the three dreaded minutes of fear, but once people are naked, they get used to it and forget they have no clothes on. Seriously, they feel dressed, and we all do the same things dressed people do, we party, hike, canoe, and hang out, we just feel more at ease, more comfortable because we do not have the clothing to restrict us, and our skin can breathe. It is the natural way; I think it is the only way, so many fear being naked, but it is irrational. People have been told to fear it, and then when they do it, they realise they have been conned by big business and organised religion. There was a time we all lived naked, we have just forgotten our roots, I live a natural life and I am not ashamed, there is nothing lewd or sexual about my body, it only becomes sexual if I chose it."

She was right, and we had all over the years come to understand that, and chosen to live our own naked lives.

Chloe sat down breathing hard with a huge smile, I patted her shoulder, I don't think this club had ever had as much fun, and Chloe had brought a unique sense of fun to them all, and judging by the noise, they were thoroughly enjoying themselves.

Before we knew it, like all good things, the time had slipped by, and it was gone twelve. We were all hot and sweaty, and tipsy, but all smiling, it really had been enormous fun. Saying goodbye was sad, we all got loads of hugs. Martha, gave us all a complimentary pass for ten visits in the New Year, and we posed for a picture, which we were assured would only remain in the club, and would be framed on the wall with the others. I saw a wall at the back filled with pictures from over the years, and was happy to know, the Curio's would not be forgotten.

Glenis and Paula walked us to the door, and wrapped in our robes, we said goodbye, and ran giggling to the car. It was more than a little bit chilly, and we all huddled together in the back shivering. Deb's who had been on coffee and fruit juice all night, started up Petal, and we drove down the driveway and out of the open gates.

We were all tired and a little bit tipsy, and huddled together as we sat back, and watched the darkness outside, there was a little light drizzle. It is funny how the ride home always feels faster than the journey there, and before we knew it, we were going through the gates, and up to the front of the house, and everything was quiet on Waterside Lane.

I stood out in the cool drizzle, just for a moment and breathed the air, the night was silent, I am not a huge fan of winter, but I do love dark quiet nights. I felt a shiver, and walked towards the door, I have no idea why, but I stopped and looked back, there was nothing there. I just felt an unpleasant feeling, and I got goose bumps, it was probably just the night chill? I walked through the door and locked it behind me, the warmth of the house surrounded me, and I smiled, back to the warmth and the cosiness of my safe place, it was good to be home.

I was covered in body paint, and headed to my room, the shower was running, Birch sat on my bed tying her hair up.

"I am having a shower to wash the paint off, are you going to join me?" I slipped off my robe, and she smiled, and got up off the bed.

Holding her hand, I followed her into the bathroom, and into the shower, she closed the glass door and pulled me close, as we stood under the hot water. She looked down on me as the water cascaded down my face.

"Tonight, was fun, I watched you all night, and I enjoyed seeing you like that, those are our kind of people, open minded and none judgemental, you looked so beautiful, like a prize flower in a bouquet of foliage."

She leaned in and kissed me softly and slowly, and I felt calm and loved, as I kissed her back. I think tonight I realised the importance of acceptance; I had never really thought that much about it. I have just been fighting for it, and stood in the club, I had understood that long before even coming home that summer, at the end of my first year of Uni. Birch had accepted me as the blue eyed, blonde, naïve, almost virgin, I was.

The important thing was, once I changed, she naturally accepted me, I think it is the first time in my life, another person has done that, she never once questioned it. I did not have to fight for it, she just looked at me and said, yep, that is who you are, and maybe that is the reason why I fell so deeply in love with her.

Birch saw me from the inside out, and accepted that. I think everyone else has seen me from the outside of who I am, the body, the hair, and the awkwardness. She saw my heart, my soul, my struggle with myself, and she just simply knew who I was, and liked it. It felt powerful to understand that.

She washed me clean, and I washed her, it was gentle and caring, it was not the lust filled jump on each other, as had often been the case, she touched me softly, and caressed me with the soapy sponge, and it felt sensual and loving.

We came out of the shower wrapped in towels and just lay together, hardly talking, saying words by just talking with our fingers and eyes, as we lay facing each other, and I have never in my life felt as loved or cared for, as I do at this moment, facing her on the bed as I do now, and it is powerful, and fulfilling.

Deb's came out of her room rubbing her hair with a towel, she sauntered along the hall towards Chloe's room, and walked in. Her shower was still running in her bathroom, she crossed the room and walked in, where she saw Chloe washing herself and humming in the shower.

"Chloe, can I borrow your dryer, mine does not seem to be working?" Chloe smiled as she rubbed herself with the sponge.

"Yeah, no worries, although I left it on the table in the kitchen, I was using it to dry off the body paint earlier."

"Thanks, I will bring it back when I am done with it, you missed some under your boobs." Chloe lifted her breasts, and had a look, she looked up at Deb's and smiled.

"Perv." Deb's giggled.

“Hey I told you, just because you are straight, it doesn’t mean I won’t look, a girl can dream.”

Deb’s came out of Chloe’s room chuckling, with the towel round her neck, and walked down the stairs towards the kitchen, she walked in and saw the hair dryer with Chloe’s brush, and picked it up. Outside the drizzle was picking up, and hail came rattling down the windows. The light flashed and she nervously looked up, as the hail pelted even harder against the glass.

The lightning flashed again, and Deb’s saw the figure of a man carrying something over his shoulder, it was only for an instant, but it was long enough.

I rolled on top of Birch kissing her softly, she wiggled and gave a soft moan, and I landed the briefest of soft kisses on her breast, she gave a soft sigh.

“Oh Deads, this is so erotic, I am so turned on.” I kissed her softly again and she caught her breath, her nipple was growing huge. “Oh Deads!” The lightening lit up the whole room.

Downstairs, there was a blood curdling scream, I sat bolt upright, as a wave of terror shot through me.

“What the hell was that?” Birch sat up.

“Whatever it is, something is very wrong.” I slid off her, and jumped onto the floor. We came out of the room and saw Chloe looking terrified her hair dripping.

“What the fuck was that?”

I shook my head, Birch was passed me, and heading down the stairs, we followed. The lights in the kitchen were out, Birch headed down the hallway, and into the kitchen. Deb’s was cowered under the table as we entered behind Birch, and she was crying, I stopped, in the darkness and gasped with shock, her face looked as white as death. Birch crouched down in front of her and reached out to her.

“Deb’s Sweetie what is wrong?” She lurched into Birch’s arms and wailed.

“Oh Birch, Birch... It was horrible... I saw someone outside carrying a body!” My skin turned instantly ice cold, and I shuddered.

Chapter 20

Safe Place.

My blood had just turned to ice, Chloe looked at me looking frightened.

"Body... What the fuck does she mean... Body?"

I was fixed on Deb's, as she wailed into Birch's shoulder, I have never in all the time I have known her, seen her that terrified, and it frightened me in ways I could not describe. Chloe was breathing hard, she gripped my arm, it hurt, and I looked at her, her eyes were wide.

"Abby I am scared, where is Edwina, we all heard that scream?"

My heart lurched, Chloe did not have to say much, I understood, she loved her sister, but was afraid, Deb's wept into Birch.

"He was out there on the patio, and he had a body over his shoulder." I was breathing harder than I realised, I looked at Chloe and grabbed her hand.

"Come on."

We both ran at high speed up the stairs, and then headed down the hall towards Edwina's room. We slid to a halt gasping, I was slightly ahead, I looked at Chloe, nodded, and turned the handle. I pushed hard, the door burst open, as we both crammed through the doorway together, and stood gasping.

Edwina was bent over, leaning on her desk with her head phones on, holding a controller. Behind her, was Luke wearing his headset, resting his controller on her back, as he slowly slid in and out of her from behind. I had never seen anything like it, Edwina was smiling and kept gasping as she tried to focus on the game, it was clear to me now why she was called Banger Bobbles.

Chloe was gasping for air, she walked over to Edwina and grabbed her head set, Edwina jerked back into Luke and gasped.

"Oh shit!"

Luke grabbed her hips, the controller slid down past her ass, he held her stable, still buried deep inside her. Chloe looked panicked, and Edwina who had turned to yell, saw her face. She stood up quickly, and Luke was expelled from her, wow he was big and thick, he had a really nice dick, I could see why Edwina was always banging him. Chloe burst into tears.

"I thought he had got you... Deb's saw a guy carrying a body on the patio, and when you did not come down, I thought it was you." Luke looked puzzled, as Edwina grabbed Chloe and pulled her close.

"I am safe baby, please don't cry, I am so sorry."

Chloe wrapped her arms round her sister and sobbed. Luke looked at me, unconcerned he was still pretty frigging huge and stiff, as it waved around in front of him like a light sabre. As much as I wanted not to, I could not help but stare at it.

"Abby what the hell happened?" I looked up at him.

"Huh?" I shook my head.

"Sorry, wow nice dick." He smiled. "Luke, Deb's was in the kitchen alone, and the lightening flashed." Outside the lightening streaked, and more hail belted down.

"She said she saw a man carrying a body, she screamed, and we all came to her, but we have not really checked. She is with Birch scared shitless and as white as a ghost, sat under the kitchen table. Chloe freaked because her sister was not there, so we rushed here to check."

He nodded grabbed Edwina's chair and sat down. The game disappeared off the screen, as he clicked open the security system.

"How long ago was this?" I was not sure, everything had happened so fast, I tried to think.

"I was with Birch, we heard the scream, we hurried down and found Deb's under the table, she broke down, and sobbed then told us. Chloe panicked, and we ran up here to see you two gamer banging, that took a moment to contemplate, and then we told you, so ten to fifteen abouts." He opened the system and a blank static screen came up. Edwina turned to see the monitor, still hugging Chloe.

"How strong is the storm?" I shrugged.

"I don't know, it's a storm, it flashes and bangs." Edwina looked at Luke, and shook her head.

"If it was that powerful it would have affected the game, what the hell is going on?" He shrugged, she turned to me. "Abby, Birch and Deb's are downstairs, yes?"

I nodded, she had a sense of urgency to her, and I was freaked out by it. She turned back to Luke.

"Do a full system diagnostic, I am going to check on Izzy, and then I'll go check the server." He nodded and started to type, Edwina released Chloe, and held her face, she wiped her eyes with her thumbs.

"Chloe sweetheart, I am fine, we need to check how Izzy is, okay, and I need you with me?" Chloe took a breath and swallowed.

"I am alright now I know you are fine." She smiled and kissed her head. "Come on then."

As Luke typed, we all came out of Edwina's room, my breathing was regulating, but my heart was still thumping in my head. It probably sounds crazy, but I saw Deb's door, and just reacted. I ran into her room, and there was her bag on the bed, I grabbed it, and tipped it upside down, the contents spilled out onto her duvet. It had tampons, condoms, two vibrators, a shit load of book tokens in it, and some chewing gum. The one thing I knew was there fell out last as I shook it harder, the taser hit the duvet, I dropped the bag and snatched it up.

When I came out of her room, Edwina and Chloe were already at Izzy's door, I saw them go in, I looked at the taser, it was small and looked like an electric razor. It had a safety lock on the back, and a power button on the side, just above the grip, it looked simple enough. I have never actually used one, so I just assumed you pushed it on to someone and hit power. I felt a little more confident.

Izzy was passed out on the bed, she held an empty glass in her hand, and on the floor was an empty whiskey bottle. Edwina grabbed her, and shook her, and patted her face.

"Izzy wake up, we need you awake come on, wake the hell up." Izzy shook limply on the bed, Chloe watched feeling nervous and scared.

"She is out cold Edwina, maybe we should leave her." She looked back.

"I want all of us together, I will not leave her here." She turned back to Izzy, and lifted her hand. "Izzy, sorry, but I need you awake." Her hand came down at a very fast pace.

SLAAAAPPP! Chloe flinched, and screwed up her eyes.

Izzy's arm shot up and gripped Edwina by the throat, she gagged, and gripped her hand, and tried to pull it off, she started to choke. Chloe grabbed Izzy and shook her.

"IZZY FOR FUCK'S SAKE WAKE UP, YOU ARE KILLING HER!"

Izzy's eyes popped open, she saw Edwina turning blue in the face, tugging at her hand and fighting for breath, and suddenly understanding, she let go. Edwina fell back gasping for air as Izzy sat up. Chloe fell to her knees as Edwina gasped and choked, red marks round her neck from Izzy's fingers. Chloe gasped as she looked back.

"Holy fuck Izzy you almost killed her with one hand." Izzy blinked, and shook her head, she looked at Edwina gasping.

"Shit... Sorry, I get weird when I am in bed, I have been attacked twice in my sleep, it is just a natural reaction." Chloe looked at Edwina.

"She is a fucking sleep ninja, if she is ever late for work, I am never ever fucking waking her up, holy shit she nearly killed you with one hand." Izzy swung her legs off the bed, and rubbed her face, she looked really rough.

"What is the big emergency anyhow?" Edwina swallowed and gasped.

"Deb's saw someone outside on the patio, she says they were carrying a body."

"What?" Chloe shrugged.

"That is what she says she saw, and honestly, she was looking so fucking terrified, I believed her." Izzy nodded.

"Where is everyone, are they safe?" Edwina nodded, and gave a cough.

"The video system has gone out in the storm, Luke is in my room rebooting it, Birch and Deb's are downstairs and Abby is...?" She looked round. "Actually, where is Abby, she was here a minute ago?"

I was walking up the hall towards the room, when Chloe came

bursting out of Izzy's room, I stopped, and she gave a sigh of relief.

"Christ, we thought we had lost you, are you alright?" I nodded.

"Is Izzy okay?" Chloe started walking towards me.

"We don't need to worry about Izzy, she is as dangerous in her sleep, as she is awake, she is a fucking sleep ninja."

"Huh?" She smiled.

"I will tell you in a bit, Jesus Abby, she is scary."

Izzy and Edwina came out of the room, and I breathed a sigh of relief. I waited for them all to meet me, and then turned with them. Edwina was croaky.

"All of you get in the library and open the security system, Luke is doing a debug, I am going to go and check the server, just get in the library, and we will restore all the cameras, and then we will take a good look round."

We split at the stairs, and headed down, Edwina stood on the landing, next to the hand rail, and watched us to make sure we went to the library, Birch was there already sat at her computer. She had already opened the system on her computer, and had a screen full of static. I pulled Deb's into my arms, and gave her a big squeeze, and then released her, and looked at her, she was as pale as paper, I won't deny, seeing her like that freaked me out.

"Are you alright, I hope you don't mind, I grabbed your taser, here." I pushed it into her hand. She gripped it tight.

"I am alright Abby, I am really scared, it was horrible, I thought it was one of us." I shook my head.

"We are all safe, Anthony went off to Michael's, so he is safe too." She nodded and gave a sigh of relief. I did not want to admit it, but I was really scared.

Edwina stood on the landing, and watched us go into the library, and then opened the door up to the Attic, and flicked on the lights. Percy was lay across the steps; she gave a sigh.

"God, is there nowhere she does not screw this frigging creepy ass thing?"

She stepped over the huge bear, with its long rubber strap on dildo, and headed up the stairs to the multi coloured Attic.

"Bloody place looks like an acid palace." She walked up the far end where the server was stationed, its lights flickered in sequence, she knelt down.

"What the hell?"

The ethernet cable was unplugged, no wonder the cameras were static, there was no internet connection. She picked it up and plugged it back in. another set of lights came to life and flashed. How it had happened she had no idea, she turned and headed back down the attic.

"Frigging Chloe I bet, rolling around with that bloody perverted toy of hers, daft bitch must have caught the cable, we will have to put a barrier round it." She stopped and looked down to the opposite end of the attic.

"OH SHIT!" The window was open just a few inches, and snow was blowing in. The thunder had brought hail, and then snow, Edwina turned and looked back down the Attic.

"Holy shit someone unplugged it on purpose."

The sudden reality of the moment hit her, someone had climbed in through the locked window, unplugged the system, and they had been seen on the patio. It took seconds to work out.

"Oh God no, it's Rodney... He has got back in, that crazy bloody maniac is loose in the house, he knows it as well as us, but who was the body, what the hell is he up too?"

She ran to the stairs, Percy was gone, and suddenly everything made sense, and it terrified her.

"Oh Christ, the sick bastard has a costume, he has frigging dressed up as Percy." Her heart leapt in her throat. "I have got to warn the others, the system will reboot, they will not see anything for a few minutes."

Birch was at her computer, Izzy was flopped back in Edwina's chair, rubbing her face. I was at my computer, Chloe sat at the spare, and Deb's was between Birch and me on the floor, when suddenly the monitor flickered, and pictures started popping onto the screen. The patio lit up in night vision, my heart filled with dread.

"Oh Christ, it is snowing!" Birch gave a beaming smile.

"I know Sweetie, isn't it wonderful, I love snow?" Deb's looked at us both.

"Seriously, we have a maniac carrying bodies round the place, and you are discussing the weather?" I felt guilty.

“Sorry, but you know how I hate the stuff.” Birch gave a big beaming smile.

“Isn’t it pretty?” She stared at the screen and her face dropped. “Why is Edwina making strange signs to the camera?” I turned and looked, Deb’s leaned in.

“She is using semaphore; it is what they use in the Guides.” Chloe suddenly stood up and backed away from the screen, she looked at us with wild looking eyes.

“She said Rodney!” Izzy, who was sat in Edwina’s chair, slowly coming round, sat up straight.

“And suddenly I am wide bloody awake… Where is he?” Chloe stared at the screen.

“She said Percy… Huh! What the fuck does that mean?” I looked at her.

“Is he in your room?” She frowned.

“He is always in my room, no one screws him only me.” I shook my head.

“Not your perverted bloody teddy, I was talking about Rodney?”

Chloe looked at the screen, only half the cameras were online, they would flick on one at a time, as they reconnected to the server. Downstairs, was coming on, the studio came into view, then the living room, both were empty, I watched trying to see if there was anything that would give us a clue as to where he was. Izzy stood up quickly, and we all jumped with fear.

“We have to find him and contain him, this is not your problem, this is mine. Jemi call the authorities and get a team here asap.” She nodded and picked up her phone, and started to dial. I looked at Izzy.

“You are not going alone, are you?” She looked back and smiled.

“Deadly, I have to deal with this.” I stood up.

“Screw that Izzy, you are one of us, and we all stand together.” I looked at the screen.

“He is not downstairs or in the cellar, he must be upstairs, Luke and Edwina are up there, so we go together.” Chloe nodded and Izzy smiled.

“Thanks girls, that really does mean a lot.”

Okay so at this point my head is screaming things like, ‘are you frigging deranged?’ and ‘what the hell is up with you?’

and honestly, I could not deny, at this moment in time, I did not understand why I was being so bloody stupid. There was a maniac upstairs, who's last sighting was carrying a body across the patio, and I did have an internal debate going on, and questioning why I was about to walk towards a complete lunatic?

We came out of the library as Birch started to talk on the phone, and stepped onto the stairs. We were not fast, and crept as quietly as we could, I was not in that big a rush to meet Rodney. Edwina came tearing down the attic stairs, and burst out through the door.

The pictures on the monitor flicked on, and as Birch talked to the hospital, she saw the frame click open on the landing, and saw Percy with his big rubber dick stood next to the attic door, Birch stood staring.

"Oh shit... Percy?" She shook her head, and spoke into the phone.

"Yeah sorry, look he is here I have him on camera, he is dressed in a costume of a teddy bear, and I think he has a weapon, you have my address now get your fucking ass here, my family are at risk. I have to go help, just hurry the gates are open and I will leave the door off the latch."

We were half way up when there was a loud crash, as the attic door opened at speed, Percy stopped it, and pushed it closed with power. It smashed into Edwina sending her reeling onto the landing, and Percy pounced. With the bang and the squeal, we felt sudden urgency, and rushed up the last half of the stairs, and came to a sudden halt.

"Huh!?"

It was really hard to describe what I saw at the top of the stairs; in fact, it made no frigging sense to me at all. Edwina was rolling around on the floor pretending to fight with Percy, who had a big knife, it was really frigging bizarre. Chloe looked and gasped, she got angry and yelled down the landing.

"WHAT THE FUCK EDWINA, YOU HAVE LUKE YOU GREEDY BITCH, LEAVE MY FUCKING PERCY ALONE!"

She kicked out, and Percy rolled off her, she scrambled backwards, squealing, the knife was stuck upright in the floor. I must admit she was brilliant at making it all look real, I wanted to applaud, and then… Percy stretched across the floor and grabbed her leg, and dragged her back towards him, and reached with his arm for the knife. Deb's, screamed out in terror making all of us jump, my heart almost exploded.

To say at this point I absolutely shit myself, is an understatement, cold bloody terror ran through me, Chloe's sex toy was alive. Deb's took two steps back, and wagged the taser in her hand.

"Okay guys something here is really frigging messed up, because I am pretty sure Percy just grabbed Edwina, and I so do not want to admit that." Chloe's eyes were wide.

"Holy fuck, I must have shagged him to life, is that even possible? Guys, this is fucking awesome, he can fuck me properly now." Yeah, she watches way too much TV. She looked over the moon, and delighted, Deb's looked at her, as Edwina kicked out at Percy, her eyes narrowed.

"That is seriously what you frigging took from that? Chloe your teddy is trying to rape or kill Edwina, oh hell, you are way messed up than I thought."

Edwina squealed and kicked out again, she was trying to crawl back, but was running out of space. I was frozen to the spot, my heart pounding and trying to understand everything properly, it was Deb's that leapt to the rescue.

Percy was up on his knees, and was about to pounce on Edwina, when Deb's ran up behind him, and shoved the taser right into what I assumed were his bollocks. Izzy appeared with a baseball bat, I had not even noticed she had disappeared, she saw what was going on and shouted at the top of her voice.

"DEB'S NO… HE REALLY ENJOYS THAT?" I looked at her in complete loss.

"HUH…!?"

It was too late, she gripped the trigger and pressed it, and Percy sat bolt upright and shook, and made a weird happy squealing sort of noise. Percy dithered, and then relaxed. I suddenly realised that Percy had been sexually stimulated, and had indeed climaxed, and honestly, I was impressed, and appalled at the same time.

Chloe suddenly, with Izzy's involvement understood what was

happening and pointed in horror, as she stared at Izzy.

"DID YOUR EX BOYFRIEND JUST CUM INSIDE MY BEAR, BECAUSE THAT IS FUCKING WELL OUT OF ORDER, ONLY I CUM WITH PERCY?"

Chloe was very pissed off, she snatched the baseball bat out of Izzy's hand, and ran at Percy. Deb's fell back looking terrified, there was a distinct smell of singed fur, and a large black hole, exposing two pink testicles. She shuddered.

"Oh hell, no one wants to see that, I am really starting to go off teddies."

Chloe waded in on Percy, as Birch hurried up the stairs, she raised the bat, and brought it down hard on the large head of Percy, and screamed as her eyes filled with tears.

"GET OUT OF MY BEAR, YOU FUCKING RAPIST, I FUCKING MEAN IT, YOU TEDDY PERVERT, LEAVE MY PERCY THE FUCK ALONE!"

She swung and battered the head again; it already had a huge oversized dint in it. Percy lay still on the floor, as Chloe lifted the bat again. She sobbed and tears streamed down her face. She was shaking violently as Birch grabbed her hand.

"Chloe Sweetie, if you hit Percy any more, he will never get erect again, he is sleeping now, so leave him." Her lip was trembling, her voice was shaky, and tears were streaming from her wide open eyes, and she was shaking violently.

"He is a rapist, Birch; he is raping my Percy."

I felt a huge surge run right through me, and gave out a loud gasp, and felt utterly and completely shocked and shaken. It suddenly hit me full on in the face, and I reeled in the shock of it, as my hand came up to my mouth, and I felt tears well up in my eyes.

"Oh my god, he violated her safe space!"

I felt the air trap in my lungs, Izzy took hold of my free hand, I turned and looked at her, as everything suddenly made complete sense.

"Percy is my archway, isn't he?" She smiled and squeezed my hand.

"We all have something we run to Abby; Percy is hers."

I nodded; I understood now. It felt so shocking and so violent,

I shook my hand free of Izzy, turned and ran. I ran down the landing, and as Birch slid the bat out of Chloe's shaking hand, I dragged her into my arms. The tears were streaming down my cheeks, as I pulled her close and held her as tight as I could.

"Chloe it is not Percy, it is a fake. Percy is safe and unharmed, he is safe Chloe, he is perfectly safe and protected, that is not him, that is a nasty bear." I squeezed her as tight as I could, Birch turned and smiled, and reached out to my cheek, her eyes filled with compassion.

"You are so amazing, you worked it out."

I felt shocked and horrified, all I wanted to do was get Chloe away, I didn't want her to see this. I pulled her back and wiped her hair from her damp face, her eyes sparkled with tears, I shook my head.

"Do not cry, he is safe." She gave a sniffle and smiled, and I smiled back.

"I promised you Chloe, no one would hurt you, and I meant it, and that also meant Percy. Come on, let's go and see how he is doing?" She nodded and I took her hand, she was trembling.

Edwina lay gasping on the floor, Birch reached out her hand, and she took it, and sat up, then got up on her shaking legs, she looked at Rodney inside Percy, and shook her head.

"I fucking hate teddies."

Birch knelt down and pulled at the large dinted head, and it slipped away, there inside was the bloody face of an unshaved Rodney, he was out cold.

I cannot say, I completely understand everything that happened, but I understood how important my archway was to me growing up. It was a security thing to me, and it helped me by being something safe, somewhere I could go when I was afraid. After that night when Martin had tried to do what he did, I had run to my archway. I had huddled in the corner, I had again the night Birch found me. I have never really been able to explain why, which is why I think in my book Sanctuary Arch, I made it the one place my persecuted vampires could go, as it was a place where they could not be harmed.

Two years ago, I spent a sunny afternoon making love to Birch there, and it had become an even more significant place to me now. If Percy was something similar for Chloe, then I understood her better than most ever would. We walked into her room and I sat her on the bed, I turned and opened the large wardrobe door and there he was, a huge teddy wearing a strap on. I lifted him out, and sat him on the bed at her side, he was really bloody heavy to lift.

“See Chloe, he is safe, he has not been violated, he is as pure as ever.” She smiled.

“I bet you think I am messed up, don’t you?” I wiped the hair from her cheek.

“Chloe, we all have a safe place or object, mine is the old archway, yours is Percy, Deb’s is Phileas, I see nothing wrong in that at all. I take it the night at the church, when you got home you cuddled Percy didn’t you?” She nodded.

“I always cuddle him when I am frightened, it helps me feel better.” I smiled.

“I see nothing wrong in that, teddy’s have been comforting to many in the past. If it helps you cope with the bad, that is a good thing. I think Rodney understood that, which is why he got a costume like Percy, I know without doubt, he is the seriously messed up one.” She smiled.

“I am so glad he did nothing to Percy, God Abby, I really wanted to kill him.”

“I understand that, oh God Chloe, you have no idea how much I understand that. Okay I am going to go and help the others; will you be alright?” She gave a sigh and smiled.

“Yeah, I will be fine now... I am sorry if I scared you Abby.” I patted her knee.

“I am fine, do not worry about it, give Percy a cuddle from me.”

I left her alone with Percy, and went back to the others, Deb’s had taken Edwina to Luke in her room, he was so busy running diagnostics on the server, he had missed the feed on the other screen opposite.

The police arrived, and I grabbed a long top for Birch and myself, as I suddenly understood we were naked, not long after, the medical team arrived. Birch talked to the police, and edited Chloe completely out of the story, she had seen enough on the screen, and had been there, and so just replaced herself with the part of Chloe.

Rodney was strapped to a stretcher and carried out; it would be a long time before he would see the light of day again. It took about two hours to sort everything out, Luke gave Terry a call, and he came over to see Chloe, he thought it might help if she had something to cuddle other than Percy, Edwina was grateful and kissed him softly.

I stood in the kitchen with a coffee, it was gone four in the morning, and the snow was still falling, it was going to be deep. I flicked on the outdoor lights and watched as the garden disappeared, it was very beautiful, I just wish it did not have to be so cold. I was tired and needed sleep, yet again, just as we started to enjoy Christmas, something else had come along to try and ruin it, and it felt like everything was against us.

I sipped my coffee, holding the mug with two slightly trembling hands, watching the large fluffy flakes fall.

"This Christmas will be the best Birch ever has if it kills me, I will not let them all steal it from her." I put my cup on the island and walked through the hall, she was bolting the door, having locked it. She smiled as she took my hand.

"It is so pretty outside, I know you hate it, but Deads Sweetie, I cannot help it, I love the snow." I held her hand tight and walked up the stairs.

"I am glad you love it, it is a reminder of your home, and that is nice." She stopped, and I turned, and looked at her, she looked so serious.

"Deads, tonight you understood the meaning of Percy, I think you realised he was to her, as your arch is to you. We all have somewhere or something, and it is the safety and security we need, just like Phileas, or even Edwina's flash drive, have you not seen how protective she is over it? Let me ask you this, where did I run to when I was afraid?"

I looked at her, and her eyes sparkled with life, she smiled, and lifted her free hand to my chest, and placed it right in the centre.

"This is my place of safety, when I am afraid, I run to you. Uppermill was where I grew up, but this, this here, you, this is my home, I thought you knew that.

Chapter 21

Snowy Surprises.

I sat in the kitchen yawning, it was midday, and Roni and William were here, as was Mum, Deb's had phoned her parents and updated them, and like all things Wotton, the news had spread.

I had not had a huge amount of sleep, Birch and myself had arrived in Birch's room, to find Deb's in our bed, she was feeling insecure, and Chloe had Terry, so she invaded us. In a way it felt a little like old times, as we all collapsed and passed out, to get what little sleep we could. I felt sorry for Izzy and Birch, they had to go into work. Deb's sent a text to Denise, and asked her to open up for her, and she would join her later. We were woken by Edwina at eleven, when everyone showed up.

Chloe showed up around a quarter to twelve, it was the latest I had ever known her get up, she was tired, but very much like her normal self. Once she had put everything into place in her mind, she was fine, and simply drank coffee and smiled, although she did have black bags under her eyes, I assumed she did more than cuddle Terry last night.

I sat with Mum as she fussed, no matter how many times I told her I was fine, although it was nice, and I had missed seeing her. Finally, that horrible man Ford had stopped staking out her house, and she was able to come over in the snow. Roni and William would be flying off tomorrow on their Christmas vacation, with Bradley and Ellen, and slipped some wrapped presents under the tree. We all sat and talked, I explained the previous night's events, and told them of how amazing Edwina, and Birch were, and also how worried I was that Birch had to work so tired.

The afternoon felt like an endless stream of interruptions, as parcels constantly arrived, we had all been shopping on line, and a long row of courier services delivered all our packages. The long table in the library was starting to pile high, as packages were placed there for each of us, all to open in private, we had been gift buying, and looking at the pile on the table, it looked like we would need a lot more space under the Christmas tree, for them.

Edwina wanted the Attic, she told me that her and Luke wanted to work on the server and the rest of G5 would be joining them. After last night she was worried that Rodney had been able to break in unnoticed and disable the cameras, I was too busy to worry, and as each of them arrived after doing their jobs, I sent them up to her.

Birch finally made it home, it was the last day of the practice, tomorrow was an office party for all the staff, so she would be going in, but her last client was done with until the New Year.

She looked really tired; she hugged her parents. I went to make coffee, and carried another forty bottles of wine down to the cellar, our wine rack was starting to fill up, and some of her wealthier clients had a good taste in wine. My mum came down, as I sorted out the different types into the rack, she smiled hugging herself, it was a bit chilly down here.

"Abby are you not cold, you are only wearing a t shirt?" I looked back at her, and shook my head.

"To be honest no, I suppose living without clothing I have got used to it. I think Chloe is the same, although running round the garden in the snow in just her boots is a bit too much for me, although I have to say mum, seeing snow angels with bum prints is funny." She smiled.

"I spoke to your father earlier." I put the bottle in the rack and turned to face her.

"Is he alright mum?" She nodded.

"For now, Graham has done a lot of damage, he is going to struggle. I know what you and Birch did Abby. I offered to sell the house to help him get his share of the cash back, and he told me, in a way, it helped save his business. Abby why, why do that, I told you be careful?" I walked across the cellar and leant in front of her, against the old table.

"I did not have the money, I could get it, I just needed two weeks. Had he given me the time, I would have paid it willingly, even now I have no issue with it. You are my mum, and that is our family home, and you belong in it, I was never going to let him sell it. Dad refused my deal because I was rude to Angela, he knew if I paid straight away, it would kill my trust fund, and he wanted to punish me, I didn't care mum, it's just money." She gave a sigh.

"That money came from both of us Abby, all your life we have both contributed, neither of us wanted you to struggle like we had in the early days." I shrugged.

"You mean more to me than that money, honestly, I would have given it him, but he would not give me time, and so Birch stepped in and put a cheque on the table, and told him she wanted the deal done by lunch time the next day. He took it, folded it neatly and left, and I was glad he went. Look mum, I am not enjoying seeing him suffer, honestly, I am not, but I have always hated watching you suffer, Birch helped me to free you, and neither of us regret it. I love dad, I still think you do in a way, but it is not enough for you mum, well you have the chance now to redo your life." She smiled.

"Wow you grew up. Abby it is not easy for me to accept this, I have always paid my own way, I do have some cash you know, let me pay back both of you." I shook my head.

"You cannot do that, I offered to pay Birch back and she refused. Birch does not want you to know, she told me this was her way of paying you back, for watching over her two years ago. She did it, because that stopped her mum and dad worrying, so you can never tell her dad told you. Mum one day that house will be mine, and I am not leaving Birch, we swore a commitment to each other, and I will honour it, because I meant it when I swore it. In a way one day we will both get the house, so stop worrying, we will be paid back in time, although I will never sell that house, that is where Birch and me began." She smiled, and nodded her head, she understood me.

"I am so proud of you Abby, you inspire me to be better, I guess I am cornered." I giggled.

"Yeah, Birch has a funny way of doing that with her grand gestures of kindness. She really loves you mum; she cares so much about all of us. Dad is an idiot to not see that, his comment hurt her so deeply, because she cared about him so much, he has a lot of making up to do, I hope he realises that now?" She shivered in the cool atmosphere.

"He has learned a lot recently, I am sure in time he will do a lot of reflecting on everything, he has some endurance to go through Abby, and he does not have the sort of support he is used to. I believe he is innocent, and when asked I will publicly support him, but I will not go to him, that is Angela's job now, if she has the stomach for it." I understood, in all honesty I was not sure Angela would stand by him, but I thought I would say little, and sit back and see.

I finished sorting the wine, and walked back up the steps to the kitchen, mum appeared happier to be in a warmer room. We sat in the kitchen, and were joined by a tired Deb's, who had left her car and trudged through the snow to the shop. As expected, there was little trade, but the weekend was coming up, and it was to be a busy one, Saturday and Sunday there was several brass bands booked to play carols, on the village green, for which there would be a host of carol singers. It was a big tradition of the village, and regardless of weather, a lot of tourists flocked in from all over. There would be food vendors, and a few side attractions, and Santa's Grotto would be at its height.

Norman and Daisy also had a thriving trade in freshly cut Christmas Trees, and had stocked up, and Mum and Anthony had made sure Norman had plenty of leaflets for all the events. Amanda Fernlee, the florist, was very well known for her designer door wreaths and cemetery pots, and she had a team of eight people working none stop creating them for sale. She was given a special licence to extend her display each year, so she could use up more of the paving to display on, and she also had a wooden cart parked in the roadway. It was decorated with fairy lights, and it was quite common for people picking up orders, to drive up, and collect them from her without getting out of their vehicles.

This was the big weekend before Christmas, and the Village of Wotton Dursley, was gearing up ready, and all of us had been called onto standby, as volunteers for the big Christmas weekend. I was dreading it, I could do rain and cold, but I really hated snow and slush, so my feelings of excitement, were somewhat diminished, whereas Chloe, Deb's and especially Birch, were becoming more and more excited, and I was starting to feel like their mum. One good thing to happen, was William bought all of us some amazing snow boots, so at least my feet would be warm and dry.

Even though we knew they were going away for a great and fun Christmas, saying goodbye and wishing them a safe flight, was really hard. I pulled Roni into a hug, and squeezed her tight.

"Have fun and enjoy the sand and the surf." Roni stood back and looked at me, she smiled.

"You have changed Abby, I see more substance to you than last time, I am very impressed, and no matter what happens, just have an amazing Christmas together." She kissed her finger and touched my nose and giggled. William dragged me into a bear like hug.

"Have a crazy and wild Christmas, you little gothic snow grinch." He kissed my cheek as I giggled.

Birch as always wept, and smiled at the same time, she hugged her mum and dad forever. Finally, she let them go, and wiped her eyes, I slipped my arms round her.

"You will see them again in two weeks, let them go and have a great time, and we will have the best Christmas ever." She turned round and faced me, and smiled.

"I know, I am really looking forward to it, I want a Christmas that is just us, but I hate them being out of the country, especially when it is snowing." I smiled.

"We have new snow boots." She gave a cheeky smile.

"I want to run naked round the garden in them, and make snow angels." Her eyes twinkled, with devilish delight. "I want you Deads, I want you naked in boots, and outside with me, looking sexy in the snow with me, and then I want you in a hot bath." I shook my head.

"Oh, Birch, please don't make me do this, I really don't like the snow." She leaned in and whispered, in a slow sensual voice in my ear.

"Have you ever had long slow, naughty sensual sex in deep snow; do you know how hot that gets me?" Oh god I am so weak, my legs dithered.

"Oh crap, I am getting naked, and grabbing my boots." She squealed with happiness, and clapped her hands.

"Me too!"

How do I let her talk me into these things? I am crazy, all she says is sex, and she is hot, and I just cave in, and now I am stood naked in my kitchen, in snow boots, shivering, as I stare out of the open door, watching Birch, Chloe and Deb's, all completely naked, running round the garden like maniacs. Birch waved.

"Sweetie... Come on, come play with me." Oh god, why did I agree with this?

I took a deep breath, and gritting my teeth, I ran outside towards her, hearing my boots crunch in the fresh snow. I did not want to stop running, because I was terrified if I stopped, I would freeze to death. I ran right past Birch and kept on, she turned with a squeal of joy and ran after me.

I looked back, and saw her crazy happy eyes, and that bothered me so much, so I ran faster, in hope of not dying from hyperthermia.

Birch in super happy mode was dangerous, especially when surrounded by several feet of fresh soft white ice cold snow. I was heading towards the back fence at high speed, with a laughing and wild Birch coming after me, and I did not realise how deep the drifting snow was here.

My legs locked, and suddenly I was falling face down in the snow, I landed with a soft thud, it was almost noiseless. I hit the white freezing cold snow, but I was so hot from running, I hardly noticed. I rolled over in the snow, as I sunk back, and Birch launched herself with a wild scream, she came hurtling onto me with a fit of giggles, and suddenly I was buried in a deep drift, with her bright sparkling eyes.

With her white skin, and her white hair, she was almost like some feral snow creature, she leaned down and kissed me, and I wrapped my arms and legs around her, more as a way of keeping them off the snow, and kissed her passionately. How could I be so hot, I was lay in the equivalent of mother nature's freezer? She moved to my neck, and kissed me softly, I could feel my skin tingle all over.

Deb's screamed, and ran away from the pool, Chloe appeared armed with snow balls, she trudged through the snow with her new boots on. A snow ball whizzed through the air and skimmed off Deb's head, she screamed and looked behind her, and another hit her right in the face, she went reeling backwards covered in snow. Chloe screamed and bounced around.

"SCORE!" Deb's lay in the snow gasping for air and laughing wildly. Chloe ran up, and leaned over her panting as she smiled, she offered a hand.

"Tag your it."

Deb's giggled, and took her hand, then pulled, Chloe over balanced, and fell over. Deb's rolled over on top of her, she sat up and grabbed a huge handful of snow, and smashed it onto her. Chloe squealed and wriggled around, Debs sat up giggling, on top of Chloe.

Somewhere towards the end of the garden, loud climatic moans rang out, Debs turned and looked towards us, as Birch writhed between my legs.

"Oh god Chloe they are having sex in the snow... Oh it's not fair, I want to have sex now." She looked back at Chloe.

"I really need to screw something Chloe." Chloe swallowed hard.

"Yeah, me too, I have never done it in the snow." Deb's looked at her.

"There is only us out here though, Jimmy is in Japan, and Terry is busy with the G5."

Chloe stared at her; Deb's leaned forward towards her. She slowly lowered her face right above Chloe's, as she sat on her waist, she got closer and closed her eyes, Chloe swallowed, was she really going to do this? Deb's moved in, and her lips were almost on Chloe's, and then SPLAT!

Snow exploded all over her, and Chloe let out a scream of joy, she twisted throwing Deb's off into the snow.

"Tag your it." She jumped up and ran off, and Deb's lay back in the snow, and gave a long disappointed sigh.

I was clawing at the snow, and it gave me no purchase, my hips were off the floor as Birch held me up, and her mouth moved on me, I was gasping for air, my heart pounding. Above me, the moon beamed down from a darkening sky, and my breath streamed up from my gasping mouth in clouds of steam.

"Oh Birch, baby I am cumming, oh god baby, don't stop... Please don't stop, OH GOODDDD!"

I exploded out into her mouth and all over the snow, and collapsed gasping for air, my skin was burning and wet, from the snow melting around me. Birch popped up with a beaming smile.

"Sweetie, your cum is so hot, it burned right through to the grass, it's frigging awesome!" I lay back exhausted, and looked at the snow surrounding me, I was so hot I had sunk lower into it, Birch sat on my waist and leaned over me.

"So, Sweetie, do you like the snow now?" I giggled.

"I concede, I will say this my white little snow monster, I love snow where I can screw you in it." She smiled.

"I can live with that Sweetie, I have never done it in the snow before, so this was special." I stared at her.

"You asked me, I thought you had done it before, I thought that was why you asked me?" She smiled and shook her head.

"I have always wanted to, but I really wanted it to be with you, although Sweetie, my tits are really numb, can we go for a bath now?" I lay back and laughed, my ass was frozen, I was not even sure if I could stand.

I staggered back through the snow, my boots felt heavier, and my legs stiffer, and I started to shiver. I was happy, as I held Birch's hand. She was smiling, and looking up at the stars, and it just felt perfect, as I looked at her as she smiled with those amazing white teeth, and her dancing happy eyes.

"I am going to run us a really hot bath, and then when you are in it, I am going to make you hotter, so you burn for days." She gave an excited giggle.

"Sweetie I am so turned on I am not sure I will last; I love snow sex; we have to have more." I glanced at her.

"Pray for more snow then." She gave an excited giggle.

Chloe and Deb's were in the kitchen wrapped in towels drinking chocolate, both had bright red faces, and happy smiles.

Thirty minutes later, we were both in a red hot bath steaming, Birch had her legs along the sides, as I held her up by her bum, and licked and sucked at her, she had her arms over the edge and her back arched as she went into the first stages of orgasm.

Feeling more and more excited, I moved faster, knowing I had her primed and ready to explode. She gasped and moaned, her head right back, she was almost there as I pushed my tongue harder into her, the moisture rushed as she stiffened, and let out a long low moan, and I felt happy, she was coming much faster than I had anticipated.

I flopped back against the taps, feeling happy, Birch sank into the hot water, her head still back on the rim of the bath, she was out of it completely, enjoying that moment of spaced out joy, from her climax. I breathed deeply and relaxed, and closed my eyes, it was like I was on a high, tonight had been everything I had never expected. Downstairs the doorbell rang, Anthony pressed the intercom.

"Hello, who is it?"

"Hi Anthony, it is Gail, are Abby and Birch home?" Michael looked at him.

"Is that the Vicar?" He nodded at Michael.

"Gail darling what a nice surprise, do come on in, I will tell Birch and Abby that you are here." He stepped back and turned to Michael. "Let her in when she gets here, I will grab those two."

I lay back drifting, when I felt Birch's foot under the water, she slid it in between my legs and started to rub me, I opened my eyes, and she smiled.

"Seriously Birch, you are going to toe me?" She chuckled.

"Have you ever been made love to by a toe?" I frowned.

"Well, no, have you?" I felt the tingle run into my legs and I twitched, she giggled.

"I have heard it can be very nice, some people find it a huge turn on." I chuckled.

"I hope you have healthy feet; I don't want athlete's chuff?" Birch gave a cackle of a laugh, and I started laughing with her.

There was a knock on the bathroom door, Birch leaned back, and looked towards her room, she saw Anthony, he looked a little embarrassed.

"I hate disturbing you whilst you are doing weird and disturbing things to each other, but Gail the Vicar is here, and she has guests with her. She wants to see you two." Birch nodded.

"Alright Anthony, could you tell her we will be there shortly." Birch turned to me. "Why is the Bell Twat here at eight at night?"

I had no idea; I was as surprised as she was.

"Why are you asking me, I have no bloody idea, let's go and find out." I stood up and grabbed a towel, and stepped out of the bath onto the thick fluffy mat, Birch stood up, her legs were still a little shaky, I gave a smile.

Five minutes later dressed in jeans and a t shirt, with wet brushed hair, we walked down the stairs to see Gail stood in the entrance hall, I smiled as she looked up at us.

"This is a surprise, what brings you here, it has been a while, Gail?" She looked round.

"This house looks stunning, I love your decorations, it is very stylish... I have something of importance to you. I was approached by someone who really needed to talk to you, I hope you don't mind Abby, but I thought we should come straight round?" I frowned; she was stood alone.

"We, Gail, I only see one of you." She smiled.

"Anthony asked my guests to relax in your living room." We reached the bottom of the stairs; she looked a little nervous.

"Abby, Birch, I take it you have not read todays National Mail." Birch sneered.

"Why would we read that rag?" She looked at us both, and she was clearly concerned.

"I know, but actually today you should read it, I will let my guest explain."

I walked round the corner of the door where a man and woman had their back to me as they spoke to Anthony, he gestured, and they turned round. I have to just say, that at this point, if you had asked me to write a list of people who would never visit my house, she would be in the top five.

I stared in disbelief, Birch had no idea who these people were, well to be honest I had no idea who the guy was either, but her, I was shocked, she looked very nervous.

"Hello Abigail." I struggled for words.

"Julia... Hi, what the hell are you doing here?" She looked very uncomfortable.

"I really need to talk with you, I take it you have not read todays Mail? I think you need to, and then we need to talk." She handed me a folded paper, she looked at Birch.

"Doctor Dixon, hello, my name is Julia Sanders, it used to be Hinkley before my divorce. We have never formally met, but I know you know of me." Birch was equally as shocked, she turned to the man. "This is my husband, Lenard." Birch smiled.

"I am glad to meet both of you, please won't you sit down?" I stared at the paper, and felt my insides squirm and twist.

"Oh god, I thought we had longer." Birch looked at the paper in my hand and started to read. Julia looked up at me from her seat.

"Abigail, I know we have not really been friends since the choir, but this is wrong. I saw it in the paper, and Len told me I should come to see you." I read the article out loud to Birch, Gail sat down next to Julia, and Anthony offered them coffee or tea.

The Face Behind The Mask Of Abigail Jennifer Watson.
By Peter Ford.

Last week we saw the shy innocent little Abigail Jennifer Watson, hit our TV screens, and wow the world, and to be quite frank it made me sick to my stomach, because when I met her on the street in her own village of Wotton Dursley two days ago, she was rude, and crude, and extremely aggressive, and nothing at all like the little innocent virginal image she presented on our screens.

I am to say the least, very disappointed, as I talk to her village neighbours, and uncover the real facts of Miss Watson, and how she really lives at home. If anything, she is a flirt and a flaunt, who uses her feminine charm to seduce men at an alarmingly fast rate, behind her long time partners back. But I shall not spare her female lover Doctor Dixon, and she is equally as bad, as she takes her work home as a sex therapist, to practice on her friends. It appears that Miss Watson and Miss Dixon are quite the tag team.

Talking to an Ex-associate who dated her house mate, the hairstylist Antonio, he revealed stories of sex parties, partner swaps, and full on orgies with various members of the band and crew of the rock group Battered Taco, and it takes very little, to understand that the Author of the lewd, crude and rude, Seeds of Summer, and the Hand of Death Vampire series, has based much of her work on her own real life sexual conquests, in what one upstanding member of the community, who has lost her seat on the local parish council, and has had her reputation blighted by Miss Watson, referred to as a Harlot, with a life of wanton debauchery and fornication.

Little is known of her past, but I am sure you will all be surprised, to find that her and her house mate, Artist Chloe Pemberton, falsely accused one of the village's most high profile and respectful members, when they levied a false accusation of attempted rape, and the well respected Choir Master lost his wife and child, as he was sentenced to prison. It is a tragic story that was told to me by newly released Martin Hinkley, a man destroyed by Miss Watson, and unable to live in the house he grew up in, which shows yet another side of this ruthless and despicable woman.

It is hardly surprising when you consider who her father is. Edwin Watson as you all know is currently being investigated for fraud and tax invasion on a mammoth scale, in a scandal that has rocked the entire financial sector of London, as I have been reporting to all of you, on a daily basis, and I for one can see that the apple has not fallen very far from the tree, as his daughter shows the same talents for deception.

Her impolite and disrespectful behaviour towards me in the street, has proven beyond doubt, that she has indeed fooled all of us, and you can take it from me, you all need to wise up, because she is not fooling me, I am on to her, as I probe deeper into her world. I expect to uncover more sordid secrets of her indecent lifestyle, which I may add, all of her readers are paying for by purchasing her work, take it from me, support another author, one who is more humane to those around her.

I looked at Birch as the tears formed in my eyes. "You know this is not true, what do we do?" Birch pulled me close, and looked at Julia.

"I am glad you brought this, it is not unexpected, but why come here, when you could have sent an email?"

Julia's husband looked at both of us, I wiped my eyes on my sleeve. He was tall, and reasonably stocky, with really kind pale blue eyes, he appeared to be talking honestly, and I felt I would be safe around him. He held Julia's hand and gave it a squeeze as he talked, which I liked. He obviously cared for her a great deal.

"I do not know you people, I saw you on the TV like most people Miss Watson, and Julia told me about what happened with him. She then told me a lot more than I think you are aware of, I felt that she should sit with you and talk to you. I realise how difficult it could possibly be, but as I told her, you two have more in common than you realise, and I think you really should hear her out." Birch leaned into me.

"I need Edwina, and Chloe should read this, keep her occupied, and give me two minutes." I nodded, and walked across the room to the sofa, and sat down facing the three of them, Gail handed me a tissue.

"I must admit Julia, I agree we were good friends at choir, as I remember, you tried to talk me out of leaving, you felt I was a better central lead vocalist? It came as a big surprise when you married Martin, and I cannot deny, I really felt like you had turned against me. I did not lie Julia, you know me better than that, I did torture myself for many years, before finding the courage to admit what he did to me, it hurt that you took his side in all of this." She swallowed hard, and looked at me, her eyes filled up slightly.

"Abigail, I was scared, he was not an easy man. Just know, it was not my choice to marry him, my parents were very forceful, and did a deal with him." Lenard held her hand and gave it another squeeze.

"Miss Watson, as I said, this is not easy for anyone here, but I really do feel it is right you speak."

Birch opened Chloe's door and leaned in, Chloe scrambled and sat up in bed and looked very embarrassed, Deb's tried to slide down out of sight. Chloe went beetroot.

"It's not what you think Birch, I never touched her." Birch shook her head.

"Guys what you do alone is your affair, and nothing to do with me... Chloe, I think you need to come downstairs, there is trouble, and you need to see and hear what is being said. Wear clothes, these people are not like us." She closed the door.

Deb's sat up and slid her legs out of bed, she put the huge dildo on the unit, Chloe looked at her.

“Birch won’t say anything... Will she, I mean it’s not gay if it’s dildo’s, right?” Deb’s turned and looked at her.

“Chloe, men have screwed you with a dildo, and now so have I, and you have screwed me with one too. Honestly, I don’t care what people think, I like you a lot, you are a great friend, and I am attracted to you, I have told you that. If this is a problem for you, I am sorry, but I have really enjoyed tonight, I needed it. Come on, we are needed, let’s get dressed... I have no clothes here, so I will run to my room.” She picked up her boots, and left, Chloe shook her head.

“Oh god, I have never cum like that with a guy, I am seriously messed up.”

Birch ran up the attic stairs, all of G5 were sat on the bean bags working on their computers, they all had leads connected to the server, she looked right at Edwina, as she looked up from her laptop.

“I need you; Ford has struck with a vengeance; it is as we predicted.” She nodded and looked at the others.

“Don’t stop we are almost there; I want this ready tonight.” She got up and walked across to Birch. “I am aware of some of it.” Birch gave a long sigh.

“He is not after taking prisoners is he, it’s an assassination piece?” She nodded.

I looked at Lenard. “I am not looking for trouble, if anything, ever since the night he was arrested, half this village has hated me. My life has been difficult since, especially with the likes of Marjorie, she has never forgiven me for catching him trying to rape Chloe.”

It was weird, as soon as I said her name she walked in, and stared with horror at Julia, her head snapped round, as she pointed back behind her.

“What the fuck is she doing here?”

“Chloe sit down, and just listen, Julia is here because Birch and I have allowed it, now shut up and read this, Julia brought it for us to read.”

I threw the paper across the seat, Chloe stared at Julia as she crossed the room, and sat down, she snatched up the paper and started to read. Julia took a deep breath.

"I am glad you are here Chloe, I tried to find you, but you had moved from the address I was given, then I heard you were here. I am not here to cause trouble, please believe me, I want to help, you need to know a lot of things." Chloe looked up from the paper.

"This is all lies and bullshit, your husband is a prick Julia." Lenard gave a cough.

"I hope you don't mean me?" Chloe looked up.

"Huh?" He smiled.

"I'm Julia's husband now, people tend to call me Len, not so much Prick." Chloe looked a little apologetic.

"Sorry, I was talking about the other one, I did not know Julia was married again, sorry Len." He smiled.

"It is fine, Chloe, we are here to try and help, although this Ford man is not an easy person to deal with, but if we can help, we will." Birch and Edwina appeared and came into the room, Birch had briefed her, she sat down at the end of the sofa.

"I am a little surprised to see you here Julia, it has taken seven years, sooner would have been more appropriate, but better late than never. We have heard he is out." She looked down.

"I was a coward and I hid away, and refused to admit a lot, Len has told me I need to deal with this and face things. I am sorry, I should have done more, as I said, I am not proud of what I have done, and I want to set the record straight." I handed Edwina the paper, she glanced at it.

"I have seen it already." I stared at her.

"When... Wow, don't you think telling me about this shit would have helped me?" She turned to me.

"How, looking at your eyes I can see I guessed right, why do you think G5 have been here all day, honestly Abby, what do you think you can do about this?" I was a little taken aback, she was pretty off handed with me.

"I don't know what I can do about this, it would have just been nice to know, that is all." Edwina turned to me and took my hand in hers, her voice softened.

"Abby I am sorry, we were going to tell you later, after his confrontation in the village with you, we have been working on a new project. Abby, you have to understand, this guy Ford is a nasty piece of work with some very influential friends, we knew the only way to take him down, was to turn those friends against him, and it has taken a lot of work. All six of us have been working none stop on this, it is almost ready, please trust us, we are on your side." I nodded, I knew that, she gave me soft smile. Edwina turned to Julia.

"We aim to take this Ford guy out, are you here to go on public record or are you wasting our time?" She looked very surprised, and looked at Len, then back to all of us.

"This man has gone too far, especially by talking to Martin, if speaking out will stop him, I will do it, but I want no mention of my new married name, I have a child, and he deserves to be protected, so does my husband."

Anthony appeared with a tray followed by Michael, and drinks, he placed it down on the table.

"I have no idea what you people want, so I brought tea, coffee and alcohol. Oh darlings, from the little I have heard, I think this is going to be a long dramatic night." Chloe smirked.

"Every bloody day in this house is dramatic, why should tonight be any different?"

Chapter 22

Coding Cube.

Julia sat at the spare computer in the library, in front of her was a large microphone, with a round mesh shield on it. Edwina sat at her desk, with headphones on, and looked at her screen, where a digital recording studio was set up.

"Alright Julia, when I give you the signal, just speak, and tell your side of the story. Everyone else, I want total silence, I want this recording as crisp and clear as possible."

I sat at my desk, and Birch hers, behind us on pillows against the bookcases sat Chloe and Deb's. Len and Gail sat either side of Julia on the chairs from under the long window table. Edwina did a test and the studio showed a good signal as small lights lit up on a display.

"Alright Julia, in your own time, and your own words, just tell us your story."

She held Len's hand tight, and took a deep breath, she looked above the monitor and right at me.

"Hello, my name is Julia Hinkley, and I am the ex wife of Martin Hinkley, the man who attempted to rape Abigail Jennifer Watson, and Chloe Pemberton, and was caught and imprisoned for it. In today's National Mail, dated Thursday the seventeenth of December, there was an article written by Peter Ford, that implied that Miss Watson and Pemberton, wrongly accused Martin, and he suffered an injustice. I am here to make it very clear, that Peter Fords article is incorrect, I know this for a fact, because Martin admitted to me it was true."

I felt a ripple run through me, and it caught my breath, Birch reached out and took my hand. Julia teared up.

"Martin admitted it, simply because, that was how I ended up pregnant and married to him. Martin raped me in the choir store room, and I was not on the pill. He snuck up on me, pinned me to a table, ripped off my underwear, and had forceful sex with me, and I got pregnant as a result. Had I not got pregnant, he would have got away with it, because he threatened me, and I was so afraid I said nothing. When my parents found out I was with child, I told them the truth, and they confronted Martin, and offered him marriage, or jail, he chose marriage."

I swallowed hard and felt the tears run down my cheeks, Birch was watching and crying too, behind me, Chloe had her head on Deb's shoulder as she quietly wept. Julia took a deep breath.

"I had no choice in the marriage, it was forced upon me to save face for my family. My life was a living misery, the only good thing to come out of it was my son. Peter Ford has lied in the most wicked of ways, I know what Abigail and Chloe endured, and it is terrifying, and took me many years of therapy to overcome it. Martin was arrested when he tried to rape Chloe, and Abigail and her friends realised, they caught him on film in the act, and it was the film footage evidence that helped get him convicted. Abigail is not a villain, she was the hero of that night, who saved her friend in an act of great bravery, I know this, because I suspected he was going to do it again, and yet I failed to act out of fear. Peter Ford should have mentioned that four other young women came forward from his previous appointment, and also pressed charges, and it was that with my last minute testimony against him, that sealed the conviction."

She took a deep breath and wiped her eyes, I understood the pictures that were going through her mind, I had lived with them for years, before finally telling Birch, I actually thought she was being very brave.

"Peter Ford came to my house, I have no idea how he found me, but he tried to get me to say I was lying about Martin. He was not aware my new husband was home, and as he threatened me, my husband confronted him, and threatened him with the police. I have a recording of that conversation, as my husband filmed it on his phone. The man is a vile evil parasite, that uses bullying and intimidation to silence people, he is no better than Martin Hinkley, and he needs to be stopped. Abigail and Chloe were the victims of a terrible crime, they should not be made victims again by this nasty lying news reporter. Thank you for listening."

Edwina raised her arm and counted down on her fingers, we all held our breath.

"DONE!" Julia looked down and started to weep.

"I am so sorry, I am so very, very sorry."

I got up and walked round the table, Gail smiled, and moved off her seat, I sat down and pulled her into my arms, and she burst into tears and threw her arms round me.

"I am so sorry Abigail, I was not a good friend to you, please forgive me." It felt painful to hear it, but I also understood the terror and fear he instilled in all of us.

"Shush Julia, this was the right thing to do, you have served your time of pain with him, and have a new life now. Julia, let this be the end of all that, the truth is now out, you are free of him, live a happy life with your new family, which is what I am doing." She looked up, and nodded at me.

"You are a better person than I am Abigail, I should have been a better friend to you." I smiled.

"I understand why you held back, and I don't hold it against you, we all have to survive the only way we know Julia. I could have done things differently, I just did not know how to back then, it takes a lot a time to overcome what he did." She gave a sniffle.

"I really am glad I came to see you tonight; I have no idea how this will help you, but I really hope it does." Edwina looked across at her.

"Julia and Len, you never admit who you made this recording with. I have a lot of friends in the cyber community that will use this to bring down Peter Ford. If you are ever asked, it was just some random computer nerd who you have never met, you must promise us that. This guy has been watched for a while by some seriously good computer wizards, and his end is about to come as the truth of him is revealed. Trust me when I say, they want to help Abby, they are big fans of her books, and we will pass this on to them for you okay?" Gail gave a giggle.

"Well, I am a member of the church, and so I cannot disclose anything, I am happy to say, this is the one time I will help protect a Pagan witch, us bell twats can be like that you know?" Birch started to chuckle.

"If you want to protect me, cut the ropes on those frigging bells." I gave a giggle, and smiled at Birch, some things never change, it is her thing you know?

Shortly after, Julia and Len, had to leave, Gail had driven them round, and was taking them home to relieve the baby sitter. We all hugged and thanked her, even Chloe, which was nice, I had not thought she would.

I sat in the library with a freshly poured glass of gin.
"So just how do we do this?" Edwina smiled a big smile.
"Do you remember the other day, when Morty turned up with a hard drive?" I nodded, I remembered it, she winked.
"He names all his hard drives so he does not get them mixed up. That drive contained everything he ripped off Peter Ford's computer, and it is a lot of very damaging stuff, emails, pictures, voice recordings, even some film footage. Guys it is a shit load of stuff, and we have all been working none stop going over it and sorting it out. That drive is the real truth, and he cannot survive if what is on it comes out, and we think it is time he was taken down." I understood that, but still could not see how that could be done.
"Okay so how will you do this?" She gave a chuckle.
"Give me a second... Last week when we set up your security system, we also set up our own VPN, which makes everything online in this house impossible to find, basically all of us are invisible online, no one can track our IP addresses. We have been building a special site, just for Peter, and it will be the first of a few from G5, but we cannot use our own name, so we decided to call our online presence after the hard drive. Guys welcome to Coding Cube."
My computer opened a new window, and there was a website, with a picture of Peter Ford on it, and above it read the words 'Coding Cube presents, 'The real truth of Peter Ford.' I started to read.
'This month Peter Ford, prestigious journalist for the National Mail Newspaper decided to attack yet another well known personality, when he wrote an article trashing Abigail Jennifer Watson. This is not the first time he has tried to destroy a well known personality he took a dislike to, and Coding Cube, decided it was time to take a look inside his computer. Guess what we found on the following celebrities he has destroyed? Yep, it was

all lies, he set them up for no other reason than they refused to talk to him, and so he went out of his way, to completely assassinate them, and hey guess what?... Pay back is a bitch.'

I saw my name and clicked the link, there was an extract which was photocopied from his article, looking like it had been ripped out of the paper, below it was a heading. 'Peter wrote this, but is it true? Let's look at the footage that was filmed of his encounter with Abigail.'

Right below it I saw the footage, where I asked him to leave me alone, and he swore at me and threatened me. Edwina watched me carefully.

"This is not live yet Abby, we will be working until late on it. I will add the sound recording of Julia, and at exactly three in the morning, your web site will get an email from Coding Cube, informing you that they have linked this site to yours, so if anyone asks, you show them the message. The same will happen on a lot of other sites, Peter's site will crash, and Coding Cube will take it over, and replace it with this one, we have also got control of the National Mail's website, and they will be doing a special feature. Tom at the Reporter, will also get a free present, there are a few things we found with Marjorie's name on it, and it appears Peter was being used by her, but he also had stuff on her, we thought it would make a nice thank you to Tom." I sat back in my seat.

"Holy shit Edwina, I knew you lot were good, but hell this goes well beyond that, you really are pro hackers." She smiled.

"Abby, we are not just helping you, look at the list, he stitched up Alison Williams the actress, Christian Besson, the writer, Helen Janis, the TV presenter, and a whole lot more, we still have a lot to add, there are bankers and politicians, and lots of ordinary good people, and he has viciously attacked them all, we are just evening up the balance, his lies, for our facts." Birch patted my hand.

"Sweetie, he has used his position of influence to hurt people, and threaten people, that is why he has a huge house and a flash car, and makes a lot of money, selling on his exclusives. He has some nasty stuff on your dad, and he has also been planning to attack my mum, it is time he was taken down and stopped for good." I understood that.

"Birch why would he attack your mum, did you know about all this?" She gave a sad smile.

"Deads Sweetie, I knew about some of it, Edwina let me see some stuff. Mum and dad had a bad patch, it was not their greatest time, he has some things I want to keep dead. My parents worked really hard to get through it, he was preparing something for her." She looked saddened by it, and I was not going to push it.

"Okay I get it, he must not be allowed to hurt your family, I love them, I do not want them hurt, as far as I am aware, I know nothing about any of this." Edwina smiled.

"Good, just watch the site when it goes live, we will unpick every word he has ever written, and I think he will be the focus of the daily newspapers for a change."

I probably had too much gin, and by the time I hit the bed, my brain felt fried, what a strange day. I felt tired and very emotional, Birch curled round me and pulled me close, and I closed my eyes and relaxed, it was seven days until Christmas, and we still had a load to do, in order to pull off Christmas, talk about an insane life?

"Birch?"

"Yes Sweetie."

"Why is everything in my life, so bloody complicated?"

"Sweetie, life is a road full of bumps, you know that."

"I thought you were in a boat?" She giggled.

"Why do you think it is so frigging bumpy?"

I started to laugh as she giggled, I felt my tummy wobbling like crazy, and I could not stop myself, she gave a cackle of a laugh, and I laughed more.

Birch and I lay in the dark, howling with laughter, and I have no idea why really, maybe we were just going insane, after all who would blame us?

Coding Cube activated at one in the morning, and went live, and it did not take long for the word to hit the streets, after all, every national newspaper and TV station, got an email notification. Peter Ford, was not as well liked by his peers, as it would have first appeared. Sure enough, Abigail's website got an email, as did the Curio's site, and Sweetie's Retreat site.

The editor at the National Mail screamed at his tech guy, as he tried to take down Peter's site and put their official one back up.

"GET THE FUCKING THING DOWN NOW!" The poor guy sat there with his arms out looking frustrated.

"I am trying, we are locked out, they have taken over the whole bloody site, do you honestly think I am not trying?" The editor raged.

"GET IT FUCKING DOWN, OR GET OUT!" The tech guy looked at him, stood up, and grabbed his coat.

"Screw this shit, you don't pay me enough to treat me like this, go screw yourself, and take your own site down." He turned and walked out.

Twenty four hour news TV was scrambling, as a team of their reporters had the site open, and were hurriedly making notes, this was the biggest scandal to hit the streets on a newspaper in years, and they were going for it full tilt. Within thirty minutes, news caster Robert Harrison, sat in his seat and smiled at the camera.

"In breaking news, tonight the website of one of the country's leading newspapers, was hacked by a group calling themselves Coding Cube, as they revealed the truth behind renown journalist Peter Ford. It appears his attack on Author, Abigail Jennifer Watson, in his piece 'The face behind the mask,' which was published on Thursday, angered the group, who have hit back, accusing him of lies, cheating, and bullying those who refused interviews with him. The site also lists lots of other celebrities including, Actress Alison Williams, who lost her court fight against the National Mail three years ago, and this site proves she was right all along. We are now going over to John Cosgrove, who is in surrey, outside Alison Williams home." Edwina leaned back into Luke with a smile.

"Screw you Ford, that is what happens when you pick on my friends." Luke put his arms round her and relaxed.

"I am knackered." She turned round and looked at him.

"We still have a lot more to do yet." He smiled.

"Hmm, but some sleep first." She started giggling.

"Oh, we are not sleeping, I am on a coding high, which can mean only one thing." She pulled down his zip, his pants were already unbuttoned, and he did not even know it, he opened one eye, and she lowered her head.

"Oh, Weena!" He closed his eyes and lay back with a smile.

Not long after I got up, I got a text from Katie, she was snowed under with calls for an interview, and had told them I was not speaking to anyone just yet, but she would inform them when I was. In a way I was glad, the last thing I wanted was yet more reporters at my door.

The morning was busy, Birch was decked out in a tinsel covered, Mrs Sexy Santa costume, and had baubles hanging from her earrings. It was Sweetie's Retreat first ever office party, and she was bubbling over with excitement. Izzy had on a deep green Santa hat with 'Fuck this shit' embroidered on it. Deb's had an ordinary Mrs Santa costume and eyed up Birch' with envy.

"Do you like have connections to some slut store I do not know about?" Birch giggled and gave a twirl, I must admit, the fish nets were getting me wet, and so seeing her with no knickers on, just got me going even more.

"Christmas is about fun, and sexy is fun." I agreed, and looked at Deb's.

"Sod that fat twat Santa, I want that coming down my chimney." She chuckled.

"If Santa looked like that, and came down our chimney, no presents would get delivered, they would be held captive here, chained to a bed." Chloe giggled.

"If Santa's dick is anything like those fat dudes at the Sun Club, and it is like a turtle's head, is it okay to be like gay for one night?" Birch chuckled and winked at Deb's, who turned scarlet. I looked at her, and she became flustered.

"I er... I got to check some stuff."

She hurried out of the kitchen, I looked at Birch, and she gave me a sweet sexy smile, and walked over to me, she leaned in revealing a lot of cleavage, God she smelt amazing, her eyes smouldered as she whispered.

"I hope you will be at my party, I will be very drunk, with low inhibitions, and looking to find something very dark, and very naughty to nibble on?" She breathed a long sexy breath towards my ear, and I swallowed hard.

"Oh hell, yeah!" She smiled.

"Don't be late Sweetie, I am already really wet, it starts at one." Chloe gave a sigh.

"Oh god I am horny now, you two need to stop this shit at breakfast, I cannot concentrate on my toast." Birch gave a giggle, and walked round behind her, and did another sexy whisper.

"Oh Chloe!" I saw her shudder and smile, Birch leaned in closer.

"Poor Aden has no one now Edwina has Luke, and Gill, Meg and Alex can get very horny, I hope you will come, and save him?" Chloe gave another shudder.

"Oh fuckin hell Birch, you have to stop this, I want to be straight, but you are putting pictures in my head, that should not be there, I think I just cheated on Abby, go to fucking work, I am too wet for this shit... But I will be there, have no doubt." She gave a smile.

"Good, you all have a box on your beds, it's a sexy Christmas outfit, call it a little sexy gift from the horny fairy." Deb's came running downstairs, she sped into the kitchen and raised her arms.

"Guys look what I found?" Chloe slurped her coffee, and coughed it all over the island.

"HOLY FUCK, IT'S TINKER SLUT!"

Deb's beamed with delight as she spun in a very short dress, which did not hide much, she had on a bright sequinned covered thong, and green fish net tights. Her green top was very revealing, especially considering her more than ample chest, and she had little tiny wings on the back, and a little tiara, which looked like it was made of glittering Vagina's. I gasped out with surprise.

"Holy shit Deb's." She gave a huge smile.

"I am a really slutty fairy; you want to rub my magic spot?" She gave a wink and giggled. I was not sure what to say.

"Deb's, you do know you work in a book shop, not on a porn shoot?" She gave a sexy wink.

"Bring a camera and we will find out." Chloe gave a giggle.

"Wow I have competition; I am defo packing a camera today."

Finally, our selection of loud noisy festive sluts, left for work, I was worried about the safety of the village. I was not certain as to whether they were leaving to spread sparkles and cheer, or to rape and pillage, and considering Birch this morning, it could go either way. As soon as the door closed, Chloe looked at me, and I read her mind instantly.

"What did we get?"

With shrieks and screams, we legged it up the stairs and headed for our rooms. As promised on my bed was a box, I gave an excited giggle as I opened it and looked inside.

"Oh, Birch you are such a naughty girl." I yanked off my t shirt, and pulled my costume out of the box.

Ten minutes later, I stood in front of the mirror, looking at myself. I was wearing a black leather satanic elf costume, it was not low cut, but was split right down to the waistband, and had red laces, all the way up, my small round mounds were visibly on display. The skirt was alternate pointed flaps of fabric in red and black, and I had on long black and red stripy, crotchless tights, and red wedged shoes.

On my head was a tiara of small sparkly bat wings, it was really sexy, and I could not deny, it was more revealing than anything I had ever worn, and yet I felt like a million dollars, and smiled as I turned to admire it. Oh yeah, it made my bum look amazing! This was without doubt, what a dark little beastie would wear at Christmas. Chloe came in and stopped, as she stared.

"Holy fuck Abby, you look fucking amazing." I turned and smiled. Chloe was wearing the sluttiest elf costume I had ever seen.

Her top was not just low cut, it had holes where her nipples poked out, onto which she had little tassels with bows attached. Her skirt was really short, and her green knickers had a piece of mistletoe embroidered on it, with an arrow pointing down that said, 'Kiss here.' She looked really sexy, as she smiled, and her elf hat, which had the words Santa's Slut written on it wobbled. She gave a giggle

"Hey watch this."

She grabbed the side of her knickers and pulled, there was a tearing sound, and they came clean off, her eyes danced with excitement.

"Abby they are Velcro, I can just rip em off, and I am primed for action." Her stripy tights like mine, were crotchless.

Chloe was very happy indeed, and I had to smile, wow Birch

knew us all so well, although there was one small snag to her plans.

“Chloe, we have to confirm the order for the veg today, we have to go and see Norman.” She shrugged.

“Okay… So, we go see Norman.” I looked at her, she was actually pretty hot in clothing.

“Chloe we will have to walk through the village dressed like this.” She shook her head.

“I am going to wear my long coat, wear your long black one, we will be fine until we get to the party… I am definitely getting laid in this, I tell you Abby, I am going to pull someone’s cracker today, I need a real guy inside me, not a girl pretending.” I frowned.

“How do you mean, I thought you bang Percy?” She looked embarrassed.

“Birch has not told you?” I shook my head.

“Told me what?” She looked really uncomfortable.

“Abby, please don’t be mad at me, I know she is your oldest friend. Last night Deb’s and me were really horny, she jumped in my bed and wanted to touch me, and she asked me to finger her, she really needed it, you know Jimmy has been gone a while and she is feeling lonely.” I was surprised.

“Wow Chloe you had sex with Deb’s, are you okay with that?” She shook her head.

“No Abby, you have got it all wrong… I won’t deny I thought about it, I mean I know what to do, I have fingered myself a million times. I told her I was not sure I was ready for it; you know she makes me confused, and I don’t know why? Anyhow I got out two dildos, and we faced each other and did each other with them.” I was not sure what to say, I mean this was Chloe.

“How was that for you?” She gave a smile.

“She made me cum loads, I am still not sure what that means, and to be honest, I really enjoyed watching her cum, her face was amazing. I didn’t do any stuff with her apart from that, although when we were done, she leaned over, and surprised me by kissing me, and I kissed her back, it felt nice. I am still sort of trying to understand that.” I sat on the bed.

“Wow been there, it took me five years to work that one out.” She nodded.

"Tell me about it... Abby is this how you were with Birch, am I going lesbian?"

Wow how do you answer that question? This was something that had been the greatest struggle of my life, I had denied it for years, and lied to myself, and everyone else about it for ages, and it almost destroyed me. She walked over and sat on the bed; I took her hand in mine.

"Chloe, I can only say that firstly, with all the guys you have had sex with, you will never qualify for the lesbian sisterhood, at best you get to wear the Bi badge. You know I really don't think it matters, and again I don't think we have to label it. I get you, I do, and the one thing I can tell you for certain is don't fight it, because it messes you up, just accept it. I mean to be honest screwing each other with dildo's is like mates helping each other."

"So, it's not gay?" I shook my head.

"Chloe, she kissed you and you liked it, you kissed her back, it is just a smooch, nothing more, how many guys have we kissed at Christmas and New Year, hundreds? I think if it made you happy, and you enjoyed it, leave it at that, and just accept it for what it was, a nice moment." She nodded and smiled.

"Abby the thing is she told me she wants to do more to me, she is really into me, I mean, you know, she finds me a huge turn on." I understood that, I remembered the first time Birch told me and I panicked.

"Chloe have you ever heard of a pillow princess?" She frowned.

"What the hell is that?" I chuckled; she knew so little about women.

"A pillow princess is a girl who will let other girls do sexual things to her, to make her cum, like she will let a girl go down on her, but she never goes down on the girl, because she is not capable. I suppose the question is, how much does Deb's want from you? That is something you two need to talk about, and then you will know just what you will and will not allow? Chloe most girls have a few girl on girl moments in their life, maybe this one is yours." She nodded and gave a sigh.

"So this could just be a one time thing with just Deb's, and I will stay the same with everyone else? I mean that does actually make a lot of sense to me." She turned and looked at me. "How did you know Birch was forever then?" I smiled.

"When she left Chloe, I wanted to die rather than be without her, the thought of never seeing her again almost destroyed me, that was when I had to grow up and be honest with myself. I was so in love with her, and pretending I wasn't, was killing me. I had to admit it, and tell her how I felt, and hope I could be with her, it was that simple... Although both of us still like to screw the odd guy, it's shameful to admit, but I love watching her have sex, it turns me on more than anything else. Hearing her moan drives me wild, I think watching someone you really like climax, is as sexy as hell... I think I am messed up." She gave a smirk.

"I really get that Abby, I really loved seeing how happy Deb's was when I made her cum, I really got off on it." It was nice to hear someone else say it, she squeezed my hand. "Abby... I have another problem, Max sent me these."

She lifted her phone, and opened her messages, there was a long column of pictures, and all of them were of Jimmy in bed with Japanese girls.

"What do I do?" I gave a long sigh.

"Oh, crap! I really wanted him to be good to her... Say nothing Chloe, let me put some feelers out with her, I know how to handle this better than you do, and it is better if it comes from me."

After another coffee, and wearing long coats, I set off with Chloe, in the direction of Norman and Daisy's. We took the short cut round the back of the village shops, and over the railway bridge. We wore our snow boots, and had our costume shoes in my bag on my back.

The nursery was really busy, and Norman had six large lads selling trees, Daisy was in the shop, and we walked in with my order, and looked at all the fresh produce. They had to buy some in, but a large percentage was organically grown on site in the long polytunnels.

We gave Daisy a sneak peep at our costumes and she went wild, she loved them a lot, and giggled when she asked me what Birch thought. I chuckled and leaned over the till.

"She has not seen it yet, but we may just christen her office today, or at least, I am hoping so." She gave me a huge smile.

"Oh, you go girl, you get her, and you go wild on her." I laughed, I loved Daisy, she was really opened minded.

She sorted out the order, and the delivery time for dinner time Dec 23rd, and I paid and left a huge tip for the staff, and we walked outside and headed for the gate.

"Abigail... Have you got a moment?" We turned and there was Tom Jennings. He smiled and raised his hands. "It is a day off, I am having a family day, this is my wife Sarah by the way."

I walked back and shook her hand, she had two little boys who nervously took her hands, Tom smiled.

"Abby, I just wanted you to know that Ford has been mauled, I am sure you have seen the site." I nodded.

"Yeah, they sent me a message telling me they had attached it to my site, obviously I had a look, to be honest Tom, I am not sorry, what he wrote on Thursday was all lies. I mean yes there are six women living in the house, and we are not nuns, we have partners, but I have never cheated on Birch, and what he wrote about Hinkley was bullshit, we caught him as you know trying to rape Chloe. If I am honest, I just want the truth out, if people will actually quote me properly, I would do more interviews, but they never do, which is why I always refuse them." He gave a sigh.

"How about you give me one in the new year, I will stay true and honest, and quote you word for word, I am looking at a shot for a national daily, and I cannot deny, an exclusive with you, would really help?"

I looked at his wife Sarah, she was watching me intently, it was clear she was hoping her husband would get it, after all, working for a national would really enhance their lives.

"Promise Sarah, you will do an honest piece, and let her sit in, and let me record it, and I will give you two hours." He smiled, and looked as my Manchester friends tell me, gob smacked.

"Really... I mean it Abby; I would walk through fire for that." I smiled.

"Promise her Tom, here and now in front of me." He turned to Sarah.

"Sarah sweetheart, I absolutely promise you that I will write a true account of all her words, no lies, no speculation and no bullshit." She nodded at me.

"Will that do for you Miss Watson?" I gave a giggle.

"It is Abby Mrs Jennings, I will email you in the New Year and set it up at my home, I will look forward to hosting you both as my guests for the afternoon." Tom looked so happy.

"Abby thanks, you have no idea how much that will help." I did actually.

"I hope your family has a lovely Christmas Tom, see you in the New Year." I turned and walked off and heard his excitement, I looked back to see him hugging his smiling wife. Chloe linked my arm.

"That was nice Abby, you are like a real Christmas fairy." I sniggered.

"Not really we already have a tinker slut in the family, one is enough, I am done with kind deeds for the year." She chuckled, and squeezed my arm tighter.

"I love you, do you know that?" I gave a giggle and smiled.

"Do I need to get a couple of dildos ready?" Chloe gave a massive laugh, and looked at me.

"You really are amazingly good looking, but for now, I will keep my dirty thoughts about you and Birch in my head, save your dildo for her." I smiled at her.

"I could never sleep with another woman, it's crazy, but I just want Birch." She snuggled into my arm.

"To be honest Abby, I actually think that is really sweet."

Chapter 23

Therapist Christmas.

The village with a good layer of snow, did look really pretty, even though the roads had been gritted, and it had turned to slush. All the roof tops were white, and I stopped and looked round, enjoying the scenery, Chloe leaned into me.

"It is a pretty place to live, isn't it?" I nodded.

"You know Chloe, it is crazy to think about it, but I really love this place. When you think of all we have been through here, the mad thing is, I have never wanted to change it, I have always wanted to preserve it as it has always been."

A van pulled up and blocked the view, I gave a sigh as I read the side of it. 'River Cable TV News.' Chloe yanked my arm, and we started walking away. The side door slid open and a camera man jumped out, followed by a young woman holding a microphone.

"Miss Watson, please could I have a brief word with you?" I gave a sigh and continued on; she ran down the street after me.

"Please Miss Watson, I just want to know if you have heard about Peter Ford?" I stopped and turned round; her camera man came panting up behind her. She took a deep breath and looked at me.

"Hi, and thanks for stopping, I am Amy Walker, could you tell me if you have heard the news about Peter Ford? I am aware he wrote a really nasty article about you." I gave a sigh.

"I don't do interviews, because of people like Peter Ford." She smiled.

"Did you know he has been fired because a malicious group of hackers took out his computer, and released all his documents to the world?" I nodded.

"I am aware of the group, they contacted me by email, and told me they had put a site up to reveal the truth, I have not really looked at it." I kept my face blank and uninterested; she was trying to work me out, but was not good enough, I lived with

Birch, I knew how to read the signs.

"Miss Watson, the site has a film clip on it which shows his aggressive treatment of you on this very street, do you know who filmed it?" I gave another long sigh.

"Miss Walker, have you any idea how many cameras get pointed at me? I cannot do anything in my home village in peace, as you can see, I cannot even walk down the street, without someone pointing a camera or microphone at me. I am sorry but you just get to a point where you no longer even react to them; you just get used to it and move on." I pointed across the green to where a guy stood with a telephoto lens on his camera. "See what I mean?" She gave me a nod.

"I would really love to sit and talk to you on camera, how about it?" I smiled.

"I like you Amy, you are respectful, and if you had asked me forty minutes ago, I may have said yes, but I have promised Tom Jennings, a full in depth exclusive early in the New Year, sorry." She gave a long sigh, and looked glum, I shrugged. "Have a nice Christmas Amy, come see me when my next book comes out." She gave me a big smile.

"I will." I turned and started to walk, she shouted. "Hey Abigail, have a great Christmas, kiss that sexy doctor for me." I heard her laugh, and raised my hand to wave behind me, we arrived at the book shop, turned and walked in.

Denise was wearing Deb's Mrs Santa costume, she did not fill it out quite as much as Deb's did, but she had enough to make it look sexy enough, Roy was in his work clothes. Deb's was at the back of the shop restocking the self awareness section, looking like Tinker Slut, I giggled as I walked up to her.

"I am actually impressed you wore that for work." She giggled.

"Is it shameful that I love it, and it turns me on to wear it?" I opened my coat and she gasped.

"Holy shit... Oh god, I am so wet, and honestly, I know we are best mates and you are with Birch, but would you consider going into the toilet with me for ten naughty minutes?" I started to laugh.

"God Deb's, if you are so horny, just screw someone, do you honestly think over there in Japan, there is no temptation?" She gave a sigh.

"Can I tell you something, and you won't get mad?" I looked at her.

"How naughty is it?" She looked at me.

"I got a message from Max, he told me things were as always." I understood.

"That does not mean he is sleeping around; didn't you once tell me you and him had an arrangement?" She gave another sigh.

"We did until we got married, he said after that he would drop the groupies, and as far as I know he has... Abby I have not been an angel either." I frowned.

"How so?" She looked down.

"Five weeks ago, Edwina came into my room looking for some notes I had written for the Curio site, I was in the shower, she came in and she was just in her panties, and I dragged her into the shower. Abby, we screwed all night, it was wild as hell. I also tried to screw Chloe yesterday, God, I wanted her so much, it was driving me insane. I really wanted to go down on her, and have her use her fingers, but she would not let me. She got two dildos' out, and we banged each other, and I am telling you, I came so God damned hard. I am way into her, even Jimmy does not make me cum that much. Am I a horrible person, Abby?" I chuckled.

"No you are not, you are just frustrated, Deb's give yourself a break, if you think Jimmy is having sex, then you need to find out for sure, I mean that is if you want to actually know." She nodded.

"I really do, I know it is crazy, but if I could find out for sure, I would not feel as guilty." I smiled, and turned.

"Hey Chloe, lend me your phone." She looked worried, as she walked towards me.

"I am not sure that is the best idea you have had Abby." She looked at Deb's.

"Max is a slut who loves to share pictures, are you really sure you can handle this?"

She nodded, and reluctantly Chloe opened her phone and showed her the pictures, Deb's took a long look, and gave a sigh of relief. Okay that was not the reaction I expected, you know, seeing your husband screwing, what looked like barely old enough Japanese girls, I would have thought would cause outrage. I looked at her.

"Are you going to be alright?" She smiled, also not what I expected.

"Abby, if he can screw, so can I."

I was not going to argue with that. Deb's grabbed Chloe by the arm, and dragged her into the toilet, I looked round the door, she had her by the head and was kissing her with a passion, and weirdly enough, Chloe was letting her. I left them to it, and walked down the shop to the till area.

Behind me there was a squeal, Chloe backed out of the toilet holding her knickers in her hand.

"Just because they are crotchless, does not mean you can use fingers." Deb's came out and giggled.

"I made you so wet, admit it, you really want me?" Chloe looked at me.

"Tell her Abby, tell her how wet I have been all day." I started to laugh.

"No idea what you are talking about Chloe, no idea at all." Denise started to giggle; Roy actually looked appalled.

It was the Friday before Christmas, and the bookshop was going to be open all day Saturday and Sunday, and so Deb's was closing early today, and opening late on Monday. Birch had invited Deb's and Denise to the party, which I also thought had a lot to do with it.

At one o'clock, Deb's locked up, and dropped her keys in her bag, and armed with two bottles of gin, we walked next door and pressed the buzzer, Gill answered.

"I am sorry, today we are only open for Christmas sluts and deviants, can you tell us which you are please?" I leaned into the intercom.

"If your boss is there, tell her, I am going to pin her to the conference table, and screw her brains out in front of all her watching staff. Is that deviant enough for this party?" I heard her gasp.

"Abby, would you really do that, I mean it's a joke right?" Deb's leaned in.

"Oh Gill, you sweet innocent child, you have no idea who you are dealing with, if you want to watch and film it, I will stand with you." There were masses of giggles.

"Oh, Sweetie I really want to do that now, you are a wicked dark little beastie, come on in." The door gave a long buzz and we entered, Denise and Roy were a little red around the cheeks. We walked in and Birch opened her arms wide.

"Sweetie's welcome, Merry Christmas come on in and join us." She looked really hot, I smiled at Gill, who was wearing a Christmas bikini, she was pretty relaxed, and I leaned over the counter and looked at her skimpy knickers.

"Wow Gill, I love the outfit, be aware Deb's is horny as hell and unsupervised." I giggled, and slipped off my coat and hung it on the rack, Birch went wild.

"OH MY GOD SWEETIE, MY DARK LITTLE BEASTIE, YOU ARE ADORABLE!"

She ran round the counter and dragged me into her arms, and kissed me passionately, I felt my heart flutter, and gasped for air. Birch broke apart and smiled, her eyes danced and sparkled with bright life, yep, she was already pissed.

In the back rooms the music was playing, I slid my arm round Birch, as she grinned from ear to ear. Gill came round and leaned into me.

"We have some medical profession guests here, watch out for their slippery hands, some of those med boys are way too confident." Chloe leaned in.

"Are they fit to screw?" Gill gave a smile.

"Does it really matter Chloe? I am sure there is plenty to amuse you?" She looked past the doorway.

"Cool, I am heading into the back." She walked through; Gill giggled.

"Do you guys want a drink, we have quite a bit?" I lifted up the two bottles, and smiled, Birch grabbed one.

"Oh Rhubarb, we have not had this since Uni, I want some."

She grabbed my hand, and dragged me behind the counter. Deb's, Denise and Roy followed. Birch poured the drinks, which is dangerous when she is sober, and bloody lethal when she is drunk. Roy opted for a can of larger, a wise, yet boring choice.

The music was banging away in the back, and we walked through to the group therapy room, the chairs were placed round the edges, and everyone was dancing, including to my surprise G5, and a lot of other men and women, who were all in some way or another, connected to the practice.

Everyone was dressed up, Rodger was wearing very short and tight leather pants, held up with tinsel braces, Pat was wearing an angel costume, which was pretty see through, and she had no underwear on at all, she had a pretty nice body and good boobs, although her wings were bent, and her halo had slipped, which was probably an accurate reflection of her motives today. Megan, had on a green bikini, with white fluffy trim, and Alex had on a golden one, it was clearly Birch who had picked them out for them. Everyone was happy and smiling, and dancing, Rodger grabbed me.

"Oh, you sexy little gothic doll, come on and dance with me, with all these hot men in the room we can protect each other." I giggled as he twirled me round.

"Oh, dear you are just too delightful, no wonder the good doctor has kept you a secret for so long." He pulled me into his arms, and then swung me out.

"I have to say, if I was straight, I would fist fight her for you."

Around me Pat was dancing with an executive, and Alex swayed in Morty's arms, Megan danced with Bongo, and Deb's was dancing with Creamy. Birch was being mauled by a drug company rep called Malc, his hands kept slipping, and she would pull his hand back.

Birch was looking a little frustrated, and as Rodger spun me round, I slapped his hand hard, as it slipped down towards her bum, he pulled back his hand and shook it, I smiled, as he scowled at me.

"Dance, but keep your hands out of the cookie jar."

Rodger gave a howl of a laugh, so did his female rep colleagues, the song ended, and Rodger released me, and gave a bow.

"I was honoured dear lady." As he bent forward, I kissed him on the forehead, and he swooned, I laughed and he gave me a big smile.

"I can see you are the reason Jemi smiles." It was a lovely compliment and I gave a curtsy.

"You honour me greatly Sire." He chuckled, as Birch grabbed me from behind, and kissed my neck, I gave a shudder and

Rodger raised his eyebrows.
"Deads, I just saw Deb's sneak off with Creamy, do you think she is doing what I think she is, shouldn't we do something?" I turned and looked at her sparkling eyes.
"Let her Birch, Jimmy is screwing everything that moves in Japan." She gave a sigh and looked sad.
"Oh Sweetie, I really wanted him to stay true to her." I nodded.
"I know, but honestly, she has decided what is good for him is good for her, let her go play. The girl is too horny to be allowed outside, she asked if I would finger her." Birch looked shocked.
"She is that horny?" I looked at her, and frowned.
"What, is that so bad, holy shit, am I on some measure for desperate women, like oh my god if she is fingering Abby she is beyond help?" Birch burst out laughing.
"I didn't mean it that way, hell Deads you are top of my list, I always want to." We walked over to the table and poured out new drinks, and stood watching everyone dance. Birch smirked.
"Some of these reps are real idiots, they are all early twenties and really full of themselves, Malc was telling me he is going to have me today, his ego is massive, he creeps me out." I turned and looked at him, he was hitting on Chloe, she smiled and then brushed him off.
"Chloe turned him down, and she is horny as hell, that is not a good sign."

I watched him move from girl to girl, he had perfect hair, and a perfect suit, and he ticked all the boxes of a perfect male, sadly he lacked the personality. I saw Aden standing and drinking alone, I looked at Birch.
"Why is Aden alone, he is a reasonably good looking guy?" She gave me a sweet smile.
"Gill is really into him; she was a little jealous when she found out he was spending time with Edwina. Honestly, I would love them to get together, they are so well suited, but Gill is shy, and Aden is far too polite, to make a move." It was sweet, and thinking about it, I could see what she meant, I saw Chloe on the prowl.
"Oh, Christ the virgin killer is moving in, Aden needs saving, here hold my drink." I walked down the room towards Chloe as

she moved on Aden, I grabbed her arm.

"Chloe, Denise looks as miserable as hell, Roy is a dead end, we need someone to liven him up, can you handle it and not bang him, he is engaged?" She looked across at him.

"Why would she want to marry someone like him, he is a stiff?" I shrugged.

"God knows, all I know is Denise is dying of boredom, at a party filled with sexual deviants, and that is not good." Chloe nodded.

"Leave it to me, I am not fucking her though." I laughed at her.

"Oh, Chloe you are so straight it's unbelievable." She looked at me with wide eyes.

"I know right." I let her go, and swerved in the direction of Aden.

I walked up and smiled, and grabbed his hand.

"Aden I really need a lift; can I borrow you for two minutes?" He smiled and gave a nod.

"Yeah, no problems."

I pulled his hand, and led him towards the door, I walked out into the corridor, and he pulled his hand free with a jerk.

"Abby you are not thinking of anything sexual, are you? I mean you are my bosses' partner, you are beautiful, but I would not do that to Jemi." I looked at him and smiled.

"Aden you are so sweet, but sadly, you do not have those gorgeous green eyes, and that long white sexy hair. Thanks for the compliment, it really is such a lovely thing and I am touched, but no, that is not what I need."

I grabbed his hand, and pulled him up the corridor, and walked towards the main reception area. I stopped near the office, and turned to look at him, and I lowered my voice a little.

"Aden, you clearly like Gill, why are you not in there with her, she is sat up front manning the phone alone, you should be there keeping her company?" He looked really awkward and uncomfortable, and started to blush.

"Abby… Yes, I like her, but she is too good for me, have you seen her, she is gorgeous?" I scowled at him.

"Aden, what the hell, don't you think it is up to her to decide, you cannot just go round deciding a girl's fate on your own? You have to let her choose for herself, my god, if you live your whole life with that attitude, you will never find a bloody girlfriend.

Aden, if you want to know if a girl likes you, ask her mates, trust me they will know, and I am telling you, that you are well in there." He looked at me stunned.

"I thought that was an urban myth." I gave a frustrated sigh.

"For a so called tech genius, you sure are a frigging idiot when it comes to life and living, look it is dead simple, do you like her enough to want to date her?"

I could not believe I was doing this, he looked like an utter drip with his glasses and his uncontrollable hair, Gill was a good looking girl, and had the IQ of Einstein, and yet here I was playing bloody cupid, dressed like I fell off the Addams Family Christmas tree. He gave a nod.

"I really like her, I am just very nervous, because I really do like her." That was enough for me, this was an office party, and that meant kissing, and alcohol. I grabbed his hand and yanked, he looked terrified.

"Okay it is Christmas, and Gill is up here all alone, so I think you need to spend some time with her and cheer her up."

I walked up the rest of the corridor, and peered round the doorway, Gill was sat by the phone, drinking alone. I yanked on Aden, who was now very white in the face, and had gone from blushing to terror. I walked into reception, Gill turned and smiled.

"Hey Gill, it's pretty wild back there, and Aden and me were talking, and thought we would bring a little party spirit up front, you know it's a party, you too are allowed some fun." She smiled.

"It's only another hour until the phone lines switch over to the holiday settings, I was going to come down then." Aden was right, she was pretty, especially in her Christmas bikini outfit. I looked up above the work station.

"Oh wow, you guys have real mistletoe, I could only get that fake plastic stuff."

Gill looked up at the large bunch hanging from the ceiling, I yanked Aden, who was trying to free himself from my iron clad grip, and pulled him round in front of me, Gill looked down.

"Aden was telling me how pretty you are, and how he hopes he will get a kiss under the mistletoe from you." He looked at me terrified, and Gill gave a smirk, I giggled, and looked at Gill.

"He really likes you but is afraid he is not good enough, so just kiss him will you and prove he is wrong." She turned a little pink, but stood up, Aden took a deep breath and I let go of his hand, and slowly withdrew, Gill moved closer.

"Merry Christmas Aden." She leaned in and kissed him, and he lifted his arms, and pulled her close. I smiled to myself, as I walked back into the corridor and left them alone.

I walked down the corridor towards the party, and Malc appeared, he gave me a smooth smile, I smirked.

"Save it big boy, I am a lesbian, chop your junk off, and we will talk when it's healed." I walked right past him, he looked instantly crushed. Birch leaned on the door frame and giggled.

"Nice line, and nice boobs, you seeing anyone you gay goddess?" I leaned on the door and looked her up and down, and then leaned into her, so my breath blew on her neck, and I lowered my voice, to sound like Bev.

"I could be, it depends on what you say next, so Snow Queen, what's it going to be, your bed or mine?" She gave a squeal, and shook her hands.

"Oh my god that is so frigging sexy, you must do that when we are in bed." I moved my face up really close, so our noses almost touched, her eyes were huge and sparkling.

"I wanna batter your biff, how about it, you wanna be my bird?" She started to shake like she was going to explode.

"Oh my god, I frigging love it when you talk like Bev."

"GUARD YOUR VAGINA!"

I looked in the room and started to laugh, Chloe and Edwina were stood with their legs crossed. Birch put her head on my shoulder, and shook with laughter.

The party was reaching a good swing, the music pumped, alcohol was flowing, and everyone was up dancing, well, except Denise. Chloe leaned on the wall next to her.

"Why are you not dancing, it's a party?" She gave a sigh, and cast her eyes left.

"Roy is not really into dancing." Chole shrugged.

"So, dance with someone else." She shook her head.

"He would not like that." Chloe leaned off the wall.

"Wow, it is probably a good job he likes breathing, because if he didn't, you would suffocate. Jesus Denise, I get your engaged, I mean, God knows why, but does he control everything you do? You need to wise up girl, watch this."

Chloe walked over to Roy and smiled, Denise watched him carefully, Chloe winked at him, and then slowly looked him up and down and smiled.

"You want to dance and rub bodies? I wouldn't mind feeling those rock hard muscles pressed against me." He looked at Chloe and smiled.

"I better not, I don't want to cause trouble with her." Chloe looked back at Denise.

"It's Christmas, dancing is allowed, let her dance with someone else, that way you are free to rub up against me." She grabbed his hand and pulled, he moved off the wall, and Chloe gave him a sexy wink, and slid into his arms.

"See it is not illegal, wow your stomach is like an iron plate, I wonder what else you have that is hard?"

She spun him round, and lifted her hand to Denise, and gave a thumbs up, she smiled, stood up and walked towards the men stood by the drinks table, Roy was too busy looking down Chloe's top to notice. Chloe carefully moved him round the floor, away from the table, where Denise was being talked to by three guys, she looked up at Roy.

"So Roy, tell me, how come you and your intended are so far apart, why are you not dancing with her?" He gave a sigh, and Chloe chuckled.

"Wow you are that bored already, and yet you asked her to spend her life with you, I get it is not really my business, but why get married at all?" He looked at her.

"It is what we do round here." She smiled.

"Not bloody me, I have seen how sad and pathetic everyone round here is, I paint and I fuck, and no one is putting a ring on this, and telling me how to live. Tell me how many girls have you slept with, and don't bullshit me, I already think I know?" He looked a little embarrassed.

"I have had a few." Chloe chuckled.

"Yeah, I was right, you have had two, and Denise has had one, and looking at the way you are looking down my top, I would say you are angling to make it three." He gave a smirk.

"I told Denise I have to go soon; you know, my flat is not far." She smiled.

"So, I could slip out on the down low, and spend the afternoon fucking at your place?" He pulled her tighter.

"Well, you know, it is Christmas, and a time to do good for each other." She gave a little friendly giggle, as she noticed Denise dance up right behind them.

"Oh Roy, as you say, we can spend all today in your bed fucking, that would be wonderful, and I bet really hot and steamy. Oh boy you have no idea how amazing and great I am in bed. Honestly, you would learn things that would make others blush." He was really interested.

"So what do you say, meet me in about fifteen next to the railway station?" Chloe gave a long happy sigh.

"Nope... Not interested, I actually think you are a twat, and Denise deserves better, she is my mate you know?"

Chloe let go of him and walked off, Roy stood there watching her, unaware Denise was stood right behind him. Chloe came over to us, and leaned against the wall.

"Roy is a twat; Denise needs to dump his ass." I turned and looked at her.

"I saw you dancing, so which move was it, meet me in the toilet, or come to my place later?" She gave a sigh.

"His place later... Why the hell did he ask her to marry him, if he still wants to play the field, it makes no sense? People like you guys are the ones that should be married, you know, you adore each other, your relationship is rock solid, and you both agree, that you can screw others with consent, now that is a fucking marriage, that I could do, not wankers like Roy." Birch took a sip of her drink.

"It is people like Roy, that have created a market for me, I am twenty seven, eight in February, and I have already seen too many broken hearts, because of broken promises from people like him. Denise is a nice girl, she needs to dump his ass, and enjoy life a little."

The alcohol was kicking in, and the music was louder, Deb's suddenly reappeared looking red and hot, I grabbed her zip and zipped the back of her dress up, and straightened her wings.

Rodger was dancing and flirting like crazy with all the men, G5 were hitting on the female reps, Alex and Morty were still nowhere to be seen, and there was a lot of kissing going on. Izzy walked in holding Malc by his tie, she smiled at us and then winked. Malc has his shirt hanging out, and was red in the face.

"He needed to be schooled. I think this naughty boy has learned his lesson." He looked exhausted, and he could barely walk, I actually felt sorry for him as he tried to sit down gingerly.

"Holy shit Izzy, what did you do to him?" She gave a wide grin.

"I pegged him, and he bloody loved it. I cleaned the cum up off the carpet, well he did, if he spits out blue fluff, that is the conference room carpet." Birch sniggered, I was caught between horrified and morbidly curious, I leaned into Birch.

"I know I sound like a complete virgin, but what does 'pegged' him mean?" Birch chuckled and whispered in my ear.

"She bent him over, and then screwed his ass with a strap on." I gave a gasp, and looked at him sat rather tenderly on the edge of the seat, feeling shocked.

"Holy shit Izzy, is he in pain?" She shook her head.

"Not really, I used plenty of lube, his hole is a lot bigger, it will take time to shrink back to the sweet little rose bud it was, but he will be fine. To be honest he loved it, I think it surprised him." I stared at him.

"It would surprise the frigging shit out of me too." Birch sniggered, I felt awful, I could not take my eyes off him, he moved so slowly and carefully, I lifted my glass, and Birch leaned over to me.

"If he farts there could be a problem... Frigging messy, I am not cleaning it up."

I sprayed my drink everywhere as I inhaled gin, and coughed and retched. Izzy laughed, and gave me a resounded slap on the back. My eyes were watering as I looked at Birch, she smiled.

"Jesus Birch, you bitch." She giggled, and her bright twinkled with joy.

By four o'clock, the dancing was slow, the music less boisterous, and I held Birch in my arms as we swayed. Around us spare food was being boxed up, and some of the couples had left. To our left Rodger was dancing with a well dressed slightly older rep, and to our right, Gill was being lovingly held by Aden, as they swayed to the music.

Chloe was in the corner making out with a guy called Dennis, and Terry was kissing a German rep named Petra. Denise was dancing slowly with John, the printer of all the flyers, Roy had left with a rep, he did not realise that Denise saw him, and Edwina was sat on Luke's lap kissing him, and being fingered, although they thought we had not noticed. It was winding down, as I held on to Birch, my head on her shoulder, and watched the room, she squeezed me tight.

"Are you alright Sweetie?" I gave a happy sigh.

"This is nice… I was thinking, look at them all, every one of them happy, kissing, holding and touching each other, all of them craving each other. Don't you think it is weird Birch? I mean, all of us are shamed for wanting sex, for wanting to be close, to hold someone, to explore that part of us, when we discover a new person, and engage in the flirting, and the love making. I find it odd, because everyone wants it, and yet if you do it, you are a slut or a whore, it is like no one can have an honest conversation about it without being shamed."

"I know, you are right, it is completely crazy Sweetie. We live in a world where sex sells everything, and people yearn for it, covet it, and in some cases are destroyed by it. I have never met a person yet that does not want to be loved, or to make love, and yet in parts of this country it is deemed distasteful, and not to be mentioned. The crazy thing is, those who shame us for it, desire it and crave it just as much. It is the contradiction of our age, so many people would have less problems if people would just sit down, grow up, and be open and honest about how they feel, and what they want." I looked up at her.

"I beat myself up for years, worrying about how I felt about you, I wish I hadn't, I really regret it Birch, I do regret not having this sooner." She smiled, and her eyes twinkled.

"Deads, there is no rush, and no need for regrets. We have forever now, but yes, it is sad that had the world been nicer, and freer, and more honest, both of us could have been more honest, as it would never have mattered. As I have always told you, that is the problem with all these so called rules of society, they were written for an age that no longer exists, and they need to be changed, the problem is, everyone is now so deeply indoctrinated by them, they fear standing up to suggest it."

"I want to go home, and get in bed with you, I really want to touch you, and hold you." She squeezed me harder.

"We will Sweetie, soon."

As the clock ticked towards five, everyone was happy and calm, and finding their second wind. Birch looked round the room, the numbers had fallen.

"Everyone, we will need to close, how about we take this party back to our place, and get back into the groove?" Chloe smiled.

"Oh god yes, naked, booze, and sex, now we are talking real party."

That pretty much swung everyone. We did a bit of a clean up, Izzy was relaxed and said she would come in tomorrow and do a bigger clean up, we packed the food, and grabbed all the booze. John who was dancing with Denise, had not been drinking, so we loaded up his car, and Denise and Deb's jumped in, the rest walked.

Wrapped in my coat shivering with Gill and Aden on the path, Birch locked up the retreat. The phones had been switched to the automated redirect, and for all the staff of Sweetie's Retreat, Christmas had begun in earnest. It was snowing again, much to the delight of the Snow Queen of Wotton, as she looked up in awe, and poked out her tongue to catch the flakes. Honestly, she is like a child.

Chapter 24

Acts of Love.

I like walking in the snow, it's pretty, but dressed as a satanic elf, with my tits two thirds exposed, and crotchless tights on, was way too breezy for my liking, and even though I had my coat pulled tightly round me, I was shivering like a drug addict, in need of a dealer.

Birch on the other hand, was practically naked, with no coat, dressed as Santa's chief slut, wearing fish net tights, no knickers, and high heels, and she was dancing around in the snow, like the fairy that found the pixie dust.

I was glad when we arrived home, and I could step into the warmth. Everyone was here, the food was being laid out on the table, and the booze was lined up, and Chloe had the music playing in the living room. I pulled off my boots, hung up my coat, and headed into the kitchen. There were a few faces I did not recognise; Chloe and Edwina had been texting.

Is it weird that all these drunken lethargic people from the practice not half an hour ago, are now loud and shaking their asses to the music like they have all had shots of acid? Gill was smiling stood by the patio door watching the snow, I walked up to her side and looked out.

"It is so much prettier when you are warm and toasty indoors, you look happy." She turned and gave a wide smile.

"I am Abby, thanks for giving him the push, he told me he was going to ask me out, he was just very nervous." I smiled.

"I like that in people, I remember Birch when we first got together, there was this moment, when I first made a move on her, and she went all shy, and embarrassed, and she looked so insanely beautiful. God Gill, I wanted her forever, just for that, that tiniest of moments, that was when I really knew how much I loved her, it was a special thing between us." She smiled, and gave a slight nod.

"Yeah, I completely get that." She turned and looked out of the window. "This snow is getting really heavy; it looks like we will have a load dumped on us tonight. I think I will ring home and see what it is like up on the hill, it could be a long wade back." I stared at the large white fluffy flakes.

"Stay here if you want, we have space, you can have my bed, I will be in with Birch, just let your parents know you are safe."

"Will that be alright; I don't want to put you out?" I shrugged.

"Recently I have hardly slept there, I spend most nights in with Birch, it is kind of strange really, we both have a room each, and share each others bed every night, we really should move into one room, I think she only does it to give me a writing space. Stay over it's no problem, and if Aden gets you drunk enough, you never know what may happen?" She gave a slightly shy giggle.

"I am not sure he will want to go that far?" I glanced at her.

"Gill look at your body in that costume, trust me, he might not have said it yet, but he has been thinking it all day. The top right hand bed unit has loads of condoms in it, Birch buys those buggers in bulk, use whatever you need. My room is the door with a bat on it." She looked at me like I was weird, I gave a smile.

"You know, I write vampire stories, it is yet many of the strange and weird things, you encounter around Birch?"

That she understood. Aden appeared with drinks, and I left them to it, and wandered into the living room.

Birch was dancing like a maniac with all the others, she waved with a big smile and danced over to me. The sofa was filled with snogging horny couples, Birch grabbed my hand and started to jive, I shook my head and joined in.

She laughed with joy, as she pulled into me, and pushed me away. She gave a twirl with a squeal of laughter, and then pulled me in close, she had that wicked glint in her eye.

"Watch this Sweetie."

With her free hand, she pushed her finger into the base of my top's laces, and then pushed me back, and as I swung away from her, she yanked hard, and my laces unthreaded, and pulled clean out of my top, she gave a wail of joy. I looked down and could see my nipples were not quite exposed, but they were very easy to access, Birch gave a huge cackle of a laugh as she spun my laces in her free hand.

"A stripper taught me that."

I could not deny, I was impressed. She pulled me back in, and threw her arms round me, I looked at her laughing, she smiled and kissed me, it was slow, soft and passionate, and I melted into her. I felt one of her hands explore under my top, and she tweaked me, I gave a sharp intake of breath, but she continued to kiss me, sucking my bottom lip. We broke apart, and both took a breath, she was still fondling my boob, and I was getting really wet.

"Birch, let's go upstairs, I really need to be alone with you right now." She gave a giggle.

"Soon Sweetie, I want you desperate for it, and you are not quite there yet, she squeezed my nipple hard, and I gasped, she giggled.

"Wow you are really poking out tonight, yummy, I am really looking forward to this." Birch's phone started to ring, she slid her hand out, and walked towards the hall, and put it to her ear.

"Hello... Yes, this is Dr Dixon... Sorry... Can you give me a minute it is a little loud here?"

She signalled to me, she had to take the call upstairs, I nodded. Deb's staggered up, and threw her arms round my neck, I smiled.

"Hey you, how are you doing, I have not seen you so much today?" She grinned and leaned into me.

"Oh god Abby, I had sex with Creamy, the first time was in the toilets at the practice, I gave him a blow job, and he is huge, and he is very creamy." She giggled.

"Holy shit Abby, the second time was in the consultation room, I did not think it would fit, he was so big, but oh my god, I have never cum like that in my life. I wanted him again, but he had to go to his sisters, so I am open to offers." She leaned back and looked at me.

"One day, I am going to bang you Abigail, you have no idea how much I want that." I smiled.

"Deb's, you are drunk. I love you, I really do, but I will never sleep with another woman while I am with Birch. I am sorry, but you have a better chance with Chloe than you ever will me." She smiled.

"I know, but a girl can dream." She swayed a little, and I held her hips, I must admit, she was taking Jimmy cheating on her far better than I thought she would.

"Deb's, are you going to be alright, you know with Jimmy and everything, I won't deny it, I worry about you a lot?" She pulled me into a hug, and held me tight.

"Abby I am fine, honestly, I am, in a way I think I knew, it sounds sort of strange, but before we were married, it worked better because we accepted we were like this. I married a rock star knowing what that life is like. I actually prefer things this way, it is more honest. I messaged him and told him I had seen the pictures, and I told him to enjoy it, because I was going to. I am going to really enjoy this Christmas, if he was here, it would be with him, but he is not, and so I will take what I can get." I held on to her.

"Just be careful and take good care of yourself."

"I am doing, honestly Abby, I really am doing." She slipped back, and smiled. "I need a drink, let's go top up."

The party was in full swing, the living room was loud and rowdy, the library had groups all gathered, Anthony was talking and laughing, and the kitchen was also very noisy, as people stood round eating the food, and topping their drinks up, Edwina had wisely locked the cellar door.

I wove through everyone, toward the kitchen unit, and the bottles of mixers and gin, it was hard to work out who was where, out on the patio, a group stood shivering and smoking, I could not really see where Birch had got to.

I topped up my drink, and started to weave my way back, Meg leaned in and kissed my cheek, 'awesome party Abby.' I smiled. Alex was making out with Morty, she had been with him all day, her blouse was open and her bikini was gone, she had nice boobs, I leaned in.

"Guys, as far as I know, the attic is empty and quiet, and there are lots of bean bags."

Morty smiled, and took her by the hand, and they slipped off up the hallway, I followed, cutting my way through back to the hallway. Edwina and Luke were talking to one of their friends, Edwina looked at me and smiled.

"Edwina, have you seen Birch?"

She shrugged, and shook her head, I moved on towards the living room, which had pretty much become a dance floor, and a sofa sex palace, where people in various stages of undress were clawing at each other, there was no sign of Birch.

The stairs were like a mine field, as couples kissed and groped each other, I made my way carefully sipping my drink, it was at times like this I liked the fact all our doors could be auto locked. Edwina had obviously triggered it, if not, every bed in the house would be full, and that was one of our house rules, no one has sex in our beds without our consent.

I made it slowly up the stairs and headed for my room, I tapped the combo lock and entered, I had hoped to find her in my bed. I put my drink on the desk, it was warm up here, and I unbuttoned my skirt, and let it fall to the floor, a top and tights was enough. I stepped out of it and picked it up, and threw it on my sofa, I lifted my glass and took a sip, and walked to the shared bathroom, and that was when I heard it, the very faint.

"Hep... Hep... Hep." I walked slowly through the bathroom, was that Birch? I arrived at her door, and was surprised to see her bed empty.

"Hep... Hep... Hep." I leaned into the room and looked round, the little tree was lit up outside, and I noticed the door to the balcony was open, I stepped into the room.

"Birch... Are you here?"

I walked, slowly looking around the room, there was no sign of her. I crossed to the bed, craning my neck, and I saw the white skinned arm of Birch, it was touching the tree, she was sat back on the balcony to the side of the door, in the snow, which was actually quite deep.

"Birch... Baby are you okay?"

As I got to the door and looked down at her, she lifted her head, her lips were trembling, and she gave a quiet sob, as tears rolled down her face.

"Hep!"

Birch was sat in the snow, she looked soaked, as the snow drifted down in waves on to her, those beautiful green eyes were filled with tears, and swollen and puffy from her crying. I stepped through the window feeling a sudden urgent pain in my chest, I dropped to my knees.

"Birch what is it, what is wrong, Baby please don't cry?" I pulled her into my arms, and she just started to shake, and then sobbed a huge painful bitter sob into me, her voice was weak.

"She has gone."

I squeezed her tight as she wailed into my shoulder, and I felt a huge wave of fear and pain course through me. Birch clamped on to me, as she shook and cried, I did not know what to do, I had never seen her like this. She had told me she was gone, but who? I felt the shiver run down my back.

"Birch Baby, I need to know, please tell me, who has gone?" She just shook, and mumbled.

"I wasn't ready to let go, not yet, I wanted her to stay longer."

She sobbed, and I held her tight and just let her cry, there was nothing I could do. I rocked her gently in my arms, unsure of whether it was for my benefit or hers. I could feel her tears turning cold as they ran down between my breasts, and she just sobbed and sobbed. I held her as close as I could, she was almost frozen, it was so cold out here. My mind felt frozen, as I held back my fear, who was gone, who was she not ready to let go of? I felt a surge of panic grow inside me.

"Birch, please tell me, who has gone?"

I was terrified she was going to say Roni, my heart was pounding like crazy, I would not be able to deal with that at all. Birch leaned back and gave a huge sniffle, and looked at me, her lip was trembling even faster, she gave a huge sob.

"Hep!"

I gazed into her broken hearted eyes, and could see her pain. I pushed her long hair back from her face, I wanted to cry, but had no idea why. I hated seeing her like this, what news had broken her heart so deeply, I was terrified of what her answer would be?

"Birch, Baby, talk to me." She bit her lip and tried to swallow; her voice was so quiet.

"She left me Deads... May has gone and left me." She shook, and her face screwed up.

"I didn't want to say goodbye yet, I loved our talks, Oh Deads she has gone, and left me." The tears flowed, and she crashed back into my shoulder, and broke down.

I felt her pain, my eyes filled with tears, we had only talked to her a few days ago, how could she be gone? Birch wailed, and I held on to her, joining in with her tears.

Her pain was so real and so genuine, I just clung to her, sobbing with her, for how long I am not sure. I lost all track of time, before she started to quieten down, she was shivering, and snow was piling up on us, I was shivering too. I stroked back her hair.

"Birch, Baby, we are going to freeze out here, you need to come inside, come on, let me run a hot bath, and we can curl up in it and talk." She slipped back and looked at me, I held her cheek.

"Will you be alright Baby?" She gave a sniffle, and nodded.

"Thanks Sweetie, I needed you, and you came to me, it feels so painful, and I don't know why?" I held her face and wiped the tear that ran from her eye with my thumb.

"You loved her, and you cared for her very deeply, that is why, when no one else understood her, you did, and she knew that. She knew you really got her, and it made a huge difference to her life. I know how that feels Birch, you did the same for me, and it saved me, just like it saved May."

Tears rolled down her cheeks, but she nodded, she understood what I meant. I tried to stand, my legs were dead with the numbness of the cold, I groaned as I stood up and reached for her arm.

"Come inside before you freeze us both to death." She took my hand, and tried to stand, she flinched as she felt the pain in her dead legs.

Slowly I hobbled backwards, and guided her to the bed, and sat her on the edge, I then reached out, and closed the patio door. Birch sat shivering, and I grabbed her shawl off the chair, and wrapped it round her. I then headed for the bathroom hobbling on numb legs, and turned on the hot water, I needed to heat her up, or she would be really ill.

Whilst the bath ran, I sat at her side, and rubbed her shoulders to get the blood flowing into her arms. I checked on the bath, and when it was full, I turned off the taps. I walked back into the bedroom and climbed on to the bed, I unzipped the back of her top, and unfastened the buttons on her skirt. I slid off the bed, and round in front of her, and slid her top up, and over her head. I then pulled her up, she was slowly coming back to life, as I slipped her skirt down, her legs looked blue. I pulled her fish nets down to the floor, and started to rub her legs vigorously.

"You are lucky you did not freeze to death; your legs are blue." She looked down at me, her face streaked from her mascara which had run.

"I am sorry Sweetie." I shook my head.

"You have nothing to be sorry about, you showed May great respect and honour." I stood up and held her face softly in my hands, and looked her straight in the eyes.

"Baby, I have always loved how big your heart is, your enormous ability to love makes you the most beautiful person I have ever known, it is why I love you so deeply." She swallowed hard, and smiled, her eyes filled with tears.

"I really love you too Deads, I really do." I leaned in and kissed her softly, she responded kissing me back, and it brought her back to life a little. I pulled away, and looked at her.

"Come and bathe with me, and talk to me Birch, tell me everything, and cry, scream, and do anything you want, but talk to me, and share it, because I want to see and know her the way you do. So, let's me and you, celebrate her by telling the world who she was." She nodded.

"I would like that, she would too."

I undressed, and then took her hand, and led her into the bathroom, her legs were frozen, and she winced as she stepped into the red hot water. I helped her lower into the bath, and then slid in behind her, biting my lip as my legs burned, Birch leaned back, and I slid my arms round her.

"Is that nice?" She relaxed into me, and gave a sigh.

"Deads, thanks for this, I got the news and just fell apart, I am really going to miss my talks with her." She started to shake, so I rested my head onto her shoulder, and just let her cry, I think she needed to let all of this out.

"Tell me about her Birch, tell me about when you first talked to her, and what that was like." She gave a sob.

"I rang Ellen, I don't really know why, but after that day when we volunteered, I kept thinking about her. I know she was diagnosed with dementia, but I thought the rudeness was a part of her true personality, and it felt like she was fighting to stay true to who she was. I suppose in a way I identified with her, and I just wanted to know if I was right. I got my mum to request a copy of her file, you know doctors' privilege and all that, I thought maybe mum could help her, and I found out, she was the mother of that corrupt MP that serves here." I knew who she meant.

"Walter Parkinson?" She nodded.

"Yeah, that twat." She turned her head to me; her eyes were full of tears.

"Deads he put her there because she was confrontational, she was rude to his rich friends, and called him a Fugazi. It means fake, fraud, pretender. Basically, there was nothing wrong with her, she was just calling him out for being the twat we know him as." Her tears rolled back onto her cheeks.

"Deads can you see, she was in that insane asylum and alone, and she was fighting with everything she had to keep herself going, by being herself. She was one of us, she was persecuted, and shamed by her own son, because she did not fit his ideal."

Her shoulders shook, and she pushed her face into me, I lifted my arm, and put it across her shoulders, as she wept, I felt a huge lump in my throat.

Birch turned in the bath, and she slid her arm behind me, as she lay on her side with her head on my shoulder, I felt wretched, and useless, all I could do was cradle her as I cried with her. Her voice was higher and croaky.

"How could he do that, she was so beautiful, such a powerful spirit, and so free? How could he cage her like that, she must have felt her sanity challenged for every second she was in there? Deads she did not deserve that, once I got to know her, she was so lovely."

Her sobs came out as wails, and they tore at my heart, I could not take her being this hurt, it was so painful to witness, and I cried just as much as she did. It took her a long time to calm back down.

"How did you get to know her, Birch?" She gave a sniffle.

"Ellen... She would let me know when her shifts were, and she would take her laptop in and set it up on the table. I sent a head set down to her, and May would put it on, so she could hear me, that place was so noisy, it was hard to hear anything." Birch lifted her head and looked at me, she smiled a beautiful smile.

"The first time she saw me, I waved and said hi Sweetie, and she smiled. She smiled Deads, and said 'Slut.' I laughed so hard, and I told her I loved it, and then I started to talk, and I told her I knew about her son, and she scowled and said 'Wanker.' I laughed so hard she chuckled, and it was such a lovely sound to hear, Deads it made her happy, she laughed, it made her so happy." She bit her lip, and sobbed.

"I knew I was right, I told her I knew what he had done, and I told her to keep fighting. I did that for weeks, and then one night I went on, and she said 'Sweetie' before I could talk, and she smiled such a lovely smile." Birch broke down again, and wept bitterly.

"I went to see her again when you came home, and your dad took you away abroad. Mum was in London, so I tagged along and hired a car. I drove up here, and sat with her, and she held my hand, and when they said I could take her for a walk in the grounds, as soon as we got outside and were alone, she looked at me and said, 'I am not mad, but I feel like I am going that way.' I told her not to give up, and she told me she was forgetting things and was afraid." She sat up and wiped her eyes.

"Deads she was fine when she went in there, it was that place that made her like that. I drove out of there, and parked up near the canal. I walked to your arch, and I sat there. I really needed you, I was missing you so much, and seeing May like that was too much. When I sent you that message, saying I miss you, while you were on holiday, that is where I was, it was the only way I could feel close to you. It was such a hard day Deads." I leaned onto her back and wrapped my arms round her.

"You should have phoned; I would have been on the next flight back." She shook her head.

"I still had years left, it would have been cruel to have you fly back, and then leave you again. When I got home, there was a letter, her son told me not to visit again, and so I talked to Ellen, and we kept up the video calls. Ellen told me she would talk normally to her and me, and to everyone else she was abusive, she fought every second she was in there and she never gave up, right up till the end. Ellen told me, that the last thing she said to the doctor, was 'piss off you posh idiot.' Even her last words were an act of defiance. God, I loved her, I loved her so much, she inspired me."

I held her tight as her shoulders shook, and she looked down into the water, I could see the rings ripple out, where her tears hit, her sobs were quiet, but each one felt just as painful to me. I allowed her the space to let out her grief, she calmed down again, I just held her.

"Birch, I hope you know you made a difference, have you any idea how important it must have been for her, just to know that one person knew the truth? Birch, I know how difficult and painful it is to be shamed and have to live alone, surrounded by people who believe all the lies about you. I lived like that when you were not here, your video calls were the only thing keeping me going, I know it sounds crazy, but I know exactly how May felt, you saved me too." She turned in the bath and looked at me.

"Deads, I love you; you are my world." I smiled.

"You are mine too, and you were also May's. Birch whichever way you look at this, these last few years have been easier on her, happier for her, before that her life was torture. Then in you walked, took one look at her, and felt that same bond you feel with all of us, because what you have done for May, you have done for Deb's, Chloe, Anthony, Edwina, and I may add Izzy. Can you not see, you are surrounded by souls who yearn to be free? We do not need this big house, you did it all in my tiny guest house, that is you, it is who you are." She gave a loud sniffle and nodded her head.

"I can understand what you are saying." I kissed her shoulder.

"Birch Baby, I honestly think that you need to decide, how you would like to honour her life. If there is going to be a service for her, we could go, or if you want something more private, and she has a marker, we can visit it. Whatever you want to do, I will be there at your side, and there if you need me." She took a deep breath.

"I would like to do something, I would like to remember her, I am not sure how, but I will mark her life one way or another." I pulled her back, and she lay back and rested with her on my front, and I held her, she put her hands on mine, and was calmer, she gave my hand a squeeze.

"I never want to lose you; I could not survive that." I kissed her shoulder.

"Celia and Lillian forever and beyond, I made the commitment to you, and aim to keep it."

"Deads?"

"Yes Baby."

"Can we go to bed and hold each other?" I kissed her shoulder.

"That is all I have wanted to do all day."

Gill was in the kitchen with Aden, and she was kissing him, and getting more than excited, she pulled back and gasped for air.

"Aden, I want more, I am so turned on right now, I have thought about this for months." He looked at her, and swallowed.

"When you say more, do you mean sleep together?" She nodded.

"I know this is technically a first date, but I want more dates, I want lots of dates. If I sleep with you, will you still be next to me when I wake up?" He wiped his mouth, and took a deep breath.

"I want to wake up with you, but it is snowing like crazy, and I live in Oxendale, it is a long way to my place by foot." She smiled.

"I am staying here tonight, Abby has let me have her room, she is sleeping with Birch. Please promise me, if we do this, you will still be here in the morning. I do not do this ever, but I really want this, do not let me down." He nodded his head, and took her hands in his.

"Gill, I want us to last, I really want this to be big for both of us, and honestly, I want to see you when I wake up. You know this is a risk for me too." She smiled.

"Okay, Aden take me upstairs and make love to me, but please go slow, I have not done this much." He smiled.

"I am so glad to hear that, I am not in a rush Gill, I want this right and at our pace."

She took his hand, and turned towards the kitchen door. Gill led Aden down the hallway, and up the stairs, towards the door with a bat on it, she turned the handle, and it swung open. The room was almost dark, the light from the bathroom cast a nice light into the room. Gill walked over to the bed, and slid open the top right hand draw, there was a huge pile of condoms, she smiled and lifted a strip out.

Aden looked nervous, she was only wearing a bikini, she took a deep breath, and reached up behind her back, and pulled open the bow, her top slipped, and Aden pulled at his shirt, and started to undo his buttons, as he looked at her naked breasts.

Gill gave a shy smile, and sat on the side of the bed, and then slid back on to it, he peeled off his shirt, and pulled his vest over his head, he was actually very nervous, Gill watched, as he undid his pants, and they fell to the floor, he took a huge breath, and slid down his boxers, he was already up for action, and she gave a big smile. He climbed onto the bed, and leaned over her.

"Oh my, gosh you are so beautiful."

Her arms slipped down her sides, and grabbed the bows tied on the side of her bottoms, she gazed down at his enlarge manhood, he was bigger than she expected, her breathing was becoming quicker, as she pulled the strings. He looked down, and slipped his fingers inside the loose fabric, and she breathed in sharply, his touch ignited her, as he pulled it away, and her womanhood was on full display to him, he smiled.

"Oh Gill, I am feeling intoxicated with you."

She reached up, and pulled him down into a kiss, he was breathing faster, and his passion was obvious, as he kissed her, her whole body was alive, as he moved onto her neck, she gasped for air.

"Oh Aden."

He kissed her slowly, and her whole body tingled, he moved slowly towards her breasts, and she lay back, breathing deeply, he made contact and she gasped, and arched slightly, he slowly sucked and her mind spun.

"OH ADEN!"

Birch lifted her head off the pillow, I had completely forgotten about Gill, I rolled over and smiled, and whispered.

"Oh crap, I completely forgot, Gill is staying in my room tonight." Birch gave a smile.

"She is with Aden?" I nodded.

"Birch I am sorry; it just slipped my mind." She lay back on the pillow and I turned to her, she turned her head and looked at me.

"I think it is nice, this is what Gill wants."

Gill was feeling things she never had before, and her body was burning up. Aden kissed under her boobs, and traced his way onto her stomach, she took a huge breath in, and gasped.

"Oh hell."

He moved slowly, and looked up at her, she was watching him, and her whole lower region was on fire and starting to tingle. He slid over her leg, and in between the two, she spread them a little to give him room.

He kissed over her tummy, and moved lower, he was just above her pelvic bone, and she gave a gasp, and started to breathe faster.

"Aden, no one has ever done that to me, I do not know what to do." He looked up and smiled.

"Just relax, I want this to be special."

She stared down at him, her heart pounding, he slid his hand under her leg, and pushed it up towards her, spreading her legs wider open, she could feel the hot liquid running out of her, and down to her bum cheeks. He slid the other leg up, and she spread wide, her eyes opened wider, as he lowered himself down to her wide open sex.

"Oh god, you really are going to do it?"

Her hands shot up above her head, and she found the headboard, his mouth made contact, and she bucked on the bed, and pulled hard on the head board.

"Oh... Oh... Oh... OH ADEN!"

I smiled, as Birch bit her lip.

"Wow he is doing pretty good, I should have known Edwina would have trained him properly."

"OH GOD.... OH GOD.... OH GOD.... OH GOD...OH, OH, OH, OH, OH, OOOOOOH!" Birch sniggered.

"One point to Aden."

Gill gripped hard to the head board, as her body shook uncontrollably, she had never felt anything like it, she lay back gasping for air, Aden moved slowly back up her body, he looked down on her, she was flushed across her face, and right down to her chest.

"Are you alright Gill?" She smiled; she had tears in her eyes.

"I have dreamed of feeling like this, I did not know, I did not know Aden I could feel this amazing." I smiled at Birch.

"That is so sweet, well done Aden." Birch slid closer, and whispered back.

"Deads Sweetie, it is making me really wet, that is not screwed up is it?" I sniggered.

"Hell no, I am soaking, how messed up is that? Listening to Gill is really turning me on." Birch gave a quiet giggle, and moved towards me, I felt her hand slide onto my stomach, she gave me a smile.

Gill smiled as he moved up to kiss her, his lips met hers, and she started to greedily, take all of him on her lips, and her passion reignited, she felt him move and his manhood touched her wet opening, she broke free.

"You have to use protection; I am not on the pill."

He moved back, he was breathing rapidly, Gill grabbed the packet and tore it open, she squinted at it in the dark.

"I want to do this."

Aden sat back on his haunches over her, and she sat up, and reached out for it, he closed his eyes, he was at full tension, and her touch made it throb slightly, she looked up and saw his face, and she smiled as she slowly rolled it down him, and he gave a gasp.

She leaned in and kissed his chest, he opened his eyes, and looked down at her, she smiled and lay back. He moved over her, she was ready, he came down towards her and she closed her eyes as she felt him enter, he slid slowly in, and her toes curled.

"OH MY GOD THAT FEELS GOOD!" She was surprised with herself, but he was pleased, she had never thought she would be so vocal.

I slid my hand over Birch as she faced me, her fingers were rubbing, and I was jittery, I slid down towards her, and she gave a little gasp as I hit her button, and bit her lip and closed her eyes, Gill moaned out loud, and I felt a pulse run down my legs, and up through my stomach, I could not believe I was this turned on.

Aden was sliding easily in, and out, he looked down at Gill as she gasped for air,

"Gill I am way too turned on; I don't think I will last very long." She smiled up at him, her heart pounded.

"Aden, I have never been this turned on, not ever, I did not know it could be like this."

He pushed a little harder and she gasped, he could feel himself building, and he wanted to push faster, he was not aware how close Gill was, he tried to focus and concentrate.

He gasped in air as he felt his hips move quicker, he was trying to hold back, but as his need grew stronger, his hips moved faster, and he pounded a little harder, it drove Gill wild, as her body built up her power, he was losing control, and he pushed harder, her hips bucked and she let out a long loud moan.

Listening to Gill and Aden, was driving Birch and myself wild, her hand was moving faster, and my body was exploding as I tried to keep pace with her, she was biting into the pillow and her legs were stretched taught as she tried to hold in her moans. I was so close, and she knew it, in the other room, Gill was close and it was driving me nuts.

"Oh, Oh, Oh, Oh, Oh, Aden, Aden, ADEN, ADENNNN!"

"OH GILL, OH, OH, OHHHHH!"

It was too much for Birch, she pushed off the duvet, push me hard onto my back, and dived down throwing her leg over me, she sat right down on my face, and buried her head between my legs, and my whole body went wild.

Gill lay flat sweating and gasping, Aden was flat on her chest breathing wildly, she brought her limp arms down, and put them round him, as she tried to regulate her breathing, and had given up trying to stop her legs shaking. Both of them lay there, slowly coming back to life. Aden slid back, and carefully removed the condom, he looked round the room, there was nowhere to put it, he slipped off the bed.

He walked into the bathroom, and saw the small bin, he pulled some toilet roll off and wrapped it up neatly, then dropped it in the bin, he went to wash his hands, and heard the long quiet moan, he stopped and panicked. He looked round towards the other door, not really sure, he walked slowly towards it, and leaned round to look, he swallowed hard and pulled back quickly.

Gill slid down the duvet and pulled it over her, Aden came in fast and jumped into bed, he slid up and she smiled, he swallowed hard.

"Gill, Abby and Jemi are having sex next door. I heard a strange noise and so looked, and they are... Well, you know, with their mouths, like I did, but at the same time. What should we do, they must have heard us?"

Gill chuckled and slid over to him, she slipped her arm under him, and pulled him close and kissed him, he gave a slight moan. She broke free and gave a smile.

"Aden, that is the best sex I have ever had, and honestly, I don't care if they heard us, the whole world can hear us, hell I will film it and show them. I loved what we did, it was perfect." He smiled and raised his eyebrows.

"Wow, best ever?" She smiled.

"Best ever, now kiss me again before I fall asleep."

Chapter 25

Snow Queen.

I leaned on the bedroom door with two cups of coffee. "Don't they look so sweet together?" Birch gave a chuckle.

"Deads they are a year younger than you, honestly, where is this motherly instinct coming from, they are not children?" I could not help it, I felt really happy.

Gill was curled up, fast asleep, Aden was behind her, and curled round her, like Birch did with me, and they looked so calm and relaxed. I think deep down inside, Gill felt very safe, I know how that feels, I have it with Birch. I walked over to the bed, and put the coffees down on the bedside unit, I sat on the edge of the bed, and looked at Gill fast asleep, I smiled as I looked at Birch. I leaned over and spoke quietly.

"Gill... Gill... Gill I have coffee, come on sweetheart, it's time to wake up." Gill stirred slightly, and opened her eyes, I smiled.

"Sweetheart it's almost twelve, I have coffee for you both." She blinked, and took a deep breath, then yawned.

"Both?" I gave a little giggle.

"Well yeah, that sleeping hunk with his arm round you needs to wake up too." She smiled.

"He stayed." I smiled at her; I could see how happy she was.

"He certainly did, somehow, I think he is going to be around for a while, and I think that is a good thing, don't you?" She gave a very happy smile.

"Thanks Abby, you did this, and I am so grateful." She slid her hand out from under the duvet, and I took it and gave it a squeeze.

"I left my kimono on the chair, as you know we don't really wear much here in the house, but I wasn't sure how you guys would feel. Megan has gone back to the practice, to collect all your clothes, all of you left them there last night, and you cannot go out in a bikini. Take your time, and when both of you are ready, there is food in the kitchen, we will be down there, so have your coffee and enjoy this morning together."

I left Gill to wake Aden, and headed downstairs, Edwina was out front organising some of the men who had stayed over, to dig out the drive, it had snowed a lot last night, I shivered just at the thought. Chloe was painting, and Deb's was back in the bookshop with Denise. Roy had been texting Denise all morning, apparently early this morning, she had sent him a picture, of him leaving the practice, with his arm round a young female sales rep, and given him the boot.

Birch was stood by the tall patio windows looking out at the snow in the back garden, as I entered the kitchen, the door to the studio door was open, and Chloe sat naked on the floor, painting. I walked up behind Birch, and slid my hands round her, and put my chin on her shoulder.

"How are you today?" She tilted her head and leaned on mine.

"I am doing fine, I feel sad, and I am still very emotional, but I listened to what you said last night, and you said a lot of things that are true. You surprised me a lot Deads, and when I needed you the most, you appeared, and it did help, thanks Sweetie."

"I hate seeing you that upset, it was awful, and it really hurt me to see it." She squeezed my hand.

"I am sorry, I got so overcome, it is not like me at all, but I just fell apart."

"Birch, you do not need to apologise, you loved her a great deal, and you did a lot for her, don't apologise for feeling love, it is one of the reasons I love you." She gave a sigh, I could feel the emotions in her, as she took a breath.

"Deads there are some people, who look ordinary, but once you get to know them, they radiate great beauty, and May was one of the most beautiful. I only spoke to her once a week, but she made my life more beautiful, and I am going to miss that a great deal." I kissed her shoulder.

All I could do was just hug her, and watch over her, and when the emotions rose within her, just be there. It is so hard at times to know what is the right thing to do. I had felt so much hurt inside myself watching her grieve last night, and the most horrible thing of all, was all I did was look at her and think back to two years ago, when she discovered the sleeping pills in my room. It had been a recurring memory ever since, the look on her face, the hurt in her eyes, the pain in her voice, I closed my eyes as I leaned on her and it all came flooding back.

"YOU CAN NEVER.... NEVER.... NEVER EVER DO THAT TO ME DEADS!"

She shook her head, as more tears rolled down her face, and her voice dropped to an almost inaudible squeak. "Not ever."

She came round the bed, reached out, and snatched me into her arms, and almost crushed me, she held me so tight. Her face buried into my shoulder and she started to sob.

"No matter what happens, you must never leave me, promise me Deads.... Promise me you will never leave me alone in this world, because I would not survive if you left me alone."

I saw that expression, and heard that tone again last night, I felt the goose bumps rise up on my arms. I came so close to doing that to her, and last night I saw a glimpse of the horrors I would have inflicted on her, and I felt ashamed of myself, for being such a coward back then.

Christmas has always been a depressing time for me, my memories run back to being a child, and playing with my presents in the front room, and listening to my dad complain. As I got older and the types of gifts I got would change, to makeup, and clothes, and again he would complain about the styles or the shades of eye makeup, he couldn't say something nice. My Christmas's from my teenage years onwards always ended the same way, with me or my mum having a row with him, which put a dampener on the rest of the day.

I really wanted this Christmas to be special, and yet at the moment, it felt like everything was going from bad to worse. Since the moment we put up the tree and lit up the house, it had felt like we were under siege, what with Rodney, and all the fear he caused, and then Ben Shepperton with his trash piece, followed by all the nasty remarks from the Shrew Crew, and my dad, and his manipulation and attacking of Birch, and then that the bloody awful Peter Ford and all his shit. It felt it was going downhill steadily, and we were only a week away.

I was worried about Chloe's breakdown, all the revelations

about Jimmy in Japan, Deb's was acting like it was okay, but I knew her well enough to know something was on her mind, and now Birch's heartbreak over May's death. I just wanted it all to stop, so we could relax and have fun, like we had been doing yesterday. I think all of us were feeling it, and we needed to just release the tension, so we could let go of all of it, and then focus on enjoying our special day.

Gill came down wrapped in the kimono and walked in yawning, I released Birch, and turned and smiled, her cup was empty, so I headed to the kettle to make more. The coffee machine was empty, I filled that up too and started a fresh new pot. At least this was one good thing to happen, Gill was really happy, and was all smiles. I turned to face her, and grinned.

"So what is it like to know he is finally yours?" She leaned her face on her hands, and just smiled.

"I am really happy Abby, last night was pretty amazing, I have never done that before, you know on a first date, but I am glad I did, I did not know I could feel like that, it was pretty mind blowing." I gave a giggle.

"Hmm, we heard." She looked down and went a little pink. "Gill it is fine, everyone here is used to the sound of orgasms, we do live with Chloe, and she is not quiet." Chloe turned in her studio and gave a big smile.

"Sex is amazing, everyone should scream and enjoy the moment." Gill gave a titter, Birch turned from the window.

"The snow is so pretty, I want to walk in it, I want to see how nature decorates everything." I turned to her.

"If you wrap up warm, I know just the place to go." She smiled, and nodded, it was nice to see her smile, and a little of the sadness in her eyes lifted. I turned to Gill.

"Meg will be back in a little while, but feel at home, use the shower or bath, hang around the house, or you know, go back to bed for a while, make the most of your time together." She looked a little flustered.

"Would that be alright; I don't want to put you out?" Birch shook her head.

"Gill, get up there, lay him on his back and sit on it, and let him watch you, as you ride him, trust me he will thank you for it. Most of the house is sound proof, although you may hear Alex, she was screwing the ass off Morty this morning when I got up, and she is not down yet, so I am assuming they are recharging for more." She looked a little red around the cheeks.

"Is that alright, I don't want to get in anyone's way." Birch shook her head.

"Gill do you want to spend the day screwing his brains out?" She swallowed and looked a little shy.

"Well yes, but..."

"Then get up there and do him, and have some bloody fun, work has finished, so enjoy yourself." She smiled an embarrassed smile. Birch headed up to her room to dress, I followed.

Ten minutes later I was ready, I had cheated, and put my crotchless tights back on under my jeans, and then a thick pair of socks. I pulled an old jumper out of my dresser, while Aden hid his nudity under the duvet, and went red as he saw me naked, I just giggled at him. With my thick coat, a woollen hat, thick scarf and gloves, I was ready and waiting. Birch appeared and smiled.

"You look toasty Sweetie."

She leaned in and kissed me, to be honest I was cooking alive, the heating in the house was set for nudity, and I had many layers on, I was actually looking forward to getting outside.

The snow had fallen all night, and on the path, it was pretty deep, the plough had cleared the road, so we walked on that, and holding her hand, I walked towards the canal. Call it a gut instinct, but knowing her love for trees, I thought this would be the best place to show her. We stood on the bridge, and looked out over the canal, and Birch gasped in awe.

"Oh Deads, it is so beautiful, I cannot believe how magical a place this has become."

I smiled looking at her bright green eyes sparkle, as her long white hair lifted on her shoulders, as it flowed out from under her hat.

"You belong here Birch, you are a like a true snow queen in this setting, you wear winter very well." She turned to me, and smiled, her eyes filled with life.

"You called me that yesterday." I nodded.

"It is the new story I am working on. To be honest I started it a while ago, I was almost finished, but I got blocked on the end of it. After we made love in the snow, I got re-inspired and made changes. You know, looking up at you, with eyes as green as the grass, and your hair like the leafless birch trees, with your pale skin as white as the snow, you were so amazingly beautiful. I had to write it down, and it became a character, named Betula, lost and alone, and yearning to find the love in the world, seeking out the truth of life. She feels cursed to protect all she loves against the winter, by covering them in her only means of protection, the snow." She swallowed hard, and took my hand in hers.

"I have never known anyone quite like you Deads, you are so inspiring to me. I don't say it often, but I love the way you use words to make everything so beautiful. I read your stories and they lifted me, they kept me going when I was alone at Uni. I missed you so much and I was so very lonely without you, and it did feel like being buried, as I curled up alone at night. I will never leave your side, you know that, don't you?" I smiled.

"I am never letting you go Birch; you are the reason I write." She smiled and her eyes filled with tears.

"I love you so much it hurts, is that mental?" I pulled her hand, and headed for the steps down, she was so delicate today, and very emotional, I felt sorry for her.

"It is not mental, it is meant to be, it is as simple as that, your white and my dark, we are like day and night, we belong together."

We walked onto the steps, I must admit I hate the snow, but I have always loved the canal covered in it. The water was dark, and yet was bright as it reflected the white of the trees either side, like a huge black mirror. All the branches that leaned out over the water, had a layer of sparkling white jewelled fluff all the way along them. The grass grew up through the thick white floor, sparkling with a thin layer of frost, and the tips hung over slightly, as the large diamond looking drops of melted water hung on, waiting until big enough to drop.

There was a silence to everything, almost like all of nature was consumed with an insulated layer of inner peace. I guess it felt the same as I do around Birch at times, when we sit or lie quietly in each others arms. Our feet crunched as the snow compacted below our boots, Birch was in tenth heaven, as she looked around, and up at all the trees, wearing a huge happy smile, I knew this place would help to heal her.

She stood in the middle of the path, her eyes dazzling like the crystals in the snow, and wearing a huge smile, I looked at the trunk leaning onto the path slightly. I lifted my leg, and using the flat of my boot soul, I slammed it into the trunk, and suddenly from above the snow broke free and fell in a stream of flakes.

Birch gave a squeal of delight, and looked up, and held out her hands, and the snow fluttered down to decorate her. It landed in her hair and on her eye lashes, and it was like she was transformed. She looked at me with a radiantly happy smile, and I gave a gasp, she was stunning, as the flakes sparkled on her, I walked up to her.

"Wow you look so stunning, and radiant." I grabbed her face and pulled her into a kiss, her arms came round me, as she pulled me in and kissed me back.

It was long and filled with love, although her nose was really cold. I sucked her bottom lip and just stared at her; with her huge green, happy eyes, which sparkled in front of me. I wanted to say something, but no words appeared to fit my intense feelings, I just looked at her, and drowned in her eyes. She smiled, and then moved in and kissed me, there was no other way to express the moment of feelings that were washing over me, and she understood that.

We walked along the picturesque pathway, and I could see Birch just drawing more and more energy from the surroundings, I regretted not bringing my camera, it was so beautiful. We walked hand in hand up to the arch, she looked up at it, dressed with snow.

"It really is the perfect sanctuary, it is funny you know Deads, because when I sat there alone, knowing you were so far away, I still felt close to you. I suppose in my head it is a symbol of you, it gave me comfort to be there."

It is so strange because it's just a lump of flat concrete, with a broken down red brick wall, with the sand stone carved arch window, and yet it is so special, so precious, I understood her completely. I have spent many nights lay in the dark remembering the view of it above me, as I lay on the floor that afternoon, in summer two years ago, making love to her. It was that day that changed my writing forever, I wrote the Shoots of Summer and Sanctuary Arch because of it, and my life changed dramatically.

There is so much we take for granted, and yet when we look back, they are iconic parts of our lives with such deep meaning. I think that day taught me the importance of those small actions, and I was reminded of that as I looked up from the path at it. There have been so many small moments between us, so many hugs, smiles, and such laughter, and all of them mean the world to me, and are precious seconds of a life I treasure, and as important as my arch was to me as a young girl.

Our noses were red, but we were toasty warm, and holding hands, we walked back quietly talking, I had been feeling a little guilty all day, and wanted to talk to her, and now we were alone, and walking at a slow pace, I plucked up the courage.

"Birch, last night was frightening for me, it made me realise how badly you would have suffered, and it showed me some of the pain you must have felt when you saw the sleeping pills. Watching you sat there freezing in the snow, I felt so wretched and guilty, and I am sorry. I remember your voice, and the fear and panic in it, when you told me I must never do that." I stopped and looked at her.

"You understand don't you, that I felt like you did last night? I honestly thought I had lost you forever, and it was unbearable. Had I known you were coming, I would have waited and left the tablets in my room in my mum's house. It has haunted me for so long, I cannot tell you of the times I have had bad dreams remembering it, and I have always felt so guilty for doing that to you, it tears me apart at times." She stopped and looked at me, her nose and cheeks were red with the cold.

"Deads, stop beating yourself up, yes it scared me, but you also have to understand, that I had missed you so much, but when I arrived, I did not really fully understand why. I asked myself did I miss our life in the little house, or the friendship and bond we shared, or was I really in love with a woman? At that moment I did not completely know, it was when I picked up those pills, and realised you either had tried, or were going to try to kill yourself, that was when I fully understood."

I was a little surprised because back then, I was so sure I loved her, I cannot deny I was not sure I could make love to her, and yet she was still working it all out, it felt strange to me. She gave a sigh.

"When I thought of a world without you in it, I knew, the feeling that surged through me, because it did shock me to see them, but in a way, it was a good thing, because that was my moment of clarity. I think faced with the reality of that moment; everything became crystal clear. I became so sure, I knew without doubt, I knew I was going to win you back, and then I was going to show you by making love to you. Deads that was also weird for me too you know, because I had no idea how to make love to a woman? I just knew that I wanted to, and when I did, I felt a huge power surge through me proving this was right for me, and that was all that mattered, and has ever since." I nodded and smiled.

"I loved your confidence, it really helped me that first night we made love, it gave me strength." She turned and frowned.

"Really?" I nodded.

"Yeah, you were so sure, and to be honest pretty good at it, I wanted it so badly, and when you did it, my whole body exploded." She gave a sigh of relief.

"Deads I was shitting myself; my brain was like don't screw this up. I was trying to think of everything guys had done to me, all the things that had made me cum. My brain was going touch her clit, wiggle your tongue on it, swirl it round, no, no, go up and down, and stuff like that, it was mad." I started to giggle, she laughed.

"Deads it was such a wonderfully bizarre and crazy time, and when you came, and my mouth was filling up, I thought I would drown. I just kept swallowing it all and hoping you would stop at some point, and I was like really happy because I drank your cum, it is so silly, and yet I will never regret it." I squeezed her hand.

"I like this, just you and me alone talking like this, it feels special and important. I wanted this Christmas to be perfect for you, and so much has happened and gone wrong." She looked up at the trees.

"We have a beautifully decorated house, I love walking up

the stairs, to be honest I never want to take them down. Our Christmas tree is the prettiest I have ever seen, and our house looks so pretty dressed in lights. All of us are together and happy, and it has snowed and made everything extra pretty, Sweetie it is already perfect. You always worry too much, we have always had people trying to put us down, did you think that would stop because it's Christmas? Deads, ignore them, they are never going to be as open minded and free thinking as we are, and that is why they hate us, we have the courage to live as we choose, they don't. I think this Christmas has been perfect so far." She stopped and looked at me.

"Deads, this here and now, walking along this idyllic snow covered canal, just you and me, I think is perfect. We looked at the arch, we held hands, you kissed me on the bridge, wow you certainly know how to spoil me. This has made me so happy today. I needed it, I needed you, and here we are, Sweetie, it's perfect to me already, stop trying so hard and enjoy it." I nodded, I guess I should have realised, Birch did not care about grand gestures, she loved the simple things in life.

"I just wanted it all right, and perfect for you."

"It is Deads, it has been since I came back." She leaned forward and kissed me, oh god I melt when she is like this, her soft kisses are such a turn on.

Deb's sat on the floor watching Chloe paint. "Honestly, I am not that bothered, to be honest, I was starting to feel like I was losing myself, I really wanted sex, oh God, I was missing it, and as long as he was missing it, I was fine. I always expected him to go off with a groupie, and when I found he had, in a way I got what I wanted, which was to go back to the arrangement I had before I was married. Chloe if I am really honest, if we do not do it this way, I don't think our marriage will work."

The gate buzzer went off, Edwina was sat with Gill and Aden, who were looking hot and sweaty, Aden was in his boxer shorts, Gill was naked, so was Alex, who had finally come down from the attic. Edwina pressed the intercom.

"Hello."

"Who is that, is Jemi or Deadly there?" Edwina looked at the studio open door, and raised her voice.

"Bev, you made it, come on in." Deb's gave a squeak.

"Guard your vagina's." Edwina laughed.

"I am wearing panties, and you guys are naked and trapped in the studio."

She chuckled, as the front door burst open, and Bev came bouncing down the hall, Edwina smiled and opened her arms.

"Bev how the hell are you doing? Merry Christmas."

Bev had bright red hair, and wrapped her arms round Edwina, she spotted the naked women in the kitchen, and gave a very large smile.

"Oh yeah, Merry Christmas, oh what do we have here, new totty? Very nice ladies, oh very nice indeed, it is a shame I am only here for a quick visit, I would like a dip in you two pretties." She looked round. "Where is Jemi and that sexy little treat Deadly?" Gill and Alex suddenly felt worried and tried to cover themselves with their arms. The studio looked empty, as Deb's and Chloe hid out of sight, as Deb's dialled.

We were walking up the steps and Birch took one last look back.

"This place is so idyllic; I have loved being here."

My phone rang, I slipped off my glove and fished it out of my pocket, it was Deb's, I lifted it to my ear and hit the button.

"Hey Deb's."

"Abby, you have to come and save us." I felt a jolt in my stomach.

"Deb's what is up, are you alright, where are you?"

"I am naked, and trapped in the studio with Chloe, and Bev is here." Birch turned.

"Guard your vagina."

"NO SHIT BIRCH!" I started to giggle.

"Deb's you will be fine, she is with Bridgette, we are on our way home, we just left the canal."

"Abby please hurry and distract her for us, she is already eyeing up the fresh meat." I frowned.

"Fresh meat?"

"Gill and Alex are naked, and hiding behind the island in the kitchen, I texted them and told them to watch out for Bev." Birch started to laugh, she leaned in.

"Deb's, Bev is a sweetheart."

"Yeah, with a sweet tooth, and she sees us all as sweet little treats, just hurry please."

"We are on our way my little sweets, just hide your yummy little selves until we get there."

"Just hurry."

Hand in hand and giggling, we skipped through the snow towards home. I was looking forward to seeing Bev, she would liven Christmas up, of that there was no doubt.

We arrived home, and she came bolting down the hall towards us, full of smiles, I noticed straight away that her hair was bright red, she pulled me into a crushing hug, as I smiled at her.

"Bev, we have missed you, it is so wonderful to see you again, I love the hair." She gave a wide smile.

"Well, you know it's Christmas, you know, I thought red was best, it sort of reminds folks of Santa and stuff." It made a weird sort of logic, but I know her, and I understand how her mind works.

Birch gave her a huge hug and took her into the living room, I walked down to the kitchen and I had to laugh. Chloe and Deb's were hiding, and Alex and Gill were still sunk low behind the island, I looked at them and gave a titter.

"Seriously guys, Bev has a long term steady girlfriend, all of you are safe enough, for god's sake come out of your hiding holes, she only looks and admires these days, she does not touch."

Bev sat on the large sofa with Birch, talking.

"Yeah, we are fine, although we are open now, I mean it had to happen, you know me? I have my regulars, and we shared a few, which was brill, but we thought it was best to keep up the long term thrill." Birch looked at her.

"Are you really okay with that, Sweetie, you know in the past, it has been a big problem for you?" She shook her head.

"This time it is different, we bang like crazy, but we need more, and so we talked about it, and this is best for us both." Birch gave a shrug.

"I can understand that, it works for a lot of people, as long as you are secure in the primary relationship, if it is working then yeah, go with it. Where is she anyhow?" Bev gave a slight smile.

“Her friends are over from her home town, she wanted to spend some time catching up, which is cool, and I wanted to see you guys, so she is waiting at the hotel for me. I am going to show them the town tomorrow, and then you can meet them all.”

I laughed at them all for being so silly, and made a hot drink, still chuckling, I headed upstairs to my room, I sat at my desk and clicked on my computer. I sat with my knees up, as it booted up, and thought about our day walking on the canal, the pictures were fresh in my mind, and I wanted to capture them.

The computer opened and I typed in the password, and when the screen loaded, I went to my documents and opened the file named ‘Snow Queen.’ I had twenty nine chapters, the last one half finished, so I opened it up, scrolled down to the last line, I knew exactly where I was in the story, and so I started to type.

Once again, this was a story like nothing else I had ever written, but it was a fun story with a lot of hidden meaning. I picked up where I left off, and took my day alone with Birch, which had meant so much to me, and wrote it into my fantasy story. Real life was becoming fantasy, but there again, who was going to know, apart from Birch and myself? Snow Queen was my vow, my love letter to Birch, but it would never openly show to anyone other than her, and that was my intention.

Chapter 26

Festive Village.

There are two problems with this morning. It is very early, and a Sunday, and we have all been drafted into helping out at the carolling and band day, which means shovelling everything that fell from the sky last night, off the pathways and green.

Yet again Santa's grotto was buried, and we would have to dig it out, which considering there were eight elves gainfully employed to run it, and had nothing to do until the pathway was clear, it felt unfair that we had to do it.

We were all up, tired, and lacking anywhere near enough coffee, wrapped up in as many layers as possible, carrying snow shovels. Mum had a clip board, and went down the list, Birch looked at me.

"I am not shovelling the Bell Twats path, from my point of view, everyone will appreciate it if the Twat cannot pull the bloody ropes." Deb's sniggered, I gave a sigh and looked at mum.

"We will do Santa; it is better if we keep Birch as far as possible from the church." She smiled.

"Thank you, Sweetie, I love that you understand me so well."

She looked happy, I just shook my head and readied my shovel, and headed for the village green. The idea was to dig a pathway through the snow about six feet wide, it looked like a daunting task, I had not seen snow this deep in Wotton ever, and whilst I hated it, Chloe, Deb's and Birch were loving it.

We shovelled the snow into wheelbarrows, and Chloe and Deb's moved it, and dumped it near the notice board. As I broke into a sweat, with Birch, it became very apparent that Chloe and Deb's were making the most of it, and as they dumped the wheelbarrow loads, they started to sculpt a snowman. Birch thought it was a lovely idea, why did that not surprise me?

It took over an hour to get the path to a reasonable standard, and build a six foot snowman. I was quite pleased with the path, we sloped the sides and smoothed it out, and it looked really neat and tidy. Chloe had an idea, and ran off to Jessop's, and returned with a hand full of water paints. Edwina turned up with coffee, which was a life saver, and we sat and drank, whilst Chloe painted Christmas flowers on the snow walls to decorate them, it actually looked really good. She also painted a bow tie and some buttons, as well as a happy face on the Snowman. The biggest problem with Sunday, happened as we sat drinking, the bells started, Birch jerked.

"What the hell, why are they so fucking loud, fucking Bell Twats, what is wrong with these people?" Chloe and Deb's sniggered, I leaned in to her.

"Birch they are louder because we are closer." She put her coffee down and covered her ears.

"It's a bloody liberty, that is what it is, that is them trying to assert their domination while trampling down everyone else's beliefs. I mean, look at us, celebrating a pagan festival that those twats stole from us. Oh yeah, they are quick to jump on a good cash generator like Christmas, but it's not is it, because actually it is Yule, the Winter Solstice, and it's been celebrated, a hell of a lot longer than Christmas? Thieving twats nicked it so they could be popular."

Deb's rolled her eyes, and I giggled, some things never change, and actually, I really like that. I kissed her cheek.

"They will be over in a minute, I do think you are adorable, do you know that?" She smiled and her eyes twinkled.

"I love you too Sweetie."

The bells ceased, and the choir could be heard in the church singing, I sat back watching the village, as it slowly came to life, at eleven o'clock the Santa's grotto opened, and all the elves came out and started to organise the early visitors. We moved on, and walked around slowly helping out, clearing snow from around the village, watching everyone else enjoy their Christmas.

Three hours later, with the paths cleared and the road ploughed, cars had arrived, and slowly the village began to fill. Deb's headed back to the bookshop to help Denise, and the brass band arrived to set up. Take out vans parked up, and prepared for business, and with a little extra help for us, the tea rooms got the road and path clear, and set tables and patio heaters outside.

Once again, the village of Wotton Dursley became a hive of activity and smiling happy faces. People in hats and scarves hurried about, as everyone made the most of the big weekend, grabbing what they would need for their own Christmas holiday. It is nice to see some many happy people and excited children, I think it one of the things that has made my home a special place over the years, knowing all of the hard work and effort put in by the villagers, and seeing the joy it brings to the visitors

The Deli was selling hot meat sandwiches, and the gift shop had extra sales stands outside the shop. The Salon was closed today, Anthony as we knew, was still tucked up safe in bed with Michael at home, the lucky bleeder. The Dress Shop was open, selling its usual old fashioned country attire, we slowed down and looked in the windows, Birch gave a shudder.

"These look too old and out of date even for the old, Christ, how do people actually think this is worth buying?" I stared at the frilly blouses, with their tiny floral print patterns.

"I have no idea; I would want someone to kill me if I ever looked in here, and thought anything was nice. Christ, what sort of old maid do you have to be to like this stuff?"

The shop door opening at my right side gave a ping, and someone came out, I wasn't really paying attention.

"Hello Abigail."

My heart skipped several beats, as I turned to see Nigel, with his poker faced wife, Primula, and she did not look at all happy. Nigel smiled as always, he had changed little over the years, it was hard to tell he was the same age as me, he had that young nerd look of a prepubescent boy, and even though his moustache was thicker, he looked just as ridiculous as always, giving him no mature credibility at all.

Primula was dressed almost the same as she did every day, her hair was in a bun, she wore a thick chequered matching skirt and jacket of wool, an Aran knitted polo neck jumper, heavy woollen tights, and sensible shoes. She had on a woollen sort of beret, and a matching scarf, it was hard to note that she was actually two years younger than me, she actually looked twenty years older, and bitchy as it sounds, she was not attractive.

I tried to smile, but it was never easy around Primula, she scowled like Marjorie, and I could feel the happiness being sucked from my soul.

"Hello Nigel, Prim, I hope you are well?" Prim turned her nose up.
"We are fine, and happily married thank you, aren't we Nigel?" He just carried on smiling like the idiot he was.
"Yes dear, we are."
Birch was watching, she had never met Prim, she had seen her from a distance, and we had mentioned her, but she had never been this close to her, she smiled at them both, and looked at Prim.
"Sweetie, do you have a stomach ache or something?" Prim frowned, and her eyes narrowed.
"Not at all, I am in peak health, why would you ask me that?" Birch shrugged.
"You look in pain, I just thought I would ask?" She appeared even more displeased, Nigel just grinned like an idiot, she was even more abrupt.
"We have errands to run, we cannot loiter with the likes of you, so I will bid you good day." She grabbed Nigel's arm and yanked him, and started to walk off, he looked back with the same gormless smile.
"Bye... Happy Christmas." She yanked on his arm.
"NIGEL!" Birch gave a long exhale.
"Wow I actually feel sorry for him, how can someone so young look and sound so old, now I understand why he never has sex, God, who the hell would want her?"

I had to agree with Birch, I watched him walk off with Prim, and she was clearly having a go at him for being nice to me, and in a strange way, I felt sorry for him. Nigel was one of those parts of my life in the village that was irritating, and always there, like a red rash, or sunburn in summer. He had asked me out a thousand times, and I had always refused him, the revelation of his collection of pictures of me, had really upset me at the time.
I hated the idea of being stalked, but even considering all that, a part of me wanted him to find some happiness, and it was

clear, Prim was not the solution. My mum had told me that his marriage was arranged and organised by Marjorie. I could see why she would approve of Prim; she was like a mini version of her, she never confronted me, but Bethany was very good at informing me of things people said about me, and Prim often called me. I was watching lost in thought, when I felt Birch lean into me.

"You know Deads, it makes you wonder, if a day will come, when Nigel ends up in a gimp suit with a dildo up his ass. It is kind of scary to watch, it is like Marjorie and Milton in their younger years." I blinked out of my thoughts.

"The thing I find strange, is he was in my year at school, he looks and acts like an idiot, but he was always the top of the year. He was head prefect, and brilliant at everything he did. He is a fully qualified geneticist, and from what I heard, he aced it all and was head hunted, but Marjorie would not let him leave home, which is why Milton bought two houses on the same piece of land. He knows nothing of normal life, or how to act, but he is not stupid, I actually feel a little sorry for him."

"He could have said no Deads, but he agreed to marry her, life is about choices, and if you do not like it, make better ones. He chose that, and if he is suffering, it was still his choice." I gave a sigh.

"Was it though? To be honest she still has half this village in her pocket, and she wields a lot of influence, not because she is respected, but because she is feared, and those people are a hell of a lot older and wiser than Nigel."

Birch took my hand, and we started to walk down the hill towards the Hunters, Chloe was a little ahead of us peering through the window of the Antique shop, she turned and looked at me.

"Do you know if someone has taken this place over?" I shook my head.

"I have not heard anything why?" We walked up to her, all the inside of the windows were papered over, Chloe was peering through a small gap.

"I can see canvasses."

That was curious, I leaned in and had a look, it was quite dark inside, but it definitely looked like there was some sort of artwork leaning against the wall. I looked at Chloe.

"They may be for the walls, you know brighten the place up, they are probably like those in the art shop at Oxendale, you know mass reproduced or motivational. I must admit I would not mind finding out who has taken it. We could use another shop, let's hope it sells something worth buying." She nodded at me.

"I suppose you are right, but that does look like a lot of pictures for the walls, if it is only for decoration, they must be selling small things, otherwise the displays would block the walls."

It made sense, I looked over the road, there were a lot of people milling around. The brass band erupted into life, with oh come all ye faithful, and with the noise of the village filled with tourists, it tweaked my memories of my childhood, walking with my mum and seeing Santa, and shopping.

It felt a little nostalgic, a feeling from the past, from a time when I was not aware of how cruel the world could be, and everything was still fresh, new, and exciting. It is sad in a way that we have to grow up and leave all that behind, life as a child is so much easier, the simple pleasures mean everything, and all the glitter and sparkles, are magical and enchanting.

I see it in Birch at times, somehow, she has managed to hold on to it, not me, my father saw to that, he could not wait to sit me down, and crash my whole experience of Christmas when I was nine, it never quite felt the same after that.

The carol singers appeared, dressed in Edwardian clothing. I cannot deny, this was a part of Christmas I have always loved in the village. The men looked so distinguished in their top hats, holding up their Victorian lanterns with candles inside. Each man stood beside a woman, dressed equally as elegant, in their period costumes, as they slowly walked singing round the Village Green. Birch was all smiles as she stood still and watched, this for her was something very new.

They came down towards us, with small children holding up collection tins, I smiled as I pulled out my purse, and took out a twenty, and slid it in the tin. The young boy smiled and tipped his hat, and Birch jumped for joy and dived into her bag. She slid out a few notes, and popped them in his tin, and he gave a very regal bow, she was so excited and happy, as she clapped and smiled with joy.

We stood back, and watched as the long line of smiling singers moved on towards the Hunters. Birch's eyes danced in her face, and each time someone made a donation, and the boys bowed, or the girls gave an elegant curtsy, she gave a little squeal of happiness, and clasped her hands together. It sounded so nice, to hear carols sung in the white covered streets of Wotton, a call back to a time long since gone, yet still alive here in my home village.

We crossed the road, and I watched Birch, as she could not take her eyes off the carol singers.

"Oh, Sweetie this is just the perfect setting for them, all this snow, and old quaint buildings, I love this village."

I smiled and linked her arm, just to ensure she did not get run over, as she was very distracted watching.

We walked slowly up the main street, everyone looked rushed and busy, as if they were on some desperate last minute search. Chloe headed into the gift shop, and we headed up towards Station Road. Mary was outside the post office, filling her racks with more cards; she made a lot of her own and they always sold well. She smiled, and we all smiled back, Peter and Mary had been very welcoming since our visit to the club. Birch gripped my arm.

"Let's go for a coffee."

I nodded, it was pretty cold, even though the sun was out, the day was getting on and it was low in the sky. We turned back onto the road, and waited for the cars pouring into the village to pass.

"Jemi... Deadly?" We turned around, Bev was coming out of the post office with a group of people, she turned to them with a smile.

"These are my best mates, Jemi and Deadly, who I was telling you about." They all offered out their hands, and I took them and shook them and said hello. Bridgette smiled at me.

"Hallo Deadly, it is nice to be seeing you again." I smiled, her English was still very broken but I loved the way it sounded, she leaned over and kissed me on both cheeks.

"It is lovely to see you too, your English is getting really wonderful." She smiled, and introduced her friends.

"This is Claire." Claire smiled and shook my hand.

"Nice to meet you." She was very English, she smiled. "Ah... Thought I was French, sorry I am a Dover girl, I live and work in France, this is my fiancée, Jon Claude."

He leaned over and kissed my cheeks, and smiled. He was tall and thin, it was hard to really see much of him as he had so many layers on, he looked good with Claire, she had a long pony tail of dark brown, hanging from the back of her woollen hat.

Bev stood smiling as Brigette introduced her other friends, two females, one was short and thin, with a narrow face, and dark piercing eyes, her name was Claudette. The other one was Alberta, she was a little taller than Claudette, but stocky, with shoulder length, blonde, very curly hair, and piercing blue eyes. She did not kiss me, she just shook my hand, and I smiled and nodded as I said hello, it may sound odd, but I think she did not trust me. Bev was bouncing with happiness.

"We are having a brill time, they love the place, they think it is a proper posh place, with the church and all the posh shops, I even bought em all a pint last night. I told em, fuck that cider shite and piss they sell over there, this is the bloody real stuff, not sure Jon Cloud got it, he looked a bit sort of weird when he tasted it, but he drank it, so fair do's." Birch smiled.

"I am happy to see you having such fun, I hope you are all coming round to see us at some point?" Bev bobbed on the spot.

"Aye, I want em all to get some good British hospitaltally, you know, a right good welcome, get em all feeling at home and stuff, have a drink and laugh and stuff. You are good mates you two, you know that? I don't blame you for fucking each other." I gave a giggle.

She was so lovely, I felt such a huge fondness for her, she was straight and direct, and to be honest pretty scary to look at when she frowned, but she was one of the kindest people I knew.

"Your guests will always be welcome Bev, and yes, we will show them some good old English hospitality, you can bank on it." She smiled.

"Mint do that is, I knew coming here was the right thing. I told Breeze I did, if we go see Jemi and Deadly we will have a right laugh, it will be the dog's bollocks of a night." She stood smiling a happy smile, Birch loved her as much as I did.

"We are looking forward to it, I like Bridgette, and it is nice to see you both so happy, I am quite looking forward to speaking to your friends, I enjoy a chance to practice my French." Bev gave a snort and wiped her nose on her sleeve.

"I am freezing me tits off, so I need to get going, we are off to that meat shop next, I told em it had frog meat in it, you know, that stuff with all the weird tasting shite in it? I figured they would love it, it's a pity there is no kebab shop here, I just fancy getting my lips on a hot kebab." She burst out laughing and Birch smirked.

"I think you have had your lips on one too many hot kebabs in the past Bev." Bev roared with laughter, she was so loud, most of the people around us stopped and stared, I put my head down and giggled.

"Aye I have, I fucking love you Jemi, I knew I would have a banging time here. Right, I will get going before this lot dies of freezer burn, I will see you all later, I am off to get some of that smelly meat for Breeze." I cringed.

She gathered her little group of bewildered tourists, and led them off. I watched her proudly pointing things out like this was her home, it reminded me very much of my first week in Uppermill, when I first met her. I smiled as I thought of my first encounter with her seven years ago, and her heavy footsteps, and feeling utterly terrified. It seems silly now, as I thought Birch would let her rape me, and yet for the rest of that week, she had been kind and caring, always making sure I was having a fun time.

I could see it again, as her French friends trusted her, and followed along happily, although I assumed Claire who appeared to be translating, would clean up her English into something a little more appropriate for them to hear. Birch gave a chuckle.

"I have not seen her so happy in a long time, I think Bridgette, has been really good for her, a steady source of love has done her good, I think she has got over some of the hurt over her mum. It amazes me Deads how parents can raise a child, and yet be so blind to how wonderful they are, it is sad that some parents can only see the negatives in a child."

Wow, she had no idea how much that resonated with me, or

did she? My dad will never accept Birch as my lover, he had no problems with her when we were not sexual, but as soon as he found out, his whole attitude changed. He went from loving her, and finding her amusingly quirky, to hate overnight. After two years, I still find it hard to understand, Birch's bright green eyes appeared in front of me, she gave me a beautiful smile.

"Hi Sweetie, are you alright? You are just staring into space lost in thought, and you looked sad." I smiled.

"Just thinking, about what you said." She understood, and pulled me into a hug.

"He will come round Sweetie, if I am honest, I think his hate for me as your lover, actually shows that down there inside all his coldness, he loves you a great deal, give him time." I snuggled into her.

"I wish he would do it soon, I am worried about him, he will be alone this Christmas." Birch gave a sigh.

"Maybe not, Angela may surprise us all and prove us wrong by supporting him, so he will have someone, and not be completely lonely." I slipped back and looked at her, her eyes were so bright and filled with life.

"How do you do that Birch; you know, you always find a way to turn something negative into a positive?" She gave a little titter.

"Deads, we have no choice, we have to always look for the good, even if it is only the slightest amount, you have to find it Sweetie, because that is where the hope for everyone lies. We have to believe that we can make a difference, otherwise what is the point of going on?" She just blows my mind, and inspires me every day.

"I hope so Birch, I really need him to understand, and see how amazing you are, and how much better I am because I am with you, I love you Birch, why can he not see that?" She shook her head.

"Oh, Sweetie he knows how much you love me, he has always seen it, everyone has. The problem is he is stuck in the ways of this village and the people who influence him, and he is caught in a fight between that, and his love for you. One day he will choose you, you have to understand that and believe in it. Look Sweetie, in many ways he is very much an adult, and yet there are parts of him that are still a little boy. It is that, which is causing him the problem, because you do bring out the child in him, he has a lot of growing up to do, just give him time." I wanted too, but it was so hard, I gave a sigh.

"How much time does he need Birch, he has had two years?" She nodded.

"Yes, he has, but for most of that time he had your mum, and his business was booming, his world was safe, well to be honest Deads, it is not so safe now. I think over the coming months your dad is going to have a lot of lessons to learn, he will do a lot of reflection on what is and what is not important. He needs this time, age is not on his side, and he is reminded of that daily, just have faith in him Deads." She leaned in, and gave me the softest of kisses. "I love you Sweetie, never forget that, no matter what happens, we will face it together."

What is it about this woman? I felt my heart flutter, her absolute belief in everything was confusing to me, but when she leaned in like this and kissed me, I felt utterly defenceless and hers. I stood in the middle of Wotton, a village that put the fear of God into me seven years ago, and yet here I was, standing exposed in the open, in front of a packed village of tourists, kissing the woman I loved, only she had the power to do that, and I had no idea why, but I loved it.

Chloe had finished shopping in the gift shop, she caught us up, and she was quite excited, to her, seeing us kiss was pretty normal, she just walked up and jumped into a conversation.

"Wow have you seen the new guy working in the gift shop, he is a hunk?" I pulled away from Birch and shook my head.

"No is he nice?" Her eyes danced.

"If that bulge in his pants is anything to go by, I want him in my collection."

Birch and I gave a chuckle. She has never changed since we had made friends, but I liked that about her, she was open and honest, swore like a sailor, and very perverted, but that was who she was, Birch sniggered.

"I hope you don't have festive ones for your cards?"

I giggled, the thought of an erect penis wearing a Santa hat sprang to mind, although now Birch had mentioned it, I would not put it past Chloe. She was quite fond of showing her picture collection off at times, much to the shock and embarrassment of the viewer. I took Birch by the hand, and looked at Chloe wrapped up to the nines with three plastic bags.

"Don't let Daisy or Norman see those bags, they will have a fit, we are heading for coffee, it is getting chilly out here, you coming?" She looked at us both and smiled.

"Yeah, I am freezing my chuff off, let's head over and get something hot." Birch giggled.

"I thought the hot stuff was in the gift shop?" We stepped onto the road, as Chloe gave a loud giggle.

"Oh, I am telling you guys, he is as sexy as fuck, I just have to sleep with him, I want to know what is going on down there." She gave a wicked giggle and rolled her eyes.

We arrived safely on the blocked off Green Street, and walked up alongside the green, it was really busy now, as it had headed well past noon, and was heading towards evening. The sky was darkening and it looked like more snow was due, all the Christmas lights were on, and it was getting really cold. The Choir had arrived in their robes, and were singing next to the brass band a little further up the street. With all the snow and the lights, it added to the Christmas atmosphere, and it felt nice.

I looked at the tea room, it was busy, there were a few empty tables outside, Louise and Stacy were clearing, and cleaning them as fast as they could, I tried to see inside, to see if any were free. I spotted one near the back, I pointed, and Birch gave a nod as we walked into the open area of pathway, through the tables that led to the doors. Birch let go of my hand, and smiled at me, her long white hair flapping on her shoulders.

"You grab the table Deads, this is on me."

Chloe happily chatted at our side, she wanted a large coffee and a pastry. We made it to the door and Birch entered, followed by Chloe, behind us an angry voice yelled out.

"ABIGAIL!"

I turned with a smile, and my heart froze. Chloe went silent, as Birch headed inside to the counter.

"Festive greetings ladies, tell me what delights do you have, to make a girl's heart flutter on Christmas?" Chloe had gone silent as she stared past my shoulder, I felt her hand slip into mine and pull back.

"Abby, come inside, whatever he wants, it is better we ignore it, if he is here, it can only mean trouble, come on, get inside, this all feels wrong to me."

Chloe looked past me, her eyes were dark and bright, and yet a little afraid, she pulled back on my arm, as she stared at him with hate.

"Fuck off Martin, we want nothing to do with you, now leave us alone."

All the customers had stopped, and were staring at Chloe and me, I took two steps back as Chloe pulled my arm. I swallowed hard, feeling the fear rising up inside me, and my voice wavered.

"Leave us alone Martin, just go home, we want no trouble."

Chapter 27

Tea Room Terrors.

I have not seen him this close to me since that night, when we caught him trying to assault Chloe sexually. The Martin I remembered was always impeccably dressed, and well groomed, he was calm and unshakable. Nothing rattled him, as his smoothness would ooze out of him, as he carefully and craftily controlled every situation.

I was staring at him, feeling shocked, scared, and really worried, as my stomach churned and twisted. He was stood facing me, about fifteen feet away, staring with hate, he wore an old dusty orange anorak, and had on dirty baggy jeans, and a thick dark jumper. He was unshaven, and his hair had grown out, and was dirty and greasy, as it hung lank round his face. The one thing that had me feeling most afraid was his eyes, they had always sparkled, with his cunning, but now they were dull, lifeless, and very frightening. I swallowed hard feeling the coldness of his stare run through me, and I shuddered.

He just stood there on the road, to a backdrop of snow, Christmas lights, and the sound of carols being sung, accompanied by a brass band, with his hands in his pockets, and I felt real terror. It grew from the pit of my stomach, and seeped out into my chest and legs.

I felt Chloe's hand tighten on mine, she pulled on it, and I stepped back, my throat was dry, and I felt myself trembling, I swallowed hard, trying to find something I could say or do. The fear was starting to surge in me, I did not understand why. He just stared at me, with eyes of malice, and I felt his hate, and it terrified me, I wanted to cry. I felt the tension in my throat, my words trembled as they came out of my mouth, Chloe was pulling me back.

"Leave us alone Martin, just go home, we want no trouble."

I felt like I could physically see the anger boiling up inside him, as his eyes locked on me, as he stared at me and his face changed, it grew creased and disfigured, as his brow furrowed, and the rage came flowing out of him.

"I HAVE NO FUCKING HOME, YOU TOOK IT, YOU TOOK EVERYTHING FROM ME, YOU WHORE!"

People stopped eating and talking, and all looked at him, I felt an overwhelming panic inside me, and my throat felt like it was tightening, as those moments of him screaming at me in the church came flooding back, I shook my head, as tears formed in my eyes, my voice was weak, and trembled more.

"Please Martin, don't do this, please just leave, you are scaring me."

The tears ran onto my face, as my lip started to tremble, he glared at me with his hating eyes, just stood there with his hands in his pockets, his legs slightly apart, and big work boots. Chloe pulled hard, and I stepped back, Birch came up at my side, and I felt her hand on my shoulder, I was shaking with fear, her voice was soft and calm.

"Deads Sweetie, go with Chloe, go inside Sweetie, it is alright, go on, get away from him. Chloe, get her the fuck inside NOW!" I felt my hand yank, and I staggered backwards.

I was losing it completely, gasping for air, as my fear built up, and I was trying to breathe, Chloe pulled me back, as I saw Birch step forward, and block the doorway. She stood there still and frozen, between him and me, her hair hanging down her back like the snow outside. I cannot explain it, but the dread seeped into my mind, this was bad, and something horrible was going to happen, I sensed it, and it terrified me, as Birch's calm voice echoed through my ears.

"Martin, you had better leave, I have alerted the police, just go, go home and we will call this a day. Whatever you are thinking, just let it go, it is not worth the trouble."

I could see him through the side of the doorway, Chloe let go of my hand, and put her arms round me in almost a bear hug, crushing me even more as I tried to breathe. Her carrier bags were hanging in front of me, and tapping me on my thighs, as they vibrated from Chloe's shaking wrists. The coldness that was growing inside me, was engulfing me, and all I could do was stare at him, feeling utterly terrified, Chloe leaned into my ear.

"Abby, please just come to the back with me, you are going to be alright, he cannot hurt you, just come with me, let Birch handle this."

I tried to nod, I understood she was right, but I could not move, I was too terrified, my legs were shaking so hard, they would not move. I felt Chloe trembling as she hung onto me, Martin took a step forward, as he looked at Birch.

"So, fucking high and mighty, doctor fucking slut, you think you are so wonderful, snogging Abigail at airports nude, or at weddings? Wow you are so full of shit, but I know what you are, I know a fucking whore when I meet one." Birch lifted her hands in a calm gesture, her bright green eyes watching, fixed on his every move.

Inside the Tea Rooms, everything had stopped, and the customers were silently staring at us, almost as if time had frozen, no body moved, and the silence was excruciating, and just added to my overwhelming fear. Birch was calm as she stood with her hands just in front of her, signalling in a calm way, that whatever he wanted, it was not going to happen.

"Martin, this is not worth the trouble you are in, you are on parole, this will not look good. Please, people came out today to enjoy their day, do not spoil it for everyone, just calmly walk away, and nothing will happen." A father sat close by with his wife and two children looked at Birch.

"If he is bothering you love, I can help him leave." Birch shook her head.

"Please do not get involved, the police are on their way, but thank you, that is very kind of you." Martin looked at him, and sneered.

"Mind your own fucking business, you nosey fucking bastard." The man twisted in his seat, as his wife slid closer to her children, he stared at Martin with an angry expression.

"These are my children; your foul language is making it my business."

Martin shook his hand in his pocket, and pulled out a small revolver, Birch gave a gasp as he pointed it at the family, the children started to cry, the guy's wife screamed, Martin stared at them, waving the gun, with a smirk.

"Not so fucking brave now, are you? Get fucking out of here."

I saw the gun and fell apart, Chloe also saw it, panicked, and yanked me hard, and dragged me back as I screamed, and I saw Birch in the doorway hold up her hands, she sounded afraid.

"Martin, please stop, please don't hurt anyone."

My heart was racing, as I saw her facing him alone, and the tears flowed into my eyes, and my voice found its way back up and whimpered out of me.

"Birch, get away, get away from him, please Birch, get away from him."

She stepped back into the shop, people all round the place were panicked in their seats, outside, the sight of a gun instilled instant terror, and people slid back their seats, grabbed their kids and fled screaming out in fear. It had all suddenly become chaos, as people stampeded in every direction, running blindly, knocking everything over. The air was filled with screams and the clashing of the metal furniture as it crashed to the floor with breaking pots. Birch was at risk, and all I could think of, was save her.

Panic engulfed me, and I fought against Chloe, and pulled out my arms, and threw them out, as terror coursed right through me, as I was reaching for Birch, wriggling, fighting, as Chloe gripped me harder and dragged me back more, and I fought to break free, screaming out her name.

"BIRCH, BIRCH NO, GET AWAY FROM HIM!"

Tables and chairs clattered in every direction as the people fled screaming and wailing away from the scene, leaving Birch alone inside the doorway, facing him with the gun. Chloe dragged me further back, she sounded as terrified as me, she pulled me to the floor, and buried her face in my shoulder.

"Abby please stay down, please don't go near him, please Abby, stay with me here, I am so scared of him too, please Abby, just stay away from him."

She was sobbing and crying, her hold was so tight on me, I could not get free, as I tried to fight free of her, and I stared at Birch who was three paces inside the Tea Rooms doorway. People were down on the floor, scrambling around making scared little moaning and panicked whimpers, as they watched with terror on their faces. Birch watched every move of Martin, her breathing had increased, and yet her voice was calm.

"Martin, you do not need a gun, this is just silly, now why don't we just calm down and talk about this in a peaceful manner?"

I could only just see her as Chloe engulfed me, I struggled to try and get free, and she just clung to me even harder crying and sobbing. I managed to get just high enough to see over the tables and out of the bottom of the window.

He stood in front of her, the gun still pointing at what was now an empty table, where the family had vacated. Tables and chairs were tipped over, and scattered on the roadway. He stared at Birch with evil eyes.

"SHE TOOK EVERYTHING, CAN YOU NOT SEE THAT?"

Birch gave a nod of recognition, her voice was calm and soft, her hands still frozen, her palms out, in a gesture of calmness.

"Martin what you were doing was wrong, you do understand that, don't you? You cannot blame Abigail, you were breaking the law and hurting people, no matter how you look at it, Martin, it was rape, and it hurt those you did it too."

Outside the Post Office Felicity stood terrified, and being forcibly held back by Peter Saxon.

"Felicity you will do no good running over there; you will get yourself or Abigail hurt. Please just stand back, the police are on the way. Getting yourself killed will not help Abigail." She stared watching in terror, tears streaming down her face, as Peter held onto her tightly.

"She is all I have Pete, I would rather he hurt me than her." Peter shook his head.

"Birch is calming him down, trust her Felicity, she loves Abby just as much as you do. She knows what she is doing, she is a professional, trust her, and just stand back, and wait for the police." Edwina arrived with Luke; she was out of breath.

"Where is Chloe?" Peter turned to her.

"She is in the Tea Rooms with Abigail, she is fine at the moment, Birch is controlling the situation." She gave a nod and stared across the street, Luke took her hand and gave it a squeeze.

"Weena, trust Birch, she will protect both of them, just like she always has, let her talk him down, it is what she does." Edwina turned and he slipped his arms round her, she had tears forming in her eyes. Martin stared at Birch with anger in his eyes.

"YOU DON'T KNOW WHAT IT IS LIKE, SHE TOOK IT ALL AWAY, MY HOME, MY WIFE, MY SON, AND NOW SHE WILL PAY!" Birch shook her head.

"No Martin, I cannot allow that, no one is being hurt today."

"SHE STOLE MY LIFE, AND NOW I WILL TAKE HERS. THAT IS FAIR, YOU HAVE NO IDEA OF HOW I SUFFERED, THE THINGS THEY DID TO ME, SHE HAS TO PAY!"

I stared at Birch through my tears, sat on the floor at the back of the room, held tightly in Chloe's grip, and shook my head, as the waves of terror coursed through me, as I sobbed.

"Birch, baby no, please come away from him, please baby, get out of his way, please baby, I cannot lose you, I cannot live without you, please baby just get away from him."

Marjorie was still sat in her seat drinking her tea, she turned and stared at me, her eyes scowling with her distaste for me.

"Oh for god's sake Abigail, shut up wailing and grow a spine, this is what you get for parading round the village like a whore. You brought all this on yourself, flaunting and flirting, what the hell did you expect?" Bethany was under the table cowering.

"Madge you really should get down." She looked down at her with utter contempt.

"What the hell for, the man is a rapist of sluts and whores, he probably has no idea even how to fire that thing?"

Birch could hear Marjorie, she did not take her eyes off Martin, who was yelling at her.

"Madge, shut the fuck up, you are not helping."

Martin raised the gun and pointed it straight at Birch, she felt her heart pound inside her chest, as the panic inside her rose up, she took a deep breath and swallowed hard, trying to remain composed.

"Martin, please, just put it down, you do not need a gun." In the distance police sirens echoed through the falling light, Martin heard them and smiled.

"More fucking law, do you think I am scared of them, do you honestly think after all the shit I have endured because of your little posh slag, I care about them?" He started to laugh. "I don't give a fuck any more, I have nothing left to lose. Don't you fucking get that?"

His arm moved to the side and... BANG!!! Birch jumped and gave a gasp of fear.

The window just above me exploded, and came raining down on me, I screamed with everything I had, as I looked up, and wailed out in terror.

"BIRCCCCCCCCCCCCCCCCHH!?"

People inside the Tea Room, and out on the street screamed in panic, and ran for cover, Peter dragged Felicity as she screamed in terror, backwards into his shop, as she fought to get free, kicking and screaming in wild panic. Edwina was screaming as Luke wrestled her back to the door of the post office, and all over the village people were screaming as they fled in every direction, it was utter chaos.

Chloe yanked me hard, and I crashed back onto the floor, as she screamed out in fear down my ear. I hit the floor hard, and she clamped round me tight. My heart was exploding as the utter terror coursed through me, and somewhere in all of it, as my ears rang from the sound of the gun shot, I heard her, she was calm, but very shaken, and her voice wavered slightly.

"Sweetie, I am fine, I am alright Sweetie, just calm down, I am alright. Deads, I am alright." I could not take much more, I was so terrified, I peered through my tears as I wept.

"Birch, please, Birch, I am so scared, I just peed myself, I am so sorry." I just shook from head to foot; her voice was calm.

"It is fine, you will be fine, just hang in there Sweetie, I will be with you soon."

Martin laughed as he waved the gun around, this was giving him a lot of pleasure.

"Awe, did I frighten poor little Abigail? Good, she should be scared, because she is going to die today." He was enjoying this far too much; he was all smiles and chuckling, as he waved the gun wildly in the air.

"Well, that is what she gets for being a bitch, that is what happens when you fuck people's lives up, and they lose everything, you get fucking scared!" Marjorie stood up.

"This has bloody well gone too far." Birch glanced at her.

"Marjorie, sit down, and stay out of this." Martin gave a giant laugh.

"Is Marjorie here, has the old battle axe decided to get involved? YOU HUNG ME OUT TO DRY YOU FUCKING BITCH!" Birch moved her hand as if to show Marjorie to stop.

"Madge you are making things worse, please sit down and stay out of this." Marjorie looked round the room, everyone was looking at her.

"This has gone too far, and it is time it was stopped, this is having an impact on the village, all this nonsense has to end."

Martin heard her, and he saw her through the net curtains, Birch turned and looked at Madge.

"MADGE SHUT THE FUCK UP, AND SIT FUCKING DOWN, HE IS NOT FOOLING AROUND!"

The police came screaming onto the main street their lights flashing, and screeched to a halt outside the Post Office, blocking the road. Two officers got out and looked at Peter Saxon.

"Okay what is going on here, we had a call about a disturbance?" Felicity was out of the Post Office in a flash, looking terrified.

"It is Martin Hinkley, he has a lot of people pinned down in the Tea Rooms, one of them is my daughter and her partner Dr Dixon. He has a gun, see there he is pointing it at Dr Dixon, she is trying to keep him calm, now hurry go and help her." The officer looked at her, and then his partner.

"Gun... No one said anything to us about a gun." Felicity nodded her head.

"He has fired it once, I don't think anyone was hit, but they are all very scared." His partner nodded.

"Okay love, I think you better get where it is safe, we do not have the kit to deal with this, we will have to radio it in." He leaned in through the open door, and grabbed the radio mic. Felicity stared at him, and pointed at the Tea Rooms.

"That is my daughter and my daughter's partner, stop bloody pissing about, and go and help calm him down!"

Birch was stood to one side of the door, she was really afraid, behind her in the Tea Rooms, people were under the tables pressed flat against the inside wall quaking, Celia and Lillian were behind the counter peering over it, Stacy and Louise were just behind Birch on the floor, both of them were as white as ghosts, and holding each other's hands.

Birch was trembling slightly, Martin stared at her, as the blue light flashed, and strobed the side of his face, making him look eviller, and more sinister, as he held the gun up.

"I won't fucking tell you again Doctor Bitch, you bring me that Abigail, or I will take everything she has away from her, so who is it going to be, her or you?" He raised the gun, and pointed it right at her. Birch shook her head, tears formed in her eyes.

"Please Martin, just stop now, hurting us will not help you." He laughed as he saw the fear on Birch's face.

"Yeah, now you have had a taste of what I have suffered, she took everything I have, and now I am going to do the same to her." He smiled pointing the gun right at Birch and his smile widened, as he gave a joyous sinister smile. Marjorie's voice echoed from inside.

"MARTIN HINKLEY, YOU JUST LISTEN TO ME, AND PUT THE GUN DOWN, AND STOP THIS NONSENSE THIS INSTANT!" Birch snapped her head round.

"Madge for fuck's sake stay out of this, you are making it worse." She scoffed.

"How can it be worse, you and your whores have been destroying the reputation of the village, since the day you arrived, it cannot get much lower?" Martin waved the gun around.

"WILL YOU JUST SHUT THE FUCK UP, YOU VICIOUS OLD BITCH!?"

He pointed the gun right at her shadowed outline behind the net curtains, and Birch realised what he was going to do, he aimed for the dark figure behind the curtain, Birch twisted, her words quiet enough for Martin not to hear.

"Oh fuck, no!"

I looked up, and saw Birch turn, run, and dive, she hit Marjorie really hard, as she screamed.

"GET DOWN MADGE..."

BANGGGG!!!

It echoed, and almost popped my ear drums it was so loud, I screamed for all I was worth, as a level of terror I had never known exploded out of me, Chloe was screaming equally as loud, as she clung to me shaking violently. Other people in the place were screaming as utter chaos and fear engulfed everything.

It felt like slow motion, as I screamed, Birch flew into the air, grabbed Madge, and twisted, her long hair flapping in a long stream behind her. Madge went sprawling backwards with a yell of objection, and collided into all the empty wooden tables and chairs, as the glass window exploded in a million pieces, and glass rained everywhere.

Birch hit the wooden table hard with a grunt, holding Madge tight in her grasp, and there was a deafening crash. The table shattered, as they both went crashing through it, chairs flew up in every direction, and came smashing down towards Chloe and me, I pulled my hands over my head and felt the agonising pain as they bounced off my arms and head, and I screamed out all my fear.

My mind swirled out of control, as everything hit high speed again, and I saw Madge roll off Birch with a loud moan. Birch lay on her side facing me, breathing in a laboured manner, she saw me staring and smiled, thick red blood ran down her face, and my world ended in a wail.

"BIRRRRRRCCCCCHHHHHH!!!"

Outside Martin wailed with laughter waving the gun, and from nowhere there was a flash of red and silver, and Bev loomed up in front of him, he looked at her and just laughed even harder.

"What the fucking hell are you?" She glared at him.

"Fucking Northern." SMACK!

She head butted him square in the middle of his forehead, and he hit the floor out cold, she looked down at him, lay sprawled out on the floor.

"Fucking wanker."

Chloe saw Birch and gasped, and her voice died in her throat.

"Fuck! He shot her."

All I could feel was a huge inner pain, churning around inside me as I tried to wipe the tears from my blurred vision. I fought and kicked with all my might, and dragged myself out of Chloe's grip, as I wailed, and scrambled over the broken glass and furniture.

"BIRCH... BIRCH BABY!" I dragged myself to her side, and lifted her up. Her eyes were closed, and there was blood everywhere.

"No, no, no, not you, it should have been me, not you Baby." There was so much blood, I pulled her into my chest and she hung limp.

"Please baby talk to me, Birch please say something, oh baby, please don't leave me.... You promised... Oh baby please say something." I unzipped my coat and pulled at my t shirt to wipe her face. My whole world was crashing into oblivion, as the reality hit me hard.

I looked up for help, at all the shocked staring faces, no one was moving, and I needed help, as the tears streamed down my face.

"Someone please, I need help, please help me... I cannot lose her; she is my life. Please someone, anyone, please help me." My eyes met Madge's as I looked around, as she lay on the floor just in front of me.

She stared at me with a strange look on her face, her arm was outstretched to me holding a clean handkerchief.

"Abigail, I am so sorry... Here."

I nodded, and reached out and took it, and looked down at Birch, her lovely white hair with black patches, had red through it, I tried to wipe it away. I shook violently in pain as I looked at her, my heart was breaking apart, as my world completely collapsed. I gave a huge sniff up as I wiped her face, but it was coming too fast, and I whimpered.

"Don't leave me Birch, please baby, I need you."

I pulled her close as my heart broke, and I felt the most unbelievable pain inside me. I held her tight and wailed, snuggling her as close as I could, everything around me felt like a haze.

Edwina came rushing in followed by Luke, the police were trying to enforce a line, as people surged forward, but Luke barged his way through dragging Edwina with him. Celia and Lillian were on the phone calling an ambulance. Edwina looked round, and saw Chloe sat dazed on the floor weeping, she tore across the room, and crashed down on her knees, snatching Chloe into her arms.

"Oh thank god, you are safe." She turned and saw me, and her breath caught in her throat.

"Oh fuck... No!"

My mum came in through the door, and looked round in panic, she saw me on the floor cradling Birch in my arms, there was blood everywhere, her hands shot to her face.

"Oh my god no!" Celia took her arm.

"Ambulances are coming."

Bev stood back held by Luke, and watched with horror, as I held her close to me, Marjorie stared at me and started to violently jerk, I could do nothing, Bev spotted it, she grabbed my mum's arm.

"Fuck me, the old cow is having a heart attack." She dragged her over towards me, and smiled. "Hang in there Deadly, she is still breathing, she ain't left you yet."

It took a second for me to understand, I looked down at Birch, she was wrapped up in her coat, I pulled at the zip, and pulled her coat open, her chest was moving, not fast, but she was breathing. I smiled and began to cry even more, the waves of relief crashing over me. I pulled her close and leaned down close to her face, my tears dripped onto her cheek.

"Hold on Baby, help is coming."

In the distance I could hear the sirens. My mum came over and cupped my face in her hands, tears were rolling down her cheeks.

"I am here Abby, he is taken care of, so you hold her close, the ambulance is on its way, hold on sweetheart, help is coming." Bev gripped her arm, and yanked her backwards.

"Deadly's mum, this one needs us more. She will be okay now, help here, it's where it is needed."

Bev tore open Marjorie's coat and placed a hand on her chest, she felt for a second, and then leaned over her mouth, to see if she could feel anything, she looked at my mum.

"Nope not breathing." She pulled off her coat and rolled it up.

"Right Deadly's mum, we are both going to fucking hate

ourselves for this, but it is the right thing to do." She grabbed her hands, and showed her how to place them.

"I need you to pump down here to get her heart going, unless you want to kiss this ugly bitch?" My mum looked panicked, and shook her head.

"Not unless I have to, I don't really know what to do, I have never done this before." Bev gave a smile.

"Aye I met a few ugly ones like this in me life, right we do thirty pumps, and then I breathe, can you handle it?" Mum nodded, Bev gave a smile, and then lifted Madge's head, and pushed the coat under her neck to rest her head back and open her airways.

"Right Mrs Deadly, off you go, nice and regular now, just like I showed you."

I held Birch close and stroked her hair back, she looked whiter than normal, whiter than snow, my insides were all over the place. I thought I had lost her, I really thought she had gone forever, and I knew, I would never survive without her. I stroked her face with the hankie trying to clean it.

"I love you so much baby, you are my whole world, just stay with me, help is coming."

Outside more police cars arrived, screaming into the village with their lights flashing, and screeching to a halt as more police jumped out, and took over the scene. Martin was face down on the floor handcuffed, with an officer crouched next to him.

Bev was counting, she shook her head.

"Oh fuck, I am going to need something much stronger than mouth wash for this bitch." She watched Flick as she grabbed Madge by the nose.

"I kissed some ugly bitches, but you, oh fuck you are ugliest, oh fuck!"

Mum gave a nod, and Bev dived in and blew, she lifted up, and took another huge gasp of air, and then locked lips and blew into her. She nodded and mum carried on, Madge twitched, she was breathing, Bev gave a gasp of relief, and nodded to mum.

"Fucking old bitch will live forever now, just to piss us off." My mum looked shocked, and completely out of it, if not a little appalled.

Two ambulances came wailing onto the high street, the police waved them down, as the crowds all watched from behind yellow tape, as the crew jumped out and came running into the tea rooms.

A young woman came to me, and a guy looked at Madge as other ambulance crews arrived. Mum and Bev were filling him in, the female ambulance attendant looked at me, she put down her bag, and smiled, and wiped my face with her blue gloved hand, her voice was soft and gentle.

“Is it okay for me to look at her, I need you to just relax and let her go?” I nodded, and gave a sniffle.

“Who is she?” My lip was still trembling, and I was shaking, Edwina crawled over.

“This is Doctor Jemima Dixon, and that is her life partner, Abigail Watson.” She smiled at me.

“I have read your books, I have wanted to meet you, under better circumstances mind.” She was busy checking Birch over. “They said there was a gun shot, do you know if she was hit?” I took a deep breath, and swallowed, my mouth was so dry.

“She dived across, and knocked Madge down, and then smashed through the table, I don’t know, it all happened so fast. It scared me so much, she means everything to me.” I started to cry again. “I don’t want her to die.” She reached into her side bag, and pulled out a packet and unwrapped it.

“Abigail, she has a nasty wound on the side of her head, I am not sure what caused it, but if I put this on there, can you hold it for me and apply gentle pressure? We are going to do everything we can to keep her with you, I also need to know, are you hurt?” I gave a nod and she smiled.

“I don’t think so, I was over there when it happened, I think I am alright... Hep... Hep... Hep!”

I sat there, my lip trembling, my nose running, watching her do a body check on Birch, as a stretcher arrived. It all felt so unreal and surreal, like it was happening to someone else, and not me. Madge was taken first, Edwina and Chloe moved in close, Chloe had eyes filled with tears, I smiled at her.

“Thanks Chloe, if it was not for you, I might have got killed, you saved me.” She shook her head.

“I was so scared Abby, I thought he had killed her, and I was

scared he would get you next, I love you guys, you know that?" I nodded.
"How much, enough for a threesome when Birch is better?" She shook her head.
"Oh, I am so straight Abby, I wish I could, but I am better off painting you a picture, of us doing that stuff. I am not sure in real life that could happen, you know those are different kinds of juices." I smiled, she looked at me and smiled, I could see how hurt she was, she was still shaking

The crew came back in, and they carefully lifted Birch, onto the stretcher, I was wet with pee, and covered in blood, Edwina helped me stand, my mum came over, Luke finally allowed her to approach me, I looked at her.
"I peed myself mum, I was so terrified." She stroked my hair back out of my face, and pulled me into a hug, and held me tight.
"Damp legs are nothing, you are alive. You go with Birch; I will get you some clean pants, and meet you at the hospital, everything will be alright sweetheart, he has gone now, you are safe, go with her, stay by her side, it is where you belong."
"Thanks mum, her mum will need to know, I will ring her as soon as they tell me anything." She squeezed me tight.
"I will be with you as fast as I can."

Walking out, at the side of the crew with Birch, cameras flashed all over the place, the word was out, and the press wanted to make the most of their latest chance for a sensation. I did not care, I held her hand, and walked with her. I stood back and they slid her in, ignoring all the yells of my name.
I jumped in behind her, and sat at her side, the female ambulance attendant was called Vanessa, she took all Birch's details. I was not sure if they were being honest with me, she was breathing with a mask on, and yet she was not awake, and the sirens were blaring. I had to ask, as I needed to know.
"Can I ask, if Birch is okay, why is she not awake, and why the sirens, I mean, normally they are only used at junctions and in road traffic?" She smiled, as she lifted a torch and checked my eyes, she was checking me over just to make sure.
"We want her at the hospital as quickly as possible, she has had

either a blow to the head, or the bullet did this, either way we want her in a hospital to check her out thoroughly." I understood, and I felt a pang in my stomach.

"She will be alright, won't she, I don't want to lose her, she is my whole world?" Vanessa smiled and patted my hand, as more tears ran down from my black streaked eyes.

"She is in good care, and we will do everything to get her back to full strength, and naked in airports again." She smiled.

Arriving at the hospital was no better than the village, the press were already waiting, and flash cameras went off everywhere. I hated them all, this was not about me, this was about taking care of Birch. It was not a bloody news story; it was the single most important thing in my life. I walked at the side of her as they rushed her up to the consultation bay.

I talked to the nurse as she filled in the paperwork, and explained how I was her life partner, and her parents were out of the country for Christmas. While I talked, they cut her clothing off, to make sure she had no shot wounds, whilst one guy, who I assumed was the head of the team, looked at the wound on the side of her head.

Once all the paperwork was done, I was shown to the waiting room, and asked to wait, I looked around at all the worried parents and partners. Everyone was staring at me, and it felt intimidating, as I sat alone trembling and afraid. I had not realised that I was covered in blood, and it was disturbing people.

I hate waiting rooms, they are oppressive, they have positive artwork, which is meaningless when you are feeling terrified, worried, and confused, because the person you love the most is in the hands of others. I leaned back, and tried to breathe properly, these places are stuffy and lack air, I felt exhausted, I leaned back and closed my eyes. I wanted this day to end, and wanted Birch to walk in and smile, and say 'Hi sweetie' just so I knew my world would not fall apart, and they were not being fast enough.

I wanted so badly to just cry, but sat there surrounded by staring strangers, even though I had my eyes closed, I could feel their eyes burning into me, and I held back the tears, and bit my lip.

My mind swirled with my insides, I was so scared, and so alone, and I had no idea what I was supposed to do, this was the most intense fear I had ever known. For the first time in a very long time, I focused my thoughts, and I prayed that she would make it through, and begged the lord for her life.

Chapter 28

Healing.

I was so tired, I am not sure if it is because of all the feelings I have experienced today, or I was just sleepy because I was up so early? Mum dropped me some dry clothes off, and brought a wash bag, which allowed me to go to the ladies, strip, and wash myself down. She offered to phone Roni for me, although I had not heard anything yet, and I had been waiting for over two hours.

For the first hour I sat with a female police officer, and was forced to relive everything, as I gave my story of what had happened. I was so tired and weary and kept bursting into tears, did no one understand that all I wanted was to see Birch? It felt like forever before they were satisfied, and finally left me alone.

Mum promised to check on Birch's progress for me, and I asked her to check on Chloe. I knew she was with Edwina, but I was worried, so I also texted Izzy, and asked her just to keep an eye on her. I sat back and rested, with my eyes closed, and drifted, as the day's events flowed through my mind. I was afraid of Martin, but actually when I saw Birch rush to help Marjorie, and then saw her on the floor bleeding, that is the single most terrifying thing I have ever known.

My mum was outside making more phone calls. I felt the huge wave of emotions inside me, and tried to hold back the tears. It was overpowering, I clenched my eyes tight and tried to calm down, I had not realised I had brought up my feet and I was sat hugging them.

"Abigail?" I opened my eyes, and looked up, it was Rev Milton Wallace, he looked down at me.

"How are you, are you doing alright dear?" I shook my head, and emotions surged up inside me.

"No... Not really." The tears I had been trying so hard to fight back, flowed onto my cheeks.

"Oh, my poor dear girl, come, come now." He sat down, and I looked at him.

"I have not heard anything, and I need to know she is fine, I have not seen her for hours."

He leaned over and pulled me close, he was so tender and so caring, as he held me, and I could not help it, I pushed my head into his shoulder, and wept like a baby. He held me, and gently rocked me, and I was really surprised by it, but I also needed it. He spoke very softly to me.

"I feel such a heavy burden, I have known you and Chloe all your lives, I christened both of you, and watched you grow. I owe both of you a massive apology. I should have done it all those years ago, but I felt such guilt, because I employed him, and he hurt people I cared for. I am so sorry Abigail, because you are such a lovely girl, and you have worked so hard to get where you are, you deserved better from me." I leaned back, and gave a sniffle and wiped my eyes on my sleeve.

"It is not your fault, he had a choice, and he chose to do that, and he got caught in the act. Rev Wallace, everyone thought he was the perfect choir master, even I did, I loved being in the choir, you cannot blame yourself." He smiled.

"You are a very kind person, I have seen it many times, I saw how you did not press charges against my son, when you had every right to. The humiliation he suffered was just, and you saw that, and felt that alone was enough. That was very Christian of you, and I was always grateful. He is my son, and he was wrong, and I pointed out how wrong his behaviour was, but I have always been grateful to you." He smiled, or at least I think he did, after all, his teeth moved.

"That is all in the past, honestly I just want that all left behind." I suddenly realised why he was there. "How is Marjorie, is she going to be alright?" He nodded.

"She is stable, and suffering a little from shock." He gave a little chuckle.

"If I am honest, I think your friend Birch surprised her a great deal, and I am not certain she knows how she should deal with that. I would like to say I am very grateful to her for what she did. I realise that may sound a little strange for you, I am aware that you all know about my club, and so yes, that must sound odd. She was not always like she is now Abigail, there was time dare I say, she was actually fun." I could not imagine Marjorie ever being fun, but in a strange way, I was glad she had recovered.

"I am glad to hear she is alright, I will not deny, she has made my life harder than it needed to be, but she did not deserve to be shot at." He sat back.

"Well, I must say Abigail, I do not think anyone honestly thought Martin was capable of that. He is back in police care, and looking at an attempted murder charge, I do not think he will pose any problems now." He took a deep breath.

"Such a terrible day for all of you, I hope you will convey my thanks, and my gratitude, to your good lady when you see her. It probably will not please her, but I have prayed for her swift recovery, but I would keep that quiet if I were you, from my perspective, I thought any help she could get would help." I had to smile; she would be incensed to know it.

"It is alright Reverend Wallace, I will keep it quiet, and I am very grateful to you."

"Miss Watson?" I turned, and saw a nurse looking my way.

"Yes, that is me." I stood, and she walked over and smiled.

"Miss Watson, we have given Dr Dixon, a full check and treated her wound, she fell on glass, which is why it has taken so long, we had to remove every piece, and make sure her wound was clear and sterile. We have sent her to the ward for overnight observation, she suffered a severe concussion." I nodded and smiled, the relief I felt was huge.

"Can I see her?" She gave me a big smile.

"It is why I am here, come on I will take you to see her." I gave a huge sigh of relief, I turned to Reverend Wallace, and took his hand and squeezed it.

"Thank you, for coming to see me, and for all your prayers, you are a good man." He smiled.

"Go to her Abigail, and hug her, I think that will recover both of you greatly." I gave him a big smile.

No one will ever understand all the feelings I have experienced today, even now walking behind the nurse knowing I was going to see her, and she would recover, and I could have her home again, they all still swirled inside me.

I walked down the cream coloured corridors, and through a set of double doors. I looked down the corridor in front of me, which appeared to branch off into wards of eight beds either side, nurses were walking around, with cloth covered pans, or paperwork. We passed all of the side wards, until we came to a door, she opened it with a smile.

"She needs rest and quiet, she has had quite a lot of pain medication, so she may be a little hazy, but go see her, and give her a hug." I smiled, and leaned round the door.

Birch was lay in the bed wearing a hospital robe, her head was bandaged up, and her lovely white hair stuck out in clumps all over the place, she was awake, if not a little woozy, but she smiled and lifted a hand, which had a drip taped on it. Her voice was soft and a little distant.

"Hi Sweetie."

I ran to the bed, as she smiled, and flopped onto her, and burst into tears, I could not control it. I did not want to cry, I really did not, but I just could not hold it back. She leaned forward and pulled me into her arms.

"Sweetie... Don't cry, I am fine, see I am alright." I felt everything exploding out of me.

"You are not fine; you have a huge bandage round your head. I thought I had lost you, I honestly thought he had shot you; I was so afraid I would never hear your voice, or look into your eyes again. Birch, I love you so much, I could not bear not knowing what was happening with you. You must never do anything that stupid again, I wanted to die with you." She stroked my hair, and held me close.

"Sweetie, it was not stupid, as much as I have no tolerance for Madge, she did not deserve to be shot by a maniac, I didn't want anyone to be hurt, especially you." I looked up, and she smiled at me, her eyes were bright and shiny.

"I could not go through that again, you know when you found those pills, you got mad at me for it, and told me never to do that again, so don't I have the right to tell you not to risk your life so carelessly again?" She gave a smile.

"You make a good point, and yes, you too have the right to stop me going overboard, and risking my life. You know when I lay there looking at you, I thought I was going to die, and I just kept saying I cannot leave her yet in my head, so you see, I was not going to leave you, I would never do that to you."

I relaxed and just enjoyed holding her, feeling her stroke my hair was wonderful, especially considering for a moment, I thought I may never feel it again, I gave a long happy sigh, and enjoyed the moment, Birch yawned.

"Oh dear, Sweetie, I am so tired, I am very sleepy." I slid back, and sat on the edge of the bed.

"Do you want me to help you lie back?" She smiled and closed her eyes.

"No Sweetie, just stay close to me, so I can sleep." I slipped off my boots, and climbed on the side of the bed, and put my arm round her, she gave a small smile, and took hold of my hand. "This is nice Sweetie."

I was so tired, and felt the absolute exhaustion flow into me, and I snuggled into her, and closed my eyes, just for a second, I could hear her soft breathing, and like waves lapping onto the beach, I felt secure in their sound.

Felicity held her phone on speaker phone as she talked to the Doctor, he knew who he was speaking to.

"Doctor Dixon it was only glass, we spent a lot of time, and we have extracted every last piece. She has four stitches, and the wound has been thoroughly cleaned and sterilised, I can assure you, she will make a rapid full recovery." Roni gave a sigh of relief.

"Thank you, Doctor, for helping my daughter, I do greatly appreciate it, today I am not a doctor, I am a mother, she may be twenty seven, but she is still my little girl, and I am a thousand miles away, and worrying myself sick." He smiled and nodded at the phone.

"Please Doctor Dixon, relax she is fine, I have recommended a few days of rest, and she has had some strong pain medication, and within a few days, it will just be a twinge. I want to keep her here simply to ensure she is fine after the concussion, there is no other reason, as long as she is fine tomorrow, I will send her home."

"Thank you, doctor, I am aware how busy you are, so I will let you go, express my thanks to all your staff for caring for Jemi."

Felicity looked at the phone.

"She is fine Roni, I will be seeing her shortly, Abby is with her at the moment, I think that alone will be a tonic for her."

"Flick I am so grateful you are there with her, Will and I will relax a little now, knowing you and Abby are with her. I will fully thank you when I get back, I will try and ring again tomorrow, I have left her a message on her phone, so I assume when the drugs wear off, she will phone me." Felicity gave a smile as she looked at the screen.

"We all love her Roni, so just relax and enjoy your break, tell Will he can stop looking at flights home, and we will see you soon enough, goodnight and sleep well."

"Night Flick, thanks, talk soon." Felicity ended the call and gave a sigh, Edwin looked at her.

"She is alright, isn't she?" Felicity looked at him and gave a nod.

"Yes, she was very lucky, she risked everything for Abby, because that was what she was doing Edwin. I was there, I heard Martin tell her it was her or Abby, and she stood her ground in front of him, she did not move. In that second, Birch made her choice, I honestly thought Birch was going to give her life to save our daughter. I cannot deny Edwin, it terrified me, because I do not care that they sleep together, she makes Abby happy, and I do regard her as a daughter, and it is about time you got your priorities right." Edwin looked at the floor, his guilt was obvious.

"We all make mistakes, and we all have regrets." She nodded and gave a sigh.

"They have every right to never forgive you for your betrayal, it is ironic isn't it, you cannot accept same sex relationships, but serial adultery is fine by you? You have a warped sense of responsibility Edwin. Well, you have time now to reflect on that, seeing as there is no hope of your business being allowed to trade until this is all over, you can use the time well." He looked up at her, his eyes looked weary and tired.

"I don't want to get into all that here Felicity, I am well aware of Graham's treachery, I came here to see Abigail, and Jemima, just to make sure they were safe and fine." Felicity turned and started to walk.

"She is in this room up here."

She walked up to the door and opened it quietly, Birch was fast asleep, and so was I, curled round her, holding her hand, Felicity smiled.

"Look at them Edwin, look at how they comfort each other, can you not see, neither of them could be apart, can you see how much they care about each other? That is not a fad, that is pure love, and you can either accept it, or continue to deny it. I will tell you this, that is not going to end, those two are together forever, I envy them, there is such strong love between them, I wish I had felt that."

Edwin stood in the doorway, he did not enter, he just stood there and looked. Birch stirred, and opened her eyes, she saw Edwin and Felicity and smiled, her eyes flickered, and she closed them, and she drifted back off to sleep, Felicity stepped back and closed the door.

"Edwin, you have a tough job, you know that don't you? Abby is not that easy to win back, you may think building your company was hard, but winning back your daughter, is a much tougher task. Hurting Birch with your rude insults is the worst thing you ever did." He took a deep breath and breathed out.

"I know, I will give it my best, and try my hardest, and try to find a way to undo what I have done." She nodded.

"She expects your all, don't fail her." He turned ready to leave.

"I have to get back, don't tell her I was here, I will explain everything when I next see her." He walked off down the corridor, and out, passing through the waiting room, where Edwina sat watching, as Deb's, Anthony, Bev, and Chloe, all sat back, resting with their eyes closed.

My dreams were disturbed and strange, and I woke with a start, Birch was stroking my hair, I felt disorientated and confused, as I looked up, she smiled, and spoke very softly.

"Hi my precious Sweetie." I swallowed hard, and sat up, and rubbed my eyes.

"Sorry I did not mean to sleep."

"Abby it is has been such an awful day, don't worry about it, we have been keeping Birch company." I blinked and saw Deb's, she smiled, as did all the others.

"When did you guys get here?" Edwina chuckled.

"We have been here, sat in the waiting room for a couple of

hours, and then they finally let us in to see Birch about thirty minutes ago." I nodded; my head still very fuzzy.

"Thanks guys." Birch rubbed the back of my neck.

"You should go home and rest, I am really sleepy with the meds, we both need a good night's sleep." I turned and looked at her.

"I don't want to leave you." She gave a smile, her eyes twinkled.

"Leave your heart here with me, and go and rest your body. Deads I am going to be fine, all I want to do is sleep, go home and rest, and then come and get me tomorrow."

We all spent another ten minutes with her, and then we had to leave, everyone hugged her, and I sat facing her, feeling wretched, I really did not want to go. I leaned in, and kissed her softly, she pulled me close as we kissed, it felt like the best kiss ever, even if she did jerk when her head twinged. I pulled out of the kiss and gave a sigh, her eyes danced as she held me.

"I really love you Sweetie; I am so sorry I scared you." I smiled.

"You came back, you came back to me Birch, that is all that matters, I love you so much, I really do." She smiled and two tears ran from her eyes.

"I was so scared Deads, I was terrified he would take you from me, I have never been that frightened in my life, it was horrible." I leaned in, and kissed the salty tears off her cheeks, then kissed her softly on the lips.

"No one will ever take me from you, not ever, do you understand Birch, I am yours always." She smiled, and gave a nod.

"I can flow with that." I smiled, as her bright eyes danced.

"I am only leaving under protest, so sleep, and get strong, and I will see you in the morning, I love you baby."

Walking out of the room was so hard, I stood at the door, and she smiled and waved, I felt it tear at me deep down inside. Chloe hung back as the others walked off, and slipped her hand into mine.

"It is going to be fine Abby; she will be home soon."

I understood that, but I still did not like it. I think it is the hardest thing about hospitals, they have visiting times. Birch means everything to me, and yes, I get it, she goes to work and I write, and we are separated all day, but she is fit and well, this is different, she is hurt, and so no, I don't want to leave her, I don't want special hours, I just want to be there at her side holding her hand.

I am quite sure if it was me, she would stand her ground and yell what a bloody liberty it is, although she does have a doctorate, and an NHS pass, so knowing her she would dig out her white coat, and sit in my room refusing to leave.

I was glad to have Chloe with me, we left through the back door, as there were still press at the front. When we got outside Deb's linked my other arm, as we walked slowly to Petal who was parked on the multistorey car park in the hospital grounds. Edwina put the ticket in the machine, and the charge came up, she looked at it whilst holding a ten pound note.

"Twelve bloody quid, are they taking the piss? This bugger needs hacking, and free parking given for everyone, robbing bloody twats."

I gave a smile, and leaned over her shoulder, and placed my card against the screen, it bleeped, and the payment was taken, and the release ticket came out of the slot, I handed it to Edwina.

"I would pay two hundred to park, and see her just for an hour." She smiled and gave a nod.

"I am sorry Abby, yeah she is worth a million times more."

I understood her, and she had a point, when you show up at a hospital, you do not care about parking. All you care about is the reason you are there, and every second you waste looking for a parking spot, and searching for change is a second wasted from a loved one you are worried about.

Making people pay and worry is wrong, and the authorities should know better than to treat people so shabbily. They are not cash cows, they are worried people, in need of seeing their loved ones. The irony was, I paid twelve pounds without a care, because I was relieved to see she was fine, maybe that was the council's hook?

Edwina drove us home, and I sat in the passenger seat, and closed my eyes, the exhaustion I felt weighed heavy on me, the others sat in the back talking quietly, and I slipped into a dream state, and pictures from the day slipped through my mind, would

I ever be free of them, I did not really know?

We were home before I knew it, and so did the press, they swarmed outside, like the predators they are, Debs slipped off her jacket and threw it over me, and as the gates opened, Edwina drove in and right up to the door.

The press screamed at me, as I ran inside, and everyone jumped out, and walked into the bright warm house, it felt nice and safe, Izzy pulled me into her arms and squeezed the life out of me.

"You okay kid?"

"I will be when she is home." She hugged me harder.

"I am a lousy substitute, but I am here if you need me, it has been a tough day, and things will play on your mind, so if you need to talk, I am in the next room." She let me go and smiled, I gave her a nod.

"I just want to sleep."

"Okay, go jump in bed."

I headed upstairs and dropped my bag of bloody clothes on the floor, then walked into Birch's room, I sat on the bed and pulled off my top, her bright little tree illuminated the whole room. I smiled, her forever tree, so small and yet so significant, surrounded by snow, and yet bright and alive, I had never realised how powerful a symbol of her it was, until now.

I slid off my pants, and then slid down the side of the bed, onto the floor, and placed my feet against the glass, and just sat there staring at it like she did. I found it strangely comforting, almost as if she was here with me, was this the power of the natural world she had told me about so many times, was this part of her spirit within the tree? I smiled, I felt it was.

Lost in thought I sat there, and the tears started to flow again, I did not want to cry again in front of her, and so I held them in, but sat here looking at her little precious tree, they flowed out, and I quietly released all the pain I still had trapped inside me.

I have no idea how long I had been there, my tears slowly stopped, and I had quietened down, when a pair of bare legs appeared, I looked up, and saw Chloe holding two coffees', she sat down at my side and handed me one.

"I thought you might want one, we never did get our drink in the Tea Room."

I took the cup and had a sip, it was really hot and strong, and the flavour tasted wonderful in my mouth, it had been hours since I had eaten or drunk anything. Chloe leaned onto me.

"Are you alright Abby, today was not just about Birch, I know I felt great fear when I saw him?" I swallowed the coffee.

"I am shaken still; I keep seeing him in my head. You were really there for me today Chloe, I froze with fear, I thought he would shoot Birch, and I could not move; you saved my ass today, I really appreciate that." She gave a sigh.

"You did the same for me, if not for you, he would have fucked me, and left me there in that room filled with his cum. I really do not know how I would have handled it. God I was so terrified back then, I was fucking terrified today, I keep hearing the shots. Deb's banged the fridge door, and I almost pissed my pants, that is alright isn't it, I mean, Abby am I really fucked up by all this?"

It was a great question, I wasn't Birch, I had no idea of what the consequences of this would be.

"Honestly Chloe, you are not alone, I am the same, I really do not know if this has screwed us up for life, or it is just a natural reaction." I turned to her, she looked as scared as I felt inside, I felt another wave of emotion inside me.

"Chloe, I am afraid to get into bed alone, it is why I am sat here, I just don't want to be alone. I didn't want to leave her; I just wanted to stay and feel her beside me." Chloe bit her lip, and her eyes filled.

"I know, it is why I am here, I am scared Abby, I know he has been taken away, but I am still secretly terrified, I am trying so hard to hide it." I wiped my eyes and gave a gasp.

"We are messed up Chloe, you know you can stay here tonight, we can be messed up together." She smiled.

"Can I? I would love that."

I got up and put my drink on the unit at the side of the bed, I slid in under the duvet, I grabbed Birch's pillow and swapped it with mine, I knew it still had her scent on it. Chloe slid in, and grabbed her cup, and sat drinking.

"We have a lot of guests arriving tonight, but I want to be away from everything, I am glad you came home, I am not sure what I would have done if you didn't." I lifted my cup and finished the last of the coffee, and then put it back, and settled down.

"I am glad you are here Chloe, I was worried about you, and you understand all this better than the others." She smiled, and put her cup down, and then slid under the duvet, and gave a sigh of relief.

"Thanks Abby."

I lay on my side and watched the tree, Chloe lay back and relaxed, and after a few moments she rolled into me and cuddled up, she slid her arm round my waist, I instinctively grabbed it and slid it up so she cupped my boob.

"Honestly it's not a kink, Birch holds it every night, and it makes me feel safe." She nuzzled into me.

"It is so warm and soft, I don't mind."

I gave a happy relaxed sigh, and closed my eyes, I could hear Chloe breathe behind me, it was different, but just as soft. My body felt utterly spent, the light from the little tree faded from sight, as I drifted, Chloe's warmth flowed into me, she was already gone, and I was not far behind.

Downstairs throughout the evening, visitors arrived, Gill and Aden brought flowers, Meg and Alex, with Morty turned up with bottles of Gin and chocolates. Rodger turned up with Pam, and Celia and Lillian arrived with a huge bunch of flowers.

Luke had called G5, and they had shown up, and helped board up the damaged windows in the Tea Rooms. They helped Stacy and Louise clean up, and move all the broken tables and chairs. Stacy had burst into tears when she saw Birch's blood on the floor, and Bongo and Creamy took over, as Lillian made strong tea for everyone.

Izzy sat and talked with all the guests, they were naturally disappointed to find Abby was in bed, but they understood it. Bev had seen Birch at the hospital, and so spent the night in the Hunters with Bridgette and her friends. Edwina, Debs and Anthony entertained the guests, and shared their fears, and in a way, it was good for everyone, and helped them all a little to get over it.

I drifted in sleep, seeing faces and red patches, and jumping and jerking, and each time I did, Chloe would squeeze my boob a little, and softly shush me, and then kiss my shoulder, and I would settle back again, and dream of that amazing smile, and those wonderful and glorious green sparkling eyes.

The process of healing had begun, although it would take a while for both Chloe and myself, she would paint it out of her system, and I would write it out of me, and through that alone, we would both heal.

Chapter 29

Heading Home.

Sleeping was not something I had expected, as my mind was filled with images, and feelings of fear, connected to years of problems surrounding Martin. I heard my dad shouting at me and felt the sting of his hand, or it was Martin's voice trembling with anticipation as he held me down, or accusing me of being a slut. Each and every time, as I started to cry in my dreams, I felt Birch, and her soft shushing voice, to ease me and comfort me. Slowly over the night, the heat from her body, and the calmness of her washed into me, sending me into the safe places of my soul, where she lived in my heart.

"Abby... Abby, Abby wake up."

I stirred, and felt warm and toasty, her body was soft, and the heat between us was strong, her hand was softly cupping my boob, I smiled, feeling safe and secure.

"Birch?" I opened my eyes to see Edwina looking at me, she gave me a smile.

"No Sweetheart, it's me, Edwina. Birch is still in the hospital Abby, but you have to be up to get her when she is ready, I brought you breakfast in bed." She held up the tray, filled with coffee and toast.

My mind slowly cleared, as I remembered last night, I was not alone in bed, I was with Chloe, and she was still fast asleep. I grabbed her hand and slid it softly away from my boob, she moaned in her sleep, and slid it back. Edwina lifted the duvet and peeped; she gave a chuckle.

"You know for a straight girl; she seems awfully attached to your boob?" I gave a little giggle.

"We understand each other, and we were both pretty insecure last night, I told her to stay, I think it made us both feel safe." Edwina smiled.

"I am glad you did; I was worried about you two, I checked in on you both a few times. I was happy to see you both being there for each other, thanks Abby, it means such a lot to me, to know she has more than me."

Chloe hugged as tightly as Birch, and it took me a while to wriggle free, Chloe rolled over and lay on her back, her legs spread wide open, Edwina sniggered.

"Look it's a natural reaction, as soon as her back hits a mattress, her legs spread wide."

I started to giggle, as Edwina walked round to the other side and knelt down, she lowered her voice.

"Chloe... Chloe sweetheart, it is time to wake up." She stirred and moaned, and rubbed her eyes, Edwina gave a titter.

"So sweetheart, how was your first lesbian experience, was Abby as good as Birch says she is?" Her eyes snapped open.

"Fucking what?" She turned and looked at me, as I sipped from my cup, I winked.

"Hey lover." She sat bolt upright, saw her legs were wide open, and snapped them shut.

"Holy fuck what have I done?" Edwina fell back on the floor laughing her head off, and holding her sides, I giggled, as I looked at the shock and horror on her face.

"Have your coffee, it replaces all the liquid you lost, and oh my god did you lose a lot, I never realised you would cum so hard." Edwina screamed out with laughter; Chloe smiled, and shook her head.

"Fuck you Abby, you would never cheat on Birch, not with me anyhow." Edwina sat up and gasped.

"Oh my god, your face was so frigging funny, I am going to pee myself, excuse me." She jumped up and ran into the bathroom, the sound of her peeing, mixed with her giggles echoed in the room. I took Chloe's hand, and gave it a squeeze.

"Thanks for last night, it really helped me." She smiled and then stretched.

"I know it sounds weird, but I liked it, you are comfy to sleep with, and I shouldn't say it, but I like how your boob felt, it was comforting, is that fucked up?" I gave a titter.

"I liked it too, I mean holy shit Chloe, I like being fondled by a straight girl, is that screwed up too?" She started to laugh, Edwina came in smiling, and still chuckling.

"I just made it in time, although I think a few rogue drops escaped." She sat on the end of the bed, where she had placed the tray of toast, we all leaned over and grabbed a slice, Chloe looked at me.

"Will she definitely come home today; it feels weird not having her in the house?" I shrugged, I had to wait for a doctor to discharge her.

"I really hope so, I hate her being there alone, I want her back where she belongs." Edwina smiled.

"She will come back with you, it's Birch, if they try to stop her, she will pull her it's a liberty, and I am a doctor routine, and walk out." I chuckled, she was right, she was potentially their biggest nightmare patient, I don't know why I worry so much.

Birch sat in bed looking glum, she hated her breakfast, it was not organic muesli, it tasted like sawdust, and the coffee was horrible, and they even offered her tea, she sat there staring at them.

"Philistines, who the hell drinks tea in a morning?"

The door opened, she looked up excitedly hoping to see a dark little beastie, her heart fell, as she stared in shock. Milton pushed a wheelchair into the room, Marjorie sat there looking as uncomfortable as Birch felt. Milton gave a smile, well his teeth moved, so Birch assumed he smiled, she smiled back.

"Oh, Birch dear, we have er... Yes, yes, we have come to see how you are doing, we hope you are feeling well, and rested after that terrible episode yesterday?"

It felt strange and surreal, and Birch was a little uncertain of what to do, the therapist in her clicked into auto pilot, and she smiled.

"Hello bel... Rev Wallace, Madge, I am glad to see you are looking well, how are you?"

Marjorie took a deep breath, this was not at all easy for her, she gave a slight nod, her face had a strange expression of confusion, and what was obviously a difficult smile, after all, smiling was not her forte around Birch, her face was somewhat accustomed to scowls.

"I am feeling much better thank you." Birch smiled.

"It may surprise you, but I am actually relieved to hear that,

Dea... Abby told me what happened, and I was concerned about you, it is nice to see you are recovering."

Neither of them really knew what to say, but even though awkward and stunted, Birch was taking the lead, and Marjorie understood the significance of that.

"You surprised me Doctor Dixon, you put your own life at risk to save mine, and I am not sure how to understand that, but my family are grateful to you, as am I." Birch smiled.

"I did not want to see you hurt, as much as that may not be in your understanding, I don't actually hate you Madge. You annoy the shit out of me, but I will not deny that I also enjoy our little digs at each other. You know, I do not want to destroy the village, none of us do, and we are not whores either, I have nowhere near as much sex as you credit me for. The truth is I do not get the sort of attention I used to, and I have never done it for money. All we want is to be a part of protecting the village, we love it as much as you do, and we want to live life our own way. I realise our ways are alien to you, yours are to us, just accept us as we are, like we do you." She actually smiled.

"I shall bear that in mind in future, the fact still remains, my family still owe you, and I would like to make a gesture of repayment." Birch understood.

"Honestly Madge, if you want to repay me, don't change, continue as you are, but I will allow you to pay for one coffee at the Tea Rooms, we missed ours, and then just stay as you are, because if you go all sweet on me, just know that the village will be damaged forever. The customers look forward to our little spats, so just don't change, I can take what you throw at me, but go easier on Abby, this has been a really difficult time for her, with her dad and his troubles, and now Martin and the press writing lies about her, she cannot take much more pressure, and she really needs a break." Marjorie nodded.

"I can do that, and I have actually held back with Abigail a lot of late, I have seen how the pressure has worn on her. I will say this for her, I saw something yesterday I never expected, I saw how deeply she cares about you, even I found it difficult to witness, it was a heart breaking thing to see." Birch bit her lip, and fought back her emotions, her eyes filled up, and her voice softened.

"I hate that I put her through that, she has suffered enough, I am glad you are well; the village would be very dull without you." Marjorie smiled.

"I think it would be dull without you too, you certainly bring a strange chaos to things." Birch gave a giggle, she agreed, life did get a little weird at times for her.

I was feeling anxious, I really wanted her to text me, and I needed to do something, I slid out of bed, and walked to the wardrobe.

"Holy shit Abby, does that not hurt?" I looked back at Chloe sat in the bed.

"What?" She pointed.

"The bruises, do they not hurt, they are all up your back and your arms?"

I opened Birch's wardrobe door, and looked at the full length mirror, I turned round twisting to look, I had a bruise on my left butt cheek, and three up my spine, and several on both the backs of my arms.

"Wow I had no idea they were there; it must have been from all the broken furniture falling and hitting me. They don't hurt at all, is that weird?"

I had clothes to pack, I went through her wardrobe, I found some awesome black bootcut jeans, I slipped them on and looked at myself, yeah, I was nicking these. I rummaged round to see what else she had? I found a great pair of bootcut jeans, with flowers embroidered up the legs, and round the bottom, I liked them too, but they were more Birch's style than mine.

I pulled out two thick vests, and a couple of jumpers, red for me, and deep blue for her, I grabbed socks from my drawers, because all mine match, unlike hers, and I grabbed boots, Chloe wandered over and leaned into the wardrobe.

"Wow Birch has some great stuff, why doesn't she wear half of this?" I stuffed her clothing into my back pack.

"She likes shopping with friends, she is a genius at picking out clothes for others, and I suppose she just gets carried away, and sees things she likes, so she buys them, yet almost never wears them. Sometimes I go rooting around and find stuff, like these black pants, and I wear them, and she hardly ever notices they were hers."

I pulled on the vest and the jumper, I needed a different coat, my thick winter coat was covered in blood, I headed downstairs to find another. Chloe followed me down, with the tray of cups and plates, I dropped the back pack at the front door, and headed for the kitchen to drink more coffee.

The kitchen table had five vases of flowers on it, Amanda at the florist shop, had done really well, I pondered as to where Birch was going to put them all. Birch loved flowers, especially ones with roots. I had picked her some once and she loved them, but told me as sweet as it was, she also felt guilty something so lovely would die because of her. Edwina handed me a cup, and I sat down, I was playing the waiting game, which I absolutely hated.

It is strange really, because I can sit at my desk for hours writing, knowing eventually that I will in time have a full manuscript for a book, but tell me you will phone, and I will pace and stomp, and drive myself insane, staring at my phone, yearning for it to ring.

Finally, she messaged me, and I felt a jolt of joy deep down inside, and suddenly, I felt really excited. “Sweetie, I can go home, please hurry I need clothes. Xxx.”

I gave a sigh of relief, gave a little giggle, and headed for the door, I grabbed my long black coat, leaned in through the living room door, and grabbed Petal’s keys from the tray. I lifted my bag off the floor, and headed out to Petal, and felt a huge ball of joy growing inside me, and I could not stop smiling no matter how much I tried.

I drove out of the gates to a barrage of flashing cameras, I hate those twats, they should allow me to run them over. They crowded around me, taking pictures like the cold blooded predators they are, I secretly wanted to run them all over as payback. I headed through the village grinning like an escaped mental patient. People must have thought I was really pleased to see them, but the truth was, I was really happy, because I could hold her, and kiss her, and pull her tightly to me. It had only been a day, and yet I had missed it so much.

I arrived at the hospital and parked up, and as I came down the steps, I could see the long row of media vans. I dodged them, and used the side door and got to her room as quickly as possible.

Birch sat on top of her bed, talking on her phone. "Mum I am fine; the doctor has signed me out... I told you, it's just four stitches... I banged my head on the table."

I slipped in through the door, with my bag on my shoulder, she saw me and waved, and smiled a huge happy smile, she looked at her phone and sighed.

"Mum, seriously, of course I had to, no one deserved that... Yeah, I know, but you know what, maybe she has learned wisdom... Oh Mum, you would not, you would have done exactly the same..."

I stood watching her, happily chatting, smiling, her eyes fixed on me, bright green, and dancing, her lovely long white hair sticking out of her bandage in clumps. Never had she looked more beautiful to me, filled with life, and the source of every good feeling I had inside. My heart beat in my chest, it was pure joy, and intense relief.

I walked up to her, and slipped my arms round her, and she leaned in, and I kissed her passionately, as she held the phone to her ear. She took the phone from her ear and kissed me back, matching my yearning, to just connect and interact. I had missed this, it was soft and slow, yet so intense, I gave a gasp, as she pulled away, and smiled, as my heart fluttered.

"Yes, she just got here... Of course, I was kissing her, I missed her." She started to giggle. "Oh Mum you can be so silly... Yes, I promise, as soon as I get home... I will!" She giggled. "Okay good point, and the doctor did say I had to go to bed." She smiled at me. "What would you do if it was dad?" She started to laugh. "So, I am just like you then?" She handed the phone to me. "Mum wants a word." I took the phone off her and held it to my ear.

"Hi Roni."

"Abby sweetheart how are you holding up?"

"I am fine now I know I can have her back." I heard her chuckle.

"Abby this would have brought up some pretty traumatic stuff, you may experience moments of panic, look do not bury it, talk to her, she understands, and if you need to, call me anytime. Take care of her Abby, she is not showing it, but she was as scared as you, and she will need you there, so she can get through this, stay close, and let her sleep and be quiet." I smiled at her, as she excitedly pulled clothing out of my bag.

"I will Roni, I am not letting her out of my sight."

"Abby put me on speaker." I clicked the button and lay the phone on the bed.

"Girls, I am very proud of you for taking care of each other, I love you both, so go home and take care of each other, and have a wonderful Christmas together. Jemi, I want a video call as soon as you have finished with Abby." She started to laugh.

"I love you girls, talk to you soon."

"Talk soon, bye." Birch pulled on her boots.

"I love these jeans, they are really pretty, when did you buy them?" I shook my head and giggled.

"I found them in your wardrobe, you bought them over a year ago." She looked down and turned her legs as she looked at them.

"I do like them, so I suppose I must have bought them, okay let's go then."

She picked up her big bag, grabbed my hand, with a big smile, and walked to the door. I had to laugh; she was in a bigger rush than I was. I felt a huge relief, and was so happy I could not stop smiling, she snuggled into my arm with a giggle. We left the room, and walked down the long corridor, she was happy and lively, smiling to everyone and saying hello, I am sure a lot of the people we passed thought she was off the nut job ward.

As we approached the doors, I saw Vanessa, sat on a seat drinking a coffee, I pulled Birch over in her direction, and smiled at her.

"Vanessa, she can go home, I just wanted to say thank you, for all you did yesterday." Birch looked at the uniform, and put two and two together.

"Deads, is this the ambulance driver?" Vanessa stood up, and looked at Birch.

"You took quite a smash, I am so glad to see you are a lot better, you really frightened your partner, it is so nice to see you two back together." Birch leaned forward and gently kissed her cheek.

"Thank you for taking care of Deads when she was so hurt, I feel I owe you so much." Vanessa smiled.

"You just paid the bill in full, not many understand what we do, seeing you both together is so nice, because when I found you both in that café, it was a pretty tragic scene, trust me. Abby loves you so much, I wish I had a love that strong in my life." I smiled at her, and felt a little shy, and embarrassed, I had not really told Birch all of it.

"She is my life, and you helped give her back to me, I will always be grateful Vanessa, Thank you so much." She smiled, and I stepped forward and pulled her into a hug, and she patted my back.

"Wow, I never expected this, you know, my little brother would die if I had a picture of you." I stepped back with a smile.

"That is easily enough done, have you got your phone on you?" Birch took her phone, and I stood beside Vanessa with a big smile, and the picture was taken, she handed the phone back to her, Birch handed her a card.

"Bring your little brother round sometime, just give me a call, and I will make sure we are home, both of you will be very welcome to join us for an afternoon, it would be nice to sit and thank you properly." Her eyes were wide as she looked at it.

"On my god he will freak when he sees this, but I will warn you, he is eighteen, and he thinks he is a bit of a lady's man, he will hit on you both, he has all the Hand of Death books." I gave a giggle.

"Don't worry about him hitting on us, we will have to muzzle one of our house mates, to keep her off him." She chuckled.

It was nice to say goodbye, and step out into the fresh air, which was crisp, and very cold, it was not nice to be confronted with an army of journalists. Camera's rattled and reporters screamed my name. 'Abigail, how does it feel to have your lover back? Is it true you fucked up Hinkley's life? Did you fuck in the hospital Abigail? Will you be paying for the damage to the building? Will you be seeing your dad when he goes to prison?'

I felt panicked, and huddled close to Birch, I felt my stomach twisting, I had not expected this, when I got to her my mind had just been focused on seeing Birch, and I had completely forgotten they were here. There was nowhere to look, the only thing stopping them mobbing me was the hand rail. Birch slipped off her coat and lifted it round us, we had to fight our way through, there was no way we were going to make it to Petal. I could feel the tears in my eyes, as I shied away from the rail, and huddled close to the wall.

"Birch I am so sorry."

A van pulled up, and the side door slid open, I saw Amy Walker, the TV reporter, I had met in the village, she smiled and waved at me.

"Jump in, I promise there are no cameras."

We hurried, and I pushed my way through, as reporters leaned over the rail, and tried to pull Birch's coat off us. There were hands everywhere reaching out, and trying to claw at us, shouting out question after question. I was so frightened, and felt a pain in my throat, and I fought to keep my head down, whilst holding Birch. One of them tried to pull the coat off Birch, and she yanked back hard on it, to stop them, I staggered as she held on to me, and felt the panic surge through me.

We reached the van and Amy helped pull us in, and slammed the door shut.

"Where is your vehicle, I take it you are in the purple Jeep?"

Reporters banged on the side of the van, I jumped in fear, and clutched Birch's arm, Birch pulled me close, and I snuggled into her shaking violently, she looked at Amy.

"It's not purple, it's Lilac, and it's not a Jeep, it's a Land Rover." I shook harder, and was fighting to breathe as I felt I was suffocating, as the banging continued, Amy looked at me.

"I am so sorry Miss Watson, after all you went through yesterday, you would think they would know better. Look give me your keys; we will grab your vehicle and drive it out for you." She leaned over the seat. "Mark head to the car park, Brett go grab the car, you know which one it is, and meet us in the Orbital car park with it."

The van moved off as the reporters banged on the sides, yelling and screaming my name. I huddled tight into Birch, shaking and trying to breathe, and closed my eyes.

I knew the Orbital; it was the large hotel, where the ring road met with the main motorway. I handed over the keys, and Brett took them, as we cowered in the back hiding our faces, as those who had chased us, continued to yell. Cameras were pushed up to the side, and back windows, it was insanity, and I cowered as low as I could fighting back the tears. The van pulled up outside the car park, and Brett jumped out, and Mark hit the gas and we drove off at speed. The reporters stopped banging as they could not keep up, and I felt myself calm a little, I looked at Amy, not quite understanding.

"Why are you doing this for us?" She smiled.

"Suspicious little vampire, aren't you? If you must know, I am aware you are giving Tom a full interview on your life and work. I would appreciate an exclusive, with you and Doctor Dixon, just to set the record straight about yesterday only, there is a lot of nasty stuff going out there. We got some film of it, all I want is to talk about yesterday, I won't step on Tom's toes, I like him, he is a good guy, look here is my card, I just want you to think about it. Abby, they have the wrong idea about you, let me set the record straight with you." I took her card and looked at it.

"We will need to talk to each other about this first, how long have we got?" Amy watched me closely.

"After today, the pictures will hit tomorrow's papers, we would need to film this soon, in order to get it on air." I understood.

"My manager will want a say in this as well, so if we say yes, she will have to be involved, she handles everything." Amy nodded and gave a sigh of relief.

"Talk to each other, and then your manager, I know Katie, so get back to me if it is a go."

I snuggled down into Birch, and could hear her heart beating, she was as scared as me, but was much better at hiding it. I looked at the floor and my thoughts drifted, as I considered what Amy had said, and before I knew it, we had arrived at the Orbital Hotel.

The van came to a halt, and she pulled on the door, and it slid open, and there was Petal pulling up at the side of the van. Brett got out and handed over the keys, and I climbed out of the van, opened Petal's door and got in behind the wheel, I was still shaking. Birch got in on the other side and I looked at her.

"I am so sorry Birch, I did not think, I forget at times those predators are everywhere I go." She grabbed my hand and squeezed it.

"Deads, I understand the way things work, I am fine, all I want is to go home and be alone with you." I turned the keys and the engine started, I waved to Amy who was still watching.

"That is all I want too, just to be alone, and quiet, and away from everyone for a while, I thought I had lost you, honestly, my need to hold you is unbelievable. Let's get home."

Amy sat in the van as we drove off, Mark was watching her.

"Will she do it?" Amy gave a sigh.

"I am not certain, but I am telling you, if the press don't back off, she will break. I am not sure she can take much more; did you see how much she was shaking?"

I headed onto the back roads, as I regulated my breathing, I constantly checked the mirrors, to make sure the road behind was clear, I just wanted to get the hell away from them. I wanted her coming out to be so nice, and I felt angry at myself, for not being more prepared, Birch leaned over in the seat.

"Deads Sweetie, we are fine, and you need to slow down, we are sixty in a forty zone, just relax, we are well away from them now." I was still trembling, and gripping the wheel tight, I looked at the speedo, and lifted my foot off the accelerator, Petal began to slow.

"I am sorry Birch, I am so sorry, I should have realised and took better care of you." She put her hand on my hand.

"Sweetie, pull over and take a moment, you need to calm down." We pulled into a small layby, and I pulled on the hand break, she unclipped her seat belt and slid over to me, I turned feeling shaky.

"Sweetie, this is for the best, this is therapy."

I frowned; she gave me a smile. Birch pulled open my seat belt, turned me round in the seat so my back was against the door, and then undid my jeans button, I looked down as she pulled on my zipper, I felt even more panicked.

"Jesus Birch it's daylight, and we are on the side of the road."

She gave a cheeky giggle as she pulled my pants and I lifted my bum, so they slid off, and down to my knees, Birch leaned over me, with a cheeky grin.

"Oh god, I need this." She unbuttoned her jeans and slid them down. I swallowed hard and looked round to make sure no one was there; my heart was racing.

Birch leaned over me and kissed me, I tilted my head back onto the glass, and started to kiss her back, I felt her hand slide between my legs and make contact, she kissed me hard and with passion, and all thoughts of worrying about if anyone was looking disappeared. I lifted my hand, and slipped it between her legs, my mind was spinning as she played, and the pulses and throbs of my lower regions, rippled through my body. I broke free of the kiss and started to breathe fast.

"Oh hell... Jesus Birch."

She slid into my neck and kissed as her breathing increased, I was trying to focus on my hand, my attention kept getting drawn to her hand, I closed my eyes, and pushed back on the glass window.

"Ohhh!... Oh, Oh, Oh, Oh god!"

I could not believe how turned on I was, this was madness and the most dangerous sex we had ever had, my body was exploding and my insides pulsating. I was not going to last, I tried finger banging her more to catch her up, my mind was drifting.

"OH GOD BIRCH!"

My legs straightened and shook, as my whole body convulsed with electric spasms, I had never come this fast in my life. She was on me kissing me, forcefully and hard, her mouth gyrating on mine, her tongue probing into me, and I banged as hard as I could, her legs were trembling and she broke from the kiss, and sat up with a wail.

"OoooooooooOOOOOOOOOOH YES, OH SWEETIE!"

I felt the gush down my wrist, she was cumming like crazy, she leaned forward, and pushed her head into my neck and spasmed. I was panting in her ear, and she shuddered hard.

"Oh god Sweetie, oh wow that was nice." She breathed in and slipped back with a smile; I shook my head.

"You are bloody insane do you know that?" She smiled, as she collapsed back against the other door and breathed hard.

"Well, you are not stressed out now, so if that is madness, give me more Sweetie." Her eyes twinkled with devilish delight, and I started to laugh.

"Oh god Birch, it was only a night, but it felt like an age, I really missed you last night." She gave a little giggle.

"I closed my eyes, thought of you and wanked like crazy last night, it is why I wanted to get out fast, the bed sheets looked like I had pissed all over them." She smiled and twitched her eye brows. "Ouch! Shit, that hurts."

I sat back with my pants round my knees, and just laughed, she was bonkers, but God, I loved her, like I never thought possible.

Chapter 30

Home Life.

We were finally home, having endured another onslaught of press at our gates, and finally got home with our hoods up, and parked petal close to the door. Feeling calmer, and in bed having arrived home, very turned on, and after all the hugs from everyone, we slid into bed, and made love properly. I lay back in the bed, as I closed my eyes, and just drifted in the feelings of joy rushing round my system.

Birch talked to her mum, and explained where the cut was, and where the stitches were located, and Roni got to see her properly, which put her mind at rest. I waved from below the duvet, so Roni could see I was there with her, she found it funny and commented.

"I said bed rest Abby, not just bed, well now you are done, you should rest... You are done, aren't you?"

Birch looked at me and winked, and we both started to giggle, Roni shook her head and started laughing, she knew when she was beat.

The call ended and we lay back and relaxed, Birch felt tired, so I turned on my side, and watched as she closed her eyes. I loved how long her eyelashes were, and the way they curled away from her eyes. It was easy to feel sorry for myself, having witnessed everything, but Birch had a huge hole in her day from when she was unconscious, and I knew her mum was right, she was hiding her fear. I slipped into lucid sleep watching her softly breathe.

Outside came a loud rev, we did not hear it, but most of the street did, a bright red Ferrari pulled up, and parked outside the house. The licence plate read, 'L35B3N' She got out of the car wearing a bright red suit, with a red vest, which considering her long coppery red hair, looked more than bright, with the snowy background. She keyed the number into the pad, and the gates swung open. Katie turned and looked at the press.

"Miss Watson will be giving one interview, and that is already arranged, and she will not be leaving the house until it has been released, so you may as well all leave, there is nothing here for any of you." She turned and walked in, and rang the doorbell.

I was still lay on my side, but was drifting in and out of a happy state of being, Birch was flat out asleep. I felt the bed move, and opened my eyes, Katie was sat on the bed staring at Birch, she looked really upset, she noticed me and smiled.

"I came as soon as I heard, you are all over the papers, the fuckers are tearing you two apart. I spoke to Amy Walker, and I am setting you both up for an interview."

"Katie, we have not talked about whether or not we want to do it." She stroked the side of Birch's face softly.

"Abby, please do this, get the fuckers away from her, they will hurt her, and I cannot bear the thought of that. Trust me please, talk to this Amy woman." I watched her carefully, and could see how upset she was, and to be honest, it really surprised me.

"I am sorry Katie, I never realised she means as much to you as she does to me, you know, it has never showed before?" She gave a sad smile.

"I am a selfish cold bitch Abby, I have always wanted her, but honestly, she was never going to come to me, and then she met you. I am happy for her, but some days it really fucking hurts. Do the interview, get the press off her, protect her for me Abby."

"Okay Katie, I will." She smiled as she looked at Birch.

"I have no idea how it must have felt for you, actually seeing it happen, I only heard about it, and it almost stopped my heart. Abby use your platform with Amy, to set the record straight. Be you, just tell it as it is, show your honesty." She took a deep breath. "I am going to head downstairs and talk to Amy, I will be there when you do it, and filming it, so if they try to edit it, we can call them out on it."

She got up and smiled, and headed out of the door, I sat there looking at Birch, as she slept, I have always wanted to protect her, I hated what had happened to her. It was heart breaking, and I honestly had no idea why the press would want to write such nasty things, it was clear most of them believed the lies of Peter

Ford.

I decided to let Birch sleep, and I got out of bed, grabbed my clothes, and wandered into my bedroom, I stood by the window and looked out at the snow. The garden looked beautiful, the sun was out, and the white blanket sparkled with millions of little twinkles.

The whole world looked peaceful and asleep, it reminded me of Birch, wild, natural, and resting, waiting for that moment to come back to life, and spring into action with a burst of life. I gave a sigh, and turned from the window, today felt hard, all I wanted was to come home and curl up with Birch, and now Katie had organised an interview, and I did not know how I felt about that.

I left Birch to sleep, and I headed downstairs, Katie walked round the library on the phone talking, I poured a coffee and walked back up the hall, and turned right in to the library and sat at my desk. Katie looked at me.

"You look knackered." I nodded and leaned back in my chair.

"Katie, I want to do something very special for her." I slid my hand inside my pocket, and pulled out a flash drive.

"I want to do this, everything you need is on the drive, it is type set and formatted, I am not sure it can be done, but if it can, I want this for her." Katie took the stick and gave me a curious look.

"How special is this?"

"This is the only way I can show all the truth of me, and I so desperately want her to see it, when I write, I express myself better than talking." It was hard to explain, but I think she understood, she nodded, and slipped it in her pocket.

I had my coffee, checked in on Birch, she was still sleeping, and headed into my room, moved to my bed, and sat down, slid back and crossed my legs. I tried to think, and really understand everything I was feeling. It had been ten years since Martin had tried to assault me, and it had hung over me for all that time, I had to wonder if it would ever be fully over. Did I need therapy like Chloe had, was I really screwed up by all this and needed to sort it all out? My mind swirled with all the possibilities, I felt like I was drowning in thoughts.

I sat there lost in my head and did not even notice Birch was awake, and had sat beside me, until she leaned in and kissed my cheek. I jumped with a start, and then realised where I was, she stroked my leg.

"Are you really alright Sweetie?" I shook my head.

"Honestly, I do not know, maybe it is just too soon to tell." She gave a sad smile and breathed in.

"Deads, after the Rodney thing, and seeing how Chloe reacted, I gave Susana Richmond a call, I heard she was looking to leave Victim Support, and I offered her a place at Sweetie's Retreat. She specialises in Trauma and Sexual Offences, and she will be starting for us after Christmas." I turned and looked at her.

"Do you think I need to see her?" She smiled, and stroked the side of my face.

"Sweetie she was the counsellor that helped Chloe, she knows all about what happened, and she really is one of the best. It is not a case of whether I think you need to see her or not, the question is, do you think she could help you? It might just help for you to speak to a neutral party, let's be honest, it won't hurt to try." She smiled. "I worry about you." I understood that.

"Is Chloe going to be seeing her?" She nodded.

"Izzy spoke to her yesterday, and she has agreed to try ten sessions, and then take it from there." I gave a sigh and I looked at her, I could see the concern in her eyes.

"I will do it under one condition, I want you to see her too." Birch gave a giggle.

"I am already having sessions with Izzy Sweetie, I arranged them when I was in the hospital. I have things I want to deal with, and I don't want you to see me break down, I am wise enough to know I need them, and she has helped me in the past."

"Alright Birch, I will do it, I want the fear of him out of my head." She leaned in and kissed me softly on the cheek.

"It is for the best for both of us, I think we both need it." I leaned on to her.

"I am just glad you are home... By the way Katie is here, she is trying to set up an interview with Amy, she wants us to do it, apparently the press have been doing a hatchet job on us... Again." Birch sat next to me with my head on her shoulder, and thought about it.

"Honestly, all I want to do is forget it, but if Katie thinks this will help you, then let's just do it and get it over with." She licked her lips. "I need a coffee, come on, let's go and get one."

The moment we told Katie, she was on the phone, and by six pm, the living room was full of lights and cameras, and Amy with her news crew. We both dressed for the interview, I had on all black with black eyes, Birch was still bandaged, and wore her flowery jeans and a green top.

The sofa was too low, so chairs were brought in, and set up by the decorated festive fireplace. Amy talked us through it. Katie had Edwina and Luke set up their camera to film all of it just in case. I was clear, the interview was to be just about the Tea Room incident, anything more, and the interview was over. Deb's Chloe, Anthony, and Michael sat in on the sofa for moral support, but were warned, they could not make a sound.

Brett set up a portable sound desk, and then helped mic us up, he gave me the wire and showed me wear to put it. I think he was afraid to touch me, for fear of freaking me out. I pulled the wire up inside my top, and he showed me how to clip it on, and then did a sound test. I felt my nervousness rising, Chloe had prepared two large gins to look like water for us, and I took a sip for Dutch courage.

Mark was ready on the cameras, he had two remote cameras on tripods, and sat at his laptop, next to the Christmas tree monitoring their feeds, Amy sat three feet in front of us and smiled.

"Both of you just answer honestly, and talk clearly, and do not be nervous, this a recording not a live feed, so if you need a break, just say so." I nodded and took a breath. Brett gave a thumbs up on the sound, and Mark looked at Amy.

"Okay in three... two... One, and go." Amy looked into the camera just off to our side.

"Hi I am Amy Walker with River TV News, at the home of Author, Abigail Jennifer Watson, who yesterday was involved in a shooting incident in her home village of Wotton Dursley. She is here with her life partner Doctor Jemima Dixon, who was badly injured, and suffered a head wound during the event." She turned and looked at both of us.

"There is a lot of speculation in all the papers, and it is clear no one really knows what has happened. How are you both today?" I swallowed hard as I saw the red light on the camera in front of me come on, Birch spoke first.

"We are very shaken, it was a very harrowing and traumatic experience for all of us, and today we are trying to make sense of all of it, but we are coping." Amy gave a slight nod.

"Gun shots were fired, and the newspapers have been saying you were shot in the head, can you give us an idea of what actually happened?" Birch looked at Amy.

"Martin Hinkley aimed his gun at one of the customers in the Tea Rooms, I tried to get the customer on the floor, and in doing so, the window fragments, from the window he shot at, embedded in the side of my head, I was not shot, just badly cut."

"You were taken to Oxendale hospital and kept there overnight, was that due to the fact that you were unconscious, or was the cut that severe?" I felt Birch squeeze my hand.

"I had a severe concussion, and there was a lot of glass to be removed, I have had several stitches just above my left ear, but I was cleared this morning to come home, as long as I get plenty of rest." Amy looked straight at me.

"Miss Watson, I believe all this happened right in front of you, that must have been a really awful thing to witness?" I gave a nod and swallowed hard, I felt a huge surge of emotion rise up inside me, Birch gripped my hand tighter.

"I was terrified, I thought he had shot her, and when I saw all the blood, I honestly thought I had lost her." My eyes filled with tears, and my voice stumbled. "I thought she was dead." I looked at the camera as I tried to gather myself, and the tears filled my eyes, I felt myself shaking. I took a deep breath as Birch squeezed my hand.

"No one will ever really understand what that is like, unless they have been through it." I gave a sob, and my voice rose even higher. "I thought he had killed her." Amy leaned forward, and handed me a hankie.

"I am sorry to put you through this, we can take a break if you need it." I wiped my eyes, and shook my head.

"I am okay, it is alright Amy, I really need to do this, I need everyone to see the lies of the papers and hear the truth from me." She patted my leg, and sat back.

"Martin Hinkley was a maniac, we did not lie. I cannot believe any reporter who was there would side with him, we did nothing wrong, we were just enjoying the Christmas festivities in the village, just like every other normal person there."

Amy gave a nod and paused a second to give me a moment to wipe my eyes.

"It is clear Miss Watson, how traumatic it was for you, so can I talk about Martin Hinkley? As you know he gave an interview to Peter Ford of the Mail, where he accused you of falsely lying about his attempted assault of you, which clearly was his motive for the events yesterday. Many of the papers today are agreeing with that article, so, what would you like to say to set the record straight?" I took a deep breath.

"He lied to Peter Ford, who should have fact checked his article with the police, it is all there as a matter of public record. When I was sixteen, after choir practice at the local church, I was tidying up the hymn books, in the store room, and he approached me from behind, and tried to rape me. I was lucky, I fought back, and by sheer luck I got away." I wiped my eyes, and swallowed hard, and looked at Amy.

"Seven years ago, he tried to rape my friend, luckily, we had all arranged to meet at the church gates, as we were going out into Oxendale for a night out. When she did not show up after all the rest of the choir left, I panicked. Jemi and myself went to find her, we caught Martin in the act, he had her pinned to a wall with her underwear torn off, and his pants round his ankles. He was just about to force his way into her, when we stopped him." Amy nodded.

"I believe it was filmed on your phone?" I nodded, and took a deep breath.

"Yes, Martin threatened me when I got away, and it scared me enough to stay quiet, Jemi was the one who thought of filming it to prove we were not lying. I froze with fear, so she gave me the phone, and I stood there filming it. It was all I could do, I was so scared, Jemi and another friend stopped him from raping her, and the police were called. Four other women came forward to say he had raped them in the same way at another church, and with the film evidence, he was convicted. He was released on parole not long ago. I had not seen him until yesterday, he apparently blamed me for it all."

"Have you seen the website Coding Cube; they published an interview with his ex-wife where she mentioned he had admitted it to her?"

"I know of the site, they sent me an email to tell me they had attached it to my site, but I have not played the interview they put on it, but I am glad she came forward. I have heard a lot of today's newspapers are saying he was right, so I would say go listen to the words of his wife, and then you will understand the truth, and all his lies. Martin Hinkley is a rapist, and that is a fact, if you don't believe me, look at the Coding Cube site, it is stuck to my site and I cannot remove it." Amy smiled.

"I take it you agree with the Coding Cube group, have you heard anything else from them?" I shook my head.

"I do not break the law, but to be honest, the press has lied so much, I felt relieved someone out there could see the injustice as well as myself. I am glad they got the proof to show what an evil man Peter Ford really is, what they have done may be illegal, but it was noble, and I shall not call them for what they have done, they got the truth out there, and I am grateful of that. It is a shame the national press do not have the same honourable ethics when reporting." Amy sat back with a smile.

"You have suffered a lot Miss Watson, more than most, and yet you still find the courage to go out and meet your fans. I believe you spent several hours meeting fans in the local bookshop the night you switched on the village lights, how was that for you?" I smiled, and took a deep breath.

"It was a little scary at first, I was so shocked when I walked on stage, and saw all those happy faces, but I have such lovely fans of my work, and in the bookshop, they were all so nice to me, it was a very special experience, one I shall never forget. It really made me very happy that I have been able to write for such lovely people." She gave me a nod and smiled.

"It has been reported that, a Mrs Wallace was injured during the shooting and taken to hospital, Dr Dixon, can you tell us what happened with her?" Birch took a breath.

"Some of it is a little fuzzy for me still. Mrs Wallace is the wife of the previous Vicar, Martin Hinkley was their choir master. She tried to get him to stop, and he lost his temper, and he aimed the gun at her. I did not want anyone hurt, I was trying to keep him calm, it happened so fast, I think I dived on her to get her out of the way, and she was injured in the fall. I remember her landing on top of me, and rolling off, not so much after that." I nodded my head.

"That was when Jemi got hurt, Mrs Wallace was lay on the floor next to Jemi, I was crying because there was so much blood, and she handed me her hankie to stop the bleeding, and then she had a heart attack, and died. She was given CPR and revived just before the ambulance arrived. I was glad about that, because she was trying to help stop Hinkley, and she suffered because of it. It is nice to know she is alright; I had some flowers and a thankyou note sent to her." Amy gave a smile.

"Mrs Wallace has been a vocal opponent of both of you has she not?" Birch gave a smile, and chuckled.

"She has been more than vocal, she has her ways and we have ours, I am not sure she will ever agree with us, but she did not deserve to be shot at by a maniac, she has done a lot in service to this village over the years. I do not agree with a lot of things she says, but I cannot fault her dedication to the preservation of this village. I saw her in the hospital and we spoke, and I was glad to see she was making a full recovery." I looked at Birch, I did not know they had spoken. She smiled and squeezed my hand.

"I am sure when she is better, she will find something else we do, a reason to complain." I giggled. Amy gave a big smile.

"Both of you have suffered with the press, they were pretty ruthless with you when you left the hospital, and I actually think very rude and inconsiderate, what do you think of their behaviour?" I looked right into the camera.

"They are the reason I do not do interviews, if they were more polite, I would talk to them, but they are not. They ask me questions, and then write lies about me. Why ask me questions, if they are not going to print my replies? I feel it is pointless to talk to them, which is unfair to my readers, it is why I have built my website, so my readers have somewhere to go to read the facts." Birch agreed.

"I deeply resent the way they think they can say anything to Abby, I see how much it hurts her, I really dislike their crude and animalistic manner. A little polite respect would go a long way, but they just have to be vulgar and insensitive, and that actually costs them, so all they do is print lies about her, and I hate them for that."

"Yet you have agreed to this, and I am aware you will be giving a full in depth interview with a local reporter in the New Year?" I nodded.

"You have been nothing but respectful Amy, which is why I agreed to this, and the same goes for my other interview, he has always shown me great respect. I like that, and so have agreed to do the interview, that is all it takes, be polite and print the truth. If the national press did that, instead of employing the likes of Peter Ford, I would happily talk more to them, because that lets me talk to my fans. I only use my website now to communicate to my readers." Amy was all smiles.

"I am aware I have boundaries for this interview, but River would love to do more with you, especially when your next book comes out. It has been a real thrill for us today, Miss Watson, and Doctor Dixon, would it be alright to ask what your plans are for Christmas?" I gave a smile.

"We are just going to spend time at home with our Curio family, and just take it easy. Normally we are all spread around the country, so this year we are staying together here. I am helping to cook dinner this year with two of my house mates, and friends and family will join us for a meal, nothing special, just a traditional Christmas."

"That sounds nice, can I just say, that you two are a really lovely couple, and I would like to wish the both of you the best for this Christmas, I am sure everyone at River will agree, you are both remarkable women." Birch smiled.

"Thank you, I think Abby needed to hear that, because she has no idea how special she is." I felt a little embarrassed as I looked at her, she gave me a smile, and leaned in and gave me a soft peck on the lips. Okay so now I was really blushing, Amy gave a chuckle.

"So adorable... Thank you so much Miss Watson for talking to us." I smiled.

"My pleasure, thank you Amy." I saw Katie beaming a big smile, she highly approved, Amy looked at the other camera.

"This is Amy Walker for River TV News." Mark lifted his hand, and then dropped it.

"That's a wrap, we have it all, it is brilliant, thanks guys."

I sat back in my chair and gave a gasp; Amy leaned forward and patted my leg.

"You did great, I am really sorry I made you cry, but to be honest, it will make for great PR for you, because it was honest and genuine." I smiled

"I am just glad it is all over; all I want to do is forget it, and not keep remembering it." She nodded.

"I think both of you are really brave, I saw what you have to deal with at the hospital, trust me, it has taught me how not to approach a person for an interview. I am sorry they are like that, I really am, they are my profession, but not all of us are like that Abby."

It took a while to take everything down, and once our mics were off, I showed Amy the rest of the downstairs of the house, we sat in the kitchen and made coffee, and were joined by the others, she loved that we all lived together, and admitted she was impressed at how organised and how clean the house was. We sat around drinking coffee, when she asked.

"Why don't all of you sit down with me sometime, and talk about the Curio Life project, you know it has grown really big and has helped a lot of young people? I would love to do a TV special on it, it would make for great viewing." I looked at Edwina and Deb's, they both shrugged, Chloe looked happy enough.

"It would be a fun thing to do, I am easy with it." Anthony nodded, and I looked at Amy.

"Talk to me in the New Year, and we will work things out." She gave me a big smile.

"I will hold you to that, I do think it will be really good to show a little of the real people behind the site, I am sure it will get a lot of viewers. I am really excited about it, yeah, you are a cool group, let's show the world how talented you all are." Chloe gave a sniff.

"I suppose I will have to wear clothes." I looked at her.

"I will buy you something special, something arty and yet slutty." She smiled.

"Okay you are on." Amy started to chuckle.

Katie was all smiles, and very pleased with our performance, she walked out with Amy once all the equipment was packed, and I relaxed on my spot on the sofa, glad it was over, all I wanted now was to look forward, and stop looking back behind me. We had another coffee, and then Katie had to leave, the good news was that the press had finally given up and gone.

I headed into the living room and curled up in my corner of the sofa. Birch came and sat down at the side of me and slid in close.

"You alright now, it's over, we can just focus on us?" I took her hand in mine.

"Can we though, we keep saying that, and yet something else just comes up and smacks us in the face? Oh god Birch, all I wanted was to stay home, and make Christmas special for you, I have got to tell you, there are times I just want to leave this country forever and never come back." She leaned in and rested on my shoulder.

"Sweetie no matter where you go now, this is the life of a famous author, and we just have to cut out all the shit, leave it at the gates, and just focus on being us here inside our home. Look here we know what we face, can you imagine going somewhere new and finding all the Marjorie's of those areas too? For now, we are better off here." It all just felt depressing.

Edwina walked in with her karaoke box and put it down next to the Christmas tree, and I watched as she switched it on, then tapped the buttons, and the large TV screen came on, as she blue toothed the connection. The track came up, and she picked up the mic, she looked at me and winked, and then smiled. The music started to play and she burst into Girlfriend by Avril, and pointed at Birch, as she shook her hips and jiggled her boobs at me.

Chloe bounced up, and joined in with her, and Deb's came rushing in, and joined in, Birch clapped her hands and laughed with utter joy, and I could not help it, as all three of them dragged Birch off the sofa, and flirted with her as they danced around her, singing at me.

I just sat there laughing, as the three of them gyrated around Birch, screaming 'Hey, Hey,' at the top of their voices, and I joined in singing along, and felt my spirits soar, God I loved these girls so much, they have no idea how precious they were to me.

Edwina was a treasure, we all needed to break the negative atmosphere, and just let go of everything, and nothing does that better than screaming out of tune, to all your favourite songs. Birch was giddy, as she wailed out to Pat Benatar, and we all became her backing singers, I don't think I have laughed like this in such a long time.

We were laughing, screaming, and dancing like maniacs, when the doorbell rang, we did not hear it, but Anthony who was in the kitchen with Michael did. It was Bev and friends, and so he buzzed them in. When Bev and friends walked in, we were grouped together singing like wild banshees into the mic, like a party of escaped mental patients.

This was the first impression of our home, for Bev's French guests, they should have looked at us like we were insane, and a bunch of feral, half dressed, or naked females, dancing around, singing at the top of our voices. They stood, watched, and smiled as we all wiggled our hips for our new audience, Bridgette appeared to be really enjoying it, and started to clap along, the others soon joined in, as we belted out the last verse.

We hit the end of the song and fell about laughing, and the mad thing was, we had only had one drink each. We were hot and sweating and out of breath, but it was such amazing fun, Bridgette and her friends were all smiles applauding, we took a bow and crashed to the floor giggling wildly, as we got our breath back. Edwina offered the mic to the new guests, Claire did not hesitate, she grabbed the mic, and went down the list of songs.

Birch gave Bev a huge hug and welcomed everyone, she took their coats and invited them all into the kitchen for a drink, I followed along breathing hard. In the kitchen Bev was all smiles and happy, her friends looked impressed with the house, and the loonies who lived here, which was all she wanted. Birch spoke fluent French as she organised drinks, which added another bonus for all of us, and the group appeared to relax pretty quickly. In the living room, a very loud Adele sounding Claire, struck up a tune.

Anthony and Michael joined in with Claire, as Deb's, Chloe and Edwina danced around the room, and Luke sat watching and laughing. Bev sat at the island as Jon Claude, Bridgette, Claudette, and Alberta headed back to the living room, I poured a fresh drink as Bev sat smiling next to Birch.

"Ta guys, that was brill when we came in, they loved it, Breeze thinks you guys are proper top, she does." Birch put her arm round her.

"Sweetie, you know us, our life is one big crazy ride, there is always something fun going on, and if it isn't, we start some." I giggled as I sat down, Bev gave me a beaming smile, I had to look a little closer, I am sure she had yet more piercings in her face.

"I knew coming here was a good idea, they love the place but it is short on fun, I mean those old shits in the pub moan if we laugh too loud." I could certainly understand that. "It is not the only reason I brought em round here, I need a bit of a favour if you like?" I looked at her.

"What kind of favour do you want Bev?" She looked a little awkward, and turned to Birch.

"It's a little bit awkward Jemi, but you know, with you being into sex and stuff for work, it is not for me, it is more for Alberty." Birch gave a nod.

"Sweetie that tells me very little, what does Alberta need?" She gave a nod and laughed.

"Oh yeah, fuck me, I said nowt, yeah, you see, we want to get her pregnant." Birch looked at me as I lifted my drink, and my jaw dropped.

"What... Bev, don't you know?" She gave a chuckle.

"Well yeah, I know how normal people do it, but you see the thing is Alberty wants to get Cloud Debt up the duff, and so far, she has failed." I gave a snigger, and looked at Birch, I knew it was wrong, but I had to ask.

"Ignore my stupidity, but when you say Alberta has tried to get Claudette pregnant, does Alberta have a dick?" Birch looked at me and tilted her head, I lifted my hands up as I smirked.

"What? She was the one said she tried to get her pregnant, I mean to me she looks female, but I don't know what is under her skirt." Bev gave a loud laugh as she suddenly understood.

"Deadly... Oh fuck that is funny... No, she used a guys cum to do it, but she does not think she did it right. Fuckin hell it would be blinding if she had a cock, she could do it herself." I was starting to understand, I had heard of this being done before, or at least I think it was done, I looked at Birch.

"Have you done this before, you know with friends?" She looked at Bev, with a sympathetic face.

"Sweetie, I have heard of it, and read about it, but I have never actually done it myself." Bev nodded looking hopeful.

"Aye, but you have read about it, so you could help us?" Birch shrugged and looked at me.

"I suppose we could help; I must admit, it will be fascinating to try." She turned to Bev. "Do you have some sperm?" She nodded.

"Aye tons." I stared at her; my morbid curiosity suddenly kicked in.

"When you say tons, just how much, I mean have you got like a bucket full?" She beamed a big smile.

"Kind of, I got it on tap."

I looked at Birch, who was watching me, her bright green eyes dancing with adventure, and suddenly I saw a moment just like I did the night Deb's asked us to shave her. She was so into this idea, and I had to wonder, what the hell was I about to get dragged into, and the what the hell does Bev mean, when she said she had it on tap?

Chapter 31

Cool Yule…ish!

"Deads, Sweetie, wake up." I groaned, I was warm and snug, I felt her hand on my shoulder, and tried to brush it away.

"Birch... I am sleeping, can we screw later?" She gave a giggle.

"Sweetie, I do not want to screw you, I just need you to wake up, it is important." I opened my eyes and gave a frustrated sigh, my head was cloudy, after all the drinking and singing we had been doing with Bev and her friends.

"Birch, I love you, honestly I do, but it is dark, if you don't want sex, go back to frigging sleep, for god's sake." I rolled over and she was dressed, and stood at the end of the bed smiling.

"Sweetie, I love you deeply too, which is why I want you to get up." I looked at the clock.

"Frigging hell it's five in the morning, if you really loved me, you would get in bed, and GO TO FRIGGING SLEEP!" She started to laugh.

"You can be a real grumpy little beastie when you want to be, look I have freshly ground coffee."

She took the top off my travel cup and wafted it around me, the aroma wafted into my nose, and my mouth that was dry started to water, my stomach groaned, and she giggled. I gave a sigh and sat up, licking my lips, her bright green eyes danced with delight, as she held it out just in front of my face. I looked at her smiling, her hair bright white in the darkness.

"You are a sadist you know that, why do I have to get up, it's the middle of the frigging night?"

She handed me the cup, and I took it both hands and lifted it to my lips, the taste exploded in my mouth, and I felt my taste buds jump wide awake. I have to admit, it tasted wonderful as I swallowed the hot liquid. Birch sat on the bed.

"I want to do something very special with you, I am a day late because I was stuck in that hell hole hospital, but I do not want to wait another year, I have planned this for a few months. Deads this would mean so much to me, will you come with me?" I sipped my coffee.

"Come with you... As in outside... At five in the frigging morning... In the snow?" She smiled.

"Please Sweetie?" I gave a long sigh, she knew I was weak and could not refuse her, especially when she gave me that bright happy glittery eyes and smile thing.

"Shit, I know I am going to regret this... But alright, what do I need to do?"

She bounced softly on the bed, and got all giddy, and I was only four large sips into my coffee. I was nowhere near awake enough for her to be uber lively yet. She got up and gathered my clothes.

"All you have to do is get dressed and just follow me."

I took another drink, yep, I was already regretting it, vague details from a woman who was always precise, meant this would be something I would regret, I thought for a second.

"We are not doing anything disturbing are we, you know like stealing bells or digging up graves?" She gave a giggle as she pulled off the duvet, and slipped a pair of thick woolly socks on my feet.

"It's too cold for grave robbing Sweetie, that is a spring to summer thing, for when the ground is warm." I looked at her as she tried to slide my jeans onto my legs.

"Why does the fact you know that bother me, and I am the gothic horror novelist?"

I put my cup down and lifted my ass off the bed, she giggled as she wiggled my pants up to my thighs.

"It is so much easier taking them off." I lay back on the bed, exposing my vagina.

"It is still not too late; she is there right in front of you." She looked at me, and bit her lip, I giggled.

"Wow you are going to pass up on my tender, juicy, succulent self, just there in front of you, begging to be adored by you?" She closed her eyes.

"Oh, Sweetie stop, just stop, you are making me dither, and I really want to do this, but I really want you now, and if I do, we will miss it, you don't play fair." I sniggered, I grabbed the top of my jeans and pulled, and my succulent little lady was hidden.

"Too late, she can stay, moist, safe, and warm in here."

I pulled up my zip and giggled, she pouted, and handed me a top and jumper. I finished my coffee and followed her downstairs, the house was silent, there was a rucksack by the door. Birch handed me my snow boots, and my thick coat, I looked at it, Birch gave me a sad look.

"I found it in that bag in your room last night and washed it, Sweetie, I don't want you having my blood all over it. I found it really upsetting seeing what you faced, I washed all your other stuff too, I don't want you keeping things like that Deads. I know you have a morbid side; I just do not want to be part of it." I nodded; it was understandable.

As I slipped on my boots and thick coat, and hunted for gloves, she went into the kitchen and refilled my cup. It took a few minutes, but finally we were ready, and she grabbed the bag, and quietly undid the door. We snook out into the cold night, and I was instantly wide awake.

"Holy shit it's freezing."

She pulled the large tarp off Petal, and we jumped in, she was driving, which worried me as the roads were icy, and she had recently had a head wound. The gates opened and we set off, the blowers doing their best to clear the windscreen and warm the cab, as I shivered. Birch turned right out of the gates and headed up Waterside Lane away from the village. We were heading up in the direction of Suttons Farm towards the high hill, which bothered me a little, as higher up it got really cold and icy, and as I was finding out, Birch drove equally as fast on ice, as she does on dry roads.

I sat back and checked my seat belt, and pushed my legs against the floor, just in case. I looked at my coffee, that presented a dilemma, because to drink it would make me alert, but the problem with that was, it was dark, icy, and I had a demonically possessed driver at the side of me. I was not that sure I wanted to be that aware of things looming out of the dark in front of us.

I opted to sip my coffee with closed eyes, it felt like the right compromise. At the top of the hill, on the road that was gritted, Birch turned off on to the ungritted top road, which was basically a thick snow drift, I only peeped for a second, but panicked, as she would simply rev the engine and plough into it, but she stopped and put the handbrake on, I opened my eyes and she was smiling at me.

"We are here." I looked out of the window; it looked bloody freezing.

"So, what do we do now?" She leaned over into the back.

"We have to walk the rest of the way." I shivered.

"Really... Oh crap." She giggled as she opened the door, and the blast that came in felt like it had come straight from the Artic, I gave a big shudder.

"I am so going to hate this, I am living with a mad woman, I will probably die, and be frozen solid, and they will find my slightly thawed corpse in Spring, half eaten by rats and deer." Birch giggled.

"Not really, the foxes will devour pretty much all of you, no one will ever know this was your last resting place." I looked at her, and got out of the cab, and the snow came up to the top of my boots, I looked across the bonnet at her.

"You can be pretty frigging creepy and scary at times; do you know that?" She tossed the rucksack over her shoulder and climbed onto the stile.

"I thought you like my naughty creepy side; you certainly liked my vampiric side at the arch two Summers ago?"

I smiled as I followed her over the stile, just the memory of that day, in the dappled shade, lay there on my back looking up at my arch, as she kissed and touched me, oh God what a memory, I was suddenly feeling a lot warmer.

We trudged along, on what I knew was a foot path, I just could not see it, as it was buried. Slowly making our way towards the crest of the hill, it was quite surprising as there was no moon, and it was full darkness, and yet it was easy to see, almost as if the snow was so white, it just ate the darkness, revealing the world to me. It was hard going in parts, I had to lift my knees up almost to my tits, just to get my leg out of the drifted snow.

Gasping for air and sweating, we arrived right on the top of the hill, far down below I could see the village street lights, and the bright coloured Christmas lights, it looked really pretty. Birch opened her pack and took out a large plastic sheet, she spread it out on the snow, and then pulled our thick travelling tartan blanket out, and placed it on the plastic. She smiled at me.

"We can sit here and wait for it." I shrugged.

"Wait for what?" She turned and pulled me close, and slid back my hood.

"Deads, I should have done this yesterday, but things got in the way. I have held you at sunset, and seen it bathe you, I have made love to you in the moonlight, we even had sex in the snow under the moon, but the one thing I have always wanted, is to see your eyes lit by the dawn of Yuletide." I felt a warmth surge inside me, she was so sincere, and her words really hit deep within me, she smiled and then softly kissed me.

"Blessed Yule my love."

Holy shit she made my toes tingle, her nose was cold, but her mouth felt like fire on my lips, God I was so turned on, I could not believe I was actually thinking of ripping her clothes off up here, in what can only be considered sub zero temperatures.

She never failed to surprise me, no matter how much I had thought I had got her worked out, she would just flip everything around, and blow me away. I came out of the kiss with a satisfied moan, and she smiled, took my hand, and led me round to the blanket.

"What is Yule actually, I have never really thought about it?" She smiled as she reached into her bag and pulled out a jar with a candle in it. And a packet of incense cones, marked Frankincense.

"Yule Sweetie, is the traditionally pagan festival, that dates back thousands of years. The Christians say it is the birth of Christ, and they celebrate it on December 25th, which is also the birth of the Roman deity Mithra. Back in 345 the pope ruled that Christmas for Christians was the 25th, so really that is how old Christmas is for them, although there was a lot of debate at the time, because as you know, the gospels of Matthew and Luke have different accounts of the birth of Christ, so I suppose the Pope ended the argument." It made sense to me, Birch lit the incense and wafted the smoke around.

"Okay so how do we know Yule is older and pagan?" She chuckled as she pulled out a flask to top up our cups with hot coffee.

"It's mainly folklore and stories passed down for thousands of years, by all the Celt races, but if you look at Roman life, there is a lot of history there to back it up." She handed me a cup of steaming coffee, I must admit, sat up here in the dark watching her, I was really interested. She relaxed and smiled.

"There is some evidence that the Romans encouraged the rise of Christianity to quell the popular supporters of Mithra, in sort of a political alliance, as Christianity was about controlled discipline, that brought order back to Rome, and its eventual downfall. Either way, it is a known fact that Christianity adopted a lot of Roman pagan religions and rituals within itself, to make it appeal more to the masses of Pagan's and help them convert. The Winter Solstice, or Yuletide, existed in the Germanic and Scandinavian lands long before the Romans took control, and there is strong evidence in Druid culture that points to celebrations of the solstice many years long before Rome was built." I cannot deny it fascinated me.

"So, sitting here in the dark waiting for the sun, that is what people in this country have done for thousands of years?" She nodded and gave a smile.

"Sweetie, I understand you were raised by Bell Twats, I am not trying to convert you, I asked you here purely out of selfish reasons. I love you for doing this I really do, because as strange as all this is, it actually is a very special part of me that I do not often show, but I wanted to show it and share it with you, this means something to me to have you here and not judge me."

"Birch, I am actually enjoying this, and I do genuinely find it all fascinating. I am a writer, stuff like this can make good material for books and stories, I also want to be here because I love you, and if this makes you happy, I want to be a part of it." She smiled and her eyes danced in her happy face.

"Choosing you was the right decision, and the best decision I ever made, I meant every word I said at Deb's wedding, I am never going to leave you." I smiled.

"My Celia." She nodded, her nose was bright red.

"My Lillian." I gave a chuckle.

"I meant it too, crazy as it may appear to others, I really want this Birch, I want you and only you." She looked to the horizon, and she gasped, and pointed.

"Look it is starting."

She stood up and took my hand, I got off the blanket and stood at her side, and together we stood silent, and watched the sun start to rise in the east. The whole of the sky had a glow along the bottom edge, and it slowly brightened and intensified as the sun made its way up to our visible horizon.

I found it stirred me inside, as the first bright beams rose into the sky, and it felt powerful and yet amazingly beautiful to observe. Birch turned her whole body to me, and grabbed my shoulder and gently turned me towards her, her beautiful green eyes watched mine, and she smiled as she saw the first light of the sun cross my face, two tears appeared in her eyes.

"I love you Abigail Jennifer Watson, my Deadly, and my life. Thank you, you are so beautiful in the first light." I felt a lump in my throat, and so emotional, it was strange, Birch was so serious, and yet it had such a powerful impact on me.

She took a deep breath, smiled and wiped her eyes, and then she pulled off her thick woollen hat, and threw it on the blanket, she had taken her bandage off, and her hair fell down across her shoulders, as the light illuminated it, and with those big green eyes that sparkled so bright, she took my breath away. I lifted my hand to her face.

"Wow you truly are the queen of the snow." She gave a shy smile, and slipped off her gloves, she faced me and swallowed hard.

"Deads... There is something really important that I need to know, if I ask, will you answer me honestly?" It seemed like such an odd question to ask, I frowned.

"You know I will, we promised, no lies, no hiding anything, and I have been true to that, just ask me Birch."

She smiled, and then crouched down in the snow, her hand came out of her pocket, and suddenly my heart began to beat really fast, no, not that, I mean, no, that would never happen right? Birch opened the box and took a huge breath, she looked terrified, I felt my breath trap in my throat, and my legs started to vibrate.

"Abigail, Deads, this was my grandmothers, it is worth a fortune and one of my most precious possessions."

I stared at the ring as it glinted in the new sunlight, my heart was pounding, and I felt my breathing increase as she looked up at me, her bright eyes fixed on mine, I was starting to tremble, and felt this huge wave of emotion wash up through me.

"Abigail, I said I would never do this, which shows how serious I am." She closed her eyes and took a huge breath, which was good, because I was frozen to the spot and not with the cold. She breathed out, swallowed hard, and opened her eyes.

"Abby I am scared shitless, but I really need to know, will you marry me?"

My breath ran out of me, and I felt tears in my eyes, I could not believe she was doing this, my head spun wildly, my heart was about to explode, she looked up at me, her eyes were bright and so full of life, she bit her lip, I was taking too long but I felt shocked.

"Birch, you better be frigging serious about this, because if this a joke I will never forgive you?" She smiled.

"Sweetie, I love you so much, and I know I swore I would never do this, but it's you... You, I could never do this with anyone else, and I will only ask once in my life, and this is it, this is the moment, I will never ask again. When I lay on the floor and I thought I would die, I knew, I knew this was what I wanted, so please for fuck's sake say yes, because I am dying here, terrified I will frighten you off forever?" I nodded, as my tears dropped on her.

"Well yeah of course I frigging will, I just never thought you would ask, I meant every word I said at the wedding, I am your Lillian, and I always will be." She burst into tears and stood up, and dragged me into a hug.

"You will not regret it, I promise, I will devote my life to making us happy, I promise Deads."

I slid my arms round her, and pulled her tight, she leaned back with a huge smile, and tears in her eyes. I have no idea how I should feel, I mean I have never had anyone like me enough to even enquire. I think I feel a little shocked, and know I am a lot happy. She leaned in and kissed me, my emotions were going crazy, but I was delighted, and a little terrified, and once again, she came right out of left field, and completely blew me away. She pulled out of the kiss, and smiled, she gave a sniffle, it was cold up here.

"Take off your glove, I am sorry I was sneaky, I measured your finger in your sleep, and got the ring altered."

I chuckled, why did that not surprise me? I looked down as she took the ring out of the box, she placed it on the end of my finger and then looked up at me, her eyes were so bright, as she smiled.

"Forever and beyond." I nodded and smiled.

"Forever and beyond, Celia and Lillian." She giggled, and slid it down my finger, I looked down at it, and it sparkled as brightly as her eyes, I swallowed hard, I felt so emotional.

"It's beautiful, I love it." She gave a giggle.

"Okay now give it back." I looked at her.

"Huh?" She giggled more with her happiness.

"I wanted to do this alone with you, but I also want to do it in front of our parents, and the guys, I want to see the shock in their eyes, so please future wifey, just wait a few more days, and then you can wear it forever. Is that okay, or am I acting screwed up, because I am really excited and want to scream my tits off?" She could do nothing but laugh, I lifted my hand, and looked at it, she snuggled in to me.

"It looks really great on you, you are happy, aren't you?" I gave a titter.

"I thought I was the insecure one, and you were the strong clever one?" She pushed her head into my shoulder.

"Honestly, I thought I was going to yerk I was so bloody terrified; I almost painted the snow, I am not sure I did not piss myself. I have your slutty tights and my wedding knickers on under these jeans."

I started to laugh, as I pulled her close, and wrapped my arms around her, I lifted my hand to her shoulder and squeezed tight, and stared at the ring on my finger. I really loved seeing it there, and oddly enough, I did not need to question it. I knew it was right for me, deep down inside, it meant I would never ever lose her, that had almost happened twice in my life, and it was never going to happen again. I suddenly thought of something.

"Birch, who is the mum and who is the dad?" She giggled.

"What do you want to be?" I sniggered.

"If I am the dad, you will become Doctor Watson." She started to giggle.

"Elementary my dear Sweetie." We both stood there like two lunatics, freezing our tits off, as the sun rose, and laughing like an irresponsible dentist, who had left the gas on.

It was really cold, and all this standing about, had just about paralysed my legs. It is strange, because now I had worn the ring, I did not really want to take it off. She looked so happy, and that was enough for me, just knowing was actually really exciting. I slid the ring off and she put it carefully back in the box. She smiled.

"Christmas Day it's yours forever." I nodded.

We both folded everything up and packed it away, Birch held her little candle in a jam jar up to the sun, which had risen quite high, and she lit it.

"I will take this home and light a bigger candle with it, as a token from the sun."

With the rucksack packed, we waded back to Petal, and I took the driver's seat, she climbed in holding her candle, which she had placed back in a jar. I started the engine, and slowly manoeuvred us round back to the road, and then headed home. As I drove down the hill, I glanced at her.

"I am frozen, how about when we get back, you take a bath with your future bride?" She gave a happy giggle.

"I really want to do that, yes let's, also I am so frigging cold, I think we will need it."

When we got home, I parked Petal whilst Birch went in, and ran upstairs to run the bath. It was weird that we had been out, and yet everyone was still in bed when we got home. I took off my coat and boots, and headed up for my room, even with thick socks on my feet were blue. I sat on my bed and rubbed them to try and get the blood flowing back in them, Birch popped her head round the doorway.

"Hey Sweetie wife, it's ready, are you coming?"

I gave a giggle, and hobbled towards the bathroom. Birch pulled me close and slipped my top off, and then slid her hands down my tummy to my jeans, I gave a little shudder and she giggled, and then pulled them down, it made me quiver a little as I felt her breath on me. I stepped out of them and she took my hand and led me to the bath, I stepped in and my legs burned, as the blood rushed back into them. I lowered myself slowly biting my lip in pain. I sat back with a gasp, and Birch sat on the edge of the bath and handed me a glass of wine.

"Jesus Birch it is only 8:30 in the morning." She slid in behind me.

"We do not have any champagne, and even if we did, I would not drink it... Yuk!"

She climbed in, leaned back and I relaxed into her, and took a sip, this was nice, I gave a happy little moan, and she stroked my shoulder.

"I love this Birch, I love our life, and all the strange things we talk about, you know like today, I knew nothing about Yule, although how do you explain Santa?" She gave a long happy sigh.

"Well, the church says it is Saint Nicolas, because he was well known for the giving of gifts and helping people. He was sainted for his kind acts, and he wore red robes, it does fit." I think I know her well enough to know her better, I took a sip and gave a giggle.

"You do not think that though do you, I know you Doctor Dixon, what strange belief do you have?" She laughed in my ear, and it was cute.

"Oh Deads, you know me too well. I did come across an ancient Siberian Shaman story once that made a lot of sense, and I actually liked it a great deal, I felt it was a more natural theory than the Christians." I giggled.

"I knew it, so tell me this crazy messed up theory you have." She slid her hand round me and cupped my boob.

"Oh yummy... In Siberia there is a red and white mushroom that the reindeers eat, and it is a psychotropic mushroom, so they get bombed like you would with shrooms, so in a sense when stoned they think they can fly." I gave a chuckle, I loved the idea of stoned reindeer, she laughed, as I took a sip of my wine.

"This mushroom apparently is pretty bloody powerful, so the local tribes used to collect the reindeers piss, and then drink it on Yule, to have a fantastic day." I gave a violent shudder.

"Oh god, I am so glad this is wine, and I do not live in Siberia, thank god we have wine and gin." I turned and looked at her. "This is wine right?" She giggled and I felt her tummy wobble as

she laughed.
"Sweetie this is serious stuff... Anyhow, here is the strange bit." I laughed.
"What drinking piss is not strange?" She squeezed my boob, and giggled.
"Sweetie please... The Shaman would collect these mushrooms, and found they only grew under pines and firs. They would collect them in early December, and place them in socks hung by the fire to dry, then on the eve of Yule, they would go round and distribute the mushrooms equally around the whole tribe. If tribe members were not home and the chimney was not smoking, he would drop it down, so the family got their fair share. So, through him, they could all get high for Yule, and have a fun day, which always ended with feasting and drinking, and lots of screwing. So, we have everything in one tale about Yule. Flying reindeer, the red and white of the mushroom, with evergreen trees, socks over the fire, gift giving, delivered down the chimney, and feasting, it pretty much all fits with the ideals of who people think Santa is." I chuckled.
"That is such a messed up folk tale, but I have to be honest, I love it, I want this crazy shaman with a sock full of hallucinogen's to be real, that is the coolest version of Santa I have ever heard. Hell Birch, he can be our Santa, that way outdoes the Bell Twats version of events."

We both started to laugh as we lay in the hot water. Chloe staggered into the bathroom rubbing her eyes.
"Guys you are aware it is only just gone nine in the morning?" Birch lifted her glass.
"Yule blessings to our perverted friend, jump in we are warming up, we have been up four hours." Chloe blinked.
"What?" I smiled.
"There is room at the bottom, jump in and pass me the bottle."
Chloe looked at us like we were mental, then grabbed the bottle and handed it to me, and climbed in and sat in the steaming hot water at the bottom of the bath. I filled my glass and handed her the bottle.
"Yule blessings my slutty friend." She smiled.
"You know we are all fucked up, don't you?" Birch looked at her.

"Well Chloe, my little sexy bath buddy, either we are messed up, or we are completely sane, and everyone else is messed up." I lifted my glass.

"I am drinking to that." Chloe started to giggle and took a mouthful from the bottle. Birch took a swig of her glass.

"Hell, if you think this is fun, wait until later, we are going to impregnate a lesbian."

Chloe spluttered and coughed up wine, she choked as we both laughed, and coughed violently.

"Birch, you bitch." She coughed up the last of the wine, and then looked up.

"Whoa hang on, what do you mean impregnate a lesbian?" I smiled.

"We are going to take one lesbian, and get her pregnant." Chloe frowned.

"Guys, you do know you are going to need a bloke for that, you kind of need sperm?" I smiled and lifted my foot out of the water, and wiggled my toes on her nipple, and laughed.

"Chloe, we have tons of it, we have it on tap." She stared at me.

"Abby, are you and Birch going to have a baby, because I would fucking love that?" Birch leaned back in the bath and gave an almighty laugh.

"A baby beastie, with a slutty baby sitter, oh god one day I want that." She leaned back and gave a massive cackle of a laugh. I turned and looked at her.

"Holy shit, I am nowhere near parent material, I would much prefer a bonkers baby Birch." She stopped laughing and sat up, and looked at me.

"You want my baby?" I pointed at her and laughed my ass off.

"Your face is a picture." She smiled.

"Screw you Deads. Oh, and by the way, I got this wine from a reindeer." I swallowed hard; Chloe frowned.

"Huh?" We both pissed our sides laughing.

"Yule Blessings Bitches."

Chapter 32

Baby Talk.

Getting up at five, and trekking up to watch the sun rise in the snow, and then getting the shock of my life, when Birch proposed, in possibly the most mind blowing way, had left me exhausted, and yet so unbelievably happy. After we got home, and Birch set up a large candle in the living room, and lit it from the candle in her jar, we chilled out in the bath, but I could hardly keep my eyes open, and so crashed out in bed. Birch slid in behind me and cuddled up, and slid her hand on my boob.

"Are you happy Deads?" I pushed back into her, and wriggled.

"I have never felt this happy in my life before, I am still a little bit in shock, because I was happy to think we would just live together, but being engaged, just makes it feel so real and truly committed. I will not deny, I have secretly wondered what it would be like to be married, I just thought it would never happen, honestly Birch, I am blown away by it." She kissed my shoulder.

"I will not deny, I was pretty terrified, because you have said to me many times, you would never marry because of your parents. The truth Deads, is I had the ring resized four months ago, but when your parents split, I was panicked, and after the other day in the Tea Rooms, I thought what the hell, I want this, I really want this, and so I took the greatest gamble of my life, you are sure now, I am not forcing this am I?"

I lay there listening to her, and just smiling to myself, I turned and looked at her, she was so happy.

"Birch, go into my room will you, and open my desk draw please?" She frowned. "Just do it." She looked really excited.

"What is it, please tell me it's an early present?" I smiled, as her eyes lit up.

"Just go see."

She gave a huge chuckle, and jumped off the bed, she ran excitedly through the bathroom happily giggling, I heard my desk draw drag open, and then silence.

I waited, and nothing happened, I had at least expected a squeal. I sat up in bed, where was she?

"Birch... Birch are you alright?"

I slid off the bed, okay so now I was panicked, I walked across the room and through the adjoining bathroom, I got to the door, and she was sat on my desk chair, with the small spot lamp on.

"Birch are you alright?" She gave a sniffle and turned to me, her eyes were full of tears, her voice was high and squeaky.

"Deads it's so beautiful." She sniffled as she held her hand under the light, I stepped into the room.

"It is supposed to be an eternity ring, it is a real diamond, it's a tiny little birch leaf, I know you like silver, but I got you platinum. To be honest I was going to give it to you Christmas Day, but I remembered that day when Kev pulled a ring out, and you backed away from him freaked out. I kind of figured it was pointless asking you to marry me, but I hoped if you misunderstood, you would think it was a proposal, but you kind of pipped me to the post, you always have been ten steps ahead of me." She wiped her eyes, as she smiled.

"Yes... Yes Sweetie, I will marry you." She giggled. "This is insane, it is so stunning Deads, I have never seen anything like it." I walked over to her and crouched down.

"You won't, I had it specially designed just for you, it is a complete one off, just like you. I am selling books Birch; I can finally afford to marry now." She giggled, and put her arms round me, and squeezed me hard.

"I am so gloriously happy, I was terrified I was pushing you into it, but I can see now, the time is right for both of us." I leaned back and looked at her.

"I do not know how you feel, but it pisses me off when people call you my girlfriend, or my partner, especially life partner. I want something more concrete, something as solid as we are, something that shows the world this is deep and has great significance. I do not want to hide it Birch, I want to say to reporters, this is my wife." She smiled and nodded her head, as she understood me.

"Yeah, I know what you mean, I want that too Deads, I will never forget this moment, this day, never, it is the happiest I have ever known." She leaned forward and kissed me softly, I held her close, and just enjoyed the moment, she pulled back and took a huge breath.

"My heart is hammering in my chest Deads." I giggled.

"Mine too, put the ring back until Christmas Day, and stop worrying about the fear of asking me, and just keep it quiet until then, and if I am honest, I think I am going to enjoy having a secret that is between just us two for a few days." She gave a nod and looked at the ring on her finger, I was so thrilled that she adored it.

I was also really relieved, I had so many doubts as to whether or not I was doing the right thing, but just watching the smile on her face, as she held her hand under the light, gave me a chance to calm down in the knowledge I had done good.

"Can I wear it for just a little longer, then put it back, it is so beautiful Deads, I cannot tell you how much I love it. If you want, go to bed and I will be with you in a few minutes, I just want to wear it a little longer."

I kissed her forehead and left her, I looked back as I reached the bathroom door, and she was sat smiling holding her hand up to stare at it.

I slipped into bed feeling happy, I could not believe she beat me, but who cared, at the end of the day, it was clear we were going the distance. I lay in bed as memories flooded into my mind, knocking on her door at Uni, and she answered naked, that first night in the guest house, after my mum screamed at me when I returned, and the night she first made love to me, I still get the shivers thinking of it.

Her eyes always watching, her white hair with black lined patches blowing off her shoulders in the breeze, so many moments of inspired joy, and the overwhelming feeling of happiness and joy I felt around her. Somewhere in all the millions of thoughts I had, they slipped into dreams, and I drifted into an exhausted sleep.

I woke, and opened my eyes, it was dark, and the little tree was shining multi colours through the window. Behind me Birch was breathing softly, her arm round me cupping my boob, the heat from her radiating into me. It felt nice and familiar, and was one of my favourite moments of every day.

I turned slightly and Birch disturbed, and gave a little moan, I giggled, she was probably having dirty dreams again. I lay there just enjoying the moment and watching the tree slightly moving in the cold breeze outside, and casting little light flickers of colour across the room. Is it weird that my bed is my most favourite place? I glanced at the clock, it was almost five o'clock, and Bev would be round at seven.

I had to get up, so I carefully wriggled free of Birch, which took ninja like qualities, slipped on my kimono, and headed downstairs, I was feeling hungry, Chloe smiled as I walked in, Deb's was cooking with her.

"I was going to wake you; did you sleep well?" I sat down and Deb's reached for the kettle.

"She had Birch clinging to her like an octopus, of course she slept well." I smiled.

"Slightly bitter tone there, Deb's." She giggled as she filled up my cup.

"I sort of miss it, you know us three in a bed in your little house, we had a fun summer, it was a crazy time for us all." Chloe shrugged.

"It's better here though, or at least I think so, admittedly it has been a bit rough this month, we have all been tested, but we are still here and all friends, that is not a bad thing."

I understood her, yes it had been hard, and I would be wrong to say it had not taken its toll, and yet this morning, my whole month had turned around. I really wanted to say something, and yell and dance a scream that she had asked, but I had to sit there holding it in.

"I am really happy here guys, especially now Anthony is with us, I think this is right for us, and let's be honest we have a lot of fun, and it's just as crazy." Deb's leaned against the cooker, and smiled.

"Yeah, we are all so lucky to have each other, I won't deny, living with Jimmy is not boring, but I love it when I come back and stay here."

Birch staggered in, looking dreamy, she smiled as she sat down and snuggled into my side, I giggled, she looked stoned.

"You okay?" She looked up at me.

"I feel happy." I slid my arm round her and smiled, Deb's rolled her eyes.

"God you two are depressing, just watching you sit together with a coffee, makes me feel like my life is lacking." Chloe sniggered.

"Says Goggle Bear." I started to laugh, she giggled.

"I love my Jimmy Bear." You had to love her, she stood there wearing a big smile, happy and relaxed, and I leaned against Birch, and she gave a happy sigh, I leaned into her ear and whispered.

"You put it on again, didn't you?" She gave a very girlie giggle, I kissed her softly on the lips, I love how happy she is over this.

Meal time was delightful, Anthony and Michael were home, so we all sat at the table, something we did not do as often as we should. Birch was just hyper happy, and everyone found her joy infectious, and so there were plenty of jokes and giggles bouncing around over the meal.

When we had finished, Birch went up to prepare the guest room, and I joined in with Anthony and Michael washing up, and cleaning the kitchen. I was happy and all smiles, Anthony picked up on it.

"Abby darling you are very happy tonight, tell me, what is going on in that inspired little brain of yours, you are not looking forward to the impregnation thing are you?" I gave a sigh, and put the stack of plates I was about to put away down.

"To be honest I am not sure how I feel about it, is it wrong that I do not want kids, am I being unreasonable?" Michael turned to me as he pulled out the plug, to drain the sink.

"I think everyone has their own choice Abby, and if they do not think something is right for them, well that is okay. The important thing to remember is that what you decide today, is not forever, you are free to change your mind at a later date. Bev's friends obviously want children, which is not an easy thing for a same sex couple, there are still a lot of people who oppose it in today's world, but there again, there are also many who do not, who are very supportive, as I said, it is up to them to talk it through and look at what is right for them." I smiled.

"Wow Michael, you are quite the little ray of sunshine at times." Anthony smiled, and leaned in and kissed him.

"Well trust me Abby darling, he has certainly brightened up my life." Stood there looking at Anthony's bright happy face was so lovely, and yes, I was really happy for him, he deserved the joy Michael had brought into his life.

Michael made me think, I wandered up to my room, and sat at my desk. Birch had asked me to marry her, and I really wanted that, but what did she want, were children in her future, I needed to know?

Her childhood had been hard, she had been forced to grow up in the shadow of her mum's fame, and as much as I hated it, any child I had, would have that same curse. The last month had shown me how hard the future could be, the press were never really going to leave me alone.

My childhood was different, my father was cold and emotionless, and because of that I had grown up watching my mum suffer a loveless life. Is it madness that because I chose Birch, I know my life will be everything my mother never had? I will have all the love I need, she is so loving, and my life will always be warm, and nurturing as it is now. If we decide to have a child, will the shadow of my fame, destroy our child and our love?

Risking Birch was too high a price to pay for me, to remain childless would ensure that never happened, and yet I felt so guilty, because let's be honest, no child could ask for a better parent than Birch. She has so much love within her, any child near her, would be blessed, oh god, why did they have to ask us to help them? If Bev had said nothing, I would not be sat here feeling these things, feeling this wretched for thinking the things I was.

Downstairs Bev arrived, and Birch greeted them all with a smile, she took them up to the guest room, and told them to settle in and get comfortable. I heard the sound of their voices, and even though I had conflicted feelings, I thought I should at least show my face, and appear helpful. I got up, and wandered out of the room, and round to the side landing and the door to the guest room.

Bev was sat on the floor emptying a bag, she had lube, plastic cups, and a large turkey baster. I saw it and shuddered, somehow the thought of having one of those shoved up me and squirted, made me feel quite queasy, and my legs wobbled.

Birch as always, appeared to take all this in her stride, Alberta looked up at me, and yet again I felt that vibe that told me she did not like me, I was not going to get involved, I smiled.

"Anyone in need of a drink, calm the nerves and all that?" Claire gave a smile; she was holding the hand of Jon Claude.

"I could really use one Abby, and I think Jon really needs one, he is nervous."

I smiled, I knew Birch and Bev would, Claudette looked very nervous, but was being fussed over by Alberta as she sat on the bed. I stepped back out of the room, and headed to the kitchen where Deb's and Chloe were sat with Edwina, I grabbed a tray and started to measure out the drinks. Deb's watched me.

"How is the grand event going, is she pregnant yet?" I glanced at her.

"Not yet they are getting ready, although that French guy Jon, he does not look like he is up to the task. If you ask me his heart is not in it." Chloe shrugged.

"His girlfriend is letting him fuck another girl, why is his heart not in it? I have seen her, she is pretty good looking, if I was a bloke, I would do her." I gave a smile.

"I don't think he is going to have sex with Claudette, they have things to put his seed in her." Chloe frowned.

"What do you mean, put in her?" She looked a little horrified.

"They have this tube with a big squeezy end, I think they use them for meat and things." Edwina grinned.

"It is probably a turkey baster, he will cum in a container, and then they suck it up in the baster, and then shove it in and squeeze out his juice." Deb's gave a violent shudder, and crossed her legs.

"Oh god, I have gone really funny feeling, that is not right, oh god that is so not right." Chloe looked appalled.

"That is really messed up, guys should screw women to make babies. They should just let him take her to bed, it would be more fun for both of them, one night of gross intense sex and hey presto, they have a little bouncing shit factory."

To be honest I was with Chloe, although I did not really see him in that light, he did little for me, but Claire should just let him do the deed, in my mind, that was the most practical solution. I filled the tray, and headed back upstairs with the drinks. Claire took the drink and gulped it down, Jon Claude was trembling, he lifted the glass to his mouth and gulped down a huge swig.

Claire took him by the hand and led him to the upstairs guest toilet carrying a cup, I watched as she slipped inside, and closed the door, well at least he was getting some action. I headed to my room, I needed space to think, and I wanted to be separate from the night's events, and to let nature take its course without me.

I sat at my desk, I felt much better by being well out of the way. I logged into my site and started to read the messages, which always cheered me up. I sat with a smile, as many of the messages expressed their concern for Birch. I sent replies back thanking them, and told them we were fine and well, and yes it had been very scary for both of us, and thanked them again.

I love my readers, they really do make my days so much better, and to be honest, I always feel a lot better after reading all their kind words. I really wanted to share my news, it felt so hard to not mention Birch's proposal. I had thought hiding it until Christmas would be fun, but actually I wanted to tell everyone. I wanted them to see how excited I was, and how much watching Birch wear the ring, and the look on her face made me so absolutely happy, but obviously I could not, and I was feeling the frustration of it.

I looked at the clock, they had been at it for an hour, and yet there was no sign of Birch, I thought I had better make an appearance, so got up and headed out into the hall, Chloe and Edwina were stood at the far end of the stairs, with drinks, I walked over to them.

"Is the deed done?" Edwina shook her head.

"Nope... It appears our supply is having problems, and production is currently very slow." Chloe shook her head.

"I told you, his heart is not in it, get them both in a room with their kit off, and he will be more than motivated." I looked back across the landing at the open door, Birch looked bored, stood with Bev, I could see Alberta fussing around.

"If you ask me, she is the problem, I have had nothing but bad vibes off her since she got here, I am telling you, she is so controlling, it has everyone on edge. Well, if she does not back down, Jon Claude will not produce, and that is their only supply of seed."

"Well not really." I turned to look at Edwina, she smiled. "I am pretty sure Luke would donate, I mean, he did say he thought it was a good cause, after all, it is not like they can do this alone is it?" I was a little surprised.

"Wow, would you be okay with that, I mean, it would be another woman having his kid?" She shrugged.

"Maybe, but it will be in France, I dated a guy with a kid three years back, his kid was okay, and the fact it was someone else's did not really bother me. I mean let's be honest, a lot of guys out there have kids with other women, I don't really have an issue with it. To be honest Abby, I would let Luke give you a kid, if it made you and Birch happy." My mind was just blown, I smiled.

"I am blown away, that is pretty cool, just don't tell Birch, if she even gets a whiff of that, she will go all gooey and start wanting kids, and I am nowhere near that at the moment, if I ever will be?"

This group never cease to amaze me, I cannot state how cool they are, just looking at Edwina as she smiled, showed what an absolutely amazing person she was, and how lucky I was to have her as a friend. The toilet door opened and Claire came out looking upset, she had tears in her eyes, she looked at us.

"He just cannot do it, I have tried everything, and my jaw is so sore, and my arm is aching. He cannot handle the pressure, what do I tell my friends, they will never forgive me?" Wow, I really felt sorry for her, I took her hand.

"Come on, take a break, you look like you need a drink, come downstairs and relax for a minute and leave him alone to his own devices, maybe it is better he does this alone."

She gave a long sigh and followed me down to the kitchen, I poured her a stiff drink and sat her at the island with Deb's. I poured Birch a drink, I knew she could use one, and smiled.

"I will just take this up to Birch, and I will be back, just relax, and everything will be fine." She nodded.

"Thanks, I really wish we had not agreed to this, it is just too stressful." I took the drink up to Birch; she saw me and came out of the room and took the glass with a smile.

"Oh, thanks Sweetie, this is nowhere as easy as it looks."

We stood next to the rail, I turned sideways on to avoid Alberta's stares, she really did not like me and I had no idea why, the toilet door opened and Chloe slipped out, with a beaming smile, I nudged Birch.

"Looks like we may have a miracle worker on our side?"

I should have known. Chloe has an unnatural talent, I walked to the corner of the stairs, she handed me the cup.

"It is okay if there is a bit of spit in it, isn't it?" Birch was at my shoulder and gave a chuckle.

"Sweetie at the moment, if it does the job, I am not that bothered, let's say, it's added lubricant." I sniggered. Edwina appeared and looked at the cup.

"What the hell is that?" I looked at her, and frowned.

"I know you have seen this stuff before, don't play coy with me." She lifted up a cup.

"I thought he couldn't, so Luke gave me some, shit we have two, what the hell do we do now?"

Birch leaned over and took her cup out of her hand, and tipped it into the one in my hand, it kind of just slopped in, and I shuddered. Birch sniggered.

"Give it a stir Deads." I felt my stomach churn, I saw the two slightly different coloured mixtures, oozing over each other. I handed the cup to Birch.

"I think I am going to yerk, here take it."

Chloe giggled. I took deep breaths, and tried to quell the weird stirrings of my insides. Birch patted my bum with a chuckle and headed to Bev who gave a big smile.

"Fucking score, right Cloud Debt, get your minge open, we have the spunk." I saw her pick up the turkey baster and push it into the cup, and my stomach twisted again.

"Yeah, that is me done; I need alcohol... A lot of alcohol!"

I headed over to my room, where my glass was on the side of my desk, Chloe grabbed the gin and the bottle of the lemon off the floor by the rail, and followed me. We entered my room and

I grabbed my glass and plopped onto the end of the bed, she sat down next to me, she looked at me.

"Is it me or is all this baby talk getting to you?" She had an odd way of understanding; I nodded and gave a sigh.

"Is it me... You know I am just not into the idea, but it is really bothering me. Chloe what if Birch wants kids, at the moment I really don't, am I being stupid?" She smiled.

"No, you are being twenty six, and in this amazing and exciting loving relationship. To be honest Abby, if I was gay and wanted to pick a partner, I would defo pick you or Birch. You guys have so much love in you, why fuck that up with something that just eats and shits for years?" I knew she would get it.

"Chloe, I love my life so much at the moment, you know I struggled for years trying to play the straight girl, and avoid my true feelings. When I went to Uni, I never expected any of this, my life was mapped out for me, I would work hard, qualify, and then move to London and write and work for a large publisher, marry the right guy and live happily in a cottage." She smiled.

"We have all had those dreams Abby, it's just life is not like that, but you know at the end of the day, you have really become a successful writer, and okay you did not get the guy, but look at the girl you got. I get it, I do, why screw it up and complicate it with kids, so go with the flow Abby, you changed your dream once, you can do it again." I frowned.

"How do you mean again?" She took a swig of her drink, and slid back up to the pillows, and rested on the head board.

"You dreamed of marrying a guy, and got Birch, you did not see that coming, in time maybe you will want kids. Look there is no rush, just enjoy now and see where it goes, I reckon you two will go the distance, so just sit back and stop beating yourself up about something that may never come up."

It made sense, maybe I was overthinking it all, I know what Birch is like, if it comes up, we will talk about it. Chloe was right, I just need to relax and enjoy the moment. I grabbed my empty glass and leaned over the bed, I lifted the gin and poured out a measure, and topped it up with lemon, and slipped onto the bed at Chloe's side.

"I take it you don't want kids either?" She took a swig of her drink.

"I am not ruling it out, but I am not in a rush either. Terry is cool, he is like my go to for sex and sleeping over. I want to see where that goes, I mean, he has what it takes if he wants that, I might consider it in a few years, but not yet, I want my art to take off first."

It felt nice that she had considered her future, I knew she would never rush into a full time relationship, but I thought it was nice she was at least thinking about it. It is funny really when I look back at those long sunny summer days, we all spent together on my first year from Uni, we were all so wild, and in a rush to explore who we were, and yet now, seven years on, even though we felt like we had not changed much, actually we had.

We had changed a lot, we had gone from teenagers to young adults without even noticing, and here I was talking about things I always thought of as grown up stuff. Back then we would jump at every chance we had to screw a guy, and yet I could not remember the last time I took a guy to bed, well apart from that weird night with Morty, when Birch had asked him to take me whilst I was pleasuring her.

In the last six months, the only sex I had, was with Birch, and I was really happy about that, we had been sexual for just over two years, and I had found I enjoyed it more and more with her, I really did not need another guy.

I had been given plenty of attention at the office party, it would have been easy to just slip off like Chloe and Deb's had, but the truth was I had not really wanted to. All I had thought of that day was finding a way to corner Birch. It was a startling thought, was this why I had spent months wondering about marriage, was I actually ready to settle down?

"Will you get married Chloe, or will you just cohabitate?" She looked at me and hunched her shoulders.

"I don't know, I guess it will depend on the guy, if they ask, I will think about it, but I am not in a rush. Abby let's be honest, I have a lot of wild creative thoughts and ideas, and not many guys will be able to handle that. Max can handle me, but he will never be that good a husband. I like him a lot, he is up for anything and I have really experimented with him, I mean hell Abby, we have done it all, he is like a male me, and that is why it will never work out between us long term."

Wow, she blew me away, she really had thought about this stuff in a way I had never thought she would. I admired her, she really understood herself enough to know who she was, I absolutely loved that about her. She gave me a smile.

"Christ, I am talking like I have it all figured out Abby, but honestly, I don't yet... What about you, we all think you and Birch will make it into the longest game of all of us?"

"You do?" I was really surprised, she nodded.

"What you don't? Shit Abby, Birch lives for you, just look at the Tea Room, she would have taken that bullet to keep you alive, she fucking worships you, and you never get over that, it lasts a lifetime." I smiled.

Yeah, she does, and if I am really honest, I worship her equally as much, I have since I first met her, it is the single most unexplainable thing in my life. I have asked myself a million times, why her, why Birch? The only answer I have ever been able to come up with, is, simply because it is Birch, and I cannot help myself. We sat together quietly talking and drinking, and hours passed us by, it was nice, and I enjoyed it, she was good company.

I am not sure really how it happened, but I ended up very drunk, naked, and asleep in bed with Chloe. She snuggled up to me and cupped my boob, and it felt nice and safe, I was lay down the middle of the bed dreaming when I felt a strange sensation on my nose. I blinked and came out of my dream world, and opened my eyes, and Birch was crouched down at the side of the bed, softly stroking my nose. I smiled.

"Hi baby?" She grinned.

"I hope you are not cheating on me with my straight friend?"

"Huh?" She chuckled, and lifted the duvet, I looked down and saw the hand cupping my boob, I looked at her.

"We got drunk, but I would never cheat on you baby, I love you too much." She smiled.

"I know Sweetie, you two look cute, is there room for one more." I smiled, and lifted the duvet.

"There is always room for you baby, you know that?"

She gave a quiet chuckle and slipped in, and lay on her side facing me, I stared into her bright sparkling eyes. She leaned forward and kissed me, it was warm and soft and loving, I gave a happy little moan, and slid my hand over to her, her body was soft and warm, as I pulled her closer, and into a deeper kiss. Oh God Chloe was so right; I was smitten with her. We broke apart and she smiled as she stroked my hair from my eyes.

"Are you alright, I am sorry it took so long, I missed you tonight?" I gave a happy sigh.

"I missed you too, but I am happy now you are here."

Birch looked into my eyes, and I could see the depth of her soul, she was so beautiful, in a way I was lucky to have her, at Uni she had always been popular, she could have had anyone, and there were plenty who offered.

"Birch, why did you pick me, you know you had a lot of others who really wanted to be with you, but you chose me instead of them, you have never told me why?" She smiled and stroked the hair softly from my face. Her voice was soft, caring, and quiet.

"Deads, I wish you could see yourself through my eyes, if you could, you would not ask that question. The truth is, you are amazingly pretty, but most of all, you inspire me, every moment we have spent together has opened my eyes to the wonder of this world. When I am with you, I feel safe, relaxed and calm, you make me believe in myself, it feels good to be simply me, no one has ever made me feel like that." I was really surprised to hear her say it, but narrowed my eyes at her.

"Really, what about Kev, you know at Uni things between you two were good, everyone thought you two would end up married?" She nodded her head.

"I will not deny, he understood me better than most, but my heart did not want what he offered, I know it took me a while to figure it all out, but my heart wanted you. It always knew that you would be the best for me, and so eventually when I accepted that, I came to you. Deads, I want this, I really do want this, I am not joking, I am absolutely serious, I want to spend every living day at your side, if you have any doubts at all tell me now." I shook my head.

"No, I want this as much as you do, but I am afraid that at the moment I do not want children. I don't want to do to a child what my parents did to me, and I don't want a child to suffer in the shadow of my fame like you did with your mum. Birch I am scared that you want them and I don't, I am really frightened I will lose you." Two tears welled up in my eyes, and she smiled.

"Oh Sweetie, you can be so silly, why have you been holding all this in, you should have sat down with me and talked about it. Deads, we are young and have so much in life we want to do, we have time to decide those kinds of things. At the moment children are the furthest things from my mind. I am so excited you know... About our secret, I have not had time to process the fact you said you would. Look over time we will work things out, we will sit and talk about every aspect of our life, whatever we decide it will be something we both want. Now dry your eyes, and just relax and enjoy the moment." She leaned in and kissed me softly.

I felt such relief, I had spent all day worrying and she was right, I needed to just relax and chill out, we had all the time in the world to work everything out. I looked at her smiling and gave a sniffle, I felt such strong emotions, and could not help it, I bit my lip, and my voice was a quiet squeaky whisper.

"I almost lost you Birch, and I was so scared, I still get scared, because I love our life so much, but he almost took you away from me, and I don't know what to do about it, I am terrified I will lose you." Her eyes clouded, and she lifted her hand to my face.

"Oh, Sweetie you have to stop worrying about that, I promised I was not leaving you, didn't I? See, look I am here and I am all well, the bandage is off, and I just have four little stitches, which will disappear into my hair. Deads please, don't let that day hold you back, all that matters is we are here, and he is gone, and we are both safe and taking care of each other." She stroked my face as she spoke quietly to me. I nodded and gave a sniffle.

"I really love you Birch; you know that right?" She gave a giggle.

"I think the thousand orgasms you gave me sort of proved the point Sweetie." I snorted a laugh, and she smiled.

"Deads, we are going to be fine; you will see."

Chapter 33

Facing Feelings.

Waking up with Chloe behind me, cupping my boob, and Birch in front of me, and me cupping her boob, was weird, but also kind of nice. I had not slept in my bed for ages, and waking up to the familiar walls and the lighting of the room, was comforting. The one thing that was not a comfort, was my head, it was banging, I had not drank that much in a while, and I should know better than to let Chloe fill my drinks.

Birch's long white with black patches hair, flowed down her back between us, it was soft and silky, and I closed my eyes and burrowed into her back, she was warm and snug, as was Chloe behind me. I did not want to move my head, and Birch's boob felt soft and smooth, I let my thumb explore, and felt her nipple start to grow. I giggled quietly as I played with it, and she started to squirm in the bed and push herself back against me, I was sure she had forgotten, Chloe was still in bed with us.

Birch gave a happy little moan, and turned over to me, she moved in close and smiled, her voice was soft and sleepy.

"Hi Sweetie."

I leaned forward and kissed her, and ran my hand down her side to her hip, she closed her eyes enjoying the feeling, I then slid down across her thigh, and headed between her legs, she smiled and opened her eyes, as my hand explored. She whispered.

"You're very naughty this morning."

I smiled as my finger began to explore, and she closed her eyes, and just smiled with contentment, as I played. She gave a little whimper, and bit down on her lip, I smiled watching her as I moved slowly and softly exploring her, just stroking her button occasionally sending shots of electric like pulses through her. She looked at me, and gave a sudden intake of breath.

"Deads, I cannot take this, I want you, I want you now."

I quietly giggled and flicked her button, she gave a jolt and breathed in heavily.

"Oh Deads... Sweetie, please I need more than this, let's go to my bed."

I giggled, and pushed a little harder, I could see the pleasure in her eyes. Birch liked to be vocal, but with Chloe in the bed, she couldn't, she turned her face into the pillow, and bit down hard on it. I flicked my wrist a little faster and harder, she whimpered into the pillow, I loved watching her being pleasured, she jerked and pushed her face down hard as she moaned.

I knew she was close, and kept my relentless attack going, I could hear her breathing into the pillow as she pushed harder into it. I pressed as hard as I could, and she began to shake, her legs went taught, and she squealed into the pillow, and snatched my wrist with her hand to stop me, she really could not take anymore. Her body shook, she lifted her head from the pillow and her face was red, I smiled, and winked at her, she rolled over onto her back, and took deep breaths, I stroked her hair back, so I could see her. She turned her head to the side, still breathing heavily, and smiled.

"You can be so naughty, what would you have done if Chloe woke up?" I smiled.

"Once my boob was free, I would have gone down on you." She giggled

"I need coffee, and a pee, I am sure Chloe is not waking any time soon, can you wiggle free, and have breakfast with me?"

I slid her hand away from my boob, and wriggled free, Chloe stirred and rolled onto her back, her legs spread and she gave a happy moan, Birch giggled.

"Even in her sleep she is perverted." We chuckled as we headed downstairs to the kitchen for breakfast.

The rest of the morning we mucked in cleaning up, I needed to wrap up the gifts I had bought for Christmas, but with Chloe asleep in my room I could not do that, I also needed gift wrap as I had forgotten it. Birch looked at me and smiled.

"Sweetie you are fooling no one you know, I know what you are doing, you have done it before." I looked at her.

"I do not know what you mean Birch?" She smiled, and reached across the island, and took my hand in hers.

"We both have to go into the village at some point Sweetie, we cannot put it off forever. I know you do not want to face it, but if we go together, we can support each other." I put my head down, she was right.

For the last three days it had been on my mind, tomorrow was Christmas Eve, and I needed wrap and gift tags, I also needed to collect some parcels from the Post Office. I was afraid, I had deliberately avoided my interview on TV last night.

Birch had watched the special, which had interviews with quite a few of the residents, Katie texted me, and was pleased Amy had kept her word, and done a true representation of everything. Katie had thought it was a really positive feature, and good PR, but I was still afraid of seeing that place where I almost lost her, was that why I was so emotional last night, had I realised I had to face up to it soon? Birch squeezed my hands.

"Deads, walk with me into the village today, hold my hand and stay at my side, and help me." I looked up at her.

"Help you... What do you mean help you?" She looked serious.

"I am afraid to go in there, hold my hand, and help me do it, I have to face this too."

I was lost for words, I did not know how to answer, she had never been afraid of anything, and she was asking me to help her find her courage, surely, she knew I was as scared as she was?

"Birch how can you be afraid, you were so cool and calm and you got everyone through it, I was the coward hiding at the back." She smiled.

"From what I saw, Chloe was finding it hard to hold you down, you were no coward Deads, you were strong, and it was your example that helped pull me through. When I turned at the counter, you were the one facing him, you were the one who stood your ground and told him to leave. I admired you, but was also afraid for you, I knew he would not harm me as much as he would you, which is why I took your place, you showed the courage I needed." I shook my head.

"Birch I was terrified."

"And yet you still faced him alone at the door, Deads, that was brave." None of it made sense to me, but I would not see her go alone, I gave a sigh and nodded.

"I will be there at your side, us girls together." She smiled.
"Thank you, Sweetie."

One hour later, we headed into the village, Edwina took Petal and parked up outside the salon, just in case, and with Birch on one side and Chloe on the other, I walked down Waterside Lane, and onto Manor Road, and turned towards the village. Birch squeezed my hand, and turned to me as we walked towards the bookshop.
"It feels like the walk of shame all over again, doesn't it?" I took a deep breath.
"Yeah, only this time we forgot the Dutch courage." She gave a small giggle.
"I have never forgotten that day Deads, the fear, the tears, and the way you held your face down, don't do that today, hold your head up for me, look at me in the eyes as you walk with me, do that for me." I nodded at her and she smiled.
"I will."

The village was busy, it was just a few days before Christmas, and everyone was getting those last little items they had forgotten. The street was packed, and I felt my stomach twist, as the three of us walked together, and people would see us and move out of our way. I kept my word and held my head high, but inside my stomach was churning, and I felt the trembles in my legs. I breathed deeply, trying to keep my composure, but across the green I could see the Tea Rooms, with all the tables outside and customers sat sipping hot chocolate.
The windows had been replaced, but the putty was still white, and the paintwork still showed signs of the damage. We arrived at the Post Office and Birch turned, Chloe let go of my hand, and stayed outside, and still holding my hand, Birch and myself approached the double doors.
The Post Office/Village store was always noisy, and today was no exception, until we both walked in, and suddenly there was silence, everyone stopped in their tracks and looked at us. I swallowed hard and walked towards the queue for the Post Office counter. Everyone in the queue moved, and silently opened the way for me to go next, I felt my legs shake. I could feel Birch

trembling slightly, I just wish someone would say something, instead of just look at us.

Mary stood behind the window, and smiled, it felt like a relief to have someone familiar to look at. I approached the counter, and swallowed hard, and took a deep breath, I looked at Mary. My throat was dry and voice my wavered slightly.

"Hi Mary... I... I believe you have some parcels for us?" She nodded.

"Yes, I do Abigail and Jemima, I do indeed, I am so happy to see you, just give me a second, and I will get them for you."

I looked down to my small shoulder bag, and reached in for my purse. I lifted out my card to pay for the gift wrap, which I also knew she had put away for me. My hand was shaking as I lifted it out, Birch moved in close and reached across me, she placed her hand on mine to steady it. I glanced at her and smiled; she looked as white as I felt.

CLAP... CLAP... CLAP... CLAP!

I jumped slightly at the sound, and turned, Marjorie stood at the back of the shop and was clapping her hands, I was not even aware she was out of hospital. It felt shocking and surreal, Peter stood behind the other counter and joined in, I stared at them, not quite knowing what to do, others joined in as I stared down the shop, and suddenly everyone was clapping.

The whole shop had come to a standstill, and everyone stood watching us, and applauding, their shopping baskets on the floor at their feet, as their hands came together. I felt a pang rush up inside me and tears filled my eyes, as I looked around, and saw people I had known all my life stood watching Birch and me, and applauding us, I never expected this, and tears rolled down my cheeks. People were smiling making little comments such as 'well done' and 'such brave girls,' it was terrifying, but it was deeply touching.

Peter came out from behind his counter with a huge smile still applauding, and walked up the aisle towards us, he gave me a big smile and handed both of us a hankie, Birch was crying too.

"You two deserve this, such bravery, both of you should know, all of us are very proud of you for what you did, a lot of people could have been hurt, and you two protected them, and we are so proud of you both, well done."

I wiped my eyes and tried to smile, I did not know what to say, people from the shop started coming up to us, they were smiling, and they nodded and took our hands and thanked us, I felt completely out of my depths. I nodded a thanks, and dabbed my eyes, both of us were speechless. Birch gave a sniffle and dried her eyes too, I wiped mine again and suddenly Marjorie was in front of me, she gave a strange sort of smile.

"Abigail... As you know, I do not approve of some of your ways, but credit where it is due, and the same to you Doctor Dixon. Both of you showed remarkable bravery, and I especially am grateful, as are many who were in there with you. Merry Christmas to both of you." She took my hand and shook it, I smiled, I think it was part fear and utter shock.

"Thank you, Marjorie, Merry Christmas to you and your family too."

She gave a brisk nod, and let go of my hand, and stepped back, quite a lot of those around us wished us Merry Christmas, and both of us responded, and then as quickly as it started, everyone picked up their baskets and went about their shopping as normal, I wiped my eyes and turned back to Mary, she was wiping her eyes too.

"There you go girls, I have put them into these new canvas shopping bags we got from Norman, they are a little token of gratitude from Peter and myself."

She handed them over and I saw the gift wrap inside, I lifted up my card to pay, and she saw my hand shaking, she reached through the hatch and took it in hers to steady it, her voice was soft and quiet.

"You two deserved that, it is about time this place recognised your efforts, it was lovely to see, and I am so happy to see you both up and about the village. This is your home, so do not be strangers in here." I smiled, and looked at Birch, she was wiping her eyes again, but smiling.

"Thanks Mary, we both hope you and Peter have a really wonderful Christmas." She gave a chuckle as I placed my card on the machine and it beeped.

"We will be turning the heating high, and enjoy it our way." Birch gave a giggle.

"Us too, Happy Christmas and Happy Nude Year." Birch beamed a big smile and Mary started to laugh, and shook her head.

"It certainly will be."

I was glad to come out of the Post Office, which was no easy feat, a lot of people stopped us and wished us well, and it was really nice, but honestly the introverted writer in me was starting to show, and so were my nerves. Outside, Chloe had several well wishers around her, I was glad she had not gone unnoticed, she too was very brave. I had not realised I had fought as hard as I had, and I could not deny, in many ways Chloe had saved me, because I would have got up, and probably been shot trying to save Birch, she too deserved the credit she got. Birch took a deep breath, and looked across the road.

"One down, and one to go, are we ready for this?" Chloe looked at us both.

"If you ask, you will never be ready, just do it guys, all girls together."

She took my hand, and I shouldered my new canvass bag and took Birch's. All three of us were filled with nerves and apprehension as we stepped onto the road. I cannot deny, this was one thing I was not looking forward to. We crossed the road, and honestly, I had no idea how I was going to react, Stacy saw us coming and scuttled into the Tea Rooms. I could see the flaked paint, and small patches where the wood had splintered and my heart began to race.

We arrived on Green Street and the wide pathway between the tables, I heard a few of the customers outside drinking whispering my name. I swallowed hard and looked at Birch, she looked really nervous, and I wished I had not looked. Chloe gave my hand a squeeze and I looked at her, she smiled.

"I love you guys, you are both like my sisters, do you know that?" I smiled.

"We love you too, thanks for being here Chloe, thanks for protecting me." She grinned.

"It was more you kicking the crap out of me, and me fighting to hang on to you, but hey, it's what we do, we handle the fucked up shit in this world." Birch gave a giggle; it did sort of fit us all.

We walked between the tables and I could see Celia and Lillian both out from behind the counter waiting for us, as I have always said, in this village, the gossip is faster than email. We approached the doors and just for a second, I faltered, it was almost as if I expected to hear his voice. Right on the doorstep I stopped, and almost as if it was instinct, I turned to look back.

Right behind me ten feet away, Edwina, Deb's, and Anthony stood watching, I did not even know they were behind us, Edwina smiled.

"Keep walking Abby, we got your back."

I nodded, and turned to look at Birch, her eyes were red and still a little watery, but she was smiling.

"Thank you, guys." Deb's snorted.

"What for, you're paying for the coffee." She grinned, and Birch gave a giggle, she turned and looked at me, and smiled.

"Thanks Sweetie, I love you, do you know that?" Chloe gave a sigh.

"Enough already you two, everyone knows you love each other, we are all freezing our chuffs off, come on."

She yanked my arm and half dragged me through the door, Birch got yanked behind me, and the others followed all giggling. We entered the shop and Celia dragged me into her arms and gave me a bone crushing hug, Lillian wrapped herself around Birch, and I am sure she copped a feel of her boob.

Hugs and loves and kind comments were all well and good, but I could not help but look. The tables had been replaced, so had the broken chairs, and the floor had been scrubbed, but I could still see her lay there in my mind.

It was a picture that was glued in my brain, and would never leave for as long as I lived, and as I stood there and looked at the spot, a cold shiver ran down my spine. Deb's noticed, and moved to my side.

"Abby, it is done with, that day has gone and it will never return. I know you, so please do not dwell on it, look she is here and at your side, and that is what really matters, that is all that matters." I breathed in, but it felt for a second like there was not enough air in the place, I looked at her bright hazel eyes.

"I know Deb's, honestly, I do, but they can clean and scrub and rebuild all of it, and that feeling I had, will still be here inside me always. Deb's, I hope you never feel what I did that day looking at her on that floor, because it took me into a realm of terror and fear I did not know existed. I never want anyone to feel that, I never want to feel it again, and yet I have since it happened." She nodded.

"Alright Abby, don't worry, we will sit up here, we will not go down there."

She took my hand and guided me to the table just a few feet away, where I had a clear view of the door. I nervously sat down, and she sat beside me, I put my bag on the seat at my side to save it for Birch, she placed the order with Edwina, and as Chloe and Anthony sat down, they came over and Birch slid in at my side and took my hand.

"How are you?" I leaned into her and she put her arm round me.

"I am scared, and remembering things I don't want to, but as Deb's reminded me, you are here at my side, and we are good, I am handling it."

I was, it was not easy, but I sat there trying not to look, and trying not to remember, and even though I could see those pictures in my mind, all I had to do was turn, and she was there, alive and well and right at my side. We had our drinks, and ate our cakes, just like we always had, one big group of people who loved and cherished each other, and yet we managed to smile and joke, and laugh, just as the Curio's had always done, and I was so glad they were there.

It sounds strange, but even if just one of them is not present, which often happens, as our lives have changed so much, with work and partners, and other things going on, the dynamic loses a little of its sparkle.

It is on those rare occasions when we are all sat round a table, or lay around the floor, that is when I really feel the nostalgia of that summer seven years ago, because around us is a magic, that only we know and feel, and it is hard to put it into words. All I can say is it is a Curio thing, and it means the world to me.

When we were finished and had wished everyone Merry

Christmas, we all walked towards Petal. Deb's gave me a hug and then hurried back to her shop, Anthony hugged me too, and went inside his shop to set up for his next appointment, and the four of us headed home, which in itself was traumatic, as Birch was driving. The temperature was falling fast, and even though the snow had melted a little, it was still freezing, and the roads were starting to ice over, and Birch was at the wheel.

For the rest of the day, we all separated and headed to our rooms, I sat on the floor surrounded by gift wrap and tape, as I made big red velvet bows, and I wrapped up my gifts, and placed them neatly in a stack, ready to be placed under the tree for Christmas day.

I locked Birch's in my wardrobe, as she was way too excited, and childlike, and I did not trust her as I knew she would try and peep. By the time I was done it was meal time, and we all sat in the living room together with our plates on our laps.

Luke, Terry, and Michael joined us, and as a group we ate and talked, and deep inside our excitement started to grow, tomorrow would be busy, we had the food arriving, a booze delivery and also, we would pile up all the presents for each other.

The house was decorated outside and in, and with crossed fingers I prayed that nothing else would go wrong. These last few weeks had been too much, and had tested us all to the limit. All we wanted now was to be left alone to live as we pleased, and actually enjoy our first full on Curio Christmas Day together, with our closest friends and family, and it would be a long day, as we had a party planned for Christmas day night.

It had felt like a hard day, and Birch took my hand earlier than normal and led me upstairs to bed. I lay in the dark, looking at her little tree, and she curled around me, as the thoughts of the day drifted through my mind. We did not speak much, both of us had a lot to think about, and all we needed was to just be close and feel each other. I drifted through memories, and into my dreams, and all I could hear was the soft sound of Birch breathing beside me, and it was enough.

Christmas Eve was madness. Deb's was up and out early, her shop was open until four, Anthony had four appointments, and the rest of us did a massive clean up. Chloe handled the washing machine and dryer, Birch and myself rocked out to Avril, as we hoovered, dusted, and polished. Izzy and Edwina sorted out the cellar for the fresh food and alcohol deliveries. Everyone was happy and smiling and giddy; the spirit of the season was running high in all of us.

The large table in the kitchen was pulled out as we had a lot of guests coming, and spare chairs were brought in from the garage. Petal and Chloe's car was parked in the garage with Edwina's, no one would be driving for a few days, and I updated my blog with Christmas messages.

Mum arrived mid day, with an overnight bag, and she helped me make up the bed with clean sheets. The deliveries arrived and we all joined in carrying crates and boxes down to the cellar, Norman and Daisy arrived with the food, and we welcomed them in and gave Daisy a herbal tea as she was driving, and a double scotch for Norman. I handed them a sack of small gifts for their little ones which were well received, and by four o'clock, we were tipsy and happy. The doorbell rang for the hundredth time as I walked down the hall.

"I WILL GET IT!" I opened the door and my breath caught in my throat.

"Dad!" He stood looking awkward, in his long heavy coat, and wrapped in a thick red scarf.

"Hello Abigail, I am not staying long, I wanted to give you these." He held up two carrier bags, I looked at them and saw the gift wrapped bottles.

"I wanted to tell you that although things are not easy between us, I hope you have a nice Christmas." I was confused and wrong footed, and a little sad, he looked older, tired and worn out, I pulled the door open more.

"Would you like to come in?" He smiled.

"I do not have long Abigail, I will have to get back soon, but I wanted to see you." He looked awkward and embarrassed.

"Abigail... I am not proud of myself; I have a hard time expressing the things other father's find easy. I understand I have let you down badly, and I regret it, I really do, you expected more of me, and I failed, but I have had a lot of time to think. I realise you will find it hard to forgive me, and that is just, as I deserve your scorn, but I want you to know I am actually very proud of what you have achieved, and how you have turned out, you are a credit to your mother."

It is crazy, there have been times in the last year, I have hated him, and looking at him stood in the cold, I felt a pang deep inside me, and I felt sorry for him? I stumbled a little, he had completely surprised me.

"Dad, you don't look well, are you alright, look come in, sit with me and talk." He smiled.

"I cannot tonight, but I would like you and Jemima to join me for a meal in London over Christmas if you could, or would. I will not blame you if you don't want to. We could talk then, I would like that very much, just me you understand, no one else." I nodded, I felt Birch's arm slip round my waste.

"Hi Ed, Merry Christmas." He looked nervous as he looked at Birch, and he also looked even more embarrassed.

"Merry Christmas Jemima, I am glad to see you recovered, I feel I owe you a deep apology. I said things to you in anger that I did not believe to be true, and for that I apologise if you will accept it?" She smiled.

"I knew that Ed, and I saw you at the hospital, and I am grateful you came to check on Abby, and I am happy to see you here, you have always been welcome, even if you did not think it."

He gave a nod and smiled, he looked nervously at me, and slipped something out of his pocket, it was a long box tied with a bow, he handed it to me.

"I know it goes against tradition, but I felt you of all people would not hold that against me. I got you both this, and I would like to know if it is suitable?"

I took the box and looked at it, and pulled on the bow, and opened the lid. Inside were two gold identity bracelets, they were high class, very expensive, and very beautiful. One had my name on it, and the other had Jemima, they both had a diamond as a full stop. I looked at Birch, she smiled.

"They are really beautiful dad, thank you." He gestured to the box.

"Turn them over, and look at the back."

I lifted the one with my name on out, and handed the box to Birch as she looked at it, I turned it over, and there on the back was engraved 'Birch.' I have no idea why, but my eyes filled with tears as I looked at it. Birch turned hers over and it read 'Deadly.' I sniffled, and my voice went really high.

"Dad they are beautiful, I don't know what to say, except I really love them, thank you." Birch stepped forward, and pulled him into a hug, which threw him completely, but he smiled and embraced her.

"Ed I cannot think of a nicer thing to receive from you, it is really lovely, not just as a gift, but as a gesture towards us, thank you so much." I wiped my eyes and Birch stepped back, I pulled him into a hug and, he squeezed me very hard.

"I do love you Abigail, it does not always show, but I do, and I am very sorry for all the pain I have caused you both." I cried, I didn't want to, I just did.

"I love you too, and I am so worried about you, are you really going to be alright?" He patted my back.

"I am fine Abigail, I have the flat, and my business has taken a bit of a hit, but I built it once and I will again. I will not be charged because I have done nothing wrong, you understand that don't you, this was not me, it was the stupidity of Graham, but that will all be resolved soon?" I gave a sniffle.

"If you need help, I will be there you know that, don't you?" He gave me a tighter squeeze.

"Spoken just like your mother, and yes, if it gets really bad, I will reach out to you." I nodded into his shoulder.

"You need to take better care of yourself." He smiled as he released me.

"Honestly I am doing, it has been a rough ride, but I am resting and sleeping, and eating properly, so stop worrying." I nodded.

"Good." Birch handed him a bag.

"This is from us two for you, Merry Christmas Ed." He looked really surprised, and I smiled.

"We would not forget you Dad, it may have felt like it, but you raised me better." He gave a smile and nodded at me.

"I have to go, let me know when you are free before new year, and I will get a booking somewhere nice for us, I still have a few strings I can pull. I hope both of you have a nice day tomorrow, and enjoy your curious Christmas together, wish everyone well for me." I nodded.

"We will… Thanks Dad for coming, I am really happy you did."
"Yeah, thanks Ed, take care of yourself, and we will see you soon."

I am not really sure why, but it hurt to watch him walk through the gate in the snow and leave. I felt a pang inside me, the truth was I did not want to see him go, which was strange because I had been so angry at him for so long, and yet stood here in the cold watching him leave alone, felt painful. Birch pulled me close and leaned onto me.

"I am glad he came Sweetie, he owed you that, and he did the bigger thing for you, a dad should. He has had a tough time, but it looks like he has done a lot of thinking, maybe the incident with Martin made him sit up and take notice. Maybe he realised a lot more than you thought, whatever it was, I am glad, you deserve better from him." I looked at the bracelet.

"I did not know he came to the hospital; I did not even know he knew you nick named me Deadly, you usually just call me Deads." His car started up and he drove off, and Birch closed the door.

"He did not come into the room, I woke up and saw him stood there with your mum, in the doorway. All that matters Deads is he was there, you were asleep on my bed, and he did not want to wake you, he just wanted to make sure you were fine, then he left."

"Why didn't you tell me?" She turned and smiled.

"It was not my place, it was up to him to make the first move, it had to come from him in person, so you understood, as you do now."

She was right, as usual, I was surprised and actually glad I had seen him, I had always thought if we met, we would fight, just like we had in the past, but deep down I was happy that we had not. It was an important gesture on his part, and I was not going to rebuke it, he raised me better than that. I put the bracelet on and Birch fastened it for me, and I looked at it on my wrist, I really like it, and it meant a lot, this is probably the first time in my life he has made Christmas feel special, and that warmed me inside.

Everyone was gathered in the kitchen; our Christmas would kick off tonight with a few friends. Gill and Aden would be coming, as was Alex, and Morty, they had been seeing each other a lot since the office party. Denise was with a guy she had met at the party, he was a supplier of pharmaceutical printed information, named John.

Terry was spending Christmas with Chloe, which was nice for her, and Megan was still hooking up with Bongo. I invited Creamy knowing he would peak Deb's interest, and so he would not be left out. Even Izzy had a date, which was a little odd, because it was Malcolm Forbes Benedict, our neighbour from number seven two doors up, and I secretly suspected he was the new owner of the club's dungeon.

We were ready for Christmas finally, everything was set and prepared, and we planned on a fun, but not rowdy evening, just hanging out and being social to ease us into Christmas. I stood by the kitchen arch watching everyone laugh and joke as we got ready for our guests to arrive, and I felt tense. I had one last thing planned and I was hoping with all my heart I could pull this one thing off, I was nervous and Birch noticed, she came up and gave me that look, it was one I knew well.

"Are you alright Sweetie? You are up to something aren't you, I know that look, trying to act all innocent and yet very nervous, what are you cooking up Miss Watson?" I giggled.

"Nothing much, I am waiting for something, actually it is really important, and it has not arrived, so I am flapping a little." She smiled that huge radiant smile.

"It's for me isn't it, nothing else would have you looking that worried?" She clapped her hands together and gave a little squeak of a giggle.

"What is it, can I know?" I was so shit at hiding things from her.

"If you must know... Yes." She bounced on the spot.

"Birch, I really need it here today; this is something I really want to do." She was all excitement and craziness and her eyes sparkled with life and happiness.

"I am so excited... Come on what is it, give me a clue."

"No!"

"Oh, Sweetie please, I want to know, I have to know, I am no good at waiting." I looked up at her wild excited face.

"Tell me about it, every time I open my desk draw the box has moved again." She had the happiest smile I had ever seen, and her eyes just danced around inside her bright happy face.

"Deads Sweetie, it's hard not to look at it, I told you, I am hopeless with secrets."

"Liar... Explain this house and Sweeties Retreat, that was a frigging big secret, and you kept that one quiet for months?" She giggled.

"That was something very special."

"So is this." She gasped.

"It's that special... Oh God, I need to know now, tell me Sweetie, tell me please?" I started to laugh, the buzzer went off and Edwina pressed it.

"Hello."

"Package for Miss Abigail Watson."

She pressed the gate release, and Birch snapped her head to the door, I knew what she was up to, and I turned and ran like hell, she came screaming behind me up the hall. I yanked open the door and scared the shit out of the poor bloke holding the box, as I snatched it into my hand, and tried to hold the door closed too behind me, whilst my insane girlfriend tugged at it, and it kept jerking my arm. He smiled.

"Sign here please, Miss O'Reilly told me, you owe her big time for this one, we ran an extra press to finish it." I pulled a twenty out of my pocket and signed for it.

"You have no idea how much this means, here, thanks I really do appreciate your long hours today." He took the note and clip board.

"My pleasure, are you sure she is your girlfriend and not a wild ten year old?" The door was constantly being jerked with wild chuckles behind it. I smiled.

"Mentally, I am not sure she is that old."

He wished me Merry Christmas and left happy with his tip, I released the door and Birch went crashing backwards onto the floor with a squeal, I stepped in and looked at her, as I held the box, with a smile.

"You can have it now, but I want you alone, when you open it."

She gave a wild excited cackle and got off the floor, her eyes were bulging with excitement as she looked at the package. I put

it behind my back.
"Bedroom now."
Birch was not waiting, she bounced up off the floor, and ran up the stairs, everyone was looking at me stood in the hall, uncertain as to what was happening. I smiled and rolled my eyes as I looked at my mum.
"I was never this bad, was I?" She giggled.
"Sometimes sweetheart."
I gave a chuckle and headed up behind my crazy maniac girlfriend. When I reached the room, she was sat on the bed bouncing around like a mental patient. I looked at her and held the box out as I slowly advanced.
"Birch for me this is very special, it is one of a kind, no other will ever see this, it is just for you and you alone, do you understand that?" She nodded rapidly, and held her hands out for it, her eyes were wild, and she was a little breathless.
"What is it, tell me?" I held out the box, and she snatched it out of my hands, faster than a piranha, and pulled it close to her.
"Oh, it's heavy."

Suddenly there was carboard everywhere as she ripped it open and lifted out the heavy, large, green, leather bound, book, she stared at the front where the gold inlaid letters read. "The Snow Queen." She swallowed and looked up at me with large eyes, and I smiled.
"This is special Birch; I will never publish this."
She placed it down carefully on the bed and ran her hand across the golden letters, my voice was soft as I sat on the bed at her side.
"Open it."
She looked at me, she was suddenly very silent and still. She opened the heavy cover, and looked at the title page.
'The Snow Queen (A letter to the love of my life) By Abigail Jennifer Watson.
I heard her breath catch in her throat, as she ran her hand over the page... She turned and looked at me with tears in her eyes, and I smiled.
"Birch there is so much I want to say to you, so many things I have struggled to get straight in my head, and at times I have not

been as eloquent as I could be. I really wanted you to know the full depths of how I feel. The truth is, when I write, I say things so much better, and so I decided to take all of those lost words I wanted to say, and put them back together in the only way I know how, I wrote you a story." She threw her arms round me and burst into tears.

"Oh, Deads, I am completely overwhelmed, I have no idea how to express what I am feeling, this is the most beautiful thing anyone has ever done for me." I held her tight, and felt the happiest I ever have; I squeezed her hard.

"Read it, and let me talk to you from my pages. I am so happy you like it. Merry Christmas Birch." She slid back and dried her eyes, and gave a sniffle, she looked down at the book.

"Can I read it now?" I gave a giggle.

"It is your book; you can read it whenever you want to."

I got up off the bed and walked to the door, and stopped and looked back, she had turned the page and was already reading with a huge happy smile on her face. I left her to it, I wanted this to be her best ever Christmas, and I think this was a great way to start. I owed Katie big time for this, she had pulled out all the stops to get it printed and bound in time.

As I walked down the stairs decorated in such a stylish way, I felt like a queen, who had saved her people, and it felt good, as I heard laughter downstairs in the kitchen, the guests were starting to arrive. Behind me alone in her room, Birch smiled and held a hankie to her mouth, and she turned the pages, and wiped her eyes, she was so happy, and that made me happy too. It really was starting to feel like Christmas this year, was going to be the best one ever.

Chapter 34

A Curious Christmas.

The night with friends was a fun and wonderful night, and as everyone said goodnight, I went up to Birch's room, where she was still sat on the bed reading. She looked up as I walked in and sniffled, her eyes were red from crying, I felt my insides twist, and walked over to the bed.

"Birch, why are you crying, it's not supposed to be sad, it is supposed to make you happy?" She gave a sniffle and smiled.

"It does make me happy." I stared at her puffy eyes.

"How, you are crying?" She nodded, and two tears ran from her eyes, onto her cheeks.

"Sweetie, it is so beautiful, it makes me cry tears of happiness." I sat on the bed.

"Birch baby, I don't want you to cry, I want you to understand how I feel inside, I don't want you upsetting yourself." She smiled and sniffled.

"Deads, I am crying because of the depth of love you feel, and all those feelings are for me, and I am so touched and so honoured. I could not help but feel the absolute beauty of your words, and cry with happiness. Sweetie, I asked you to marry me, and now I see it was the right thing to do."

Honestly, she is mental, she looks at life in the strangest of ways, and she still makes it unbelievably wonderful to be around her, I leaned into her and kissed her on the cheek.

"Told you, I love you." I smiled and got off the bed, and started to undress. "Don't read all night, it is Christmas tomorrow."

I slipped into bed at her side, and lay back watching her, she was sat with a smile, reading the story of her and me. I have no idea when she finally went to sleep, I was tired and nodded off, and just assumed that she eventually put the book down, after all she had been reading for over seven hours. I woke briefly in the night, and she was curled around me cupping my boob, it felt nice, snug, and safe, so I closed my eyes and drifted back into happiness and sleep.

"GUYS WAKE UP.... GUYS GET UP IT'S CHRISTMAS, COME ON WE ALL WANT TO SEE WHAT SANTA BROUGHT!"

I opened one eye, and Chloe was bouncing on the bed, Deb's was behind her wearing a huge smile, I gave a sigh.

"What time is it?"

"It is eight o'clock." I groaned, and nudged Birch.

"Honey, get up, the kids want you." Chloe gave a giggle.

"Abby we are excited, come on, we have loads of presents." Birch let go of me, and sat bolt upright with her eyes closed.

"I love presents." I rolled on to my back, and gave a sigh, and patted her leg.

"The kids are awake baby, go feed them or something, I will be down in a few hours." Her head turned slowly round to me; she opened her eyes.

"Hi Sweetie, it's Christmas." I giggled.

"I know, we spent weeks preparing for it, and it is only eight am." She gave a bright smile.

"OOO! We have all day to play with our prezzies." I closed my eyes again.

"Oh Christ, you are going to be louder than they are, aren't you? Just don't wake my mum up, she is in the next room." Deb's shook her head.

"No she is not, she is in the kitchen helping Edwina cook breakfast, she was the one who sent us up for you two." I groaned.

"Oh god, what is the point of the hell that is puberty, to grow up and be an adult, if you still get dragged out of bed early on Christmas morning by your mum? Birch at your place last year, we did not get up until eleven."

She leaned over and gave me a long slow passionate kiss, I felt my toes curl, Chloe leaned back and looked at Deb's.

"Whoa, is it fucked up that I am turned on about now?" She rolled her eyes.

"You will get wet just pulling a cracker, so no not really." Birch stopped kissing me, and looked back at Deb's.

"Do we have crackers to pull, I love Christmas crackers?" And that was the end of my kiss, as Birch bounced out of bed, and grabbed her kimono.

"Sweetie, get up, it's Christmas and we are having crackers."

I gave a long sigh, and sat up, it was too late now, they had lit Birch's crazy fuse, and she was going to fizzle all day. I slid my legs out of bed, Deb's gave a squeal, and ran for the door, Chloe and Birch followed, and ran down stairs like ten year olds screaming, and I dropped my legs to the floor, I was going to need a lot of coffee. I stared at the open door and listened to the squeals on the stairs.

"We have always had crackers; the whole bloody house is filled with people who are crackers."

I arrived in the kitchen where Anthony, Michael, Deb's, Chloe, and Birch were sat at the table eating like hungry cannibals, and talking at high speed. Luke and Terry were still asleep, the lucky sods, I sat at the island and Edwina placed a coffee in front of me, and kissed my head.

"Merry Christmas Abby."

I nodded and lifted my cup; I loved that Edwina understood me, and expected nothing from me in the morning. Izzy was frying eggs, and mum was handling beans and sausages, she smiled from the stove, she too knew me well enough. I sat and drank coffee and felt life ooze into my body, Edwina placed a plate down with two slices of toast on it, I smiled, my routine never changed, even at Christmas.

With breakfast over, we headed towards the living room, well I walked with a coffee in my hand, accompanied by Edwina and Anthony, Deb's Chloe, and Birch ran. We had a rule of one gift only, and I had cheated already, as I gave her the book early.

By the time I arrived at the living room, Birch was in melt down, her eyes were so bright I thought they were going to go super nova and explode. She was vibrating at a higher frequency than a tuning fork, as Chloe dragged out presents from under the tree, and passed them round. She sat down like a child, and pulled the paper off her presents, and she was loud, and crazy and absolutely lovely. This was her first real Christmas, and I was not going to stop her enjoying herself. Chloe placed a pile of presents in front of me, and kissed my cheek.

"Merry Christmas Abby." I smiled, and kissed her back on the cheek, I looked at her.

"Chloe why are you wearing Gill's bikini?" She giggled.

"It's not, I liked hers so much I ordered myself one, and I got Deb's one too, I figured being naked today may cause problems, so I covered up." Hers was red with white trim, Deb's was green and white, and I could not argue with her logic. Although as to covered up, there was not a huge amount of fabric, and it just about hid their womanly bits, and I mean just!

Birch gave a squeal and pushed a pair of bootcut leather pants in front of me from Deb's, they were really nice. I grabbed Deb's gift and unwrapped it to find a matching pair, I held them up and Birch gave a yelp of delight, within seconds, paper was ripping and landing in my lap, as she grabbed another gift, I looked at mum and shook my head, she smiled, she was having as much fun watching Birch as I was.

Birch was surrounded with gifts of clothes, perfume, sweets, and booze, and she was delighted, it was like her birthday times ten for her, and I had spent so much time watching her love the morning, I was a little behind. She bent down and grabbed a gift and held it up with a beaming smile, I looked at it, and her excitement was bubbling like a cauldron.

"Open mine... Come on hurry, I am way too excited, Deads, come on, open it." I giggled and took it, and she slid up close next to me, she reached for the paper to pull it off, and I pulled it away.

"Birch behave, this is mine, control your hands."

She giggled excitedly and gripped my arm with both hands, and rested her head on my shoulder. I pulled on the paper and peeled it away slowly, just to annoy her, she bobbed about at my side, as I revealed a book cover, and it was an old one. As I peeled the paper off it, I realised it was the back cover, it was a cream colour, so I turned it over and saw the illustration of a sphinx like looking beast, and knew straight away what it was. I turned and looked at her, I felt my breath trapped in my throat.

"Birch this is a first edition." She smiled and kissed my cheek.

"I know how much you love it, open it."

My hands trembled, Deb's stopped what she was doing and stood up, and was staring at it. I opened the cover and gasped as

I read the print. 'The Time Machine, H.G. Wells.' It was signed, I could not believe my eyes, Deb's walked slowly across the room, staring at me like I was holding the holy grail, she gave a long flow of breath out of her lips.

"Holy shit Abby, have you any idea what that is worth?" I looked up at her with her wide eyes, and nodded, Birch giggled.

"Are you happy Sweetie?" I was lost for words, for me this was like lifting the crown jewels, I met her bright shiny eyes, and I felt tears.

"Birch this is too much, I mean this is just mind blowing." She smiled, and leaned in.

"Happy Christmas Sweetie." She kissed me softly, Deb's was on her knees in front of me staring at the book. I looked at her and she smiled.

"If that is not true love, nothing is Abby. I mean hell, that is the coolest gift I have ever seen anyone get. Please can I hold it just for a minute?" As a steam punk fan, this was the ultimate in books, and I held it out, she cradled it in her hands.

"Wow Abby, this was printed in a whole different era, the people who read this, actually dressed the same as the characters in this book, it is like the bible of steam punk, this really is where sci fi began."

Birch exploded and dragged me into her arms, she pinned me to the sofa, and her face came close to mine, her eyes looked like a crazy person's, she giggled.

"You cheated; I have not seen your present to me yet." I smiled.

"I know, I hid it in my robes." She gave a squeal, and pulled at my kimono, I started to laugh and giggle.

"Birch wait, you are tickling me."

It had slipped between my legs, and she was groping me looking for it. I gave a squeal, and her hand rubbed up against me as she slid between my thighs and found it. She yanked it out and held it up with victory, I lay back looking at her giggling, my mum was laughing so hard at us.

Birch sat back with excitement, and pulled at the gift wrap, to reveal a long black box, she looked at me and giggled with excitement, and opened the box, she gave a gasp and turned to me.

"It matches." I smiled, and she filled up. "Deads, they are so beautiful." My mum leaned over and gave a smile.

Inside the box was a necklace of diamond birch leaves, with a small platinum Birch tree hanging from it, and there was a bracelet to match the ring I had bought her, my mum looked at me.

"Is that platinum and diamonds?" I nodded my head and she smiled.

"Wow Abby, that is one hell of a gift, I take it you had it custom done?" Birch looked at me, with tears in her eyes.

"There was a time when everyone forgot I was Birch, and I missed it so much, and now I am her again. This is so perfect, because this is who I want to be, and you have made something that says that." I pulled her close and kissed her cheek.

"Merry Christmas Birch, I want this to be the best day ever for you." She stared at her necklace and bracelet.

"I have felt so much love today, and I am so happy, thank you everyone, thank you so much, this really is wonderful." She burst into tears and bawled like a baby.

For Birch this was the most amazing thing that had ever happened to her, and in a way, it was sad, because her parents were very practical. Her birthday as a child, from what I gather, was always a massive event, but I felt good inside knowing she was experiencing this for the first time. She lifted out the jewellery and put it on, and I was right, it sparkled as brightly as her eyes.

I finally unwrapped my gifts, Chloe bought me black dungarees, Izzy got me a set of mixed gothic horror books, Edwina gave me a collection of different dictionaries, which had slang, gothic, and old world terms. Anthony bought me a beautiful brush and comb set with little bats on the back, and mum bought me a really beautiful black satin frilly skirt. Terry, Michael and Luke bought me booze and chocolates. Dad bought us all bottles of alcohol, I got raspberry gin, but what made me laugh was he bought mum Rhubarb gin, all these years, he actually knew what was hidden behind the flour bags.

After presents, came the big clean up, and Birch who was just buzzing with happiness, set up her laptop so she could talk to her mum, they were in the Bahamas with Bradley and Ellen, so she set the laptop on a small side table so that it faced the sofa on which we would all sit.

Edwina did a quick stint in the kitchen, getting the turkey prepared, and in the oven. It was still pretty early, so I made coffee's and nipped up to my room, and put on my black jeans and a long black top, and slipped my ring into the jeans pocket. I ran back to the kitchen and poured out the drinks.

Everyone gathered again, and Birch clicked the button, it was eleven am here, and six in the Bahamas, so they had all got up extra early to talk to us. The link connected and the four of them sat on a sofa came into view, behind them was a big window, and I could see the tall palms swaying in the breeze, it looked amazing.

They all waved, and screamed 'Merry Christmas' and even though we were all crammed onto one sofa, we waved like hooligans. Birch slid with Deb's onto the floor just in front of the screen to see their parents better. They both chatted away to their parents, Birch talked of what it was like, she told her mum of the special book and cried a little, everyone looked at me, obviously they knew nothing about it, and realised I had cheated. I suddenly felt really nervous as Birch called me over, she stepped back a little from the screen and looked at her parents.

"Mum, Dad, I have been thinking a lot lately, and after a lot of thought there is something, I need to know." Roni smiled.

"What is it Jemi, just ask?"

I swallowed hard as she slid down onto one knee, and looked up at me, her eyes shone with joy, I noticed Roni suddenly stiffen, and lean towards the computer. Birch took a deep breath, it is crazy we had done this already, but I felt just as terrified and started to tremble.

Deb's, suddenly noticed what she was doing, and gave a huge and very loud gasp, her eyes went huge, and she pulled her hands to her mouth. Chloe and Edwina stood frozen watching; I think they were holding their breath.

Birch smiled, as she lifted up a box and opened it revealing the ring, I felt my legs trembling and my stomach wobble.

"Deads… Abigail Jennifer Watson." She stumbled a little as Deb's held her hands to her face, she was literally a foot away, my mum stared with shock.

"Abby, Sweetie, will you marry me, and please answer quickly, I am terrified because my mum is watching?"

I had already done this, but it still felt as powerful. I looked at her, the hope, the joy, the wild and wonderful shine to her eyes. My eyes filled with tears, as she smiled, she looked so nervous, I mean it is crazy, Deb's swallowed hard.

"Abby for god's sake say yes, it's killing me with suspense." Birch giggled and I nodded at her.

"Yes... Yes Jemima Dixon, I will marry you, but we have problem." Deb's, gasped out in shock.

"Problem, what problem? Abby there is no problem, say yes, and put the bloody ring on." Birch giggled; I pulled my ring out of my pocket.

"The problem Birch, is I wanted to ask you." Deb's, screamed and bounced on the floor as I knelt down, she looked at Birch.

"Stand the hell up Birch!"

I giggled as she rose off her knees, and stood in front of me. I held up the open box, and she looked down and swallowed hard, she too was trembling. Edwina and Chloe stood together watching hugging each other, Anthony was already in tears hugging Michael.

"Doctor Jemima Dixon, I have said yes to you, so will you say yes to me?" She jiggled on the spot, and gave a huge cackle of a laugh.

"I will, I will, I most definitely will." Deb's and Chloe both exploded and screamed with delight, and for a moment I went deaf.

We both took the rings out of our boxes, and slid them on to each others fingers, tears were streaming down her face, as she smiled and lifted up her hand. I was suddenly surrounded by thick bushy brown hair as Deb's screamed out, and pulled me into a huge hug, she was bawling her eyes out, as she hung from my neck. The room went mental, and suddenly both of us were swamped, we had pulled it off, and could now openly admit it to everyone.

It took a few minutes before Birch dragged me into her arms and kissed me, and then pulled me down to the screen where

Roni was wiping her eyes, so was Ellen, I smiled as I looked at Will's big smile.

"Are you guys okay with this?" Roni gave a sniffle and leaned forward; she was crying.

"I want to hug you both so much at the moment, and I am so happy for you both, oh Abby, you have no idea how thrilled we are. Hold the rings closer to the camera and let us see them." We both held our hands up and got them where they could see them, William was all smiles.

"Jemi, Abby, I am so happy for both of you, and Jemi, I highly approve of your choice for my new daughter in law."

She giggled, and pulled me close, I felt so amazingly happy, and Roni and Will were on our side, and that was all that mattered to me, that her parents approved. We moved back so Deb's could talk with her parents, as Roni needed more hankies, I walked over to my mum, she was wiping her eyes, she smiled as she pulled me into her arms.

"You listened to me the day you moved out, remember I told you, hold on to her, oh Abby I am so unbelievably happy for you. She is such a lovely person, and she risked her life to protect you, which says everything doesn't it?" I smiled.

"I have loved her for a long time, although I am not sure Dad will be happy about this. I mean, he is pretty old fashioned." She gave a sigh.

"Abby you cannot live your life for his feelings, he has two choices, support you or lose you, and I am not sure he is stupid enough to lose you forever." I nodded and Birch came over and my mum hugged her hard.

"In my head you are already my daughter, but I am glad you made it official." Birch held up her hand.

"Look how pretty it is, it's a birch leaf." Her eyes were dancing with joy, it felt so wonderful seeing this day just get so much better for her, Edwina squeezed in, and pulled me into a hug.

"We thought you two would never get here, but I am so glad you have. Abby, this is so right for both of you. I hate saying this, but we have a meal to cook and we will need you in a minute to help." I nodded and she kissed my cheek. "God I am jealous, give Luke a nudge for me." I giggled.

"I will, let's hope he took the hint."

As fun as it was, the truth was, a meal had to be prepared, and I was on the cooking shift. I left Birch and Deb's to talk to their parents, and joined Chloe and Edwina, and we got stuck in with a full traditional meal. I arrived in the kitchen and Chloe handed me a glass; she smiled as she raised it.

"To happiness, and Birch and you."

I took a swig and smiled, she was such a good friend, it is so hard now to look back and believe we had ever considered each other enemies at one time. I felt so happy as Chloe looked at the ring on my finger.

"That is a pretty old ring you know, it is worth a few quid, I like the idea of Birch giving you something so special." She looked me right in the eyes. "So, tell me Abby, when did she really propose?" I started to giggle.

"How did you spot it?" She shrugged.

"You did not look anywhere near as terrified as I thought you would. You did it the other morning didn't you, I knew you two were way to happy to be in the bath drinking wine at that time?"

As I peeled the potatoes and she prepared the veg, we stood side by side and I told her of how Birch took me up to the top of the hill for sunrise, and as the sun came up, she went down on one knee and proposed. I also told her how I bought the ring as an eternity ring because I was afraid to ask, and hoped she would misunderstand enough to say yes. Edwina and Chloe looked all dreamy as they peeled and chopped.

The meal was finally underway, and the house was filled with laughter, and guests started to arrive, and the house got loud and noisy. Bev and her party arrived, followed shortly after by Delphine, and when the Pemberton's arrived I took charge whilst Chloe and Edwina hugged their mum and dad. Birch came into the kitchen looking happy, she slid her arms round me, you would have thought she was drunk she was so happy, but she had not had a drink yet.

"Deads, thanks, this has been the most amazing day, and I am so happy with my story and my ring." She held out her hand, and I looked at it, I was so happy, I turned round and pulled her close.

"I wanted this day to be so special for you, I am glad you have enjoyed it." She smiled.

"You are so special Sweetie, so precious to me, mum and dad are delighted, my mum cried so much, I have never seen her like that before. See, didn't I tell you, all the bad things that have happened, they mean nothing Deads, it might have felt like everything was going wrong, but just look at us."

She was right, everything had gone crazy and scary, and I had been so afraid, and yet here I was looking into her bright green eyes, surrounded by that amazing snow white hair, and holding her in my arms, and she was going to be my wife, or female husband, I frowned.

"Birch what will we be, I mean will we be a wife, wife couple, or will one of us have to be manly, oh hell, I am not being the bloke my voice is way too high?" She giggled.

"We can be whatever we want to each other, I definitely want to introduce you as my wife. I think we can choose whatever we want, we will do a lot of talking before we do it, and find a way that suits us. I want something that is exactly what we want... I am going to put some clothes on, I cannot run around in a kimono today." She leaned in a kissed me slowly and passionately, and I gave a happy little moan, I had secretly wanted another all day.

"Good grief, not engaged more than an hour, and you are already at it, just don't burn the dinner." I pulled away and turned with a smile.

"Hatty!" I ran round the island, and launched into her arms and pulled her tight.

"I have missed you so much." She gave a chuckle, as she held me tightly.

"I have missed you both as well, although I have seen you have been living up to my standards, and wrecking the village, how are you both, I came to the hospital, but you were both out cold?" I held her tightly.

"We are fine, it was scary, but we are okay." She patted my back and I released her, and looked into her eyes. "You look amazing, and very happy." She smiled.

"I am, I really am." I smiled.

"I want you to be happy, but tell Clive we need to see more of you." She giggled.

"I will, we have something for you all, and if you can stay

separated long enough from your wild woman over there, I want both of you to join us all."

She took my hand, and a hand of Birch, and she led us into the library, where Clive stood looking very happy indeed. On the long table was a big heavy looking wooden box. Chloe, Edwina, Deb's and Anthony were all waiting, behind them everyone else was gathered, Clive gave a proud smile, as Hatty slid her arm round his waist.

"I have to admit, what we have for you all was a challenging project for us, I have used all of Harriot's pictures, so I really hope you like this gift from us to you."

Clive slid a crow bar out of his belt, and with Hatty's assistance, he carefully prized the lid off the box. He gently placed it on the floor, and then carefully prized one of the sides off, and lifted it carefully away. All of us watched not completely sure what he had, as the sides came off, there was a huge pile of packing straw. Hatty carefully lifted the straw out of the way to reveal something covered in a white heavy cloth, she turned and smiled.

"You guys have been an inspiration to all of us, and one way or another, all of you have had a big impact on us as people, so I wanted something very special for all of you to show you how much we love you, and how special you truly are." She lifted the cloth and revealed what was underneath.

I have to say I was not expecting anything like what I saw, I felt a huge wave of emotion rise up inside me as the whole room gave a gasp, I felt tears in my eyes, as I looked at Hatty.

"It's us." She smiled.

There we were modelled in stone, one foot high, the six of us stood together holding hands. Birch was on her knees level with it, her eyes streaming with tears, Deb's was at her side, I looked at the small figure of Birch, and me and all the others, and it was perfect. Clive looked really pleased.

"Do you like it guys?" All of us were speechless, I wanted to talk but I was so filled with emotion, I couldn't, all I could do was cry, Birch spoke first.

"It's beautiful, you have Deads spot on." I wiped my eyes.

"Clive, I do not know what to say, it is perfect, it's beautiful, you are an amazing sculptor." I walked over to him and pulled him into a hug.

"Thank you so much." Chloe wiped the tears from her eyes.

"Wow I feel really cheap now, I only bought you guys' wine." Clive gave a giggle.

"I very much like wine Chloe thank you." She smiled.

"You are an amazing talent; do you know that?" He smiled.

"From an artist of your standing, that is praise indeed, and I am honoured by your comment."

Everyone crowded round to look at it, and sadly I had to head back to the kitchen, with Edwina and Chloe. I had this huge ball of emotion deep inside me, and it was bubbling away, I kept feeling like I wanted to cry.

The room was heating up, and Anthony appeared with Deb's to lay out the big table, it was a good job we had a table big enough, there was a lot to seat. We got busy with bubbling pans, and stacking plates ready, it was a good job we had such a huge range to cook on, with enough hobs, and double the oven space, the turkey was a monster.

I washed as we went, to keep every surface as free as possible, and was starting to envy Chloe in her bikini with just an apron over it, she opened the oven door, and slid out the turkey to baste it, and I felt a sudden pang of horror run through me, I pointed in complete alarm.

"Where the hell did you get that from?" Chloe looked up and frowned at me.

"What the turkey baster?" I felt waves of utter panic run through me, just saying its name freaked the hell out of me, Chloe looked at it.

"It was in the draw." I shook my head.

"Chloe, we don't have one, we had to spoon the beef remember?" She frowned. I had a million emotions surging through me, and all of them were being led by the pied piper of utter panic.

"Abby, we have one I am using it, if we did not have one why would I have found it in the draw?" Untold horrors were ripping through my body, as Edwina turned and looked at my white terrified face.

"Abby what is the big deal about a baster?" I was finding it hard to breathe, I held my hand to my chest, breathing rapidly, and looked round, Anthony and Deb's had not noticed my panic.

"Guys we have only used a baster once this year, and it was not for frigging meat."

Edwina looked confused, and then suddenly she understood me, she turned to Chloe, who was squirting juice all over the bird.

"OH FUCK!"

I looked at Chloe who was still squatting, and squirting even more fat across the turkey. The baster made a weird squirty noise, and my stomach churned.

"Chloe for Christ's sake stop that, it is screwed up, and honestly, I think I am about to have a panic attack." She gave a sigh.

"Abby what the fuck is your problem, it's just juice from the bird?" Edwina smirked.

"Well, we are both used to juice from a bird, the question is, will the guests be okay with it, although it's not just the birds juice?" I stared at her feeling mortified, and panic surging through every nerve of my being.

"How the hell can you joke about it?" She smirked.

"Abby relax, it's not like we have not sucked a few in our time, and swallowed what came out of it, hell I have taken pints off Luke." Chloe suddenly stopped squirting and looked at the baster, she looked up at my white face and started to laugh.

"Is that where this came from, holy fuck?" Edwina started to giggle.

"Congrats Chloe, you just successfully impregnated the turkey." I looked at them both laughing, my heart was hammering in my chest.

"Guys this is not frigging funny that thing has had Luke and Jon Claude inside it."

Chloe sat back and started to laugh really hard, Edwina held onto the side, as she giggled wildly. Chloe poked it in to the juice, and sucked up a batch, she then stabbed the end of the turkey and gave the baster a full on squirt. Edwina shrieked with laughter, and Chloe giggled.

"Well, this one is well and truly done, I am going to name it Claudette." Edwina crossed her legs as she howled, I just stared in abject horror.

"Guys this is frigging serious, everyone who eats turkey will be eating Luke and Jon Claude." Edwina stamped her foot, and shrieked, Chloe smiled.

"Been there." Chloe shrugged, and giggled.

"Abby, chill the fuck out, there is not a woman alive that hasn't swallowed some during their life." I looked at her, feeling a sense of shock and horror.

"Oh yeah, well what about your dad, has he? Think about it, if Luke ever marries your sister, today he will be eating his future grandchildren." Edwina roared with laughter.

"I am going to piss myself, excuse me." She ran out of the kitchen howling with laughter. I took a deep breath.

"What are we going to do Chloe?" She slid the turkey back in the oven with a smirk, and closed the door, and stood up.

"Abby if we throw the turkey away, Christmas dinner is ruined, it has been cooked well, so the way I see it, we say nothing and serve it up. I mean, no one knows right, and it is not poisonous, so we are fine. Hell, I blew Luke a year or so back, and swallowed some, and I got a bit of Jon the other night, and I am still alive, so what is the big deal?"

I leaned back on the island, sweating and breathing hard, as my heart hammered away inside me.

"Chloe, I trust you, I really do, but I am freaked the hell out at the moment." She giggled at me.

"Abby chill out, have another drink, and just think that in that other room, there is an amazing sexy woman, who just asked you to marry her, and she wants a turkey dinner, even if the meat does taste a little salty." She burst out laughing, and hugged me. "Calm down and have a drink."

My heart was racing, I took a deep breath, and tried to breathe slower, I was sweating like crazy, it was really hot in here. I poured another drink and stood sipping as I came down a little. Chloe winked and checked all the veg. Edwina returned chuckling, and began the process of getting ready for service, it would not be much longer now. The table was set and decorated with candles, red bows and holly, it looked stunning, Birch came in and looked at her watch, she glanced at Edwina.

"How long before service?" She smiled.

"About fifteen, twenty minutes, and we will be ready to go."

Birch took my hand.

"Can I borrow you?" She walked me down the hall, it was a little cooler out here, Birch turned and looked at me.

"Sweetie, I have planned an extra guest, Izzy is getting them now, it is a surprise, so can you keep Anthony busy in the kitchen?" I nodded, and she smiled and then slid closer.

"I love you wifey." She giggled, and then kissed me, softly. Oh, I melted into her, and just enjoyed our moment alone in our crazy house. Separating was hard, she gave an excited giggle, and bounced around.

"This is going to be such fun, today is amazing already, but it is just getting better." She headed for the door, and I turned back to the kitchen, to hold Anthony captive. I cornered him near the studio, and he smiled as he looked at me.

"Abby darling, I love you and Birch so much, and I am so happy for you two. But if I am honest, I am happiest for you, although I feel as a brother, because you are like my sister, I should warn you. Abby darling, you are marrying a crazy person, always drive when your married, she is not to be trusted on a road." He smiled and pulled me close, and it felt nice, I wrapped my arms round him, and snuggled into him.

"I see you as a brother too, I really do, I love you so much Anthony, and I know she is bonkers, but I need her madness in my life, and yes, I will always drive." He held me so close.

"Seriously Abby, she is the only one for you, I know we talked a long time ago, and you had doubts, but look at how bad it got without her. I used to spend nights lay awake, worrying about you, you have no idea how glad I was when she came home to you." I looked up at him and saw how serious he was.

"I never meant to worry you Anthony." He smiled.

"Abby, worrying about a friend of your calibre, is a worthwhile thing, trust me on that." I smiled; I really did love him with all my heart. Birch appeared with a giggle in the kitchen doorway.

"I say Anthony, are you trying to steal my intended?" He gave a snort.

"Oh, Birch darling, you can trust me, there is no hope of that happening, I am way too sane for her tastes." I giggled as he let me go, and looked at Birch as her eyes sparkled with excitement, she gave a big grin.

"Anthony, we have a special extra guest for dinner, I hope that is alright with you?" She moved out of the doorway. "Everyone, this is Linda, she is Anthony's..."

"MUM!" He ran up the kitchen and dragged her into his arms, and burst into tears, she wrapped her arms round him, and smiled.

"Merry Christmas Anthony love." Birch walked down the kitchen towards me with a smile, I wiped the tear from my eye.

"Birch that is the sweetest thing you have ever done." She smiled as we stood together and watched Anthony, as his mum talked to him quietly.

"I am so happy for him, he has always been the most isolated one of us, it feels like the Curio family are complete now. I take it his father still refuses to talk to him?" Birch gave a sigh.

"His father's pride is stupid, his mum loves and misses him, and this is his home, she should be a visitor, I hope from now on she will be."

As I have always said, some days Birch just blows me away, she just pops up, and does the most unbelievable acts of kindness, and without understanding, she changes the world around herself for the better. It was time to get moving, we had a crowd to please. Birch walked up the kitchen.

"Edwina how are we doing?" She looked up from the oven door, and saw me watching.

"It's cumming along nicely, and we are heading for the climax." Chloe snorted and almost dropped the pan of potatoes, as she burst out laughing, Edwina stabbed a fork into the back of the turkey.

"I just gave it a good poke, and fuck this bird is moist." Even I sniggered, as I saw Chloe kick Edwina, and laugh harder.

I joined the two girls, and we went into action stations. The plates were on the table, and we started to dish everything out onto serving platters, and into bowls so people could help themselves. We had home made cranberry sauce and stuffing, roast and mashed potatoes, carrots, sprouts, and swede, and three boats of gravy. The turkey was placed on a large silver tray, and sat at the head of the table, and everyone took their seats.

Luke and Michael, opened several bottles of Champagne, and filled all the glasses, and as the man of the house, Anthony was given the honour of carving the turkey. It was a lavish spread, and there was more than enough food, it had felt like cooking for an army. Mum stood up and tapped her glass with her knife, she smiled at everyone.

"Girls, Anthony, thank you for opening your home to us all today, your table is divine and beautiful, and the love in your hearts is overwhelming for all of us, and it is a privilege to be here. I think everyone here feels a part of your Curio family, and we all feel blessed to be included. Will all of you raise your glasses in a toast to such a unique and wonderful group of people, who have worked so hard to make today happen. Thank you, and Merry Christmas Curio's"

We all lifted our glasses and yelled out 'Merry Christmas.' Birch patted my leg as she sipped her drink and screwed up her eyes. "Yuk!"

I giggled, she smiled, and raised her glass to me.

"To us, together forever and beyond." I clinked my glass on hers, and sipped, she screwed up her eyes.

"Yuk!" I giggled, we had pulled it off, and Christmas was finally going great, she gave an evil grin.

"We have crackers." She clapped her hands together. "I WANT TO PULL A CRACKER!" Chloe sniggered.

"You already have, and put a ring on her."

Everyone chuckled, and suddenly all around us crackers were snapping, and lame jokes were being told, and Birch lifted her bright purple paper crown, and slid it over her snow white hair, as she giggled at all the stupid jokes. Bev shovelled more turkey off the platter onto her plate.

"This is a banging bird, it's well moist."

I put my head down, and so did Chloe and Edwina, as we sniggered, I wonder if we will ever tell them, no doubt Chloe will, she is shit at keeping secrets?

Chapter 35

Looking Ahead.

The Christmas dinner went down really well, Edwina made a home made Christmas pudding out of plums, and served it up on a platter covered in brandy and burning, it felt amazing and exciting. We all ate our fill, and staggered into the living room, fully sated, and Izzy led the charge on pot washing, with Birch, who wore pink rubber gloves to keep her ring dry. Deb's and Michael, covered for Anthony, who was loving having his mum round. He gave her a tour of the house, and told her all about his life, and it was so sweet to see it.

For the rest of the afternoon, we sat around and played music, and talked, I think it is the first time the living room has been truly full, and every seat was taken. As we moved towards the evening, we needed to change, as we had a Christmas Day party planned, and a lot of guests had been invited. Most of the guests at the office party would be arriving, Paula from the Sun Club was coming, with a few friends, Gail was coming with a few friends, Michael had been allowed a few of his friends to join us, so once again it was going to be a full house.

The Pemberton's left at six, and thanked all of us, they had really enjoyed themselves, and Mr Pemberton actually stayed awake all day, much to Chloe's joy. It was nice to see her with her dad, and she really is a daddy's girl, it is clear how much she loves him.

Linda shed a few tears as we all hugged her, she was so amazed at our home, and the life we lived, she took Birch's hands in hers and smiled.

"Thank you, it has been such a lovely day, and I feel so relieved seeing how well cared for he is by such good friends. You are all so nice, I have really enjoyed it today, it has been my best Christmas for a long time." Birch pulled her close.

"Linda you are Anthony's mum, which means our door is never

closed to you, so please, be a regular visitor, he does actually need you, so come any time you want to see him."

Anthony walked her to the taxi we ordered, Izzy had been on the Scotch, so we took the safe route to ensure his mum was safe. Hatty hugged the life out of us as she said goodbye, so did mum, she was going round to Hatty's for the evening. It was so nice seeing her, and really nice to see how happy she was, but I cannot deny, there has been a few days, where I have really missed having her around.

We had to change and get ready, so I headed to my room, to get my slutty vamp elf costume. I slipped off my pants, and top, and lay back on the bed and relaxed, I felt tired, it had been a long day of excitement. I held up my hand and looked at my ring, and felt that little burst of happiness inside me, it felt strange to know it was official now.

I lay back on my bed and heard a little titter, I lifted my head up, and looked round, no one was to be seen. I sat up and slipped off the bed, and walked towards the bathroom, I heard it again. I gave a smile, I knew what she was up to, I peered round the doorframe and I was right. Birch sat on the bed with her book open, and she was reading it, she sat looking at the pages with a hand on her mouth, she would read and take a deep breath and titter, I smiled and leaned round the doorway.

"You are supposed to be getting ready, not reading." She looked up, with a smile on her face.

"It is your fault, I am addicted, Sweetie it is so beautiful, I love it so much, I cannot leave it alone." I walked into the room.

"Birch, we have to get ready, as the home owners we are the hosts, we should be there when the guests arrive." She gave a sigh and closed the book.

"I would rather be here reading, but if you insist, but as soon as it is all going smoothly, I am slipping away. Sweetie, I have to know what happens, I have to read on, Betula is aligned with Nightshade, the dark spirit, and has fallen so deeply for her, I have to know if her light will win over the day."

I had to chuckle, had she not realised this was my love letter to her, I thought considering our own story, the ending was actually quite predictable? I loved how much she was captivated by it, but we had a party to host, and we were running behind.

I headed back to my room, and dressed in my slutty vampire elf dress and realised the laces were still missing, I had no idea what Birch had done with them. I walked back through to her room where she was dressed as a slutty Miss Santa, and sat reading her book again. I looked at her and she looked up, and smiled, I shook my head.

“Birch what did you do with my lace?”

She closed the book and got off the bed, and came over to me with a twinkle in her eye, she looked at the long split that ran down to my navel, and ran her finger down it. I gave a shudder, and she grinned.

“I think I prefer it without a lace, it gives me better access.” She slid her hand in and started to play, I felt the pulse run through me.

“Birch people will be arriving any moment, please don’t, we do not ha... Oh god!”

We were late to the party, it was in full swing when we finally made it downstairs, and everyone was crowded into the house drinking and dancing, I had never seen so many guests.

The Curio Christmas party became a three day long event, as we drank made love and passed out, slept, and started again. It was crazy, and the best party I have ever seen. People would disappear, and then arrive again with stacks of beer, and yet more people. On the fourth day, and still slightly inebriated, we took a train to London and met with my dad, who had been tipped off by mum, about our engagement.

We dined in a high class restaurant, and talked, and I talked to him like I have not done in years. His fall from grace had sent ripples through his world, he liquidated a lot of assets and kept his company and staff in full employment, after all, his fees were so high, even with only half his client base, he was still pretty well off. Photographers were everywhere, and even during the meal, there was the occasional series of flashes.

We talked until late, and dad booked us a room, so we could stay in London, and return home the following day. We had breakfast in bed, and had a long bath together before we checked out. Before going for the train, we decided to do a little shopping, and walked hand in hand along the streets looking at shops and talking about what our life would become.

It had been a long time since we were this alone without interruption, and for myself, having this time away felt like a luxury. Just Birch and myself, this was what my life would be with her, and we laughed, giggled, and messed around. It was early evening when we stood on the platform waiting for the train to come in, Birch was linking my arm, and leaning into me talking quietly and giggling.

"Excuse me, Miss Watson... It is Miss Watson, isn't it?" I turned to see a young girl with long dark hair and all black clothing, I smiled.

"Yes, that is me." She looked excited.

"I do not want to be rude, but I saw you, and I just could not resist, please would you sign my book, I would be so grateful?" She pulled a dog eared tatty copy of Seeds of Summer out of her pocket, and handed it to me with a pen. I smiled as I looked at it, the book had seen much better days.

"It looks like you have almost read all the print off this, how many times have you read it?" She gave a little chuckle.

"About forty or fifty times, I have lost count to be honest, I really love it." She leaned over as I opened the book.

"Would you sign it to Ruth please?" I wrote an inscription and signed it, she smiled. "Again, I know I am cheeky, but would your doctor sign it too, she is after all Willow?" Birch gave a happy chuckle and took the book, she signed it and handed it back, Ruth looked at her hand and gasped.

"Are you guys engaged?" Birch smiled.

"Yes, we are, I proposed at Yule." She looked at me with a wildly excited face.

"I am so happy for you, congratulations, I knew it, I knew you were Bram." I could not deny it.

"Ruth I am the author, there is a part of me in every character I create, although there are parts of the book that do reflect some of my own life." She looked so happy.

"I just want to say thank you for stopping and talking with me, and signing my book. I will cherish it, and keep writing stuff like this as well as your gothic stuff, you two are really lovely people,

I hope you will be really happy." She held her book tight, and walked off towards her other friends, who were all taking pictures with their phones.

Our train rolled in and we boarded, and sat together, it was nice to be heading home, but there was a part of me that did not want to. I had really enjoyed the alone time, it felt like the guest house all over again, and I had not realised how much I had missed it.

It was six pm when we pulled into the station at Wotton, I laughed as we walked out of the gates towards Petal, where Edwina sat waiting. The memory of being nineteen with black hair and red tips, coming home from my first summer term, at the end of my first Uni year, and the fear and panic I felt washed over me. It was crazy to think how much my life had changed in seven years.

I think this year more than any, and especially over Christmas, I have begun to notice the changes in all of us. We were all hard workers, who are employed, which took us away from each other, we had to a degree matured, although if you saw us party you would doubt that. We did not fall out or have as much drama in our lives, but maybe that was because we shared all our experiences, and so therefore have a lot of people, to give us opinions. That has helped all of us make better decisions, and most importantly, we have all looked at our futures more seriously, something we did not do at all back then, we were too busy living in the moment.

We can still be spontaneous; we just do it with a lot more knowledge behind us. The one thing that still surprises me, is when I look back at nineteen year old me, I loved sex, I craved it, and it was a pretty meaningless act. These days I prefer to be sexual with Birch, it fulfils me more, we do have the occasional mix up for fun, but it is nowhere near as often as it used to be.

We arrived home, and I took my bag upstairs to my room, I dropped it and felt glad to be home. I looked round my room, which still reminded me of the guest house, I looked above my bed and the large oil painting of Birch, Deb's and me, that Hatty painted, it was such an important moment in my life, and in many ways, it was a turning point for a better future.

Downstairs was a high pitched squeal, I turned sharply, and headed for the door, I hurried to the top of the stairs and looked down, to see Birch hugging her mum, as Will stood smiling. I ran down the stairs and Will gave a huge smile, as I jumped into his arms, and he squeezed me hard.

"I have missed you guys." He smiled.

"I missed you too Abby." He looked tanned and healthy, he held my hands and looked at me, and he noticed my ring and lifted my left hand up to look at it, and he had a huge smile on his face.

"I am so delighted for you Abby, I will not deny, I was unsure you would admit a lot of what was happening inside you, but I am so glad you found your way, and it matched with Jemi. I can boast of having the two most amazing daughters in the country now." I giggled.

"I am above average; Jemi is well above average." He winked.

"Not in my book." I chuckled and felt myself tugged, and suddenly Roni was squeezing me to death.

"I am so relieved one of you asked, I thought neither of you would. I have missed my daughter's dark little beastie, oh Abby I am so happy, you have no idea."

We had lots of hugs, and all the others joined in, they were both pretty jetlagged, and so told us they would not spend long. They had only been home an hour, and were dying to see us, but after a coffee they wanted to head back to Bradley's and sleep, Deb's was already there. They stayed for just an hour, but it felt like five minutes, and soon we hugged again, and looked forward to the next day, after they had slept.

That night I sat with Birch on her bed, she was reading again, she gave a gasp and shut the book.

"Oh God, I cannot take it." I frowned at her.

"What is up?" She looked frightened and upset.

"Sweetie, Nightshade has been mortally wounded, and Betula is falling apart out of fear, oh please tell me you did not kill her, oh God if she dies, I am not sure how I will handle it?" I started to laugh, the whole book was based on us, how could she even think she would die?

"Birch just read it, you cannot stop now, you are almost through the whole book, if you stop, you will spend your life questioning it."

She looked at the book, and then the unit at the side of the bed, she leaned over and grabbed the tissue box, and put it at the side of the book. She took a deep breath, and then carefully opened it at the book mark.

I sat watching, as she held her breath, and started to read, her eyes never left the page, but her arm crept slowly to the side, and found the tissue box, she pulled out the tissue and held it ready, I started to chuckle and slipped off the bed.

"I will make a fresh coffee."

I knew what was coming, so I scarpered fast. Ten minutes later armed with coffee and chocolates on a tray, I entered her room, she sat cross legged on the bed, surrounded by a circle of tissues, bawling her eyes out. I sniggered as she looked up at me with tear filled red eyes. I stood there holding the tray, smirking, she wiped her eyes.

"Oh Sweetie, I cannot take this book, it's heart breaking, I just want to sit in the shower and cry."

I put the tray down and sat at her side, and took her hand, and held it. Birch sniffled, and blew her nose, and she looked at me with swollen red puffy eyes.

"I love this book, it is so beautiful, but Sweetie, I have experienced every emotion I have ever had in one week, it is better than therapy, but it is killing me."

I could not help giggling, I really tried not to, but just looking at her face, made me want to laugh, she looked emotionally drained, maybe it was a good thing I was not going to publish it? I would probably emotionally destroy my fan base. I looked at the book, and giggled.

"Birch, you have about ten pages left, just read them, and close the book." She shook her head.

"I am still afraid to... If it is a sad ending, I may throw myself out of the attic window." I giggled, and leaned over and pulled her close, and kissed her cheek.

"I am glad that it has touched you deeply, but just finish it Birch; I think it is worth it." She nodded and took a deep breath.

"I am going to have my coffee then run a bath, so I will be here if you feel suicidal." I giggled, and grabbed my cup.

She looked down at the book, and started to read again, I watched her eyes follow the line, and she bit her lip, her hand waiting to turn the page so she did not miss a moment, she looked so cute, as she made little gasps. She turned the page and held her breath, I could almost hear her heart beating, she gave a little soft smile, I put my coffee down and slid off the bed.

In the bathroom I turned on the taps and watched the water fill the large bath, I checked the towel rack to make sure we had enough, and then headed back for my drink, Birch was holding one hand to her heart, as she turned the next page, I picked up my coffee and walked to her dresser and lifted her brush, and ran it through my hair, then swirled my long locks through my fingers, and pinned it up. I grabbed a new bath bomb, and walked back towards the bathroom to check on the water level, I tossed the bomb in and watched it fizz. I waited for the tub to fill, and turned off the taps.

I walked back out of the bathroom, and Birch was lay face down on the bed, with her head buried in the pillow, as she shook, which I presumed, as I know her so well, was because she was bawling her brains out again. I sat on the bed and touched her shoulder; I think I broke her.

I placed my hand on her shoulder, and gave it a gentle squeeze. Birch rolled over hugging the book, God, she looked a right mess, her eyes had streaked, and ran, and they were swollen and very red. The book was gripped to her chest, with both hands, she sniffled and took a deep breath, and then she screwed up her eyes and burst back into tears, and bawled her brains out.

“You really love me... Deads you love me even more than I thought.” She rolled towards me, and I pulled her close as she sobbed into my leg. It was funny, but I understood her feelings and so hid my smile, I stroked her hair as she settled slightly.

“Birch of course I love you, that is why I accepted your marriage proposal, I want to spend my life with you, and I really wanted you to know how much you mean to me. I wrote this book just for you, so I could show you the truth of why I said yes to you. I am not going to publish it, because they will never fully understand the story, well not like you do.” She sat up and sniffed up, and took a breath.

“Deads, this is the most amazing and wonderful thing I have

ever read; you have no idea how good you are at writing. Wow this did not just speak to me, it wrapped its arms around me, and took me on a journey through my inner self, I have realised so much about me and my feelings. I am telling you; it has drained me to read it, but that is a seriously good thing. I love you so much, and I always felt I loved you more, but not now, I want to marry you ten times more than when I asked you." I put my arm round her and pulled her close.

"I have shown you my depth, I wanted to, and I am glad you liked it so much. Come on, jump in the bath with me." She nodded and smiled, I chuckled.

"The book is not water proof; you will have to leave it behind." She gave a giggle, and put it carefully down on the bed.

New Year's Eve was potentially another important milestone for all of us. Mum was round with Roni and Will, and Bradley and Ellen had joined us. The big news was Jimmy was back, and Deb's was busy in the bedroom, Chloe climbed all over Max until Terry arrived, and much to our surprise, she moved towards Terry, and Max was left out in the cold.

It was early evening, and I was sat in the kitchen with Birch and Roni. Maybe it was because it was New Year, but everyone's mind was on the future. Roni was talking about her company, the Dixon Group, which to be honest, apart from the bit that helps me put books out, I don't really know a huge amount about how it operates.

"Girls I have been thinking about the business, when you take into account the online services, the videos, the books I sell, and the practice, which have all done very well, to be honest better than any of us expected. Then add to that the ten percent stake in Sweeties Retreat, plus the inclusion of Abby's book sales through our publishing arm, and the other authors we now work with, the company has grown beyond belief."

I saw Birch focused on her mum, her eyes noting everything, Roni put her cup down.

"Katie was a massive addition, letting her buy in at a fifteen percent stake was a good move, but I have reached fifty years old, and whilst we were away, on what is the first holiday in a long time, I have realised that I want to slow things down a little, and spend a little more time with Will."

I understood that, she did look more relaxed and happier than I had seen her in a long time, Birch glanced at her mum, she knew her better than I did.

"What are you thinking mum?" She lifted her drink.

"Well firstly, you sweetheart, have a twenty percent stake in the company, and your dad has ten, which will pass to you if he dies, I hold fifty five percent, and when you both get married, I want to transfer twenty percent of my shares to Abby." I sat up and paid more attention.

"I don't want them, well not just for getting married, I don't know anything about therapy, that is Birch's future not mine, I am a writer." She agreed.

"Yes, Abby you are, and I may add, one who has contributed massive revenues to the company, your books have earned you a large place in our firm, and that is why you should be a stake holder. Look one day you two will manage this company, either by yourselves, or as board members, it is time. I want to hand half my clients over to Shelley, she covers them for me when I am on the road, so to be honest they all know her, and she is one of the best I have trained. Abby, I want a little more time to write and I would like to hit the stage more, less time at the practice will allow that." Birch sat back.

"What does Steven think, he manages the practice, I know he was not pleased with me starting the retreat away from the Dixon Group, at the end of the day he is the one who will take the brunt of not having you there, and I am not giving Izzy back, she is brilliant with her management of my operation?" She gave a sigh.

"Jemi, at the end of the day, he is an employee, he is not on the board, he will not give me any problems, he knows I watch everything, and that won't change." Roni looked at Birch. "You know, you once planned to hit the road, why have you not put a toe in the water yet?"

I nodded, I remember that night here, when she planned a more interactive event, she did it brilliantly. Birch took a sip of her drink.

"It has taken a while to build things up here, I have thought of something I would like to try, I do have a concept I am toying with, but it is not for the retreat. Well, it is and it isn't, I have something in mind for Curio Life, it has grown very large."

I was surprised to hear her say that, but actually why, this is after all Birch, and her mind never stops? She smiled at her mother.

"Aden and Edwina have fitted a bigger server over this holiday, and are moving all of it over before next week. It has grown to the point where we have had to double its size, and the money it has raised has helped pay for Aden, and has been spent on a lot of good causes. We are supporting over two hundred separate causes now, and I want to bring them together." Roni looked at her.

"Bring them together, you mean in one place?" She nodded.

"Mum, we use help groups all over the place, but what if we could have several places, where people who have been hit the worse can go, you know like a residential treatment centre? A place just like those residential spar and gyms, but for mental health, we could have on the ground hands on help and support, it has got to be better than all the online services we use?"

I looked at her, and I was blown away, how could she go from the blubbering mess she was last night over a book, to this inspired genius?

"Birch, if there could be a place like that, it would make a huge difference, if something like that had existed when I was alone here, I would have used it." Birch took my hand in hers.

"That is what made me think of it, you were so isolated and alone here, and I asked myself, how many others are in that situation, and what would have helped her the most?" Roni took a sip of her drink.

"It is an ambitious project Jemi, how would you finance it, because it will require more money than it is currently raising, and you cannot just cut off all those you help?" Birch gave a nod.

"The development won't be a problem, we can use Bradley, but we will need to make some big fund raising event. I thought why not take the Curio's on the road, let the rest of the country meet them, and do an international event." I frowned.

"International, you mean flying?" She shook her head.

"No, live stream, we use the modern technology to broadcast it live from the Curio site, or a TV network if we can get one. We do the first in the UK, then maybe a year or two later do the US, and then maybe Canada. We have a large following in all three, if we can fund raise three events, we may be able to bring in a massive amount of finance, on a global level."

Once again Birch was taking things forward with a modern approach, and putting a new twist on Roni's traditional way of doing things, she looked like she intended to bring the Dixon Group into the digital age. As I sat back and listened to them both talk, it was clear, that Birch was best placed to do it.

She had Edwina, and G5, a close bond with Katie, and a working business relationship with Bradley, and her mother. Everything she would require was already at her finger tips, including the original Curio's. If anyone could pull it off, it was Birch, because that is what she did, she thought, planned, and then came at you from left field, it was one of her things, it is her thing.

I left them to talk, Hatty and Clive had arrived, and they were delighted to see the figurine of all of us had pride of place in the centre of our mantle. Everyone sat back with drinks, as the clock slowly ticked through the last day of the year. Outside in the village, the snow had finally melted with rain, and the Christmas lights were illuminated for the last few days of the festive season, and the village was quiet and peaceful.

I sat on the sofa with Chloe and Deb's, Ellen sat with mum on the other side of the room whispering, Clive, Will and Bradley were also in deep conversation, and Hatty was chatting to Luke, Anthony and Edwina. We were all in various stages of conversation, when Roni and Birch came in. Birch smiled, and wriggled in between Deb's and me, and snuggled into me, mum and Ellen suddenly looked up, Michael had arrived talking to Terry and Jimmy, and everyone was gathered, Mum cleared her throat.

"Everyone, can I have your attention please?"

We all stopped talking and looked at her, she was using her Parish Council voice, she looked round the room, everyone was silent, she stood up and walked to the fire place, and faced us all.

"I have two items of news which I want to share, the first is, I have been invited out on a date." I smiled.

"Mum that is amazing, who is it?" She looked a little embarrassed.

"Patrick my solicitor has asked me to accompany him for a meal several times, and I have been thinking a lot about him lately, so I decided to take a leaf out of my daughters' book and follow my heart. I do like him, he is fun, so I have agreed to a date." She gave a very girlie giggle and everyone suddenly spoke wishing her well, Chloe leaned forward and smirked.

"Trust a divorce lawyer to screw both sides at the same time." I sniggered, and Birch giggled. Mum looked disapprovingly at Chloe, which made us laugh more. She faced us all again.

"I have also decided that considering the amount of free time I have, to invest in a business opportunity. We have waited until tonight to share this news, because most of you are probably not aware, but Ellen has left her job at the care home." We all gasped, even Deb's, my mum smiled.

"Ellen was wasted there, she has a good head for business, and so we have joined our capital, and we have bought the empty shop in the village, we aim to open an art dealership, and gallery."

There were even bigger gasps, and even though I was surprised, I really got it, mum knew art like the back of her hand, she was also a very talented painter, if anyone could run a gallery it was her. I gave her a huge smile.

"Mum that is awesome, will you be selling your own art?" She looked really proud.

"We aim to sell whatever art we can trade, so Hatty, Clive and Chloe, would you like to be featured by Waterside Galleries?" Hatty smiled; Chloe gave a huge gasp.

"You want to sell my art for me?" Ellen gave a giggle.

"Yes Chloe, you have an amazing talent, as does Harriet and Clive, and so we would like to invite you to offer pieces for sale, we will obviously take a commission for the sale, and we will work all of that out with you, but yes, we would love to feature the creative abilities of this village, especially you three." Chloe looked blown away and she nodded with a huge smile.

"You can take what you want, just get people looking, and that will be fine by me, I really need to get my profile up in the art world." Ellen smiled at her.

"Leave it with us Chloe, we aim to get you lots of exposure." I was so delighted, just the look on Chloe's face was enough, she was so happy, William stood up.

"I do believe we should have a toast, and celebrate."

Those were the words to launch a party, and the drinks flowed, we toasted Ellen and my mum, and soon the mood was lifted and the frolicking began. It was New Year's Eve, and the whole house felt filled with hope for a new year, and a new start, our spirits were running high and we were happy, and close. Oh, we were so close, we were not just friends who met on the village green to talk anymore, we were house mates, no scratch that, we were family, one big happy family.

As midnight approached, and everyone counted down at the top of their voices, I stood with Birch staring into her bright green eyes, as she smiled. Everyone screamed as the clock hit midnight, but I was not really that aware of them, all I could see was this amazingly talented and deeply loving woman before me. She had the most intense green eyes, the kindest face, of snow white skin, and long white hair that had bars and patches of black, to look like the bark of a birch tree. I smiled at her.

"Happy New Year, I love you Baby." She smiled and her eyes twinkled.

"Happy New Year, Sweetie, thank you for the most amazing Christmas of my life." I giggled.

"We got stalked by a lunatic dressed as a teddy with a dildo strapped onto them, hounded and trashed by the press, attacked by the Shrew Crew, and you were almost shot by a rapist, it is possibly the strangest Christmas I have ever known." She smiled.

"You missed ate turkey with the possible additive of semen." I giggled.

"I take it Chloe confessed?" She gave a chuckle.

"She ran into my room when I was reading feeling wretched and told me, but you know what, we also have the worlds most perverted Christmas house lights, and a beautiful tree, a lovely house, and you gave me the most amazing book and a forever tree, I love you so much Deads, you gave me the best Christmas ever."

She leaned in, and as everyone around us went bonkers, I enjoyed the feeling of being in her arms and feeling her soft warm lips on mine, oh God I was so wet it was unbelievable.

My mum once said that life was not easy, and there would always be bumps in the road, and in the last month, I had felt like my road was paid for by Oxendale District Council, because the bumps felt bigger, and more often than most other roads.

It was the start of another year, and a time to take stock of the years past, and plan for the year to come. I have spent a lot of time recently facing trials I never expected, and looking back down the road I had travelled, and there in the distance I saw fear, isolation, terror, and death.

I had come so far away from them, and not just in my life, but the life of all the Curio's had changed so much from those days when we were just getting to really know each other, sat in my dad's guest house across the road from my current home.

We had been gelled as a group because none of us felt we belonged, the truth was, there was no place in Wotton life for us at that time, we were shamed and shunned, and tried to avoid facing those who wronged us. Our lives had changed so much, some of it was luck, and some hard work, but the one thing in common we all shared, was our love for one person.

She was a crazy, mega clever, pagan, naturist with a hatred of Bell Twats, who had a knack for creating chaos. I was stood holding her in my arms, and she was as clueless now as she was back then, about how powerfully influential and driven she was. Birch was the standard we had united around, and under her watchful eye, we had carved out a place that we belonged in, and she called it family.

So many people say that family is about blood, it's not, it is about love and support, having each other's back, and sharing the bad and the good, and we had done that for seven years. The bonds we have forged were stronger than family, they were deep and strong like the roots of an oak, and they had grown from an idea that we could reject the labels of society, and shun them as society had shunned us.

It did not matter to us who we liked or loved, or made love to, just caring enough to be around someone, and to learn from them, and learn about them, was all we desired. We were to say the least, a curious lot, and from that was hatched our philosophy which we now referred to as Curio.

We chose our own label, and we pushed back to create enough

space, so that we too could survive the bullies of our world. Normally at this time of year, we were all scattered around other families, separated and feeling out of place. We had decided that for at least one year, we would defy the odds, and stay together, and form an even deeper bond, if that was even possible?

It had not been easy, we had certainly faced more than our fair share of problems, and faced many hurdles to climb over, but we stood together, and finally overcame it, and I cannot deny, as hard and as fun as it had been, it had without doubt, been the most curious Christmas I had ever known, and I had absolutely loved it.

"Birch?"

"Yes Sweetie."

"Birch I am not sure about the church for our..."

"Oh Sweetie, Bell Twats were banned long before I proposed to you. I have something in mind, something a little more us."

"How do you mean... Us?"

"Sweetie, just trust me, it will not be boring."

"You said that about living here, and it's been chaos at times."

"Yeah... About that... It has been different, but fun though, hasn't it?"

"Yeah, and suddenly I am nervous about my wedding day."

"Sweetie, relax, it will be fine, I have some really great ideas."

"Oh crap, I knew it!"

More Author's

From

Violet Circle Publishing

Mike Beale. (Children's Book)

Crumble's Adventures.
ISBN: 978-1-910299-06-7
Digital ISBN: 978-1-910299-08-1

Colin Smith (Play)

Heaven knows I'm Miserable Now
ISBN: 978-1-910299-16-6
Digital ISBN: 978-1-910299-23-4

Ted Morgan. (Poetry and verse)

Wordsmith's Wanderings.
ISBN: 978-1-910299-04-3
Digital ISBN: 978-1-910299-09-8
Peregrinations of the Wordsmith
ISBN: 978-1-910299-18-0
Digital ISBN: 978-1-910299-21-0
Silhouette Soldiers
ISBN: 978-1-910299-19-7
Digital ISBN: 978-1-910299-22-7
A Menu of Memories
Digital ISBN: 978-1-910299-32-6
Digital ISBN: 978-1-910299-33-3

Robin John Morgan. (Fiction/Fantasy/Slice of Life)

Heirs to the Kingdom.

Book One, The Bowman of Loxley.

ISBN: 978-1-910299-00-5

Digital ISBN: 978-1-910299-10-4

Book Two, The Lost Sword of Carnac.

ISBN: 978-1-910299-01-2

Digital ISBN: 978-1-910299-11-1

Book Three, The Darkness of Dunnottar.

ISBN: 978-1-910299-02-9

Digital ISBN: 978-1-910299-12-8

Book Four, Queen of the Violet Isle.

ISBN: 978-1-910299-03-6

Digital ISBN: 978-1-910299-13-5

Book Five, Crystals of the Mirrored Waters.

ISBN: 978-1-910299-05-0

Digital ISBN: 978-1-910299-14-2

Book Six, Last Arrow of the Woodland Realm.

ISBN: 978-1-910299-07-4

Digital ISBN: 978-1-910299-15-9

Book Seven, Bridge Of Sequana.

ISBN: 978-1-910299-17-3

Digital ISBN: 978-1-910299-20-3

Book Eight, The Circle of Darkness.

ISBN: 978-1-910299-26-5

Digital ISBN: 978-1-910299-29-6

The Curio Chronicles.

Part One, Abigail's Summer.

ISBN: 978-1-910299-27-2

Digital ISBN: 978-1-910299-28-9

Part Two, Curio's Summer.

ISBN: 978-1-910299-34-0

Digital ISBN: 978-1-910299-35-7

Part Three, Curio's Christmas.

ISBN: 978-1-910299-38-8

Digital ISBN: 978-1-910299-39-5

Other Works.

Rise Of The Raven
ISBN: 978-1-910299-30-2
Digital ISBN: 978-1-910299-31-9

Han's Cottage.
ISBN: 978-1-910299-36-4
Digital ISBN: 978-1-910299-37-1

Violet Circle Publishing Manchester UK

Ltd.

3
4B/2786